FYODOR DOSTOYEVSKY was born in Moscow on October 30, 1821. He was educated in Moscow and at the School of Military Engineers in St. Petersburg, where he spent four years. In 1844 he resigned his Commission in the army to devote himself to literature. In 1846, he wrote his first novel, *Poor Folk;* it was an immediate critical and popular success. This was followed by short stories and a novel, *The Double.* While at work on *Netochka Nezvanova,* the twenty-seven-year-old author was arrested for belonging to a young socialist group. He was tried and condemned to death, but at the last moment his sentence was commuted to prison in Siberia. He spent four years in the penal settlement at Omsk; then he was released on the condition that he serve in the army. While in the army he fell in love with and married Marie Isaeva. In 1859 he was granted full amnesty and allowed to return to St. Petersburg. In the next few years he wrote his first full-length novels: *The Friend of the Family* (1859) and *The Insulted and the Injured* (1862). *Notes from Underground* (1864) was in many ways his most influential work of this period, containing the wellsprings of his mature philosophy: the hope of gaining salvation through degradation and suffering. At the end of this literary period, his wife died. Plagued by epilepsy, faced with financial ruin, he worked at superhuman speed to produce *The Gambler,* dictating the novel to eighteen-year-old Anna Grigorievna Snitkina. The manuscript was delivered to his publisher in time. During the next fourteen years, Dostoyevsky wrote his greatest works: *Crime and Punishment, The Idiot, The Possessed,* and *The Brothers Karamazov.* The latter book was published a year before his death on January 28, 1881.

FYODOR DOSTOYEVSKY

THE
BROTHERS KARAMAZOV

Translated by CONSTANCE GARNETT

Edited and with a Foreword by
MANUEL KOMROFF

Revised and Updated Bibliography

A SIGNET CLASSIC

NEW AMERICAN LIBRARY

For the many days and nights of work and for many
important suggestions in preparing this new edition for the
American reader, the editor here acknowledges
with gratitude, the invaluable assistance
of his wife, Odette Komroff.

SIGNET, SIGNET CLASSIC, MENTOR, PLUME, MERIDIAN AND NAL
BOOKS are published by New American Library,
1633 Broadway, New York, New York 10019

23 24 25 26 27 28 29 30 31

PRINTED IN THE UNITED STATES OF AMERICA

CONTENTS

Book VIII: Dmitri

Book IX: The Preliminary Investigation

PART FOUR

Book X: The Boys

Book XI: Ivan

Book XII: A Judicial Error

Epilogue

FOREWORD

A Note about Dostoyevsky and a Key to His Work

Dostoyevsky was born in 1821. The sixty years of his life were spent in a Russia that was emerging from a long darkness and reaching out toward enlightenment and the promise of a unique destiny. During these sixty years he worked and produced those books which have won for him the distinction of being the world's greatest novelist.

Only nine years before Dostoyevsky's birth, Napoleon and his *Grande Armée* had been driven from Russian soil. The French forces had been torn apart. The destruction had been complete and the joy and pride in this victory filled the hearts of all Russians. The young Tzar Alexander had dictated the terms of peace at the Congress of Vienna. Russia, in a flood of patriotism, felt itself superior to Europe. Yet, serfdom still existed, a ruthless nobility ruled, the powerful church clung to the past and its darkness, and the people were gripped in ignorance, illiteracy, and poverty. The concepts of personal liberty long established in England, France and America were only beginning to infiltrate.

It was a troubling time of social and political change. The first stirrings of political freedom were in the air and Russia was entering a new era. It was a period of nervous discomfort which finally culminated in that social upheaval which completely broke with the past—the Russian Revolution of 1917.

Dostoyevsky lived his life in this changing Russia. He was deeply influenced by this nervous, restless time. He distilled the ideas of this period and presented them in his writings. No other writer revealed his people so completely as Dostoyevsky. And although a full century has passed since he first began to write, and great political and economic changes have taken place in Russia, the soul of the Russian people as revealed by Dostoyevsky remains the same. If one wants to understand Russia and the Russian people, one must read Dostoyevsky. There is no better source. He is Russia.

Dostoyevsky was one of seven children. His father was a staff doctor in a military hospital in Moscow, and the entire family lived in two rooms in a wing of the hospital. The doctor and his wife slept in one room while the children and several servants slept in the other. They were poor and had only seven servants. Serfs in Russia were plentiful and cheap. A wealthy family usually had sixty or more servants.

Dostoyevsky's mother died when he was sixteen and his father then moved to the country where he owned two small villages. There he surrounded himself with a harem. He was constantly drunk and tyrannized his serfs. In all he owned 150 souls of which about 30 were male workers; the rest were women, children and old people. The doctor was so cruel and brutal that one night his serfs murdered him. But the family did not report his murder to the authorities, for had they done so all the men of both villages would have been sent to Siberia and the family would have lost its source of income.

Dostoyevsky was eighteen years old and attending school in St. Petersburg when his father was murdered. This murder left a deep impression on the young man. In his last book, *The Brothers Karamazov*, written forty years later, he used the concept of this murder and modeled the horrible and lecherous old Karamazov—who drank life like brandy—after his own father.

Two years after the death of his father, Dostoyevsky became a second lieutenant in the engineers. He remained in the army for four years, acquired extravagant and reckless habits, and was constantly in debt. He was always waiting for money to arrive from the estate. The character Dmitri, in *The Brothers Karamazov*, has these same traits.

After leaving the army in 1846, Dostoyevsky wrote his first novel, *Poor Folk*. This work was deeply influenced by Gogol and tells the story of a frustrated love between a poor old clerk and a young girl. It appeared serially and was an immediate success, bringing Dostoyevsky the highest critical praise. *Poor Folk* was followed by a group of short stories and two short novels, *The Double*, a keen psychological study of a split personality, and *The Landlady*, another psychological study. Two years later Dostoyevsky began writing *Nyetochka Nyezvanova*, the diary of an adolescent girl. The work, which began appearing serially, attracted wide attention, but it was never finished because Dostoyevsky was suddenly arrested for being a member of a young socialist group.

Dostoyevsky was twenty-nine at the time of his arrest. Together with a number of other young liberals he was tried and condemned to die. But at the last moment his life was spared. As he stood with the other prisoners waiting for the firing squad and watching the first men being tied to the stakes, the sentence was suddenly commuted, by the kindness of the Tzar, to prison and exile in Siberia. Two of the prisoners went insane from this harrowing experience.

Dostoyevsky spent the next four years as a prisoner in Siberia. He was in the constant company of murderers, robbers and other criminals. "They are rough, angry, embittered men," he wrote to his brother. "Their hatred of the nobility is boundless. They would devour us if only they could." Pride and caste allowed Dostoyevsky to count himself as a member of the nobility. Yet, his close contact with criminals produced some good. Siberia was a unique training school for a novelist.

When Dostoyevsky's prison term ended, he was still forced to remain in exile in Siberia. During this time he married the widow of a minor official. She has been described as a pretty blonde of middle height, thin, tubercular, passionate, irresponsible—an hysterical woman with a strong streak of cruelty. Years later he confessed: "We were unhappy together . . . but we could not cease to love one another. The more unhappy we were the more we became attached to each other." Dostoyevsky used her as a model for Lise in *The Brothers Karamazov*.

Three years after his marriage, Dostoyevsky was pardoned by the Tzar and permitted to return to Russia. For nine years he had been in Siberia without writing a word and now he went to St. Petersburg to resume his literary work. He was free again, but with this freedom came a new kind of bondage which was to last to the end of his days: epilepsy, gambling and poverty. The epilepsy which had been latent in him since childhood now attacked him with violence. Gambling became a passion. And from this time on he was always in debt and under the pressure of delivering manuscript for serialization. Sometimes three chapters were already published, the fourth in type, the fifth in the mail, while the sixth and remaining chapters were unwritten and only roughly thought out. But in spite of all difficulties he worked on. During the next few years, besides journalistic work and two short stories, he wrote his first full-length novels: *The House of the Dead* and *The Insulted and Injured*.

It was at the end of this period of writing that Dostoyevsky's wife died after a long illness. Her death closes the second part of his life. He was now forty-five. His prospects could not have been worse, for besides his ill health and other misfortunes, he now found himself faced with ruin and a probable second term of imprisonment—this time for debt. He had signed a hard contract with a dishonest publisher and seemed unable to produce the work he had promised. If he could only deliver a novel within the stipulated time then all might be saved. But he had delayed working on it so long that it was almost too late.

It was at this critical moment that the eighteen year old Anna made her appearance. By an odd coincidence she had been nicknamed after the child heroine of Dostoyevsky's unfinished novel, *Nyetochka Nyezvanova*, written just before his imprisonment and exile in Siberia. She knew shorthand and could take rapid dictation. And so, on the fourth of October, 1866, Dostoyevsky began dictating to Anna. After working day and night for three weeks he completed the novel, *The Gambler*. It was delivered in time and he was saved. Thus began his third period, his truly important period. He and Anna were married and a new life now opened for him.

During the fourteen years of their married life, Dostoyevsky created his four important novels, his masterpieces: *Crime and Punishment, The Idiot, The Possessed*, and *The Brothers Karamazov*. Anna made it possible for him to surmount his difficulties—his poverty, his constant epileptic fits, his inner suffering, his feelings of guilt and humiliation. She had no great charms, no talents, no wealth, no wit. She was ordinary. Her lips were thick, her nostrils too far apart. But she was devoted to Dostoyevsky, recognized his genius, understood the fever of his creation and softened his torments with affection and care. She made a home for him and bore him children. She was practical and efficient. She possessed all that his starved nature required. In a short time she rescued him from his most pressing debts, took charge of the finances, drove off the money-lenders, his begging relations and other leeches. She alone made it possible for his genius to unfold and develop. She even published and acted as book-seller of his later books so that he could secure a fair share from his labor. Without Anna there would have been no Dostoyevsky as we know him today.

Dostoyevsky was not an easy man to have for a husband. His passion for gambling, his epilepsy, his financial difficulties and his infidelities continued throughout the years of their married life. Nor was his character agreeable. Turgeniev once said that he was "the most evil Christian I have ever met in my life." And when Dostoyevsky died one of Tolstoi's friends wrote of him: "I cannot consider Dostoyevsky either a good or a happy man. He was wicked, envious, vicious, and spent the whole of his life in emotions and irritations. . . . In Switzerland he treated his servant, in my presence, so abominably that the offended servant cried out: 'I too am a human being!' " But all this the faithful Anna denied. The fourteen years of their life together, she has recorded in her memoirs, convinced her that Dostoyevsky was the purest being on earth. And now after a century nothing matters except his genius and the rich heritage he has left us.

Dostoyevsky died a year after the publication of *The Brothers Karamazov*. He was sixty years old and the year was 1881. Immediately following his death the Tzar honored his genius and his memory by bestowing a small pension upon Anna. Added to this, his books had a wide sale and so Anna enjoyed a long period of comfort. However, during the Revolution her property was confiscated. She died of privation in 1920, thirty-nine years after Dostoyevsky's death.

Dostoyevsky is the most Russian of all Russian novelists, and his novels follow the Russian form. Unlike English novels, which are biographical, Dostoyevsky's novels are built on a theme charged with a moral philosophy that binds the characters to the action and induces in them a compelling emotional drive.

In *Crime and Punishment,* Dostoyevsky presents a simple theme: Thou shalt not kill. In the development of this theme he presents the philosophy that even when death benefits everyone, it is forbidden by moral law. In support of this the murderer is condemned by his deed and brought to his ruin by the weight of his own conscience.

The theme of *The Idiot* is the failure of virtue, sacrifice and saintliness in a world of thorny reality. The Christ-like hero of this novel surrenders pride, egotism, ambition only to become a wise but lovable fool. Morality is weighed in a balance and Western culture is challenged.

In *The Possessed,* Dostoyevsky deals with the theme of revolution. He discloses the dangers of nihilism and socialism and the extreme ruthlessness of the revolutionary character as well as the stupidity, ignorance and incompetence of government officials who try to combat new ideas. Between revolutionary ruthlessness and conservative stupidity man is caught and crushed.

In *The Brothers Karamazov,* the last and greatest of Dostoyevsky's novels, the theme and philosophy are clearly stated in one of the early chapters: "The awful thing is that beauty is mysterious as well as terrible. God and the Devil are fighting there and the battlefield is the heart of man." This duel is more than a simple encounter. It is a duel unto death. God and the Devil fight for the soul of man. And Dostoyevsky asks: "Who is laughing at mankind?" And he answers by showing that the laughter comes from within man himself: "In every man a demon lies hidden."

The theme and philosophy of *The Brothers Karamazov* occupied Dostoyevsky's mind for many years. In a letter to a friend he writes: "The chief problem dealt with throughout this particular work is the very one which has, my whole life long, tormented my conscious and subconscious being: The question of the existence of God." What if God does not exist? Then for Dostoyevsky the world is nothing but a "vaudeville of devils" and "all things are lawful," even crime.

To illustrate this theme and philosophy, Dostoyevsky introduces us to the Karamazov family. We meet a lecherous and corrupt father and four sons. The eldest son, Dmitri, symbolizes the flesh, the second son, Ivan, represents the intellect, the youngest son, Alyosha, the spiritual side of man, and the illegitimate son, Smerdyakov, represents the "insulted and injured, the disinherited." These characters are caught in a web of moral philosophy, the strands of which are so strong that none can escape. God and the Devil battle for possession of their souls. The fight is furious. It rages from the first page to the last page. The characters are all involved in a murder, and as they stamp across the stage they reveal their emotions, conscious and subconscious, with terrifying clarity.

In that famous chapter "The Grand Inquisitor," certainly the most famous chapter in all literature, Christ himself returns to our sorry earth and is challenged by organized religion. Here Christianity is weighed with critical bitterness. And the questions are asked: "Can man live by Christ's teachings? Would not the Devil, that 'wise and mighty spirit of the wilderness' support mankind in a better manner? And why must man choose between freedom and bread?" "The Grand Inquisitor" is more than a chapter in a novel. It presents a whole philosophy of history in literary form. In this chapter God and the Devil wage a fierce encounter. And in the end God seems vanquished and the Devil the proud victor: Christianity is condemned. This theme is again restated towards the end of the novel in another famous chapter. Here Ivan holds a dialogue with the Devil and they weigh Western morality in life's battered scales.

These two chapters present the arguments for the denial of God. The affirmation of God is contained in chapters dealing with Alyosha and the Elder, Father Zossima. In these chapters Dostoyevsky attempts to show the making of a saint and the power of Christ-like love. Dostoyevsky believes that Christ-like love wins in the end. But does he prove it? He is a master in dealing with crime and the unlawful heart of man, but how well he succeeds with goodness, of which Father Zossima and Alyosha are the symbols, the reader must decide for himself. In the face of the miscarriage of justice, who is the winner, God or the Devil?

The very inconclusiveness of the book and its ideas, which remain unsolved, seems to add power to the story and the reader becomes deeply involved in the emotions and philosophy. Before long he must surrender being a simple reader, for he becomes part of the Karamazov world. The reader starts out as an innocent bystander and ends up by taking sides and becoming involved in the battle between God and the Devil. And whether he enjoys the experience or not one thing is certain: he emerges from this experience a different person from when he first opened the book. He has been tried by fire. He has been made to think and to reach decisions about many problems which are his personal problems too. The Karamazovs and those who associate with them are terrifying people to the reader because they display boldly certain characteristics which are deeply hidden in our own hearts and which we try hard to deny.

Dostoyevsky is supreme as a novelist of ideas. Throughout his works he is concerned and occupied with four R's. Revelation of Man's secret heart, Revolution, Russia and Religion.

Dostoyevsky's revelations in the field of psychology are enormous. They anticipated many of the principles later established by trained psychologists.

Born half a century before Freud, Dostoyevsky records in the pages of his novels astonishing observations in the field of human emotions. He writes in detail about exhibitionism, the Oedipus complex and perversions involving adolescents. He noted that dreams stem from the subconscious and contain erotic symbolism, that they are "induced not by reason but by desire." He observed that laughter reveals a hidden and secret side of personality, that it is an unconscious unmasking. He described the "accidental family" in which each member is separated from the others and lives an independent and isolated life. *The Brothers Karamazov* illustrates such a family. He discovered that there is a tendency to despotism, a "will to power," inherent in man. He found that love contains among its elements the desire to exercise power over the beloved, and that if this desire is not gratified then the loved one can be hated and loved at the same time. This principle is also clearly displayed in the pages of *The Brothers Karamazov*.

In Dostoyevsky's observations of the love for self-torture and punishment as a guilt-cleansing device, he anticipated our modern theory of "death-instinct" and Freud's "beyond the pleasure principle."

Dostoyevsky contributed all this to our modern world of psychology—all this and more. He even recorded in detail the workings of the "split personality." He described it in its fairly mild as well as its extreme pathological manifestations. There is hardly an important character in all his works who is not a divided personality. He has one of his characters in *The Possessed* say: "I am capable of desiring to do something good and of feeling pleasure from it: at the same time I desire evil and feel pleasure from that too." But no better examples of "split personalities" can be found than in *The Brothers Karamazov*. There are for instance Dmitri, Katerina with her love-hate, the young girl Lise, and Ivan whose two selves come to clash in that famous chapter in which he encounters the Devil.

Dostoyevsky was not only a psychologist but also a visionary and prophet. He wrote about extra-sensory perception (mental telepathy as well as clairvoyance) and his observations contributed to our present day theories of psychical research. His observations regarding gambling, for which he had an abnormal passion, are only recently being confirmed and may in time be incorporated in our modern theories of chance. He believed, for instance, that personal distractions destroyed the power to win and for that reason he never brought his wife with him to the roulette wheel. He believed in a will to win. "I still retain the conviction," he once wrote, "that in games of chance, if one has perfect control of one's will . . . one cannot fail to overcome the brutality of chance." This theory he illustrates in his short novel *The Gambler*.

The second R with which Dostoyevsky was concerned was Revolution. While many observations on revolution are scattered through his books, the main text of this subject is contained in his novel *The Possessed*, written almost fifty years before the advent of the Revolution. In this work he anticipates many of the elements of the Communist Revolution. Contrary to general belief at the time, he foresaw that the Revolution would involve only Russia and not the world; that its nationalism would in time become religious; that its early leaders would not emerge from the workers; that these leaders would become ruthless and distort even history to glorify their cause. All this and more. He foresaw the horrors of the "cell" system and predicted that revolution in Russia "starting from unlimited freedom" would "arrive at unlimited despotism."

Goodness and glory were bound to Dostoyevsky's third R— Russia. For him everything Russian was fine and wonderful. In his eyes the soul of the Russian peasant was beautiful, and from the soil of Russia watered by the tears of those who suffered, would spring the flower of a new world. He felt that Europe and Western civilization were already degenerate. He pokes fun at Germans, Frenchmen and Englishmen. He loathes Poles and Jews. He hates Europe and America. He speaks of Europe as a corpse. Moscow is his Holy City, his "new Jerusalem." At heart he is a monarchist and loves the Russian Tzars. Everything that was Russian he loved. Russia, he felt, had nothing to learn from the West: the West had everything to learn from Russia. Dostoyevsky's patriotism knew no limits.

Religion, Dostoyevsky's fourth R, permeates his other three R's. He is a deeply religious man, the most religious of all great novelists. In the narrower sense he considers all religions false except the Russian Orthodox with its roots deep in the Byzantine Empire. "Christ lives in the Orthodox Church alone," he says. In the wider sense he is preoccupied with Good and Evil, God and the Devil, with Man and his Salvation regardless of nationality and race. He believes passionately in Love, Christ-like Love. He asks, "What is Hell?" And one of his characters, Father Zossima, replies, "It is the suffering of being unable to love."

Due to the pressure of his existence, Dostoyevsky's books suffer from serious technical defects. But in the face of his great genius these defects are trifling. Dostoyevsky towers above all other novelists, for no other novelist has ever presented so many vital ideas—ideas that have revolutionized our thinking and our lives. As a novelist he has brought to life a whole gallery of people; people of bone, flesh and blood all caught in a web of circumstance. He has the power to engulf his characters in dramatic situations and drive them headlong with passionate desperation. And while his characters are caught in the agony of life, he plumbs deep and lays bare their secret hearts. We understand these hearts for they are not unlike our own. The Dostoyevsky heart is universal. And the people that he gave life to a century ago are living today and will live on for centuries to come. Their blood is warm, red and their hearts beat on.

—Manuel Komroff

PART ONE

BOOK I: THE HISTORY OF A FAMILY

1. Fyodor Karamazov

ALEXEY KARAMAZOV WAS THE THIRD SON of Fyodor Karamazov, a landowner well known in our district in his own day, and still remembered among us because of his gloomy and tragic death, which happened thirteen years ago, and which I shall describe in its proper place. For the present I will only say that this "landowner"—for so we used to call him, although he hardly spent a day of his life on his own estate—was a strange person, yet one fairly frequently to be met with, a despicable, vicious man and at the same time senseless. But he was one of those senseless people who are very capable of looking after their affairs, and, apparently, after nothing else. Fyodor Karamazov, for instance, began with next to nothing; his estate was of the smallest; he ran to dine at other men's tables, fastened on to them as a toady, and at his death had a hundred thousand roubles in hard cash. At the same time, he was always one of the most senseless, fantastic men in the whole district. I repeat, it was not stupidity—the majority of these fantastic men are shrewd and intelligent enough—but just senselessness, and a peculiar national form of it.

He was married twice, and had three sons, the eldest, Dmitri, by his first wife, and two, Ivan and Alexey, by his second. Fyodor Karamazov's first wife, Adelaïde, belonged to a fairly rich and distinguished noble family, also landowners in our district, the Miusovs. How it happened that an heiress, who was also a beauty, and moreover one of those vigorous, intelligent girls, so common in this generation, but sometimes also to be found in the last, could have married such a worthless wretch, as we all called him, I won't attempt to explain.

I knew a young lady of the last "romantic" generation who after some years of a strange passion for a gentleman, whom she might easily have married at any moment, invented countless obstacles to their union, and ended by throwing herself one stormy night into a deep river from a high bank, almost a precipice. And so she died, entirely to satisfy her own whim, and to be like Shakespeare's Ophelia. If this precipice, a chosen and favorite spot of hers, had been less picturesque, if there had been a prosaic flat bank in its place, most likely the suicide would never have taken place. This is a fact, and there probably have been a few similar cases in the last two or three generations. Adelaide Miusov's marriage was also, no doubt, an echo of other people's ideas, and was due to the irritation caused by lack of mental freedom. She wanted, perhaps, to show her feminine independence, to override class distinctions and the despotism of her family. And her imagination persuaded her, we must suppose, for a brief moment, that Fyodor Karamazov, in spite of his parasitic position, was one of the bold and ironical spirits of that progressive age, though he was, in fact, an ill-natured buffoon and nothing more. What gave the marriage piquancy was that it was preceded by an elopement, and this greatly captivated Adelaide's fancy.

Fyodor Karamazov's position at the time made him specially eager for such an undertaking, for he was passionately anxious to advance himself in one way or another. To attach himself to a good family and obtain a dowry was an alluring prospect. As for mutual love it did not exist apparently, either in the bride or in him, in spite of Adelaide's beauty. This was, perhaps, unique in the life of Fyodor Karamazov, who was always of a sensuous nature, and ready to run after any female on the slightest encouragement. Adelaide seems to have been the only woman who had no particular appeal for him.

Immediately after the elopement Adelaide discovered that she had no feeling for her husband but contempt. The marriage showed itself in its true colors with extraordinary speed. Although the family accepted the elopement quickly and apportioned the runaway bride her dowry, the husband and wife began to lead a most disorderly life, and there were everlasting scenes between them.

It was said that the young wife showed infinitely more generosity and dignity than Fyodor Karamazov, who, as is now known, got hold of all her money up to twenty-five thousand roubles as soon as she received it, so that those thousands were lost to her forever. The little village and the rather fine town house which formed part of her dowry he did his best for a long time to transfer to his name, by means of some deed of conveyance. He would probably have succeeded, merely from Adelaide's moral fatigue and desire to get rid of him, and from the contempt and loathing he aroused by his persistent and shameless demands. But, fortunately, Adelaide's family intervened and checked his greediness.

It is known for a fact that frequent fights took place between the husband and wife, but rumor had it that Fyodor Karamazov did not beat his wife but was beaten by her, for she was a hot-tempered, bold, dark-browed, impatient woman, possessed of remarkable physical strength. Finally, she left the house and

18

ran away from Fyodor Karamazov with a destitute divinity student, leaving Dmitri, a child of three years old, in her husband's hands.

Immediately following this Fyodor Karamazov introduced a regular harem into the house, and abandoned himself to orgies of drunkenness. In the intervals he used to drive all over the province, complaining tearfully to everybody of Adelaide's having left him, going into details too disgraceful for a husband to mention in regard to his own married life. What seemed to gratify him and flatter his self-love most was to play the ridiculous part of the injured husband, and to parade his woes with embellishments.

"One would think that you'd got a promotion, Fyodor Karamazov, you seem so pleased in spite of your sorrow," some said making fun of him. Many even added that they thought he was glad of a new chance to play the buffoon, and that it was simply to make it funnier that he pretended to be unaware of the spectacle he was making of himself. But, who knows, it may have been simplicity.

At last he succeeded in getting on the track of his runaway wife. The poor woman turned out to be in Petersburg, where she had gone with her divinity student, and where she had thrown herself into a life of complete freedom. Fyodor Karamazov at once began bustling about, making preparations to go to Petersburg, but with what object he could not himself have said. He would perhaps have really gone; but having determined to do so he felt at once entitled to fortify himself for the journey by another bout of drinking. And just at that time his wife's family received the news of her death in Petersburg. She had died quite suddenly in a garret, according to one story, of typhus, or as another version had it, of starvation.

Fyodor Karamazov was drunk when he heard of his wife's death, and the story is that he ran out into the street and began shouting with joy, raising his hands to Heaven: "Lord, now lettest Thou Thy servant depart in peace." But others say he wept without restraint like a little child, so much so that people were sorry for him, in spite of the repulsion he aroused. It is quite possible that both versions were true, that he rejoiced at his release, and at the same time wept for her who released him. As a general rule, people, even the wicked, are much more naive and simple-hearted than we suppose. And we ourselves are, too.

2. He Gets Rid of His Eldest Son

YOU CAN EASILY IMAGINE what a father such a man would be and how he would bring up his children. His behavior as a father was exactly what might be expected. He completely abandoned the child of his marriage with Adelaide, not from spite nor because of his matrimonial grievances, but simply because he forgot him. While he was wearying everyone with his tears and complaints, and turning his house into a sink of debauchery, a faithful servant of the family, Gregory, took the three-year old Dmitri into his care. If this servant hadn't looked after him there would have been no one even to change the child's little shirt.

It happened moreover that the child's relatives on his mother's side forgot him too at first. His grandfather was no longer living. His widow, Dmitri's grandmother, had moved to Moscow and was seriously ill, while their daughters were married. So Dmitri stayed for almost a whole year in old Gregory's charge and lived with him in the servant's cottage. But even if his father had remembered him (he could not have been altogether unaware of his existence) he would have sent him back to the cottage, as the child would only have been in the way of his wild parties.

At this time, very fortunately, a cousin of little Dmitri's mother, Peter Miusov, happened to return from Paris. He lived abroad for many years afterwards, but was at that time quite a young man, and distinguished among the Miusovs as a man of enlightened ideas and of European culture, who had traveled widely. Toward the end of his life he became a Liberal of the type common in the forties and fifties. In the course of his career he had come into contact with many of the most Liberal men of his time, both in Russia and abroad. He had known Proudhon and Bakunin personally, and in his old age was very fond of describing the three days of the Paris Revolution of February, 1848, hinting that he himself had almost taken part in the fighting on the barricades. This was one of the most grateful recollections of his youth. He had an independent property of about a thousand serfs, to reckon in the old style. His fine estate lay on the outskirts of our little town and bordered on the lands of our famous monastery, with which Peter Miusov began an endless lawsuit, almost as soon as he came into his inheritance, concerning fishing rights in the river or wood-cutting in the forest, I don't know exactly which. He regarded it as his duty as a citizen and a man of culture to open an attack upon the "clericals." Hearing all about Adelaide, whom he, of course, remembered, and in whom he had at one time been interested, and learning of the existence of the child Dmitri, he intervened, in spite of all his contempt for Fyodor Karamazov. He met Karamazov for the first time, and told him at once that he wanted to undertake the child's education. Long afterwards he used to tell as a characteristic touch, that when he began to speak of little Dmitri, Fyodor Karamazov looked as though he did not understand what child he was talking about, and even as though he was surprised to hear that he had a little son in the house. The story may have been exaggerated, yet there must have been some truth in it.

Fyodor Karamazov was all his life fond of acting, of suddenly playing an unexpected part, sometimes without any motive for doing so, and even to his own direct disadvantage, as, for instance, in the present case. This habit, however, is characteristic of a very great number of people, some of them very clever ones, not like Fyodor Karamazov.

Peter Miusov carried the business through boldly, and was appointed, with Fyodor Karamazov, as joint guardian of the child, who had a small property, a house and land, left to him by his mother. Little Dmitri did, in fact, pass into this cousin's keeping. But as Peter Miusov had no family of his own, and after securing the revenues of his estates was in a hurry to return to Paris, he left the boy in charge of one of his cousins, a lady living in Moscow. It came to pass that, settling permanently in Paris he, too, forgot the child, especially when the revolution of February broke out making an impression on his mind that he remembered all the rest of his life. In time the Moscow lady died, and Dmitri passed into the care of one of her married daughters. I believe he changed his home a fourth time later on. I won't go into that now, as I shall have a lot to tell later of Fyodor Karamazov's firstborn, and must confine myself now to the most essential facts about him, without which I could not begin my story.

In the first place, Dmitri was the only one of Fyodor Karamazov's three sons who grew up in the belief that he had property, and that he would be independent on coming of age. He spent a confused boyhood and youth. He did not finish his high school; he entered a military school, then went to the Caucasus, was promoted, fought a duel, and was degraded to the ranks, earned promotion again, led a wild life, and spent a great deal of money. He did not begin to receive any income from his father until he came of age, and until then got into debt.

He saw and knew his father, Fyodor Karamazov, for the first time on coming of age, when he visited our neighborhood for the purpose of settling with him about his property. He did not seem to like his father. He did not stay long with him, and hurried to get away. At this time he only succeeded in obtaining a sum of money, and entering into an agreement for future payments from his estate. He was unable to learn from his father anything about the revenues and value of his estate, a fact worthy of note. Fyodor Karamazov remarked for the first time then (this, too, should be noted) that Dmitri had a vague and exaggerated idea of his property. Fyodor Karamazov was very well satisfied with this, as it fell in with his own designs. He gathered only that the young man was frivolous, unruly, of violent passions, impatient, and dissipated, and that if he could only obtain ready money he would be satisfied, although only, of course, for a short time.

So Fyodor Karamazov began to take advantage of this fact, sending Dmitri from time to time small installments. In the end, when four years later, Dmitri, losing patience, came a second time to our little town to settle up once and for all with his father, it turned out to his amazement that he had nothing. It was impossible even to get an accounting. It seemed that he had received the whole value of his property in sums of money from his father, and was perhaps even in debt to him, that by various agreements into which he had, of his own desire, entered at various previous dates, he had no right to expect anything more, and so on, and so on.

Dmitri was bewildered, suspected deceit and cheating, and was almost beside himself. And it was this that led to the disaster which is the subject of my first introductory story, or rather the external side of it. But before I pass to that story I must say a little of Fyodor Karamazov's other two sons.

3. The Second Marriage and the Second Family

VERY SHORTLY after getting his four-year old Dmitri off his hands Fyodor Karamazov married a second time. His second marriage lasted eight years. He took this second wife, Sophia, also a very young girl, from another province, where he had gone on some business with a Jew. Though Fyodor Karamazov was a drunkard and morally corrupt, he never neglected investing his capital, and managed his business affairs very successfully, though not over scrupulously.

Sophia was the daughter of an obscure deacon, and was left from childhood an orphan without relatives. She grew up in the house of a general's widow, a wealthy old lady of good position, who was at once her benefactress and tormentor. I do not know the details, but I have only heard that the orphan girl, a meek and gentle creature, was once cut down from a halter in which she was hanging from a nail in the attic, so terrible were her sufferings from the cruelty and everlasting nagging of this old woman, who was apparently not bad-hearted but had become a tyrant through idleness.

Fyodor Karamazov proposed to her; inquiries were made about him and he was refused. But again, as in his first marriage, he planned an elopement with the orphan girl. There is very little doubt that she would not have married him if she had known a little more about him. But she lived in another province; besides what could a girl of sixteen feel, except that she would be better at the bottom of the river than remaining with her benefactress. So the poor girl exchanged a benefactress for a benefactor.

Fyodor Karamazov did not get a penny this time, for the general's widow was furious. She gave them nothing and cursed them both. But he had not counted on a dowry. What attracted him was the remarkable beauty of the girl, above all her innocent appearance. It had a peculiar attraction for this immoral wretch, who had before this admired only the coarser types of feminine beauty.

"Those innocent eyes slit my soul like a razor," he used to say afterwards, with his loathsome snicker. . . . In a man so depraved this might, of course, mean no more than sensual attraction.

As he had received no dowry and had, so to speak, taken Sophia "from the halter," he did not stand on ceremony with her. Making her feel that she had "wronged" him, he took advantage of her meekness and submissiveness to trample on the ordinary decencies of marriage. He gathered loose women into his house, and held orgies in her presence. To show what things had come to, I may mention that Gregory, the gloomy, stupid, obstinate, argumentative servant, who had always hated his first mistress, Adelaide, took the side of his new mistress. He championed her cause, abusing Fyodor Karamazov in a manner little befitting a servant, and, on one occasion broke up the wild party and drove all the disorderly women out of the house.

In the end this unhappy Sophia, kept in terror from her childhood, fell into that kind of nervous disease which is most frequently found in peasant women who are said to be "possessed by devils." At times after terrible fits of hysterics she even lost her reason. Yet she bore Fyodor Karamazov two sons, Ivan and Alexey, the eldest in the first year of marriage and the second three years later. When she died, little Alexey was in his fourth year, and, strange as it seems, I know that he remembered his mother all his life, like a dream, of course.

At her death almost exactly the same thing happened to the two little boys as had happened to their elder brother, Dmitri. They were completely forgotten and abandoned by their father. They were looked after by the same Gregory and lived in his cottage, where they were found by the tyrannical old lady who had brought up their mother. She was still alive, and had not, all those eight years, forgotten the insult done her. All that time she was getting information about Sophia. And hearing of her illness and hideous surroundings she declared aloud two or three times to her servants: "It serves her right. God has punished her for her ingratitude."

Exactly three months after Sophia's death the general's widow suddenly appeared in our town, and went straight to Fyodor Karamazov's house. She spent only half an hour in the town but she did a great deal. It was evening. Fyodor Karamazov, whom she had not seen for eight years, was drunk. The story is that instantly upon seeing him, without any sort of explanation, she gave him two good, resounding slaps on the face,

23

seized him by a tuft of hair, and shook him three times. Then, without a word, she went straight to the servant's cottage to the two boys. Seeing, at a glance, that they were unwashed and in dirty clothes, she promptly gave Gregory a box on the ear. And announcing that she would carry off both children, she wrapped them just as they were in a rug, put them in the carriage, and drove off to her own town.

Gregory accepted the blow like a devoted slave, without a word. And when he escorted the old lady to her carriage he bowed low and pronounced impressively that, "God would repay her for the orphans."

"You are a blockhead all the same," the old lady shouted at him as she drove away.

Fyodor Karamazov, thinking it over, decided that it was a good thing, and did not refuse the general's widow his formal consent to any proposition in regard to his children's education. As for the slaps she had given him, he drove all over the town telling the story.

It happened that the old lady died soon after this. She left the boys in her will a thousand roubles each "for their instruction, and to be spent on them exclusively, with the condition that it be so divided as to last till they are twenty-one for it is more than adequate provision for such children. If other people think fit to throw away their money, let them." I have not read the will myself, but I heard there was something queer about it.

The principal heir, Yefim Polenov, the Marshal of Nobility of the province, turned out, however, to be an honest man. Writing to Fyodor Karamazov, and realizing at once that he could get nothing from him for his children's education (though Karamazov never directly refused but only delayed as he always did in such cases, and was over-sentimental), Yefim Polenov took a personal interest in the orphans. He became especially fond of the younger boy, Alexey, who lived for a long time as one of his family. I beg the reader to note this from the beginning. And to Yefim Polenov, a man of a generosity and humanity rarely to be met with, the two young boys were more indebted for their education and bringing up than to anyone else. He kept the two thousand roubles left to them by the general's widow intact, so that by the time they came of age their money had been doubled by the accumulation of interest. He educated them both at his own expense, and certainly spent far more than a thousand roubles on each of them.

I won't go into a detailed account of their boyhood and youth, but will only mention a few of the most important events. Of the elder, Ivan, I will only say that he grew into a somewhat morose and reserved, though far from timid boy. At ten years of age he had realized that he and his brother were not living in their own home but on other people's charity, and that their father was a man of whom it was disgraceful to speak.

Ivan began very early, almost in his infancy (so they say at least), to show a brilliant and unusual aptitude for learning. I don't know exactly why, but he left the family of Yefim Polenov when he was hardly thirteen, entering a Moscow school, and boarding with an experienced and well-known teacher, an old friend of Yefim Polenov. Ivan used to say afterwards that this was all due to the "ardor for good works" of Yefim Polenov, who was captivated by the idea that his genius should be trained by a teacher of genius.

Neither Yefim Polenov nor this teacher was living when Ivan finished at the school and entered a university. As Yefim Polenov had made no provision for the payment of the tyrannical old lady's legacy, which had grown from one thousand to two, it was delayed, owing to formalities inevitable in Russia, and Ivan was in great straits for the first two years. He was forced to support himself all the time he was studying. It must be noted that he did not even attempt to communicate with his father, perhaps from pride, perhaps from contempt for him, or perhaps from his cool common sense, which told him that from such a father he would get no assistance.

However that may have been, Ivan was by no means despondent and succeeded in getting work, at first giving lessons and afterward getting paragraphs on street incidents into the newspapers under the signature of "Eye-Witness." These paragraphs, it was said, were so interesting that they were quickly accepted. This alone showed Ivan's practical and intellectual superiority over the masses of needy and unfortunate students of both sexes who hang about the offices of the newspapers and journals, unable to think of anything better than everlasting entreaties for copying and translating from French.

Having once been in touch with the editors Ivan kept up his connection with them, and in his latter years at the university he published brilliant reviews of books upon various subjects, so that he became known in literary circles. But it was only in his last year that he suddenly succeeded in attracting the attention of a far wider circle of readers, so that a great many people noticed and remembered him. It was a rather curious incident.

He had just graduated from the university and was preparing to go abroad using his two thousand roubles when he published in one of the more important journals a strange article, which attracted general notice. It was on a subject of which Ivan might have been supposed to know nothing, as he was a student of natural science. The article dealt with a problem which was being debated everywhere at the time—the position of the ecclesiastical courts. After discussing several opinions on the subject he went on to explain his own view. What was most striking about the article was its tone, and its unexpected conclusion. Many of the Church party regarded him unquestioningly as on their side. And yet atheists joined in the applause. Finally some wiser people said that the article was nothing but an impudent satirical burlesque.

I mention this incident particularly because this article penetrated into the famous monastery in our neighborhood, where the monks, being very interested in the question of the ecclesiastical courts, were completely bewildered by it. Learning the author's name, they were interested in his being a native of the town and the son of "that Fyodor Karamazov." And it was just then that Ivan, the author himself, made his appearance among us.

Why Ivan had come, I remember asking myself at the time with a certain uneasiness. This fateful visit, which was the first step leading to so many events, I never fully explained to myself. It seemed strange that a young man so educated, so proud, and apparently so cautious, should suddenly visit such an infamous house and a father who had ignored him all his life. It seemed strange that he should visit his father who hardly knew him, never thought of him, and would not under any circumstances have given him money (Karamazov was always afraid that his sons Ivan and Alexey, like Dmitri, would also come to ask him for money). And here Ivan was staying in the house of such a father, had been living with him for two months, and they were on the best possible terms.

This last fact was a cause of wonder to many others as well as to me. Peter Miusov, of whom I have spoken already, the cousin of Fyodor Karamazov's first wife, happened to be in the neighborhood again on a visit to his estate. He had come from Paris, which was his permanent home. I remember that he was more surprised than anyone else when he met Ivan, who interested him extremely, and with whom he sometimes argued and secretly compared himself.

"He is proud," he used to say, "he will never be in want of money; he has money enough to go abroad now. What does he want here? Everyone can see that he hasn't come for money, for his father would never give him any. He has no taste for drink or dissipation, and yet his father can't do without him. They get on so well together!"

That was the truth. The young man had an unmistakable influence over his father, who really appeared to be behaving more decently. He even seemed at times ready to obey Ivan, though he was often extremely and even spitefully perverse.

It was only later that we learned that Ivan had come partly at the request of, and in the interests of, his elder half-brother, Dmitri, whom he met for the first time on this visit, though he had before leaving Moscow been in correspondence with him about an important matter of more concern to Dmitri than himself. What that business was the reader will learn in due time. Yet even when I did know of this special circumstance I still felt that Ivan was a puzzling person, and thought his visit rather strange.

I may add that Ivan acted at the time as a mediator between his father and his elder brother Dmitri, who was quarreling with his father and even planning to bring a lawsuit against him.

The family was now united for the first time, some of its members now met for the first time in their lives. The younger brother, Alexey, had been a year already among us, having been the first of the three to arrive. It is of the brother Alexey I find it most difficult to speak at this time. Yet I must give an account of him, if only to explain one queer fact, which is that I have to introduce my hero to the reader wearing the cassock of a novice. Yes, he had been for the last year in our monastery, and seemed willing to be cloistered there for the rest of his life.

4. The Third Son, Alyosha

ALEXEY WAS ONLY TWENTY, his brother Ivan was in his twenty-fourth year at the time, while their elder half-brother Dmitri was twenty-seven. First of all, I must explain that this young man Alexey, or Alyosha as we fondly called him, was not a fanatic and in my opinion, at least, was not even a mystic. I may as well give my full opinion from the beginning. He was simply a lover of humanity, and that he adopted the monastic life was because at that time it struck him as the ideal escape for his soul struggling from the darkness of worldly wickedness to the light of love. And the reason this life struck him in this way was that he found in it at that time, as he thought, an extraordinary being, our celebrated elder, Zossima, to whom he became attached with all the warm first love of his ardent heart.

I do not deny that he was very strange even at that time, and had been so indeed from his cradle. I have mentioned already, by the way, that although he lost his mother in his fourth year he remembered her all his life—her face, her caresses, "as though she stood living before me." Such memories may persist, as everyone knows, from an even earlier age, even from two years old, but they seldom stand out through a whole lifetime like spots of light out of darkness, like a corner torn out of a huge picture which has all faded and disappeared except that fragment. That is how it was with him.

He remembered one still summer evening, an open window, the slanting rays of the setting sun (he recalled this most vividly of all); in a corner of the room the holy image, before it a lighted lamp, and on her knees before the image his mother, sobbing hysterically with cries and moans, snatching him up in both arms, squeezing him close till it hurt, and praying for him to the Mother of God, holding him out in both arms to the image as though to put him under the Mother's protection . . .

and suddenly a nurse runs in and snatches him from her in terror. That was the picture! And Alyosha remembered his mother's face at that minute. He used to say that it was frenzied but beautiful. But he rarely cared to speak of this memory to anyone.

In his childhood and youth he was by no means forthcoming and he talked very little, but not from shyness or sullenness; quite the contrary, from something different, from a sort of inner preoccupation entirely personal and unconcerned with other people. This preoccupation was so important to him that he seemed, as it were, to forget others on account of it. Still he was fond of people. He seemed throughout his life to put implicit trust in people; yet no one ever looked on him as a simple or naive person. There was something about him which made one feel at once (and it was so all his life afterwards) that he did not care to be a judge of others—that he would never take it upon himself to criticize and would never condemn anyone for anything. He seemed, indeed, to accept everything without the least condemnation though often grieving bitterly. And this was so much so that no one could surprise or frighten him even in his earliest youth.

Coming, when he was twenty, to his father's house which was a sink of debauchery, he, chaste and pure as he was, simply withdrew in silence when to look on was unbearable. He did this without the slightest sign of contempt or condemnation. His father, who had once been in a dependent position, and so was sensitive and ready to take offense, met him at first with distrust and sullenness. "He does not say much," he used to say, "and he thinks too much." But soon, within two weeks, he took to embracing him and kissing him terribly often, with drunken tears, with sentimentality. Yet it should be noted that he evidently felt a real and deep affection for him, such as he had never been capable of feeling for anyone before.

Everyone, indeed, loved Alyosha wherever he went, and it was so from his earliest childhood. When he went to live with his benefactor, Yefim Polenov, he won the hearts of all the family, so that they looked on him as their own child. Yet he entered the house at such an early age that he could not have done so from design nor cunning. So that the quality of making himself loved directly and unconsciously was inherent in him, in his very nature so to speak. It was the same at school, one might have thought that he was the kind of child who would be distrusted, sometimes ridiculed, and even disliked by his schoolfellows. He was dreamy, for instance, and rather solitary. From his earliest childhood he was fond of creeping into a corner to read, and yet he was a general favorite all the while he was at school. He was rarely playful or gay, but anyone could see at the first glance that this was not from sullenness. On the contrary he was bright and good-tempered. He never tried to show off among his schoolfellows. Perhaps because of this, he

28

was never afraid of anyone, yet the boys immediately understood that he was not proud of his fearlessness and seemed to be unaware that he was bold and courageous. He never resented an insult. It often happened that an hour after the offense he would address the offender or answer some question with as trustful and candid an expression as though nothing had happened between them. And it was not that he seemed to have forgotten or intentionally forgiven the affront, but simply that he did not regard it as an affront, and this completely conquered and captivated the boys.

He had one characteristic, however, which made all his schoolfellows from the bottom class to the top want to make fun of him, not from malice but because it amused them. This characteristic was a wild fanatical modesty and chastity. He could not bear to hear certain words and certain conversations about women. There are "certain" words and conversations unhappily impossible to eradicate in schools. Boys pure in mind and heart, almost children, are fond of talking in school among themselves, and even aloud, of things, pictures, and images of which even soldiers would sometimes hesitate to speak. More than that, much that soldiers have no knowledge or conception of is familiar to quite young children of our intellectual and higher classes. There is, however, in this no moral depravity, no real corrupt inner cynicism, but there is the appearance of it, and it is often looked upon among schoolboys as something subtle, daring, and worthy of imitation.

Seeing that Alyosha Karamazov put his fingers in his ears when they talked of "that," his schoolfellows sometimes crowded around him, pulled his hands away, and shouted nastiness into both his ears, while he struggled, slipped to the floor, tried to hide himself without uttering one word of abuse, enduring their insults in silence. But at last they gave up doing this. They left him alone and gave up teasing him about being a "regular girl." And what's more they began to look upon his modesty with compassion, as a weakness. He was always one of the best in the class but was never first.

At the time of Yefim Polenov's death Alyosha had two more years to complete at school. The widow went almost immediately after his death for a long visit to Italy with her whole family, which consisted only of women and girls. Alyosha went to live in the house of two distant relatives of Yefim Polenov, ladies whom he had never seen before. On what terms he lived with them he did not know himself. It was very characteristic of him that he never cared at whose expense he was living. In that respect he was a striking contrast to his elder brother Ivan, who struggled with poverty for his first two years in the university, supported himself, and had from childhood been bitterly conscious of living at the expense of his benefactor. But this strange trait in Alyosha's character must not, I think, be criticized too severely, for at the slightest acquaintance with

29

him one recognized that he was one of those youths, almost of the type of religious enthusiast, who, if they were suddenly to inherit a large fortune, would not hesitate to give it away for the asking, either for good works or to some schemer. He seemed scarcely to know the value of money; not, of course, in a literal sense. When he was given pocket-money, which he never asked for, he was either terribly careless with it so that it was gone in a moment, or he kept it for weeks not knowing what to do with it.

In later years Peter Miusov, a man very sensitive on the subject of money and bourgeois honesty, pronounced the following judgment after getting to know Alyosha: "Here is perhaps the one man in the world whom you might leave alone without a penny, in the center of an unknown town of a million inhabitants, and he would not come to harm. He would not die of cold and hunger, for he would be fed and sheltered at once; and if he were not, he would find a shelter for himself, and it would cost him no effort or humiliation. And to shelter him would be no burden, but, on the contrary, would probably be looked on as a pleasure."

Alyosha did not finish his schooling. A year before graduation, he suddenly announced to the ladies that he was going to see his father about a plan which had occurred to him. They were sorry and unwilling to let him go. The journey was not an expensive one, and the ladies would not let him pawn his watch, a parting present from his benefactor's family. They provided him with money and even bought him new clothes. But he returned half the money they gave him, saying that he intended to go third class.

On his arrival in the town he did not answer his father's first inquiry why he had come before completing his studies, and he seemed unusually thoughtful. It soon, however, became clear that he was looking for his mother's grave. He practically confessed at the time that that was the only object of his visit. But this can hardly have been the whole reason. It is more probable that he himself did not understand and could not explain what had suddenly arisen in his soul, and drawn him irresistibly into a new, unknown, but inevitable path.

His father, Fyodor Karamazov, could not show him where his second wife was buried, for he had never visited her grave since he had thrown earth upon her coffin, and in the course of years had entirely forgotten the place. He, by the way, had for some time not been living in our town. Three or four years after his wife's death he had gone to the south of Russia and finally turned up in Odessa, where he spent several years. He made the acquaintance at first, in his own words, "of a lot of low Jews, Jewesses, and Jewkins," and ended by being received by "Jews high and low alike." It may be presumed that at this period he developed a peculiar faculty for making and hoarding money.

He finally returned to our town only three years before Alyosha's arrival. His former acquaintances found him looking terribly aged, although he was by no means an old man. He behaved not exactly with more dignity but with more effrontery. The former buffoon showed an insolent ability for making buffoons of others. His depravity with women was not simply what it used to be, but even more revolting.

In a short time he opened a great number of new taverns in the district. It was evident that he had perhaps a hundred thousand roubles or not much less. Many of the inhabitants of the town and district were soon in his debt, and, of course, had given good security. Of late, too, he looked somehow bloated and seemed more irresponsible, more uneven, had sunk into a sort of incoherence, used to begin one thing and go on with another, as though he were letting himself go altogether. He was more and more frequently drunk. And, if it had not been for his servant Gregory, who by that time had aged considerably too, and used to look after him, Fyodor Karamazov might have gotten into serious trouble. Alyosha's arrival seemed to affect even his moral side, as though something had awakened in this prematurely old man which had long been dead in his soul.

"Do you know," he often said, looking at Alyosha, "that you are like her, the 'crazy woman' "—that was what he used to call his dead wife, Alyosha's mother.

It was Gregory who pointed out the "crazy woman's" grave to Alyosha. He took him to our town cemetery and showed him in a remote corner a cast-iron tombstone, cheap but decently kept, on which were inscribed the name and age of the deceased and the date of her death, and below a four-lined verse, such as are commonly used on old-fashioned middle-class tombs. To Alyosha's amazement all this turned out to be Gregory's doing. He had put it up on the poor "crazy woman's" grave at his own expense, after Fyodor Karamazov, whom he had often pestered about the grave, had gone to Odessa, abandoning the grave and all its memories.

Alyosha showed no particular emotion at the sight of his mother's grave. He only listened to Gregory's minute and solemn account of the crection of the tombstone; he stood with bowed head and walked away without uttering a word. It was perhaps a year before he visited the cemetery again.

But this little episode was not without an influence upon Fyodor Karamazov—and a very original one. He suddenly took a thousand roubles to our monastery to pay for requiems for the soul of his wife; but not for the second, Alyosha's mother, the "crazy woman," but for the first, Adelaide, who used to beat him. In the evening of the same day he got drunk and abused the monks to Alyosha. He was far from being religious; he had probably never put a penny candle before the image of a saint. Strange impulses of sudden feeling and sudden thought are common in such people.

31

I have mentioned already that he looked bloated. His appearance at this time bore traces of something that testified unmistakably to the life he had led. Besides the long fleshy bags under his little, always insolent, suspicious, and ironical eyes; besides the multitude of deep wrinkles in his little fat face, his Adam's apple hung below his sharp chin like a great, fleshy goitre. It gave him a peculiar, repulsive, sensual appearance. He had besides a long rapacious mouth with full lips, between which could be seen little stumps of black decayed teeth. He slobbered every time he began to speak. He liked to make fun of his own face, though, I believe, he was well satisfied with it. He often pointed to his nose, which was not very large, but very delicate and conspicuously aquiline. "A regular Roman nose," he used to say, "with my goitre I look like an ancient Roman patrician of the decadent period." He seemed proud of it.

Not long after visiting his mother's grave Alyosha suddenly announced that he wanted to enter the monastery, and that the monks were willing to receive him as a novice. He explained that this was his strongest desire. He solemnly asked his father's consent. The old man knew that the elder Zossima, who was living in the monastery hermitage, had made a special impression upon his "gentle boy."

"That is the most honest monk among them, of course," he observed, after listening in thoughtful silence to Alyosha, and seeming scarcely surprised at his request. "H'm! . . . So that's where you want to be, my gentle boy?"

He was half drunk, and suddenly he grinned his slow half-drunken grin, which was not without a certain cunning and slyness. "H'm! . . . I had an idea that you would end in something like this. Would you believe it? You were making straight for it. Well, to be sure you have your own two thousand. That's a dowry for you. And I'll never desert you, my angel. And I'll pay what's wanted for you there, if they ask for it. But, of course, if they don't ask, why should we worry them? What do you say? You know, you spend money like a canary, two grains a week. H'm! . . . Do you know that near one monastery there's a place outside the town where every baby knows there are none but 'the monks' wives' living, as they are called. Thirty women, I believe. I have been there myself. You know, it's interesting in its own way, of course, as a variety. The worst of it is it's awfully Russian. There are no French women there. Of course they could get them fast enough, they have plenty of money. If they get to hear of it they'll come along. Well, there's nothing of that sort here, no 'monks' wives,' and two hundred monks. They're honest. They keep the fasts. I admit it. . . . H'm! . . . So you want to be a monk? And do you know I'm sorry to lose you, Alyosha; would you believe it, I've really grown fond of you? Well, it's a good opportunity. You'll pray for us sinners; we have sinned too much here. I've always been wondering who would pray for me, and whether there was anyone in the world who would do it. My dear boy, I'm awfully stupid about that. You wouldn't believe it. Awfully. You see, however stupid I am about it, I keep thinking, I keep thinking —from time to time, of course, not all the while. It's impossible, I think, for the devils to forget to drag me down to hell with their hooks when I die. Then I wonder—hooks? Where would they get them? What of? Iron hooks? Where do they forge them? Have they a foundry there of some sort? The monks in the monastery probably believe that there's a ceiling in hell, for instance. Now I'm ready to believe in hell, but without a ceiling. It makes it more refined, more enlightened, more Lutheran that is. And, after all, what does it matter whether it has a ceiling or not? But, do you know, there's a damnable question involved in it? If there's no ceiling there can be no hooks, and if there are no hooks it all breaks down, which is unlikely again, for then there would be none to drag me down to hell, and if they don't drag me down what justice is there in the world? They would have to invent them, those hooks, on purpose for me alone, for, if you only knew, Alyosha, what a despicable person I am."

"But there are no hooks there," said Alyosha, looking gently and seriously at his father.

"Yes, yes, only the shadows of hooks. I know, I know. That's how a Frenchman described hell. 'I saw the shadow of a coachman that together with the shadow of a brush polished the shadow of a coach!' ... How do you know there are no hooks? When you've lived with the monks you'll sing a different tune. But go and get at the truth there, and then come and tell me. Anyway it's easier going to the other world if one knows what there is there. Besides, it will be more proper for you to be with the monks than here with me, with a drunken old man and young whores ... though you're like an angel, nothing touches you. And I think nothing will touch you there. That's why I let you go, because I hope for that. You've got all your wits about you. You will burn and you will burn out; you will be healed and come back again. And I will wait for you. I feel that you're the only creature in the world who has not condemned me. My dear boy, I feel it, you know. I can't help feeling it."

And he began blubbering. He was sentimental. He was evil and sentimental.

5. Elders

SOME OF MY READERS may imagine that Alyosha was a sickly, ecstatic, poorly developed creature, a pale, consumptive dreamer. On the contrary, he was at this time a well-grown, clear-eyed young man of nineteen, radiant with health. He was very handsome, too, graceful, moderately tall, with dark brown hair, with a regular, rather long, oval-shaped face, and wide-set dark gray eyes. He was very thoughtful and very serene.

I shall be told, perhaps, that radiant health is not incompatible with fanaticism and mysticism; but I believe that Alyosha was more of a realist than anyone. Oh! no doubt, in the monastery he fully believed in miracles, but, to my thinking, miracles are never a stumbling-block to the realist. It is not miracles that prompt realists to belief. The genuine realist, if he is an unbeliever, will always find strength and ability to disbelieve in the miraculous, and if he is confronted with a miracle as an irrefutable fact he would rather disbelieve his own senses than admit the fact. Even if he admits it, he admits it as a fact of nature till then unrecognized by him. Faith does not, in the realist, spring from the miracle but the miracle from faith. If the realist once believes, then he is bound by his very realism to admit the miraculous also. The Apostle Thomas said that he would not believe till he saw, but when he did see he said: "My Lord and my God!" Was it the miracle that forced him to believe? Most likely not, but he believed solely because he desired to believe and possibly he fully believed in his secret heart even when he said: "I do not believe till I see."

I shall be told, perhaps, that Alyosha was stupid, undeveloped, had not finished his studies, and so on. That he did not finish his studies is true, but to say that he was stupid or dull would be a great injustice. I'll simply repeat what I have said above. He entered upon this path only because, at that time, it alone struck his imagination and seemed to him to offer an ideal means of escape for his soul from darkness to light. Add to that that he was to some extent a youth of our past generation—that is, honest in nature, desiring the truth, seeking for it and believing in it, and seeking to serve it at once with all the strength of his soul, seeking for immediate action, and ready to sacrifice everything, even life itself. These young men unhappily fail to understand that the sacrifice of life is, in many cases, the easiest of all sacrifices. They fail to understand that to sacrifice five or six years of their seething youth to hard and tedious study, if only to multiply ten-fold their powers of serving the truth and the cause they have set before them as their goal, is utterly beyond the strength of many of them.

The path Alyosha chose was a path going in the opposite direction, but he chose it with the same thirst for swift achievement. As soon as he reflected seriously he was convinced of the existence of God and immortality, and at once he instinctively said to himself: "I want to live for immortality, and I will accept no compromise." In the same way, if he had decided that God and immortality did not exist, he would at once have become an atheist and a socialist. For socialism is not merely the labor question, it is before all things the atheistic question, the question of the form taken by atheism today. It is the question of the tower of Babel built without God, not to mount to Heaven from earth but to set up Heaven on earth. Alyosha would have found it strange and impossible to go on living as before. It is written: "Give all that thou hast to the poor and follow Me, if thou wouldst be perfect."

Alyosha said to himself: "I can't give two roubles instead of 'all,' and only go to mass instead of 'following Him.' " Perhaps his memories of childhood brought back our monastery, to which his mother may have taken him to mass. Perhaps the slanting sunlight and the holy image to which his poor "crazy" mother had held him up still worked upon his imagination. Brooding on these things he may have come to us perhaps only to see whether here he could sacrifice all or only "two roubles," and in the monastery he met this elder.

I must digress to explain what an "elder" is in Russian monasteries, and I am sorry that I do not feel very competent to do so. I will try, however, to give a superficial account of it in a few words. Authorities on the subject assert that the institution of "elders" is of recent date, not more than a hundred years old in our monasteries, though in the orthodox East, especially in Sinai and Athos, it has existed over a thousand years. It is maintained that it existed in ancient times in Russia also, but through the calamities which overtook Russia—the Tatars, civil war, the interruption of relations with the East after the destruction of Constantinople—this institution fell into oblivion. It was revived among us towards the end of the last century by one of the great "ascetics," as they called him, Passy Velitchkovsky, and his disciples. But to this day it has been adopted by only a few monasteries, and has sometimes been almost persecuted as an innovation in Russia. It flourished especially in the celebrated Kozelski Optin Monastery. When and how it was introduced into our monastery I cannot say. We had already had three such elders and Zossima was the last of them. But he was almost dying of weakness and disease, and there was no one to take his place. The question for our monastery was an important one, for it had not been distinguished by anything in particular till then: it had neither relics of saints, nor wonder-working ikons, nor glorious traditions, nor historical claims. Our monastery had flourished and been glorious all over Russia only because of its elders. And pilgrims had flocked for thousands of miles, from all parts, to see and hear them.

What was such an elder? An elder was one who took your soul, your will, into his soul and his will. When you choose an elder, you renounce your own will and yield it to him in complete submission, complete self-abnegation. This novitiate, this terrible school of abnegation, is undertaken voluntarily, in the hope of self-conquest, of self-mastery, in order, after a life of obedience, to attain perfect freedom, that is, from self; to escape the lot of those who have lived their whole life without finding their true selves in themselves. This institution of elders is not founded on theory, but was established in the East from the practice of a thousand years. The obligations due to an elder are not the ordinary "obedience" which has always existed in our Russian monasteries. The obligation involves confession to the elder by all who have submitted themselves to him, and an indissoluble bond between him and them.

The story is told, for instance, that in the early days of Christianity a novice, failing to fulfill some command laid upon him by his elder, left his monastery in Syria and went to Egypt. There, after great deeds he was found worthy at last to suffer torture and a martyr's death for the faith. When the Church, regarding him as a saint, was burying him, suddenly at the deacon's command: "Depart all ye unbaptized," the coffin containing the martyr's body left its place and was cast forth from the church. This took place three times. And only later they learnt that this holy man had broken his vow of obedience and left his elder and, therefore, could not be forgiven without the elder's absolution in spite of his great deeds. Only after this could the funeral take place. This, of course, is only a legend. But here is a recent instance.

A monk was suddenly commanded by his elder to leave Athos, which he loved as a sacred place and a haven of refuge, and to go first to Jerusalem to do homage to the Holy Places and then to the north to Siberia: "There is the place for thee and not here." The monk overwhelmed with sorrow went to the Ecumenical Patriarch at Constantinople and besought him to release him from his obedience. But the Patriarch replied that not only was he unable to release him, but that there was no power on earth which could release him except the elder who had himself laid the duty upon him. This shows how the elders are endowed in certain cases with unbounded authority. And that is why in many of our monasteries the institution was at first resisted almost to persecution. But in time the elders began to be highly esteemed among the people. Masses of the ignorant as well as men of distinction flocked, for instance, to the elders of our monastery to confess their doubts, their sins, and their sufferings, and ask for counsel and admonition. Seeing this, the opponents of the elders declared that the sacrament of confession was being arbitrarily and frivolously degraded, though the continual opening of the heart to the elder by the monk or the layman had nothing of the character of the sacrament. In the end, however, the institution of elders has been retained and is becoming established in Russian monasteries. It is true, perhaps, that this practice which had stood the test of a thousand years for the moral regeneration of a man from slavery to freedom and to moral perfection may be a two-edged weapon and that it may lead some not to humility and complete self-control but to the most Satanic pride, that is, to bondage and not to freedom.

The elder Zossima was sixty-five. He came of a family of landowners, had been in the army in his early youth, and had served in the Caucasus as an officer. He had impressed Alyosha by some peculiar quality of his soul. Alyosha lived in the cell of the elder, who was very fond of him and let him wait upon him. It must however be noted that Alyosha was bound by no obligation and could go where he pleased and be absent for whole days. Though he wore the monastic dress it was voluntarily, not to be different from others. He liked to do so. Possibly his youthful imagination was deeply stirred by the power and fame of his elder. It was said that so many people had for years past come to confess their sins to Father Zossima and to entreat him for words of advice and healing, that he had acquired the keenest intuition and could tell from a stranger's face what he wanted, and what was the suffering on his conscience. He sometimes astonished and almost alarmed his visitors by his knowledge of their secrets before they had spoken a word.

Alyosha noticed that many, almost all, went in to the elder for the first time with apprehension and uneasiness, but came out with bright and happy faces. He was particularly struck by the fact that Father Zossima was not at all stern. On the contrary, he was always almost gay. The monks used to say that he was more drawn to those who were more sinful, and the greater the sinner the more he loved him.

There were, no doubt, up to the end of his life, among the monks some who hated and envied him. But they were few in number and they were silent. Among them however were some of great dignity in the monastery, one, for instance, of the older monks distinguished for his strict keeping of fasts and vows of silence. But the majority were on Father Zossima's side and many of them loved him with all their hearts, warmly and sincerely. Some were almost fanatically devoted to him, and declared, though not quite aloud, that he was a saint, that there could be no doubt of it, and, seeing that his death was near, they anticipated miracles and great glory to the monastery in the immediate future from his relics.

Alyosha had unquestioning faith in the miraculous power of the elder, just as he had unquestioning faith in the story of the coffin that flew out of the church. He saw many who came with sick children or relatives and besought the elder to lay hands on them and to pray over them, return shortly after— some the next day—and, falling in tears at the elder's feet, thank him for healing their sick.

Whether they had really been healed or were simply better in the natural course of the disease was a question which did not exist for Alyosha. He fully believed in the spiritual power of his teacher and rejoiced in his fame, in his glory, as though it were his own triumph. His heart throbbed, and he glowed, as it were, all over when the elder came out to the gates of the hermitage into the waiting crowd of pilgrims of the humbler class who had flocked from all parts of Russia to see him and obtain his blessing. They fell down before him, wept, kissed his feet, kissed the earth on which he stood, and wailed, while the women held up their children to him and brought him the sick "possessed with devils." The elder spoke to them, read a brief prayer over them, blessed them, and dismissed them.

Of late he had become so weak because of illness that he was sometimes unable to leave his cell, and the pilgrims often waited several days for him to come out. Alyosha did not wonder why they loved him so, why they fell down before him and wept merely at seeing his face. Oh! he understood that for the humble soul of the Russian peasant, worn out by grief and toil, and still more by everlasting injustice and everlasting sin, his own and the world's, it was of the greatest need and comfort to find someone or something holy to fall down before and worship.

"Among us there is sin, injustice, and temptation, but yet, somewhere on earth there is someone holy and exalted. He has the truth. He knows the truth. So truth is not dead upon the earth; it will come one day to us, too, and rule over all the earth according to the promise."

Alyosha knew that this was just how the people felt and even reasoned. He understood it, but that the elder Zossima was this saint and custodian of God's truth—of that he had no more doubt than the weeping peasants and the sick women who held out their children to the elder. The conviction that after his death the elder would bring extraordinary glory to the monastery was even stronger in Alyosha than in any one there, and, of late a kind of deep flame of inner ecstasy burnt more and more strongly in his heart. He was not at all troubled at this elder's standing as a solitary example before him.

"He is holy. He carries in his heart the secret of renewal for all: that power which will, at last, establish truth on the earth. All men will then be holy and love one another. And there will be no more rich nor poor, no exalted nor humbled, but all will be as the children of God, and the true Kingdom of Christ will come." That was the dream in Alyosha's heart.

The arrival of his two brothers made a great impression on Alyosha. He made friends more quickly with his half-brother Dmitri (though he arrived later) than with his own brother Ivan, whom he scarcely knew. He was extremely interested in his brother Ivan, but after Ivan had been two months in our town, though they had met fairly often, they were still not intimate. Alyosha was naturally silent, and he seemed to be expecting something, ashamed about something, while his brother Ivan, though Alyosha noticed at first that he looked long and curiously at him, seemed soon to have stopped thinking of him. Alyosha noticed it with some embarrassment. He attributed his brother's coolness at first to the difference in their age and education. But he also wondered whether the absence of curiosity

38

and sympathy in Ivan might be due to some other cause entirely unknown to him. He kept thinking that Ivan was absorbed in something—something inward and important—that he was striving toward some goal, perhaps very hard to attain, and that that was why he had no thought for him. Alyosha wondered, too, whether there was not some contempt on the part of Ivan for him—a foolish novice. He was certain that his brother was an atheist. He could not take offense at this contempt, if it existed; yet, with an uneasy embarrassment which he did not himself understand, he waited for his brother to come nearer to him.

Dmitri used to speak of Ivan with the deepest respect and with a peculiar earnestness. From him Alyosha learnt all the details of the important affair which had of late formed such a close and remarkable bond between these two half-brothers. Dmitri's enthusiasm for Ivan was the more striking in Alyosha's eyes since Dmitri was, compared with Ivan, almost uneducated, and the two were such a contrast in personality and character that it would be difficult to find two men more unlike.

It was at this time a meeting, or, rather gathering of the members of this discordant family took place in the cell of the elder who had such an extraordinary influence on Alyosha. The pretext for this gathering was a false one. It was at this time that the trouble between Dmitri and their father seemed at its most acute stage and their relations had become dangerously strained.

Fyodor Karamazov seems to have been the first to suggest, apparently as a joke, that they should all meet in Father Zossima's cell. He said that without appealing to his direct intervention, they might more decently come to an understanding under the conciliating influence of the elder's presence.

Dmitri, who had never seen the elder, suspected that his father was trying to intimidate him, but, as he secretly blamed himself for his outbursts of temper with his father on several recent occasions, he accepted the proposal. It must be noted that he was not, like Ivan, staying with his father, but living at the other end of the town. It happened that Peter Miusov, who was staying in the district at the time, favored the idea. A Liberal of the forties and fifties, a freethinker and atheist, he may have been led on by boredom and the hope of diversion. He was suddenly seized with the desire to see the monastery and the holy man. As his lawsuit with the monastery still dragged on, he made it the pretext for seeing the Superior, in order to attempt to settle it amicably. A visitor coming with such laudible intentions might be received with more attention and consideration than if he came from simple curiosity.

And so influences from within the monastery were brought to bear on the elder, who of late had scarcely left his cell, and had been forced by illness to deny even his ordinary visitors. In the end he consented to see them, and the day was fixed.

"Who has made me a judge over them?" was all he said, smiling to Alyosha.

Alyosha was very disturbed when he heard of the proposed visit. Of all the wrangling, quarrelsome group, Dmitri was the only one who could possibly regard the interview seriously. All the others would come from unworthy motives, perhaps insulting to the elder. Alyosha was well aware of that. Ivan and Miusov would come from curiosity, perhaps of the coarsest kind, while his father might be planning some piece of buffoonery. Though he said nothing, Alyosha thoroughly understood his father. The young man, I repeat, was far from being so simple as everyone thought him.

Alyosha awaited the day with a heavy heart. He undoubtedly wondered how the family troubles could be ended. But his chief anxiety concerned the elder. He trembled for him, for his glory, and dreaded any affront to him, especially the refined, courteous irony of Miusov and the supercilious half-utterances of the highly educated Ivan. He even wanted to warn the elder, telling him something about them, but, on second thought, said nothing. He only sent word the day before, through a friend, to his brother Dmitri, that he loved him and expected him to keep his promise. Dmitri wondered, for he could not remember what he had promised. However, he answered by letter that he would do his utmost not to let himself be provoked "by vileness," but that, although he had a deep respect for the elder and for his brother Ivan, he was convinced that the meeting was either a trap for him or some degrading joke.

"Nevertheless I would rather bite out my tongue than be lacking in respect to the sainted man whom you reverence so highly," he wrote in conclusion. But Alyosha was not greatly cheered by this letter.

BOOK II: AN UNFORTUNATE GATHERING

1. They Arrive at the Monastery

IT WAS A WARM, BRIGHT DAY at the end of August. The interview with the elder had been fixed for half-past eleven, immediately after late mass. Our visitors did not take part in the service, but arrived just as it was over.

First an elegant open carriage, drawn by two fine horses, drove up with Miusov and a distant relative of his, a young man of twenty, called Peter Kalganov. This young man was preparing to enter a university. Miusov, with whom he was staying, was trying to persuade him to go abroad to the university of Zurich or Jena. The young man was undecided. He was thoughtful and absent-minded. He was nice-looking, strongly built, and rather tall. He had a strange fixed gaze at times. Like all very absent-minded people he would sometimes stare at a person without seeing him. He was silent and rather awkward, but sometimes, when he was alone with someone he became talkative and effusive, and would laugh at anything or nothing. But his animation vanished as quickly as it appeared. He was always well and even elegantly dressed. He had already some independent fortune and expectations of much more. He was a friend of Alyosha's.

In a shabby, jolting, but roomy hired carriage, with a pair of old pinkish-gray horses, a long way behind Miusov's carriage, came Fyodor Karamazov with his son Ivan. Dmitri was late, though he had been informed of the time the evening before.

The visitors left their carriage at the hotel outside the grounds, and went to the gates of the monastery on foot. Except for the old Karamazov, none of the party had ever seen the monastery; Miusov had probably not even been to church for thirty years. He looked about him with curiosity and assumed ease. But, except for the church and the domestic buildings, though these too were ordinary enough, he found nothing of interest in the interior of the monastery.

The last of the worshippers were coming out of the church, bareheaded and crossing themselves. Among the humbler people were a few of higher rank—two or three ladies and a very old general. They were all staying at the hotel. Our visitors were at once surrounded by beggars, but none of them gave them anything, except young Kalganov, who took a ten-kopeck piece out of his purse and nervous and embarrassed—God knows why!—hurriedly gave it to an old woman, saying: "Divide it equally." No one remarked about it, so that he had no reason to be embarrassed; but noticing this he was even more uncomfortable.

It was strange that their arrival did not seem expected, and that they were not received with special honor. One of them, the old Karamazov, had recently made a donation of a thousand roubles, while another, Peter Miusov, was a very wealthy and highly cultured landowner, upon whom all in the monastery were in a sense dependent. The decision of his lawsuit might at any moment put their fishing rights in his hands. Yet no official person met them.

Miusov looked absent-mindedly at the tombstones around the church. He was on the point of saying that the dead buried here must have paid a pretty penny for the right of lying in this "holy place," but he refrained. His liberal irony was rapidly changing almost into anger.

"Who the devil is there to ask in this place? We must find

out, for time is passing," he observed suddenly, as though speaking to himself.

All at once a bald-headed man appeared. He was an elderly man with ingratiating little eyes, wearing a full, summer overcoat. Lifting his hat, he introduced himself with a honeyed lisp as Maximov, a landowner of Tula. He at once entered into our visitors' difficulty.

"Father Zossima lives in the hermitage, apart, four hundred yards from the monastery, the other side of the grove."

"I know it's the other side of the grove," observed Fyodor Karamazov, "but we don't remember the way. It is a long time since we've been here."

"This way, by this gate, and straight across the grove . . . the grove. Come with me, won't you? I'll show you. I have to go . . . I am going myself. This way, this way."

They went through the gate and turned toward the grove. Maximov, a man of sixty, ran rather than walked, turning sideways to stare at them all, with an incredible degree of nervous curiosity. His eyes bulged out of his head.

"You see, we have come to the elder upon private business," observed Miusov sternly. "His eminence has granted us an audience so to speak, and so, though we thank you for showing us the way, we cannot ask you to accompany us."

"I've been there. I've already been there. A perfect cavalier!" and Maximov snapped his fingers in the air.

"Who is a cavalier?" asked Miusov.

"The elder, the splendid elder, the elder! The honor and glory of the monastery, Zossima. Such an elder!"

But his incoherent talk was cut short by a very pale, wan-looking monk of medium height, wearing a monk's cap, who overtook them. Fyodor Karamazov and Miusov stopped.

The monk, with an extremely courteous, profound bow, announced: "The Father Superior invites all of you gentlemen to dine with him after your visit to the hermitage. At one o'clock, not later. And you also," he added, addressing Maximov.

"That I certainly will, without fail," cried Fyodor Karamazov, greatly delighted at the invitation. "And, believe me, we've all given our word to behave properly here. . . . And you, Peter Miusov, will you go, too?"

"Yes, of course. What have I come for but to study all the customs here? The only obstacle to me is your company. . . ."

"Yes, Dmitri has not arrived as yet."

"It would be a wonderful thing if he didn't turn up. Do you think I like all this business, and in your company, too? So we will come to dinner. Thank the Father Superior," he said to the monk.

"No, it is my duty now to conduct you to the elder," answered the monk.

"If so I'll go straight to the Father Superior—to the Father Superior," babbled Maximov.

"The Father Superior is engaged just now. But as you please. . . ." the monk hesitated.

"Impertinent old man!" Miusov observed aloud, while Maximov ran back to the monastery.

"He's like Von Sohn," Fyodor Karamazov said suddenly.

"Is that all you can think of? . . . In what way is he like Von Sohn? Have you ever seen Von Sohn?"

"I've seen his portrait. It's not the features, but something indefinable. He's a second Von Sohn. I can always tell from the physiognomy."

"Ah, I dare say you are a connoisseur in such things. But look here, Fyodor Karamazov, you said just now that we had given our word to behave properly. Remember it. I advise you to control yourself. But, if you begin to play the fool I don't intend to be associated with you here. . . . You see what a man he is!" He turned to the monk. "I'm afraid to go among decent people with him." A smile, not without a certain slyness, came to the pale, bloodless lips of the monk, but he made no reply, and was evidently silent from a sense of his own dignity.

Miusov frowned more than ever. "Oh, the devil take them all! An outer show built up through centuries, and nothing but charlatanism and nonsense underneath," flashed through Miusov's mind.

"Here's the hermitage. We've arrived," cried Fyodor Karamazov. "The gates are shut." And he repeatedly made the sign of the cross to the saints painted above and on the sides of the gates. "When you go to Rome you must do as the Romans do. Here in this hermitage there are twenty-five saints being saved. They look at one another, and eat cabbages. And not one woman goes in at this gate. That's what is remarkable. And that really is so. But I did hear that the elder receives ladies," he remarked suddenly to the monk.

"Women of the people are here even now, lying in the portico there waiting. But for ladies of higher rank two rooms have been built adjoining the portico, but outside the grounds—you can see the windows—and the elder goes out to them by an inner passage when he is well enough. They are always outside the grounds. There is a Harkov lady, Madame Hohlakov, waiting there now with her sick daughter. Probably he has promised to come out to her, though of late he has been so weak that he has hardly shown himself even to the people."

"So then there are loopholes, after all, to creep out of the hermitage to the ladies. Don't suppose, holy father, that I mean any harm. But do you know that at Athos not only the visits of women are not allowed, but no creature of the female sex—no hens, nor turkey-hens, nor cows."

"Fyodor Karamazov, I warn you I shall go back and leave you here. They'll turn you out when I'm gone."

"But I'm not interfering with you, Peter Miusov. Look," he

cried suddenly, stepping within the grounds, "what a vale of roses they live in!"

Though there were no roses blooming then, there were rare and beautiful autumn flowers growing wherever there was space for them, evidently tended by a skillful hand. There were flower-beds around the church and between the tombs. And the one-storied wooden house where the elder lived was also surrounded with flowers.

"And it was like this in the time of the last elder, Varsonofy? He didn't care for such elegance. They say he used to jump up and beat even ladies with a stick," observed Fyodor Karamazov as he went up the steps.

"The elder Varsonofy did sometimes seem rather strange, but a great deal that's told about him is nonsense. He never beat anyone," answered the monk. "Now, gentlemen, if you will wait a minute I will announce you."

"Fyodor Karamazov, for the last time, your promise, do you hear? Behave properly or I will get even with you!" Miusov had time to mutter again.

"I can't think why you are so upset," Fyodor Karamazov said sarcastically. "Are you uneasy about your sins? They say he can tell by one's eyes what one has come about. And what a lot you think of their opinion! You, a Parisian, and so advanced. I'm surprised at you."

But Miusov had no time to reply to this sarcasm. They were asked to come in. He walked in, somewhat irritated. "Now, I know myself, I am annoyed, I shall lose my temper and begin to quarrel—and lower myself and my ideas," he reflected.

2. The Old Buffoon

THEY ENTERED THE ROOM almost at the same moment that the elder came in from his bedroom. There were already in the cell, awaiting the elder, two monks of the hermitage, Father Joseph the librarian, and Father Paissy, a very learned man, so they said, in delicate health though not old. There was also a tall young man, who looked about two and twenty, standing in the corner throughout the interview. He had a broad, fresh face, and clever, observant, narrow brown eyes, and was wearing ordinary dress. His name was Rakitln. He was a divinity student, living under the protection of the monastery. His expression was one of unquestioning, but self-respecting, reverence. Being in a subordinate and dependent position and therefore not on equal terms with the guests, he did not greet them with a bow.

Father Zossima was accompanied by Alyosha and a novice. The two monks rose and greeted him with a very deep bow, touching the ground with their fingers. Then they kissed his hand. Blessing them, the elder replied with as deep a reverence to them, and asked their blessing.

The whole ceremony was performed very seriously and with an appearance of feeling, not like an everyday rite. But Miusov imagined that it was all done with intentional impressiveness. He stood in front of the other visitors. He ought—he had reflected upon it the evening before—from simple politeness, since it was the custom here, to have gone up to receive the elder's blessing, even if he did not kiss his hand. But when he saw all this bowing and kissing on the part of the monks he instantly changed his mind. With dignified gravity he made a rather deep, conventional bow and moved away to a chair. Fyodor Karamazov did the same, mimicking Miusov like an ape. Ivan bowed with great dignity and courtesy, but he too kept his hands at his sides, while Kalganov was so confused that he did not bow at all.

The elder let fall the hand raised to bless them, and bowing to them again, asked them all to sit down. The blood rushed to Alyosha's cheeks. He was ashamed. His forebodings were coming true.

Father Zossima sat down on a very old-fashioned mahogany sofa, covered with leather, and made his visitors sit down in a row along the opposite wall on four mahogany chairs, covered with shabby black leather. The monks sat, one at the door and the other at the window. Rakitin, the divinity student, Porfiry the novice, and Alyosha remained standing.

The cell was not very large and had a faded look. It contained nothing but the most necessary furniture, of coarse and poor quality. There were two pots of flowers in the window, and a number of holy pictures in the corner. Before one huge ancient ikon of the Virgin a lamp was burning. Near it were two other holy pictures in shining settings and next to them carved cherubim, china eggs, a Catholic cross of ivory with a Mater Dolorosa embracing it, and several foreign engravings from the great Italian artists of past centuries. Next to these fine engravings were several of the roughest Russian prints of saints and martyrs, such as are sold for a few pennies at fairs. On the other walls were portraits of Russian bishops, past and present.

Miusov took a quick glance at all these "conventional" surroundings and then looked intently upon the elder. He had a high opinion of his own insight, a weakness excusable in him as he was fifty, an age at which a clever worldly man can hardly help taking himself rather seriously. He did not like Zossima. There was, indeed, something in the elder's face which many people besides Miusov might not have liked. He was a short, bent, little man, with very weak legs, and though

45

he was only sixty-five, he looked at least ten years older. His face was very thin and covered with a network of fine wrinkles, particularly about his eyes, which were small, light-colored, quick, and shining like two bright points. He had a sprinkling of gray hair about his temples. His pointed beard was small and scanty and his lips, which smiled frequently, were as thin as two threads. His nose was not long but sharp like a bird's beak.

"To all appearances a malicious soul, full of petty pride," thought Miusov. He felt altogether dissatisfied with having come.

A cheap little clock on the wall hurriedly struck twelve and served to begin the conversation.

"We are precisely on time," cried Fyodor Karamazov. "But no sign of my son, Dmitri. I apologize for him, sacred elder!" (Alyosha shuddered all over at "sacred elder.") "I am always punctual myself, minute for minute, remembering that punctuality is the courtesy of kings . . ."

"But you are not a king, anyway," Miusov muttered, losing his self-restraint at once.

"Yes, that's true. I'm not a king and would you believe it, I was aware of that myself. But, there! I always say the wrong thing. Your reverence," he cried, with sudden pathos, "you behold before you a buffoon! I introduce myself as such. It's an old habit, alas! And if I sometimes talk nonsense it's with an object, with the object of amusing people and making myself agreeable. One must be agreeable, mustn't one? . . . I was seven years ago in a little town where I had business, and I made friends with some merchants there. We went to the captain of police because we had to see him about something and we asked him to dine with us. He was a tall, fat, fair, sulky man, the most dangerous type in such cases. It's their liver. I went straight up to him, and with the ease of a man of the world, you know: 'Mr. Ispravnik,' said I, 'be our Napravnik.' 'What do you mean by Napravnik?' said he. I saw, at the first half-second, that my joke had missed fire. He stood there so glum. 'I wanted to make a joke,' said I, 'for the general diversion, as Mr. Napravnik is our well-known Russian orchestra conductor and what we need for the harmony of our undertaking is someone of that sort.' And I explained my comparison very reasonably, didn't I? 'Excuse me,' said he, 'I am an Ispravnik, and I do not allow puns to be made on my calling.' He turned and walked away. I followed him, shouting, 'Yes, yes, you are an Ispravnik, not a Napravnik.' 'No,' he said, 'since you called me a Napravnik I am one.' And would you believe it, it ruined our business! And I'm always like that, always like that. Always injuring myself with my politeness. . . . Once, many years ago, I said to an influential person: 'Your wife is a ticklish lady,' in an honorable sense, of the moral qualities, so to speak. But he asked me, 'Why, have you tickled her?' I thought I'd be polite, so I couldn't help saying 'Yes.' And he gave me a fine tickling on the spot. It happened long ago, so I'm not ashamed to tell the story. I'm always injuring myself like that."

"You're doing it now," muttered Miusov with disgust.

Father Zossima studied them both in silence.

"Am I? Would you believe it, I was aware of that, too, Peter Miusov. And let me tell you I foresaw I would as soon as I began to speak. And do you know I foresaw, too, that you'd be the first to remark about it. . . . The minute I see my joke isn't coming off, your reverence, both my cheeks feel as though they were drawn down to the lower jaw and there is almost a spasm in them. It's been that way since I was young, when I had to tell jokes for my living in noblemen's families. I am an inveterate buffoon and have been so from my birth, your reverence. It's as though it were a craze in me. I daresay it's a devil within me. But only a little one. A more serious one would have chosen another lodging. But not your soul, Peter Miusov; you're not a lodging worth having either. But I do believe—I believe in God, though I have had doubts of late. But now I sit and await words of wisdom. I'm like the philosopher, Diderot, your reverence. Did you ever hear, most Holy Father, how Diderot went to see the Metropolitan Platon, in the time of the Empress Catherine? He went in and said straight out, 'There is no God.' To which the great Bishop lifted up his finger and answered, 'The fool has said in his heart there is no God.' And Diderot fell down at his feet on the spot. 'I believe,' he cried, 'and will be christened.' And so he was. Princess Dashkov was his godmother and Potyomkin his godfather."

"Fyodor Karamazov, this is unbearable! You know you're telling lies and that that stupid anecdote isn't true. Why are you playing the fool?" cried Miusov in a shaking voice.

"I suspected all my life that it wasn't true," Fyodor Karamazov cried with conviction. "But I'll tell you the whole truth, gentlemen. Great elder! Forgive me, the last thing about Diderot's christening I made up just now. I never thought of it before. I made it up to add spice. I play the fool to make myself agreeable. Though I really don't know myself, sometimes, what I do it for. And as for Diderot, I heard as far as 'the fool hath said in his heart' twenty times from the gentry about here when I was young. I heard your aunt, Peter Miusov, tell the story. They all believe to this day that the infidel Diderot came to argue about God with the Metropolitan Platon. . . ."

Miusov got up, forgetting himself in his impatience. He was furious and conscious of being ridiculous.

What was taking place in the cell was really incredible. For forty or fifty years past, from the times of former elders, no visitors had entered that cell without feelings of the profoundest veneration. Almost everyone admitted to the cell felt that a great favor was being shown him. Many remained kneeling during the whole visit. Of those visitors, many had been men of high rank and learning, some even freethinkers, attracted by curiosity. But all without exception had shown the most profound reverence and delicacy, for here there was no question of money, but only, on the one side love and kindness, and on the other penitence and an eager desire to decide some spiritual problem or crisis. So that such buffoonery amazed and bewildered those present, or at least some of them. The monks, with unchanged expressions, waited with earnest attention to hear what the elder would say. They seemed on the point of standing up, like Miusov. Alyosha stood, with hanging head, on the verge of tears. What seemed to him strangest of all was that his brother Ivan, on whom alone he had rested his hopes, and who alone had such influence on his father that he could have stopped him, sat quite unmoved, with downcast eyes, apparently waiting with interest to see how it would end as though he had nothing to do with it. Alyosha did not dare to look at Rakitin, the divinity student, whom he knew almost intimately. He alone in the monastery knew Rakitin's thoughts.

"Forgive me," began Miusov addressing Father Zossima, "for perhaps I seem to be taking part in this shameful scene. I made a mistake in believing that a man like Fyodor Karamazov would understand what was due on a visit to so honored a person. I did not think I would have to apologise simply for having come with him. . . ." Peter Miusov could say no more, and was about to leave the room overwhelmed with confusion.

"Don't distress yourself, I beg." The elder rose to his feeble legs and taking Peter Miusov by both hands made him sit down again. "I beg you not to disturb yourself. I particularly beg you to be my guest." And with a bow he went back and sat down again on his little sofa.

"Great elder, speak! Do I annoy you by my talk?" Fyodor Karamazov cried suddenly, clutching the arms of his chair in both hands as though ready to leap up from it if the answer were unfavorable.

"I earnestly beg you, too, not to disturb yourself, and not to be uneasy," the elder said earnestly. "Do not trouble. Make yourself quite at home. And, above all, do not be so ashamed of yourself, for that is at the root of it all."

"Quite at home? To be my natural self? Oh, that is much too much, but I accept it gratefully. Do you know, blessed father, you'd better not invite me to be my natural self. Don't risk it. . . . I will not go so far as that myself. I warn you for your own sake. Well, the rest is still plunged in the mists of uncertainty, though there are people who'd be pleased to describe me for you. I mean that for you, Peter Miusov. But as

48

for you, holy being, let me tell you, I am filled with ecstasy."

He got up and throwing up his hands, called out, "Blessed be the womb that bore thee, and the paps that gave thee suck —the paps especially. When you said just now 'Don't be so ashamed of yourself for that is at the root of it all,' you pierced right through me by that remark, and read me to the core. Indeed, I always feel when I meet people that I am lower than all, and that they all take me for a buffoon. So I say: 'Let me really play the buffoon. I am not afraid of your opinion, for you are every one of you worse than I am.' That is why I am a buffoon. It is from shame, great elder, from shame; it's simply over-sensitiveness that makes me rowdy. If I had only been sure that everyone would accept me as the kindest and wisest of men, oh, Lord, what a good man I would have been! Teacher!" He fell suddenly on his knees. "What must I do to gain eternal life?"

It was difficult even now to decide whether he was joking or really moved.

Father Zossima, lifting his eyes, looked at him and said with a smile: "You have known for a long time what you must do. You have sense enough. Don't give way to drunkenness and incontinence of speech. Don't give way to sensual lust. And, above all, to the love of money. And close your taverns. If you can't close all, at least two or three. And, above all— don't lie."

"You mean about Diderot?"

"No, not about Diderot. Above all, don't lie to yourself. The man who lies to himself and listens to his own lie comes to such a point that he cannot distinguish the truth within him, or around him, and so loses all respect for himself and for others. And having no respect he ceases to love. And in order to distract himself without love he gives way to passions and coarse pleasures and sinks to bestiality in his vices—all this from continual lying to other men and to himself. The man who lies to himself can be more easily offended than anyone else. You know it is sometimes very pleasant to take offense, isn't it? A man may know that nobody has insulted him, but that he has invented the insult for himself, has lied and exaggerated to make it picturesque, has caught at a word and made a mountain out of a molehill—he knows that himself, yet he will be the first to take offense, and will revel in his resentment till he feels great pleasure in it. And so he will pass to genuine vindictiveness. . . . But get up. Sit down, I beg you. All this, too, is deceitful posturing . . ."

"Blessed man! Give me your hand to kiss."

Fyodor Karamazov went up quickly and imprinted a kiss on the elder's thin hand. "It is, it is pleasant to take offense. You said that better than I ever heard it before. Yes, I have all my life taken offense, to please myself. Taken offense on aesthetic grounds, for it is not so much pleasant as distinguished

49

sometimes to be insulted—that you had forgotten, great elder, it is distinguished! I shall make a note of that. But I have been lying, lying my whole life long, every day and hour of it. Of a truth, I am a lie, and the father of lies. Though I believe I am not the father of lies. I am getting mixed in my texts. Say, the son of lies, and that will be enough. Only . . . my angel . . . I may sometimes talk about Diderot! Diderot will do no harm, though sometimes a word will do harm. . . . Great elder, by the way, I was forgetting, though I had been meaning for the last two years to come here on purpose to ask and to find out something. Only tell Peter Miusov not to interrupt me. Here is my question: Is it true, great Father, that the story is told somewhere in the 'Lives of the Saints' of a holy saint martyred for his faith who, when his head was cut off at last, stood up, picked up his head, and, 'courteously kissing it,' walked a long way, carrying it in his hands. Is that true or not, honored Father?"

"No. It is untrue," said the elder.

"There is nothing of the kind in all the lives of the saints. What saint do you say the story is about?" asked the Father Librarian.

"I don't know what saint. I don't know and can't tell. I was deceived. I was told the story. I had heard it, and do you know who told it? Peter Miusov here, who was so angry just now about Diderot. He told the story."

"I have never told it to you. I never speak to you at all."

"It is true you did not tell me, but you told it when I was present. It was three years ago. I mentioned it because by that ridiculous story you shook my faith, Peter Miusov. You didn't realize it but I went home with my faith shaken, and I have been getting more and more shaken ever since. Yes, Peter Miusov, you were the cause of a great fall. That was not a Diderot!"

Fyodor Karamazov got excited. It was perfectly clear to everyone by now that he was playing a part again. Yet Miusov was stung by his words.

"What nonsense. It is all nonsense," he muttered. "I may really have told it, sometime or other . . . but not to you. It was told to me. I heard it in Paris from a Frenchman. He told me it was read at our mass from the 'Lives of the Saints' . . . He was a very learned man who had made a special study of Russian statistics and had lived a long time in Russia. . . . I have not read the 'Lives of the Saints' myself, and I am not going to read them . . . All sorts of things are said at dinner—we were dining then."

"Yes, you were dining then, and so I lost my faith!" said Fyodor Karamazov, mimicking him.

"What do I care for your faith?" Miusov was on the point of shouting. But he suddenly checked himself, and said instead with contempt: "You defile everything you touch."

The elder suddenly rose from his seat. "Excuse me, gentlemen, for leaving you a few minutes," he said, addressing all his guests. "I have visitors awaiting me who arrived before you. . . . And don't tell lies," he added, turning to Fyodor Karamazov with a good-humored face.

He was about to leave the cell. Alyosha and the novice ran to escort him. Alyosha was breathless. He was glad to get away, but he was glad, too, that the elder was not offended. Father Zossima was going to the portico to bless the people waiting for him there. But Fyodor Karamazov stopped him at the door of the cell.

"Blessed man!" he cried, with feeling. "Allow me to kiss your hand once more. Yes, with you I could still talk, I could still get on. Do you think I always lie and play the fool like this? Believe me, I have been acting like this all the time on purpose to try you. I have been testing you all the time to see whether I could get on with you. Is there room for my humility beside your pride? I am ready to give you a testimonial that one can get on with you! But now, I'll be quiet. I will keep quiet all the time. I'll sit in a chair and hold my tongue. Now it is for you to speak, Peter Miusov. You are the principal person left now for two minutes."

3. Peasant Women Who Have Faith

NEAR THE PORTICO which was attached to the wall that enclosed the monastery grounds, there was a crowd of about twenty peasant women. They had been told that the elder was at last coming out and they gathered together in anticipation. Two ladies, Madame Hohlakov and her daughter, had also come out into the portico to wait for the elder, but in a separate part of it set aside for women of rank.

Madame Hohlakov was a wealthy lady, still young and attractive, and dressed with taste. She was rather pale and had lively black eyes. She was not more than thirty-three and had been a widow for the last five years. Her daughter, a girl of fourteen, was partially paralyzed. The poor child had not been able to walk for the last six months and was wheeled about in a long reclining chair. She had a charming little face, rather thin from illness, but full of gaiety. There was a gleam of mischief in her big dark eyes with their long lashes. Her mother had intended to take her abroad ever since spring, but they had been detained all summer by business connected with their estate. They had been staying a week in our town, where they had come more for business than devotion, but had visited Father Zossima once already, three days before. Though they knew that the elder scarcely saw anyone, they had now

51

suddenly turned up again, and urgently begged for "the happiness of looking once again on the great healer."

The mother was sitting by the side of her daughter's wheel chair, and close by her stood an old monk. He was not from our monastery but a visitor from an obscure religious order in the far north. He too sought the elder's blessing.

But Father Zossima, on entering the portico, went straight to the peasants who were crowded at the foot of the three steps at the entrance. He stood on the top step with Porfiry and Alyosha close behind him. He put on his stole, and began blessing the women who thronged about him. One crazy woman was led up to him. As soon as she caught sight of the elder she began shrieking and writhing as though in the pains of childbirth. Laying the stole on her forehead, he read a short prayer over her, and she was at once soothed and quieted.

I do not know how it is now, but in my childhood I often saw and heard these "possessed" women in the villages and monasteries. They used to be brought to mass. They would squeal and bark like a dog so that they were heard all over the church. But when the sacrament was carried in and they were led up to it, the "possession" ceased, and the sick women were soothed for a time. I was greatly impressed and amazed at this as a child. But then I heard from country neighbors and from my town teachers that the whole illness was induced to avoid work, and that it could always be cured by suitable severity. Various examples were given to confirm this. But later on I learnt with astonishment from doctors that there is no pretense about it, that it is a terrible illness to which women are subject. It is especially prevalent among us in Russia and is due to the hard lot of our peasant women. It is a disease, I was told, arising from exhausting toil too soon after hard, abnormal and unassisted labor in childbirth, and from the hopeless misery, from beatings, and so on, which some women are not able to endure. The strange and instant healing of the frantic and struggling woman as soon as she was led up to the holy sacrament, which had been explained to me as due to the trickery of the "clericals," probably came in the most natural manner. Both the women who supported her and the "possessed" one herself fully believed that the evil spirit in possession of her could not hold out if she were brought to the sacrament and made to bow down before it. And so, with a nervous and psychically deranged woman, a sort of convulsion of the whole body always took place, and was bound to take place, at the moment of bowing down to the sacrament, aroused by the expectation of the miracle of healing and the implicit belief that it would come to pass. And it did come to pass, though only for a moment. It was exactly the same now as soon as the elder touched the sick woman with the stole.

Many of the women in the crowd were moved to tears of

ecstasy by the effect of the moment. Some tried to kiss the hem of his garment. Others cried out in singsong voices.

He blessed them all and talked with some of them. The "possessed" woman he knew already. She came from a village only six miles from the monastery and had been brought to him before.

"But here is one from afar." He pointed to a woman by no means old but very thin and wasted, with a face not merely sunburnt but almost blackened by exposure. She was kneeling and gazing with a fixed stare at the elder. There was something almost frenzied in her eyes.

"From afar off, Father, from afar off! From two hundred miles from here. From afar off, Father, from afar off!" the woman began in a singsong voice as though she were chanting a dirge, swaying her head from side to side with her cheek resting in her hand.

There is silent and long-suffering sorrow to be met with among the peasantry. It withdraws into itself and is still. But there is a grief that breaks out, and from the minute it bursts into tears and finds vent in wailing. This is particularly common with women. But it is no lighter a grief than the silent. Lamentations comfort only by lacerating the heart still more. Such grief does not desire consolation. It feeds on the sense of its hopelessness. Lamentations spring only from the constant craving to re-open the wound.

"You are of the tradesman class?" said Father Zossima, looking curiously at her.

"Townfolk we are, Father, townfolk. Yet we are peasants though we live in town. I have come to see you, oh Father! We heard of you, Father, we heard of you. I have buried my little son and I have come on a pilgrimage. I have been in three monasteries, but they told me, 'Go, Nastasha, go to them'—that is to you. And so I have come. Yesterday I was at the service, and today I have come to you."

"Why are you weeping?"

"I'm grieving for my little son, Father. He was three years old—three years all but three months. For my little boy, Father. I'm in anguish for my little boy. He was the last one left. We had four, my Nikita and I, and now we've no children. Our dear ones have all gone. I buried the first three without grieving overmuch, and now that I have buried the last I can't forget him. He seems always standing before me. He never leaves me. He has withered my heart. I look at his little clothes, his little shirt, his little boots, and I weep. I lay out all that is left of him, all his little things. I look at them and weep. I say to Nikita, my husband, let me go on a pilgrimage, master. He is a driver. We're not poor people, Father, not poor; he drives his own horse. It's all our own, the horse and the carriage. But what good is it all to us now? My Nikita has begun drinking while I am away. He's sure to. It used to be so before.

53

As soon as I turn my back he gives way to it. But now I don't think about him. It's three months since I left home. I've forgotten him. I've forgotten everything. I don't want to remember. And what would our life be like now if we were together? I'm through with him. I'm finished. I'm done with them all. I don't want to look upon my house and my goods. I don't want to see anything at all."

"Listen, mother," said the elder. "Once in olden times a holy saint saw in the Temple a mother like you weeping for her little one, her only one, whom God had taken. 'Knowest thou not,' said the saint to her, 'how bold these little ones are before the throne of God? Verily there are none bolder than they in the Kingdom of Heaven. "Thou didst give us life, oh Lord," they say, "and scarcely had we looked upon it when Thou didst take it back again." And so boldly they ask and ask again that God gives them at once the rank of angels. Therefore,' said the saint, 'thou too, oh mother, rejoice and weep not, for thy little one is with the Lord in the fellowship of the angels.' That's what the saint said to the weeping mother of old. He was a great saint and he could not have spoken falsely. Therefore you too, mother, know that your little one is surely before the throne of God, is rejoicing and happy, and praying to God for you, and therefore weep not, but rejoice."

The woman listened to the elder, looking down with her cheek in her hand. She sighed deeply.

"My Nikita tried to comfort me with the same words as you. 'Foolish one,' he said, 'why weep? Our son is no doubt singing with the angels before God.' He says that to me, but he weeps himself. I see that he cries like me. 'I know, Nikita,' said I. 'Where could he be if not with the Lord God? Only, he is not here with us as he used to be before.' And if only I could look upon him once more, if only I could peep at him, without going up to him, without speaking . . . If I could be hidden in a corner and only see him for one little minute, hear him playing in the yard, calling in his little voice, 'Mummy, where are you?' If only I could hear him pattering with his little feet about the room just once, only once; for so often, so often I remember how he used to run to me and shout and laugh . . . If only I could hear his little feet! . . . But he's gone, Father, he's gone, and I shall never hear him again. Here's his little sash, but him I shall never see or hear now."

She drew out her boy's little embroidered sash. And as soon as she looked at it she began shaking with sobs, hiding her eyes with her fingers through which the tears flowed

"It is Rachel of old," said the elder, "weeping for her children. And she will not be comforted because they are not. Such is the lot set on earth for you mothers. Be not comforted. Consolation is not what you need. Weep and be not consoled, but weep. Only every time that you weep be sure to remember that your little son is one of the angels of God, that he looks

54

down from there at you and sees you, and rejoices at your tears, and points at them to the Lord God. . . . A long while yet will you keep that great mother's grief. But it will turn in the end into quiet joy. And your bitter tears will be only tears of sorrow that purify the heart and deliver it from sin. And I shall pray for the peace of your child's soul. What was his name?"

"Alexey, Father."

"A sweet name. After Alexey, the man of God?"

"Yes, Father."

"What a saint he was! I will remember your child, mother, and your grief in my prayers. And I will also pray for your husband's health. It is a sin for you to leave him. Your little one will see from heaven that you have forsaken his father and will weep over you. Why do you trouble his happiness? He is living, for the soul lives forever, and though he is not in the house he is near you, unseen. How can he go into the house when you say that the house is hateful to you? To whom is he to go if you are not together, his father and mother? He comes to you in dreams now, and you grieve. But then he will send you gentle dreams. Go to your husband, mother; go this very day."

"I will go, Father, at your word. I will go. Your words have touched my heart. . . . My Nikita, my Nikita, you are waiting for me," the woman began in a sing-song voice.

The elder had already turned toward a very old woman, dressed like a person from town, not like a pilgrim. Her eyes showed that she had come with an object. She said she was the widow of a non-commissioned officer and lived close by in the town. Her son Vasenka was in the commissariat service and had gone to Irkutsk in Siberia. He had written twice from there. But now a whole year had passed since he had last written. She wanted to inquire about him, but she did not know the proper place to inquire.

"Only the other day Stephanie—she's a rich merchant's wife—said to me, 'You go and put your son's name down for prayer in the church, and pray for the peace of his soul as though he were dead. His soul will be troubled,' she said, 'and he will write you a letter.' And Stephanie told me it was a sure thing which had been tried many times. Only I am in doubt. . . . Oh, you light of ours! Is it true or false? And would it be right?"

"Don't think of it. It's shameful to ask the question. How is it possible to pray for the peace of a living soul? And his own mother too! It's a great sin, like sorcery. Only for your ignorance it is forgiven you. Better pray to the Queen of Heaven, our swift defense and help, for his good health, and that she may forgive you for your error. And another thing I will tell you. Either he will soon come back to you, your son, or he will be sure to send a letter. Go, and henceforward be in peace. Your son is alive, I tell you."

"Dear Father. God reward you. Our benefactor who prays for all of us and for our sins!"

But the elder had already noticed in the crowd two glowing eyes fixed upon him. An exhausted, consumptive-looking, though young peasant woman was gazing at him in silence. Her eyes besought him but she seemed afraid to approach.

"What is it, my child?"

"Absolve my soul, Father," she said softly and slowly. She sank on her knees and bowed down at his feet. "I have sinned, Father. I am afraid of my sin."

Father Zossima sat down on the lower step. The woman crept closer to him, still on her knees.

"I am a widow these three years," she began in a half-whisper, with a sort of shudder. "I had a hard life with my husband. He was an old man. He used to beat me cruelly. He lay ill. I thought looking at him, if he were to get well . . . If he were to get up again, what then? And then the thought came to me . . ."

"Stay!" said the elder, and he put his ear close to her lips.

The woman went on in a low whisper so that it was almost impossible to hear anything. She was soon finished.

"Three years ago?" asked the elder.

"Three years. At first I didn't think about it. But now I've begun to be ill, and the thought never leaves me."

"Have you come from far?"

"Three hundred miles away."

"Have you told it in confession?"

"I have confessed it. Twice I have confessed it."

"Have you been admitted to Communion?"

"Yes. I am afraid. I am afraid to die."

"Fear nothing and never be afraid. And don't worry. If only your penitence fail not, God will forgive all. There is no sin, and there can be no sin on all the earth, which the Lord will not forgive to the truly repentant! Man cannot commit a sin so great as to exhaust the infinite love of God. Can there be a sin which could exceed the love of God? Think only of repentance, continual repentance, but dismiss fear altogether. Believe that God loves you as you cannot conceive; that He loves you with your sin, in your sin. It has been said of old that over one repentant sinner there is more joy in heaven than over ten righteous men. Go, and fear not. Be not bitter against men. Be not angry if you are wronged. Forgive the dead man in your heart what wrong he did you. Be reconciled with him in truth. If you are penitent, you love. And if you love you are of God. All things are atoned for, all things are saved by love. If I, a sinner even as you are, am tender with you and have pity on you, how much more will God have pity upon you. Love is such a priceless treasure that you can re-

56

deem the whole world by it, and cleanse not only your own sins but the sins of others."

Father Zossima made the sign of the cross over her three times. Then he took from his own neck a little ikon and put it upon her. She bowed down to the earth without speaking.

He got up and looked cheerfully at a healthy peasant woman with a tiny baby in her arms.

"From Vyshegorye, dear Father."

"You have dragged yourself with the baby five miles. What do you want?"

"I've come to look at you. I have been to you before—or have you forgotten? You've no great memory if you've forgotten me. They told us you were ill. So I thought, I'll go and see him for myself. Now I see you, and you're not ill! You'll live another twenty years. God bless you! There are plenty to pray for you; how can you be ill?"

"I thank you for all, daughter."

"By the way, I have a thing to ask, not a great one. Here are sixty pennies. Give them, dear Father, to someone poorer than me. I thought as I came along, better give through him. He'll know whom to give to."

"Thank you, my dear. Thank you! You are a good woman. I love you. I will certainly do so. Is that your little girl?"

"Yes, my little girl, Father."

"May the Lord bless you both, you and your babe! You have gladdened my heart, mother."

Then speaking to all gathered before him, he said: "Farewell, dear children. Farewell, dear ones." He blessed them all and bowed low to them.

4. A Lady of Little Faith

MADAME HOHLAKOV witnessing the elder's conversation with the peasants and his blessing of them shed silent tears and wiped them away with her handkerchief. She was sentimental and of a genuinely good disposition in many respects. When the elder, still followed by Porfiry and Alyosha, went up to her at last she met him enthusiastically.

"Ah, how I have felt looking on at this touching scene! . . ." She could not go on for emotion. "Oh, I understand the people's love for you. I love the people myself. I want to love them. And who could help loving them, our splendid Russian people, so simple in their greatness!"

"How is your daughter's health? You wanted to talk to me again?"

"Oh, I have been urgently begging for it, I have prayed for it! I was ready to fall on my knees and kneel for three days at your windows until you let me in. We have come, great healer, to express our deep gratitude. You have healed my Lise, healed her completely, merely by praying over her last Thursday and laying your hands upon her. We have hurried here to kiss those hands, to pour out our feelings and our homage."

"What do you mean by healed? She is still lying down in her chair."

"But her fevers at night have stopped completely since Thursday," she said nervously. "And that's not all. Her legs are stronger. This morning she got up feeling well. She had slept all night. Look at her pink cheeks, her bright eyes! She used to cry all the time but now she laughs and is gay and happy. This morning she insisted on my letting her stand up. And she stood up for a whole minute without any support. She insists that in two weeks she'll be dancing. I've called in Doctor Herzenstube. He shrugged his shoulders and said: 'I am amazed. I can make nothing of it.' And would you ask us not to come here to disturb you, not to fly here to thank you? Lise, thank the elder! Thank the elder!"

Lise's pretty little laughing face became suddenly serious. She rose in her chair as far as she could and, looking at the elder, clasped her hands before him. But suddenly she could not restrain herself any longer and broke into laughter.

"It's him," she said, pointing to Alyosha, with childish vexation at herself for not being able to repress her laughter.

If anyone had looked at Alyosha standing a step behind the elder, he would have seen his cheeks flush crimson. His eyes shone and he looked down.

"She has a message for you. How are you?" the mother went on, holding out her beautifully gloved hand to Alyosha.

Father Zossima turned round and looked at Alyosha. Alyosha then went up to Lise and, smiling in a strangely awkward way, held out his hand. Lise assumed an important air.

"Katerina has sent you this through me." She handed him a little note. "She particularly begs you to go and see her as soon as possible. She hopes that you will not disappoint her, but will be sure to come."

"She asks me to go and see her? Me? What for?" Alyosha said, surprised. He looked worried.

"Oh, it's all about your brother Dmitri and—what has happened lately," the mother explained hurriedly. "Katerina has made up her mind, but she must see you about it. . . . Why, of course, I can't say. But she wants to see you at once. And you will go to her, of course. It is a Christian duty."

"But I have only seen her once," Alyosha protested.

"Oh, she is such a fine, wonderful creature! If only for her suffering . . . Think what she has gone through, what she is enduring now! Think what awaits her! It's all terrible, terrible!"

"All right. I will go," Alyosha decided, after quickly read-

58

ing Katerina's brief note, which consisted of an urgent plea that he should come. She gave no explanation.

"Oh, how sweet and generous that is of you!" cried Lise with sudden animation. "I told Mamma you wouldn't go. I said you were saving your soul. How good you are! I've always thought you were good. How glad I am to tell you so!"

"Lise!" said her mother emphatically, though she smiled after she had said it.

"You seem to have forgotten us, Alyosha," she said. "You never come to see us. Yet Lise has told me twice that she is never happy except with you."

Alyosha raised his downcast eyes and flushed again. And again he smiled without knowing why. But the elder was no longer watching him. He had begun talking to the monk who, as mentioned before, had been waiting by Lise's chair. He was obviously a monk of the humblest, that is of the peasant, class, of a narrow outlook but a true believer, and, in his own way, a stubborn one. He said that he had come from the far north, from Obdorsk, from Saint Sylvester, and was a member of a poor monastery of only ten monks. The elder gave him his blessing and invited him to come to his cell whenever he liked.

"How can you presume to do such deeds?" the monk asked suddenly, pointing significantly at Lise. He was referring to her "healing."

"It's too early, of course, to speak of that. Relief is not complete cure and may come from different things. But if there has been any healing, it is by no power but God's will. It's all from God. Visit me, Father," he added to the monk. "It's not often I can see visitors. I am ill and I know that my days are numbered."

"Oh, no, no! God will not take you from us. You will live a long, long time yet," cried Madame Hohlakov. "And in what way are you ill? You look so well, so gay and happy."

"I am much better today. But I know that it's only for a moment. I understand my illness thoroughly. If I seem happy to you . . . You could never say anything that would please me more. For men are made for happiness, and anyone who is completely happy has a right to say to himself, 'I am doing God's will on earth.' All the righteous, all the saints, all the holy martyrs were happy."

"Oh, how you speak! What bold and beautiful words!" cried Madame Hohlakov. "Your words are so penetrating. And yet —happiness, happiness—where is it? Who can say of himself that he is happy? Oh, since you have been so good as to let us see you once more today, let me say what I could not say last time, what I dared not say. I have been suffering for so long! I am suffering! Forgive me! I am suffering!"

And in a rush of emotion she clasped her hands before him.

"You are suffering? From what are you suffering?"

"I suffer . . . from lack of faith."

"Lack of faith in God?"

"Oh, no, no! I dare not even think of that. But life after death—it is such an enigma! And no one, no one can solve it. Listen! You are a healer, you are deeply versed in the human soul, and of course I dare not expect you to believe me entirely, but I assure you on my word of honor that I am not speaking lightly now. The thought of life beyond the grave fills me with anguish, with terror. And I don't know to whom to appeal, and have not dared to all my life. And now I am bold enough to ask you! Oh, God! What will you think of me now?"

She again clasped her hands.

"Don't worry about my opinion of you," said Father Zossima. "I believe in the sincerity of your suffering."

"Oh, how thankful I am to you! You see, I shut my eyes and ask myself, if everyone has faith where did it come from? They say that it all comes from terror at the menacing phenomena of nature, and that none of it is real. And I say to myself: 'What if I've been believing all my life, and when I come to die there's nothing but weeds growing on my grave?' I read that in a book. It's awful! How—how can I get back my faith? I only believed when I was a little child, mechanically, without thinking of anything. How, how is one to prove it? I have come now to lay my soul before you and to ask you about it. If I let this chance slip, no one all my life will be able to give me the answer. How can I prove it? How can I convince myself? Oh, how unhappy I am! I stand and look about me and see that scarcely anyone else cares; no one troubles his head about it. I'm the only one who can't stand it. It's deadly—deadly!"

"No doubt. But there's no proving it, though you can be convinced of it."

"How?"

"By the experience of active love. Strive to love your neighbor actively and constantly. In so far as you advance in love you will grow surer of the reality of God and of the immortality of your soul. If you attain perfect self-forgetfulness in the love of your neighbor, then you will believe without doubt. Doubt will no longer be able to enter your soul. This has been tried. This is certain."

"In active love? There's another question—another question! You see, I so love humanity that—would you believe it I often dream of forsaking all that I have, leaving Lise, and becoming a sister of mercy. I close my eyes and think and dream, and at that moment I feel full of strength. I have strength enough to overcome all obstacles! No wounds, no festering sores could at that moment frighten me. I would bind them up and wash them with my own hands. I would nurse the afflicted. I would be ready to kiss such wounds."

"It is well that your mind is full of such dreams and not

60

others. Sometime, unawares, you may do a good deed in reality."

"Yes. But could I endure such a life for long?" Madame Hohlakov went on fervently, almost frantically. "That's the main question—that's my most agonizing question. I shut my eyes and ask myself: 'Would you persevere long on that path? And if the patient whose wounds you are washing did not meet you with gratitude, but worried you with his whims, without valuing or remarking upon your kindness, began abusing you and rudely commanding you, and complaining to the authorities about you—which often happens when people are in great suffering—what then? Would you persevere in your love, or not?' And do you know, I came with horror to the conclusion that, if anything could dissipate my love for humanity, it would be ingratitude. In short, I am a hired servant, I expect my payment at once—that is, praise, and the repayment of love with love. Otherwise I am incapable of loving anyone."

She was in the throes of self-castigation. And concluding she looked with defiant determination at the elder.

"It's just the same story a doctor once told me," observed the elder. "He was a man getting on in years, and undoubtedly clever. He spoke as freely as you, though in sarcasm, in bitter sarcasm. 'I love humanity,' he said, 'but I wonder at myself. The more I love humanity in general, the less I love man in particular. In my dreams,' he said, 'I often make plans for the service of humanity, and perhaps I might actually face crucifixion if it were suddenly necessary. Yet I am incapable of living in the same room with anyone for two days together. I know from experience. As soon as anyone is near me, his personality disturbs me and restricts my freedom. In twenty-four hours I begin to hate the best of men: one because he's too long over his dinner, another because he has a cold and keeps on blowing his nose. I become hostile to people the moment they come close to me. But it has always happened that the more I hate men individually the more I love humanity.'"

"But what can be done? What can one do in such a case? Must one despair?"

"No. It is enough that you are distressed. Do what you can and it will be reckoned unto you. Much is done already in you since you can so deeply and sincerely know yourself. If you have been talking to me so sincerely, simply to gain approval as you did from me just now, then of course you will not attain real love; you will get no further than dreams, and your whole life will slip away like a phantom. In that case you will naturally stop thinking of life everlasting too and will grow calmer after a fashion."

"You have crushed me! Only now, as you speak, I understand that I was really only seeking your approval for my sincerity when I told you I could not endure ingratitude. You

61

have revealed me to myself. You have seen through me and explained me to myself!"

"Are you speaking the truth? Well, now, after such a confession, I believe that you are sincere and good at heart. If you do not attain happiness, always remember that you are on the right road, and try not to leave it. Above all, avoid falsehood, every kind of falsehood, especially falseness to yourself. Watch over your own deceitfulness and look into it every hour, every minute. Avoid being scornful, both to others and to yourself. What seems to you bad within you will grow purer from the very fact of your observing it in yourself. Avoid fear, too, though fear is only the result of falsehood. Never be frightened at your own faint-heartedness in attaining love. Don't be too frightened even at your evil actions. I am sorry I can say nothing more consoling to you, for love in action is a harsh and dreadful thing compared with love in dreams. Love in dreams is greedy for immediate action, rapidly performed and in the sight of all. Men will even give their lives if only the ordeal does not last long but is soon over, with all looking on and applauding as though on the stage. But active love is labor and fortitude, and for some people too, perhaps, a complete science. But I predict that just when you see with horror that in spite of all your efforts you are getting further from your goal instead of nearer to it—at that very moment I predict that you will reach it and behold clearly the miraculous power of the Lord who has been all the time loving and mysteriously guiding you. Forgive me for not being able to stay longer with you. They are waiting for me. Good-by."

Madame Hohlakov was weeping.

"Lise, Lise! Bless her—bless her!" she cried suddenly.

"She does not deserve to be loved. I have seen her naughtiness all along," the elder said jokingly. "Why have you been laughing at Alyosha?"

Lise had in fact been teasing him all the time. She knew that Alyosha was shy and tried not to look at her, and she found this very amusing. She waited to catch his eye. Alyosha, unable to endure her persistent stare, was forced to glance at her, and at once she smiled triumphantly at him. At this Alyosha was even more disconcerted. At last he turned away from her altogether and hid behind the elder's back. After a few minutes, however, drawn by an irresistible force, he turned again to see whether he was being looked at or not, and found Lise almost hanging out of her chair staring sideways at him, eagerly waiting to attract his attention. Catching his eye, she laughed. Father Zossima could not help saying: "Why do you make fun of him like that, naughty girl?"

Lise suddenly and quite unexpectedly blushed. Her eyes flashed and her face became quite serious. She began speaking quickly and nervously in a warm and resentful voice: "Why! Has he forgotten everything then? Has he forgotten those days in Moscow? He used to carry me around when I was little. We used to play together. He used to teach me to read. Two years ago, when he went away, he said that he would never forget me, that we were friends forever, forever, forever! And now he's afraid of me all at once. Am I going to eat him? Why doesn't he want to come near me? Why doesn't he talk? Why won't he come and see us? It's not that you won't let him. We know that he goes everywhere. It's not good manners for me to invite him. He ought to have thought of it first, if he hasn't forgotten me. No, now he's saving his soul! Why have you put that long gown on him? If he runs he'll fall."

And suddenly she hid her face in her hand and broke into uncontrolled, prolonged, nervous laughter. The elder listened to her with a smile, and blessed her tenderly. She stopped laughing. As she kissed his hand she suddenly pressed it to her eyes and began crying.

"Don't be angry with me. I'm silly and . . . And perhaps Alyosha's right, very right, in not wanting to come and see such a ridiculous girl."

"I will certainly send him," said the elder

5. So Be It! So Be It!

FATHER ZOSSIMA'S ABSENCE FROM HIS CELL had lasted for about twenty-five minutes. It was more than half past twelve, but Dmitri, on whose account they had all gathered, had still not appeared. He seemed almost forgotten, and when the elder entered his cell again, he found his guests talking eagerly. Ivan and the two monks led the conversation and Miusov, too, was trying eagerly to take part in it. But he was unsuccessful. He was evidently in the background, and his remarks were treated with neglect, which irritated him. He had had intellectual encounters with Ivan before and he could not endure a certain indifference Ivan showed toward him.

"In the past I have stood in the front ranks of all that is progressive in Europe, and here the new generation ignores me," he thought.

Fyodor Karamazov, who had given his word to sit still and be quiet, had actually been quiet for some time, but he watched his neighbor Miusov with an ironical little smile, obviously enjoying his discomfort. He had been waiting for some time to pay off old scores, and now he could not let the opportunity slip. Bending over, he began teasing Miusov in a whisper.

"Why didn't you go away after the 'courteously kissing'? Why did you consent to remain in such unseemly company?

It was because you felt insulted. You remained to vindicate yourself by showing off your intelligence. Now you won't go till you've displayed your intellect to them."

"You again? . . . I'm just about to leave."

"You'll be the last, the last of all to go!" Fyodor Karamazov delivered him another thrust, almost at the moment of Father Zossima's return.

The discussion died down for a moment. But the elder, seating himself in his former place, looked at them all as though inviting them to go on. Alyosha, who knew every expression of his face, saw that he was fearfully exhausted and making a great effort. Of late he had been prone to fainting. His face had the pallor that was common before such attacks, and his lips were white. But he evidently did not want to break up the gathering. He seemed to have some special object of his own in keeping them. What object? Alyosha watched him intently.

"We are discussing this gentleman's most interesting article," said Father Joseph, the librarian, addressing the elder, and indicating Ivan. "He presents much that is new, but I think the argument cuts both ways. It is an article written in answer to a book by a church authority on the question of the ecclesiastical court, and the scope of its jurisdiction."

"I'm sorry I have not read your article, but I've heard of it," said the elder, looking keenly at Ivan.

"He takes a most interesting position," continued the Father Librarian. "As far as Church jurisdiction is concerned he is apparently quite opposed to the separation of Church from State."

"That's interesting. But in what sense?" Father Zossima asked.

Ivan answered him, not condescendingly, as Alyosha feared, but with modesty and reserve, with evident goodwill and apparently without the slightest arrière-pensée.

"I start from the position that this confusion of elements, that is, of the essential principles of Church and State, will, of course, go on forever in spite of the fact that it is impossible for them to fuse. The confusion of these elements cannot lead to any consistent or even normal results, for there is falseness at the very foundation. Compromise between the Church and State in such questions as, for instance, jurisdiction, is to my thinking impossible in any real sense. My clerical opponent maintains that the Church holds a precise and defined position in the State. I maintain, on the contrary, that the Church ought to include the whole State and not simply to occupy a corner of it. And if this is for some reason impossible at present, then it ought in reality to be set up as the direct and chief aim of the future development of Christian society!"

"Perfectly true," Father Paissy, the silent and learned monk, agreed with decision.

"The purest Ultramontanism!" cried Miusov impatiently, crossing and recrossing his legs.

"Oh, well, we have no mountains," cried Father Joseph. And turning to the elder he continued: "Observe the answer he makes to the following 'fundamental and essential' propositions of his opponent, who is, you must note, an ecclesiastic. First, that 'no social organization can or ought to arrogate to itself power to dispose of the civic and political rights of its members.' Secondly, that 'criminal and civil jurisdiction ought not to belong to the Church, and is inconsistent with its nature, both as a divine institution and as an organization of men for religious purposes.' And finally, in the third place, 'the Church is a kingdom not of this world.' "

"A most unworthy play upon words for an ecclesiastic!" Father Paissy could not refrain from breaking in again. "I have read the book which you have answered," he added, addressing Ivan, "and was astounded at the words 'the Church is a kingdom not of this world.' If it is not of this world then it cannot exist on earth at all. In the Gospel, the words 'not of this world,' are not used in that sense. To play with such words is indefensible. Our Lord Jesus Christ came to set up the Church upon earth. The Kingdom of Heaven, of course, is not of this world but in Heaven; but it is only entered through the Church which has been founded and established upon earth. And so a frivolous play upon words in such a connection is unpardonable and improper. The Church is, in truth, a kingdom and ordained to rule, and in the end must undoubtedly become the kingdom ruling over all the earth. For that we have the divine promise."

He stopped speaking suddenly as though checking himself.

After listening attentively and respectfully to Father Paissy, Ivan went on, addressing the elder with perfect composure and as before with obvious friendliness. "The whole point of my article lies in the fact that during the first three centuries Christianity only existed on earth in the Church and was nothing but the Church. When the pagan Roman Empire desired to become Christian, it inevitably happened that, by becoming Christian, it included the Church but remained a pagan State in very many ways. This was bound to happen. But Rome as a State retained too much of the pagan civilization and culture, as, for example, in the very objects and fundamental principles of the State. The Christian Church entering into the State could, of course, surrender no part of its fundamental principles—the rock on which it stands. It could pursue no other aims than those which have been ordained and revealed by God Himself, among them that of drawing the whole world and therefore the ancient pagan State itself into the Church. In this way (that is, with a view to the future) it is not the Church that should seek a definite position in the State, like 'every social organization,' or as 'an organization of men for religious purposes' (as my opponent calls the Church). On the contrary, every earthly State should be, in the end, completely transformed into the Church and should become nothing else but a Church, rejecting every purpose incongruous with the aims of the Church. All this will not degrade it in any way or diminish its honor and glory as a great State, nor lessen the glory of its rulers. All this will only turn it from a false, still pagan, and mistaken path to the true and rightful path which alone leads to the eternal goal. This is why the author of the book 'On the Foundations of Church Jurisdiction' would have judged correctly if, in seeking and laying down those foundations, he had looked upon them as only a temporary compromise inevitable in our sinful and imperfect days. But as soon as the author ventures to declare that the foundations which he predicates now, part of which Father Joseph just enumerated, are the permanent, essential, and eternal foundations, he is going directly against the Church and its sacred and eternal vocation. That is the gist of my article."

"That is, in brief," Father Paissy began again laying stress on each word, "according to certain theories only too clearly formulated in the nineteenth century, the Church ought to be transformed into the State, as though this would be an advance from a lower to a higher form, so as to disappear into it, making way for science, for the spirit of the age, and civilization. And if the Church resists and is unwilling, some corner will be set apart for her in the State, under control—and this will be so everywhere in all modern European countries. But Russian hopes and ideals demand not that the Church should pass from a lower into a higher order, the State, but on the contrary, that the State should end by being worthy of becoming the Church and nothing else. So be it! So be it!"

"Well, I confess you've reassured me somewhat," Miusov said, smiling, again crossing his legs. "So far as I understand then, the realization of such an ideal is infinitely remote, at the second coming of Christ. That's how you want it. It's a beautiful Utopian dream of the abolition of war, diplomacy, banks, and so on—something after the fashion of socialism, I'd say. But I imagine that it is all meant seriously, and that the Church may now be going to try criminals, and sentence them to beating, prison, and even death."

"But if there were none but the ecclesiastical court, the Church would not even now sentence a criminal to prison or to death," Ivan said calmly. "Crime and the way of regarding it would inevitably change, not all at once of course, but fairly soon."

"Are you serious?" Miusov looked intently at him.

"If everything became the Church, the Church would exclude all the criminal, and disobedient, and would not cut off their heads," Ivan went on. "I ask you, what would become of the excluded? He would be cut off then not only from

66

men, as now, but from Christ. By his crime he would have transgressed not only against men but against the Church of Christ. This is so even now, of course, strictly speaking, but it is not clearly stated, and very, very often the criminal of today compromises with his conscience: 'I steal,' he says, 'but I don't go against the Church. I'm not an enemy of Christ.' That's what the criminal of today is continually saying to himself, but when the Church takes the place of the State it will be difficult for him, in opposition to the Church all over the world, to say: 'All men are mistaken, all in error, all mankind are the false Church. I, a thief and murderer, am the only true Christian Church.' It will be very difficult for a criminal to say this to himself; it requires a rare combination of unusual circumstances. Now, on the other hand, take the Church's own view of crime: is it not bound to renounce the present almost pagan attitude, and to change from a mechanical cutting off of its tainted member for the preservation of Society, as at present, into completely and honestly adopting the idea of the regeneration of the man, of his reformation and salvation?"

"What do you mean? I fail to understand," Miusov interrupted. "Is this again some sort of dream? Something shapeless and even incomprehensible? What is excommunication? What sort of exclusion? I suspect you are simply amusing yourself, Ivan."

"Yes, but you know, in reality it is so now," said Father Zossima suddenly. All turned to him at once. "If it were not for the Church of Christ there would be nothing to restrain the criminal from evil-doing, no real punishment. The mechanical punishment spoken of just now, in the majority of cases only embitters the heart. It is not the real punishment. The only effectual one, the only deterrent and softening one, lies in the recognition of sin by conscience."

"How is that, may one inquire?" asked Miusov, with curiosity.

"Why," began the elder, "all these sentences to exile with hard labor, and formerly with flogging also, reform no one, and what's more, deter hardly a single criminal. The number of crimes does not diminish but is continually on the increase. You must admit that consequently the security of society is not preserved, for, although the dangerous member is mechanically cut off and sent far away out of sight, another criminal always comes to take his place at once, and often two of them. If anything does preserve society, even in our time, and does regenerate and transform the criminal, it is the law of Christ speaking in his conscience. . . . It is only by recognizing his wrong-doing as a son of a Christian society—that is, of the Church—that he recognizes his sin against society—that is, against the Church. So that it is only against

67

the Church, and not against the State, that the criminal of to-day can recognize that he has sinned.

"If society, as a Church, had jurisdiction then it would know whom to bring back and to re-unite to itself. Now the Church having no real jurisdiction, but only the power of moral condemnation, withdraws of her own accord from actively punishing the criminal. She does not excommunicate him but simply persists in fatherly exhortation of him. What is more, the Church even tries to preserve all Christian communion with the criminal. She admits him to church services, to the holy sacrament, gives him charity, and treats him more as a captive than as a convict. And what would become of the criminal, O Lord, if even Christian society—that is, the Church—were to reject him as the civil law rejects him and cuts him off. What would become of him if the Church punished him with her excommunication as the direct consequence of the secular law? There could be no more terrible despair, at least for a Russian criminal, for Russian criminals still have faith. Though, who knows, perhaps then a fearful thing would happen, perhaps the despairing heart of the criminal would lose its faith and then what would become of him? But the Church, like a tender, loving mother, holds aloof from active punishment herself, as the sinner is too severely punished already by the civil law, and there must be at least someone to have pity on him. The Church holds aloof, above all, because its judgment alone contains the truth, and therefore cannot practically and morally be united to any other judgment even as a temporary compromise. She can enter into no compact about that.

"The foreign criminal, they say, rarely repents, for the very doctrines of today confirm him in the idea that his crime is not a crime, but only a reaction against an unjustly oppressive force. Society cuts him off completely by a force that triumphs over him mechanically and (so at least they say of themselves in Europe) accompanies this exclusion with hatred, forgetfulness, and the most profound indifference as to the ultimate fate of the erring brother. In this way, it all takes place without the compassionate intervention of the Church, for in many cases there are no churches there at all, for though ecclesiastics and splendid church buildings remain, the churches themselves have long ago passed from Church into State and disappeared completely. So it seems at least in Lutheran countries. As for Rome, it was proclaimed a State instead of a Church a thousand years ago. And so the criminal is no longer conscious of being a member of the Church and sinks into despair. If he returns to society, often it is with such hatred that society itself instinctively cuts him off. You can judge for yourself how it must end. In many cases it would seem to be the same with us, but the difference is that besides the established law courts we have the Church too, which always keeps

68

up relations with the criminal as a dear and still precious son. And besides that, there is still preserved, though only in thought, the judgment of the Church, which though no longer existing in practice is still living as a dream for the future, and is, no doubt, instinctively recognized by the criminal in his soul.

"What was said here just now is true too, that is, that if the jurisdiction of the Church were introduced in practice in its full force, that is, if the whole of the society were changed into the Church, not only the judgment of the Church would have influence on the reformation of the criminal such as it never has now, but possibly also the crimes themselves would be incredibly diminished. And there can be no doubt that the Church would look upon the criminal and the crime in many cases quite differently and would succeed in restoring the excluded, in restraining those who plan evil, and in regenerating the fallen. It is true," said Father Zossima, with a smile, "Christian society is at present not ready and is only resting on some seven righteous men. But as they are never lacking, it will continue unshaken in expectation of its complete transformation from a society almost heathen in character into a single universal and all-powerful Church. So be it, so be it. Even though it is long delayed, until the end of the ages, it is ordained to come to pass! And there is no need to be troubled about times and seasons, for the secret of the times and seasons is in the wisdom of God, in His foresight, and His love. And what in human reckoning seems still afar off, may by Divine ordinance be close at hand, on the eve of its appearance. And so be it, so be it!"

"So be it, so be it!" Father Paissy repeated austerely and reverently.

"Strange, extremely strange!" Miusov said, not so much with anger as with latent indignation.

"What strikes you as so strange?" Father Joseph inquired cautiously.

"Why, it's beyond anything!" cried Miusov, suddenly breaking out. "The State is eliminated and the Church is raised to the position of the State. It's not simply Ultramontanism, it's arch-Ultramontanism! It's even beyond the dreams of Pope Gregory the Seventh!"

"You are completely misunderstanding it," said Father Paissy sternly. "You must understand that the Church is not to be transformed into the State. That is Rome and its dream. That is the third temptation of the devil. On the contrary, the State is to be transformed into the Church, will ascend and become a Church over the whole world—which is the complete opposite of Ultramontanism and Rome, and your interpretation, and is only the glorious destiny ordained for the Orthodox Church. This star will arise in the East!"

Miusov was silent. His whole figure expressed extreme per-

69

sonal dignity. A supercilious and condescending smile played on his lips.

Alyosha watched it all with a throbbing heart. The whole conversation had stirred him profoundly. He glanced at the divinity student, Rakitin, who was standing immovable by the door listening and watching intently though with downcast eyes. And from the color in his cheeks Alyosha guessed that Rakitin was probably no less excited, and he knew what had caused his excitement.

"Allow me to relate one little anecdote, gentlemen," Miusov said impressively, with a majestic air. "Some years ago, soon after the December uprising, I happened to be calling in Paris on an extremely influential person in the Government, and I met a very interesting man in his house. This individual was not precisely a detective but was a sort of superintendent of a whole regiment of political detectives—a rather powerful position in its own way. I was prompted by curiosity to seize the opportunity of conversation with him. And as he had not come as a visitor but as a subordinate official bringing a special report, and as he saw the reception given me by his chief he spoke with some openness, to a certain extent only, of course. He was rather more courteous than open, as Frenchmen know how to be especially with a foreigner. But I understood him. The subject was the socialist revolutionaries who were at that time persecuted. I will quote only one curious remark dropped by this person. 'We are not particularly afraid,' said he, 'of all these socialists, anarchists, infidels, and revolutionists; we keep watch on them and know all their doings. But there are a few peculiar men among them who believe in God and are Christians, but at the same time are socialists. Those are the people we are most afraid of. They are dreadful people! The socialist who is a Christian is more to be dreaded than a socialist who is an atheist.' These words struck me at the time, and now they have suddenly come back to me, gentlemen."

"You apply them to us, and look upon us as socialists?" Father Paissy asked directly, without evading the issue.

But before Peter Miusov could think of an answer, the door opened, and the guest so long expected, Dmitri Karamazov, came in. They had, in fact, given up expecting him, and his sudden appearance caused surprise for a moment.

6. Why Is Such a Man Alive?

DMITRI, A YOUNG MAN OF TWENTY-EIGHT, of medium height and agreeable appearance, looked older than he was. He was muscular and strong. Yet there was something not healthy about his face. It was rather thin, his cheeks were hollow and his complexion sallow. His large, prominent, dark eyes had an expression of determination, and yet there was a vague look in them, too. Even when he was excited and talking irritably, his eyes somehow did not follow his mood, but betrayed something else, sometimes quite incongruous with what he was saying. "It's hard to tell what he's thinking," many said. People who saw something pensive and sullen in his eyes were startled by his sudden laugh, which revealed light-hearted thoughts while his eyes seemed so gloomy. A certain strained look in his face was easy to understand at such a moment. Everyone knew, or had heard of the restless and dissipated life which he had been leading of late, as well as of the violent anger which he had displayed in his quarrels with his father. There were several stories in the town about it. It is true that he was excitable by nature, "of an unstable and unbalanced mind," as our justice of the peace, Katchalnikov, described him.

He was fashionably dressed in a frock coat. He wore black gloves and carried a top hat. Having only recently left the army, he still had a mustache but no beard. His dark brown hair was cropped short, and combed forward on his temples. He had the long determined stride of a military man.

As soon as he entered Father Zossima's cell he glanced at everyone and then went straight up to the elder, guessing him to be the host. He made him a low bow, and asked his blessing. Father Zossima, rising in his chair, blessed him. Dmitri kissed his hand respectfully and with intense feeling, almost anger, he said: "Be so generous as to forgive me for having kept you waiting so long, but Smerdyakov . . . my father sent his valet, Smerdyakov, to me twice to tell me that the appointment was for one o'clock. Now I suddenly learn . . ."

"Don't upset yourself," interrupted the elder. "It does not matter. You are a little late. It's of no consequence. . . ."

"I'm very grateful to you. I expected no less from your goodness."

Saying this, Dmitri bowed once more. Then, turning suddenly toward his father he also bowed respectfully to him. He had evidently considered it beforehand, and made this bow in all seriousness, thinking it his duty to show his respect and good intentions.

Although the old Karamazov was taken by surprise, he was equal to the occasion. He jumped up from his chair and bowed to his son in return. His face was suddenly solemn and impressive. He had a malignant look.

Dmitri now bowed generally to all present, and without a word walked to the window with his long stride, sat down on the only empty chair near Father Paissy, and bending forward prepared to listen to the conversation he had interrupted.

Dmitri's entrance had taken no more than two minutes, and the conversation was resumed. But this time Miusov thought

71

it unnecessary to reply to Father Paissy's persistent and almost irritable question.

"Allow me to withdraw from this discussion," he observed with a certain well-bred nonchalance. "It's a subtle question, too. Here Ivan is smiling at us. He must have something interesting to say. Ask him."

"Nothing special, except one little remark," Ivan replied at once. "European liberals in general, and even our liberal dilettanti, often mix up the final results of socialism with those of Christianity. This wild notion is, of course, a characteristic feature. But it's not only liberals and dilettanti who mix up socialism and Christianity, but in many cases it appears, the police—the foreign police of course—do the same. Your Paris anecdote is rather to the point, Peter Miusov."

"I ask your permission to drop this subject altogether," Miusov repeated. "I will tell you instead, gentlemen, another interesting and rather characteristic anecdote about Ivan himself. Only five days ago, in a gathering here, principally of ladies, he solemnly declared in argument that there was nothing in the whole world to make men love their neighbors. That there was no law of nature that men should love mankind, and that, if there had been any love on earth before this, it was not owing to a natural law, but simply because men have believed in immortality. Ivan added in parenthesis that the whole natural law lies in that faith, and that if you were to destroy in mankind the belief in immortality, not only love but every living force maintaining the life of the world would at once be dried up. Moreover, nothing then would be immoral, everything would be lawful, even cannibalism. That's not all. He ended by asserting that for every individual who does not believe in God or immortality, the moral law of nature must immediately be changed into the exact contrary of the former religious law. He said that egoism, even to crime, must become, not only lawful but recognized as the inevitable, the most rational, even honorable outcome. From this, gentlemen, you can judge about the rest of our eccentric and paradoxical friend Ivan's theories."

"Excuse me," Dmitri cried suddenly. "If I've heard correctly, crime must not only be permitted but even recognized as the inevitable and the most rational outcome for every infidel! Is that so or not?"

"Quite so," said Father Paissy.

"I'll remember it."

Having said these words Dmitri stopped speaking as suddenly as he had begun. Everyone looked at him, puzzled.

"Is that really your conviction as to the consequences of the disappearance of the faith in immortality?" Father Zossima now asked Ivan.

"Yes. That was my contention. There is no virtue if there is no immortality."

"You are blessed in believing that, or else most unhappy."

"Why unhappy?" Ivan asked, smiling.

"Because, in all probability you yourself don't believe in the immortality of your soul, nor in what you have written in your article on Church jurisdiction."

"Perhaps you are right! . . . But I wasn't altogether joking." Ivan suddenly and strangely confessed, flushing quickly.

"You were not altogether joking. That's true. The question is still bothering your heart; it is still unanswered. But the martyr sometimes likes to divert himself with his despair, as if driven to it by despair itself. Meanwhile, in your despair, you, too, divert yourself with magazine articles and discussions in society though you don't believe your own arguments, and with an aching heart mock at them inwardly. . . . That question you have not answered. And this is your great grief for it clamors for an answer."

"But can it be answered by me? Answered in the affirmative?" Ivan went on asking strangely, still looking at the elder with the same inexplicable smile.

"If it can't be decided in the affirmative, it will never be decided in the negative. You know that that is the peculiarity of your heart, and all its suffering is due to it. But thank the Creator who has given you a heart capable of such suffering; of thinking and seeking higher things, for our dwelling is in the heavens. God grant that your heart will attain the answer on earth. And may God bless your path."

The elder raised his hand and would have made the sign of the cross over Ivan from where he was. But Ivan rose from his chair, went up to Father Zossima, received his blessing, and kissing his hand went back to his place in silence. His face was set and earnest. This act and all the preceding conversation, which was so surprising coming from Ivan, impressed everyone by its strangeness and created a certain solemnity. All were silent for a moment, and there was a look almost of apprehension on Alyosha's face. But then suddenly Miusov shrugged his shoulders and Fyodor Karamazov jumped up from his chair.

"Most pious and holy elder," he cried, pointing to Ivan. "That is my son, flesh of my flesh, the dearest of my flesh! He is my most dutiful Karl Moor, so to speak, while this son who has just come in, Dmitri, against whom I am seeking justice from you, is the undutiful Franz Moor—they are both out of Schiller's *Robbers*. And so I am the reigning Count von Moor! Judge and save us! We need not only your prayers but your prophecies!"

"Speak without buffoonery, and don't begin by insulting the members of your family," answered Father Zossima, in a faint, exhausted voice. He was obviously getting more and more tired, and his strength was failing.

"It is all a farce which I foresaw when I came here!" cried

Dmitri. He too jumped up. "Forgive it, reverend Father," he added, addressing the elder. "I am not a cultured man, and I don't even know how to address you properly, but you have been deceived and you have been too good-natured in letting us meet here. All my father wants is to make a scene. Why he wants it only he can tell. He always has some motive. But I believe I know why . . ."

"They all blame me, all of them!" cried Fyodor Karamazov. "Peter Miusov here blames me too. You have been blaming me, Miusov, haven't you?" he turned suddenly to him, although Miusov was not dreaming of interrupting him. "They all accuse me of having hidden my children's money in my boots, and of having cheated them. But isn't there a court of law? There they will figure out for you, Dmitri, from your notes, your letters, and your agreements, how much money you had, how much you have spent, and how much you have left. . . . Why does Miusov refuse to pass judgment? Dmitri is not a stranger to him. He refuses to pass judgment because they are all against me, while Dmitri is in debt to me, and not a little, but some thousands of which I have documentary proof. The whole town is echoing with his debaucheries. And where he was stationed before, he several times spent a thousand or two for the seduction of some respectable girl; we know all about that, Dmitri, in its most secret details. I'll prove it. . . . Would you believe it, holy Father, he has won the heart of the most honorable of young ladies, a girl of good family and fortune. She is the daughter of a colonel, formerly his superior officer, who had received many honors and had the Anna Order on his breast. Dmitri compromised the girl by his promise of marriage. Now she is an orphan and here in our town. She is engaged to him, yet before her very eyes he is dancing attendance on a certain enchantress. And although this enchantress has lived in, so to speak, common law marriage with a respectable man yet she is independent, an unapproachable fortress for everybody, just like a legal wife—for she is virtuous, yes, holy Father, she is virtuous. Dmitri wants to open this fortress with a golden key, and that's why he is insolent to me now, trying to get money from me, though he had wasted thousands on this enchantress already. He's continually borrowing money for this purpose. From whom do you think? Shall I tell, Dmitri?"

"Keep quiet!" cried Dmitri. "Wait till I'm gone. Don't you dare in my presence to destroy the good name of an honorable girl! That you should speak a word about her is an outrage, and I won't permit it!"

He was breathless.

"Dmitri! Dmitri!" cried old Karamazov hysterically, squeezing out a tear. "And is your father's blessing nothing to you? If I curse you, what then?"

"Hypocrite!" exclaimed Dmitri in fury.

"He says that to his father! His father! How would he behave with others? Gentlemen, would you believe it; there's a
poor but honorable man living here, burdened with a large
family, a captain who got into trouble and was discharged
from the army, but not by court-martial, with no slur on his
honor. And three weeks ago, Dmitri grabbed him by the
beard in a tavern, dragged him out into the street and beat him
publicly. And all because this poor man is an agent in a little
business of mine."

"It's all a lie! Outwardly it's the truth, but inwardly, a lie!"
Dmitri was trembling with rage. Then turning to his father he
continued. "I don't justify my action. Yes, I confess, I behaved
like a brute to that captain. And I regret it now. And I'm disgusted with myself for my brutal rage. But this captain, this
agent of yours, went to that lady whom you call an enchantress . . . You sent him to suggest to her that she should take
I.O.U.s of mine which were in your possession, and should
sue me for the money so as to get me into prison if I persisted in claiming an account from you of my property. Now
you reproach me for having a liking for that lady when you
yourself incited her to captivate me! She told me so to my
face. . . . She told me the story and laughed at you. . . . You
wanted to put me in prison because you are jealous of my
friendship with her, because you'd begun to force your atten-
tions upon her. I know all about that, too. She laughed at you
for that as well—you hear—she laughed at you as she described it. So here you have this man, this father who reproaches his son! Gentlemen, forgive my anger, but I foresaw
that this crafty old man had only brought you together to
create a scene. I had come prepared to forgive him if he held
out his hand. To forgive him and ask forgiveness! But as he
has just this minute insulted not only me, but an honorable
young lady for whom I feel such respect that I dare not take
her name in vain, I have made up my mind to expose him,
even though he is my father. . . ." He could not go on. His
eyes were glittering and he breathed with difficulty.

Everyone in the cell was stirred. All except Father Zossima
got up from their chairs uneasily. The monks looked austere
and waited for guidance from the elder. He sat still, pale, not
from excitement but from the weakness. An imploring smile
lighted up his face. From time to time he raised his hand, as
though to check the storm. A word from him would have been
enough to end the scene, but he seemed to be waiting for
something. He watched them intently as though trying to make
out something which was not perfectly clear to him. At last
Miusov felt completely humiliated and disgraced.

"We are all to blame for this scandalous scene," he said in
anger. "But I did not foresee it when I came, though I knew
with whom I had to deal. It must be stopped at once! Believe me, your reverence, I had no knowledge of the details

that have just come to light. I was unwilling to believe them, and I learn for the first time. . . . A father is jealous of his son's relations with a woman of loose behavior and intrigues with this creature to get his son into prison! This is the company in which I have been forced to be present! I was deceived. I declare to you all that I was as much deceived as anyone."

"Dmitri!" yelled the old Karamazov suddenly, in an unnatural voice. "If you were not my son I would challenge you this instant to a duel . . . With pistols, at three paces . . . across a handkerchief." He stamped with both feet.

With old liars who have been acting all their lives there are moments when they enter so completely into their part that they tremble or shed real tears, although at that very moment or a second later, they are able to whisper to themselves, "You know you are lying, you shameless old sinner! You're acting now, in spite of your 'holy' wrath."

Dmitri frowned painfully. And he looked with unutterable contempt at his father.

"I thought . . . I thought," he said in a soft and, as it were, controlled voice, "that I was coming to my native place with the angel of my heart, my fiancée, to cherish my father's old age . . . And I find nothing but a depraved, a despicable clown!"

"A duel!" yelled the old wretch again, breathless and spluttering at each syllable. "And you, Miusov, let me tell you that there has never been in all your family a loftier, and more honest—you hear—more honest woman than this 'creature,' as you have dared to call her! And you, Dmitri, have abandoned your fiancée for that 'creature,' so you must yourself have thought that your fiancée couldn't hold a candle to her. That's the woman called a 'creature'!"

"Shameful!" cried Father Joseph.

"Shameful and disgraceful!" Kalganov cried in a boyish voice, trembling with emotion and flushing crimson. He had been silent till that moment.

"Why is such a man alive?" Dmitri, beside himself with rage, growled in a hollow voice, hunching up his shoulders till he looked almost deformed. "Tell me, can he be allowed to go on defiling the earth?" He looked round at everyone and pointed at his father. He spoke evenly and deliberately.

"Listen, listen, monks, to the parricide!" cried the old man, rushing up to Father Joseph. "That's the answer to your 'shameful'! What is shameful? That 'creature,' that 'woman of loose behavior' is perhaps holier than you are yourselves, you monks who are seeking salvation! She fell perhaps in her youth, ruined by her environment. But she loved much, and Christ himself forgave the woman 'who loved much.' "

"It was not for such love Christ forgave her," broke impatiently from the gentle Father Joseph.

"Yes, it was for such love, monks, it was! You save your

76

souls here, eating cabbage, and think you are righteous. You eat a gudgeon a day, and you think you bribe God with this little fish."

"It's a disgrace!" was heard on all sides in the cell.

This scene was suddenly cut short in a most unexpected way. Father Zossima rose from his seat. Almost distracted with anxiety for the elder, Alyosha supported him by the arm. Father Zossima moved toward Dmitri and reaching him sank on his knees before him. Alyosha thought that he had fallen from weakness, but this was not so. The elder distinctly and deliberately bowed down at Dmitri's feet till his forehead touched the floor. Alyosha was so astonished that he failed to help him when he got up again.

"Good-by! Forgive me, all of you!" Father Zossima then said, bowing on all sides to his guests. There was a faint smile on his lips.

Dmitri stood for a few moments, amazed. Bowing down to him—what did it mean? Suddenly he cried aloud, "Oh God!" hid his face in his hands and rushed out of the room. Everyone ran out after him, in their confusion not saying good-by, or bowing to Father Zossima. Only the monks went up to him for a blessing.

"What did it mean, falling at his feet, like that? Was it symbolic or what?" said Fyodor Karamazov, suddenly quieted and trying to reopen conversation without addressing anybody in particular. They were all going out of the hermitage at the moment.

"I can't answer for a madhouse and for madmen," Miusov answered, irritated. "But I will spare myself your company, Fyodor Karamazov, and trust me, forever. Where's that monk?"

"That monk," that is, the monk who had invited them to dine with the Superior, did not keep them waiting. He met them as soon as they came down the steps from the elder's cell, as though he had been waiting for them all the time.

"Reverend Father, kindly do me a favor. Convey my deepest respect to the Father Superior and apologize for me personally, Miusov, to his reverence. Kindly tell him that I deeply regret that owing to unforeseen circumstances I am unable to have the honor of being present at his table, greatly as I should desire to do so," Miusov said to the monk.

"And that unforeseen circumstance, of course, is myself," Fyodor Karamazov cut in immediately. "Do you hear, Father, this gentleman doesn't want to remain in my company or else he'd come." Then turning to Miusov he said: "You shall go, Miusov. Pray go to the Father Superior and good appetite to you. I will decline the invitation, not you. Home, home, I'll eat at home. I don't feel equal to it here, Miusov, my amiable relative."

"I am not your relative and never have been, you contemptible man!"

"I said it on purpose to madden you, because you always disclaim the relationship, though you really are a relative in spite of your shuffling. I'll prove it by the church calendar. As for you, Ivan, stay if you like. I'll send the horses for you later. . . . Propriety requires you to go to the Father Superior, Miusov, to apologize for the disturbance we've been making."

"Is it true that you are going home? Are you lying?"

"Peter Miusov! How could I dare after what's happened! Forgive me, gentlemen, I was carried away. And upset besides! And I am ashamed. Gentlemen, one man has the heart of Alexander of Macedon and another the heart of the little dog Fido. Mine is that of the little dog Fido. I am abashed! After such a scene how can I go to dinner, to gobble up the monastery's sauces. I am ashamed, I can't. You must excuse me!"

"The devil only knows if he is going to deceive us," thought Miusov, still hesitating, and watching the retreating buffoon with mistrust. The old wretch turned round, and noticing that Miusov was watching him, blew him a kiss.

"Well, are you coming to the Superior?" Miusov asked Ivan abruptly.

"Why not? I was especially invited yesterday."

"Unfortunately I feel I must go to this confounded dinner," said Miusov with irritation, regardless of the fact that the monk was listening. "We should at least apologize for the disturbance, and explain that it was not our doing. What do you think?"

"Yes, we must explain that it wasn't our doing. Besides, father won't be there," observed Ivan.

"Well, I should hope not! Confound this dinner!"

They all walked on. The monk listened in silence. On the road through the grove he made one observation however—that the Father Superior had been waiting a long time, and that they were more than half an hour late. He received no answer.

Miusov looked with hatred at Ivan.

"Here he is, going to the dinner as though nothing had happened," he thought. "A brazen face, and the conscience of a Karamazov!"

7. A Young Man Bent on a Career

ALYOSHA HELPED FATHER ZOSSIMA to his bedroom and seated him on his bed. It was a little room furnished with the bare necessities. There was a narrow iron bedstead, with a strip of felt for a mattress. In the corner, under the ikons, was a reading desk with a cross and the Gospel lying on it. The elder sank exhausted on the bed. His eyes glittered and he breathed hard. He looked intently at Alyosha, as though considering something.

"Go, my dear boy, go. Porfiry is enough for me. Hurry, you are needed there, go and wait at the Father Superior's table."

"Let me stay here," Alyosha begged.

"You are more needed there. There is no peace there. You will wait, and be of service. If evil spirits rise up, repeat a prayer. And remember, my son (the elder liked to call him that), this is not the place for you in the future. When it is God's will to call me, leave the monastery. Go away for good."

Alyosha stared.

"What is it? This is not your place for the time. I bless you for great service in the world. Yours will be a long pilgrimage. And you will have to take a wife, too. You will have to bear *all* before you come back. There will be much to do. But I have trust in you, and so I send you forth. Christ is with you. Do not abandon Him and He will not abandon you. You will see great sorrow, and in that sorrow you will be happy. This is my last message to you: in sorrow seek happiness. Work, work unceasingly. Remember my words, for although I shall talk with you again, not only my days but my hours are numbered."

Alyosha's face betrayed his emotion. The corners of his mouth quivered.

"What is it?" Father Zossima asked, smiling gently. "The worldly may follow the dead with tears, but here we rejoice over the father who is departing. We rejoice and pray for him. Leave me. I must pray. Go. Hurry. Be near your brothers. And not near one only, but near both."

Father Zossima raised his hand to bless him. Alyosha could not protest, though he had a great longing to remain. He longed, moreover, to ask the significance of the elder's bowing to Dmitri. This question was on the tip of his tongue, but he dared not ask it. He knew that the elder would have explained it unasked if he had wanted to. But evidently it was not his wish. That act had made a terrible impression on Alyosha. He believed blindly in its mysterious significance. Mysterious, and perhaps awful.

As he hurried out of the hermitage to go to the monastery to serve at the Father Superior's dinner he felt a sudden pang at his heart. He stopped short. He seemed to hear again Father Zossima's words, foretelling his approaching end. What he had foretold so exactly must infallibly come to pass. Alyosha believed that implicitly. But how could he be left without him. How could he live without seeing and hearing him? Where should he go? He had told him not to weep, and to leave the monastery. Oh God! It was long since Alyosha had known such anguish. He hurried through the grove that divided the monastery from the hermitage, and unable to bear the burden of his thoughts, he gazed at the ancient pines beside the path. He had not far to go—about five hundred yards. He expected to meet no one at that hour, but at the first turn in the path he saw the divinity student Rakitin. He was waiting for someone.

"Are you waiting for me?" asked Alyosha.

"Yes," grinned Rakitin. "You are hurrying to the Father Superior, I know. He is having a banquet. There hasn't been such a banquet since the Superior entertained the Bishop and General Pahatov. Do you remember? I won't be there, but you go and serve the sauces . . . Tell me one thing, Alyosha, what does that vision mean? That's what I want to ask you."

"What vision?"

"That bowing to your brother, Dmitri. And didn't he touch the ground with his forehead, too!"

"Are you speaking of Father Zossima?"

"Yes, of Father Zossima."

"Touched the ground?"

"What does that vision mean?"

"I don't know what it means," said Alyosha.

"I knew he wouldn't explain it to you! There's nothing wonderful about it! It's only the usual holy nonsense. But there was a reason for Father Zossima doing it; all the pious people in the town will talk about it and spread the story through the province, wondering what it meant. To my thinking the old man really has a keen nose! He sniffed a crime. Your house stinks of it."

"What crime?"

Rakitin evidently had something he was eager to speak about. They walked on together.

"It'll be in your family, this crime. Between your brothers and your rich old father. So Father Zossima flopped down to be ready for what may turn up. If something happens later on, it'll be: 'Ah, the holy man foresaw it, prophesied it!' Though it's a poor sort of prophecy, flopping down like that. 'Ah, but it was symbolic,' they'll say, 'an allegory.' And the devil knows what else they'll say! It'll be remembered to his glory: 'He predicted the crime and marked the criminal!' That's always the way with fanatics; they cross themselves at the tavern and throw stones at the temple. Like your elder, Father Zossima, who takes a stick to a just man and falls at the feet of a murderer."

"What crime? What murderer? What do you mean?"

Alyosha stopped dead. Rakitin stopped, too.

"What murderer? As though you didn't know! You've thought of it. That's interesting, too, by the way. Listen, Alyosha, you always speak the truth, though you're always between two stools. Have you thought of it or not? Answer."

"I have," answered Alyosha in a low voice. Even Rakitin was startled.

"What? Have you really?" he cried.

"I . . . I've not exactly thought of it," muttered Alyosha. "But as you began speaking, I realized I had thought of it myself."

"You see? Looking at your father and your brother Dmitri today you thought of a crime. Then I'm not wrong."

"But wait, wait a minute," Alyosha broke in uneasily. "What has led you to see all this? Why does it interest you? That's the first question."

"Two questions, disconnected, but natural. I'll deal with them separately. What led me to see it? I wouldn't have seen it, if I hadn't suddenly understood your brother Dmitri, seen right into the very heart of him all at once. I caught his whole character from one trait. These very honest but passionate people have a line which mustn't be crossed. If it is . . . He'll run at your father with a knife . . . But your father's a drunken and shameless man who can never draw the line—if they both let themselves go, they'll both come to grief."

"No. No. If that's all you think, you've reassured me! It won't come to that."

"But why are you trembling? Let me tell you why. Your Dmitri may be honest (he is stupid, but honest) but he's sensual. That's the definition and inner essence of him. It's your father who handed him on his low sensuality. Do you know, I wonder at you, Alyosha, how you can have kept your purity. You're a Karamazov too, you know! In your family sensuality is carried to a disease. But now, these three sensualists are watching one another, with their knives in their belts. The three of them are knocking their heads together, and you may be the fourth."

"You are mistaken about that woman. Dmitri despises her," said Alyosha with a shudder.

"Grushenka? No, he doesn't despise her. Since he has openly abandoned his fiancée for her, he doesn't despise her. There's something there, Alyosha, that you don't understand yet. A man will fall in love with some beauty, with a woman's body, or even with a part of a woman's body and he'll abandon his own children for her, sell his father and mother, and his country, Russia, too. If he's honest, he'll steal; if he's humane, he'll murder; if he's faithful, he'll deceive. Pushkin, the poet of women's feet, sung of their feet in his verse. Others don't sing their praises, but they can't look at a woman's feet without a thrill—and it's not only their feet. Contempt's no help here, Alyosha. Even if Dmitri did despise Grushenka . . . He does, but he can't tear himself away."

"I understand that," Alyosha said suddenly.

81

"You do? Well, I guess you do since you blurt it out like that," said Rakitin maliciously. "It escaped you unawares. Your confession is revealing. So it's a familiar subject; you've thought about it already, about sensuality, I mean! Oh, you virgin soul! You're a quiet one, Alyosha, you're a saint, I know, but the devil only knows what you're thinking about, and what you know already! You are pure, but you've been down into the depths. . . . I've been watching you a long time. You're a Karamazov yourself; you're a thorough Karamazov—birth and heredity have shaped you. You're a sensualist from your father, a crazy saint from your mother. Why do you tremble? Is it true, then? Do you know, Grushenka has been begging me to bring you to her house. 'I'll pull off his cassock,' she says. You can't imagine how she begs me to bring you. I wondered why she takes such an interest in you. Do you know, she's an extraordinary woman too!"

"Thank her and say I'm not coming," said Alyosha, with a strained smile. "Finish what you were saying. I'll tell you what I think after."

"There's nothing to finish. It's all clear. It's the same old tune. If even you are sensual at heart what of your brother, Ivan? He's a Karamazov, too. What is at the root of all you Karamazovs is that you're all sensual, grasping and crazy! Your brother Ivan writes theological articles as a joke, for some idiotic, unknown motive of his own, though he's an atheist, and he admits it's a fraud. That's your brother Ivan! He's trying to get Dmitri's fiancée for himself, and I think he'll succeed, too. And what's more it's with Dmitri's consent. For Dmitri will give Ivan his fiancée just to be rid of her. Then he'll be free to go to Grushenka. And he's ready to do this in spite of all his nobility. Remember that. Those are the most fatal people! Who the devil can make you out? Dmitri recognizes how base he is and still he goes on with it! Let me tell you, too, the old man, your father is standing in Dmitri's way now. He has suddenly gone crazy over Grushenka. His mouth waters at the sight of her. It's simply because of her that he made that scene in the cell just now, simply because Miusov called her an 'abandoned creature.' He's worse than a tom cat in heat. At first she was only employed by him in connection with his taverns and in some other shady business, but now he has suddenly realized all she is and has gone wild about her. He keeps pestering her with his offers, not honorable ones, of course. And they'll have a head-on collision, the precious father and son, on that path! But Grushenka does not care for either of them, she's playing with them, and teasing them both, and waiting to see which she can get most out of. For though she could get a lot of money from your father he wouldn't marry her. And he might turn stingy in the end, and keep his purse shut. That's where Dmitri comes in, he has no money, but he's ready to marry her. Yes, ready to marry her! To abandon his fiancée, the beautiful Katerina who's rich, and the daughter of a colonel! He's ready to abandon her and marry Grushenka, who has been the mistress of a dissipated old merchant, Kuzma Samsonov, a coarse, uneducated provincial mayor. Some murderous clash can result from all this, and that's what your brother Ivan is waiting for. It would suit him perfectly. He'll carry off Katerina and pocket her dowry of sixty thousand. That's very alluring to start with, for a man of no consequence and a beggar. And, remember, he won't be wronging Dmitri but doing him a favor. For I know as a fact that Dmitri only last week when he was drunk with some gypsy girls in a tavern, cried out that he was unworthy of Katerina, but brother Ivan, he was the man who deserved her. And Katerina will not in the end refuse such a fascinating man as Ivan. She's hesitating between the two of them already. And how has Ivan won you all, so that you all worship him? He is laughing at you, and enjoying himself at your expense."

"How do you know? How can you speak so confidently?" Alyosha asked, frowning.

"Why do you ask? Are you frightened at my answer? It shows that you know I'm speaking the truth."

"You don't like Ivan. Ivan wouldn't be tempted by money."

"Really? And the beauty of Katerina? It's not only the money, though a fortune of sixty thousand is an attraction."

"Ivan is above that. He wouldn't play up to anyone for money. It is not money, it's not comfort Ivan is seeking. Perhaps it's suffering he is seeking?"

"What wild dream is that? Oh, you—aristocrats!"

"Ah, Ivan has a stormy spirit. His mind is in bondage. He is haunted by a great, unsolved doubt. He is one of those who don't want millions, but an answer to their questions."

"That's plagiarism, Alyosha. You're quoting Father Zossima. Ah, Ivan is a problem to you!" cried Rakitin, with undisguised malice. His face changed, and his lips twitched. "And the problem's a stupid one. It is no good guessing at it. Rack your brains—you'll understand it. His article is absurd and ridiculous. And did you hear his stupid theory just now: if there's no immortality of the soul, then there's no virtue, and everything is lawful? And by the way, do you remember how your brother Dmitri cried out: 'I will remember!' An attractive theory for scoundrels! . . . I'm being abusive, that's stupid. Not for scoundrels, but for pedantic fakers, 'haunted by profound, unsolved doubts.' He's showing off, and what it all comes to is, 'on the one hand we cannot but admit' and 'on the other it must be confessed!' His whole theory is a fraud! Humanity will find in itself the power to live for virtue even without believing in immortality. It will find it in love for freedom, for equality, for fraternity."

Rakitin could hardly restrain his emotions, but, suddenly, as though remembering something he stopped short.

"Well, that's enough," he said, with a twisted smile. "Why are you laughing? Do you think I'm a fool?"

"No, I never think of you as a fool. You are clever but . . . Never mind. I was silly to smile. I understand your getting irritated about it. And I suspect from your behavior that you are not indifferent to Katerina yourself. I've suspected that for a long time. That's why you don't like my brother Ivan. Are you jealous of him?"

"And greedy for her money, too? Won't you add that?"

"I'll say nothing about money. I am not going to insult you."

"I believe it, since you say so, but damn you, and your brother Ivan with you. Don't you understand that one might very well dislike him, apart from Katerina? And why the devil should I like him? He condescends to abuse me, you know. Why haven't I a right to abuse him?"

"I never heard him saying anything about you, good or bad. He doesn't speak of you at all."

"But I heard that the day before yesterday at Katerina's he was abusing me for all he was worth—you see what an interest he takes in your humble servant. And who is the jealous one after that, I can't say. He was so good as to say that, if I don't become a monk I will certainly go to Petersburg and become a reviewer on a magazine. And he said that I will write for the next ten years, and in the end become the owner of the magazine, and bring it out on the liberal and atheistic side, with a socialistic tinge, with a tiny gloss of socialism, but keeping a sharp lookout all the time, that is, keeping in with both sides and hoodwinking the fools. According to your brother's account, the tinge of socialism won't hinder me from laying by the profits and investing them under the guidance of some Jew, till at the end of my career I build a great house in Petersburg and move my publishing offices into it, and rent out the upper floors to lodgers. He has even chosen the place for it, near the new stone bridge across the Neva, which they say is to be built in Petersburg."

"Ah, Rakitin, that's just what will really happen, every word of it," cried Alyosha, unable to restrain a good-humored smile.

"You are pleased to be sarcastic, too, Alyosha."

"No, no, I'm fooling, forgive me. I've something quite different in my mind. But, excuse me, who told you all this? You can't have been at Katerina's yourself when he was talking about you?"

"I wasn't there, but Dmitri was; and I heard him tell it with my own ears. If you want to know, he didn't tell me, but I overheard him. I was sitting in Grushenka's bedroom and I couldn't go away because Dmitri was in the next room."

"Oh yes, I'd forgotten she was a relative of yours."

"A relative! That Grushenka a relative of mine!" cried

Rakitin, turning crimson. "Are you mad. You're out of your mind!"

"Why, isn't she a relative of yours? I heard so."

"Where can you have heard it? You Karamazovs brag of being an ancient, noble family, though your father used to run about playing the buffoon at other men's tables, and was only admitted to the kitchen as a favor. I may be only a priest's son, and dirt in the eyes of noblemen like you, but don't insult me. I have a sense of honor, too, Alyosha, I couldn't be a relation of Grushenka, a common whore. I want you to understand that!"

Rakitin was very irritated.

"Forgive me. For goodness' sake, I had no idea . . . Besides . . . How can you call her a whore. Is she . . . that sort of woman?" Alyosha flushed suddenly. "I tell you again, I heard that she was a relative of yours. You often go to see her, and you told me yourself you're not her lover. I never dreamed that you of all people had such contempt for her! Does she really deserve it?"

"I may have reasons of my own for visiting her. That's not your business. But as for relationship, your brother, or even your father is more likely to make her your relative than mine. Well, here we are." Rakitin and Alyosha had finally reached the Father Superior's where Alyosha was to help serve at dinner. "You'd better go to the kitchen," said Rakitin. Then suddenly he cried out: "Hullo! What's wrong! What is it? Are we late? They can't have finished dinner so soon! Have the Karamazovs been making trouble again? They probably have. There's your father and your brother Ivan running after him. They've left the Father Superior's. And look, Father Isidor's shouting something after them from the steps. And your father's shouting and waving his arms. He's swearing. And there goes Miusov driving away in his carriage. You see, he's going. And there's old Maximov running! There must have been a fight. There can't have been any dinner. Surely they've not been beating the Father Superior! Or have they, themselves, perhaps, been beaten? It would serve them right!"

There was reason for Rakitin's excitement. There had been a disgraceful, an unprecedented scene. It had all come from the impulse of a moment.

8. The Disgraceful Scene

Miusov, as a man of breeding and delicacy, could not but feel some inward qualms, when he reached the Father Superior's with Ivan. He felt ashamed of having lost his temper. He felt that he ought to have disregarded that despicable wretch, Fyodor Karamazov, and not have allowed himself to be upset by him in Father Zossima's cell. "The monks were not to blame, in any case," he reflected, on the steps. "And if they're people of birth here (and the Father Superior, I understand, is a nobleman) why not be friendly and courteous with them? I won't argue. I'll fall in with everything. I'll win them by politeness, and . . . and . . . show them that I've nothing to do with that Aesop, that buffoon, that Pierrot, and have been dragged into this affair, just as they have."

He determined to drop his litigation with the monastery, and relinquish his claims to the wood-cutting and fishery rights at once. He was the more ready to do this because the rights had become much less valuable, and he had not the vaguest idea where the wood and river in question were.

These excellent intentions were strengthened when Miusov entered the Father Superior's dining room, though, strictly speaking, it was not a dining room, for the Father Superior had only two rooms altogether. These rooms were, however, much larger and more comfortable than Father Zossima's. But there was no great luxury about the furnishings either. The furniture was of mahogany, covered with leather, in the old-fashioned style of 1820. The floor was not even stained, but everything was shining with cleanliness, and there were beautiful flowers in the windows. The most sumptuous thing in the room was, of course, the dinner table. The cloth was clean, the service shone. There were three kinds of well-baked bread, two bottles of wine, two of excellent mead, and a large glass jug of beer. Both the mead and the beer were made in the monastery and were famous in the neighborhood. There was no vodka. Rakitin related afterwards that there were five dishes: fish soup served with little fish patties, then boiled fish served in a special way, then salmon cutlets, sherbet and compote, and finally, a blanc-mange.

Rakitin found out about all these good things because he went into the kitchen, where he had a footing. He had a footing everywhere, and got information about everything. He was of an uneasy and envious temper. He was well aware of his abilities, and nervously exaggerated them in his self-conceit. He felt confident that he would someday play a prominent part of some sort. But Alyosha, who was attached to him, was distressed to see that his friend Rakitin was dishonorable, and quite unconscious of being so. He felt, on the contrary, that because he would not steal money left on a table that he was a man of the highest integrity. Neither Alyosha nor anyone else could have convinced him otherwise.

Rakitin, of course, was a person of too little importance to be invited to the dinner, to which Father Joseph, Father Paissy, and only one other monk were invited. They were already waiting when Miusov, Kalganov, and Ivan arrived. The other guest, Maximov, stood a little aside, waiting also. The

Father Superior stepped into the middle of the room to receive his guests. He was a tall, thin, but still vigorous old man, with black hair streaked with gray, and a long, grave, ascetic face. He bowed to his guests in silence. They approached to receive his blessing. Miusov even tried to kiss his hand, but the Father Superior graciously drew it back in time to avoid letting Miusov humble himself. But he allowed Ivan and Kalganov to do so. They went through the ceremony in the most simple-hearted and complete manner, as peasants do.

"We must apologize most humbly, your reverence," began Miusov speaking in a dignified and respectful tone. "Forgive us for having come alone without the gentleman you invited, Fyodor Karamazov. He felt obliged to decline the honor of your hospitality, and not without reason. In the reverend Father Zossima's cell he was carried away by an unhappy disagreement with his son, and let fall words which were quite out of keeping . . . In fact, quite unseemly . . . As your reverence is, no doubt, already aware." He glanced at the monks. "And recognizing that he had been to blame, he felt sincere regret and shame, and begged me, and his son Ivan to convey to you his apologies and regrets. In brief, he hopes and desires to make amends later. He asks your blessing, and begs you to forget what has taken place."

As Miusov spoke the last word he completely recovered his self-complacency. All traces of his former irritation disappeared. He fully and sincerely loved humanity again.

The Father Superior listened to him with dignity. And with a slight bend of the head, he replied: "I sincerely deplore his absence. Perhaps at our table he might have learned to like us, and we him. Pray be seated, gentlemen."

The Father Superior stood before the holy image, and began to say grace, aloud. All bent their heads reverently. And Maximov clasped his hands before him, with peculiar fervor.

It was at this moment that Fyodor Karamazov played his last prank. It must be noted that he really had meant to go home. He really had felt the impossibility of going to dine with the Father Superior as though nothing had happened, after his disgraceful behavior in the elder's cell. Not that he was so very much ashamed of himself—quite the contrary perhaps. But still he felt it would be unseemly to go to dinner. Yet his creaking carriage had hardly been brought forward, and he had hardly got into it, when he suddenly stopped short. He remembered his own words in the elder's cell: "I always feel when I meet people that I am lower than they, and that they all take me for a buffoon. So I say let me play the buffoon, for you are, every one of you, more stupid and lower than I." He longed to revenge himself on everyone for his own shortcomings. He suddenly recalled how he had once been asked: "Why do you hate so and so, so much?" And he had answered in his shameless way, "I'll tell you. He has done me no harm.

But I played him a dirty trick, and ever since then I have hated him."

Remembering that now, he smiled quietly and maliciously, hesitating for a moment. His eyes gleamed, and his lips quivered. "Well, since I have begun, I may as well go on," he decided. His predominant sensation at that moment might be expressed in the following words: "Well, there is no rehabilitating myself now. So let me shame them for all I am worth. I will show them I don't care what they think—that's all!"

He told the coachman to wait. Then quickly he returned to the monastery and went straight to the Father Superior's. He had no clear idea what he would do, but he knew that he could not control himself, and that the slightest thing might drive him to the limits of obscenity, but only to obscenity, to nothing criminal, nothing for which he could be legally punished. In the last resort, he could always restrain himself; he had marveled at this power sometimes.

He appeared in the Father Superior's dining room, at the moment when the prayer was over. Standing in the doorway, he scanned the company, and laughing maliciously, looked them all boldly in the face. "You thought I had gone, and here I am again!" he cried to the whole room.

For a moment everyone stared at him without a word. At once everyone felt that something revolting, grotesque, positively scandalous, was about to happen. Miusov changed from the most benevolent frame of mind to the most savage. All the feelings that had subsided and died down in his heart revived instantly.

"No! This I cannot endure!" he cried. "I absolutely cannot! And . . . I certainly cannot!"

The blood rushed to his head. He stammered. He forgot his manners. He grabbed his hat.

"What is it he cannot?" cried Fyodor Karamazov. "What is it he absolutely cannot and certainly cannot? Your reverence, am I to come in or not? Will you receive me as your guest?"

"You are welcome with all my heart," answered the Superior. "Gentlemen!" he added, "I beg you most earnestly to lay aside your dissensions, and to be united in love and family harmony—with prayer to the Lord at our humble table."

"No, no, it is impossible!" cried Miusov.

"Well, if it is impossible for Miusov, it is impossible for me, and I won't stop. That is why I came. I will stay with him everywhere now. If you will go away, Miusov, I will go away too: if you remain, I will remain. . . . You stung him by what you said about family harmony, Father Superior. He does not admit he is my relative." Then suddenly turning to Maximov he asked: "That's right, isn't it, Von Sohn? Here's Von Sohn. How are you, Von Sohn?"

"Do you mean me?" muttered Maximov, puzzled.

"Of course I mean you," cried old Karamazov. "Who else? The Father Superior could not be Von Sohn."

"But I am not Von Sohn either. I am Maximov."

"No, you are Von Sohn. Your reverence, do you know who Von Sohn was? It was a famous murder case. He was killed in a house of prostitution. I believe that is what such places are called among you. He was killed and robbed, and in spite of his venerable age, he was nailed up in a box and sent from Petersburg to Moscow in the luggage van. And while they were nailing him up the prostitutes sang songs and played the harp, that is to say, the piano. So this is that very Von Sohn. He has risen from the dead, hasn't he, Von Sohn?"

"What is happening? What's this?" asked the monks.

"Let us go," cried Miusov, addressing Kalganov.

"No, excuse me," Fyodor Karamazov broke in shrilly, taking another step into the room. "Allow me to finish. There in the cell you blamed me for behaving disrespectfully just because I spoke of eating gudgeon. Miusov, my relative, prefers to have more nobility than sincerity in his words, but I prefer in mine to have more sincerity than nobility and . . . Damn nobility! That's right, isn't it, Von Sohn? Allow me, Father Superior, though I am a buffoon and play the buffoon, yet I am the soul of honor, and I want to speak my mind. Yes, I am and nothing else. I came here, perhaps to have a look and speak my mind. My son Alyosha is here being saved. I am his father. I care for his welfare, and it is my duty to care. While I've been playing the fool, I have been listening and watching. And now I want to give you the last act of the performance. You know how things are with us? As a thing falls, so it lies. As a thing once has fallen, so it must lie forever. Not a bit of it! I want to get up again. Holy Father, I am indignant with you. Confession is a great sacrament, before which I am ready to bow down reverently; but there in the cell, they all kneel down and confess aloud. Can it be right to confess aloud? It was ordained by the holy fathers to confess in secret: then only will your confession be a mystery. So it was of old. But how can I explain before everyone that I did this and that . . . Well, you understand what—sometimes it would not be proper to talk about certain things. . . . So it is really a scandal! No, fathers, one might be carried along with you to the Flagellants, I dare say . . . at the first opportunity I shall write to the Synod, and I shall take my son, Alyosha, home."

It must be noted here that Fyodor Karamazov knew where to look for the weak spot. There had been rumors which had even reached the Archbishop (regarding our monastery and others where the institution of elders existed) that too much respect was paid to the elders, even to the detriment of the authority of the Superior; that the elders abused the sacrament of confession and so on and so on—absurd charges which had died away of themselves everywhere. But the spirit of evil, which had caught up Fyodor Karamazov and was carrying him into lower and lower depths of disgrace, prompted him to revive this old slander. He did not understand a word of it, and he did not even express it sensibly, for no one had been kneeling and confessing aloud in the elder's cell, so that he could not have seen anything of the kind. He was only speaking from the confused memory of old slanders. And as soon as he had delivered his tirade, he felt he had been talking absurd nonsense, and at once longed to prove to his audience and above all to himself, that he had not been talking nonsense. And, though he knew perfectly well that with each word he would be adding more and more absurdity, he could not restrain himself, and plunged forward blindly.

"How shocking!" cried Miusov.

"Pardon me!" said the Father Superior. "It was said of old 'Many have begun to speak against me and have uttered evil sayings about me. And hearing it I have said to myself: it is the correction of the Lord and He has sent it to heal my vain soul.' And so we humbly thank you, honored guest!" and the Father Superior bowed to Fyodor Karamazov.

"Tut—tut—tut—sanctimoniousness and stock phrases! Old phrases and old gestures. The old lies and formal prostrations. We know all about them. A kiss on the lips and a dagger in the heart, as in Schiller's *Robbers*. I don't like falsehood, fathers, I want the truth. But the truth is not to be found in eating gudgeon and that I proclaim aloud! Father monks, why do you fast? Why do you expect reward in heaven for that? Why, for a reward like that I will come and fast too! No, saintly monk, you try being virtuous in the world, do good to society, without shutting yourself up in a monastery at other people's expense, and without expecting a reward up aloft for it—you'll find that a bit harder. I can talk sense, too, Father Superior." He stopped short. Then going up to the table he said: "What have they got here? Old port wine, mead brewed by the Eliseyev Brothers. Fie, fie, fathers! That is something beyond gudgeon. Look at the bottles the fathers have brought out, he! he! he! And who has provided it all? The Russian peasant, the laborer, brings here the pennies earned by his horny hand, wringing them from his family and the tax-gatherer! You bleed the people, holy fathers!"

"This is too disgraceful!" said Father Joseph.

Father Paissy kept obstinately silent. Miusov rushed from the room and Kalganov followed him.

"Well, Father, I will follow Miusov! I am not coming to see you again. You may beg me on your knees, I won't come. I sent you a thousand roubles. I am taking my revenge for my youth, for all the humiliation I endured." He thumped the table with his fist in a false display of feeling. "This monastery has played an important part in my life! It has cost me many bitter tears. You used to set my wife, the crazy one, against me. You cursed me with 'bell and book.' You spread stories about me all over the place. Enough, fathers! This is the age of Liberalism, the age of steamers and railways. Neither a thousand, nor a hundred roubles; no, not even a hundred pennies will you get out of me!"

It must be noted again that our monastery never had played any great part in his life, and he never had shed a bitter tear owing to it. But he was so carried away by his own acting, that he was for one moment almost believing it himself. He was so touched he was almost in tears. But at that very instant, he felt that it was time to draw back.

The Father Superior bowed his head at the old wretch's malicious lie, and again spoke impressively: "It is written: 'Bear circumspectly and gladly dishonor that cometh upon thee by no act of thine own. Be not confounded and hate not him who hath dishonored thee.' And so will we."

"Tut, tut, tut! And the rest of your rigmarole. I go, fathers. But I will take my son, Alyosha, away from here forever. Ivan, my most dutiful son, permit me to order you to follow me. Von Sohn, what have you to stay for? Come with me now to town. It is fun there. It is only one short mile. Instead of lenten oil, I will give you sucking-pig and kasha. We will have dinner with some brandy and liqueur and . . . I've cloudberry wine. Hey, Von Sohn, don't lose your chance." He went out, shouting and waving his arms.

It was at that moment that Rakitin saw him and pointed him out to Alyosha.

"Alyosha!" old Karamazov shouted, from far off, catching sight of his youngest son. "You come home to me today, for good, and bring your pillow and mattress. Leave no trace behind."

Alyosha stood rooted to the spot, watching in silence.

Fyodor Karamazov got into the carriage and Ivan was about to follow him without even turning to say good-by to Alyosha. But at this point another almost incredible scene of grotesque buffoonery gave the finishing touch to the episode. Maximov suddenly appeared by the side of the carriage. He ran up, panting, afraid of being too late. He was in such a hurry that in his impatience he put his foot on the step on which Ivan's left foot was still resting, and clutching the carriage he kept trying to jump in. "I am going with you!" he kept shouting, laughing a thin laugh with a look of glee on his face. "Take me, too."

"There!" cried the old Karamazov, delighted. "Did I not say he was Von Sohn. It is Von Sohn himself, risen from the dead. Why, how did you tear yourself away? What did you *vonsohn* there? And how could you get away from the dinner? You must be a brazen-faced fellow! I am that myself, but I am surprised at you! Jump in, jump in! Let him in, Ivan. It will be fun. He can lie somewhere at our feet. Will you lie at our feet, Von Sohn? Or perch on the box with the coachman. Jump up on to the box, Von Sohn!"

But Ivan, who had by now taken his seat, without a word gave Maximov a violent punch in the chest and sent him flying. It was only by chance he did not fall.

"Drive on!" Ivan shouted angrily to the coachman.

"Why, what are you doing? What are you doing? Why did you do that?" his father protested.

But the carriage had already started off. Ivan made no reply.

"Well you are a fine one," his father said. Then after a pause he added, looking askance at his son: "Why, it was you that got up all this monastery business. You urged it, you approved of it. Why are you angry now?"

"You've talked enough. You might rest a bit now," Ivan answered sullenly.

Fyodor Karamazov was again silent.

"A drop of brandy would be nice now," he at length observed. But Ivan did not answer him.

"You shall have some, too, when we get home."

Ivan was still silent.

Fyodor Karamazov waited a few minutes.

"But I shall take Alyosha away from the monastery, even though you disapprove, most honored Karl von Moor."

Ivan shrugged his shoulders and turning away in contempt stared at the road. And they did not speak again all the way home.

BOOK III: THE SENSUALISTS

1. *In the Servants' Quarters*

THE KARAMAZOVS' HOUSE was far from being in the center of town, but it was not quite outside of town either. It was a pleasant-looking old house of two stories, painted gray, with a red iron roof. It was roomy and snug, and would still last many years. It had all sorts of unexpected little cupboards and closets and staircases. There were rats in it, but Fyodor Karamazov did not altogether dislike them. "One doesn't feel so isolated when one's left alone in the evening," he used to say. It was his habit to send the servants away to the lodge for the night and to lock himself up alone.

The lodge was a roomy and solid building in the yard. Fyodor Karamazov used to have the cooking done there, although there was a kitchen in the house. He did not like the smell of cooking, and, winter and summer alike, the dishes were carried in across the courtyard. The house was built for a large family; there was room for five times as many, with their servants. But at the time of our story there was no one living in the house but Fyodor Karamazov and his son Ivan. And in the lodge there were only three servants: old Gregory, and his old wife Marfa, and a young man called Smerdyakov.

Of these three we must say a few words. Of old Gregory we have said something already. He was firm and determined and went blindly and obstinately toward his object if he believed that it was right, even though his reasons were often very illogical. He was honest and could not be corrupted. His wife, Marfa, had obeyed her husband's will implicitly all her life, yet she had pestered him terribly after the emancipation of the serfs. She was set on leaving Fyodor Karamazov and opening a little shop in Moscow with their small savings. But Gregory decided then, once and for all that "the woman's talking nonsense, for every woman is dishonest," and that they should not leave their old master, whatever he might be, for "that was now their duty."

"Do you understand what duty is?" he asked Marfa.

"I understand what duty means, Gregory, but why it's our duty to stay here I shall never understand," Marfa answered firmly.

"Well, don't understand then. But that's how it's going to be. And you hold your tongue." And so it was. They did not go away, and Fyodor Karamazov promised them a small wage, and paid it regularly.

Gregory knew that he had a strong influence over his master. It was true, and he was aware of it. Karamazov was an obstinate and cunning buffoon, yet, though his will was strong enough "in some of the affairs of life," as he expressed it, he found himself, to his surprise, extremely feeble in facing certain other emergencies. He knew his weaknesses and was afraid of them. There are positions in which one has to keep a sharp lookout. And that's not easy without a trustworthy man, and Gregory was a most trustworthy man.

Many times during his life Fyodor Karamazov had only just escaped a beating through Gregory's intervention, and on each occasion the old servant gave him a good lecture. But it wasn't only beatings that Karamazov was afraid of. There were more serious occasions, and very subtle and complicated ones, when he could not have explained the extraordinary craving for someone faithful and devoted, which unaccountably and suddenly came over him. It was almost a morbid condition.

Corrupt and often cruel in his lust, like some poisonous insect, Fyodor Karamazov was sometimes, in moments of drunkenness, overcome by superstitious terror and a moral convulsion which took an almost physical form. "My soul simply quakes in my throat at those times," he used to say.

At such moments he liked to feel that there was near at hand, in the lodge if not in the room, a strong, faithful man, virtuous and unlike himself . . . One who had seen all his vices and knew all his secrets, but was ready in his devotion to overlook everything, not to oppose him and above all, not to reproach him or threaten him with anything either in this world or in the next, and, in case of need, to defend him—from whom? From somebody unknown, but terrible and dangerous. What he needed was to feel that there was *another* man, an old and tried friend, whom he might call in his sick moments merely to look at or merely to exchange some quiet words with. And if the old servant were not angry, he felt comforted, and if he were angry, he was more dejected. It happened even (very rarely however) that Fyodor Karamazov went at night to the lodge to wake Gregory and bring him back to the house for a moment. Then he would begin talking about the most trivial matters, and would soon let Gregory go again, sometimes even with a joke. And after he had gone, Karamazov would get into bed with a curse and sleep the sleep of the just.

Something of the sort had happened to Fyodor Karamazov when his son Alyosha arrived. Alyosha "pierced his heart" by "living with him, seeing everything and blaming nothing." Moreover, Alyosha brought with him something his father had never known before: a complete absence of contempt for him and a consistent kindness, a perfectly natural, unaffected devotion to the old man who deserved it so little. All this was a complete surprise to the old wretch who had dropped all family ties. It was a new and surprising experience for him, who had till then loved nothing but "evil." And when Alyosha had left him to join the monastery, he confessed to himself that he had learned something he had not till then been willing to learn.

I have mentioned already that Gregory had detested Adelaide, the first wife of Fyodor Karamazov and the mother of Dmitri, and that he had, on the other hand, protected Sophia, the poor "crazy woman" against his master and anyone else who chanced to speak ill or lightly of her. His sympathy for the unhappy wife had become something sacred to him, so that even now, twenty years later, he could not bear a slighting allusion to her from anyone, and would at once protest. Externally, Gregory was cold, dignified and reserved, and spoke, weighing his words, without frivolity. It was impossible to tell at first sight whether he loved his meek, obedient wife, Marfa. But he really did love her, and she knew it.

Marfa was by no means foolish, she was probably more clever than her husband or, at least, more prudent than he in worldly affairs. Yet she had given in to him in everything without question or complaint ever since her marriage and she respected him for his spiritual superiority. It was remarkable how little they spoke to one another in the course of their lives; they spoke only of the most necessary daily affairs. The reserved

Gregory thought over all his cares and duties alone, so that Marfa had long grown used to knowing that he did not need her advice. She felt that her husband respected her silence, and took it as a sign of her good sense. He had never beaten her but once, and then only slightly. Once during the year after Fyodor Karamazov's marriage with Adelaide, the village girls and women—at that time serfs—were called together before the house to sing and dance. They were beginning *In the Green Meadows,* when Marfa, at that time a young woman, skipped forward and danced "the Russian Dance." She danced it, not in the village fashion but as she had danced it when she was a servant in the service of the rich Miusov family, in their private theater, where the actors were taught to dance by a dancing master from Moscow. Gregory saw how his wife danced, and, an hour later, at home in their cottage he gave her a lesson, pulling her hair a little. But there it ended. The beating was never repeated, and Marfa gave up dancing.

God had not blessed Gregory and Marfa with children. One child was born but it died. Gregory was fond of children, and was not ashamed of showing it. When Adelaide ran away, Gregory took Dmitri, then a child three years old, combed his hair and washed him in a tub with his own hands, and looked after him for almost a year. Later he looked after Ivan and Alyosha, for which the general's widow had rewarded him with a slap in the face. But I have already related all that. . . . The only happiness his own child brought him was in the anticipation of its birth. When it was born, he was overwhelmed with grief and horror. The baby had six fingers. Gregory was so crushed by this, that he was not only silent till the day of the christening, but spent most of his time in the garden. It was spring, and he spent three days digging the kitchen garden. The third day was fixed for christening the boy. In the meantime Gregory had reached a conclusion. Going into the cottage where the priest and visitors had assembled, including Fyodor Karamazov, who was to stand godfather, he suddenly announced that the baby "ought not to be christened at all." He announced this quietly, briefly, forcing out his words, and gazing with dull intentness at the priest.

"Why not?" asked the priest with good-humored surprise.

"Because it's a monster," muttered Gregory.

"A monster? What monster?"

Gregory was silent for a time. "It's a confusion of nature," he muttered vaguely but firmly, obviously unwilling to say more.

They laughed, and of course christened the poor baby. Gregory prayed earnestly at the font, but his opinion of the newborn child remained unchanged. Yet he did not interfere in any way.

As long as the sickly infant lived Gregory scarcely looked at it, tried not to notice it, and most of the time kept out of the cottage. But when, at the end of two weeks the baby died of thrush, he himself laid it in its little coffin. He looked at it in profound grief, and later when they were filling up the shallow little grave he fell on his knees and bowed down to the earth. He did not for years afterwards mention his child, nor did Marfa speak of the baby before him. Even if Gregory were not present, she never spoke of it above a whisper.

Marfa observed that, from the day of the burial, Gregory devoted himself to "religion," and took to reading the "Lives of the Saints," for the most part sitting alone and in silence, and always putting on his big, round, silver-rimmed spectacles. He rarely read aloud, only perhaps during Lent. He was fond of the Book of Job, and had somehow acquired a copy of the sayings and sermons of "the God-fearing Father Isaac the Syrian." He read this persistently for years on end, understanding very little of it but perhaps prizing and loving it the more for that. Of late he had begun to listen to the doctrines of the sect of Flagellants settled in the neighborhood. He was evidently shaken by them, but judged it unfitting to go over to the new faith. His habit of religious reading gave him an expression of still greater gravity.

Gregory was perhaps predisposed to mysticism. And the birth and death of his deformed child had, as though by special design, been accompanied by another strange and marvelous event which, as he said later, had left a "stamp" upon his soul. It happened that on the very night after the burial of his child, Marfa was awakened by the wail of a newborn baby. She was frightened and called her husband. He listened and said he thought it was more like someone groaning, "it might be a woman." He got up and dressed. It was a rather warm night in May. As he went down the steps, he distinctly heard groans coming from the garden. But the gate from the yard into the garden was locked at night, and there was no other way of entering it, because it was enclosed all around by a strong, high fence.

Going back into the house, Gregory lighted a lantern, took the garden key, and ignoring the hysterical fears of his wife, who was certain that she heard a baby crying, and that it was her own baby crying and calling for her, he went into the garden in silence. There he heard at once that the groans came from the bathhouse that stood near the garden gate, and that they were the groans of a woman.

Opening the door of the bathhouse, he saw a sight which petrified him. An idiot girl, who wandered about the streets and was known to the whole town by the nickname of Lizaveta Smerdyastchaya (Stinking Lizaveta), had gotten into the bathhouse and had just given birth to a child. She lay dying with the baby beside her. She said nothing, for she had never been able to speak. But her story needs a chapter to itself.

2. Lizaveta

THERE WAS ONE THING which struck Gregory particularly, and confirmed a very unpleasant and revolting suspicion. This Lizaveta was a dwarfish creature, "not five foot within a wee bit," as many of the pious old women said pathetically about her, after her death. Her broad, healthy, red face had a look of blank idiocy and the fixed stare in her eyes was unpleasant, in spite of their meek expression. She wandered about, summer and winter alike, barefooted, wearing nothing but a rough smock. Her coarse, almost black hair curled like lamb's wool, and formed a sort of huge cap on her head. It was caked with mud, and had leaves, bits of sticks and shavings clinging to it, as she always slept on the ground and in the dirt.

Her father, a homeless, sickly drunkard, had lost everything and lived many years as a workman with some well-to-do tradespeople. Her mother had long been dead. Spiteful and diseased, her father used to beat Lizaveta inhumanly whenever she returned to him. But she rarely did so, for everyone in the town was ready to look after her as being an idiot, and so specially dear to God. Her father's employers and many others in the town, especially of the tradespeople, tried to clothe her better, and always gave her high boots and a sheepskin coat for the winter. But, although she let them dress her up without resisting, she usually went away, preferably to the cathedral porch, and taking off all that had been given her—kerchief, sheepskin, skirt or boots—she left them there and walked away barefoot in her smock as before.

It happened on one occasion that a new governor of the province, making a tour of inspection in our town, saw Lizaveta, and was deeply moved. And although he was told she was an idiot, he said that for a young woman of twenty to wander about in nothing but a smock was a breach of propriety and must not occur again. But the governor went his way, and Lizaveta was left as she was.

At last her father died, which made her even more acceptable in the eyes of the religious people of the town, because she was now an orphan. In fact, everyone seemed to like her; even the boys did not tease her, and the boys of our town, especially the schoolboys, are a mischievous set. She would walk into strange houses, and no one drove her away. Everyone was kind to her and gave her something. If she were given a penny, she would take it, and at once drop it in the alms box of the church or prison. If she were given a roll or bun in the market, she would hand it to the first child she met. Sometimes she would stop one of the richest ladies in the town and give it to her, and the lady would be pleased to take it. She herself never tasted anything but black bread and water. If she went into an expensive shop, where there were costly goods or money lying about, no one kept watch on her, for they knew that if she saw thousands of roubles she would not have touched a penny.

She scarcely ever went to church. She slept either on the church porch or climbed over a low fence into a kitchen garden. At least once a week she used to turn up "at home," that is at the house of her father's former employers, and in the winter she went there every night, and slept either in the passage or the cowhouse. People were amazed that she could stand such a life, but she was accustomed to it and, although she was very tiny, she was strong and healthy. Some of the townspeople declared that she did all this only from pride, but that is hardly credible. She couldn't speak, and only from time to time uttered an inarticulate grunt. How could she have been proud?

It happened one clear, warm, moonlight night in September (many years ago) that five or six drunken men were returning from the club at a very late hour. They passed through the "back way," which led between the back gardens of the houses, with low fences on either side. This way leads out onto the bridge over the long, stagnant pool which we call a river. Among the weeds under a low fence these men saw Lizaveta asleep. They stopped to look at her, laughing, and began joking in a very vulgar way. It occurred to one of them to ask whether any man could possibly look upon such an animal as a woman, and so forth. . . . They all said that it was impossible. But Fyodor Karamazov, who was among them, declared that it was by no means impossible, and that, indeed, there was a certain attraction about it, and so on. . . . It is true that at that time he was overdoing his part as a buffoon. He wanted to put himself forward and entertain the company, on equal terms, of course, though in reality he was on a servile footing with them. It was just at the time when he had received the news of his first wife's death in Petersburg, and, with crepe upon his hat, was drinking and behaving so shamelessly that even the most open-minded among us were shocked at the sight of him.

His drunken companions, of course, laughed at this unexpected opinion. And one of them even began challenging Karamazov to act upon it. The others, however, rejected the idea, and went on their way. Later on, Fyodor Karamazov swore that he had gone with them, and perhaps it was so. No one knows for certain. No one ever knew. But five or six months later, all the town was talking, with intense and sincere indignation, of Lizaveta's condition, and trying to find out who had wronged her. Then suddenly a terrible rumor was all over town that it was no other than Fyodor Karamazov. Who set the rumor going? Of that drunken band five had left the town and the only one still among us was an elderly and much respected civil councillor, the father of grown-up daughters, who could

98

hardly have spread the tale, even if there had been any foundation for it. But rumor pointed straight at Fyodor Karamazov, and persisted in pointing at him. Of course this was no great sorrow to him, he would not have troubled to contradict tradespeople. In those days he was proud, and did not condescend to talk except in his own circle of the officials and nobles, whom he entertained so well.

At the time, Gregory stood up for his master. He provoked quarrels in defense of him and succeeded in bringing some people round to his side. "It's the wench's own fault," he asserted, and he said that the culprit was Karp, a dangerous convict, who had escaped from prison and whose name was well known to us, as he had hidden in our town. This sounded plausible, for it was remembered that Karp had been in the neighborhood just at that time in the autumn, and had robbed three people.

But this talk did not change popular sympathy from the poor idiot. She was better looked after than ever. A well-to-do merchant's widow arranged to take her into her home at the end of April, meaning not to let her go out until after the confinement. They kept a constant watch over her, but in spite of their vigilance she escaped on the very last day, and made her way into Fyodor Karamazov's garden. How, in her condition, she managed to climb over the high, strong fence remained a mystery. Some said that she must have been lifted over by somebody; others hinted at something more uncanny. The most likely explanation is that it happened naturally—that Lizaveta, accustomed to clambering over low fences to sleep in gardens, had somehow managed to climb this high fence, in spite of her condition, and had jumped down, injuring herself.

Gregory, finding her in the bathhouse, rushed to Marfa. He sent her to Lizaveta while he ran to fetch an old midwife who lived close by. They saved the baby, but Lizaveta died at dawn. Gregory took the baby, brought it home, and making Marfa sit down, he put it on her lap. "A child of God—an orphan is related to all," he said, "and to us above others. Our little lost one has sent us this, who has come from the devil's son and a holy innocent. Nurse him and weep no more."

So Marfa brought up the child. He was christened Pavel, to which people were not slow in adding "son of Fyodor." Fyodor Karamazov did not object to any of this. He thought it amusing, though he persisted in denying his responsibility. The townspeople were pleased at his adopting the foundling. Later on, Fyodor Karamazov invented a surname for the child, calling him Smerdyakov, "The Stinker," after his mother's nickname.

So in time this Smerdyakov became Fyodor Karamazov's second servant. He was living in the lodge with Gregory and Marfa at the time our story begins. He was employed as cook and valet. I ought to say something of this Smerdyakov, but I am ashamed of keeping my readers' attention so long occupied with these servants. And so I will go back to my story, hoping in time to say more of Smerdyakov.

3. The Confession of a Passionate Heart—in Verse

ALYOSHA REMAINED UNDECIDED for some time after hearing the command his father shouted to him from the carriage. But in spite of his uneasiness he did not stand still. That was not his way. He went at once to the kitchen to find out what his father had been up to. Then he set off for his father's house, trusting that on the way he would find an answer to the doubt tormenting him. I want to add that his father's shouts, commanding him to return home "with his mattress and pillow" did not frighten him in the least. He understood perfectly that such shouts were merely "a flourish" to produce an effect. In the same way a tradesman in our town who was celebrating his name-day with a party of friends, getting angry at being refused more vodka, smashed up his own china and furniture and tore his own and his wife's clothes, and finally broke his windows, all for the sake of effect. Next day, of course, when he was sober, he regretted the broken cups and saucers. Alyosha knew that his father would let him go back to the monastery next day, possibly even that evening. Moreover, he was fully convinced that his father might hurt anyone else, but he would not hurt him. Alyosha was certain that no one in the whole world ever would want to hurt him, and, what is more, he knew that no one could hurt him. This was for him an axiom, assumed once and for all without question. And he went his way without hesitation, relying on it.

Alyosha was not worried about his father and himself but he was worried about something else. He was worried about a woman, Katerina, who had so urgently begged him in the note handed to him by Madame Hohlakov to come and see her about something. This had aroused an uneasy feeling in his heart, and this feeling had grown more and more painful all morning in spite of the scenes at the hermitage and at the Father Superior's. Alyosha was not uneasy because he did not know what Katerina would speak about and what he must answer. And he was not afraid of her simply as a woman. Though he knew little of women, he had spent his life, from early childhood till he entered the monastery, entirely with women. He was simply afraid of Katerina. He had been afraid of her from the first time he saw her. He had only seen her two or three times, and had only said a few words to her. He thought of her

100

as a beautiful, proud, domineering girl. But it was not her beauty which troubled him. It was something else. And the vagueness of his fear increased his apprehension. Katerina's aim was noble, he knew that. She was trying to save his brother Dmitri through generosity, although he had behaved very badly to her. Alyosha recognized and did justice to all these fine and generous sentiments, yet a chill came over him every time he drew near her house.

He reasoned that he would not find Ivan, who was an intimate friend, with her, for Ivan was certainly now with his father. He was even more certain not to find Dmitri there, and he had a foreboding of the reason. And so his conversation would be with her alone. He had a great longing to run and see his brother Dmitri before that fateful interview. Without showing him the letter, he could talk to him about it. But Dmitri lived a long way off, and he was sure to be away from home. Standing still for a minute, Alyosha reached a decision. Crossing himself with a rapid and accustomed gesture, and smiling, he turned and started toward his dreaded interview with Katerina.

He knew her house. If he went down the High Street and then across the market-place, it was a long way around. Though our town is small, it is scattered, and the houses are far apart. And meanwhile his father was expecting him, and perhaps had not yet forgotten his command. He might be unreasonable, and so Alyosha felt he had to hurry to get there and back. So he decided to take a short cut through the back way, for he knew every inch of the ground. This meant climbing over low fences, and crossing other people's back yards, where everyone he met would know him and greet him. But in this way he could reach the High Street in half the time.

He had to pass the garden adjoining his father's, and belonging to a little tumbledown house with four windows. The owner of this house, as Alyosha knew, was a bedridden old woman living with her daughter, who had been a maid in generals' families in Petersburg. Now she had been at home a year looking after her sick mother. She always dressed up in fine clothes, though her old mother and she had sunk into such poverty that they went every day to Fyodor Karamazov's kitchen for soup and bread, which Marfa gave them. Yet, though the young woman came for soup, she had never sold any of her dresses, and one of these even had a long train—a fact which Alyosha had learned from Rakitin, who always knew everything that was going on in town. He had forgotten it as soon as he heard it, but now, on reaching the garden, he remembered the dress with the train, raised his head and came upon something quite unexpected.

Over the low garden fence he saw Dmitri waving violently, beckoning to him, obviously afraid to utter a word for fear of being overheard. Alyosha ran up to the fence.

"It's a good thing you looked up. I was about to shout at you," Dmitri said in a happy hurried whisper. "Climb over the fence quickly! How lucky that you've come! I was just thinking of you!"

Alyosha was happy too. But he did not know how to get over the fence. Dmitri put his powerful hand under his elbow to help him jump. Tucking up his cassock, Alyosha then jumped over the fence with the ease of a bare-legged street urchin.

"Well done! Now come along," said Dmitri in a whisper.

"Where?" whispered Alyosha, looking about him and finding himself in a deserted garden with no one near. The garden was small. The house was at least fifty yards away.

"There's no one here. Why do you whisper?" asked Alyosha.

"Why do I whisper? The devil take it!" cried Dmitri at the top of his voice. "You see what silly tricks nature plays. I am here in secret, and on the watch. I'll explain later on, but, knowing it's a secret, I began whispering like a fool, when there's no need to whisper. Let's go. Over there. Till then be quiet. I want to hug you.

> Glory to God in the world,
> Glory to God in me . . .

I was just repeating these lines, sitting here, before you came."

The garden was about three acres and planted with trees along the fence at the four sides. There were apple trees, maples, limes and birch trees. The middle of the garden was an empty grass space, from which several hundred pounds of hay was cut in the summer. The garden was rented out for a few roubles each summer. There were also bushes of raspberries, currants and gooseberries. A kitchen garden had recently been planted near the house.

Dmitri led Alyosha to the most secluded corner of the garden. There, in a thicket of lime trees and old bushes of black currant, elder, snowball, and lilac, there stood a tumbledown green summer house, blackened with age. Its walls were of lattice work, but there was still a roof which could give shelter. God knows when this summer house was built. It was said that it had been put up some fifty years before by a retired colonel who owned the house at that time. It was all falling apart, the floor was rotting, the planks were loose, the wood smelled musty. Inside there was a green wooden table fixed in the ground and around it were some benches upon which it was still possible to sit.

Alyosha had noticed that Dmitri seemed overstimulated and on entering the summer house he saw half a bottle of brandy and a wineglass on the table.

"That's brandy," Dmitri laughed. "I see your look: 'He's drinking again!' Distrust the apparition.

Distrust the worthless, lying crowd,
And lay aside thy doubts.

I'm not drinking, I'm only 'indulging,' as that pig, your Rakitin, says. He'll be a civil councillor one day, but he'll always talk about 'indulging.' Sit down. I could take you in my arms, Alyosha, and press you to my heart till I crush you, for in the whole world—in reality—in re-al-i-ty—(can you take it in?) I love no one but you!"

He spoke the last words in a sort of exaltation.

"No one but you and one 'jade' I have fallen in love with, to my ruin. But being in love doesn't mean loving. You may be in love with a woman and yet hate her. Remember that! I can talk about it freely still. Sit down here by the table and I'll sit beside you and look at you, and go on talking. You will keep quiet and I'll go on talking, for the time has come. But on second thought, you know, I'd better speak quietly, for here—here—you can never tell who is listening. I will explain everything. As they say, 'the story will be continued.' Why have I been longing for you? Why have I been thirsting for you all these days, and just now? (It's five days since I've cast anchor here.) Because it's only to you I can tell everything; because I must, because I need you, because tomorrow I shall fly from the clouds, because tomorrow life is ending and beginning. Have you ever felt, have you ever dreamed of falling down a precipice into a pit? That's just how I'm falling, but not in a dream. And I'm not afraid, and you mustn't be afraid. At least, I am afraid, but I enjoy it. It's not pleasure though, but ecstasy. Damn it all, whatever it is! A strong spirit, a weak spirit, a womanish spirit—whatever it is! Let us praise nature; you see what sunshine, how clear the sky is, the leaves are all green, it's still summer; four o'clock in the afternoon and the stillness! . . . Where were you going?"

"I was going to father's, but I meant to go to Katerina first."

"To her, and to father! Oh! What a coincidence! Why was I waiting for you? Hungering and thirsting for you in every cranny of my soul and even in my ribs? Why, to send you to father and to her, Katerina, so as to be finished with her and with father. To send an angel. I might have sent anyone, but I wanted to send an angel. And here you are on your way to see father and her."

"Did you really mean to send me?" cried Alyosha in distress.

"Wait! You knew it! And I see you understand it all. But be quiet, be quiet for a while. Don't be sorry and don't cry."

Dmitri stood up, thought a moment, and put his finger to his forehead.

"She's asked you, written you a letter or something. That's why you're going to her? You wouldn't be going except for that?"

"Here is her note." Alyosha took it out of his pocket. Dmitri looked through it quickly.

"And you were going the back way! Oh, gods, I thank you for sending him by the back way. He came to me like the golden fish to the silly old fishermen in the fable! Listen, Alyosha, listen, brother! Now I will tell you everything, for I must tell someone. An angel in heaven I've told already; but I want to tell an angel on earth. You are an angel on earth. You will hear and judge and forgive. And that's what I need, that someone above me should forgive. Listen! If two people break away from everything on earth and fly off into the unknown, or at least if one of them does . . . Before flying off or going to ruin he comes to someone else and says, 'Do this for me'—some favor never asked before that could only be asked on one's deathbed—would that other refuse, if he were a friend or a brother?"

"I will do it. But tell me what it is. And hurry," said Alyosha.

"Hurry! H'm! . . . Don't be in a hurry, Alyosha. You hurry and worry yourself. There's no need to hurry now. Now the world has taken a new turning. Ah, Alyosha, what a pity you can't understand ecstasy. But what am I saying to you? As though you didn't understand . . . What an ass I am. What am I saying: 'Be noble, oh, man!' Who says that?"

Alyosha decided to stay with Dmitri. He felt that, perhaps, his duty lay here. Dmitri sank into thought for a moment, with his elbow on the table and his head in his hand. Both were silent.

"Alyosha," said Dmitri at length, "you're the only one who won't laugh. I should like to begin—my confession—with Schiller's 'Hymn to Joy.' I don't know German. I only know it's called that. Don't think I'm talking nonsense because I'm drunk. I'm not a bit drunk. Brandy's all very well, but I need two bottles to make me drunk:

> *Silenus with his rosy phiz*
> *Upon his stumbling ass.*

But I haven't drunk a quarter of a bottle, and I'm not Silenus. I'm not Silenus, though I am strong, for I've made a decision once and for all. Don't be uneasy. I'm not stretching it out. I'm talking sense, and I'll come to the point in a minute. I won't keep you in suspense. Stay. How does it go?"

He raised his head, thought a moment, and began with enthusiasm:

> *"Wild and fearful in his cavern*
> *Hid the naked troglodyte*
> *And the homeless nomad wandered*
> *Laying waste the fertile plain.*
> *Menacing with spear and arrow*
> *In the woods the hunter strayed. . . .*

> *Woe to all poor wretches stranded*
> *On those cruel and hostile shores!*

> *"From the peak of high Olympus*
> *Came the mother Ceres down,*
> *Seeking in those savage regions*
> *Her lost daughter Proserpine.*
> *But the Goddess found no refuge,*
> *Found no kindly welcome there,*
> *And no temple bearing witness*
> *To the worship of the gods.*

> *"From the fields and from the vineyards*
> *Came no fruits to deck the feats,*
> *Only flesh of blood-stained victims*
> *Smouldered on the altar-fires,*
> *And where'er the grieving goddess*
> *Turns her melancholy gaze,*
> *Sunk in vilest degradation*
> *Man his loathesomeness displays."*

Dmitri broke into tears and grabbed Alyosha's hand.

"Alyosha! Alyosha! In degradation, in degradation now, too. There's a terrible amount of suffering for man on earth, a terrible lot of trouble. Don't think I'm only a brute in an officer's uniform, wallowing in dirt and drink. I hardly think of anything but of that degraded man—if only I'm not lying. I pray God I'm not lying and showing off. I think about that man because I am that man myself.

> *Would he purge his soul from vileness*
> *And attain to light and worth,*
> *He must turn and cling forever*
> *To his ancient Mother Earth.*

But the difficulty is how am I to cling forever to Mother Earth. I don't kiss her. I don't cling to her bosom. Am I to become a peasant or a shepherd? I go on and I don't know whether I'm going into darkness or to light and joy. That's the trouble. Everything in the world is a riddle! And whenever I've happened to sink into the vilest degradation (and it's always been happening) I always read that poem about Ceres and man. Has it reformed me? Never! For I'm a Karamazov. For when I do leap into the pit, I go headlong with my heels up, and I am pleased to be falling and pride myself on it. And in the very depths of that degradation I begin a hymn of praise. Let me be accursed. Let me be vile and base, only let me kiss the hem of the veil in which my God is shrouded. Though I may be following the devil, I am Thy son, O Lord, and I love Thee. And I feel the joy without which the world cannot stand.

> *Joy everlasting fosters*
> *The soul of all creation*

It is her secret ferment fires
The cup of life with flame.
'Tis at her beck the grass hath turned
Each blade towards the light
And solar systems have evolved
From chaos and dark night,
Filling the realms of boundless space
Beyond the sage's sight.

At bounteous nature's kindly breast,
All things that breathe drink Joy,
And birds and beasts and creeping things
All follow where She leads.
Her gifts to man are friends in need,
The wreath, the foaming must,
To angels—vision of God's throne,
To insects—sensual lust.

But enough poetry! I am in tears; let me cry. It may be foolishness that everyone would laugh at. But you won't laugh. Your eyes are shining, too. Enough poetry. I want to tell you now about the insects to whom God gave 'sensual lust.'

To insects — sensual lust.

I am that insect, Alyosha, and it is said of me especially. All we Karamazovs are such insects. And angel as you are, that insect lives in you, too, and will stir up a tempest in your blood. Tempests, because sensual lust is a tempest—worse than a tempest! Beauty is a terrible and awful thing! It is terrible because it has not been fathomed and never can be fathomed, for God sets before us nothing but riddles. Here the boundaries meet and all contradictions exist side by side. I am not an educated nor cultured man, Alyosha, but I've thought a lot about this. It's terrible what mysteries there are! Too many riddles weigh men down on earth. We must solve them as we can, and try to keep a dry skin in the water. Beauty! I can't bear the thought that a man of lofty mind and heart begins with the ideal of the Madonna and ends with the ideal of Sodom. What's still more awful is that a man with the ideal of Sodom in his soul does not renounce the ideal of the Madonna, and his heart may be on fire with that ideal, genuinely on fire, just as in his days of youth and innocence. Yes, man is broad, too broad. I'd have him narrower. The devil only knows what to make of it! What to the mind is shameful is beauty and nothing else to the heart. Is there beauty in Sodom? Believe me, that for the immense mass of mankind beauty is found in Sodom. Did you know that secret? The awful thing is that beauty is mysterious as well as terrible. God and the devil are fighting there and the battlefield is the heart of man. But a man always talks of his own ache. Listen now, let's come to facts."

4. The Confession of
a Passionate Heart—in Anecdote

"I WAS LEADING A WILD LIFE THEN. Father said just now that I spent several thousand roubles in seducing young girls. That's a swinish invention, and there was no truth in it. And if there was, I didn't need money simply for *that*. With me money is an accessory, the overflow of my heart, the framework. Today it would be a lady; tomorrow a wench out of the streets. I entertained them both. I threw away money by the handful on music, wild parties and gypsies. Sometimes I gave it to the ladies, too, for they'll take it easily, that must be admitted, and be pleased and thankful for it. Ladies used to be fond of me; not all of them, but it happened, it happened. But I always liked side paths, little dark back alleys behind the main road—there one finds adventures and surprises, and precious metal in the dirt. I am speaking figuratively, Alyosha. In the town I was in, there were no such back alleys in the literal sense, but morally there were. If you were like me, you'd know what that means. I loved vice, I loved the dishonor of vice. I loved cruelty. Am I not a bug, am I not a poisonous insect? In fact I'm a Karamazov! . . . Once we went, a whole lot of us, for a picnic, in seven sleighs. It was dark, it was winter, and I began squeezing a girl's hand, and forced her to kiss me. She was the daughter of an official, a sweet, gentle, submissive creature. She allowed me, she allowed me much in the dark. She thought, poor thing, that I would come next day to propose (I was looked upon as a good match). But I didn't say a word to her for five months. I used to see her in a corner at dances (we were always having dances), her eyes watching me. I saw how they glowed with fire—a fire of indignation. This game only tickled that insect lust I cherished in my soul. Five months later she married an official and left the town, still angry, and still, perhaps, in love with me. Now they live happily. But remember, Alyosha, that I didn't tell anyone. I didn't boast of it. Though I'm full of baseness, and love what's low, I'm not dishonorable. You're blushing. Enough of this filth with you. And all this was nothing much—wayside blossoms *à la* Paul de Kock—though the cruel insect had already grown strong in my soul. I've an album of memories, Alyosha. God bless them, the darlings. I tried to break with them without quarreling. And I never gave them away. I never bragged of one of them. But that's enough. You don't suppose I brought you here simply to talk of such nonsense. No, I'm going to tell you something curious. And don't be surprised that I'm glad to tell you, instead of being ashamed."

"You say that because I blushed," Alyosha said suddenly. "I

wasn't blushing at what you were saying or at what you've done. I blushed because I am the same as you are."

"You? That's going a little too far!"

"No, it's true," insisted Alyosha (obviously the idea was not a new one). "The ladder's the same. I'm at the bottom step, and you're above, somewhere about the thirteenth. That's how I see it. But it's all the same. Absolutely the same. Anyone on the bottom step is bound to go up to the top one."

"Then one should not step on the first rung at all."

"Anyone who can help it had better not."

"But can you?"

"I don't think so."

"Hush, Alyosha, hush! I could press your hand, you move me so. . . . That rogue Grushenka has an eye for men. She told me once that she'd devour you one day. There, there, I won't! From this field of corruption fouled by flies, let's pass to my tragedy, also befouled by flies, that is by every sort of vileness. Although father told lies about my seducing innocent girls, there really was something of the sort in my tragedy, though it was only once and then it did not come off. The old man who has reproached me with what never happened does not even know about it. I never told anyone about it. You're the first, except Ivan, of course—Ivan knows everything. He knew about it long ago. But Ivan's a tomb."

"Ivan's a tomb?"

"Yes."

Alyosha listened carefully.

"I was a lieutenant in a line regiment, but still I was under supervision, like a kind of convict. Yet I was awfully well received in the little town. I spent money right and left. Everyone thought I was rich; I thought so myself. But I must have pleased them in other ways too. Although they shook their heads about me, they liked me. But my colonel, who was an old man, took a sudden dislike to me. He was always down on me but I had powerful friends and, besides, all the town was on my side. So he couldn't do me much harm. I was at fault for not treating him with proper respect. I was proud. This obstinate old fellow, who was really a very good sort, kind hearted and hospitable, had had two wives, both dead. His first wife, who was of a humble family, left a daughter as unpretentious as herself. She was a young woman of twenty-four when I was there, and was living with her father and an aunt, her mother's sister. The aunt was simple and illiterate: the niece was simple but lively. I like to say nice things about people. I never knew a woman of more charming personality. And she wasn't bad looking either: tall, with a full figure, and beautiful eyes, though a rather coarse face. She had not married, although she had had two suitors. She refused them, but was as cheerful as ever. I was intimate with her. Not in 'that' way, it was pure friendship. I have often been friendly with women quite innocently. I used to talk to

108

her with great frankness, and she only laughed. Many women like such freedom, and she was inexperienced too, which made it very amusing. She and her aunt lived in her father's house with a sort of voluntary humility, not putting themselves on the same footing with other people. She was popular and of use to everyone, for she was a good dressmaker. She had a talent for it. She sewed for everyone without asking for money, but if anyone offered her money, she didn't refuse.

"The colonel, of course, was a very different matter. He was one of the most important people in the district. He kept open house, entertained the whole town, gave suppers and dances. At the time I arrived and joined the battalion, all the town was talking of the expected return of the colonel's second daughter, a great beauty, who had just left a fashionable school in the capital. This second daughter is Katerina. She was the child of the second wife, who belonged to a distinguished general's family; although, as I learned on good authority, this wife also brought the colonel no money. She had connections, and that was all. There may have been expectations, but they had come to nothing.

"Yet, when Katerina came from boarding school on a visit, the whole town revived. The most distinguished ladies—two 'Excellencies' and a colonel's wife—and all the rest following their lead, at once gave parties in her honor. She was the belle of the balls, and they got up entertainments for the benefit of distressed governesses. I took no notice. I went on as wildly as before. And one of my exploits at the time set all the town talking.

"I saw Katerina's eyes looking me over one evening at the battery commander's, but I didn't go up to her. I acted as though I didn't care to make her acquaintance. However, I did go up and speak to her at a party not long after. She scarcely looked at me. She was almost scornful. 'Just you wait. I'll have my revenge,' I thought. I behaved like an awful fool on many occasions at that time, and I was conscious of it. What made it worse was that I felt that Katerina was not an innocent boarding-school girl, but a person of character, proud and really high-principled. Above all, she had education and intellect, and I had neither. You think I meant to propose to her? No, I just wanted to get revenge because I was such a hero and she didn't seem to feel it.

"Meanwhile, I spent my time in drink and wild parties until the lieutenant-colonel put me under arrest for three days. Just at that time father sent me six thousand roubles in return for my sending him a deed giving up all claims upon him—settling our accounts, so to speak, and saying that I wouldn't expect anything more. I didn't understand a word of it at the time. Until I came here, Alyosha, till the last few days, perhaps even now, I haven't been able to make head or tail of my account with father. But never mind that, we'll talk of it later.

"Just as I received the money, I got a letter from a friend telling me something that interested me very much. The authorities, I learned, were dissatisfied with our lieutenant-colonel. He was suspected of irregularities; in fact they were preparing a surprise for him. And then the commander of the division arrived, and kicked up a hell of a mess. Shortly afterwards the lieutenant-colonel was ordered to retire. I won't tell you how it all happened. He had enemies certainly. Suddenly there was a marked coolness in the town toward him and all his family. His friends all turned their backs on him. Then I took my first step. I met Katerina's half-sister with whom I'd always kept up a friendship and said, 'Do you know there's a deficit of 4500 roubles of government money in your father's accounts?'

"'What do you mean? What makes you say so? The general was here not long ago, and everything was all right.'

"'Then it was, but now it isn't.'

"She was terribly scared. 'Don't frighten me!' she said. 'Who told you?'

"'Don't worry,' I said, 'I won't tell anyone. You know I won't talk. I only wanted to add that when they demand the 4500 roubles from your father . . . if he can't produce it, he'll be tried, and made to serve as a common soldier in his old age, unless you want to send Katerina to me secretly. I've just received some money. I'll give her 4500, if you like, and keep the secret religiously.'

"'Oh you cad!' That's what she said. 'You cad! How dare you!'

"She went away absolutely furious, while I shouted after her once more that the secret would be kept sacred. Those two simple creatures, Katerina's half-sister and her aunt, I may as well admit, behaved like perfect angels all through this business. They really adored Katerina and thought her far above them, and waited on her hand and foot. But she was told of our conversation. I found that out afterwards. Her half-sister told her. And of course that was all I wanted.

"Suddenly the new major arrived to take command of the battalion. The old lieutenant-colonel was taken ill at once, couldn't leave his room for two days, and didn't hand over the government money. The doctor said that he really was ill. But I knew for a fact, and had known for a long time, that for the last four years the money had never been in the colonel's hands except when the commander made his visits of inspection. He used to lend the money to a merchant, an old widower, with a big beard and gold-rimmed glasses. This man used to go to the fair, do a profitable business with the money, and return the whole sum to the colonel, bringing with it a present from the fair, as well as interest on the loan. But this time (I heard all about it quite by chance from the merchant's son and heir, a miserable youth and one of the most vicious in the world)— this time, I say, the merchant brought nothing back from the

110

fair. The lieutenant-colonel flew to him. 'I've never received any money from you, and couldn't possibly have received any.' That was all the answer he got. So now our lieutenant-colonel is confined to the house, with a towel round his head, while all three women are busy putting ice on it. All at once an orderly arrives on the scene with the book and the order to 'hand over the battalion money immediately, within two hours.' The colonel signed the book (I saw the signature in the book afterward), stood up, saying he would put on his uniform, ran to his bedroom, loaded his double-barreled gun with a service bullet, took the boot off his right foot, fixed the gun against his chest, and began feeling for the trigger with his foot. But Katerina's half-sister, remembering what I had told her, had her suspicions. She stole up and looked into the room just in time. She rushed in, flung herself upon him from behind, threw her arms around him, and the gun went off, hit the ceiling, but hurt no one. The others ran in, took away the gun, and held him by the arms. I heard all about it afterward. . . . I was at home, it was getting dark, and I was just getting ready to go out. I had dressed, brushed my hair, scented my handkerchief, and taken up my cap, when suddenly the door opened, and facing me in the room stood Katerina.

"It's strange how things happen sometimes. No one had seen her in the street, so that no one knew of it in the town. I roomed with two decrepit old ladies, who looked after me. They were most obliging, ready to do anything for me, and were as silent afterwards as two cast-iron posts. Of course I grasped the situation at once. Katerina walked in and looked straight at me, her dark eyes determined, even defiant, but on her lips and around her mouth I saw uncertainty.

" 'My sister told me,' she began, 'that you would give me 4500 roubles if I came to you for it—myself. I have come . . . give me the money!'

"She couldn't keep it up. She was breathless, frightened, her voice failed her, and the corners of her mouth quivered. . . . Alyosha, are you listening, or are you asleep?"

"Dmitri, I know you will tell the whole truth," said Alyosha, disturbed.

"I am telling the truth. If I tell the whole truth just as it happened I won't spare myself. My first idea was a—Karamazov one. Once I was bitten by a centipede and laid up for two weeks with fever. Well, I felt a centipede biting at my heart then—a poisonous insect, you understand? I looked at her up and down. You've seen her? She's a beauty. But she was beautiful in another way then. At that moment she was beautiful because she was noble, and I was a cad; she in all the grandeur of her generosity and sacrifice for her father, and I—a bug! And scoundrel as I was, she was altogether at my mercy, body and soul. She was hemmed in. I tell you frankly that thought, that venomous thought, so possessed my heart that I was almost overcome. It seemed as if there could be no resisting it; as though I should act like a bug, like a venomous spider, without a spark of pity. I could scarcely breathe. Understand, I would have gone the next day to ask for her hand, so that it might end honorably, so to speak, and so that nobody would or could know. For though I'm a cad, I'm honest. And at that very second some voice seemed to whisper in my ear, 'But when you come tomorrow to make your proposal, that girl won't even see you; she'll order her coachman to kick you out of the yard. "Publish it through all the town," she will say, "I'm not afraid of you."' I looked at Katerina. My voice had not deceived me. That is how it would be. There could be no doubt of it. I could see from her face that I would be turned out of the house. I became spiteful. I wanted to play the nastiest swinish trick; to look at her with a sneer, and on the spot where she stood before me to stun her with a tone of voice that only a shopman could use. I wanted to say: 'Four-thousand-five-hundred! What do you mean? I was joking. You've been counting your chickens too easily. Two hundred, if you like, with all my heart. But four-thousand-five-hundred is not a sum to throw away. You've gone to a lot of trouble for nothing.' But I did not say these words.

"I would have lost out, of course. She'd have run away. But it would have been an infernal revenge. It would have been worth it all. . . . Would you believe it, it has never happened to me with any other woman, not one, to look at her at such a moment with hatred. But I swear, I looked at Katerina for three seconds, or five perhaps, with fearful hatred—that hate which is only a hairsbreadth from love, from the maddest love!

"I went to the window, put my forehead against the frozen pane, and I remember the ice burnt my forehead like fire. I did not keep her long, don't be afraid. I turned round, went up to the table, opened the drawer and took out a banknote for five thousand roubles (it was lying in a French dictionary). Then I showed it to her in silence, folded it, handed it to her, opened the door into the hall and stepping back, I bowed. I bowed a most respectful, a most impressive bow, believe me! She trembled all over, gazed at me for a second, turned horribly pale—white as a sheet, in fact—and all at once, not impetuously but softly, gently, bowed down to my feet—not a boarding-school curtsy, but a Russian bow, with her forehead to the floor. Then she jumped up and ran away. I was wearing my sword. I drew it and nearly stabbed myself with it on the spot; why, I don't know. It would have been stupid, of course. I suppose it was from pleasure. Can you understand that one might kill oneself from pleasure? But I didn't stab myself. I only kissed my sword and put it back in the scabbard—which I didn't have to tell you, by the way. And I think that in telling you about my inner conflict I have laid it on in order to glorify myself. But let it

112

pass, and to hell with all who pry into the human heart! Well, so much for that 'adventure' with Katerina. So now Ivan knows about it, and you—no one else."

Dmitri got up, took a step or two, pulled out his handkerchief and mopped his forehead. Then he sat down again, not in the same place as before, but on the opposite side, so that Alyosha had to turn around to face him.

5. The Confession of a Passionate Heart—"Heels Up"

"Now," said Alyosha, "I understand the first half."

"You understand the first half. That half is a drama, and it was played out there. The second half is a tragedy, and it is being acted here."

"I understand nothing of that second half so far," said Alyosha.

"And I? Do you suppose I understand it?"

"Stop, Dmitri. There's one important question. Tell me, you were engaged. Are you still engaged?"

"We weren't engaged at once, not for three months after that encounter. The next day I told myself that the incident was closed, concluded, that there would be no sequel. It seemed to me caddish to propose to her. On her side she gave no sign of life for the six weeks that she remained at home, except for one thing. The day after her visit a maid came round with an envelope. I tore it open. It contained the change out of the banknote. Only 4500 was needed, but there was a charge of about 200 for changing it. She sent back about 260 roubles, I don't remember exactly, but not a note, not a word of explanation. I searched the envelope for a pencil mark—nothing! Well, I spent the rest of the money on such a wild party that the new major had to reprimand me.

"Well, the lieutenant-colonel produced the battalion money, to the astonishment of everyone, for nobody believed that he had the money untouched. He'd no sooner paid it than he fell ill, took to his bed, and, three weeks later, softening of the brain set in, and he died five days afterwards. He was buried with military honors, for he had not had time to receive his discharge. Ten days after his funeral, Katerina, with her aunt and half-sister, went to Moscow. And on the very day they went away (I hadn't seen them, didn't see them off or say good-by) I received a tiny note, a sheet of thin blue paper, and on it only one line in pencil: 'I will write to you. Wait. K.' And that was all.

"I'll explain the rest now, in two words. In Moscow their fortunes changed with the swiftness of lightning and the unexpectedness of an Arabian fairy tale. That general's widow, their

113

nearest relative, suddenly lost the two nieces who were her heiresses and next-of-kin—both died in the same week of smallpox. The old lady, prostrated with grief, welcomed Katerina as a daughter, as her one hope, clutched at her, and altered her will in Katerina's favor. But that concerned the future. In the meantime she gave her eighty thousand roubles as a marriage portion, to do what she liked with. She was an hysterical woman. I saw something of her in Moscow, later.

"Well, suddenly I received by mail four-thousand-five-hundred roubles. I was speechless. Three days later came the promised letter. I have it with me now. I always keep it, and shall keep it till I die. Shall I show it to you? You must read it. She offers to be my wife, offers herself to me. 'I love you madly,' she says, 'even if you don't love me, never mind. Be my husband. Don't be afraid. I won't hinder you in any way. I will be your chattel. I will be the carpet under your feet. I want to love you forever. I want to save you from yourself.' Alyosha, I am not worthy to repeat those lines in my vulgar words and in my vulgar tone, my everlastingly vulgar tone, that I can never cure myself of. That letter stabs me even now. Do you think I don't mind—that I don't mind still? . . . I wrote her an answer at once, as it was impossible for me to go to Moscow. I wrote to her with tears. One thing I shall be ashamed of forever, I referred to her being rich and having a dowry while I was only a stuck-up beggar! I mentioned money! I ought to have borne it in silence, but it slipped from my pen. Then I wrote at once to Ivan, and told him all I could about it in a six page letter and I asked him to go to see her. . . . Why do you look like that? Why are you staring at me? Yes, Ivan fell in love with her; he's in love with her still. I know that. I did a stupid thing, in the world's opinion; but perhaps that one stupid thing may be the saving of us all now. Oh! Don't you see how much she thinks of Ivan, how she respects him? When she compares us, do you suppose she can love a man like me, especially after all that has happened here?"

"But I'm convinced that she does love a man like you, and not a man like him."

"She loves her own *virtue*, not me." The words broke involuntarily and almost maliciously from Dmitri. He laughed. But a minute later his eyes gleamed, he flushed crimson and struck the table with his fist.

"I swear, Alyosha," he cried, with intense anger at himself, "as God is holy and as Christ is God, I swear that though I smiled at her lofty sentiments just now, I know that I am a million times baser in soul than she. I swear that these lofty sentiments of hers are as sincere as a heavenly angel's. That's the tragedy of it—that I know that for certain. What if someone does show off a bit? Don't I do it myself? And yet I'm sincere, I'm sincere. As for Ivan, I can understand how he must be cursing nature now—with his intellect, too! To see the prefer-

114

ence given—to whom, to what? To a monster who, though he is engaged and all eyes are fixed on him, can't control his vices—and before the very eyes of his fiancée. A man like me is preferred, while he is rejected. And why? Because a girl wants to sacrifice her life and destiny out of gratitude. It's ridiculous! I've never said a word of this to Ivan, and Ivan of course has never hinted about it to me. But destiny will win and the best man will hold his ground while the undeserving one will vanish into his back alley forever—his filthy back alley, his beloved back alley, where he is at home and where he will sink in filth and stench through his own free will and with pleasure. I've been talking foolishly. I've no words left. I use them at random, but it will be as I have said. I will drown in the back alley, and she will marry Ivan."

"Stop, Dmitri," Alyosha interrupted with anxiety. "There's one thing you haven't made clear yet: you are still engaged, aren't you? How can you break off the engagement if she, Katerina, doesn't want to?"

"Yes, formally and solemnly engaged. It was all done on my arrival in Moscow, with great ceremony, with ikons, all in fine style. The general's wife blessed us, and—would you believe it?—congratulated Katerina. 'You've made a good choice,' she said, 'I see right through him.' And, would you believe it, she didn't like Ivan, and hardly spoke to him? I had a long talk with Katerina in Moscow. I told her about myself—sincerely, honorably. She listened to everything.

There was sweet confusion,
There were tender words.

Though there were proud words, too. She forced me to promise to reform. I gave my promise, and here . . ."

"What?"

"Why, I called you and brought you here today, this very day—remember—to send you—this very day again—to Katerina, and . . ."

"What?"

"To tell her that I will never go to see her again. Say: 'He sends you his compliments.' "

"But is that possible?"

"That's just the reason I'm sending you, in my place, because it's impossible. And, how could I tell her this myself?"

"And where are you going?"

"To the back alley."

"To Grushenka!" Alyosha exclaimed. "Did Rakitin really tell the truth? I thought that you had just visited her, and that was all."

"Can an engaged man pay such visits? Is such a thing possible and with such a fiancée, and before the eyes of all the world? Damn it, I have some honor! As soon as I began visiting Grushenka, I stopped being engaged and I stopped being an honest

115

man. Why do you look at me? You see, I went to see Grushenka the first time to beat her. I had heard, and I know for a fact now, that that captain, father's agent, had given Grushenka an I.O.U. of mine so that she could sue me, so that she could put an end to me. Father wanted to scare me. I went to beat her. I had had a glimpse of her before. She doesn't strike one at first sight. I knew about her old merchant, who's lying ill now, paralyzed; but he's leaving her some money. I knew, too, that she was fond of money, that she hoarded it, and lent it out at a cruel rate of interest, that she's a merciless cheat and swindler. I went to beat her, and I stayed. The storm broke. It struck me down like the plague. I'm still plague-stricken and I know that everything is over, that there will never be anything more for me. The cycle of the ages is accomplished. That's my position. And though I'm a beggar, as fate would have it, I had three thousand just then in my pocket. I drove with Grushenka to Mokroe, a place twenty-five miles from here. I got gypsies and champagne and made all the peasants there drunk on it, and all the women and girls. I sent the money flying. In three days' time I was stripped bare, but a hero. Do you suppose the hero had gained his end? Not a sign of it from her. I tell you that tramp, Grushenka, has a supple curve all over her body. You can see it in her little foot, even in her little toe. I saw it, and kissed it, but that was all I swear! 'I'll marry you if you like,' she said, 'you're a beggar you know. Say that you won't beat me, and will let me do anything I choose, and perhaps I will marry you.' She laughed, and she's laughing still!"

Dmitri jumped up in a sort of fury. It seemed all at once as though he were drunk. His eyes became suddenly bloodshot.

"And do you really mean to marry her?"

"At once, if she will. And if she won't . . . I'll be the porter at her gate. Alyosha!" he cried. He stopped short before Alyosha and grabbing him by the shoulders began shaking him. "Do you know, you innocent boy, that this is all delirium, senseless delirium, and there's a tragedy in it. Let me tell you that I may be a low man, with low and degraded passions, but a thief and a pickpocket Dmitri Karamazov never can be. Well, then; let me tell you that I am a thief and a pickpocket. That very morning, just before I went to beat Grushenka, Katerina sent for me, and in strict secrecy (why I don't know, I suppose she had some reason) asked me to go to the chief town of the province to mail three thousand roubles to her half-sister in Moscow. She wanted me to mail it from there so that nothing would be known about it in this town. So I had Katerina's three thousand roubles in my pocket when I went to see Grushenka, and it was this money we spent at Mokroe. Afterwards I pretended to Katerina that I had been to the town, but did not show her any post office receipt. I said I had sent the money and would bring the receipt, and so far I haven't brought it. I've forgotten it. Now what do you think you're going to say to her today. 'He sends his compliments.' And she'll ask you, 'What about the money?' You might say to her: 'He's degraded and a low creature, with uncontrolled passions. He didn't send your money but wasted it because like a brute, he couldn't control himself.' And you might add: 'He isn't a thief though. Here is your three thousand; he sends it back. Send it yourself to your sister. . . . He told me to say, he sends his compliments. And she'll ask, 'But where is the money?' "

"Dmitri, you are unhappy! But not as unhappy as you think. Don't drive yourself to death with despair."

"What, do you think I'd shoot myself because I can't get three thousand roubles to pay back to Katerina? That's just it. I won't shoot myself. I haven't the strength now. Afterwards, perhaps. But now I'm going to Grushenka. I don't care what happens."

"And what then?"

"I'll be her husband if she will have me, and when lovers come, I'll go into the next room. I'll clean her friends' galoshes, light their samovar, run their errands."

"Katerina will understand it all," Alyosha said solemnly. "She'll understand how great this trouble is and will forgive. She has compassion, and no one could be more unhappy than you. She'll see that herself."

"She won't forgive everything," said Dmitri, with a grin. "There's something in it, Alyosha, that no woman can forgive. Do you know what would be the best thing to do?"

"What?"

"Pay back the three thousand."

"Where can we get it? I have two thousand. Ivan will give you another thousand—that makes three. Take it and pay it back."

"And when will you receive your two thousand? You're not of age. Besides you must—you absolutely must—take my farewell to Katerina today, with the money or without it, for I can't go on any longer, things have come to such a pass. Tomorrow is too late. . . . I will send you to father."

"To father?"

"Yes, to father first. Ask him for three thousand."

"But, Dmitri, he won't give it."

"As though he would! I know he won't. Do you know the meaning of despair, Alyosha?"

"Yes."

"Listen. Legally he owes me nothing. I've received my share from him, I know that. But morally he owes me something, doesn't he? You know he started with twenty-eight thousand roubles of my mother's money and made a hundred thousand with it. Let him give me back only three out of the twenty-eight thousand, and he'll draw my soul out of hell, and it will atone for many of his sins. For that three thousand—I give you my word—I'll settle for everything, and he will hear nothing more of me. For the last time I give him the chance to be a father. Tell him God Himself sends him this chance."

"Dmitri, he won't give it to you."

"I know he won't. I know it perfectly well. Now, especially. That's not all. I know something more. Now, only a few days ago, perhaps only yesterday he found out for the first time *in earnest* that Grushenka is really not joking, and really means to marry me. He knows her, he knows the cat. And do you think he's going to give me money to help me marry her when he's crazy about her himself? And that's not all, either. I can tell you more than that. I know that for the last five days he has had three thousand roubles, changed into notes of a hundred roubles, packed into a large sealed envelope and tied with a pink ribbon. You see I know all about it! On the envelope is written: 'A present of three thousand roubles for my angel, Grushenka, when she will come to me.' He scrawled it himself in secret, and no one knows that the money's there except his cook and valet, Smerdyakov, whom he trusts like himself. He's been expecting Grushenka for the last three or four days; he hopes she'll come for the money. He has sent her word about it, and she has sent him word that perhaps she'll come. And if she does go to the old man, can I marry her after that? You understand now why I'm hiding here and what I'm watching for."

"For her?"

"Yes, for her. Foma has a room in the house of these sluts here. Foma was a soldier in my regiment. He does jobs for them. He's watchman at night and goes grouse shooting in the daytime. That's how he lives. I sometimes stay in his room. But neither he nor the women of the house know the secret— that is, that I am on the watch here."

"No one but Smerdyakov knows, then?"

"No one else. He will let me know if Grushenka goes to the old man."

"He told you about the money?"

"Yes. It's a dead secret. Even Ivan doesn't know about the money, or anything. The old man is sending Ivan to Tchermashnya on a two or three days' trip. A buyer has turned up for the woodland; he'll give eight thousand for the timber. So the old man keeps asking Ivan to help him by going to arrange it. It will take him two or three days. That's what the old man wants, so that Grushenka can come while he's away."

"Then he's expecting Grushenka today?"

"No, she won't come today; there are signs. She's certain not to come," cried Dmitri suddenly. "Smerdyakov thinks so, too. . . . Father's drinking now. He's sitting at table with Ivan. Go to him, Alyosha, and ask him for the three thousand roubles."

"Dmitri, what's the matter with you?" cried Alyosha, jumping up and looking at his brother's frenzied face. For one moment the thought struck him that Dmitri was mad.

"What is it? I'm not insane," said Dmitri, looking intently

118

and earnestly at him. "Don't be afraid. I am sending you to father, and I know what I'm saying. I believe in miracles."

"In miracles?"

"In a miracle of Divine Providence. God knows my heart. He sees my despair. He sees the whole picture. Surely He won't let something awful happen, Alyosha. I believe in miracles. Go!"

"I'm going. Tell me, will you wait for me here?"

"Yes. I know it will take time. You can't ask him point blank. He's drunk now. I'll wait three hours—four, five, six, seven. Only remember you must go to Katerina today, even if it's at midnight, *with the money or without the money,* and say: 'He sends his compliments to you.' I want you to say that to her: 'He sends his compliments to you.' "

"Dmitri! And what if Grushenka comes today—if not today, tomorrow, or the next day?"

"Grushenka? I will see her. I will rush out and prevent it."

"And if . . . ?"

"If there's an if, it will be murder. I couldn't endure it."

"Who will be murdered?"

"The old man. I won't kill her."

"Dmitri, what are you saying!"

"Oh, I don't know. . . . I don't know. Perhaps I won't kill him, and perhaps I will. I'm afraid that he will suddenly become so loathsome to me at that moment . . . I hate his ugly throat, his nose, his eyes, his shameless snicker. I feel a physical repulsion. That's what I'm afraid of. That's what may be too much for me."

"I'll go, Dmitri. I believe that God will order things for the best, that nothing awful will happen."

"And I will sit and wait for the miracle. And if it doesn't come to pass . . ."

Alyosha went toward his father's house.

6. Smerdyakov

ALYOSHA DID IN FACT FIND HIS FATHER still at the dinner table. Though there was a dining room in the house, the table was laid as usual in the drawing room, which was the largest room, and furnished with old-fashioned ostentation. The furniture was white and very old, upholstered in red, silky material. In the spaces between the windows there were mirrors in elaborate white and gilt carved frames. On the walls, covered with white paper which was torn in many places, there hung two large portraits—one of some prince who had been governor of the district thirty years before, and the other of some bishop, long since dead. In the corner opposite the door there were several ikons, before which a lamp was lighted at nightfall, not so much for devotional purposes as to light the room. Fyodor Karamazov used to go to bed very late, at three or four o'clock in the morning, and he would wander about the room at night or sit in an armchair, thinking. This had become a habit with him. He usually slept alone in the house, sending his servants to the lodge; but sometimes Smerdyakov remained on a bench in the hall.

When Alyosha came in, dinner was over, but coffee and dessert had been served. Fyodor Karamazov liked sweet things with brandy after dinner. Ivan was with him at table, sipping coffee. The servants, Gregory and Smerdyakov, were standing by. Both the gentlemen and the servants seemed in unusually good spirits. The old Karamazov was roaring with laughter. Before he entered the room, Alyosha heard the laugh he knew so well, and he could tell from the sound of it that his father had only reached the good-humored stage, and was far from being completely drunk.

"Here he is! Here he is!" yelled the old man, highly delighted at seeing Alyosha. "Join us. Sit down. Coffee is a lenten dish, but it's hot and good. I won't offer you brandy, you're keeping the fast. But would you like some? No. I'd better give you some of our famous liqueur. Smerdyakov, go to the cupboard, the second shelf on the right. Here are the keys. Wake up!"

Alyosha began refusing the liqueur.

"Never mind. If you won't have it, we will," said his father, beaming. "But stay—have you had dinner?"

"Yes," answered Alyosha, who had in truth only eaten a piece of bread and drunk a glass of beer in the Father Superior's kitchen. "Though I would be glad to have some hot coffee."

"Bravo, my darling! He'll have some coffee. Does it need heating? No, it's boiling. It's good coffee. Smerdyakov made it. My Smerdyakov's an artist at coffee and at fish patties, and at fish soup, too. You must come some day and have some fish soup. Let me know beforehand. . . . But wait! Didn't I tell you this morning to come home with your mattress and pillow and everything? Have you brought your mattress? He, he, he!"

"No, I haven't," said Alyosha smiling.

"Oh, but you were frightened. You were frightened this morning, weren't you? There, my darling, I wouldn't do anything to upset you. Do you know, Ivan, I can't resist the way he looks one straight in the face and laughs? It makes me laugh all over. I'm so fond of him. Alyosha, let me give you my blessing —a father's blessing."

Alyosha rose. But Fyodor Karamazov had already changed his mind.

"No, no," he said. "I'll just make the sign of the cross over you, for now. Sit still. Now we've a treat for you, in your own line, too. It'll make you laugh. Balaam's ass has begun talking to us here—and how he talks! How he talks!"

Balaam's ass, it appeared, was the servant Smerdyakov. He was a young man of about twenty-four, remarkably unsociable and self-contained. Not that he was shy or bashful. On the contrary, he was conceited and seemed to despise everybody.

We must pause to say a few words about him now. He was brought up by Gregory and Marfa. But he grew up "with no sense of gratitude," as Gregory expressed it. He was an unfriendly boy, and seemed to look at the world with suspicion. In his childhood he liked to hang cats and bury them with great ceremony. He used to dress up in a sheet as though it were a surplice, and sing and wave some object over the dead cat as though it were a censer. All this he did on the sly, with the greatest secrecy. Gregory caught him once and beat him. He shrank into a corner and sulked there for a week. "He doesn't care for you or me, the beast," Gregory used to say to Marfa. "He doesn't care for anyone." Then speaking directly to the boy, he asked: "Are you a human being? You're not a human being. You grew from the mildew in the bathhouse. That's what you are." Smerdyakov, it appeared afterwards, could never forgive Gregory those words. Gregory taught him to read and write, and when he was twelve years old, began teaching him the Scriptures. But this teaching came to nothing. At the second or third lesson the boy suddenly grinned.

"What are you grinning for?" asked Gregory, looking at him threateningly from under his glasses.

"Oh, nothing. God created light on the first day, and the sun, moon, and stars on the fourth day. Where did the light come from on the first day."

Gregory was thunderstruck. The boy looked sarcastically at his teacher. There was something positively condescending in his expression. Gregory could not restrain himself. "I'll show you where!" he cried, and gave the boy a slap on the cheek. The boy took the slap without a word, but withdrew into his corner again for some days. A week later he had his first attack of the disease to which he was subject all the rest of his life—epilepsy.

When Fyodor Karamazov heard of it, his attitude toward the boy changed at once. Until then he had taken no notice of him. He never scolded him, but always gave him a penny when he met him. Sometimes, when he was in good humor, he would send the boy something sweet from his table. But as soon as he heard of Smerdyakov's illness, he showed an active interest in him. He sent for a doctor, and tried remedies, but the disease turned out to be incurable. The fits occurred, on an average, once a month, but at various intervals. The fits varied too, in violence. Some were light: some were very severe. Fyodor Karamazov then strictly forbade Gregory to beat the boy, and began allowing him to come upstairs to him. He forbade him to be taught anything whatever for a time. One day when the boy was about fifteen, Fyodor Karamazov noticed him lingering by the bookcase, and reading the titles through the glass. Old Karamazov had a fair number of books—over a hundred—but no one ever saw him reading. He at once gave Smerdyakov the key to the bookcase. "Come, read. You shall be my librarian. You'll be better sitting reading than hanging about the yard. Come, read this," and Fyodor Karamazov gave him *Evenings in a Cottage near Dikanka*.

Smerdyakov read a little, but didn't like it. He did not once smile, and ended by frowning.

"Why? Isn't it funny?" asked Fyodor Karamazov.

Smerdyakov did not answer.

"Answer, stupid!"

"It's all untrue," mumbled the boy.

"Then go to the devil! You have the soul of a lackey. Wait. Here's a book, *Universal History*. It's all true. Read it."

But Smerdyakov did not get through ten pages of the history. He found it dull. So the bookcase was closed again.

Shortly afterwards Marfa and Gregory reported to Fyodor Karamazov that Smerdyakov was beginning to show an extraordinary fastidiousness. He would sit before his soup, take up his spoon and look into the soup, bend over it, examine it, take a spoonful and hold it to the light.

"What is it? A beetle?" Gregory would ask.

"A fly, perhaps," Marfa would observe.

The squeamish youth never answered. But he did the same with his bread, his meat, and everything he ate. He would hold a piece on his fork to the light, examine it, and only after long deliberation put it in his mouth.

"Ach! What fine gentleman's airs!" Gregory would mutter looking at him.

When Fyodor Karamazov heard of this he determined to make Smerdyakov his cook, and sent him to Moscow to be trained. He spent some years there and came back remarkably changed in appearance. He looked extraordinarily old for his age. His face had grown wrinkled, yellow, and strangely effeminate. But in character he seemed almost exactly the same as before he went away. He was just as unsociable, and showed not the slightest inclination for companionship. In Moscow, too, as we heard afterwards, he had always been reserved. Moscow itself had little interest for him; he saw very little there, and took scarcely any notice of anything. He went once to the theater, but returned silent and displeased with it. On the other hand, he came back to us from Moscow well dressed, in a clean coat and clean linen. He brushed his clothes most scrupulously twice a day and was very fond of cleaning his smart calf boots with a special English polish, so that they shone like mirrors.

He turned out to be a first-rate cook. Fyodor Karamazov paid him a salary, almost the whole of which Smerdyakov spent on clothes, pomade, perfumes, and such things. But he seemed to have as much contempt for the female sex as for men; he was discreet, almost unapproachable, with them. Fyodor Karamazov began to regard him rather differently. His fits were becoming more frequent, and on the days he was ill Marfa cooked, which did not suit Fyodor Karamazov at all.

"Why are your fits getting worse?" asked Fyodor Karamazov, looking at his new cook. "Would you like to get married? Shall I find you a wife?"

But Smerdyakov turned pale with anger, and did not reply. Karamazov left him with an impatient gesture. The great thing was that he had absolute confidence in his honesty. It happened once, when the old man was drunk, that he dropped in the muddy yard three hundred-rouble notes. He only missed them next day, and was just searching his pockets when he saw the notes lying on the table. Where had they come from? Smerdyakov had picked them up and brought them in the day before.

"Well, my lad, I've never met anyone like you," Fyodor Karamazov said and he gave him ten roubles. We may add that Karamazov not only believed in his honesty, but had, for some reason, a liking for him, although the young man looked as morosely at him as at everyone else and was always silent. He rarely spoke.

If it had occurred to anyone to wonder at the time what the young man was interested in, and what was on his mind, it would have been impossible to tell by looking at him. Yet he would sometimes stop suddenly in the house, or in the yard or street, and stand still for ten minutes, lost in thought. Studying his face one would have said that there was no thought in it, no reflection, but only a sort of contemplation.

There is a remarkable picture called *Contemplation*. It shows a forest in winter and on a roadway through the forest, in absolute solitude, stands a peasant in a torn kaftan and bark shoes. He stands, as it were, lost in thought. Yet he is not thinking: he is "contemplating." If anyone touched him he would start and look bewildered. It's true he would come to himself immediately; but if he were asked what he had been thinking about, he would remember nothing. Yet probably he has hidden within himself, the impression which dominated him during the period of contemplation. Those impressions are dear to him and he probably hoards them imperceptibly, and even unconsciously. How and why, of course, he does not know. He may suddenly, after hoarding impressions for many years, abandon everything and go off to Jerusalem on a pilgrimage. Or he may suddenly set fire to his native village. Or he may do both.

There are a good many "contemplatives" among our peasants. And Smerdyakov was probably one of them. And he was probably greedily hoarding up his impressions, hardly knowing why.

7. *The Controversy*

BUT BALAAM'S ASS HAD SUDDENLY SPOKEN. The subject was a strange one. Gregory had gone marketing in the morning and had heard from a shopkeeper the story of a Russian soldier which had appeared in the newspaper that day. This soldier had been taken prisoner in some remote part of Asia, and was threatened with an immediate agonizing death if he did not renounce Christianity and follow the Mohammedan faith. He refused to deny his faith and was tortured and died, praising and glorifying Christ. Gregory told the story while he was serving at the dinner table. Fyodor Karamazov always liked, over the dessert after dinner, to laugh and talk, if only with Gregory. This day he was in a particularly good-humored and expansive mood. Sipping his brandy and listening to the story, he remarked that they ought to make a saint of a soldier like that and take his skin to some monastery. "That would make the people gather, and bring the money in."

Gregory frowned, seeing that his master was by no means touched, but, as usual, was beginning to scoff. At that moment, Smerdyakov, who was standing by the door, smiled. Smerdyakov often waited at table toward the end of dinner, and since Ivan's arrival in our town he had done so every day.

"What are you grinning at?" asked the old Karamazov, catching the smile and knowing that it referred to Gregory.

"Well, my opinion is," Smerdyakov began suddenly, and unexpectedly, in a loud voice, "that if that soldier's exploit was so very great there would have been, to my thinking, no sin in it if he had in such an emergency renounced, so to speak, the name of Christ and his own christening. By doing this he could have saved his life, for good deeds. And through these good deeds he could, through the years, have atoned for his cowardice."

"How could it not be a sin? You're talking nonsense. For that you'll go straight to hell and be roasted like mutton," put in Fyodor Karamazov.

It was at this point that Alyosha came in, and his father, as we have seen, was highly delighted at his appearance.

"We're on your subject, your subject," he chuckled, making Alyosha sit down to listen.

"As for mutton, that's not so. There'll be nothing in hell . . . And there shouldn't be either, if it's according to justice," Smerdyakov maintained stoutly.

"How do you mean 'according to justice'?" old Karamazov cried gleefully, nudging Alyosha with his knee.

"He's a fool, that's what he is!" said Gregory. He looked Smerdyakov angrily in the face.

"As for being a fool, wait a little, Gregory," answered Smerdyakov with perfect composure. "You'd better consider yourself that, once I am taken prisoner by the enemies of the Christian race, and they demand that I curse the name of God and renounce my holy christening. . . . I am fully entitled to act by my own reason, since there would be no sin in it."

"But you've said that before. Don't waste words. Prove it," cried Fyodor Karamazov.

"Soup-maker!" muttered Gregory contemptuously.

"As for being a soup-maker, wait a bit, too, and consider yourself, Gregory, without abusing me. For as soon as I say to those enemies: 'No, I'm not a Christian, and I curse my true God,' then at once, by God's high judgment, I become accursed and am cut off from the Holy Church. It is exactly as though I were a heathen. At that very instant, not only when I say it aloud, but when I think of saying it, before a quarter of a second has passed, I am cut off. Is that so or not, Gregory?"

He addressed Gregory with obvious satisfaction, though he was really answering Fyodor Karamazov's questions. He was well aware of this and was only pretending that Gregory had asked the questions.

"Ivan," cried the old Karamazov suddenly, "stoop down, I want to whisper to you. . . . He's got this all up for your benefit. He wants you to praise him. Praise him."

Ivan listened with perfect seriousness to his father's excited whisper.

"Wait, Smerdyakov, be quiet a minute," cried Fyodor Karamazov once more. "Ivan, your ear again."

Ivan bent down again with a perfectly serious face.

"I love you as I do Alyosha. Don't think I don't love you. Some brandy?"

"Yes," said Ivan looking steadily at his father and thinking that he was drunk. The old man was watching Smerdyakov with great curiosity.

"You're accursed, as it is," Gregory suddenly cried out. "And how dare you argue, you fool, after that, if . . ."

"Don't scold him, Gregory, don't scold him," Fyodor Karamazov cut him short.

"You should wait, Gregory, and listen, for I haven't finished all I had to say. For at the very moment I become accursed, at that same highest moment, I become exactly like a heathen, and my christening is taken off me and becomes of no avail. Isn't that so?"

"Hurry up and finish, my boy," Fyodor Karamazov urged him, sipping from his wineglass with relish.

"And if I've ceased to be a Christian, then I told no lie to the enemy when they asked whether I was a Christian or not a Christian. I had already been relieved by God Himself of my

Christianity by reason of the thought alone, before I had time to utter a word to the enemy. And if I have already been discharged, in what manner and with what sort of justice can I be held responsible as a Christian in the other world for having denied Christ, when, through the very thought alone, before denying Him I had been relieved of my christening? If I'm no longer a Christian, then I can't renounce Christ, for I've nothing then to renounce. Who will hold an unclean Tatar responsible, Gregory, even in heaven, for not having been born a Christian? And who would punish him for that, considering that you can't take two skins off one ox? For God Almighty Himself, even if He did make the Tatar responsible when he dies would give him the smallest possible punishment, I imagine (since he must be punished) judging that he is not to blame if he has come into the world an unclean heathen, from heathen parents. The Lord God surely can't take a Tatar and say he was a Christian? That would mean that the Almighty would be lying. And can the Lord of Heaven and Earth tell a lie?"

Gregory was thunderstruck and looked at Smerdyakov, his eyes bulging out of his head. Though he did not clearly understand what was said, he had caught something of it and he stood looking like a man who has just hit his head against a wall. Fyodor Karamazov emptied his glass and went off into his shrill laugh.

"Alyosha! Alyosha! What do you say to that! . . . He must have been with the Jesuits somewhere, Ivan. Oh, you stinking Jesuit, who taught you? But you're talking nonsense, nonsense, nonsense, nonsense. Don't cry, Gregory, we'll reduce him to smoke and ashes in a moment. Tell me this, oh, ass; you may be right before your enemies, but you have renounced your faith all the same in your own heart, and you say yourself that in that very hour you became accursed. And if once you're accursed they won't pat you on the head for it in hell. What do you say to that, my fine Jesuit?"

"There is no doubt that I have renounced it in my own heart, but there was no special sin in that. Or if there was sin, it was the most ordinary."

"How's that the most ordinary?"

"You lie, accursed one!" cried Gregory.

"Consider, Gregory," Smerdyakov went on, staid and unruffled, conscious of his triumph but, as it were, generous to the vanquished foe. "Consider, Gregory, it is said in the Scripture that if you have faith, even as a mustard seed, and bid a mountain move into the sea, it will move without the least delay. Well, Gregory, if I'm without faith and you have so great a faith that you are continually swearing at me, you try telling this mountain, not to move into the sea for that's a long way off, but even to our stinking little river which runs at the bottom of the garden. You'll see for yourself that it won't budge, but will stay just where it is no matter how much you shout at

126

it. And that shows, Gregory, that you haven't faith in the proper manner, and only abuse others about it. Again, taking into consideration that no one in our day, not only you, but actually no one, from the highest person to the lowest peasant can shove mountains into the sea—except perhaps some one man in the world, or, at most, two, and they are most likely saving their souls somewhere in the Egyptian desert, so you wouldn't find them—if all the rest have no faith, will God curse all the rest? That is, the population of the whole earth, except two hermits in the desert . . . And in His well-known mercy will He not forgive one of them? And so I believe that though I may once have doubted I shall be forgiven if I shed tears of repentance."

"Wait!" cried old Karamazov with delight. "So you think there are two hermits who can move mountains? Ivan, make a note of it. Write it down. There you have the Russian all over!"

"You're quite right in saying it's characteristic of the people's faith," Ivan agreed with a smile.

"You agree. Then it must be so, if you agree. It's true, isn't it, Alyosha? That's the Russian faith all over, isn't it?"

"No. Smerdyakov has not the Russian faith at all," said Alyosha firmly and gravely.

"I'm not talking about his faith. I mean those two hermits in the desert. Surely that's Russian, isn't it?"

"Yes, that's purely Russian," said Alyosha smiling.

"Your words are worth a gold piece, oh, ass, and I'll give it to you today. But as to the rest you talk nonsense, nonsense, nonsense. Let me tell you, stupid, that we here are all of little faith, only from carelessness, because we haven't time. Things are too much for us and, in the second place, the Lord God has given us so little time, only twenty-four hours in the day, so that one hasn't even time to get sleep enough much less to repent of one's sins. While you have denied your faith to your enemies when you had nothing else to think about but to show your faith! So I believe that it constitutes a sin."

"Constitute a sin it may, but consider . . . If I had believed then in truth, as I ought to have believed, then it really would have been sinful if I had not faced tortures for my faith, and had gone over to the pagan Mohammedan faith. But, of course, it wouldn't have come to torture then, because I would only have had to say at that instant to the mountain 'move and crush the tormentor,' and it would have moved and crushed him like a black beetle. And I would have walked away as though nothing had happened, praising and glorifying God. But, suppose at that very moment I had tried all that, and cried to that mountain: 'Crush these tormentors,' and it hadn't crushed them, how could I have helped doubting at such a time and at such a dread hour of mortal terror? And apart from that, I should know already that I could not attain to the fullness of the Kingdom of Heaven (for since the mountain had not moved at my word, they could not think very much of my faith up above and there could be no very great reward awaiting me in the world to come). So why should I let them torture me? For, even though they had flayed my skin half off my back, even then the mountain would not have moved at my word or at my cry. And at such a moment not only doubt might come over one but one might lose one's reason from fear, so that one would not be able to think at all. And, therefore, why should I be particularly to blame if not seeing my advantage or reward there or here, I should, at least, save my skin? And so trusting fully in the grace of the Lord I should cherish the hope that I might be altogether forgiven."

8. Over the Brandy

THE ARGUMENT WAS OVER. But strange to say Fyodor Karamazov, who had been so agreeable, suddenly began frowning. He frowned and gulped brandy, and it was already a glass too much.

"Get along you Jesuits!" he cried to the servants. "Go away, Smerdyakov. I'll send you the gold piece I promised you, but go away! Don't cry, Gregory. Go to Marfa. She'll comfort you and put you to bed. The rascals won't let us sit in peace after dinner," he snapped peevishly as the servants quickly withdrew.

"Smerdyakov always pokes himself in now, after dinner. It's you he's so interested in, Ivan. What have you done to fascinate him?" he added.

"Nothing whatever," answered Ivan. "He likes to think well of me. He's a lackey and a low person. Raw material for revolution when the time comes."

"Revolution?"

"There will be others and better ones. But there will be some like him as well. His kind will come first, and better ones after."

"And when will the time come?"

"The rocket will go off and fizzle out. So far the peasants are not very interested in listening to these soup-makers."

"Ah, but a Balaam's ass like that thinks and thinks, and only the devil knows what he's thinking."

"He's storing up ideas," said Ivan smiling.

"You see, I know he can't stand me, nor anyone else, even you, Ivan, though you think that he has a high opinion of you. Worse still with Alyosha. He despises Alyosha. But he doesn't steal, that's one thing. And he's not a gossip. He holds his tongue and doesn't talk about us in public. He makes excellent fish pies too. But, damn him, is he worth talking about so much?"

"Of course he isn't."

"And as for the ideas he may be hatching, the Russian peasant, generally speaking, needs beating. That I've always maintained. Our peasants are swindlers, and don't deserve to be pitied, and it's a good thing they're still flogged sometimes. Russia is rich in birches. If they destroyed the forests, it would be the ruin of Russia. I stand up for the clever people. We've given up beating the peasants, we've grown so clever, but they go on beating themselves. And a good thing too. 'For with what measure ye mete it shall be measured to you again,' or how does it go? Anyhow, it will be measured. But Russia's all swinishness. If you only knew how I hate Russia. . . . That is, not Russia, but all this vice! But maybe I mean Russia. . . . Do you know what I like? I like wit."

"You've had another glass. That's enough."

"Wait a minute. I'll have one more, and then another, and then I'll stop. No wait, you interrupted me. At Mokroe I was talking to an old man, and he told me: 'There's nothing we like so much as sentencing girls to be whipped, and we always give young men the job of beating them. And the girl he has whipped today, the young man will marry tomorrow. So it suits the girls, too,' he said. There's a set of de Sades for you! But it's clever, anyway. Shall we go over and have a look at it, eh? Alyosha, are you blushing? Don't be bashful, child. I'm sorry I didn't stay to dinner at the Superior's and tell the monks about the girls at Mokroe. Alyosha, don't be angry that I offended your Superior this morning. I lost my temper. If there is a God, if He exists, then, of course, I'm to blame, and I will have to answer for it. But if there isn't a God at all, what do they deserve, your fathers? It's not enough to cut their heads off, for they keep back progress. Would you believe it, Ivan, that idea torments me? No, I see from your eyes that you don't believe me. You believe what people say, that I'm nothing but a buffoon. Alyosha, do you believe that I'm nothing but a buffoon?"

"No, I don't believe it."

"And I believe you don't, and that you speak the truth. You look sincere and you speak sincerely. But not Ivan. Ivan's arrogant. . . . I'd make an end of your monks, though, all the same. I'd take all that mystic stuff and suppress it, once and for all, all over Russia, so as to bring all the fools to reason. And the gold and the silver that would flow into the mint!"

"But why suppress it?" asked Ivan.

"That Truth may prevail. That's why."

"Well, if Truth were to prevail, you know, you'd be the first to be robbed and suppressed."

"Ah! I daresay you're right. Ah, I'm an ass!" cried the old Karamazov striking himself lightly on the forehead.

"Well, your monastery may stand then, Alyosha, if that's how it is. And we clever people will sit snug and enjoy our brandy. You know, Ivan, it must have been so ordained by the Almighty Himself. Ivan, speak, is there a God or not? Speak the truth, speak seriously. Why are you laughing?"

"I'm laughing because you made a clever remark just now about Smerdyakov's belief in the existence of two saints who could move mountains."

"Why, am I like him?"

"Very much."

"Well, that shows I'm a Russian, too, and I have a Russian character. And you may be caught in the same way, though you are a philosopher. Shall I catch you? What do you bet that I'll catch you tomorrow. Speak, all the same: is there a God, or not? Only, be serious. I want you to be serious now."

"No, there is no God."

"Alyosha, is there a God?"

"There is."

"Ivan, and is there immortality of some sort, just a little, just a tiny bit?"

"There is no immortality either."

"None at all?"

"None at all."

"There's absolute nothingness then. Perhaps there is just something? Anything is better than nothing!"

"Absolute nothingness."

"Alyosha, is there immortality?"

"There is."

"God and immortality?"

"God and immortality. In God is immortality."

"H'm! It's more likely Ivan's right. Good God! To think what faith, what force of all kinds, man has lavished for nothing on that dream, and for how many thousands of years. Who is it laughing at man? Ivan! For the last time, once and for all, is there a God or not? I ask for the last time."

"And for the last time I say there is no God."

"Who is laughing at mankind, Ivan?"

"It must be the devil," answered Ivan smiling.

"And the devil? Does he exist?"

"No, there's no devil either."

"It's too bad. . . . Damn it all, what wouldn't I do to the man who first invented God! Hanging on a bitter aspen tree would be too good for him."

"There would have been no civilization if they hadn't invented God," said Ivan.

"Wouldn't there have been? Without God?"

"No. And there would have been no brandy either. But I must take your brandy away from you."

"Stop, stop, stop, one more little glass. . . . I've hurt Alyosha's feelings. You're not angry with me, Alyosha? My dear little Alyosha!"

"No, I am not angry. I know your thoughts. Your heart is better than your head."

"My heart better than my head, is it? Oh Lord! And that from you. Ivan, do you love Alyosha?"

"Yes."

"You must love him." (The old Karamazov was by this time very drunk.) "Listen, Alyosha, I was rude to your elder this morning. But I was excited. But there's wit in that elder, don't you think, Ivan?"

"Possibly."

"There is, there is. He's a Jesuit, a Russian one, that is. But since he's an honorable person there's a hidden indignation boiling within him at having to pretend holiness."

"But he believes in God."

"No. Didn't you know? Why, he tells everyone himself. That is, not everyone, but all the clever people who come to him. He said straight out to Governor Schultz not long ago: 'Credo, but I don't know in what.' "

"Really?"

"He really did. But I respect him. There's something of Mephistopheles about him, or rather of 'The hero of our time.' . . . Arbenin, or what's his name? . . . You see, he's sensual. He's so sensual that I would be afraid for my daughter or my wife if they went to confess to him. You know, when he begins telling stories. . . . The year before last he invited us to tea, tea with liqueur (the ladies send him liqueur) and he began telling us about old times till we nearly split our sides. . . . Especially how he once cured a paralyzed woman. 'If my legs were not bad I know a dance I could dance for you,' he said. What do you think of that? 'I've played plenty of tricks in my time,' he said. He did Demidov, the merchant, out of sixty thousand."

"What, he stole it?"

"Demidov brought him the money as a man he could trust, saying: 'Take care of it for me, friend, there'll be a police search at my place tomorrow.' And he kept it. 'You have given it to the Church,' he declared. I said to him: 'You're a scoundrel.' 'No,' said he, 'I'm not a scoundrel, but I'm broadminded.' . . . But that wasn't Father Zossima, that was someone else. I've confused him with someone else . . . without noticing it. Come, another glass and that's enough. Take away the bottle, Ivan. I've been telling lies. Why didn't you stop me, Ivan, and tell me I was lying?"

"I knew you'd stop by yourself."

"That's a lie. You did it from spite, from spite against me. You despise me. You have come to me and you despise me in my own house."

"Well, I'm going away. You've had too much brandy."

"I've begged you for Christ's sake to go to Tchermashnya for a day or two, and you don't go."

"I'll go tomorrow if you're so set on it."

"You won't go. You want to keep an eye on me. That's what you want. You're spiteful. That's why you won't go."

The old man persisted. He had reached that state of drunkenness when the drunkard who has till then been inoffensive tries to pick a quarrel and to assert himself.

"Why are you looking at me? Why do you look like that? Your eyes look at me and say: 'You ugly drunkard!' Your eyes are mistrustful. They're contemptuous. . . . You've come here with some plot. Alyosha, here, looks at me and his eyes shine. Alyosha doesn't despise me. Alyosha, you mustn't love Ivan."

"Don't be angry with Ivan. Stop attacking him," Alyosha said emphatically.

"Oh, all right. Ugh, my head aches. Take away the brandy, Ivan. It's the third time I've told you."

He sat in silence thinking for a while. Then a slow, cunning grin spread over his face.

"Don't be angry with a feeble old man, Ivan. I know you don't love me, but don't be angry all the same. You've nothing to love me for. You go to Tchermashnya. I'll come to you myself and give you something nice. I'll show you a little wench there. I've had my eye on her a long time. She's still running around barefoot. Don't be afraid of barefooted wenches—don't despise them—they're pearls!" And he kissed his hand with a smack.

"To my thinking," he continued and he revived at once, seeming to grow sober the moment he touched on his favorite topic. "To my thinking . . . Ah, you boys! You children, little sucking pigs. . . . To my thinking . . . I never thought a woman ugly in my life—that's been my rule! Can you understand that? How could you understand it? You've milk in your veins, not blood. You're not out of your shells yet. My rule has been that you can always find something interesting in every woman that you wouldn't find in any other. Only, one must know how to find it, that's the point! That's a talent! To my mind there are no ugly women. The very fact that she is a woman is half the battle . . . But how could you understand that? Even in old maids, even in them you can find something that makes you wonder that men have been such fools as to let them grow old without noticing them. Barefooted girls or unattractive ones, you must take by surprise. Didn't you know that? You must surprise them till they're fascinated, upset, ashamed that such a gentleman should fall in love with such a little slut. It's a good thing that there always are and will be masters and slaves in the world. And so there always will be a little maid-of-all-work and her master, and you know, that's all that's needed for happiness. Wait . . . listen, Alyosha, I always used to surprise your mother, but in a different way. I paid no attention to her at all, but all at once, when the minute came, I'd be all devotion to her, crawl on my knees, kiss her feet, and I always, always—I remember it as though it were today—reduced her to that tinkling, quiet, nervous queer little laugh. It was peculiar to her. I knew her attacks always used to begin like that. The next day she would begin shrieking hysterically. You see, that little laugh was not a sign of delight; it was only a counterfeit. That's the great thing, to know how to take everyone. Once Belyavsky—he was a handsome fellow, and rich and he used to come here and hang around her—suddenly gave me a slap in the face in front of her. And she who was always such a mild sheep—why, I thought she was going to knock me down. How she pounced on me! 'You're beaten, beaten!' she said. 'You've let him hit you. You have been trying to sell me to him,' she said. . . . 'And how dared he strike you in my presence! Don't dare come near me again, never, never! Run at once, challenge him to a duel!' . . . I took her to the monastery to bring her to her senses. The holy Fathers prayed her back to reason. But I swear, by God, Alyosha, I never insulted the poor crazy girl! Only once, perhaps, in the first year; then she was very fond of praying. She used to keep the feasts of Our Lady particularly and used to keep me out of her room then. I'll knock that mysticism out of her, I thought! 'Here,' I said, 'you see your holy ikon. Here it is. Here I take it down. You believe it's miraculous, but here, I'll spit on it and nothing will happen to me!' . . . When she saw it, good Lord! I thought she would kill me. But she only jumped up, wrung her hands, then suddenly hiding her face in them she began trembling all over and fell on the floor . . . fell in a heap. Alyosha, Alyosha, what's the matter?"

The old man jumped up frightened. From the time he had begun speaking about Alyosha's mother, a change had come over Alyosha's face. He grew crimson, his eyes glowed, his lips quivered. The old wretch had gone spluttering on, noticing nothing, till something very strange happened to Alyosha. Precisely what he was describing in the crazy woman was suddenly repeated with Alyosha. He jumped up exactly as his mother was said to have done, wrung his hands, hid his face in them, and fell back in his chair, shaking all over in an hysterical convulsion of violent, silent weeping. His extraordinary resemblance to his mother particularly impressed the old man.

"Ivan, Ivan! Water, quickly! It's like her, exactly as she used to be. His mother. Spurt some water on him from your mouth, that's what I used to do to her. He's upset about his mother. His mother," he muttered to Ivan.

"But she was my mother, too. Wasn't she?" said Ivan, with anger and contempt.

The old man shrank before Ivan's burning eyes.

Then something very strange happened, though only for a second; it seemed to escape the old man's mind that Alyosha's mother actually was the mother of Ivan too.

"Your mother?" he muttered, not understanding. "What do you mean? What mother are you talking about? Was she? . . . Why, damn it! Of course she was yours too! Damn it! My mind has never been so muddled before. Excuse me. Why, I was thinking Ivan . . . He, he, he!" He stopped. A broad, drunken, half-senseless grin spread over his face.

At that moment a terrible commotion was heard in the hall. There were shouts. Then the door was flung open and Dmitri burst into the room. The old man rushed to Ivan in terror.

"He'll kill me! He'll kill me! Don't let him get at me!" he screamed, clinging to Ivan's coat.

9. The Sensualists

GREGORY AND SMERDYAKOV RAN INTO THE ROOM after Dmitri. They had been struggling with him in the hallway. They had tried to prevent him from coming in, acting on instructions given them by Fyodor Karamazov some days before.

Taking advantage of the fact that Dmitri paused on entering the room to look about him, Gregory ran round the table, closed the double doors on the opposite side of the room leading to the other rooms. He stood before the closed doors, stretching wide his arms, prepared to defend the entrance, so to speak, with the last drop of his blood. Seeing this, Dmitri screamed and rushed at Gregory.

"Then she's there! She's hidden there! Out of my way!"

He tried to pull Gregory away, but the old servant pushed him back. Beside himself with fury, Dmitri then struck out and hit Gregory with all his might. The old man fell like a log, and Dmitri, leaping over him broke in the doors. Smerdyakov stood pale and trembling at the other end of the room. He huddled close to his master.

"She's here!" shouted Dmitri. "I saw her turn toward the house just now, but I couldn't catch her. Where is she? Where is she?"

That shout, "She's here!" produced an indescribable effect on Fyodor Karamazov. All his terror left him.

"Hold him! Hold him!" he cried, and he dashed after Dmitri. Meanwhile Gregory got up from the floor but he still seemed stunned. Ivan and Alyosha ran after their father. Something fell on the floor with a ringing crash; it was a large glass vase —not an expensive one—which Dmitri had upset as he ran past.

"Hold him!" shouted the old man. "Help!"

Ivan and Alyosha caught their father and tried to pull him back.

"Why do you run after him? He'll murder you," Ivan cried.

"Ivan! Alyosha! She must be here. Grushenka's here. He said he saw her himself, running."

He was choking. He was not expecting Grushenka at the time, and the sudden news that she had come roused him. He was trembling all over. He seemed frantic.

"But you've seen for yourself that she hasn't come," cried Ivan.

"But she may have come by that other entrance."

"You know that entrance is locked, and you have the key."

Dmitri suddenly reappeared in the drawing room. He had, of course, found the other entrance locked, and the key actually was in his father's pocket. The windows of all the rooms were also closed so Grushenka could not have come in anywhere nor have run out anywhere.

"Hold him!" shrieked Fyodor Karamazov as soon as he saw Dmitri again. "He's been stealing money in my bedroom." And tearing himself from Ivan he rushed again at Dmitri.

Dmitri threw up both hands and clutched the old man by two tufts of hair that remained on his temples. He tugged at them, and then flung him on the floor. He kicked him in the face two or three times with his heel. The old man moaned. Ivan, though not so strong as Dmitri, threw his arms around him, and with all his might pulled him away. Alyosha helped him, holding Dmitri in front.

"You've killed him!" cried Ivan.

"Serves him right!" shouted Dmitri breathlessly. "If I haven't killed him, I'll come again and kill him. You can't save him!"

"Dmitri! Go away at once!" commanded Alyosha.

"Alyosha! You tell me. It's only you I can believe; was she here just now, or not? I saw her myself coming this way by the fence from the lane. I shouted. She ran away."

"I swear she hasn't been here, and that no one expected her."

"But I saw her. . . . So she must . . . I'll find out where she is. . . . Good-by, Alyosha! Not a word about the money. But go to Katerina at once and be sure to say, 'He sends his compliments to you!' Compliments, his compliments! Just compliments and farewell! Describe the scene to her."

Meanwhile Ivan and Gregory had raised old Karamazov from the floor and had seated him in an armchair. His face was covered with blood, but he was conscious and listened greedily to Dmitri's words. He still believed that Grushenka really was somewhere in the house. Dmitri glared at him with hatred as he went out.

"I'm not sorry for shedding your blood!" he cried. "Beware, old man, beware of your dream, for I have my dream, too. I curse you, and disown you altogether."

He ran out of the room.

"She's here. She must be here. Smerdyakov! Smerdyakov!" the old man wheezed, scarcely audibly, beckoning with his finger.

"No, she's not here, you old fool!" Ivan shouted at him angrily. "Here, he's fainting! Water! A towel! Hurry, Smerdyakov!"

Smerdyakov ran for water. At last they got the old man undressed, and put him to bed. They wrapped a wet towel round his head. Exhausted by the brandy, by his violent emotion, and the blows he had received, he shut his eyes and fell asleep as soon as his head touched the pillow.

Ivan and Alyosha went back to the drawing room. Smerdyakov removed the fragments of the broken vase, while Gregory stood by the table looking gloomily at the floor.

"Shouldn't you put a wet bandage on your head and go to bed, too?" Alyosha said to Gregory. "We'll look after father. Dmitri gave you a terrible blow—on the head."

"He's insulted me!" Gregory said gloomily and distinctly.

"He's 'insulted' his father, not only you," observed Ivan with a forced smile.

"When he was little I used to wash him in a tub. He's insulted me," repeated Gregory.

"Damn it all, if I hadn't pulled Dmitri away he might have murdered father. It wouldn't take much to kill him, would it?" whispered Ivan to Alyosha.

"God forbid!" cried Alyosha.

"Why should He forbid?" Ivan went on in the same whisper, with a smile. "One reptile will devour the other. And it will serve them both right, too."

Alyosha shuddered.

"Of course I won't let him be murdered. . . . Stay here, Alyosha. I'm going outside for some fresh air. My head's aching."

Alyosha went to his father's bedroom and sat by his bedside behind a screen for about an hour. The old man suddenly opened his eyes and gazed for a long while at Alyosha, evidently remembering and meditating. All at once he grew very excited.

"Alyosha," he whispered apprehensively. "Where's Ivan?"

"In the yard. He's got a headache. He's on the lookout."

"Give me that looking glass. It's over there. Give it to me."

Alyosha gave him a little round folding looking glass which stood on the chest of drawers. The old man looked at himself in it. His nose was quite swollen, and on the left side of his forehead there was a large crimson bruise.

"What does Ivan say? Alyosha, my dear, my only son, I'm afraid of Ivan. I'm more afraid of Ivan than of Dmitri. You're the only one I'm not afraid of. . . ."

"Don't be afraid of Ivan either. He is angry, but he'll defend you."

"Alyosha, and what of the other? He's run to Grushenka. Tell me the truth, was she here just now or not?"

"No one has seen her. It was a mistake. She has not been here."

"You know Dmitri wants to marry her, to marry her."

"She won't marry him."

"She won't. She won't. She won't. She won't under any circumstances!"

The old man glowed with joy, as though nothing more comforting could have been said to him. In his delight he seized Alyosha's hand and pressed it warmly to his heart. Tears glittered in his eyes.

"That ikon of the Mother of God about which I was telling you just now," he said. "Take it and keep it for yourself. And I'll let you go back to the monastery. . . . I was joking this morning. Don't be angry with me. My head aches, Alyosha . . . Alyosha, comfort my heart. Be an angel and tell me the truth!"

"You're still asking whether she has been here or not?" Alyosha said sadly.

"No, no, no. I believe you. I'll tell you what I want. You go to Grushenka yourself, or see her somehow. Hurry and ask her. See for yourself who she means to choose, him or me. Eh? What? Can you?"

"If I see her I'll ask her," Alyosha muttered embarrassed.

"No, she won't tell you," the old man interrupted. "She's a rogue. She'll begin kissing you and saying that it's you she wants. She's a deceitful, shameless hussy. You mustn't go to her, you mustn't!"

"No, father, and it wouldn't be right, it wouldn't be right at all."

"Where was he sending you just now? He shouted 'Go' as he ran away."

"To Katerina."

"For money? To ask her for money?"

"No. Not for money."

"He has no money; not a penny. I'll settle down for the night and think things over, and you can go. Perhaps you'll meet her. . . . Only be sure to come to me tomorrow morning. Be sure to. I have something to say to you tomorrow. Will you come?"

"Yes."

"When you come, pretend you've come of your own accord to ask after me. Don't tell anyone I told you to come. Don't say a word to Ivan."

"Very well."

"Good-by, my angel. You stood up for me, just now. I shall never forget it. I've something to say to you tomorrow—but I must think about it."

"And how do you feel now?"

"I'll get up tomorrow and go out, perfectly well, perfectly well!"

Crossing the yard Alyosha found Ivan sitting on the bench at the gateway. He was sitting writing something in pencil in his notebook. Alyosha told Ivan that their father was awake and conscious and that he had let him go back to sleep at the monastery.

"Alyosha, I would be very glad to meet you tomorrow morning," said Ivan cordially, standing up. His cordiality was a complete surprise to Alyosha.

"I shall be at the Hohlakovs' tomorrow," answered Alyosha, "I may be at Katerina's, too, if I don't find her at home now."

"You're going to her now? For that 'compliments and farewell,' " said Ivan smiling. Alyosha was disconcerted.

"I think I understand his words now and part of what went on before. Dmitri has asked you to go to her and say that he—well, in fact—takes his leave of her?"

"Ivan, how will all this horror end between father and Dmitri!" exclaimed Alyosha.

"One can't tell for sure. Perhaps in nothing; it may all fizzle out. That woman is a beast. Anyway we must keep the old man at home and not let Dmitri into the house."

"Ivan, let me ask you one thing more: has any man a right to look at other men and decide which is worthy to live?"

"Why bring in the question of worth? The matter is most often decided in men's hearts on other grounds much more natural. And as for rights—who has not the right to wish?"

"Not for another man's death?"

"Why not for another man's death? Why lie to oneself since all men are like this and perhaps cannot help being like this. Are you referring to what I said before—that one reptile will devour the other? In that case let me ask you something. Do you think I'm like Dmitri, capable of shedding his blood, murdering him, eh?"

"What are you saying, Ivan? Such an idea never crossed my mind. I don't think Dmitri is capable of it, either."

"Thank you," smiled Ivan. "Be sure, I will always defend him. But I reserve for myself full freedom in my wishes. Goodby till tomorrow. Don't condemn me, and don't look on me as a villain," he added with a smile.

They shook hands warmly as they had never done before. Alyosha felt that his brother Ivan had taken the first step toward him. But he felt that he had done this with some definite motive.

10. Both Together

ALYOSHA LEFT HIS FATHER'S HOUSE feeling even more exhausted and dejected than when he had entered it. His mind seemed shattered and unhinged. He felt afraid to put together the disjointed fragments and form a general idea from all the agonizing and conflicting experiences of the day. He felt something bordering upon despair, which he had never known till then.

Towering like a mountain above all the rest stood the fatal insoluble question: How would things end between his father and his brother Dmitri and this terrible woman? He had himself been witness to it; he had been present and seen them face to face. Yet only his brother Dmitri could be made unhappy, terribly, completely unhappy. There was trouble awaiting him. It appeared too that there were other people involved, far more so than Alyosha could have supposed. There was something mysterious in it, too. Ivan had made a step toward him, which was what Alyosha had been long desiring. But now he felt for some reason frightened at it. And these women? Strange to say, that morning he had set out for Katerina's in the greatest embarrassment; now he felt nothing of the kind. On the contrary, he was hurrying to her as though expecting to find guidance from her. Yet to give her this message was obviously more difficult than before. The problem of the three thousand roubles was now decided irrevocably and Dmitri, feeling himself dishonored and losing his last hope, might sink to any depth. Dmitri had, moreover, told him to describe to Katerina the scene which had just taken place with his father.

It was by now seven o'clock, and it was getting dark as Alyosha entered Katerina's very spacious and comfortable house on the High Street. Alyosha knew that she lived with two aunts. One of them, a woman of little education, was the aunt of her half-sister who had looked after her in her father's house when she came from boarding school. The other aunt was a Moscow lady of style and consequence, though in straitened circumstances. It was said that they both gave way in everything to Katerina and that she only kept them with her as chaperones. Katerina herself gave way to no one but her benefactress, the general's widow, who had been kept by illness in Moscow, and to whom she wrote twice a week a full account of all her doings.

When Alyosha entered the hall and asked the maid to take his name up, it was obvious that Katerina and her aunts were already aware of his arrival. Possibly he had been seen from the window. At least, Alyosha heard a noise, caught the sound of hurrying footsteps and rustling skirts. Two or three women had run out of the room. He thought it strange that his arrival should cause such excitement.

Alyosha was shown into the drawing room at once. It was a large room, elegantly and amply furnished, not at all in provincial style. There were many sofas, settees, big and little tables. There were pictures on the walls, vases and lamps on the tables, masses of flowers, and even an aquarium in the window. It was twilight and rather dark. Alyosha saw a silk cape on the sofa, where people had evidently just been sitting. And on a table in front of the sofa were two unfinished cups of chocolate, cakes, a glass saucer with raisins, and another with candy. Alyosha saw that he had interrupted visitors, and frowned. But at that instant the portiere was raised, and with rapid footsteps Katerina came in, holding out both hands to Alyosha with a radiant smile of delight. At the same time a servant brought in two lighted candles and set them on the table.

"Thank God! At last you have come! I've been praying for you all day! Sit down."

Alyosha had been struck by Katerina's beauty when, three weeks before, Dmitri had first brought him at Katerina's request to be introduced to her. There had been no conversation between them at that interview, however. Thinking Alyosha was very shy, Katerina had talked all the time to Dmitri. Alyosha had been silent, but he had seen a great deal very clearly. He was struck by Katerina's proud ease, self-confidence and haughtiness. It was all evident. Alyosha felt that he was not exaggerating. He thought her great glowing black eyes were very fine, especially with her pale, even rather sallow, longish face. But in those eyes and in the lines of her lips there was something with which his brother might well be passionately in love, but which perhaps could not be loved for long. He expressed this thought almost plainly to Dmitri when, after the visit, his brother asked and insisted that he should tell him his impression of Katerina.

"You'll be happy with her, but perhaps—not peacefully happy."

"That's possible. Such people remain always the same. They don't yield to fate. So you think I won't love her forever."

"No. Perhaps you will love her forever. But perhaps you won't always be happy with her."

Alyosha had given his opinion at the time, blushing, and angry with himself for having given in to his brother's pleas and put such "foolish" ideas into words. For his opinion had struck him as awfully foolish immediately after he had spoken it. He felt ashamed too of having given so confident an opinion about a woman. It was with the more amazement that he felt now, at the first glance at Katerina as she ran in to him, that he had perhaps been completely mistaken. This time her face was beaming with good-natured kindliness and warm-hearted sincerity. The "pride and haughtiness," which had struck Alyosha so much before, was only betrayed now in a frank, generous energy and a sort of bright strong faith in herself. Alyosha realized at the first glance, at the first word, that all the tragedy of Katerina's position in relation to the man she loved so dearly was no secret to her; that she perhaps already knew everything, absolutely everything. And yet, in spite of that, there was such brightness in her face, such faith in the future. Alyosha felt at once that he had wronged her in his thoughts. He was captivated immediately. Besides all this, he noticed at her first words that she was very excited. Her excitement was so intense that it almost approached ecstasy.

"I was so eager to see you, because you can tell me the whole truth—you and no one else."

"I have come," muttered Alyosha in confusion. "I—he sent me."

"Oh, he sent you! I thought he would. Now I know every-thing—everything!" cried Katerina, her eyes flashing. "Wait a moment, I'll tell you why I've been longing to see you. You see, I know perhaps far more than you do yourself, and there's no need for you to tell me anything. I'll tell you what I want from you. I want to know your last impression of him. I want you to tell me directly, plainly, coarsely even, what you thought of him just now and of his attitude. That will be better than if I had a talk with him, as he does not want to come to me. Do you understand what I want from you? Now, tell me simply, tell me every word of the message he sent."

"He told me to give you his compliments—and to say that he would never come again—but to give you his compliments."

"His compliments? Was that what he said—his own expres-sion?"

"Yes."

"Perhaps he made a mistake in the word, perhaps he did not use the right word?"

"No. He told me precisely to repeat that word. He begged me two or three times not to forget it."

Katerina flushed.

"Help me, Alyosha. I really need your help. I'll tell you what I think, and you must say whether it's right or not. Listen! If he had sent me his compliments in passing, without insisting on your repeating the words, without emphasizing them, that would be the end of everything! But if he particularly insisted on those words, if he particularly told you not to forget to re-peat them to me, then perhaps he was excited, beside himself. He had made his decision and was frightened at it. He wasn't walking away from me with a determined step, but leaping headlong. The emphasis on that phrase may have been simply bravado."

"Yes, yes!" cried Alyosha. "I believe that is so."

"And, if so, he's not altogether lost. I can still save him. Wait! Did he tell you anything about money—about three thousand roubles?"

"He did speak about it, and it's that more than anything else that's crushing him. He said he had lost his honor and that nothing matters now," Alyosha answered, feeling a rush of hope in his heart and believing that there really might be a way of escape and salvation for his brother. "But do you know about the money?" he added.

"I've known about it for a long time. I telegraphed to Mos-cow to inquire, and heard long ago that the money had not ar-rived. He didn't send the money, but I said nothing. Last week I learned that he still needed money. My only object in all this was that he should know to whom to turn, and who was his true friend. No, he won't recognize that I am his truest friend; he regards me merely as a woman. I've been tormented all week, trying to think how to prevent him from being ashamed to face me because he spent that three thousand. Let him feel ashamed of himself, let him be ashamed of other people's knowing, but not of my knowing. He can tell God everything without shame. Why is it he still does not understand how much I am ready to bear for his sake? Why, why doesn't he know me? How can he not know me after all that has happened? I want to save him. Let him forget me as his fiancée. . . . And he's afraid that he is dishonored in my eyes. Why, he wasn't afraid to speak freely with you, Alyosha. How is it that I don't deserve the same confidence?"

She spoke the last words in tears.

"I must tell you," Alyosha began, his voice trembling, "what happened just now between him and my father."

And he described the whole scene, how Dmitri had sent him to get the money, how Dmitri had broken in, knocked his father down, and how after that he had again specially begged him to take his compliments and farewell to her. Then Alyosha added softly: "He went to that woman."

"And do you imagine that I can't put up with that woman? Does he think I can't? But he won't marry her," she suddenly laughed nervously. "Could such a passion last forever in a Karamazov? It's passion, not love. He won't marry her because she won't marry him." Again Katerina laughed strangely.

"He may marry her," said Alyosha looking down.

"He won't marry her, I tell you. That girl is an angel. Do you know that? Do you know that?" Katerina exclaimed suddenly with extraordinary warmth. "She is one of the most fantastic of fantastic creatures. I know how bewitching she is, but I also know that she is kind, firm and noble. Why do you look at me like that, Alyosha? Perhaps you are puzzled at my words. Perhaps you don't believe me? . . . My angel!" she cried suddenly to someone in the next room. "Come in to us. This is a friend. This is Alyosha. He knows all about us. Come."

"I've only been waiting behind the curtain for you to call me," said a soft, one might even say sugary, feminine voice.

The portiere was raised and Grushenka, smiling and cheerful, came up to the table. A violent revulsion passed over Alyosha. He fixed his eyes on her and could not take them off. Here she was, that awful woman, the "beast," as Ivan had called her half an hour before. And yet one would have thought the creature standing before him a simple, good-natured, kind woman, handsome certainly, but so like other handsome ordinary women! It is true she was very, very good-looking with that Russian beauty so passionately loved by many men. She was a rather tall woman, though a little shorter than Katerina, who was exceptionally tall. She had a full figure, with soft, as it were, noiseless movements, softened to a peculiar oversweetness, like her voice. She moved, not like Katerina with a vigorous, bold step, but noiselessly. Her feet made absolutely no sound on the floor. She sank softly into a low chair, rustling her sumptuous black silk dress, and delicately nestling her milk-white neck and broad shoulders in a costly black cashmere shawl.

Grushenka was twenty-two years old and her face looked exactly that age. She had very white skin with a pale pink tint on her cheeks. The modeling of her face might be said to be too broad, and the lower jaw was set a trifle forward. Her upper lip was thin, but the slightly prominent lower lip was at least twice as full and looked pouting. But her magnificent, abundant dark brown hair, her sable-colored eyebrows and charming gray-blue eyes with their long lashes would have made the most indifferent person, meeting her casually in a crowd in the street, stop at the sight of her face and remember it long after.

What struck Alyosha most about Grushenka's face was its expression of childlike good nature. There was a childlike look in her eyes, a look of delight. She seemed as though expecting something with childish, impatient curiosity. The light in her eyes made one happy—Alyosha felt that.

There was something else about Grushenka which Alyosha could not understand, or would not have been able to define, and which yet perhaps unconsciously affected him. It was that softness, that voluptuousness of her bodily movements, that catlike noiselessness. Yet it was a vigorous, ample body. Under the shawl could be seen full broad shoulders and a high girlish bosom. Her figure suggested the lines of *Venus de Milo,* though in somewhat exaggerated proportions. Connoisseurs of Russian beauty could have foretold that this fresh, still youthful, beauty would lose its harmony by the age of thirty, would "spread"; that her face would become puffy, and that wrinkles would very soon appear upon her forehead and around her eyes; her complexion would grow coarse and red. She had the beauty of the moment, the fleeting beauty which is so often met with in Russian women. Alyosha, of course, did not think of this. And although he was fascinated, yet he wondered with an unpleasant sensation, and regretfully, why she drawled in that way and could not speak naturally. She did so evidently feeling there was a charm in the exaggerated, honeyed modulation of the syllables. It was, of course, only a bad habit that showed a lack of education and a false idea of good manners. And yet this intonation and manner of speaking impressed Alyosha as almost incredibly incongruous with the childishly simple and happy expression of her face, the soft, babyish joy in her eyes.

Katerina bent over Grushenka's chair and kissed her several times. She seemed quite in love with her.

"This is the first time we've met, Alyosha," she said. "I wanted to know her, to see her. I wanted to go to her, but I'd no sooner expressed the wish than she came to me. I knew we would settle everything together—everything. My heart told me so—I was begged not to do it, but I felt it would be a way out of

143

the difficulty, and I was not mistaken. Grushenka has explained everything to me, told me all she means to do. She flew here like an angel of goodness and brought us peace and joy."

"You did not look down upon me, my dear," drawled Grushenka in her sing-song voice, still with the same charming smile of delight.

"Don't say such things, you sorceress! Look down upon you! Here I kiss you once more. Look how she laughs. Alyosha! It does one's heart good to see the angel!"

Alyosha flushed. And faint, imperceptible shivers kept running through him.

"You make so much of me, my dear. Perhaps I am not at all worthy of your kindness."

"Not worthy! She's not worthy of it!" Katerina cried. Then speaking indirectly of Grushenka she said: "You know, Alyosha, we're fanciful, we're self-willed, but proudest of the proud in our little heart. We're noble, we're generous. We have only been unfortunate. We were too ready to make every sacrifice for an unworthy, perhaps a fickle man. There was one man—one, an officer too, we loved him, we sacrificed everything for him. That was long ago, five years ago, and he has forgotten us, he has married. Now he is a widower. He has written, he is coming here. And, do you know, we've loved him, none but him, all this time, and we've loved him all our life! He will come and Grushenka will be happy again. For the last five years she's been wretched. But who can reproach her, who can boast of her favors? Only that bedridden old merchant, but he is more like her father, her friend, her protector. He found her in despair, in agony, deserted by the man she loved. She was ready to drown herself but the old merchant saved her—saved her!"

"You defend me very kindly, my dear. You are in a great hurry about everything," Grushenka drawled again.

"Defend you! Is it for me to defend you? Should I dare to defend you? Grushenka, angel, give me your hand. Look at that charming soft little hand, Aylosha! Look at it! It has brought me happiness and has lifted me up, and I'm going to kiss it, outside and inside. Here, here, here!"

And three times she kissed the certainly charming, though rather plump hand of Grushenka who with a musical, nervous little laugh, watched Katerina. She obviously liked having her hand kissed.

"This is rather too much," thought Alyosha. He blushed. He felt a peculiar uneasiness.

"You won't make me blush, my dear, kissing my hand like this before this gentleman."

"Do you really think I meant to make you blush?" said Katerina, somewhat surprised. "Oh, how little you understand me!"

"Yes, and you too perhaps quite misunderstand me, my

dear. Maybe I'm not so good as I seem to you. I've an evil heart; I'm headstrong. I fascinated poor Dmitri that day simply for fun."

"But now you'll save him. You've given me your word. You'll explain it all to him. You'll tell him that you have long loved another man, who is now offering you his hand."

"Oh, no! I didn't give you my word to do that. It was you kept talking about that. I didn't give you my word."

"Then I didn't quite understand you," said Katerina slowly, turning a little pale. "You promised . . ."

"Oh no, my dear, I've promised nothing," Grushenka interrupted softly and evenly, still with the same gay and simple expression. "You see now, my dear, what a willful wretch I am compared with you. If I want to do something I do it. I may have promised you something. But now I'm thinking I will see Dmitri again. I liked him very much once—liked him for almost a whole hour. . . . Maybe I will now go and tell him to stay with me from this day on. You see, I'm so changeable."

"Just now you said—something quite different," Katerina whispered faintly.

"Oh, just now! But, you know, I'm such a soft-hearted, silly creature. Only think what he's gone through because of me! What if when I go home I feel sorry for him? What then?"

"I never expected . . ."

"Oh, my dear, how good and generous you are compared with me! Now perhaps you won't care for a silly creature like me, now that you know my character. Give me your sweet little hand, my dear," she said tenderly. And with a sort of reverence she took Katerina's hand.

"Here, my dear, I'll take your hand and kiss it as you did mine. You kissed mine three times, but I ought to kiss yours three hundred times to be even with you. Well, but let that go. And then it shall be as God wills. Perhaps I will be your slave and want to do your bidding like a slave. Let it be as God wills, without any agreements and promises. What a sweet hand—what a sweet hand you have! You dear, you incredible beauty!"

She slowly raised the hand to her lips, with the object of "being even" with her in kisses.

Katerina did not take her hand away. She listened with timid hope to the last words, although Grushenka's promise to do her bidding like a slave was very strangely expressed. She looked intently into her eyes. She still saw in those eyes the same simple-hearted, confiding expression, the same bright gaiety.

"She's maybe too naïve," thought Katerina with hope.

Grushenka meanwhile seemed enthusiastic over the "sweet hand." She raised it deliberately to her lips. But she held it for a moment near her lips, as though reconsidering something.

"Do you know, my dear," she suddenly drawled in an even more soft and sugary voice. "Do you know, after all, I don't think I'll kiss your hand?" And she laughed a little gay laugh.

"As you like. What's the matter with you?" said Katerina suddenly.

"So that you may remember that you kissed my hand, but I didn't kiss yours."

There was a sudden glare in her eyes. She looked with awful intentness at Katerina.

"Insolent creature!" cried Katerina, as though suddenly grasping something. She flushed all over and jumped up from her chair.

Grushenka got up too but without hurrying.

"So I shall tell Dmitri how you kissed my hand, but I didn't kiss yours. And how he will laugh!"

"Vile slut! Go away!"

"Ah, for shame, my dear! Ah, for shame! That's unbecoming for you, my dear, a word like that."

"Go away! You're a creature for sale!" screamed Katerina. Anger distorted her face.

"For sale! You used to visit gentlemen in the evening for money once. You brought your beauty for sale. You see, I know."

Katerina shrieked. She would have rushed at Grushenka but Alyosha held her with all his strength.

"Not a word more!" he cried. "Don't speak. Don't answer her. She'll go away—she'll go at once."

At that instant Katerina's two aunts and a maid ran into the room. They had heard her shriek. All hurried to her.

"I will go away," said Grushenka, taking her cape from the sofa. "Alyosha, darling, see me home!"

"Go away—go away, hurry!" cried Alyosha imploringly.

"Dear little Alyosha, see me home! I've got a story to tell you on the way. I created this scene for your benefit, Alyosha. See me home, dear, you'll be glad of it afterwards."

Alyosha turned away. Grushenka ran out of the house, laughing.

Katerina went into hysterics. She sobbed and was shaken with convulsions. Everyone fussed around her.

"I warned you," said the elder of her aunts. "I tried to prevent your doing this. You're too impulsive. How could you do such a thing? You don't know these creatures, and they say she's worse than any of them. You are too self-willed."

"She's a tigress!" yelled Katerina. "Why did you hold me back, Alyosha! I'd have beaten her—beaten her!"

She could not control herself in front of Alyosha. Perhaps she did not care to.

"She ought to be flogged in public!"

Alyosha went toward the door.

"But, my God!" cried Katerina, clasping her hands. "He! He! He could be so dishonorable, so inhuman! Why, he told that creature what happened on that fatal, accursed day!

146

'You brought your beauty for sale, my dear.' She knows it! Your brother's a scoundrel, Alyosha."

Alyosha wanted to say something, but he couldn't find the words. His heart ached.

"Go away, Alyosha! It's shameful, it's awful for me! Tomorrow, I beg you on my knees, come tomorrow. Don't condemn me. Forgive me. I don't know what I shall do now!"

Alyosha walked out into the street. His head was reeling. He could have wept as she did. Suddenly he was overtaken by the maid.

"My young lady forgot to give you this letter from Madame Hohlakov. It's been with us since dinnertime."

Alyosha took the little pink envelope mechanically and put it into his pocket.

11. *Another Reputation Ruined*

IT WAS NOT MUCH MORE THAN THREE-QUARTERS OF A MILE from the town to the monastery. Alyosha walked quickly along the road, at that hour deserted. It was almost night, and too dark to see anything clearly at a distance. There were cross-roads halfway. A figure came into sight under a solitary willow at the cross-roads.

As soon as Alyosha reached the cross-roads the figure rushed at him, shouting savagely: "Your money or your life!"

"It's you, Dmitri," cried Alyosha surprised and startled.

"Ha, ha, ha! You didn't expect me? I wondered where to wait for you. By her house? But I might have missed you. At last I thought of waiting here, because you had to pass here. There's no other way to the monastery. Come, tell me the truth. Crush me like a beetle. . . . But what's the matter?"

"Nothing, Dmitri—it's just that you frightened me. Oh, Dmitri! Father's blood just now." (Alyosha began to cry. He had been on the verge of tears for a long time, and now something seemed to snap in him.) "You almost killed him—cursed him and now—here—you cry: Your money or your life!"

"Well, what of it? It's not right—is that it? Not proper in my position?"

"No—I only . . ."

"Wait. Look at the night. You see what a dark night, what clouds, what a wind has risen. I hid here under the willow waiting for you. And as God's above, I suddenly thought, why go on in misery any longer? What is there to wait for? Here I have a willow, a handkerchief, a shirt, I can twist them into a rope in a minute . . . Why go on burdening the earth, dishonoring it with my presence. And then I heard you coming—Heavens, it was as though something flew down to me suddenly. Here is a man whom I love. Here he is, that man, my brother, whom I love more than anyone in the world. The only one I love in the world. And I loved you so much, so much at that moment that I thought: 'I'll embrace him at once.' Then a stupid idea struck me, to scare you. I shouted, like a fool, 'your money!' Forgive my fooling—it was only nonsense. There's nothing evil in my soul. . . . Damn it all, tell me what's happened. What did she say? Don't spare me! Was she furious?"

"No, not that. . . . There was nothing like that, Dmitri. There—I found them both there."

"Both?"

"Grushenka at Katerina's."

Dmitri was struck dumb.

"Impossible!" he cried. "You're mad! Grushenka with her?"

Alyosha described all that had happened from the moment he went in to Katerina's. He took a long time telling his story. He didn't tell it fluently and consecutively, but he seemed to make it clear, not omitting any word or action of significance, and vividly describing his own sensations. Dmitri listened in silence, looking at him with a terrible fixed stare. But it was clear to Alyosha that he understood it all.

As the story went on, Dmitri's face became gloomy and threatening. He scowled, he clenched his teeth, and his fixed stare became still more rigid, more concentrated, more terrible. Then suddenly his savage face changed and he broke into uncontrolled laughter. He literally shook with laughter. For a long time he could not speak.

"So she wouldn't kiss her hand! So she didn't kiss it. So she ran away!" he kept exclaiming with delight; insolent delight it might have been called, if it had not been so spontaneous. "So the other one called her a tigress! And a tigress she is! So Grushenka ought to be flogged! Yes, yes, she should. That's just what I think. She should have been flogged long ago. It's like this, Alyosha, let her be punished, but I must get better first. I understand the queen of impudence. That's her all over! You saw her all over in that hand-kissing, the she-devil! She's the queen of all she-devils you can imagine in the world! She's magnificent in her own way! So she ran home? I'll go—ah—I'll run to her! Alyosha, don't blame me. I agree that hanging is too good for her."

"But Katerina!" exclaimed Alyosha.

"I see her, too! I see right through her, as I've never done before! It's the discovery of the four continents of the world, that is, of the five! What a thing to do! That's just like Katerina, who was not afraid to face a coarse, unmannerly officer and risk a deadly insult on a generous impulse to save her father! But the pride, the recklessness, the defiance, the unbounded defiance! You say her aunt tried to stop her. That aunt, you know, is overbearing, herself. She's the sister of the general's widow in Moscow, and even more haughty than Ka-

148

terina. But her husband was caught stealing government money. He lost everything, his estate and all, and the proud wife had to lower her colors, and hasn't raised them since. So she tried to prevent Katerina but she wouldn't listen to her! She thinks she can overcome everything, that everything will give way to her. She thought she could bewitch Grushenka. She believed she could; she plays a part to herself, and whose fault is it? Do you think she kissed Grushenka's hand first, on purpose, with a motive? No, she really was fascinated by Grushenka, that's to say, not by Grushenka, but by her own dream, her own delusion—because it was *her* dream, *her* delusion! Alyosha, how did you escape from them, those women? Did you pick up your cassock and run? Ha, ha, ha!"

"Dmitri, you don't seem to understand how you've insulted Katerina by telling Grushenka about that day. And she flung it in her face just now. She accused her of having gone to gentlemen in secret to sell her beauty! What could be worse than that insult?"

What worried Alyosha more than anything was that, incredible as it seemed, his brother appeared pleased at Katerina's humiliation.

Dmitri frowned and struck his forehead with his hand. He only now realized what he had done.

"Yes, perhaps, I really did tell Grushenka about that 'fatal day,' as Katerina calls it. Yes, I did tell her, I remember! It was that time at Mokroe. I was drunk, the gypsies were singing. . . . But I was sobbing. I was sobbing then, kneeling and praying to Katerina's image, and Grushenka understood it. She understood it all then. I remember, she cried herself. . . . Damn it all! . . . Then she cried, but now it's a 'dagger in the heart'! That's how women are."

He looked down and sank into thought.

"Yes, I am a scoundrel, a thorough scoundrel!" he said in a gloomy voice. "It doesn't matter whether I cried or not, I'm a scoundrel! Tell her I accept the name, if that's any comfort. Come, that's enough. Good-by. It's no use talking! It's not amusing. You go your way and I'll go my way. And I don't want to see you again except as a last resource. Good-by, Alyosha!"

He pressed Alyosha's hand. Then still looking down, without raising his head, as though tearing himself away, he quickly turned toward the town.

Alyosha looked after him, unable to believe he would go away so abruptly.

"Wait, Alyosha, one more confession to you alone!" cried Dmitri, suddenly turning back. "Look at me. Look at me. You see here, here—there's terrible disgrace in store for me." (As he said "here," Dmitri struck his chest with his fist with a strange air, as though the dishonor lay precisely on his chest, in some spot, in a pocket, perhaps, or hanging round his neck.)

"You know me now, a scoundrel, a sworn scoundrel. But let me tell you that I've never done anything before and never will again, anything that can compare in baseness with the dishonor which I bear now at this very minute on my breast. Here, here, a dishonor which will come to pass, though I'm perfectly free to stop it. I can stop it or carry it through, remember that. Well, let me tell you, I will carry it through. I won't stop it. I told you everything just now, but I didn't tell you this, because even I am not bold enough. I can still prevent it. If I do, I can give back the full half of my lost honor tomorrow. But I won't prevent it. I will carry out my plan, and you can bear witness that I told you so beforehand. Darkness and destruction! No need to explain. You'll find out in time. The filthy back alley and the she-devil. Good-by. Don't pray for me, I'm not worth it. And there's no use, no use at all . . . I don't need it! Good-by!"

And he suddenly went off.

Alyosha turned toward the monastery. "What? I shall never see him again! What is he saying?" he wondered wildly. "Why, I shall certainly see him tomorrow. I shall look him up. I shall make a point of it. What does he mean?"

Alyosha went around the monastery and crossed the pine wood to the hermitage. The door was opened to him, although there was a rule that no one should be admitted at that hour. There was a tremor in his heart as he went into Father Zossima's cell.

"Why, why, had he gone forth? Why had Father Zossima sent him into the world? Here in the hermitage was peace. Here was holiness. But out in the world there was confusion, there was darkness in which one lost one's way. . . ."

In the cell Alyosha found the novice Porfiry and Father Paissy, who came every hour to inquire after Father Zossima. And he learned with alarm that the elder was getting weaker and weaker. His usual discourse with the brothers had not taken place that day.

As a rule every evening after service the monks flocked into Father Zossima's cell and confessed aloud their sins of the day, their sinful thoughts and temptations; even their disagreements, if there had been any. Some confessed kneeling. Their elder absolved, reconciled, exhorted, imposed penance, blessed, and dismissed them. It was against this general "confession" that the opponents of "elders" protested, maintaining that it profaned the sacrament of confession, that it was almost a sacrilege. These opponents even claimed that such confessions attained no good object, but actually to a large extent led to sin and temptation. Many of the brothers disliked going to the elder, and went against their own will because everyone went, and for fear they should be accused of pride and rebellious ideas. People said that some of the monks agreed beforehand, saying, "I'll confess I lost my temper with you this morning, and you confirm it," simply in order to have something to say. Alyosha knew that this actually happened sometimes. He knew, too, that there were among the monks some who deeply resented the fact that letters from relatives were brought to the elder, to be opened and read by him before being seen by those to whom they were addressed.

It was assumed, of course, that all this was done freely, and in good faith, by way of voluntary submission and salutary guidance. But, in fact, there was sometimes insincerity, and much that was false and strained in this practice. Yet the older and more experienced of the monks adhered to their opinion, arguing that "for those who have come within these walls sincerely seeking salvation, such obedience and sacrifice will certainly be of great benefit. Those, on the other hand, who find it irksome, and complain, are not true monks, and have made a mistake in entering the monastery—their proper place is in the world. Even in the temple one cannot be safe from sin and the devil."

"Father Zossima is weaker, a drowsiness has come over him," Father Paissy whispered to Alyosha, as he blessed him. "It's difficult to rouse him. And he must not be roused. He woke up for five minutes, sent his blessing to the brothers, and begged their prayers for him at night. He intends to take the sacrament again in the morning. He remembered you, Alyosha. He asked whether you had gone away, and was told that you were in the town. 'I blessed him for that work,' he said, 'his place is there, not here, for a while.' Those were his words about you. He remembered you lovingly, with anxiety; do you understand how he honored you? But how is it that he has decided that you must spend some time in the world? He must have foreseen something! But understand clearly, Alyosha, that if you return to the world, it must be to do the duty laid upon you by your elder, and not for frivolous vanity and worldly pleasures."

Father Paissy went out. Alyosha now realized that Father Zossima was dying, though he might live another day or two. And he firmly and ardently resolved that in spite of his promises to his father, the Hohlakovs and Katerina, he would not leave the monastery next day, but would remain with his elder to the end. His heart glowed with love, and he reproached himself bitterly for having been able for one instant to forget him whom he had left in the monastery on his deathbed, and whom he honored above everyone in the world. He went into Father Zossima's bedroom. He knelt down, and bowed to the ground before his elder, who slept quietly without stirring, with regular, hardly audible breathing and a peaceful face.

Later Alyosha returned to the other room, where Father Zossima had received his guests in the morning. Taking off his boots, he lay down on the hard, narrow, leathern sofa, which he had long used as a bed, bringing nothing but a pillow. The mattress, about which his father had shouted to him that morning, he had long forgotten to lay on. He took off his cassock, which he used as a covering. But before going to bed, he fell on his knees and prayed a long time. In his fervent prayer he did not beseech God to lighten his darkness. He only thirsted for the joyous emotion, which always visited his soul after the praise and adoration, of which his evening prayer usually consisted. That joy always brought him light untroubled sleep.

But this night as he was praying, he suddenly felt in his pocket the little pink note the servant had handed him as he left Katerina's. He was disturbed, but finished his prayer. Then, after some hesitation, he opened the envelope. In it was a letter to him, signed by Lise, the young daughter of Madame Hohlakov, who had laughed at him before the elder that very morning.

"Alyosha," she wrote,

I am writing to you without anyone's knowledge, even mother's, and I know how wrong it is. But I cannot live without telling you about the feeling in my heart. And this no one but us two must know for a time. But how am I to say what I want so much to tell you? Paper, they say, does not blush, but I assure you it's not true and that it's blushing just as I am now. Dear Alyosha, I love you. I've loved you from my childhood, since our Moscow days, when you were very different from what you are now, and I shall love you all my life. My heart has chosen you, to unite our lives, and pass them together till our old age. Of course, on condition that you will leave the monastery. As for our age we will wait for the time fixed by the law. By that time I shall certainly be quite strong. I shall be walking and dancing. There can be no doubt of that.

You see how I've thought of everything. There's only one thing I can't imagine; what you'll think of me when you read this? I'm always laughing and being naughty. I made you angry this morning, but I assure you before I took up my pen, I prayed before the Image of the Mother of God, and now I'm again praying—and almost crying.

My secret is in your hands. When you come tomorrow, I don't know how I shall look at you. Ah, Alyosha, what if I can't restrain myself and begin laughing when I look at you as I did today? You'll think I'm nasty and making fun of you, and you won't believe my letter. And so I beg you, darling, if you've any pity for me, when you come tomorrow, don't look me straight in the face, for if I meet your eyes I will surely laugh, especially as you'll be wearing that long gown. I feel cold all over when I think of it, so when you come, don't look at me at all for a time. Look at mother or at the window....

Here I've written you a love letter. Oh, dear, what have I done? Alyosha, don't despise me. And if I've done something very horrid and hurt you, forgive me. Now the secret of my reputation, ruined perhaps forever, is in your hands.

I shall certainly cry today. Good-by till our meeting, our *awful* meeting.
　　　　　　—Lise.
　P.S.—Alyosha! You must, must, must come!
　　　　　　　　　　　—Lise.

Alyosha read the note in amazement. He read it through twice, thought a little, and then laughed a soft, sweet laugh. He started. That laugh seemed to him sinful. But a minute later he laughed again just as softly and happily. He slowly replaced the note in the envelope, crossed himself and lay down.

The trouble in his heart passed away at once. "God have mercy upon all of them. Hold all these unhappy and turbulent souls in Thy keeping, and set them on the right path. All ways are Thine. Save them according to Thy wisdom. Thou art love. Thou wilt send joy to all!" he murmured, crossing himself again, and falling into peaceful sleep.

PART TWO

BOOK IV: LACERATIONS

1. Father Ferapont

ALYOSHA GOT UP EARLY, before daybreak. Father Zossima woke up feeling very weak, but nevertheless he wanted to get out of bed and sit up in a chair. His mind was clear; his face looked very tired, yet bright and almost happy. It had an expression of gaiety, kindness and cordiality. "Maybe I shall not live through the coming day," he said to Alyosha. Then he wanted to confess and take the sacrament. He always confessed to Father Paissy. After taking communion, the service of extreme unction followed. The monks assembled and the cell was gradually filled up by the members of the hermitage. In the meantime the daylight grew stronger. People began coming from the monastery. After the service was over the elder wanted to take leave of everyone. As the cell was small the earlier visitors withdrew to make room for others. The elder was seated in an arm chair and Alyosha stood beside him. He talked as much as he could. Though his voice was weak, it was fairly steady.

"I've been teaching you for so many years, and I've been talking aloud for so many years, that I'm in the habit of talking, so much so that it's almost more difficult for me to hold my tongue than to talk. Even now, I cannot stop talking in spite of my weakness, dear Fathers and brothers," he said with humor, looking at the group round him.

Alyosha remembered afterwards something of what Father Zossima said to them. But although he spoke out distinctly and his voice was fairly steady, his thoughts were somewhat disconnected. He spoke of many things. He seemed anxious before death to say everything he had not said in his life, and not simply for the sake of instructing them, but as though thirsting to share with all men and all creation his joy and ecstasy, and once more in his life to open his whole heart.

"Love one another, Fathers," said Father Zossima, as far as Alyosha could remember afterwards. "Love God's people. Because we have come here and shut ourselves within these

154

walls, we are no holier than those that are outside, but on the contrary, from the very fact of coming here, each of us has confessed to himself that he is worse than others, than all men on earth. . . . And the longer the monk lives in his seclusion, the more keenly he must recognize this fact. Else he would have had no reason to come here. When he realizes that he is not only worse than others, but that he is responsible to all men for all and everything, for all human sins, national and individual, only then can the aim of our seclusion be attained. For know, dear ones, that every one of us is undoubtedly responsible for all men and everything on earth, not merely through the general sinfulness of creation, but each one personally for all mankind and every individual man. This knowledge is the crown of life for the monk and for every man. For monks are not a special sort of men, but only what all men ought to be. Only through that knowledge, our heart grows soft with infinite, universal, inexhaustible love. Then every one of you will have the power to win over the whole world by love and to wash away the sins of the world with your tears. . . . Each of you keep watch over your heart and confess your sins to yourself unceasingly. Be not afraid of your sins, even when perceiving them, if only there be penitence, but make no conditions with God. Again I say: Be not proud. Be proud neither to the little nor to the great. Hate not those who reject you, who insult you, who abuse and slander you. Hate not the atheists, the teachers of evil, the materialists—and I mean not only the good ones—for there are many good ones among them, especially in our day—hate not even the wicked ones. Remember them in your prayers thus: Save, O Lord, all those who have none to pray for them. Save too all those who will not pray. And add: It is not in pride that I make this prayer, O Lord, for I am lower than all men. . . . Love God's people. Let not strangers draw away the flock, for if you slumber in your slothfulness and disdainful pride, or worse still, in covetousness, they will come from all sides and draw away your flock. Expound the Gospel to the people unceasingly . . . Be not mercenary. . . . Do not love gold and silver; do not hoard them. . . . Have faith. Cling to the banner and raise it on high."

But the elder's words were more rambling than Alyosha reported them afterwards. Sometimes he broke off altogether, as though to take breath and recover his strength.

Father Zossima was in a sort of ecstasy. Those who stood about heard him with emotion, though many wondered at his words and found them obscure. . . . Still afterwards all remembered what he said.

When Alyosha happened for a moment to leave the cell, he was struck by the excitement and suspense of the monks who were crowding about. All were expecting that some miracle would happen immediately after the elder's death. This anticipation showed itself in some by anxiety, in others by devout solemnity. Their suspense was, from one point of view, almost frivolous, but even the most austere of the monks were affected by it. Father Paissy's face looked the gravest of all.

Alyosha was suddenly called by a monk to see the divinity student, Rakitin, who had arrived from town with a letter for him from Madame Hohlakov. In it she informed Alyosha of a strange incident. It appeared that among the women who had come on the previous day to receive Father Zossima's blessing, there had been an old woman from the town, a sergeant's widow. She had inquired whether she might pray for the soul of her son who had gone to Irkutsk, and had sent her no news for over a year. To this Father Zossima had answered sternly, forbidding her to do so, and saying that to pray for the living as though they were dead was a kind of sorcery. He afterwards forgave her because of her ignorance, and added "as though reading the book of the future" (this was Madame Hohlakov's expression): "that her son was certainly alive and would either come himself very shortly or send a letter, and that she was to go home and expect him." And "would you believe it," wrote Madame Hohlakov enthusiastically, "the prophecy has been fulfilled literally indeed, and more than that." Scarcely had the old woman reached home when they gave her a letter from Siberia which had been awaiting her. But that was not all; in the letter written on the road from Ekaterinburg, her son said that he was returning to Russia with an official, and that in three weeks he hoped "to embrace his mother."

Madame Hohlakov entreated Alyosha to report this new "miracle of prediction" to the Superior and all the brotherhood. "All, all, ought to know of it!" she concluded. The letter had been written in haste and her excitement was apparent in every line. But Alyosha did not need to tell the monks, for all knew about it already. Rakitin had asked the monk who brought his message "to inform most respectfully his reverence Father Paissy, that he, Rakitin, has a matter to speak of with him, of such gravity that he dare not delay it for a moment, and humbly begs forgiveness for his presumption." As the monk had given this message to Father Paissy before handing the letter to Alyosha, there was nothing left for Alyosha to do but to hand it to Father Paissy in confirmation of the story.

And even that austere and cautious man, though he frowned as he read the news of the "miracle," could not completely suppress some inner emotion. His eyes glistened and a grave and solemn smile came to his lips. "We shall see greater things!" he said.

"We shall see greater things, greater things yet!" the monks around repeated.

But Father Paissy, frowning again, begged all of them at least for a time, not to speak of the matter "until it be more fully confirmed, seeing there is so much readiness to believe any rumor among those of this world. This marvel may have happened naturally," he added prudently, as though to satisfy his conscience. But he scarcely believed his own disavowal, a fact his listeners very clearly recognized.

Within the hour the "miracle" was of course known to the whole monastery and to many visitors who had come for mass. No one seemed more impressed by it than the monk who had come the day before from St. Sylvester, from the little monastery of Obdorsk in the far North. It was he who had been standing near Madame Hohlakov the previous day and had asked Father Zossima earnestly, referring to the "healing" of the lady's daughter, "How can you presume to do such things?"

He was now puzzled and did not know whom to believe. The evening before he had visited Father Ferapont in his cell, behind the apiary, and had been awed by his visit. This Father Ferapont was that aged monk so devout in fasting and observing silence who has been mentioned already, as antagonistic to Father Zossima and the whole institution of "elders," which he regarded as a pernicious and frivolous innovation. He was a very forceful opponent, although from his practice of silence he scarcely spoke a word to anyone. What made him forceful was that a number of monks shared his feeling, and many of the visitors looked upon him as a great saint and ascetic, although they knew that he was crazy. But it was just his craziness that attracted them.

Father Ferapont never went to see the elder. And although he lived in the hermitage his superiors did not make him keep its regulations. He was excused because they thought he was crazy. He was seventy-five or more, and he lived in a corner beyond the apiary in an old decaying wooden cell which had been built long ago for another great ascetic, Father Iona, who had lived to be a hundred and five, and of whose saintly doings many curious stories were still spoken of in the monastery and the neighborhood.

Father Ferapont had moved into this same solitary cell seven years before. It was simply a peasant's hut, though it looked like a chapel, for it contained an extraordinary number of ikons with lamps perpetually burning before them—which people brought to the monastery as offerings to God. Father Ferapont had been appointed to look after them and keep the lamps burning.

It was said (and indeed it was true) that he ate only two pounds of bread in three days. The beekeeper used to bring him the bread, and even to this man who waited upon him, Father Ferapont rarely uttered a word. The four pounds of bread, together with the sacrament bread, regularly sent him on Sundays after the late mass by the Father Superior, made up his weekly rations. The water in his jug was changed every day. He rarely appeared at mass. Visitors who came to do him homage saw him sometimes kneeling all day long at prayer without looking around. If he addressed them, he was brief, abrupt, strange, and almost always rude. On very rare occasions, however, he would talk to visitors. But what he said was often a complete riddle. And no pleading would induce him to add a word of explanation. He was not a priest, but a simple monk. There was a strange belief, chiefly however among the most ignorant, that Father Ferapont had communication with heavenly spirits and would only converse with them, and was therefore silent with men.

The monk from Obdorsk, having been shown the way to the apiary by the beekeeper, who was also a very silent and surly monk, went to the corner where Father Ferapont's cell stood. "Maybe he will speak as you are a stranger but on the other hand you may get nothing out of him," the beekeeper had warned. The monk, as he related afterwards, approached with apprehension. It was rather late in the evening. Father Ferapont was sitting at the door of his cell on a low bench. A huge old elm was lightly rustling overhead. There was an evening freshness in the air. The monk from Obdorsk bowed down before the saint and asked his blessing.

"Do you want me to bow down to you, monk?" said Father Ferapont. "Get up!"

The monk got up.

"Blessing, be blessed! Sit beside me. Where have you come from?"

What struck the poor monk most was the fact that in spite of his strict fasting and great age, Father Ferapont still looked vigorous. He was tall, held himself erect, and had a thin but fresh and healthy face. There was no doubt that he still had considerable strength. He was of athletic build. In spite of his great age he was not even quite gray, and still had very thick hair and a full beard, both of which had once been black. His eyes were gray, large and luminous, but strikingly prominent. He spoke with a broad accent. He was dressed in a peasant's long reddish coat of coarse convict cloth (as it used to be called) and had a stout rope around his waist. His throat and chest were bare. Beneath his coat, his shirt of the coarsest linen showed almost black with dirt, not having been changed for months. They said that he wore irons weighing thirty pounds under his coat. His bare feet were in old slippers almost falling to pieces.

"From the little Obdorsk monastery, from St. Sylvester," the monk answered humbly, while his keen and inquisitive, but rather frightened little eyes kept watch on the hermit.

"I have been at Sylvester's. I used to stay there. Is Sylvester well?"

The monk hesitated.

"You are a senseless lot at Sylvester's! How do you keep the fasts?"

"Our diet is according to the ancient conventual rules. During Lent there are no meals on Monday, Wednesday, and Friday. For Tuesday and Thursday we have white bread, stewed fruit with honey, wild berries, or salt cabbage and wholemeal cereal. On Saturday white cabbage soup, noodles with peas, kasha, all with hemp oil. On weekdays we have dried fish and kasha with the cabbage soup. From Monday till Saturday evening, six whole days in Holy Week, nothing is cooked, and we have only bread and water, and that sparingly; if possible not taking food every day, just the same as is ordered for first week in Lent. On Good Friday nothing is eaten. In the same way on the Saturday we have to fast till three o'clock, and then take a little bread and water and drink a single cup of wine. On Holy Thursday we drink wine and have something cooked without oil or not cooked at all; inasmuch as the Laodicean council lays down for Holy Thursday: 'it is unseemly by remitting the fast on the Holy Thursday to dishonor the whole of Lent!' This is how we keep the fast. But what is that compared with you, holy Father," added the monk, growing more confident, "for all the year round, even at Easter, you take nothing but bread and water, and what we eat in two days lasts you a full seven. It's truly marvelous—marvelous."

"And mushrooms?" asked Father Ferapont, suddenly.

"Mushrooms?" repeated the surprised monk.

"Yes. I can give up their bread, not needing it at all, and go into the forest and live there on mushrooms and berries. But they can't give up their bread here; they are in bondage to the devil. Nowadays the unclean deny that there is need of such fasting. Haughty and unclean is their judgment."

"Ah, true," sighed the monk.

"And have you seen devils among them?" asked Ferapont.

"Among them? Among whom?" asked the monk timidly.

"I went to the Father Superior on Trinity Sunday last year, I haven't been since. I saw a devil sitting on one man's chest hiding under his cassock; only his horns poked out. Another had one peeping out of his pocket with such sharp eyes, he was afraid of me. Another devil settled in the unclean belly of one. Another was hanging round a man's neck and he was carrying him about without seeing him."

"You—can see spirits?" the monk asked.

"I tell you I can see, I can see through them. When I was coming out from the Superior's I saw one hiding from me behind the door. He was a big one, a yard and a half or more high, with a thick long gray tail. And the tip of his tail was in the crack of the door and I was quick and slammed the door, pinching his tail in it. He squealed and began to struggle, and I made the sign of the cross over him three times. And he died on the spot like a crushed spider. He must have rotted there in the corner and he must be stinking. But they don't see, they don't smell. It's a year since I have been there. I reveal it to you, as you are a stranger."

"Your words are terrible! But, holy and blessed Father,"

159

said the monk, growing bolder and bolder, "is it true, as they noise abroad even to distant lands, that you are in continual communication with the Holy Ghost?"

"He does fly down at times."

"How does he fly down? In what form?"

"As a bird."

"The Holy Ghost in the form of a Dove?"

"There's the Holy Ghost and there's the Holy Spirit. The Holy Spirit can appear as other birds—sometimes as a swallow, sometimes a goldfinch and sometimes as a blue-tit."

"How do you know him from an ordinary tit?"

"He speaks."

"How does he speak, in what language?"

"Human language."

"And what does he tell you?"

"Why, today he told me that a fool would visit me and would ask me silly questions. You want to know too much, monk."

"Terrible are your words, most holy and blessed Father." The monk shook his head. But there was a doubtful look in his frightened little eyes.

"Do you see this tree?" asked Father Ferapont after a pause.

"I do, blessed Father."

"You think it's an elm, but for me it has another shape."

"What sort of shape?" inquired the monk.

"It happens at night. You see those two branches? In the night it is Christ holding out His arms to me and seeking me with those arms. I see it clearly and tremble. It's terrible, terrible!"

"What is there terrible if it's Christ Himself?"

"Why, He'll snatch me up and carry me away."

"Alive?"

"In the spirit and glory of Elijah, haven't you heard? He will take me in His arms and bear me away."

Though the monk returned to the cell he was sharing with one of the brothers, in a bewildered state, he still cherished at heart a greater reverence for Father Ferapont than for Father Zossima. He was strongly in favor of fasting, and it was not strange that one who kept so rigid a fast as Father Ferapont should "see marvels." His words seemed certainly queer, but God only could tell what was hidden in those words. And were not stranger words and acts commonly seen in those who have sacrificed their intellects for the glory of God? The pinching of the devil's tail he was ready and eager to believe, and not only in the figurative sense. Besides, he had, before visiting the monastery, a strong prejudice against the institution of "elders" which he only knew of by hearsay and which he believed to be an evil innovation. Before he had been long at the monastery he had detected the secret mur-

murings of some shallow brothers who disliked the institution. He was, besides, a meddlesome, inquisitive man, who poked his nose into everything. This was why the news of the fresh "miracle" performed by Father Zossima reduced him to extreme perplexity.

Alyosha remembered afterward how their inquisitive guest from Obdorsk had been continually flitting to and fro from one group to another, listening and asking questions among the monks that were crowding within and without the elder's cell. But Alyosha did not pay much attention to him at the time, and only remembered it afterward. He had no time to spare thinking of the visiting monk, for when Father Zossima, feeling tired again, had gone back to bed and was closing his eyes, and sent for Alyosha, Alyosha ran at once.

There was no one else in the cell but Father Paissy, Father Joseph, and the novice Porfiry. The elder, opening his weary eyes and looking steadily at Alyosha, asked him: "Are your people expecting you, my son?"

Alyosha hesitated.

"Haven't they need of you? Didn't you promise someone yesterday to see them today?"

"I did promise—to my father—my brothers—others too."

"You see, you must go. Don't grieve. Be sure I shall not die without your being to hear my last word. To you I will say that word, my son, it will be my last gift to you. To you, dear son, because you love me. But now go keep your promise."

Alyosha obeyed although it was hard for him to leave. But the promise that he should hear his elder's last word on earth, that it should be a last gift to him, Alyosha, filled his soul with rapture. He hurried so that he might finish what he had to do in the town and return quickly.

Father Paissy, too, spoke some words which moved and surprised Alyosha greatly. He spoke as they left the cell together.

"Remember always, young man," Father Paissy began, without preface, "that science which has become a great power in the last century, has analyzed everything divine handed down to us in the holy books. After this cruel analysis the learned of this world have nothing left of all that was sacred. But they have only analyzed the parts and overlooked the whole, and indeed their blindness is marvelous. Yet the whole still stands steadfast before their eyes, and the gates of hell shall not prevail against it. Has it not lasted nineteen centuries? Is it not still a living, a moving power in the individual soul and in the masses of people? It is still strong and living even in the souls of atheists, who have destroyed everything! For even those who have renounced Christianity and attack it still follow the Christian ideal. And neither their subtlety nor the ardor of their hearts has been able to create a higher ideal of man and of virtue than the ideal given by Christ of old. When it has been attempted, the result has been only grotesque. Remember this especially, young man, since you are being sent into the world by your departing elder. Maybe, remembering this great day, you will not forget my words, spoken from the heart for your guidance because you are young and the temptations of the world are great and beyond your strength to endure. Well, now go, my orphan."

With these words Father Paissy blessed him.

And as Alyosha left the monastery, thinking them over, he suddenly realized that he had met a new and unexpected friend, a warmly loving teacher, in this austere monk who had before this always treated him sternly. It was as though Father Zossima were bequeathing Father Paissy to him. And "perhaps that's just what had passed between them," Alyosha thought suddenly.

The philosophic reflections Alyosha had just heard so unexpectedly testified to the warmth of Father Paissy's heart. He was eager to arm the boy's mind for conflict with temptation and to guard the young soul left in his charge with the strongest defense he could imagine.

2. At His Father's

ALYOSHA WENT TO HIS FATHER'S HOUSE. On the way he remembered that his father had insisted the day before that he should come without his brother Ivan seeing him. "Why?" Alyosha wondered. "Even if father has something to say to me alone, why should I go in unseen? Most likely in his excitement yesterday he meant to say something different," he decided.

Yet he was very glad when Marfa, who opened the garden gate to him (Gregory was ill in bed in the lodge), told him that Ivan had gone out two hours before.

"And my father?"

"He is up, taking his coffee," Marfa answered somewhat dryly.

Alyosha went in. The old man was sitting alone at the table, wearing slippers and an old overcoat of yellow cotton. He was amusing himself by looking through some accounts. He was alone in the house for Smerdyakov had gone out marketing. Though he had gotten up early he looked tired and weak. His forehead, upon which huge purple bruises had come out during the night, was bandaged with a red handkerchief. His nose was swollen and there were some small bruises on it. This gave his whole face a peculiarly spiteful and irritable look. The old man was aware of this. He turned a hostile glance on Alyosha as he came in.

"The coffee is cold," he cried harshly. "I won't offer you any. I've ordered nothing but a Lenten fish soup, and I won't invite anyone to share it. Why have you come?"

"To find out how you are," said Alyosha.

"Yes. Besides, I told you to come yesterday. But it's not important. You didn't need to bother. I knew you'd come poking your nose in."

He said this with belligerence. At the same time he got up and looked anxiously in the looking glass (perhaps for the fortieth time that morning) at his nose. He also arranged his red handkerchief more attractively on his forehead.

"Red's better. It's just like the hospital in a white one," he observed. "Well, how are things over there? How is your elder?"

"He is very ill. He may die today," answered Alyosha sadly. But his father had not listened and had already forgotten his own question.

"Ivan's gone out," he said suddenly. "He is doing his best to carry off Dmitri's fiancée. That's what he is staying here for," he added maliciously and twisting his mouth he looked at Alyosha.

"Surely he did not tell you so?" asked Alyosha.

"Yes, he did, long ago. Would you believe it, he told me three weeks ago? You don't think he also came to murder me, do you? He must have had some object in coming."

"What do you mean? Why do you say such things?" said Alyosha troubled.

"He doesn't ask for money, it's true, but yet he won't get a penny from me. I intend living as long as possible, you may as well know, my dear Alyosha, and so I need every cent. And the longer I live, the more I shall need it," he continued, pacing from one corner of the room to the other, keeping his hands in the pockets of his loose greasy overcoat. "I can still pass for a man of fifty-five but I want to pass for one for another twenty years. As I get older, you know, I won't be a pretty object. The wenches won't come to me of their own accord, so I will need my money. So I am saving up more and more, simply for myself, my dear son. You may as well know. For I mean to go on in my sins to the end, let me tell you. For sin is sweet. All abuse it but all men live in it. The only difference is that others do it on the sly and I do it openly. And so all the other sinners fall upon me for being so simple. And your paradise, Alyosha, is not to my taste, let me tell you that. It's not the proper place for a gentleman, your paradise, even if it exists. I believe that I fall asleep and don't wake up again, and that's all. You can pray for my soul if you like. And if you don't want to, don't, damn you! That's my philosophy. Ivan talked well here yesterday, though we were all drunk. Ivan is a conceited fool. He has no particular learning . . . nor education either. He sits silent and smiles without speaking—that's what pulls him through."

Alyosha listened to his father in silence.

"Why won't he talk to me? If he does speak, he puts on airs. Your Ivan is a scoundrel! And I'll marry Grushenka in a minute if I want to. For if you've got money, Alyosha, you can have anything you want. That's what Ivan is afraid of. He is on the watch to prevent me getting married and that's why he is egging on Dmitri to marry Grushenka. He hopes to keep me from Grushenka, as though I would leave him my money if I don't marry her! Besides if Dmitri marries Grushenka, Ivan will carry off his rich fiancée. That's what he's counting on! He is a scoundrel, your Ivan!"

"How angry you are. It's because of yesterday. You had better lie down," said Alyosha.

"There! You say that," the old man observed suddenly, as though it had struck him for the first time, "and I am not angry with you. But if Ivan said it, I would be angry with him. It is only with you I have good moments. All the rest of the time you know I am ill-natured."

"You are not ill-natured, but distorted," said Alyosha with a smile.

"Listen, I meant this morning to get that ruffian Dmitri locked up and I don't know now what I shall do about it. Of course in these modern days fathers and mothers are looked upon as a prejudice. But even now the law does not allow you to drag your old father about by the hair, to kick him in the face in his own house, and brag of murdering him outright—all in the presence of witnesses. If I liked, I could crush him and could have him locked up at once for what he did yesterday."

"Then you don't mean to do it?"

"Ivan has persuaded me not to. I shouldn't pay attention to Ivan, but there's another thing."

And bending down to Alyosha, he went on in a confidential half-whisper.

"If I send the ruffian to prison, she'll hear of it and run to see him at once. But if she hears that he has beaten me, a weak old man, within an inch of my life, she may give him up and come to me. . . . For that's her way, everything by contraries. I know her through and through! . . . Won't you have a drop of brandy? Take some cold coffee and I'll pour a quarter of a glass of brandy into it. It's delicious, my boy."

"No, thank you. But I'll take that roll with me if I may," said Alyosha. And taking a French roll he put it in the pocket of his cassock. "And you'd better not have brandy, either," he suggested looking into the old man's face.

"You are quite right, it irritates my nerves instead of soothing them. Only one little glass. I'll get it out of the cupboard."

He unlocked the cupboard, poured out a glass and drank it.

Then he locked the cupboard and put the key back in his pocket.

"That's enough. One glass won't kill me."

"You see you are in a better humor now," said Alyosha smiling.

"Um! I love you even without the brandy, but with scoundrels I am a scoundrel. Ivan is not going to Tchermashnya—why? He wants to find out how much I give Grushenka if she comes. They are all scoundrels! But I don't recognize Ivan. I don't know him at all. Where does he come from? He is not one of us in soul. As though I'd leave him anything! I won't leave a will at all, you may as well know. And I'll crush Dmitri like a beetle. I squash black beetles at night with my slipper; they squelch when you tread on them. And your Dmitri will squelch too. *Your* Dmitri; you love him. Yes, you love him and I am not afraid of your loving him. But if Ivan loved him I would be afraid. But Ivan loves nobody. Ivan is not one of us. People like Ivan are not our sort, my boy. They are like a cloud of dust. When the wind blows, the dust will be gone . . . I had a silly idea in my head when I told you to come today; I wanted to find out from you about Dmitri. If I were to give him a thousand roubles or maybe two, would the wretch agree to go off altogether for five years or, better still, thirty-five, and without Grushenka, and give her up once and for all, eh?"

"I—I'll ask him," muttered Alyosha. "If you would give him three thousand, perhaps he . . ."

"That's nonsense! You needn't ask him now, no need! I've changed my mind. It was a stupid idea of mine. I won't give him anything, not a penny, I want my money myself," cried the old man, waving his hand. "I'll crush him like a beetle without it. Don't say anything to him or else . . . There's nothing for you to do here, you don't need to stay. Is that fiancée of his, Katerina, whom he has kept so carefully hidden from me all this time, going to marry him or not? You went to see her yesterday, didn't you?"

"Nothing will induce her to abandon him."

"There you see how dearly these fine young ladies love a rake and a scoundrel. They are poor creatures I tell you, those pale young ladies, very different from . . . Ah, if I had his youth and the looks I had then (for I was better looking than he at twenty-eight) I'd have been a conquering hero just as he is. He is a cad! But he won't get Grushenka, anyway. He won't! I'll crush him!"

His anger had returned with the last words.

"You can go. There's nothing for you to do here today," he said harshly.

Alyosha went up to say good-by to him, and kissed him on the shoulder.

"What's that for?" The old man was a little surprised. "We'll see each other again, or do you think we won't?"

"I didn't mean anything."

"Neither did I, I didn't mean anything," said the old man, looking at him. "Listen, listen," he shouted after him. "Hurry and come again and I'll have a fish soup for you, a good one, not like today. Be sure to come! Come tomorrow, do you hear, tomorrow!"

And as soon as Alyosha had gone out of the door, he went to the cupboard again and poured out another half glass of brandy.

"I won't take any more!" he muttered, clearing his throat. And again he locked the cupboard and put the key in his pocket. Then he went into his bedroom, lay down on the bed, exhausted, and in one minute he was asleep.

3. A Meeting with the Schoolboys

"THANK GOODNESS HE DIDN'T ASK ME about Grushenka," thought Alyosha, as he left his father's house and turned towards Madame Hohlakov's. "I might have had to tell him of my meeting with Grushenka yesterday."

Alyosha felt painfully that since yesterday both his father and Dmitri had renewed their energies, and that their hearts had grown hard again. "Father is spiteful and angry, he's made some plan and will stick to it. And what of Dmitri? He too will be harder than yesterday, he too must be spiteful and angry, and he too, no doubt, has made some plan. Oh, I must find him today, whatever happens."

But Alyosha did not have long to think of these things. An incident occurred on the road which made a great impression on him. Just after he had crossed the square and turned the corner coming out into Mihailovsky Street, which is divided by a small ditch from the High Street (our whole town is intersected by ditches), he saw a group of schoolboys between the ages of nine and twelve. They were going home from school, some with their bags on their shoulders, others with leather satchels; some in short jackets, others in overcoats. Some even had those high boots with creases round the ankles, such as little boys spoilt by rich fathers love to wear. The whole group was talking eagerly about something, apparently holding a council. Alyosha had never been able to pass children without taking notice of them, and although he was particularly fond of children of three or thereabouts, he liked schoolboys of ten and eleven too. And so, anxious as he was that day, he wanted to talk to them. He looked into their excited faces. Then he noticed that all the boys had stones in their hands. Behind the ditch some thirty yards away, there was another schoolboy standing by a fence. He too had a school bag at his side. He was about ten years old, pale, delicate looking and with sparkling black eyes. He kept an anxious watch on the other six with whom he had evidently been feuding.

Alyosha went up and speaking to a fair, curlyheaded boy in a black jacket observed: "When I used to carry a school bag like yours, I always carried it on my left side, so as to have my right hand free. But you've got yours on your right side. So it will be awkward for you to get at it."

Alyosha had no design in beginning with this practical remark. But it is the only way for a grown-up person to get at once into a child's confidence or still more into the confidence of a group of children. One must begin in a serious business-like way so as to be on a perfectly equal footing. Alyosha understood this by instinct.

"But he is left-handed," a fine healthy-looking boy of eleven answered promptly. All the others stared at Alyosha.

"He even throws stones with his left hand," observed a third.

At that moment a stone fell into the group. It just grazed the left-handed boy. It was thrown by the boy standing on the other side of the ditch.

"Give it to him, hit him back, Smurov," they all shouted. But Smurov, the left-handed boy, needed no telling, and at once revenged himself. He threw a stone, but it missed the boy and hit the ground.

The boy on the other side of the ditch, the pocket of whose coat was visibly bulging with stones, flung another stone at the group. This time it flew straight at Alyosha and hit him on the shoulder.

"He aimed it at you. He meant it! You are Kamarazov, Karamazov!" the boys shouted laughing. "Come, let's all throw stones at him!" And six stones flew at the boy. One struck the boy on the head and he fell down. But he jumped up at once and began returning their fire. Both sides threw stones.

"What are you doing! Aren't you ashamed? Six against one! Why, you'll kill him," cried Alyosha.

He ran forward to protect the solitary boy. Three or four of the boys stopped throwing for a minute.

"He began first!" cried a boy in a red shirt in an angry childish voice. "He is a beast, he stabbed Krassotkin in class the other day with a penknife. It bled. Krassotkin wouldn't report him, but he must be beaten."

"But what for? I suppose you tease him."

"There, he threw another stone at you. He knows you," cried the boys. "It's you he is throwing at now, not us. Come, all of you, attack. Don't miss, Smurov!" And again a fire of stones began. The boy on the other side of the ditch was hit in the chest. He screamed, began to cry and ran away uphill toward Mihailovsky Street. They all shouted: "Aha, he's a coward. He is running away. Wisp of tow!"

"You don't know what a beast he is, Karamazov. Killing is too good for him," said the boy in the black jacket, with flashing eyes. He seemed to be the eldest.

"What's wrong with him?" asked Alyosha. "Is he a tell-tale or what?"

The boys looked at one another.

"Are you going that way, to Mihailovsky?" the same boy went on. "Catch up with him . . . You see he's stopped again. He is waiting and looking at you."

"He is looking at you," the other boys chimed in.

"Ask him if he likes a wisp of tow. Do you hear, ask him that!"

There was a burst of laughter. Alyosha looked at the boys and they at him.

"Don't go near him. He'll hurt you," cried Smurov in warning.

"I won't ask him about the wisp of tow, because I think you tease him with that question somehow. But I'll find out from him why you hate him so."

"Find out then. Find out," cried the boys laughing.

Alyosha walked uphill by the fence, straight toward the boy.

"You'd better look out," the boys called after him. "He won't be afraid of you. He will stab you in a minute as he did Krassotkin."

The boy waited for Alyosha without budging. Coming up to him, Alyosha saw facing him a child of about nine years old. He was an undersized weak boy with a thin pale face and large dark eyes that gazed at him vindictively. He was dressed in a shabby old overcoat, which he had outgrown. His bare arms stuck out beyond his sleeves. There was a large patch on the right knee of his trousers, and in his right boot just at the toe there was a big hole in the leather, carefully blackened with ink. Both the pockets of his great coat were weighed down with stones. Alyosha stopped two steps in front of him.

The boy, seeing at once from Alyosha's eyes that he wouldn't beat him, became less defiant, and began to speak. "I am alone, and there are six of them. I'll beat them all, alone!" he said suddenly.

"I think one of the stones must have hurt you badly," observed Alyosha.

"But I hit Smurov on the head!" cried the boy.

"They told me that you know me, and that you threw a stone at me on purpose," said Alyosha.

The boy scowled at him.

"I don't know you. Do you know me?" Alyosha continued.

"Leave me alone!" the boy cried, but he did not move, as though he were expecting something. There was a vindictive light in his eyes.

"All right. I am going," said Alyosha. "Only I don't know you and I don't tease you. They told me how they tease you, but I don't want to tease you. Good-by!"

"Monk in silk trousers!" cried the boy, following Alyosha with the same vindictive and defiant expression. He threw himself into an attitude of defense, feeling sure that now Alyosha would attack him. But Alyosha turned and walked away. He had not gone three steps, however, before the biggest stone the boy had in his pocket hit him painfully on the back.

"So you'll hit a man from behind! They tell the truth, then, when they say that you are underhand," said Alyosha, turning round again. This time the boy aimed a stone right at Alyosha's face. But Alyosha had time to guard himself and the stone struck him on the elbow.

"Aren't you ashamed? What have I done to you?" he cried.

The boy waited in silent defiance, certain that now Alyosha would attack him. But seeing that even now he would not, his rage was like a wild beast's. He flew at Alyosha and before Alyosha had time to move, he seized his left hand and bit his middle finger. He fixed his teeth in it. Alyosha cried out with pain and pulled his finger away with all his might. The child let go and retreated. Alyosha's finger had been badly bitten to the bone, close to the nail. It began to bleed. Alyosha took out his handkerchief and bound it tightly round his injured finger. He was a full minute bandaging it. The boy stood waiting all the time. At last Alyosha raised his gentle eyes and looked at him.

"Well," he said. "You see how badly you've bitten me. That's enough, isn't it? Now tell me what have I done to you?"

The boy stared.

"Though I don't know you and it's the first time I've seen you," Alyosha went on with the same serenity, "yet I must have done something to you—you wouldn't have hurt me like this for nothing. So what have I done? How have I wronged you, tell me?"

Instead of answering, the boy broke into a loud tearful wail and ran away.

Alyosha walked slowly after him toward Mihailovsky Street, and for a long time he saw the child running in the distance as fast as ever, not turning his head, and still keeping up his tearful wail. And he made up his mind to seek out the boy as soon as he had time and solve the mystery. Just now he did not have the time.

4. At the Hohlakovs'

ALYOSHA SOON REACHED Madame Hohlakov's house, a handsome stone house of two stories, one of the finest in our town. Though Madame Hohlakov spent most of her time in another province where she had an estate, or in Moscow, where she had a house of her own, yet she had an estate in our district and a house in our town too, inherited from her family. Her estate in our district was the largest of her three properties, yet she had been very little in our province before this time. She ran out to Alyosha in the hall.

"Did you get my letter about the new miracle?" She spoke rapidly and nervously.

"Yes."

"Did you show it to everyone? He restored the son to his mother!"

"He is dying today," said Alyosha.

"I have heard, I know. Oh, how I long to talk to you, to you, or someone about all this. No, to you, to you! And how sorry I am I can't see him! The whole town is excited. They are all in suspense. But now—do you know Katerina is here now?"

"Ah, that's lucky," cried Alyosha. "Then I shall see her. She told me yesterday to be sure to come and see her today."

"I know, I know. I've heard exactly what happened yesterday—and the atrocious behavior of that—creature. It's tragic. And if I'd been in her place I don't know what I would have done. And your brother Dmitri, what do you think of him?— my goodness! Alyosha, I am forgetting. Your brother is in there with her now, not that dreadful brother who was so shocking yesterday, but the other, Ivan. He is sitting with her talking. They are having a serious conversation. If you could only imagine what's passing between them now—it's awful. I tell you it's lacerating; it's like some incredible tale of horror. They are ruining their lives for no reason anyone can see. They both recognize it and revel in it. I've been watching for you! I've been thirsting for you! It's too much for me, that's the worst of it. I'll tell you all about it later but now I must speak of something else, the most important thing—I had forgotten what's most important. Tell me; why has Lise been crying hysterically? As soon as she heard you were here, she became hysterical!"

"Mother, it's you who are hysterical now, not I," Lise called through a crack in the door. Her voice sounded as though she wanted to laugh. But she was doing her best to control it.

Alyosha noticed the crack. Lise was peeping through it, but that he could not see.

"And no wonder, Lise, no wonder . . . your whims will make me hysterical too. But she is so ill, Alyosha, she has been so ill all night, feverish and moaning! I could hardly wait for the morning and for Doctor Herzenstube to come. He says that he can make nothing of it, that we must wait. Herzenstube always comes and says that he can make nothing of it. . . . As soon as you approached the house, she screamed, became hysterical and insisted on being wheeled back into this room here."

"Mother, I didn't know he had come. It wasn't because of him that I wanted to be wheeled into this room."

"That's not true, Lise. Julia ran to tell you that Alyosha was coming. She was on the lookout for you."

"My darling mother, it's not at all clever of you. But if you want to make up for it and say something very clever, mother, you'd better tell our honored visitor, Alyosha, that he has shown his want of wit by coming here after what happened yesterday. Everyone is laughing at him."

"Lise, you go too far. I shall have to be severe with you. Who laughs at him? I am so glad he has come, I need him, I can't do without him. Oh, Alyosha, I am so unhappy!"

"But what's the matter with you, mother darling?"

"Oh Lise, your whims, your illness, that awful night of fever, that awful everlasting Doctor Herzenstube. Everlasting, everlasting, that's the worst of it! Everything, in fact, everything. . . . Even that miracle, too! Oh, how it has upset me. How it has shattered me, that miracle. Dear Alyosha! And that tragedy in the drawing room, it's more than I can bear, I warn you. I can't bear it. A comedy, perhaps, not a tragedy. Tell me, will Father Zossima live till tomorrow? Will he? Oh, my God! What is happening to me? I close my eyes and see that it's all nonsense, all nonsense."

"I should be very grateful," Alyosha interrupted suddenly, "if you could give me a clean rag to bind up my finger. I have hurt it, and it's very painful."

Alyosha unbound his bitten finger. The handkerchief was soaked with blood.

Madame Hohlakov screamed and shut her eyes. "Good heavens, what a wound, how awful!"

But as soon as Lise saw Alyosha's finger through the crack she flung the door wide open.

"Come, come here," she cried. "No nonsense now! Good heavens, why did you stand there saying nothing about it all this time? He might have bled to death, mother! How did you do it? Water, water! You must wash it first of all, simply hold it in cold water to stop the pain, and keep it there, keep it there. . . . Hurry, mother, some water in a basin. Hurry," she finished nervously. She was frightened at the sight of Alyosha's finger.

"Shouldn't we send for Herzenstube?" cried Madame Hohlakov.

"Mother, you'll be the death of me. Your Doctor Herzenstube will come and say that he can make nothing of it! Water, water! Mother, for goodness' sake go get it yourself. Julia is such a slowpoke! Hurry, mother, or I shall die."

"Why, it's nothing much," cried Alyosha, frightened at this alarm.

Julia ran in with water and Alyosha put his finger in it.

"Some cotton, mother, for heaven's sake, bring some cotton and that caustic lotion. What's it called? We've got some. You know where the bottle is, mother. It's in your bedroom in the right-hand cupboard, there's a big bottle of it there."

"I'll bring everything in a minute, Lise, only don't scream and don't fuss. You see how bravely Alyosha bears it. How did this happen, Alyosha?"

Madame Hohlakov hurried away. This was all Lise was waiting for.

"First of all, answer the question, where did you get hurt like this?" she asked Alyosha quickly. "And then I'll talk to you about something quite different. Well?"

Instinctively feeling that the time of her mother's absence was precious for her, Alyosha hurried to tell her of his meeting with the schoolboys. Lise clasped her hands at his story.

"How can you, and in that dress too, associate with schoolboys!" she cried angrily, as though she had a right to order him about. "You are nothing but a boy yourself if you can do such things, a perfect boy! But you must find out for me about that horrid boy and tell me all about it, for there's some mystery in it. Now for the second thing, but first a question: does the pain prevent you talking about unimportant things, but talking sensibly?"

"Of course not. I don't feel much pain now."

"That's because your finger is in the water. It must be changed at once for it will get warm in a minute. Julia, bring some ice from the cellar and another basin of water. Now she is gone, I can speak. Will you give me the letter I sent you yesterday, dear Alyosha—be quick for mother will be back in a minute and I don't want . . ."

"I haven't got the letter."

"That's not true, you have. I knew you would say that. You've got it in that pocket. I've been regretting my joke all night. Give me back the letter at once. Give it to me."

"I've left it at home."

"But you can't consider me as a child, a little girl, after that silly joke! I am sorry for that silliness, but you must bring me the letter, if you really haven't got it—bring it today, you must, you must."

172

"Today! I can't possibly because I am going back to the monastery. And I won't come and see you for the next two days—three or four perhaps—for Father Zossima . . ."

"Four days, what nonsense! Listen. Did you laugh at me very much?"

"I didn't laugh at all."

"Why not?"

"Because I believed all you said."

"You are insulting me!"

"Not at all. As soon as I read it, I thought that all you said would come to pass, for as soon as Father Zossima dies, I am to leave the monastery. Then I shall go back and finish my studies, and when you reach the legal age we will be married. I will love you. Though I haven't had time to think about it, I don't believe I could find a better wife than you. And Father Zossima tells me I must marry."

"But I am a cripple, wheeled about in a chair," laughed Lise, flushing crimson.

"I'll wheel you about myself. But I'm sure you'll be well by then."

"But you are mad," said Lise nervously, "to take a joke so seriously! Here's mother. Mother, how slow you always are. How can you be so slow! And here's Julia with the ice!"

"Oh, Lise, don't scream, above all things don't scream. That scream drives me . . . How can I help it when you put the cotton in another place. I've been hunting and hunting—I think you did it on purpose."

"I couldn't tell that he would come with a bad finger, or else perhaps I might have done it on purpose. My darling mother, you say really funny things."

"Never mind my being funny. But I must say you show strange feeling for Alyosha's suffering! Oh, my dear Alyosha, what's killing me is no one thing in particular, not Herzenstube, but everything together, that's what is too much for me."

"That's enough, mother, enough about Herzenstube," Lise laughed gaily. "Hurry with the cotton and lotion, mother. That's simply Goulard's water, Alyosha, I remember the name now, but it's a good lotion. Would you believe it, mother, on the way here he had a fight with boys in the street, and it was a boy who bit his finger. Isn't he a child, a child himself? Is he fit to get married after that? For would you believe it, he wants to get married, mother. Just think of him married, wouldn't it be funny, wouldn't it be awful?"

And Lise kept laughing her thin hysterical giggle, looking at Alyosha.

"But why married, Lise? What makes you talk of such a thing? It's quite out of place—and perhaps the boy was rabid."

"Why mother! As though there were rabid boys!"

"Why not, Lise, as though I had said something stupid! The

boy might have been bitten by a mad dog and he would become mad and bite anyone near him. How well she has bandaged it, Alyosha. I couldn't have done it. Do you still feel the pain?"

"It's nothing much now."

"You don't feel afraid of water?" asked Lise.

"Come, that's enough, Lise. Perhaps I really was rather too quick talking of the boy being rabid. . . . Katerina has only just heard that you are here, Alyosha. She's dying to see you, dying!"

"Oh, mother. He can't go just now, he is in too much pain."

"Not at all. I can go," said Alyosha.

"What! Are you going away? Is that what you are saying?"

"Well, when I've seen Katerina and Ivan I'll come back here and we can talk as much as you like. But I want to see Katerina at once, because I am very anxious to be back at the monastery as soon as I can."

"Mother, take him away quickly. Alyosha, don't bother to come and see me afterwards, but go straight back to your monastery. I want to sleep. I didn't sleep all night."

"Ah, Lise, you are only joking. But how I wish you would sleep!" cried Madame Hohlakov.

"I don't know what I've done. . . . I'll stay another three minutes, five if you like," muttered Alyosha.

"Even five! Take him away quickly, mother, he is a monster."

"Lise, you are crazy. Let us go, Alyosha, she is too difficult today. I am afraid to cross her. Oh, the trouble one has with nervous girls! Perhaps she really will be able to sleep after seeing you. How quickly you have made her sleepy, and how fortunate it is."

"Oh mother, how sweetly you talk. I must kiss you, mother."

"And I kiss you too, Lise. . . . Listen, Alyosha," Madame Hohlakov began mysteriously in a whisper. "I don't want to suggest anything, I don't want to lift the veil, you will see for yourself what's going on. It's appalling. It's the most fantastic thing. She loves your brother, Ivan, and she is doing her best to persuade herself that she loves your brother, Dmitri. It's appalling! I'll go in with you, and if they don't turn me out, I'll stay to the end."

5. A Laceration in the Drawing Room

IN THE DRAWING ROOM the conversation was already over. Katerina was greatly excited, though she looked determined. At the moment Alyosha and Madame Hohlakov entered, Ivan stood up to leave. His face was pale. And Alyosha looked at him anxiously, for this moment was to solve a doubt, a harassing enigma which had for some time haunted him. During the preceding month it had been several times suggested to him that his brother Ivan was in love with Katerina, and what was more, that he meant "to carry her off" from Dmitri. Until quite lately the idea seemed to Alyosha monstrous, though it worried him extremely. He loved both his brothers, and dreaded such rivalry between them. Meantime, Dmitri had said outright on the previous day that he was glad that Ivan was his rival. It was a great help to him. In what way did it help him? To marry Grushenka? But that Alyosha considered the worst thing possible. Besides all this, Alyosha had till the evening before believed that Katerina had a steadfast and passionate love for Dmitri; but he had only believed it till the evening before. He had also believed that she was incapable of loving a man like Ivan, and that she did love Dmitri, and loved him just as he was, in spite of all the strangeness of such a passion.

But during yesterday's scene with Grushenka another idea had struck him. The word "lacerating," which Madame Hohlakov had just spoken, almost made him start, because half waking up toward daybreak that day he had cried out: "Laceration, laceration," probably applying it to his dream. He had been dreaming all night of the previous day's scene at Katerina's. Now Alyosha was impressed by Madame Hohlakov's blunt and persistent assertion that Katerina was in love with Ivan, and only deceived herself through some sort of pose, from "self-laceration," and tortured herself by her pretended love for Dmitri from some fancied duty of gratitude. "Yes," he thought, "perhaps the whole truth lies in those words." But in that case what was Ivan's position? Alyosha felt instinctively that a character like Katerina's must dominate, and she could only dominate someone like Dmitri, and never a man like Ivan. For Dmitri might at last submit to her domination "for his own happiness" (which was what Alyosha would have liked), but Ivan . . . No, Ivan could not submit to her. Such submission would not give him happiness. Alyosha could not help believing that of Ivan. And now all these doubts and reflections flitted through his mind as he entered the drawing room. Another idea, also, forced itself upon him: "What if she loved neither of them—neither Ivan nor Dmitri?"

It must be noted that Alyosha had felt ashamed of his thoughts and had blamed himself when they kept recurring to him during the last month. "What do I know about love and women and how can I decide such questions?" he asked himself reproachfully. And yet it was impossible for him not to think about it. He felt instinctively that this rivalry was of immense importance in his brothers' lives and that a great deal depended upon it.

"One reptile will devour the other," Ivan had said the day before, speaking in anger of his father and Dmitri. So Ivan looked upon Dmitri as a reptile. He had perhaps looked upon him this way for a long time. Was it since he had known Katerina? These words had, of course, escaped Ivan unawares yesterday, but that only made them more important. If he felt like that, what chance was there of peace? Were there not, on the contrary, new grounds for hatred and hostility? And with whom was Alyosha to sympathize? And what was he to wish for each of them? He loved them both, but their desires were conflicting. He might go astray in this maze, and his heart could not endure uncertainty, because his love was always of an active kind. He was incapable of passive love. If he loved anyone, he wanted at once to help him. And to do so he must know what he was aiming at. It was natural for him to help both Ivan and Dmitri. But instead of a definite aim, he found nothing but uncertainty on all sides. "It was lacerating," as was just said. But what could he understand even in this "laceration"? He did not understand the first word in this perplexing maze.

Seeing Alyosha, Katerina said quickly and happily to Ivan, who had already gotten up to go, "A minute! Stay another minute! I want to hear what Alyosha thinks. I trust him absolutely. . . . Don't go away," she added, addressing Madame Hohlakov. She made Alyosha sit down beside her. Madame Hohlakov sat beside Ivan.

"You are all my friends, all I have in the world, my dear friends," she began warmly, in a voice which quivered with genuine tears of suffering. Alyosha's heart warmed to her at once. "You, Alyosha, were witness yesterday of that dreadful scene, and you saw what I did. You did not see it, Ivan, he did. What he thought of me yesterday I don't know. I only know one thing, that if it were repeated today, this minute, I would express the same feelings again as yesterday—the same feelings, the same words, the same actions. You remember my actions, Alyosha; you checked me in one of them" . . . (as she said that, she flushed). "I must tell you that I can't get over it. Listen, Alyosha. I don't even know whether I still love *him*. I feel *pity* for him, and that is a poor sign of love. If I loved him, if I still loved him, perhaps I wouldn't be sorry for him now, but would hate him."

Her voice trembled and tears glittered on her eyelashes. Alyosha shuddered inwardly. "She is truthful and sincere," he thought. "And she does not love Dmitri any more."

"That's true, that's true," cried Madame Hohlakov.

"Wait, dear. I haven't told you about the final decision I came to during the night. I feel that perhaps my decision is a terrible one—for me. But I foresee that nothing will induce me to alter it—nothing. It will stand all my life. My dear, ever-faithful and generous adviser, the one friend I have in the world, Ivan, with his deep insight into the heart, approves my decision. He knows it."

"Yes, I approve of it," Ivan said in a subdued but firm voice.

"But I should like Alyosha, also, to tell me whether I am right. I feel instinctively that you, Alyosha," she said, taking his cold hand in hers, "I feel that your decision, your approval, will bring me peace, in spite of all my sufferings. After your words, I shall be calm and submit—I feel that."

"I don't know what you are asking me," said Alyosha, flushing. "I only know that I love you and at this moment wish for your happiness more than my own! . . . But I know nothing about such affairs," something impelled him to add hurriedly.

"In such matters, Alyosha, in such matters, the main thing is honor and duty and something higher—I don't know what— but higher perhaps even than duty. I am conscious of this irresistible feeling in my heart, and it compels me. But it may all be put in two words. I've already decided, even if he marries that—creature (she began solemnly), whom I never, never can forgive, *even then I will not abandon him.* I will never, never abandon him!" she cried, breaking into a sort of pale, hysterical ecstasy. "Not that I would run after him, get in his way and worry him. Oh, no! I will go away to another town— any place—but I will watch over him all my life—I will watch over him all my life without rest. When he becomes unhappy with that woman, and that is bound to happen, let him come to me and he will find a friend, a sister. . . . Only a sister, of course, and so forever; but he will learn at least that that sister is really his sister, one who loves him and has sacrificed her life to him. I will gain my point. I will insist on his knowing me and confiding entirely in me, without reserve," she cried, in a sort of frenzy. "I will be a god to whom he can pray. He owes me that for his treachery and for what I suffered yesterday because of him. And let him see that all my life I will be true to him and the promise I gave him, in spite of his being untrue and betraying me. I will—I will become nothing but a means for his happiness, or—how shall I express it?—an instrument for his happiness. For my whole life, my whole life. And he will see it all his life! That's my decision. Ivan fully approves."

She was breathless. She had perhaps intended to express her idea with more dignity, art and naturalness, but her speech was hurried and crude. It was impulsive. It betrayed that she was still smarting from yesterday's insult, and that her pride craved satisfaction. She recognized this herself. Her face suddenly darkened. An unpleasant look came into her eyes. Alyosha saw it and felt a pang of sympathy. His brother Ivan made it worse by adding: "From anyone else, Katerina, such words would have been affected and overstrained, but from you— no. Any other woman would have been wrong, but you are right. I don't know how to explain it, but I see that you are absolutely sincere and, therefore, you are right."

"But that's only for the moment. And what does this mo-

177

ment stand for? Nothing but yesterday's insult." Madame Hohlakov had not intended to interfere, but she could no refrain from this reasonable comment.

"You're right. You're right," cried Ivan, with peculiar eagerness, obviously annoyed at being interrupted. "In anyone else this moment would be only due to yesterday's impression and would be only a moment. But with Katerina that moment will last all her life. What for anyone else would be only a promise is for her an everlasting, burdensome, grim perhaps, but unflagging duty. And she will be sustained by the feeling of this duty being fulfilled. Your life, Katerina, will be spent in painful brooding over your own feelings, your own heroism, and your own suffering. But in the end that suffering will be softened and will pass into contemplation of the fulfillment of a bold and proud design. Yes, proud it certainly is, and desperate in any case, but a triumph for you. And the consciousness of it will at last be a source of complete satisfaction and will make you resigned to everything else."

This was unmistakably said with some malice and obviously with intention. He spoke ironically.

"Oh, dear, how wrong it all is!" Madame Hohlakov cried.

"Alyosha, speak. I want dreadfully to know what you think!" cried Katerina bursting into tears. Alyosha got up from the sofa.

"It's nothing, nothing!" she went on through her tears. "I'm upset. I didn't sleep last night. But with two such friends as you and your brother I feel strong—for I know—you two will never desert me."

"Unfortunately, I must return to Moscow—perhaps tomorrow—and leave you for a long time. It's unavoidable," Ivan said suddenly.

"Tomorrow—to Moscow!" Katerina's face was suddenly contorted. "But—but how fortunate," she cried in a voice suddenly changed. In one instant there was no trace left of her tears. She underwent a transformation, which amazed Alyosha. Instead of a poor, insulted girl, weeping in a sort of "laceration," he saw a woman completely self-possessed and even exceedingly pleased, as though something agreeable had just happened.

"Oh, not fortunate that I am losing you, of course not," she corrected herself suddenly, with a charming society smile. "Such a friend as you are could not think that. I am only too unhappy at losing you." She rushed impulsively at Ivan, and seizing both his hands, pressed them warmly. "But what is fortunate is that in Moscow you will be able to see my aunt and sister and tell them all the horror of my present position. You can speak freely to my sister, but spare my aunt. You will know how to do that. You can't believe how miserable I was yesterday and this morning, wondering how I could write them that dreadful letter—for one can never tell such things in a letter. . . . Now it will be easy for me to write, for you will see them and explain everything. Oh, how glad I am! But I am only glad of that, believe me. Of course, no one can take your place. . . . I will run at once to write the letter," she finished suddenly, and took a step as though to go out of the room.

"And what about Alyosha and his opinion, which you were so desperately anxious to hear?" cried Madame Hohlakov. There was a sarcastic, angry note in her voice.

"I have not forgotten," cried Katerina. "And why are you so antagonistic?" she added reproachfully. "What I said, I repeat. I must have his opinion. More than that, I must have his decision! As he says, so it shall be. You see how anxious I am for your words, Alyosha. . . . But what's the matter?"

"I wouldn't have believed it. I can't understand it!" Alyosha cried in distress.

"What? What?"

"He is going to Moscow, and you cry out that you are glad. You said that on purpose! And you begin explaining that you are not glad of that but sorry to be—losing a friend. But that was acting—you were playing a part—as in a theater!"

"In a theater? What? What do you mean?" exclaimed Katerina, astonished, flushing crimson, and frowning.

"Though you assure him you are sorry to lose a friend in him, you persist in telling him to his face that it's fortunate he is going," said Alyosha breathlessly. He was standing at the table and did not sit down.

"What are you talking about? I don't understand?"

"I don't understand myself. . . . I seemed to see . . . I know I am not saying it properly, but I'll say it anyway," Alyosha went on in a shaking and broken voice. "What I see is that you don't love Dmitri at all . . . and never have, from the beginning. . . . And Dmitri has never loved you . . . and only respects you. . . . I really don't know how I dare to say all this, but somebody must tell the truth . . . for nobody here will tell the truth."

"What truth?" cried Katerina. There was an hysterical ring in her voice.

"I'll tell you," Alyosha went on with desperation, as though he were jumping from the top of a house. "Call Dmitri. I will bring him—and let him come here and take your hand and take Ivan's and join your hands. For you're torturing Ivan, simply because you love him—and torturing him because you love Dmitri through 'self-laceration'—with an unreal love—because you've persuaded yourself."

Alyosha broke off and was silent.

"You . . . you . . . you are a little religious idiot—that's what you are!" Katerina snapped. Her face was white and her lips were moving with anger.

Ivan suddenly laughed and got up. His hat was in his hand.

"You are mistaken, my good Alyosha," he said, with an expression Alyosha had never seen on his face before—an expression of youthful sincerity. "Katerina has never cared for me! She has known all the time that I cared for her—though I never said a word of my love to her—she knew, but she didn't care for me. I have never been her friend either, not for one moment. She is too proud to need my friendship. She kept me at her side as a means of revenge. She revenged with me and on me all the insults which she has been continually receiving from Dmitri ever since their first meeting. For that first meeting has rankled in her heart as an insult—that's what her heart is like! She has talked to me of nothing but her love for him. . . . I am going now. But, believe me, Katerina, you really love him. And the more he insults you, the more you love him—that's your 'laceration.' You love him just as he is. You love him for insulting you. If he reformed, you'd give him up at once and stop loving him. But you need him so as to contemplate continually your heroic fidelity and reproach him for infidelity. And it all comes from your pride. Oh, there's a great deal of humiliation and self-abasement about it, but it all comes from pride. . . . I am too young and I've loved you too much. I know that I ought not to say this, that it would be more dignified on my part simply to leave you, and it would be less offensive for you. But I am going far away, and shall never come back. . . . It is forever. I don't want to sit beside a 'laceration.' . . . But I don't know how to speak now. I've said everything. . . . Good-by, Katerina. You can't be angry with me, because I am a hundred times more severely punished than you, if only by the fact that I shall never see you again. Good-by! I don't want your hand. You have tortured me too deliberately for me to be able to forgive you at this moment. I will forgive you later, but now I don't want your hand. 'Your thanks, lady, I do not desire,' " he added in German with a forced smile, showing, however, that he could read Schiller, and read him till he knew him by heart—which Alyosha would never have believed. He went out of the room without saying good-by even to his hostess, Madame Hohlakov.

"Ivan!" Alyosha cried desperately. "Come back, Ivan! . . . No, nothing will induce him to come back now!" he said regretfully. "It's my fault, my fault. I began it! Ivan spoke in anger. Unjustly and angrily. He must come back here. He must."

Katerina suddenly went into the next room.

"You have done no harm. You behaved beautifully, like an angel," Madame Hohlakov whispered ecstatically to Alyosha. "I will do my best to prevent Ivan from going to Moscow."

Her face beamed with delight, to Alyosha's great distress.

Katerina suddenly returned. She had two hundred-rouble notes in her hand.

"I have a great favor to ask of you, Alyosha," she began

with a calm and even voice, as though nothing had happened. "A week—yes, I think it was a week ago—Dmitri did a very ugly thing. There is a certain tavern here in town and in it he met that discharged officer, that captain, whom your father used to employ. Dmitri somehow lost his temper with this man, grabbed him by the beard and dragged him out into the street in that insulting fashion. And I am told that the captain's son, a little boy who is at the school here, ran beside them crying and begging for his father, appealing to everyone to defend him. But everyone laughed. You must forgive me, Alyosha, but I cannot think calmly of that disgraceful action of his . . . one of those things of which only Dmitri would be capable . . . I can't even describe it . . . I can't find words. I've made inquiries about the captain and find he is a poor man. His name is Snegiryov. He did something wrong in the army and was discharged. I can't tell you what. And now he has sunk into destitution, with his family—an unhappy family of sick children, and, I believe, an insane wife. He has been living here a long time; he used to work as a copy clerk, but now he is doing nothing. I thought if you . . . That is I thought . . . I don't know. I am so confused. You see, I wanted to ask you, my dear Alyosha, to go to him, to find some excuse to go to them—I mean to that captain—oh, goodness, how badly I explain it!—and carefully, as only you know how to, manage to give him these two hundred roubles. He will be sure to take it. . . . I mean, persuade him to take it. . . . Or, rather, what do I mean? You see it's not by way of compensation to stop him from filing charges against Dmitri (for I heard he meant to) but simply as a token of sympathy. As Dmitri's fiancée I would like to help him. But you know. . . . I would go myself, but you'll know how to do it ever so much better. He lives on Lake Street. Please, Alyosha, do it for me, and now . . . Now I am rather . . . tired. Good-by!"

She turned and disappeared so quickly behind the portiere that Alyosha did not have time to say a word, though he wanted to speak. He longed to beg her pardon, to blame himself, to say something, for his heart was full. He could not bear to leave without speaking. But Madame Hohlakov took him by the hand and drew him along with her. In the hall she stopped him and whispered as before: "She is proud, she is struggling with herself; but kind, charming, generous. Oh, how I love her, especially sometimes, and how glad I am again of everything! Dear Alyosha, you didn't know, but I must tell you, that we all, all—both her aunts, I and all of us, Lise, even—have been hoping and praying for nothing for the last month but that she may give up your brother Dmitri, who takes no notice of her and does not care for her, and marry Ivan. He is such an educated and cultivated young man. He loves her more than anything in the world. We are plotting to bring it about. I am actually staying here because of it."

"But she has been crying—she has been wounded again," said Alyosha.

"Never trust a woman's tears, Alyosha. I am never for the women in such cases. I am always on the side of the men."

"Mother, you are spoiling him," Lise's voice cried from behind the door.

"No, it was all my fault. I am horribly to blame," Alyosha repeated unconsoled, hiding his face in his hands in an agony of remorse.

"On the contrary. You behaved like an angel, like an angel. I am ready to say so a thousand times over."

"Mother, how has he behaved like an angel?" Lise's voice was heard again.

"I somehow felt all at once," Alyosha went on as though he had not heard Lise, "that she loved Ivan, and so I said that stupid thing. . . . What will happen now?"

"To whom, to whom?" cried Lise. "Mother, you really want to be the death of me. I ask you questions and you don't answer."

At that moment the maid ran in. "Miss Katerina is ill. . . . She is crying, struggling . . . hysterics."

"What is the matter?" cried Lise anxiously. "Mother, I will be having hysterics, too!"

"Lise, please don't scream. Don't persecute me. At your age one can't know everything that grown-up people know. I'll come and tell you everything you ought to know. Oh, mercy on us! I am coming, I am coming. . . . Hysterics are a good sign, Alyosha. It's an excellent thing that she is hysterical. That's just as it ought to be. In such cases I am always against the woman, against all these feminine tears and hysterics. . . . Run and say, Julia, that I'll fly to her. . . . As for Ivan going away like that, it's her own fault. But he won't go away. Lise, for heaven's sake, don't scream! Oh, yes; you are not screaming. It's I who am screaming. Forgive your mother. . . . But I am delighted, delighted, delighted! Did you notice, Alyosha, how young, how young Ivan was just now when he went out, when he said all that and went out? I thought he was so educated, such a scholar, and all of a sudden he behaved so warmly, openly, and with such youthful inexperience. It was all so like you. . . . And the way he repeated that German line, it was just like you! But I must fly, I must fly! Alyosha, hurry to the captain with Katerina's money and then hurry back here. Lise, do you want anything now? For heaven's sake, don't keep Alyosha a minute. He will come back to you later."

Madame Hohlakov at last ran off.

Before leaving, Alyosha wanted to open the door to see Lise.

"On no account," cried Lise. "On no account now. Speak through the door. How have you come to be an angel? That's the only thing I want to know."

"For an awful piece of stupidity, Lise! Good-by!"

182

"Don't dare to go away like that!" Lise was beginning.

"Lise, I have a real sorrow! I'll be back later. I have a great, great sorrow!"

And he ran out of the hall.

6. A Laceration in the Cottage

ALYOSHA WAS GRIEVED in a way he had seldom been before. He had rushed in like a fool, and meddled in what? In a love affair. "But what do I know about it? What can I tell about such things?" he repeated to himself for the hundredth time, flushing crimson. "Oh, being ashamed would be nothing. Shame is only the punishment I deserve. The trouble is I have caused more unhappiness . . . And Father Zossima sent me to reconcile and bring them together. Is this the way to bring them together?" Then he suddenly remembered how he had suggested joining their hands, and he felt fearfully ashamed again. "Though I acted sincerely, I must be more sensible in the future," he concluded.

Katerina's errand took Alyosha to Lake Street. His brother Dmitri lived close by. And Alyosha decided to go to see him before going to the captain, though he had a feeling that he would not find his brother at home. He suspected that Dmitri would keep out of his way now, but he felt he must find him anyhow. Time was passing. And the thought of his dying elder had not left Alyosha for one minute from the time he set off from the monastery.

There was one point which interested him particularly about Katerina's errand; when she had mentioned the captain's son, the little schoolboy who had run beside his father crying, the idea had at once struck Alyosha that this must be the schoolboy who had bitten his finger. Now Alyosha felt certain of this, though he could not have said why. Thinking of another subject was a relief, and he decided to think no more about the "harm" he had done, not to torture himself with remorse, but to do what he had to do, let come what may. At that thought he was completely comforted.

Turning into the street where Dmitri lived he felt hungry. Taking out of his pocket the roll he had brought from his father's, he ate it. It made him feel stronger.

Dmitri was not at home. The people of the house, an old cabinetmaker, his son, and his old wife, looked with positive suspicion at Alyosha. "He hasn't slept here for the last three nights. Maybe he has gone away," the old man said in answer to Alyosha's inquiries. Alyosha felt that the old man was answering in accordance with instructions. When he asked whether his brother were at Grushenka's or in hiding at Foma's

183

(Alyosha spoke freely on purpose), all three looked at him in alarm. "They are fond of him, they are doing their best for him," thought Alyosha. "That's good."

At last Alyosha found the captain's house on Lake Street. It was a decrepit little house, sunk on one side, with three windows looking into the street, and with a muddy yard, in the middle of which stood a solitary cow. He crossed the yard and found the door opening into the passage. On the left of the passage lived the old woman, who owned the house, with her old daughter. Both were deaf. In answer to his repeated inquiry for the captain, one of them at last understood and pointed to a door across the passage.

The captain's place turned out to be one room. Alyosha had his hand on the iron latch to open the door, when he was struck by the strange hush within. Yet he knew from Katerina's words that the man had a family. "Either they are all asleep or they have heard me coming and are waiting for me to open the door. I'd better knock first." He knocked. An answer came, not at once, but after an interval of perhaps ten seconds.

"Who's there?" shouted a man in a loud and angry voice.

Alyosha opened the door and crossed the threshold. He found himself in a regular peasant's room. It was large and cluttered with belongings of all sorts. There were several people in it. On the left was a large Russian stove. From the stove to a window was a string with rags hanging on it. There was a bed against the wall on each side, right and left, covered with knitted quilts. On the one to the left was a pyramid of four print-covered pillows, each smaller than the one beneath. On the other bed there was only one very small pillow. The opposite corner of the room was screened off by a curtain or sheet hung on a string. Behind this curtain could be seen bedding made up on a bench and a chair. A rough square table of plain wood stood in front of the middle window. The three windows, each of four tiny greenish mildewy panes were shut, so that the room was not very light and rather stuffy. On the table was a frying pan with the remains of some fried eggs, a half-eaten piece of bread, and a small bottle with a few drops of vodka.

A woman of refined appearance, wearing a cotton dress, was sitting on a chair by the bed on the left. Her face was thin and yellow and her sunken cheeks betrayed at the first glance that she was ill. But what struck Alyosha most was the expression in the poor woman's eyes—a look of surprised inquiry and yet of haughty pride. While he was talking to her husband, her big brown eyes moved from one speaker to the other with the same proud and questioning expression. Beside her at the window stood a young girl, rather plain, with scanty reddish hair, poorly but very neatly dressed. She looked disdainfully at Alyosha as he came in. Beside the other bed sat

184

another female figure. She was a very sad sight, a young girl of about twenty, but hunchback and crippled "with withered legs," as Alyosha was told afterwards. Her crutches stood in the corner. The strikingly beautiful and gentle eyes of this poor girl looked with mild serenity at Alyosha. A man of forty-five was sitting at the table, finishing the fried eggs. He was small and weakly built. He had reddish hair and a scanty light-colored beard, very much like a wisp of tow (this comparison and the phrase "a wisp of tow" flashed at once into Alyosha's mind). It was obviously this man who had shouted to him when he knocked on the door. Seeing Alyosha, the man got up from the bench on which he was sitting, and wiping his mouth with a ragged napkin, came up to him.

"It's a monk come to beg for the monastery. A nice place to come to!" the girl standing in the left corner said aloud. The man looked toward her and answered in an excited and breaking voice. "No, Varvara, you are wrong. Allow me to ask," he turned again to Alyosha, "what has brought you to —our retreat?"

Alyosha looked at him. There was something angular, flurried and irritable about him. Though he had obviously just been drinking, he was not drunk. There was extraordinary impudence in his expression, and yet, strange to say, at the same time there was fear. He looked like a man who had long been kept in subjection and had submitted to it, and now had suddenly turned and was trying to assert himself. Or, better still, like a man who wants to hit you but is horribly afraid you will hit him. In his words and in the intonation of his shrill voice there was a sort of crazy humor, at times spiteful and at times cringing, and continually shifting from one tone to another. The question about "our retreat" he had asked as it were quivering all over, rolling his eyes, and coming up so close to Alyosha that Alyosha instinctively drew back a step. He was dressed in a very shabby dark cotton coat, patched and spotted. He wore checked trousers of a light color, long out of fashion, and of very thin material. They were so wrinkled and so short that he looked as though he had grown out of them like a boy.

"I am Alexey Karamazov," Alyosha began.

"I understand that, sir," the man answered at once to assure Alyosha that he already knew who he was. "I am Captain Snegiryov, sir, but I would still like to know what has brought you . . ."

"Oh, nothing special. I wanted to have a word with you—if only you allow me."

"In that case, here is a chair, sir. Kindly be seated. That's what they used to say in the old comedies, 'kindly be seated.' " And with a quick movement he seized an empty chair (it was a rough wooden chair, not upholstered) and set it for him almost in the middle of the room. Then, taking another rough

185

wooden chair for himself, he sat down facing Alyosha, so close to him that their knees almost touched.

"Nicholas Snegiryov, sir, formerly a captain in the Russian infantry, degraded for his vices, but still a captain. Though I might not be one now because of the way I talk; for the last half of my life I've learned to say 'sir.' It's a word you use when you've come down in the world."

"That's very true," smiled Alyosha. "But do you use it involuntarily or on purpose?"

"As God's above, it's involuntary! I didn't use the word 'sir' all my life, but as soon as I sank into low water I began to say 'sir.' It's the work of a higher power. . . . But why, may I ask, have you come? You can see our home is very humble and not a place for entertaining."

"I've come—about that business."

"About what business?" the captain asked.

"About your meeting with my brother Dmitri," Alyosha blurted out awkwardly.

"What meeting, sir? You don't mean that meeting? About my 'wisp of tow'?" He moved closer so that his knees knocked against Alyosha. His lips were strangely compressed like a thread.

"What wisp of tow?" muttered Alyosha.

"He is come to complain of me, father!" cried a voice familiar to Alyosha—the voice of the schoolboy—from behind the curtain. "I bit his finger." The curtain was pulled back, and Alyosha saw the schoolboy lying on a little bed made up on the bench and the chair in the corner under the ikons. The boy was covered with his coat and an old wadded quilt. He was evidently sick, and, judging by his glittering eyes, he had a fever. He looked at Alyosha without fear, as though he felt that being at home he could not be touched.

"What! Did he bite your finger?" The captain jumped up from his chair. "Was it your finger he bit?"

"Yes. He was throwing stones with other schoolboys. There were six of them against him alone. I went up to him, and he threw a stone at me and then another at my head. I asked him what I had done to him. And then he rushed at me and bit my finger. I don't know why."

"I'll punish him, sir, at once—this minute!" The captain jumped up from his chair.

"But I am not complaining, I am simply telling you. . . . I don't want him to be punished. Besides, he seems to be ill."

"And do you think I'd punish him? That I'd take my Ilusha and beat him before you for your satisfaction? Would you like it done at once, sir?" said the captain, suddenly turning to Alyosha, as though he were going to attack him. "I am sorry about your finger, sir. But instead of beating Ilusha, would you like me to chop off my four fingers with this knife here before your eyes to satisfy your anger? I should think four

186

fingers would be enough to satisfy your thirst for vengeance. You won't ask for the fifth one too?" He stopped short with a catch in his throat. Every feature in his face was twitching and working. He looked defiant. He was in a sort of frenzy.

"I think I understand it all now," said Alyosha gently and sorrowfully, still keeping his seat. "So your boy is a good boy. He loves his father, and he attacked me as the brother of your . . . Now I understand it," he repeated thoughtfully. "But my brother Dmitri regrets what he did, I know that. And if only it is possible for him to come to you, or better still, to meet you in that same place, he will apologize before everyone—if you wish it."

"After pulling out my beard, you mean, he will apologize? And he thinks that will be a satisfactory finish, does he?"

"Oh, no! On the contrary, he will do anything you like and in any way you like."

"So if I were to ask his highness to go down on his knees before me in that very tavern—'The Metropolis' it's called—or in the market place, he would do it?"

"Yes, he would even go down on his knees."

"You've pierced me to the heart, sir. Touched me to tears and pierced me to the heart! I am only too aware of your brother's generosity. Let me introduce my family: my two daughters and my son—my litter. If I die, who will care for them, and while I live who but they will care for a wretch like me? That's a thing the Lord has ordained for every man of my sort, sir. For there must be someone able to love even a man like me."

"Oh that's perfectly true!" exclaimed Alyosha.

"Oh, stop playing the fool! Some idiot comes in, and you put us to shame!" cried the girl by the window, suddenly turning to her father with contempt.

"Wait a minute, Varvara!" cried her father, speaking emphatically but looking at her quite approvingly. "That's her character," he said, addressing Alyosha again.

> "And in all nature there was naught
> That could find favor in his eyes

or rather in her eyes: *That could find favor in her eyes*. But now let me present you to my wife, Arina. She is crippled, she is forty-three; she can move, but very little. She is of humble origin. Arina, compose yourself. This is Alexey Karamazov." He took Alyosha by the hand and with unexpected force pulled him up. "You must stand up to be introduced to a lady. It's not the Karamazov, mother, who . . . h'm . . . but his brother, radiant with modest virtues. Come Arina, come mother, first your hand to be kissed." And he kissed his wife's hand respectfully and even tenderly.

The girl at the window turned her back on the scene.

A very friendly expression came over the inquiring face of

the woman. "Good morning! Sit down, Mr. Tchernomazov," she said.

"Karamazov, mother, Karamazov," he whispered.

"Well, Karamazov, or whatever it is. But I always think of Tchernomazov. ... . Sit down. Why has he pulled you out of your chair? He calls me crippled but I am not, only my legs are swollen like barrels, but the rest of me is shriveled up. I used to be so fat, but now I'm so thin."

"We are of humble origin," the captain muttered.

"Oh, father, father!" the hunchback girl, who had till then been silent, said suddenly, as she hid her eyes in her handkerchief.

"Buffoon!" blurted out the girl at the window.

"Have you heard our news?" said the mother, pointing at her daughters. "It's like clouds coming over; the clouds pass and we have music again. When we were with the army, we used to have many such guests. I don't mean to make any comparisons; everyone to their taste. The deacon's wife used to come then and say: 'Alexander is a man of the noblest heart, but Nastasya,' she would say, 'is of the brood of hell.' 'Well,' I said, 'that's a matter of taste. But you are a little spitfire.' 'And you need to be put in your place,' says she. 'You black sword,' said I. 'Who asked you to teach me?' 'But my breath,' says she, 'is clean, and yours is unclean.' 'You ask all the officers whether my breath is unclean.' And ever since then I have had it on my mind. Not long ago I was sitting here as I am now, when I saw that very General come in who came here for Easter, and I asked him: 'Your Excellency,' said I, 'can a lady's breath be unpleasant?' 'Yes,' he answered. 'You ought to open a window or open the door, for the air is not fresh here.' And they all go on like that! And what is my breath to them? The dead smell worse still! 'I won't spoil the air,' said I, 'I'll order some slippers and go away.' My darlings, don't blame your mother! Nicholas, how is it I can't please you? There's only Ilusha who comes home from school and loves me. Yesterday he brought me an apple. Forgive your mother —forgive a poor lonely creature! Why has my breath become unpleasant to you?"

And the poor mad woman broke into sobs. Tears streamed down her cheeks. The captain rushed up to her.

"Mother, mother, my dear! You are not lonely. Everyone loves you, everyone adores you." He began kissing both her hands and tenderly stroking her face. Then taking the trayed dinner napkin, he began wiping away her tears.

"There, you see, you hear?" The captain turned with a sort of fury to Alyosha, pointing to the poor imbecile.

"I see and hear," muttered Alyosha. He felt that he too had tears in his eyes.

"Father, father, how can you—with him! Let him alone!"

cried the boy, sitting up in his bed and gazing at his father with glowing eyes.

"Stop fooling. Stop showing off. Your silly antics never lead to anything!" shouted Varvara, stamping her foot.

"Your anger is quite justified this time, Varvara, and I'll stop at once. Come, put on your cap, sir, and I'll put on mine. We will go out. I want to speak to you, but not here. This girl sitting here is my daughter Nina. I forgot to introduce her to you. She is a heavenly angel incarnate . . . who has flown down to us mortals, . . . if you can understand."

"There he is shaking all over, as though in convulsions!" Varvara went on indignantly.

"And she there stamping her foot at me and calling me a fool, she is a heavenly angel incarnate too. And she has good reason to call me a fool. Come along, sir."

And, taking Alyosha's hand, he led him out of the room into the street.

7. And in the Open Air

"THE AIR OUT HERE IS FRESH, but in my home it is not fresh in any sense of the word. Let us walk slowly, sir. I would be glad of your attention."

"I too have something important to say to you," observed Alyosha, "only I don't know how to begin."

"To be sure you must have business with me, otherwise you would never have come. Unless you came simply to complain of the boy, and that's hardly likely. And, by the way, about the boy; I could not explain to you in there, but now I will describe what happened. My tow was thicker a week ago—I mean my beard. That's the nickname they give to my beard, the schoolboys most of all. Well, your brother Dmitri was pulling me by my beard. I'd done nothing. He was in a rage and happened to come upon me. He dragged me out of the tavern into the market place. At that moment the boys were coming out of school, and with them my son, Ilusha. As soon as he saw what was happening he rushed up to me. 'Father,' he cried, 'father!' He caught hold of me, hugged me, tried to pull me away, crying at your brother, 'Let go, let go, it's my father, forgive him!'—yes, he actually cried 'forgive him.' He clutched at your brother's hand, that very hand, with his little hands and kissed it. . . . I remember his little face at that moment. I haven't forgotten it and I never will!"

"I swear," cried Alyosha, "that my brother will apologize, even if he has to go down on his knees in that same market place. . . . I'll make him or he is no brother of mine!"

"Aha, then it's only a suggestion! And it does not come from

189

him but simply from the generosity of your heart. You should have said so. No, in that case let me tell you of your brother's chivalrous generosity, for he did express it at the time. He stopped dragging me by my beard and let go of me: 'You are an officer,' he said, 'and I am an officer. If you can find a decent man to be your second send me your challenge. I will give you satisfaction, though you are a scoundrel.' That's what he said. A chivalrous spirit indeed. . . . I went off with Ilusha, but that scene is imprinted forever on Ilusha's soul. No, it's not for us to claim the privileges of noblemen. Judge for yourself. You've just been in our mansion, what did you see there? Three ladies, one a cripple and weak-minded, another a cripple and hunchback and the third not crippled but far too clever. She is a student, dying to get back to Petersburg, to work for the emancipation of the Russian woman on the banks of the Neva. I won't speak of Ilusha, he is only nine. I am alone in the world, and if I die, what will become of all of them? I ask you that. And if I challenge him and he kills me on the spot, what then? What will become of them? And worse still, if he doesn't kill me but only cripples me; I couldn't work, but I would still be a mouth to feed. Who would feed it and who would feed them all? Must I take Ilusha from school and send him to beg in the streets? That's what it means for me to challenge him to a duel. It's silly talk and nothing else."

"He will apologize. He will bow down at your feet in the middle of the market place," cried Alyosha again.

"I did think of bringing charges against him," the captain went on. "But could I get much compensation for personal injury? And then Agrafena Svyetlov, whom everyone calls Grushenka, sent for me and shouted at me: 'Don't dare dream of it! If you bring charges against him, I'll tell everyone that he beat you for your dishonesty, and then you will be prosecuted.' I call God to witness whose dishonesty it was. Did I not act at her orders and at the orders of your father, Fyodor Karamazov? 'And what's more,' she went on, 'I'll dismiss you for good and you'll never earn another penny from me. I'll speak to my merchant too (that's what she calls her old man) and he will also dismiss you!' And if he dismisses me, what can I earn then? Those two are all I have now, because your father has not only dismissed me, for another reason, but he means to make use of papers I've signed to go to law against me. And so I kept quiet. And you have seen our home. But now let me ask you, did Ilusha hurt your finger much? I didn't like to go into it in our mansion before him."

"Yes, very much. He was in a fury. He was avenging you on me as a Karamazov, I see that now. But if only you had seen how he was throwing stones at his schoolfellows! It's very dangerous. They might kill him. They are children and stupid. A stone may be thrown and break somebody's skull."

"That's just what has happened. He was hit by a stone today.

Not on the head but on the chest, just above the heart. He came home crying and now he is ill."

"And you know he attacks them first. He is bitter against them because of you. They say he stabbed a boy called Krassotkin with a penknife not long ago."

"I've heard about that too. It's not good. Krassotkin is an official here, we may hear more about it."

"I would advise you," Alyosha went on in a friendly way, "not to send him to school at all for a time till he is calmer ... and his anger has passed."

"Anger!" the captain repeated. "That's just what it is. He is a little fellow but it's a mighty anger. You don't know all, sir. Let me tell you more. Since that incident all the boys have been teasing him about the 'wisp of tow.' Schoolboys are a merciless lot. Individually they are angels, but together, especially in schools, they are often cruel. Their teasing has stirred up Ilusha. An ordinary boy, a weak son, would have submitted, have felt ashamed of his father, sir, but Ilusha stands up for me against them all. For his father and for truth and justice. For what he suffered when he kissed your brother's hand and cried to him: 'Forgive father, forgive him,'—that only God knows—and I, his father. For our children—not your children, but ours—the children of the poor looked down upon by everyone—know what justice means, sir, even at nine years of age. How should the rich know? They don't explore such depths even once in their lives. But at that moment when Ilusha kissed your brother's hand, at that moment he grasped all that justice means. That truth entered into him and crushed him forever, sir," the captain said with a sort of frenzy. And he struck his right fist against his left palm as though he wanted to show how "that truth" crushed Ilusha.

"That very day, sir, he fell ill with fever and was delirious all night. All that day he hardly said a word to me, but I noticed he kept watching me from the corner, though he turned to the window and pretended to be learning his lessons. But I could see his mind was not on his lessons. Next day I got drunk to forget my troubles and I don't remember much. Mother began crying, too—I am very fond of mother —well, I spent my last penny drowning my troubles. Don't despise me for that, sir. In Russia the best men drink. The best men among us are the greatest drunkards. I lay down and I don't remember about Ilusha, though all that day the boys had been teasing him at school. 'Wisp of tow,' they shouted. 'Your father was pulled out of the tavern by his wisp of tow. And you ran by and begged forgiveness.'

"On the third day when he came back from school, I saw he looked pale and miserable. 'What is it?' I asked. He wouldn't answer. Well, there's no talking in our mansion without mother and the girls taking part in it. What's more the girls had heard about it the very first day. Varvara had begun snarling: 'You

191

fools and buffoons, can you ever do anything rational?' 'You're right,' I said. 'Can we ever do anything rational?' For the time I passed it off like that. So in the evening I took the boy out for a walk. We go for a walk every evening, always the same way. The way we are going now—from our gate to that great stone which lies in the road under the fence that marks the beginning of the town pasture. A beautiful and lonely spot, sir. Ilusha and I walked along hand in hand as usual. He has a little hand, his fingers are thin and cold—he suffers with his chest, you know. 'Father,' he said, 'father!' 'Well?' said I. I saw his eyes flashing. 'Father, how he treated you then!' 'It can't be helped, Ilusha,' I said. 'Don't forgive him, father, don't forgive him! At school they say that he has paid you ten roubles for it.' 'No, Ilusha,' said I, 'I would not take money from him for anything.' Then he began trembling all over, took my hand and kissed it. 'Father,' he said. 'Father, challenge him to a duel. At school they say you are a coward and won't challenge him, and that you'll accept ten roubles from him.' 'I can't challenge him to a duel, Ilusha,' I answered. And I told him briefly what I've just told you. He listened. 'Father,' he said, 'anyway don't forgive him. When I grow up I'll call him out myself and kill him.' His eyes shone and glowed. And of course I am his father, and I had to put in a word: 'It's a sin to kill,' I said, 'even in a duel.' 'Father,' he said, 'when I grow up, I'll knock him down, knock the sword out of his hand. I'll fall on him, wave my sword over him and say: "I could kill you, but I forgive you, so there!" ' You see what the workings of his little mind have been during these two days. He must have been planning that vengeance all the time and raving about it at night.

"But he began to come home from school badly beaten. I found out about it the day before yesterday, and you are right, I won't send him to that school any more. I heard that he was standing up against all the class alone and defying them all, that his heart was full of resentment, of bitterness—I was alarmed about him. We went for another walk. 'Father,' he asked, 'are rich people stronger than anyone else on earth?' 'Yes, Ilusha,' I said, 'there are no people on earth stronger than the rich.' 'Father,' he said, 'I will get rich, I will become an officer and conquer everybody. The Tsar will reward me. I will come back here and then no one will dare. . . .' Then he was silent but his lips trembled. 'Father,' he said, 'what a horrid town this is.' 'Yes, Ilusha,' I said, 'it isn't a very nice town.' 'Father, let us move into another town, a nice one,' he said, 'where people don't know about us.' 'We will move, we will, Ilusha,' I said, 'only I must save up for it.' I was glad to be able to turn his mind from painful thoughts. And we began to dream of how we would move to another town, how we would buy a horse and cart. 'We will put mother and your sisters inside, we will cover them up and we'll walk. You will

192

have a lift now and then, but I'll walk, for we must take care of our horse. We can't all ride. That's how we'll go.' He was enchanted at that, most of all at the thought of having a horse and driving him. For of course a Russian boy is born among horses. We talked a long while. Thank God, I thought, I have diverted his mind and comforted him.

"That was the day before yesterday, in the evening, but last night everything changed. He had gone to school in the morning. He came back depressed, terribly depressed. In the evening I took him by the hand and we went for a walk. He would not talk. There was a wind blowing and no sun, and a feeling of autumn. Twilight was coming on. We walked along, both of us depressed. 'Well, my boy,' I said, 'how about our setting off on our travels?' I thought I might bring him back to our talk of the day before. He didn't answer, but I felt his fingers trembling in my hand. Ah, I thought, it's not good; there's something new. We had reached the stone where we are now. I sat down on the stone. And in the air there were lots of kites flapping and whirling. There were as many as thirty in sight. Of course, it's just the season for kites. 'Look, Ilusha,' I said, 'it's time we got out our last year's kite again. I'll mend it. Where have you put it?' My boy made no answer. He looked away and turned sideways. And then a gust of wind blew up the sand. He suddenly fell on me, threw both his little arms around my neck and held me tight. You know, when children are silent and proud, and try to keep back their tears when they are in great trouble and suddenly break down, their tears fall in streams. With those warm streams of tears, he wet my face. He sobbed and shook as though he were in convulsions, and squeezed up against me as I sat on the stone. 'Father,' he kept crying, 'dear father, how he insulted you!' And I cried too. We sat shaking in each other's arms. 'Ilusha,' I said to him, 'Ilusha darling.' No one saw us then. God alone saw us. I hope he will record it to my credit. You must thank your brother, sir. No, sir, I won't beat my boy for your satisfaction."

He had gone back to his original tone of resentful buffoonery. Alyosha felt though that he trusted him, and that if there had been someone else in his, Alyosha's, place, the man would not have spoken so openly and would not have told what he had just told. This encouraged Alyosha whose heart was trembling and who was on the verge of tears.

"Ah, how I would like to make friends with your boy!" he cried. "If you could arrange it . . ."

"Certainly, sir," muttered the captain.

"But now listen to something quite different!" Alyosha went on. "I have a message for you. That same brother of mine, Dmitri, has also insulted his fiancée. She is a very fine young woman of whom you have probably heard. I have a right to tell you how he insulted her; I ought to do so, in fact, for hear-

193

ing of the insult done to you and learning all about your unfortunate position, she asked me at once—just now—to bring you this help from her—but only from her alone, not from Dmitri, who has abandoned her. Nor from me, his brother, nor from anyone else, but from her, only from her! She begs you to accept her help. . . . You have both been insulted by the same man. She thought of you only when she had just received a similar insult from him—similar in its cruelty, I mean. She comes like a sister to help a brother in misfortune. . . . She told me to persuade you to take these two hundred roubles from her, as from a sister, knowing that you are in such need. No one will know of it, it can give rise to no unjust slander. Here are the two hundred roubles, and I swear you must take them unless—unless all men are to be enemies on earth! But there are brothers even on earth. . . . You have a generous heart. . . . You must see that, you must." Alyosha held out two new rainbow-colored hundred-rouble notes.

They were both standing at the time by the great stone close to the fence, and there was no one near. The notes made a tremendous impression on the captain. He started from astonishment. Such a conclusion to their conversation was the last thing he expected. Nothing could have been further from his dreams than help from anyone—and such a sum!

He took the notes. For a minute he was almost unable to answer. A new expression came to his face.

"That for me? So much money—two hundred roubles! Good heavens! Why, I haven't seen so much money for the last four years! Mercy on us! And she says she is a sister . . . And is that the truth?"

"I swear that all I told you is the truth," cried Alyosha.

The captain flushed red.

"Listen, listen. If I take it, I won't be behaving like a scoundrel? In your eyes, sir, I won't be a scoundrel? No, sir, listen, listen," he hurried, touching Alyosha with both his hands. "You are persuading me to take it, saying that it's a sister sends it. But inwardly, in your heart won't you feel contempt for me if I take it?"

"No, no, on my salvation I swear I won't! And no one will ever know but me—I, you and she, and one other lady, her friend."

"Never mind the lady! Listen, sir, at a moment like this you must listen, for you can't understand what these two hundred roubles mean to me." The poor captain went on rising gradually into a sort of incoherent, almost wild enthusiasm. He talked extremely fast as though afraid he would not be allowed to say all he had to say.

"Besides it's being honestly acquired from a 'sister,' so highly respected and revered, do you know that now I can look after mother and Nina, my hunchback angel daughter?

Doctor Herzenstube came from the kindness of his heart and examined them both for a whole hour. 'I can make nothing of it,' said he, but he prescribed a mineral water which is sold by a druggist here. He said it would be sure to do her good, and he ordered baths, too, with some medicine in them. The mineral water costs thirty cents, and she'd need to drink about forty bottles. So I took the prescription and laid it on the shelf under the ikons, and there it lies. And he ordered hot baths for Nina with something dissolved in them, morning and evening. But how can we carry out such a cure in our mansion, without servants, without help, without a bath, and without water? Nina is rheumatic all over, I don't think I told you that. All her right side aches at night. She is in agony. And, would you believe it, the angel bears it without groaning for fear of waking us. We eat what we can get, and she'll only take the leavings, what you'd scarcely give to a dog. 'I am not worth it. I am taking it from you. I am a burden to you,' that's what her angel eyes try to express. We wait on her, but she doesn't like it. 'I am a useless cripple, no good to anyone.' As though she were not worth it, when she is the saving of all of us with her angelic sweetness. Without her, without her gentle word it would be hell among us! She softens even Varvara. And don't judge Varvara harshly either. She is an angel too. She, too, has suffered wrong. She came to us for the summer, and she brought sixteen roubles she had earned by lessons and saved up, to go back with to Petersburg in September, that is now. But we took her money and lived on it, so now she has nothing to go back with. Though she couldn't go back anyway because she has to work for us like a slave. She is like an overdriven horse with all of us on her back. She waits on us all, mends and washes, sweeps the floor, and puts mother to bed. And mother is difficult and tearful and insane! And now I can get a servant with this money, you understand, sir. I can get medicines for my family. I can send Varvara to Petersburg. I can buy beef. I can feed them properly. Good Lord, but it's a dream!"

Alyosha was delighted that he had brought him such happiness and that the poor captain had consented to be made happy.

"Wait, sir, wait." The captain again began to talk with frenzied speed carried away by a new daydream. "Do you know that Ilusha and I will perhaps really carry out our dream. We will buy a horse and cart, a black horse, he insists on its being black, and we will set off as we pretended the other day. I have an old friend, a lawyer in K. province, and I heard through someone that if I were to go he'd give me a job as clerk in his office. So who knows, maybe he would. So I'd just put mother and Nina in the cart, and Ilusha could drive, and I'd walk, I'd walk. . . . Why, if I only succeed in getting one

195

debt paid that's owing me, I would have perhaps enough for that too!"

"There would be enough!" cried Alyosha. "Katerina will send you as much more as you need. And you know, I have money too. Take what you want, as you would from a brother, from a friend. You can give it back later. . . . You'll get rich, you'll get rich! And you know you couldn't have a better idea than to move to another province! It would be the salvation of you, especially of your boy—and you ought to go quickly, before the winter, before the cold. You must write to us when you are there, and we will always be brothers. . . . No, it's not a dream!"

Alyosha could have hugged him, he was so pleased. But glancing at him he stopped short. The man was standing with his neck outstretched, his lips protruding, and with a pale and frenzied face. His lips were moving as though trying to say something; no sound came, but still his lips moved. It was uncanny.

"What is it?" asked Alyosha, startled.

"Sir . . . I . . . You," muttered the captain, faltering and looking at him with a strange fixed stare, an air of desperate resolution. At the same time there was a sort of grin on his lips. "I . . . you, sir . . . Wouldn't you like me to show you a little trick I know?" he murmured, suddenly, in a firm rapid whisper, his voice no longer faltering.

"What trick?"

"A trick," whispered the captain. His mouth was twisted on the left side. His left eye was screwed up. He still stared at Alyosha.

"What trick?" Alyosha cried, now thoroughly alarmed.

"Why, look," squealed the captain suddenly. And showing him the two notes which he had been holding by one corner between his thumb and forefinger during the conversation, he crumpled them up savagely and squeezed them tight in his right hand. "Do you see, do you see?" he shrieked, pale and infuriated. And suddenly flinging up his hand, he threw the crumpled notes on the sand. "Do you see?" he shrieked again, pointing to them. "Look there!"

And with fury he began trampling them under his heel, gasping and exclaiming as he did so: "So much for your money! So much for your money! So much for your money! So much for your money!"

Suddenly he drew himself up before Alyosha. His whole figure expressed unutterable pride.

"Tell those who sent you that the 'wisp of tow' does not sell his honor," he cried, raising his arm in the air. Then he turned quickly and began to run. But he had not run five steps before he turned completely around and threw a kiss to Alyosha. He ran another five yards and then turned around for the last time. This time his face was not contorted but quivering all over with tears. In a faltering, sobbing voice he cried: "What would I say to my boy if I took money from you for our shame?"

And then he ran on without turning. Alyosha looked after him grieved. Oh, he understood that till the very last moment the captain had not known he would crumple up and fling away the notes. He did not turn back. Alyosha knew he would not. He would not follow him and call him back, he knew why.

When the captain was out of sight, Alyosha picked up the two notes. They were very much crushed and crumpled, and had been pressed into the sand, but were uninjured. They even rustled like new ones when Alyosha smoothed them out. He put them in his pocket and went to Katerina to report on the success of her errand.

BOOK V: PRO AND CONTRA

1. The Engagement

MADAME HOHLAKOV was again the first to meet Alyosha. She was flustered. Something had happened. Katerina's hysterics had ended in a fainting fit, and then "a terrible, awful weakness had followed. She lay with her eyes turned up and was delirious. Now she had a fever." They had sent for Herzenstube; they had sent for the aunts. The aunts had already arrived, but Herzenstube had not yet come. They were all sitting in her room, waiting. She was unconscious now, and "what if it turned to brain fever!"

Madame Hohlakov was deeply alarmed. "This is serious, serious," she added at every word, as though nothing that had happened to her before had been serious. Alyosha listened with distress. Then he tried to tell of his experience but she interrupted him at the first words. She had not time to listen. She begged him to sit with Lise and wait for her there.

"Lise," she whispered almost in his ear, "Lise has greatly surprised me just now, dear Alyosha. She touched me, too, and so my heart forgives her everything. Would you believe it, as soon as you had gone, she began to be truly sorry for having laughed at you today and yesterday; though she was not really laughing at you, but only joking. But she was seriously sorry for it, almost ready to cry, so that I was quite surprised. She has never been really sorry for laughing at me, but has only made a joke of it. And you know she is laughing at me every minute. But this time she was in earnest. She thinks a great deal of you, Alyosha, so don't take offense if you can help it. I am never

197

hard on her, for she's such a clever little thing—would you believe it? She said just now that you were a friend of her childhood, 'the greatest friend of her childhood'—just think of that —'greatest friend'—and what about me? She has very strong feelings and memories, and, what's more, she uses these phrases, most unexpected words, which come out all of a sudden when you least expect them. She recently spoke about a pine-tree, for instance; there used to be a pine-tree standing in our garden in her early childhood. It's probably standing there still; so there's no need to speak in the past tense. Pine trees are not like people, Alyosha, they don't change quickly. 'Mother,' she said, 'I remember that pine tree as in a dream.' Only she said something so original about it that I can't repeat it. Besides, I've forgotten it. Well, good-by! I am so worried I feel I shall go out of my mind. Oh! Alyosha, I've been out of my mind twice in my life. Go to Lise, cheer her up, as you always do. . . . Lise," she cried, going to the door, "here I've brought you Alyosha, whom you insulted so. He is not at all angry, I assure you. On the contrary, he is surprised that you could think so."

"Thank you, mother. Come in, Alyosha."

Alyosha went in. Lise looked rather embarrassed, and at once flushed crimson. She was evidently ashamed of something, and, as people always do in such cases, she began immediately talking of other things, as though they were of absorbing interest to her at the moment.

"Mother has just told me all about the two hundred roubles, Alyosha, and your taking them to that poor captain . . . And she told me all the awful story of how he has been insulted . . . And you know, although mother gets everything mixed up . . . She always rushes from one thing to another . . . I cried when I heard it. Well, did you give him the money and how is the poor man getting on?"

"The fact is I didn't give it to him, and it's a long story," answered Alyosha, as though he, too, could think of nothing but his regret at having failed. Yet Lise saw perfectly well that he, too, looked away, and that he, too, was trying to talk of other things.

Alyosha sat down and began to tell his story. At the first words he lost his embarrassment and gained the whole of Lise's attention as well. He spoke with deep feeling and told his story well. In the old days in Moscow he had been fond of coming to Lise and describing to her what had just happened to him, what he had read, or what he remembered of his childhood. Sometimes they had made daydreams and woven whole romances together—generally cheerful and amusing ones. Now they both felt suddenly transported to the old days in Moscow. Lise was extremely touched by his story. Alyosha described Ilusha with warm feeling. And when he finished describing how the luckless captain stamped on the money, Lise could not help clasping her hands and crying out: "So you didn't give him the money! So you let him run away! Oh, you should have run after him!"

"No, Lise. It's better that I didn't run after him," said Alyosha, getting up from his chair and walking thoughtfully across the room.

"Why? How is it better? Now they are without food and hopeless."

"Not hopeless, for the two hundred roubles will still be theirs. The captain'll take the money tomorrow. Tomorrow he will be sure to take it," said Alyosha, pacing up and down. "You see, Lise," he went on, stopping suddenly before her, "I made one blunder, but that, even that, is all for the best."

"What blunder, and why is it for the best?"

"I'll tell you. He is a man of weak and timid character. He has suffered so much and is very good-natured. I keep wondering why he took offense so suddenly, for I assure you, up to the last minute, he did not know that he was going to trample on the money. And I think now that there was a great deal to offend him . . . And it could not have been otherwise in his position. . . . To begin with, he was angry at himself for having been so glad of the money in my presence and for not having concealed it from me. If he had been pleased, but not so much; if he had not shown it; if he had pretended scruples and difficulties, as other people do when they take money, he might still have taken it. But he was too genuinely delighted, and that was mortifying. Ah, Lise, he is a good and truthful man—that's the worst of the whole business. All the time he talked, his voice was so weak, so broken. He talked so fast, so fast. He kept laughing or perhaps he was crying—yes, I am sure he was crying, he was so delighted—and he talked about his daughters—and about the job he could get in another town. . . . And when he had poured out his heart, he felt ashamed at having shown me his inmost soul like that. So he began to hate me. He is one of those awfully sensitive people. What made him feel most ashamed was that he had given in too soon and accepted me as a friend, you see. At first he almost flew at me and tried to intimidate me, but as soon as he saw the money he began embracing me. He kept touching me with his hands. This must be why he came to feel so humiliated, and then I made that blunder, a very important one. I suddenly said to him that if he didn't have enough money to move to another town, we would give it to him; I myself would give him as much as he wanted of my own money. That struck him all at once. Why, he wondered, did I offer to help him? You know, Lise, it's awfully hard for a man who has been injured, when other people look at him as though they were his benefactors. . . . I've heard that. Father Zossima told me so. I don't know how to say it, but I have often seen it myself. And I feel like that myself too. And the worst of it was that though he did not know, up to the very last minute, that he would trample on the money, he had a kind

199

of presentiment of it, I am sure of that. . . . And though it's so dreadful, it's all for the best. In fact, I believe nothing better could have happened."

"Why, why could nothing better have happened?" cried Lise, looking with great surprise at Alyosha.

"Because if he had taken the money, in an hour after getting home, he would be crying with mortification. That's just what would have happened. And most likely he would have come to me early tomorrow, and flung the notes at me and trampled on them as he did just now. But now he has gone home proud and triumphant, even though he knows he has 'ruined himself.' So now nothing could be easier than to make him accept the two hundred roubles tomorrow, for he has already vindicated his honor, tossed away the money, and trampled it under foot. . . . He didn't know when he did it that I would bring it to him again tomorrow, and yet he is in terrible need of that money. Though he is proud of himself now, yet even today he'll be thinking of what he has lost. He will think of it more than ever at night, will dream of it, and by tomorrow morning he may be ready to run to me. It's just then that I'll appear. 'Here, you are a proud man,' I will say. 'You have shown yourself to be proud. But now take the money and forgive us!' And then he will take it!"

Alyosha was carried away as he spoke the last words: "And then he will take it!"

Lise clapped her hands. "Ah, that's true! I understand it perfectly now. Oh, Alyosha, how do you know all this? So young and yet he knows what's in the heart. . . . I should never have worked it out."

"The main thing now is to persuade him that he is on an equal footing with us, in spite of his taking money from us," Alyosha went on in his excitement, "and not only on an equal, but even on a higher footing."

"On a higher footing is charming, Alyosha. But go on, go on!"

"You mean there isn't such an expression as 'on a higher footing'? But it doesn't matter because . . ."

"Oh, no, of course it doesn't matter. Forgive me, Alyosha, dear. . . . You know, I scarcely respected you till now—that is I respected you but on an equal footing. But now I shall begin to respect you on a higher footing. Don't be angry, dear, at my joking," she put in at once, with strong feeling. "I am absurd and small, but you, you! Listen, Alyosha. Isn't there in all our analysis—I mean your analysis. . . . No, better call it ours—aren't we showing contempt for him, for that poor captain—in analyzing his soul like this, as it were, from above? In deciding so certainly that he will take the money?"

"No, Lise, it's not contempt," Alyosha answered, as though he had prepared himself for the question. "I was thinking of that on the way here. How can it be contempt when we are all

200

like him, when we are all just the same as he is. For you know we are just the same, no better. If we are better, we should have been just the same in his place. . . . I don't know about you, Lise, but I feel that I have a sordid soul in many ways, and that his soul is not sordid. On the contrary, it's full of fine feeling. . . . No, Lise, I have no contempt for him. Do you know, Lise, my elder told me once to care for most people exactly as one would for children, and for some of them as one would for the sick in hospitals."

"Oh, Alyosha, dear, let us care for people as we would for the sick!"

"Let us, Lise; I am ready. Though I am not altogether ready in myself. I am sometimes very impatient and at other times I don't see things. It's different with you."

"Oh, I don't believe it! Alyosha, how happy I am."

"I am so glad you say so, Lise."

"Alyosha, you are wonderfully good, but you are sometimes so formal. . . . And yet you are not a bit formal really. Go to the door, open it gently, and see whether mother is listening," said Lise, in a nervous, hurried whisper.

Alyosha went, opened the door, and reported that no one was listening.

"Come here, Alyosha," Lise went on, flushing redder and redder. "Give me your hand—that's right. I have to make a confession. I didn't write to you yesterday in joke, but in earnest," and she hid her eyes with her hand. It was obvious that she was ashamed of the confession.

Suddenly she kissed his hand three times.

"Oh, Lise!" cried Alyosha joyfully. "You know, I was perfectly sure you were in earnest."

"Sure?" She put aside his hand, but did not let go of it. She blushed and laughed a little happy laugh. "I kiss his hand and he says, 'Oh, Lise!'"

But her reproach was undeserved. Alyosha, too, was greatly overcome.

"I should like to please you always, Lise, but I don't know how to do it," he muttered.

"Alyosha, dear, you are cold and rude. Don't you see? You have chosen me as your wife and you are settled about it. You are sure I was in earnest. What a thing to say! Why, that's impertinence—that's what it is."

"Why was it wrong of me to feel sure?" Alyosha asked, laughing suddenly.

"Oh, Alyosha, on the contrary, it was delightfully right," cried Lise, looking tenderly and happily at him.

Alyosha stood still, holding her hand in his. Suddenly he stooped down and kissed her on her lips.

"Oh, what are you doing?" cried Lise. Alyosha was terribly embarrassed.

"Oh, forgive me if I shouldn't. . . . Perhaps I'm awfully

stupid. . . . You said I was cold, so I kissed you. . . . But I see it was stupid."

Lise laughed, and hid her face in her hands. "And in that dress!" she said. But she suddenly stopped laughing and became serious, almost stern.

"Alyosha, we must put off kissing. We are not ready for that yet, and we shall have a long time to wait," she ended suddenly. "Tell me rather why you who are so clever, so intellectual, so observant, choose a little idiot, an invalid like me? Oh, Alyosha, I am awfully happy for I don't deserve you a bit."

"You do, Lise. I shall be leaving the monastery in a few days. If I go into the world, I must marry. I know that. Father Zossima told me to marry. Whom could I marry better than you—and who would have me except you? I have been thinking it over. In the first place, you've known me since we were children and you've a great many qualities I haven't. You are more lighthearted than I am; above all, you are more innocent than I am. I have been brought into contact with many, many things already. . . . Oh, you don't know, but I, too, am a Karamazov. What does it matter if you do laugh and make jokes, and at me, too? Go on laughing. I am so glad you do. You laugh like a little child, but you think like a martyr."

"Like a martyr? How?"

"Yes, Lise, your question just now; whether we weren't showing contempt for that poor man by dissecting his soul—that was the question of a sufferer. . . . You see, I don't know how to express it, but any one who thinks of such questions is capable of suffering. Sitting in your invalid chair you must have thought over many things already."

"Alyosha, give me your hand. Why are you taking it away?" murmured Lise in a failing voice, soft with happiness. "Listen, Alyosha. What will you wear when you come out of the monastery? What sort of suit? Don't laugh. Don't be angry. It's very, very important to me."

"I haven't thought about it, Lise. But I'll wear whatever you like."

"I would like you to have a dark blue velvet coat, a white piqué waistcoat, and a soft gray felt hat. . . . Tell me, did you think that I didn't care for you when I said I didn't mean what I wrote?"

"No, I didn't believe it."

"Oh, you dreadful person. You are impossible!"

"You see, I knew that you cared for me, but I pretended that you didn't care for me to make it—easier for you."

"That makes it worse! Worse and better! Alyosha, I am awfully fond of you. Just before you came this morning, I tried my fortune. I decided I would ask you for my letter, and if you brought it out calmly and gave it to me (as might have been expected from you) it would mean that you did not love me at all, that you felt nothing, and were simply a stupid boy, good for nothing, and that I was ruined. But you left the letter at home and that makes me happy. You left it behind on purpose, so as not to give it back, because you knew I would ask for it? That is it, isn't it?"

"Oh, Lise, it's not so. I have the letter with me now. I had it this morning too. In this pocket. Here it is."

Alyosha pulled the letter out laughing, and showed it to her from a distance.

"But I am not going to give it to you. Look at it from here."

"Why, then you told a lie? You, a monk, told a lie!"

"I told a lie if you like," Alyosha laughed. "I told a lie so as not to give you back the letter. It's very precious to me," he added suddenly, with strong feeling. And again he flushed. "It always will be, and I won't give it up to anyone!"

Lise looked at him happily. "Alyosha," she murmured again. "Look at the door. Isn't mother listening?"

"All right, Lise, I'll look. But wouldn't it be better not to look? Why suspect your mother of such meanness?"

"What meanness? As for her spying on her daughter, it's her right, it's not meanness!" cried Lise, flaring up. "You may be sure, Alyosha, that when I am a mother, if I have a daughter like myself I shall certainly spy on her!"

"Really, Lise? That's not right."

"Oh, my goodness! What has meanness to do with it? If she were listening to some ordinary worldly conversation, it would be meanness, but when her own daughter is shut up with a young man . . . Listen, Alyosha, do you know I shall spy upon you as soon as we are married. And let me tell you I shall open all your letters and read them, so you may as well be prepared."

"Yes, of course, if . . ." said Alyosha. "Only it's not right."

"Oh, how contemptuous! Alyosha, dear, we mustn't quarrel the very first day. I'd better tell you the whole truth. Of course it's very wrong to spy on people, and, of course, I am not right and you are, only I will spy on you all the same."

"Do, then. You won't find out anything," laughed Alyosha.

"And Alyosha, will you give in to me? We must decide that too."

"I shall be delighted to, Lise, and certain to, only not in the most important things. Even if you don't agree with me, I will do my duty in the most important things."

"That's right. But let me tell you that I am ready to give in to you not only in the most important matters, but in everything. And I am ready to promise to do so now—in everything. And for all my life!" cried Lise fervently. "And I'll do it gladly, gladly! What's more I'll swear never to spy on you, never once, never to read one of your letters. For you are right and I am not. And although I shall be awfully tempted to spy, I know that I won't do it since you consider it dishonorable. You are my conscience now . . . Listen, Alyosha, why have you been so sad lately—both yesterday and today? I know you have a lot of worry and trouble, but I am afraid that you have some special grief besides, some secret one, perhaps?"

"Yes, Lise, I have a secret one, too," answered Alyosha mournfully. "I see you love me, since you guessed that."

"What grief? Can you tell me?" asked Lise timidly.

"I'll tell you later, Lise—afterwards," said Alyosha confused. "You wouldn't understand it now—and perhaps I couldn't explain it."

"I know, your brothers and your father are worrying you?"

"Yes, my brothers . . ." murmured Alyosha.

"I don't like your brother Ivan, Alyosha," said Lise suddenly.

He heard this remark with some surprise, but did not answer it.

"My brothers are destroying themselves," he went on. "My father, too. And they are destroying others with them. It's 'the primitive force of the Karamazovs,' as Father Paissy said the other day. A crude, unbridled, earthly force. Does the spirit of God move above that force? Even that I don't know. I only know that I, too, am a Karamazov. . . . Me a monk, a monk! Am I a monk, Lise? You said just now that I was."

"Yes, I did."

"But perhaps I don't even believe in God."

"You don't believe? What is the matter?" asked Lise quietly and gently. But Alyosha did not answer. There was something too mysterious, too subjective in these last words of his. Their meaning was perhaps obscure even to him but yet it tormented him.

"And now on top of it all, my friend, the best man in the world is going, is leaving the earth! If you knew, Lise, how bound up in soul I am with him! And then I shall be left alone. . . . I shall come to you, Lise. . . . For the future we will be together."

"Yes, together, together! We shall be always together, all our lives! Listen, kiss me."

Alyosha kissed her.

"Come, now go. Christ be with you!" and she made the sign of the cross over him. "Hurry back to *him* while he is still alive. I see I've kept you cruelly. I'll pray today for him and you. Alyosha, we shall be happy! Shall we be happy, shall we?"

"I believe we shall, Lise."

Alyosha thought it better not to go in to Madame Hohlakov and was about to leave the house without saying good-by to her. But no sooner had he opened the door than he found Madame Hohlakov standing before him. From the first word Alyosha guessed that she had been waiting for him.

"Alyosha, this is awful. This is all childish nonsense and ridiculous. I hope you won't dream . . . It's foolishness, nothing but foolishness!" she said, attacking him at once.

204

"Only don't tell her that," said Alyosha, "or she will be upset. And that's bad for her now."

"Sensible advice from a sensible young man. Am I to understand that you only agreed with her from compassion for her condition, because you didn't want to irritate her by contradicting her?"

"Oh no, not at all. I was quite serious in what I said," Alyosha declared.

"To be serious about it is impossible, unthinkable. In the first place I will never be at home to you again, and I will take her away. You may be sure of that."

"But why?" asked Alyosha. "It's all so far off. We may have to wait another year and a half."

"Ah, Alyosha, that's true, of course. And you'll have time to quarrel and separate a thousand times in a year and a half. But I am so unhappy! Though it's such nonsense, it's a great shock to me. I feel like Famusov in the last scene of *Sorrow from Wit*. You are Tchatsky and she is Sophia and I've run down to meet you on the stairs. In the play the fatal scene takes place on the staircase. I heard it all. I almost dropped. So this is the explanation of her dreadful night and her hysterics of late! It means love to the daughter but death to the mother. I might as well be in my grave right now. And what is this letter she has written? Show it to me at once, at once!"

"No, there's no need. Tell me, how is Katerina now? I must know."

"She is still delirious. She has not regained consciousness. Her aunts are here but they do nothing but sigh. Herzenstube came, and he was so alarmed that I didn't know what to do for him. I nearly sent for a doctor to look after him. He was driven home in my carriage. And on the top of it all, you and this letter! It's true nothing can happen for a year and a half. In the name of all that's holy, in the name of your dying elder, show me that letter, Alyosha. I'm her mother. Hold it in your hand, if you like, and I will read it that way."

"No, I won't show it to you. Even if Lise said I should, I wouldn't. I am coming tomorrow, and if you like, we can talk over many things. But now good-by!"

And Alyosha ran out into the street.

2. *Smerdyakov with a Guitar*

ALYOSHA HAD NO TIME TO LOSE. Even while he was saying good-by to Lise, the thought had struck him that he must find his brother Dmitri, who was evidently keeping out of his way. It was getting late, nearly three o'clock. Alyosha's whole soul turned toward the monastery, toward his dying saint, but the necessity of seeing Dmitri outweighed everything.

The conviction that a great catastrophe was about to happen grew stronger in Alyosha's mind with every hour. What that catastrophe was, and what he would say at that moment to his brother, he could perhaps not have said definitely. "Even if Father Zossima dies without me . . . I won't have to reproach myself all my life with the thought that I might have saved something and didn't, but passed by and hurried home. If I do as I plan I will be following my elder's great precept."

Alyosha's plan was to catch his brother Dmitri unawares, to climb over the fence, as he had the day before, get into the garden and sit in the summerhouse. If Dmitri were not there, thought Alyosha, he would not announce himself to Foma, the ex-soldier and watchman, or the women of the house, but would stay hidden in the summerhouse, even if he had to wait there till evening. But if, as before, Dmitri were lying in wait for Grushenka, he would undoubtedly come to the summerhouse. Alyosha did not, however, give much thought to the details of his plan, but decided to act upon it, even if it meant not getting back to the monastery that day.

Everything happened without trouble; he climbed over the fence almost in the same spot as the day before, and stole into the summerhouse unseen. He did not want to be seen. The women of the house and Foma too, if he were there, might be loyal to his brother and obey his instructions. They might refuse to let Alyosha into the garden, or they might warn Dmitri.

There was no one in the summerhouse. Alyosha sat down and began to wait. He looked round the summerhouse, which somehow struck him as a great deal more dilapidated than before. Though the day was just as fine as yesterday, it seemed a wretched place this time. There was a stain on the table from the glass of brandy having been spilled the day before.

Foolish and irrelevant ideas strayed about Alyosha's mind, as they always do in a time of tedious waiting. He wondered, for instance, why he had sat down precisely in the same place as before, why not in the other seat. At last he felt very depressed—depressed by suspense and uncertainty. But he had not sat there more than a quarter of an hour, when he suddenly heard the thrum of a guitar somewhere quite close. People were sitting, or had only just sat down, somewhere in the bushes not more than twenty yards away. Alyosha suddenly remembered that on coming out of the summerhouse the day before, he had caught a glimpse of an old garden seat among the bushes on the left, by the fence. The people must be sitting on it now. Who were they?

A man, accompanying himself on the guitar, suddenly began singing in a sugary falsetto:

"With invincible force
I am bound to my dear.

206

> *Oh, Lord, have mercy*
> *On her and on me!*
> *On her and on me!*
> *On her and on me!"*

The voice stopped. It was a lackey's tenor and a lackey's song. Another voice, a woman's, suddenly asked insinuatingly and bashfully, though with mincing affectation: "Why haven't you been to see us for so long, Pavel? Why do you always look down upon us?"

"Not at all," answered a man's voice politely, but with emphatic dignity. It was clear that the man had the best of the position, and that the woman was making advances.

"I believe the man is Smerdyakov!" thought Alyosha. "And the other must be the daughter of the house here, the one who was a maid and wears the dress with the train and goes to Marfa for soup."

"I am awfully fond of verses of all kinds, if they rhyme," the woman's voice continued. "Why don't you go on?"

The man sang again:

> *"What do I care for royal wealth*
> *If but my dear one be in health?*
> *Lord have mercy*
> *On her and on me!*
> *On her and on me!*
> *On her and on me!"*

"It was even better last time," observed the woman's voice. "You sang, 'If my darling be in health.' It sounded more tender."

"Poetry is rubbish!" said Smerdyakov curtly.

"Oh, no! I am very fond of poetry."

"So far as it's poetry, it's rubbish. Consider, who ever talks in rhyme? And if we were all to talk in rhyme, even though it were decreed by the government, we wouldn't say much, would we? Poetry is no good, Maria."

"How clever you are! How is it you've gone so deep into everything?" The woman's voice was more and more insinuating.

"I could have done better than that. I could have known more than that, if it had not been for the circumstances of my birth. I would have been capable of shooting a man in a duel if he called me names because I am descended from a stinking beggar and have no father. And they used to call me a stinking, bastard in Moscow. It had reached them from here, thanks to Gregory. Gregory blames me for rebelling against my birth, but I would have welcomed their killing me before I was born so that I might not have come into the world at all. They used to say in the market, and your mother too, that my mother's hair was like a mat on her head, and that she was short of five foot by a 'wee bit.' Why talk of a 'wee bit' when they might say 'a little bit'? They wanted to make it touching, a regular peasant's feeling. Can a Russian peasant be said to feel, in comparison with an educated man? He can't be said to have feeling at all, in his ignorance. From my childhood up when I hear 'a wee bit,' I am ready to burst with rage. I hate all Russia, Maria."

"If you'd been a cadet in the army, or a young hussar, you wouldn't talk like that, but would draw your sabre to defend all Russia."

"I don't want to be a hussar and what's more I'd like to abolish all soldiers."

"And when an enemy comes, who is going to defend us?"

"There's no need of defense. In 1812 there was a great invasion of Russia by Napoleon, first Emperor of the French, father of the present one, and it would have been a good thing if they had conquered us. A clever nation would have conquered a very stupid one and annexed it. We would have had quite different institutions."

"Are the French so much better than we are? I wouldn't change someone I know for three young Frenchmen," observed Maria tenderly, accompanying her words with a languishing glance.

"That's as one prefers."

"But you are just like a foreigner—just like a most gentlemanly foreigner. I tell you that, though it makes me blush."

"If you care to know, the folks there and ours here are just alike in their vices. They are swindlers, only abroad the scoundrel wears polished boots and here he grovels in filth and sees no harm in it. The Russian people need beating, as Fyodor Karamazov said very truly yesterday, though he is mad, and all his sons, too."

"You said you had such respect for Ivan!"

"But he said I was a stinking lackey. He thinks that I might get out of hand. But he's mistaken there. If I had a certain sum of money in my pocket, I would have left long ago. . . . Dmitri is lower than any lackey in his behavior, in his mind, and in his poverty. He doesn't know how to do anything, and yet he is respected by everyone. I may be only a soup maker, but with luck I could open a café in Moscow. My cooking is something special. And there's no one in Moscow except foreigners, whose cooking is anything special. Dmitri is nothing but a beggar, but if he were to challenge the son of the first count in the country, that nobleman's son would fight him. Though in what way is he better than I am? He is more stupid than I am. Look at the money he has wasted!"

"It must be lovely, a duel," Maria observed suddenly.

"Why?"

"It must be so dreadful and so brave, especially when young officers with pistols in their hands pop at one another for the

208

sake of some lady. A perfect picture! Ah, if only girls were allowed to look on, I'd give anything to see one!"

"It's all right when you are firing at someone, but when he is firing straight at you, you must feel pretty silly. You'd be glad to run away, Maria."

"You don't mean you would run away?" But Smerdyakov did not deign to reply.

After a moment's silence the guitar tinkled again, and Smerdyakov sang again in the same falsetto:

> *"Whatever you may say,*
> *I shall go far away.*
> *Life will be bright and gay*
> *In the city far away.*
> *I shall not grieve,*
> *I shall not grieve at all.*
> *I don't intend to grieve at all."*

Then something unexpected happened. Alyosha suddenly sneezed. Smerdyakov and Maria were silent. Alyosha got up and walked toward them. He found Smerdyakov dressed up and wearing polished boots, his hair pomaded and curled. The guitar lay on the garden seat. Maria was wearing a light blue dress with a train two yards long. She was young and would not have been bad-looking except that her face was so round and terribly freckled.

"Will my brother Dmitri be back soon?" asked Alyosha with as much ease as he could.

Smerdyakov got up slowly. Maria rose too.

"How should I know about Dmitri? I'm not his keeper," answered Smerdyakov quietly, distinctly and superciliously.

"But I simply asked whether you know?" Alyosha explained.

"I know nothing of his whereabouts and don't want to."

"But my brother told me that you let him know all that goes on in the house; that you promised to let him know when Grushenka comes."

Smerdyakov fixed a deliberate, unmoved glance on Alyosha. "And how did you get in here? The gate was bolted an hour ago," he asked.

"I came in from the back alley, over the fence, and went straight to the summerhouse. I hope you'll forgive me," he added, addressing Maria. "I was in a hurry to find my brother."

"Ach, as though we could take it amiss in you!" drawled Maria, flattered by Alyosha's apology. "Your brother often goes to the summerhouse that same way. We don't know he is here and he is sitting in the summerhouse."

"I am very anxious to find him, or to learn from you where he is now. It's on business of great importance to him."

"He never tells us," lisped Maria.

"Though I come here as a friend," Smerdyakov began, "Dmitri pesters me in a merciless way even here with his incessant questions about your father. 'What news?' he'll ask. 'What's going on in there now? Who's coming and going? Can't you tell me something more?' Twice already he's threatened to kill me."

"To kill you?" Alyosha exclaimed in surprise.

"Do you suppose he'd think much of that, with his temper, which you had a chance of observing for yourself yesterday? He says if I let Grushenka in and she spends the night there with your father, I'll suffer for it. I am terribly afraid of him. I ought to tell the police. God only knows what he might do!"

"Your brother said to him the other day, 'I'll pound you in a mortar!' " added Maria.

"Oh, if it's pounding in a mortar, it may be only talk," observed Alyosha. "When I see him, I might speak to him about that too."

"Well the only thing I can tell you is this," said Smerdyakov, as though thinking better of it; "I am here as an old friend and neighbor, and it would be odd if I didn't come. On the other hand, Ivan sent me first thing this morning to your brother's place on Lake Street, without a letter, but with a message. Ivan wants Dmitri to dine with him at the restaurant here, in the market place. I went, but didn't find Dmitri at home, though it was eight o'clock. 'He's been here, but he is gone,' those were the very words his landlady said. It's as though there was an understanding between them. Perhaps at this moment he is in the restaurant with Ivan because Ivan has not been home to dinner and your father dined alone an hour ago. He has now gone to lie down. But don't speak of me and of what I have told you, because he'd kill me."

"Ivan invited Dmitri to a restaurant today?" repeated Alyosha quickly.

"Yes."

"The Metropolis tavern in the market place?"

"Yes."

"That's possible," cried Alyosha, much excited. "Thank you, Smerdyakov. That's important. I'll go there at once."

"Don't betray me," Smerdyakov called after him.

"Oh, no, I'll go to the tavern as though by chance. Don't worry."

"But wait a minute, I'll open the gate to you," cried Maria.

"No. I'll climb over the fence again."

Alyosha ran to the tavern. It was impossible for him to go into the tavern in his cassock but he could inquire at the entrance for his brothers and call them out. But just as he reached the tavern, an upper window was flung open, and his brother Ivan called to him.

"Alyosha, can't you come up here to me? I will be awfully grateful."

"I don't quite know whether in this dress . . ."

210

"But I am in a private room. Come up the steps; I'll run down to meet you."

A minute later Alyosha was sitting beside his brother. Ivan was dining alone.

3. The Brothers Make Friends

IVAN WAS NOT, HOWEVER, IN A PRIVATE ROOM, but only in a place closed off by a screen. It was the first room after the entrance and it had a buffet along the wall. Waiters were continually coming and going. The only person in the room was an old retired military man drinking tea in a corner. But there was the usual bustle going on in the other rooms of the tavern. There were shouts for the waiters, the sound of popping corks, the click of billiard balls and the drone of an organ. Alyosha knew that Ivan did not usually visit this tavern and disliked taverns in general. So he must have come here, as Smerdyakov had said, simply to meet Dmitri. Yet Dmitri was not there.

"Shall I order fish or something for you? You don't live on tea alone, I hope," cried Ivan, apparently delighted at having gotten hold of Alyosha. He had finished dinner and was drinking tea.

"Let me have soup, and tea afterwards, I am hungry," said Alyosha.

"And cherry jam? They have it here. You remember how you used to love cherry jam when you were little?"

"You remember that? Let me have jam too, I still like it."

Ivan called the waiter and ordered soup, jam and tea.

"I remember everything, Alyosha. I remember you till you were eleven. I was nearly fifteen. There's such a difference between fifteen and eleven that brothers are never companions at those ages. I don't know whether I even liked you. When I went away to Moscow, for the first few years, I never thought of you at all. Then, when you came to Moscow yourself, we only met once somewhere, I believe. And now I've been here more than three months, and so far we have scarcely said a word to each other. Tomorrow I am going away. And I was just wondering as I sat here how I could see you to say good-by. And just then you passed."

"Were you very anxious to see me?"

"Very, I want to get to know you once and for all, and I want you to know me. And then we will say good-by. I believe it's always best to get to know people just before leaving them. I've noticed how you've been looking at me these three months. There has been a continual look of expectation in your eyes, and I can't endure that. That's why I've kept away from you. But in the end I have learned to respect you. The little man

211

stands firm, I thought. Though I am laughing, I am serious. You do stand firm, don't you? I like people who are firm like that whatever it is they stand by, even when they are such little fellows as you. Your expectant eyes stopped annoying me. I grew fond of them in the end, those expectant eyes. You seem to love me for some reason, Alyosha?"

"I do love you, Ivan. Dmitri says of you—Ivan is a tomb! I say of you, Ivan is a riddle. You are a riddle to me even now. But I understand something in you that I did not understand till this morning."

"What's that?" laughed Ivan.

"You won't be angry?" Alyosha laughed too.

"Well?"

"That you are just as young as other young men of twenty-three; that you are young and fresh and nice, green in fact! Now, have I insulted you?"

"On the contrary, I am struck by a coincidence," cried Ivan good-humoredly. "Would you believe it that ever since that scene with Katerina, I have thought of nothing else but my youthful greenness. And just as though you guessed that, you begin talking about it. Do you know I've been sitting here thinking to myself: that if I didn't believe in life, if I lost faith in the woman I love, lost faith in the order of things, were convinced in fact that everything is a disorderly, damnable, and perhaps devil-ridden chaos, if I were struck by every horror of man's disillusionment—still I should want to live. Having once tasted of the cup, I would not turn away from it till I had drained it! At thirty though, I shall be sure to leave the cup, even if I've not emptied it, and turn away—where I don't know. But till I am thirty, I know that my youth will triumph over everything —every disillusionment, every disgust with life. I've asked myself many times whether there is in the world any despair that could overcome this frantic thirst for life. And I've come to the conclusion that there isn't, that is till I am thirty. Some driveling consumptive moralists—and poets especially—call that thirst for life base. It's a feature of the Karamazovs it's true, that thirst for life regardless of everything. You probably have it too. But why is it base? The centripetal force on our planet is still fearfully strong, Alyosha. I have a longing for life, and I go on living in spite of logic. Though I may not believe in the order of the universe, yet I love the sticky little leaves as they open in spring. I love the blue sky. I love some people, whom one loves you know sometimes without knowing why. I love some great deeds done by men, though I've long ceased perhaps to have faith in them. Yet from habit one's heart prizes them. . . . Here they have brought the soup for you. Eat it. It will do you good. It's excellent soup. They know how to make it here. . . . I want to travel in Europe, Alyosha. And yet I know that I am only going to a graveyard, but it's a most precious graveyard, that's what it is! Precious are the dead that lie there.

212

Every stone over them speaks of such burning life in the past, of such passionate faith in their work, their truth, their struggle and their science. I know I shall fall on the ground and kiss those stones and weep over them even though I'm convinced in my heart that it's long been nothing but a graveyard. And I shall not weep from despair, but simply because I shall be happy in my tears. I shall steep my soul in my emotion. I love the sticky leaves in spring, the blue sky—that's all it is. It's not a matter of intellect or logic, it's loving with one's inside, with one's stomach. One loves the first strength of one's youth. Do you understand anything of what I am saying, Alyosha?" Ivan laughed suddenly.

"I understand too well, Ivan. One longs to love with one's inside, with one's stomach. You said that so well and I am awfully glad that you have such a longing for life," cried Alyosha. "I think everyone should love life above everything in the world."

"Love life more than the meaning of it?"

"Certainly. Love it, regardless of logic as you say. It must be regardless of logic. It's only then one can understand the meaning of it. I have thought so a long time. Half your work is done, Ivan. You love life. Now you've only to do the second half and you are saved."

"You are trying to save me, but perhaps I am not lost! And what does your second half mean?"

"Why, one has to raise up your dead, who perhaps have not died after all. Come, let me have the tea! I am so glad of our talk, Ivan."

"You are inspired. I am awfully fond of such professions of faith from such—novices. You are a steadfast person, Alyosha. It is true that you mean to leave the monastery?"

"Yes, my elder sends me out into the world."

"We shall see each other then in the world. We shall meet again before I am thirty, when I shall begin to turn aside from the cup. Father doesn't want to turn aside from his cup till he is seventy. He dreams of hanging on to eighty in fact, so he says. He means it seriously, although he is a buffoon. He stands on a firm rock, too. He stands on his sensuality—after we are thirty there may be nothing else to stand on. . . . But to hang on until seventy is wrong, better only until thirty. One may retain 'a shadow of nobility' by deceiving oneself. . . . Have you seen Dmitri today?"

"No, but I saw Smerdyakov." And Alyosha quickly described his meeting with Smerdyakov. Ivan listened carefully and questioned him.

"But he begged me not to tell Dmitri that he had told me about him," added Alyosha.

Ivan frowned.

"Are you frowning because of Smerdyakov?" asked Alyosha.

213

"Yes. Damn him. I did want to see Dmitri, but now there's no need," said Ivan reluctantly.

"But are you really going so soon, Ivan?"

"Yes."

"What of Dmitri and father? How will it end?" asked Alyosha anxiously.

"You are always harping on it! What have I to do with it? Am I my brother Dmitri's keeper?" Ivan asked irritably. And then he smiled bitterly. "Cain's answer about his murdered brother, wasn't it? Perhaps that's what you're thinking at this moment? Well, damn it all, I can't stay here to be their keeper, can I? I've finished what I had to do, and I am going. Do you imagine I am jealous of Dmitri, that I've been trying to steal his beautiful Katerina for the last three months. Nonsense. I had business of my own. I finished it. I am going. I finished it just now, you were witness."

"At Katerina's?"

"Yes. And I've released myself once and for all. And after all, what have I to do with Dmitri? Dmitri doesn't enter into it. I had my own business to settle with Katerina. You know, on the other hand, that Dmitri behaved as though there was an understanding between us. I didn't ask him to do it, but he handed her over to me and gave us his blessing. It's all too funny. Oh, Alyosha, if you only knew how light my heart is now! Would you believe it, I sat here eating my dinner and was nearly ordering champagne to celebrate my first hour of freedom. It's been going on nearly six months, and all at once I've thrown it off. I could never have guessed even yesterday, how easy it would be to put an end to it if I wanted."

"Are you speaking of your love, Ivan?"

"Of my love, if you like. I fell in love with her, I worried over her and she worried me. I sat watching over her. . . . And all at once it's collapsed! I spoke this morning with passion, but I went away and roared with laughter. Would you believe it? Yes, it's the truth."

"You seem very happy about it now," observed Alyosha, looking into Ivan's face which had suddenly grown brighter.

"But how could I tell that I didn't care for her! Ha-ha! It appears after all I didn't. And yet how she attracted me! How attractive she was when I made my speech! And do you know she attracts me awfully even now, yet how easy it is to leave her. Do you think I am boasting?"

"No, only perhaps it wasn't love."

"Alyosha," laughed Ivan, "don't make reflections about love, it's unseemly for you. How you rushed into the discussion this morning! I've forgotten to thank you for it. . . . But how she tormented me! It certainly was sitting by a 'laceration.' She knew how I loved her! She loved me and not Dmitri," Ivan insisted. "Her feeling for Dmitri was simply a self-laceration. All I told her was perfectly true. But the worst of it is, it may

214

take her fifteen or twenty years to find out that she doesn't care for Dmitri but loves me whom she torments. She may never find it out at all, in spite of her lesson today. Well, it's better this way. Like this I can go away for good. By the way, how is she now? What happened after I left?"

Alyosha told him Katerina had been hysterical, and that when he left she was unconscious and delirious.

"Isn't Madame Hohlakov exaggerating?"

"I don't think so."

"I must find out. But nobody dies of hysterics. God gave woman hysterics as a relief. I won't go to her. Why push myself forward again?"

"But you told her that she had never cared for you."

"I did that on purpose. Alyosha, shall I call for some champagne? Let us drink to my freedom. Ah, if only you knew how glad I am!"

"No, Ivan, we had better not drink," said Alyosha suddenly. "Besides I somehow feel depressed."

"Yes, you've been depressed a long time, I've noticed it."

"Have you decided to go tomorrow morning then?"

"Morning? I didn't say I would go in the morning. . . . But perhaps it may be the morning. Would you believe it, I dined here today only to avoid dining with father, I loathe him so. I would have left long ago, so far as he is concerned. But why are you so worried about my going away? We've plenty of time before I go, an eternity!"

"If you are going away tomorrow, what do you mean by an eternity?"

"But what does it matter to us?" laughed Ivan. "We've time enough for our talk, for what brought us here. Why do you look so surprised? Answer. Why have we met here? To talk of my love for Katerina, of father and Dmitri? Of travel abroad? Of the fatal position of Russia? Of the Emperor Napoleon? Is that it?"

"No."

"Then you know what for. It's different for other people. But we in our green youth have to settle the eternal questions first of all. That's what we care about. Young Russia is talking about nothing but the eternal questions now. Just when the older generation is all taken up with practical questions. Why have you been looking at me in expectation for the last three months? To ask me 'what do you believe, or don't you believe at all?' That's what your eyes have been meaning for these three months, haven't they?"

"Perhaps so," smiled Alyosha. "You are not laughing at me, now, Ivan?"

"Me laughing! I don't want to hurt my little brother who has been watching me with such expectation for three months. Alyosha, look straight at me! Of course I am just as much of a little boy as you are, only not a novice. And what have Russian boys been doing up till now, some of them, I mean? In this filthy tavern, for instance, here they meet and sit in a corner. They've never met in their lives before and when they go out of the tavern, they won't meet again for forty years. And what do they talk about during that short time in the tavern? Of the eternal questions, of the existence of God and immortality. And those who do not believe in God talk of socialism or anarchism, of the transformation of all humanity on a new pattern, so that it all comes to the same. They're the same questions turned inside out. And masses, masses of the most original Russians do nothing but talk of the eternal questions! Isn't it so?"

"Yes, for real Russians the questions of God's existence and of immortality, or, as you say, the same questions turned inside out, come first and foremost. And of course they should," said Alyosha, still watching his brother with the same gentle and inquiring smile.

"Well, Alyosha, it's sometimes very unwise to be a Russian at all. But anything more stupid than the way Russians spend their time one can hardly imagine. But there's one Russian youth called Alyosha I am awfully fond of."

"How nicely you put that in!" Alyosha laughed suddenly.

"Well, tell me where to begin, give your orders. The existence of God?"

"Begin where you like. You declared yesterday at father's that there was no God." Alyosha looked searchingly at his brother.

"I said that yesterday at dinner on purpose to tease you. But now I've no objection to discussing this question with you, and I say so very seriously. I want to be friends with you, Alyosha, because I have no friends and want to try it. Well, would you believe it, perhaps I too accept God," laughed Ivan. "That's a surprise for you, isn't it?"

"Yes, of course, if you are not joking now."

"Joking? I was told at the elder's yesterday that I was joking. You know, Alyosha, there was an old sinner in the eighteenth century who declared that, if there were no God, he would have to be invented. And man has actually invented God. And what's strange, what would be marvelous, is not that God should really exist; the marvel is that such an idea, the idea of the necessity of God, could enter the head of such a savage, vicious beast as man. So holy is it, so touching, so wise and so great a credit is it to man. As for me, I've long resolved not to think whether man created God or God man. And I won't go through all the axioms laid down by Russians on that subject, all stemming from European hypotheses; for what's a hypothesis there, is an axiom with Russians. Not only with the young Russians but with their teachers too, for our Russian professors are often just the same themselves. And so I omit all the hypotheses. For what are we aiming at now? I am trying to ex-

216

plain as quickly as possible my essential nature, that is what manner of man I am, what I believe in, and for what I hope. That's it, isn't it? And therefore I tell you that I accept God simply. But you must note this: if God exists and if He really did create the world, then, as we all know, He created it according to the geometry of Euclid and the human mind, with the conception of only three dimensions in space. Yet there have been and still are mathematicians and philosophers who doubt whether the whole universe, or to speak more widely the whole of being, was only created in Euclid's geometry. They even dare to dream that two parallel lines, which according to Euclid can never meet on earth, may meet somewhere in infinity. I have come to the conclusion that, since I can't understand even that, I can't expect to understand about God. I acknowledge humbly that I have no faculty for settling such questions. I have a Euclidian earthly mind and so how can I solve problems that are not of this world? And I advise you never to think about it either, Alyosha, especially about God, whether He exists or not. All such questions are utterly inappropriate for a mind created with an idea of only three dimensions. And so I accept God and am glad to, and what's more I accept His wisdom, His purpose—which is completely beyond our knowledge. I believe in the underlying order and the meaning of life. I believe in the eternal harmony in which they say we shall one day be blended. I believe in the Word to Which the universe is striving, and Which Itself was 'with God,' and Which Itself is God and so on, and so on, to infinity. There are all sorts of phrases for it. I seem to be on the right path, don't I? Yet would you believe it, in the final result I don't accept this world of God's. Although I know it exists, I don't accept it at all. It's not that I don't accept God, you must understand, it's the world created by Him I don't and cannot accept. Let me make it plain. I believe like a child that suffering will be healed and made up for. I believe that all the humiliating absurdity of human contradictions will vanish like a mirage, like the despicable fabrication of the impotent and infinitely small Euclidian mind of man. I believe that at the world's end, at the moment of eternal harmony, something so precious will come to pass that it will suffice for all hearts, for the comforting of all resentments, for the atonement of all the crimes of humanity, of all the blood that has been shed. I believe that it will not only be possible to forgive but to justify all that has happened—but though all that may come to pass, I don't accept it. I won't accept it. Even if parallel lines do meet and I see it myself, I will see it and say that they've met, but still I won't accept it. That's what's at the root of me, Alyosha. That's my creed. I mean what I say. I began our talk as stupidly as I could on purpose, but I've led up to my confession, for that's all you want. You didn't want to hear about God; you only wanted to know what the brother you love lives by. And so I've told you."

217

Ivan concluded with marked and unexpected feeling.

"And why did you begin 'as stupidly as you could'?" asked Alyosha, looking dreamily at him.

"To begin with, for the sake of being Russian. Russian conversations on such subjects are always carried on stupidly. And secondly, the more stupid one is, the closer one is to reality. The more stupid one is, the clearer one is. Stupidity is brief and artless, while intelligence squirms and hides itself. Intelligence is unprincipled, but stupidity is honest and straightforward."

"Will you explain why you don't accept the world?" asked Alyosha.

"Yes I will. It's not a secret. That's what I've been leading up to. But Alyosha, I don't want to corrupt you or to turn you from your stronghold. Perhaps I even want to be healed by you." Ivan smiled suddenly like a gentle child. Alyosha had never seen such a smile on his face before.

4. Rebellion

"I MUST MAKE ONE CONFESSION," Ivan began. "I could never understand how one can love one's neighbors. It's just one's neighbors, to my mind, that one can't love, though one might love those who live at a distance. I once read somewhere of the saint, John the Merciful. When a hungry, frozen beggar came to him, he took him into his bed, held him in his arms, and began breathing into his mouth, which was putrid and loathsome from some awful disease. I am convinced that he did that from "self-laceration," from the self-laceration of falseness, for the sake of the charity imposed by duty, as a penance laid on him. For anyone to love a man, he must be hidden, for as soon as he shows his face, love is gone."

"Father Zossima has talked of that more than once," observed Alyosha. "He, too, said that the face of a man often hinders people not practiced in love, from loving him. But yet there's a great deal of love in mankind, an almost Christ-like love. I know that myself, Ivan."

"Well, I know nothing of it so far, and can't understand it, and the mass of mankind are with me there. The question is, whether this lack of ability to love is due to men's bad qualities or whether it's inherent in their nature. To my thinking, Christ-like love for men is a miracle impossible on earth. He was God. But we are not gods. Suppose I, for instance, suffer intensely. Another can never know how much I suffer, because he is another and not I. And what's more, a man is rarely ready to admit another's suffering. Why won't he admit it, do you think? Because I smell unpleasant, because I have a stupid face, because I once trod on his foot. Besides there is suffering and suffering; degrading, humiliating suffering such as humbles me—hunger, for instance. But when you come to higher suffering—for an idea, for instance—he will very rarely admit it, perhaps because my face he thinks is not the face of a man who suffers for an idea. And so he deprives me instantly of his favor, and not at all from badness of heart. Beggars, especially genteel beggars, should never show themselves, but ask for charity through the newspapers.

"One can love one's neighbors in the abstract, or even at a distance, but at close quarters it's almost impossible. If it were as on the stage, in the ballet, where if beggars come in, they wear silken rags and tattered lace and beg for alms dancing gracefully, then one might enjoy looking at them. But even then we should not love them. But enough of that. I simply wanted to show you my point of view. I meant to speak of the suffering of mankind generally. But we had better confine ourselves to the sufferings of children. That reduces the scope of my argument to a tenth of what it would be. Still we'd better keep to children, though it does weaken my case. But, in the first place, children can be loved even at close quarters, even when they are dirty, even when they are ugly. The second reason why I won't speak of grown-up people is that, besides being disgusting and unworthy of love, they have a compensation—they've eaten the apple and know good and evil, and they have become 'like god.' They go on eating it still. But children haven't eaten anything, and are innocent. Are you fond of children, Alyosha? I know you are, and you will understand why I prefer to speak of them. If they, too, suffer horribly on earth, they must suffer for their fathers' sins, they must be punished for their fathers, who have eaten the apple. But that reasoning is of the other world and is incomprehensible for the heart of man here on earth. The innocent must not suffer for another's sins, and especially such innocents! You may be surprised at me, Alyosha, but I am awfully fond of children, too. And remember, cruel people, the violent, the rapacious, the Karamazovs are sometimes very fond of children. Children while they are quite little—up to seven, for instance—are so remote from grown-up people; they are different creatures, as it were, of a different species. I knew a criminal in prison who had murdered whole families, including several children. But when he was in prison, he had a strange affection for them. He spent all his time at his window watching the children playing in the prison yard. He trained one little boy to come up to his window and made friends with him. . . . You don't know why I am telling you all this, Alyosha? My head aches and I am sad."

"You speak in such a strange way," observed Alyosha uneasily, "as though you were not quite yourself."

"By the way, a Bulgarian I met lately in Moscow," Ivan went on, seeming not to hear his brother's words, "told me about the crimes committed by Turks and Circassians in Bulgaria through fear of a general uprising of the Slavs. They burned villages, murdered, outraged women and children, they nailed their prisoners by the ears to the fences, left them till morning, and in the morning they hanged them—all sorts of things you can't imagine. People talk sometimes of bestial cruelty, but that's a great injustice and insult to the beasts; a beast can never be so cruel as a man, so artistically cruel. The tiger only tears and gnaws, that's all he can do. He would never think of nailing people by the ears, even if he were able to do it. These Turks took pleasure in torturing children, too; cutting the unborn child from the mother's womb, and tossing babies up in the air and catching them on the points of their bayonets before their mother's eyes. Doing it before the mother's eyes was what gave zest to the amusement. Here is another scene that I thought very interesting. Imagine a trembling mother with her baby in her arms, a circle of invading Turks around her. They've planned a game; they pet the baby, laugh to make it laugh. They succeed, the baby laughs. At that moment a Turk points a pistol four inches from the baby's face. The baby laughs, holds out its little hands to the pistol, and the Turk pulls the trigger in the baby's face and blows out its brains. Artistic, wasn't it? By the way, Turks are particularly fond of sweet things, they say."

"Ivan, what are you driving at?" asked Alyosha.

"I think if the devil doesn't exist, then man has created him. He has created him in his own image and likeness."

"Just as man created God, then?" observed Alyosha.

" 'It's wonderful how you can turn words,' as Polonius says in *Hamlet*," laughed Ivan. "You turn my words against me. Well, I am glad. Yours must be a fine God, if man created Him in His image and likeness. You asked just now what I was driving at. You see, I like to collect certain facts, and, would you believe, I even copy anecdotes of a certain sort from newspapers and books. I've already got a fine collection. The Turks, of course, are included, but they are foreigners. I have Russian examples that are even better than the Turks. You know we prefer beating—rods and scourges—that's our national institution. Nailing ears is unthinkable for us, for we are, after all, Europeans. But the rod and the scourge we have always with us and they cannot be taken from us. Abroad now they scarcely do any beating. Manners are more humane, or laws have been passed, so that they don't dare to flog men now. But they make up for it in another way just as national as ours. It is so national that it would be practically impossible among us, though I believe we are being inoculated with it, since the religious movement began in our aristocracy.

"I have a charming pamphlet translated from the French describing how, quite recently, five years ago, a murderer, Richard, was executed—a young man, I believe, of twenty-three, who repented and was converted to the Christian faith at the

220

scaffold. This Richard was illegitimate and had been given as a child of six by his parents to some shepherds on the Swiss mountains. They brought him up to work for them. He grew up like a wild beast among them. The shepherds taught him nothing, and scarcely fed or clothed him, but sent him out at seven to herd the flock in cold and wet, and no one hesitated to treat him in this way. On the contrary, they thought they had every right, for Richard had been given to them as chattel, and they did not even see the necessity of feeding him. Richard himself described how in those years, like the Prodigal Son in the Gospel, he longed to eat of the mash given to the pigs, which were fattened for sale. But they wouldn't even give him that, and beat him when he stole from the pigs. And that was how he spent all his childhood and his youth, till he grew up and was strong enough to go away and be a thief. The savage began to earn his living as a day laborer in Geneva. He drank what he earned, he lived like a brute, and finished by killing and robbing an old man. He was caught, tried, and condemned to death. They are not sentimentalists there. And in prison he was immediately surrounded by pastors, members of Christian brotherhoods, philanthropic ladies, and the like. They taught him to read and write in prison, and expounded the Gospel to him. They exhorted him, worked upon him, drummed at him incessantly, till at last he solemnly confessed his crime. He was converted. He wrote to the court himself that he was a monster, but that in the end God had given him light and shown grace.

"All Geneva was excited about him—all philanthropic and religious Geneva. All the aristocratic and well-bred society of the town rushed to the prison, kissed Richard and embraced him: 'You are our brother, you have found grace.' And Richard did nothing but weep with emotion: 'Yes, I've found grace! All my youth and childhood I was glad of pigs' food, but now even I have found grace. I am dying in the Lord.' 'Yes, Richard, die in the Lord; you have shed blood and must die. Though it's not your fault that you knew not the Lord, when you coveted the pigs' food and were beaten for stealing it (which was very wrong of you, for stealing is forbidden); but you've shed blood and you must die.' And on the last day, Richard, perfectly limp, did nothing but cry and repeat every minute: 'This is my happiest day. I am going to the Lord.' 'Yes,' cried the pastors and the judges and philanthropic ladies. 'This is the happiest day of your life, for you are going to the Lord!' They all walked or drove to the scaffold behind the prison van. At the scaffold they called to Richard: 'Die, brother, die in the Lord, for even thou hast found grace!' And so, covered with his brothers' kisses, Richard was dragged to the scaffold, and led to the guillotine. And they chopped off his head in brotherly fashion, because he had found grace. Yes, that's characteristic. That pamphlet is translated into Russian by some Russian philanthropists of aristocratic rank and evangelical aspirations, and has been distributed gratis for the enlightenment of our people.

"Richard's case is interesting because it's national. Though to us it's absurd to cut off a man's head, because he has become our brother and has found grace, yet we have our own specialty, which is worse. Our historical pastime is the direct satisfaction of inflicting pain. There are lines in Nekrassov describing how a peasant lashes a horse on the eyes, 'on its meek eyes,' everyone must have seen it. It's typically Russian. He describes how a feeble little nag had foundered under too heavy a load and could not move. The peasant beats it, beats it savagely, beats it at last not knowing what he is doing in the intoxication of cruelty. He thrashes it mercilessly over and over again. 'However weak you are, you must pull, even if you die doing it.' The nag strains, and then he begins lashing the poor defenseless creature on its weeping, on its 'meek eyes.' The frantic beast tugs and draws the load, trembling all over, gasping for breath, moving sideways, with a sort of unnatural spasmodic action —it's awful. But that's only a horse, and God has given horses to be beaten. So the Tatars have taught us, and they left us the knout as a remembrance of it.

"But men, too, can be beaten. A well-educated, cultured man and his wife beat their own child with a birch rod, a girl of seven. I have an account of it. The father was glad that the birch was covered with twigs. 'It stings more,' said he, and so he began stinging his daughter. I know for a fact that there are people who at every blow are worked up to sensuality, to literal sensuality, which increases progressively at every blow they inflict. They beat for a minute, for five minutes, for ten minutes, more often and more savagely. The child screams. At last the child cannot scream, it gasps, 'Daddy! daddy!' By some diabolical unseemly chance the case was brought into court. A lawyer is engaged. The Russian people have long called a lawyer 'a conscience for hire.' The lawyer protests in his client's defense. 'It's such a simple thing,' he says, 'an everyday occurrence. A father punishes his child. To our shame be it said, it is brought into court.' The jury, convinced by him, give a favorable verdict. The public roars with delight that the torturer is acquitted. Ah, pity I wasn't there! I would have proposed to raise a subscription in his honor! . . . Charming pictures.

"But I've still better things about children. I've collected a great, great deal about Russian children, Alyosha. There was a little girl of five who was hated by her father and mother, 'most worthy and respectable people, of good education and breeding.' You see, I must repeat again, it is a peculiar characteristic of many people, this love of torturing children, and children only. To all other types of humanity these torturers behave mildly and kindly, like cultivated and humane Europeans. But they are very fond of tormenting children. It's just their defenselessness that tempts the tormentor, just the angelic confi-

222

dence of the child who has no refuge and no appeal, that sets the tormentor's vile blood on fire. In every man, of course, a demon lies hidden—the demon of rage, the demon of lustful heat at the screams of the tortured victim, the demon of lawlessness let off the chain, the demon of diseases that follow on vice, gout, kidney disease, and so on.

"This poor child of five was subjected to every possible torture by those cultivated parents. They beat her, kicked her for no reason till her body was one bruise. Then, they went to greater refinements of cruelty—shut her up all night in the cold and frost in a privy, because she didn't ask to be taken up at night (as though a child of five sleeping its sound sleep could be trained to wake and ask), they smeared her face and filled her mouth with excrement. It was her mother, her mother who did this. And that mother could sleep, hearing the poor child's groans! Can you understand why a little creature, who can't even understand what's done to her, should beat her little aching heart with her tiny fist in the dark and the cold, and weep her meek unresentful tears to dear, kind God to protect her? Do you understand that, Alyosha, you pious and humble novice? Do you understand why this infamy must be and is permitted? Without it, I am told, man could not have existed on earth, for he could not have known good and evil. Why should he know that diabolical good and evil when it costs so much? Why, the whole world of knowledge is not worth that child's prayer to 'dear, kind God'! I say nothing of the sufferings of grown-up people, they have eaten the apple, damn them, and the devil take them all! But these little ones! . . . I am making you suffer, Alyosha. I'll stop if you like."

"Never mind. I want to suffer too," muttered Alyosha.

"One picture, only one more, because it's so curious, so characteristic, and I have only just read it in some collection of Russian antiquities. I've forgotten the name. I must look it up. It was in the darkest days of serfdom at the beginning of the century, and long live the Liberator of the People! There was in those days a general of aristocratic connections, the owner of great estates, one of those men—somewhat exceptional, I believe, even then—who, retiring from the service into a life of leisure, are convinced that they've earned absolute power over the lives of their subjects. There were such men then. So our general, settled on his property of two thousand souls, lives in pomp, and dominates his poor neighbors as though they were dependents. He has kennels of hundreds of hounds and nearly a hundred dog-boys—all mounted, and in uniform. One day a serf boy, a little child of eight, threw a stone in play and hurt the paw of the general's favorite hound. 'Why is my favorite dog lame?' He is told that the boy threw a stone that hurt the dog's paw. 'So you did it.' The general looked the child up and down. 'Take him.' He was taken—taken from his mother and kept shut up all night. Early the next morning the general comes out on horseback, with the hounds, his dependents, dog-boys, and huntsmen, all mounted around him in full hunting parade. The servants are summoned for their edification, and in front of them all stands the mother of the child. The child is brought forward. It's a gloomy cold, foggy autumn day, a perfect day for hunting. The general orders the child to be undressed. The child is stripped naked. He shivers, numb with terror, not daring to cry. . . . 'Make him run,' commands the general. 'Run, run!' shout the dog-boys. The boy runs. . . . 'At him!' yells the general, and he sets the whole pack of hounds after the child. The hounds catch him, and tear him to pieces before his mother's eyes! . . . I believe the general was afterwards declared incapable of administering his estates. Well—what did he deserve? To be shot? To be shot for the satisfaction of our moral feelings? Speak, Alyosha!"

"To be shot," murmured Alyosha, lifting his eyes to Ivan with a pale, twisted smile.

"Good!" cried Ivan delighted. "If even you say so . . . You're a pretty monk! So there is a little devil sitting in your heart, Alyosha Karamazov!"

"What I said was absurd, but . . ."

"That's just the point that 'but'!" cried Ivan. "Let me tell you, novice, that the absurd is only too necessary on earth. The world stands on absurdities, and perhaps nothing would have come to pass in it without them. We know what we know!"

"What do you know?"

"I understand nothing," Ivan went on, as though delirious. "I don't want to understand anything now. I want to stick to the facts. I made up my mind long ago not to understand. If I try to understand anything, I will be false to the facts and I have determined to stick to the facts."

"Why are you testing me?" Alyosha cried. "Will you say what you mean?"

"Of course, I will. That's what I've been leading up to. You are dear to me. I don't want to let you go. And I won't give you up to your Zossima."

Ivan was silent for a minute. His face became all at once very sad.

"Listen! I spoke of children only to make my case clearer. Of the other tears of humanity with which the earth is soaked from its crust to its center, I will say nothing. I have narrowed my subject on purpose. And I recognize in all humility that I cannot understand why the world is arranged as it is. Men are themselves to blame, I suppose: they were given paradise, they wanted freedom, and stole fire from heaven, though they knew they would become unhappy. So there is no need to pity them. With my earthly, Euclidian understanding, all I know is that there is suffering and that there are none guilty; that cause follows effect, simply and directly; that everything flows and finds its level—but that's only Euclidian nonsense, I know that, and I can't consent to live by it! What comfort is it to me that there are none guilty and that cause follows effect simply and directly, and that I know it—I must have justice, or I will destroy myself. And not justice in some remote infinite time and space, but here on earth. Justice that I can see myself. I have believed in it. I want to see it. And if I am dead by then, let me rise again, for if it all happens without me, it will be too unfair. Surely I haven't suffered, simply that I, my crimes and my sufferings, may manure the soil of future harmony for somebody else. I want to see with my own eyes the lamb lie down with the lion and the victim rise up and embrace his murderer. I want to be there when everyone suddenly understands what it has all been about. All the religions of the world are built on this longing, and I am a believer.

"But then there are the children, and what am I to do about them? That's a question I can't answer. For the hundredth time I repeat, there are numbers of questions, but I've only taken the children, because in their case what I mean is so unanswerably clear. Listen! If all must suffer to pay for eternal harmony, what have children to do with it? Tell me, please. It's beyond all comprehension why they should suffer and why they should pay for the harmony. Why should they, too, furnish material to enrich the soil for the harmony of the future? I understand solidarity in sin among men. I understand solidarity in retribution, too; but there can be no such solidarity with children. And if it is really true that they must share responsibility for all their fathers' crimes, such a truth is not of this world and is beyond my comprehension. Some jester will say, perhaps, that the child would have grown up and have sinned, but you see he didn't grow up, he was torn to pieces by the dogs, at eight years of age.

"Oh, Alyosha, I am not blaspheming! I understand, of course, what an upheaval of the universe it will be, when everything in heaven and earth blends in one hymn of praise and everything that lives and has lived cries aloud: 'Thou art just, O Lord, for Thy ways are revealed.' When the mother embraces the fiend who threw her child to the dogs, and all three cry aloud with tears, 'Thou art just, O Lord!' then, of course, the crown of knowledge will be reached and all will be made clear. But what troubles me is that I can't accept that harmony. And while I am on earth, I hurry to take my own measures. You see, Alyosha, perhaps it really may happen that if I live to that moment, or rise again to see it, I, too, perhaps, may cry aloud with the rest, looking at the mother embracing the child's torturer: 'Thou art just, O Lord!' But I don't want to cry aloud then. While there is still time, I want to protect myself and so I renounce the higher harmony altogether. It's not worth the tears of that one tortured child who beat itself on the breast with its little fist and prayed in its stinking outhouse, with its tears to 'dear, kind God'! It's not worth it, because those tears are unatoned for. They must be atoned for, or there can be no harmony. But how? How are you going to atone for them? Is it possible? By their being avenged? But what do I care for avenging them? What do I care for a hell for oppressors? What good can hell do, since those children have already been tortured? And what becomes of harmony, if there is hell? I want to forgive. I want to embrace. I don't want more suffering. And if the sufferings of children go to swell the sum of sufferings which was necessary to pay for truth, then I protest that the truth is not worth such a price. I don't want the mother to embrace the oppressor who threw her sons to the dogs! She dare not forgive him! Let her forgive him for herself, if she will. Let her forgive the torturer for the immeasurable suffering of her mother's heart. But the sufferings of her tortured child she has no right to forgive; she dare not forgive the torturer, even if the child were to forgive him! And if that is so, if they dare not forgive, what becomes of harmony? Is there in the whole world a person who would have the right to forgive and could forgive? I don't want harmony. From love for humanity I don't want it. I would rather be left with unavenged suffering. I would rather remain with my unavenged suffering and unsatisfied indignation, *even if I were wrong*. Besides, too high a price is asked for harmony; it's beyond our means to pay so much. And so I give back my entrance ticket, and if I am an honest man I give it back as soon as possible. And that I am doing. It's not God that I don't accept, Alyosha, only I most respectfully return the ticket to Him."

"That's rebellion," murmured Alyosha, looking down.

"Rebellion? I am sorry you call it that," said Ivan earnestly. "One can hardly live in rebellion, and I want to live. Tell me yourself, I challenge you—answer. Imagine that you are creating a fabric of human destiny with the object of making men happy in the end, giving them peace and rest at last. Imagine that you are doing this but that it is essential and inevitable to torture to death only one tiny creature—that child beating its breast with its fist, for instance—in order to found that edifice on its unavenged tears. Would you consent to be the architect on those conditions? Tell me. Tell the truth."

"No, I wouldn't consent," said Alyosha softly.

"And can you accept the idea that the men for whom you are building would agree to receive their happiness from the unatoned blood of a little victim? And accepting it would remain happy forever?"

"No, I can't admit it," said Alyosha suddenly, with flashing eyes. "But, Ivan, you asked just now, is there a person in the whole world who has the right to forgive and can forgive? But there is a Being and He can forgive everything, all and for all, because He gave His innocent blood for all and everything. You have forgotten Him, and on Him is built the edifice, and it is to Him they cry aloud: 'Thou art just, O Lord, for Thy ways are revealed!' "

"Ah! The One without sin and His blood! No, I have not forgotten Him. On the contrary I've been wondering all the time how it was you did not bring Him in before, for usually all arguments on your side put Him in the foreground. Do you know, Alyosha—don't laugh! I wrote a poem about a year ago. If you can waste another ten minutes, I'll tell it to you."

"You wrote a poem?"

"Oh, no, I didn't write it," laughed Ivan. "I've never written two lines of poetry in my life. But I made up this poem in prose and I remember it. I was carried away when I made it up. You will be my first reader—that is, listener. Why should an author forego even one listener?" smiled Ivan. "Shall I tell it to you?"

"Yes. I am listening," said Alyosha.

"My poem is called 'The Grand Inquisitor.' It's a ridiculous thing, but I want to tell it to you."

5. *The Grand Inquisitor*

EVEN THIS MUST HAVE A PREFACE—that is, a literary preface," laughed Ivan, "and I am a poor hand at such things. You see, my story takes place in the sixteenth century. At that time, as you probably learned at school, it was customary in poetry to bring down heavenly powers on earth. Dante was not the only one to do this. In France, clerks, as well as monks in monasteries, used to give regular performances in which the Madonna, the saints, the angels, Christ, and God Himself were brought on the stage. In those days it was done in all simplicity. In Victor Hugo's *Notre Dame de Paris* an edifying and gratuitous spectacle was provided for the people in the Hotel de Ville of Paris in the reign of Louis XI in honor of the birth of the dauphin. It was called 'The good judgment of the very saintly and gracious Virgin Mary,' and she appears herself on the stage and pronounces her 'good judgment.' Similar plays, based on the Old Testament, were occasionally performed in Moscow too, up to the time of Peter the Great. But besides plays there were all sorts of legends and ballads scattered about the world, in which the saints and angels and all the powers of Heaven took part when required.

"In our monasteries the monks busied themselves in translating, copying, and even composing such poems—even under the Tatars. There is, for instance, one such poem (of course, from the Greek), *The Wanderings of Our Lady through Hell*, with descriptions as bold as Dante's. Our Lady visits Hell, and the Archangel Michael leads her through the torments. She sees the sinners and their punishment. There she sees among others a set of sinners in a burning lake. Some of them sink to the bottom of the lake so that they can't swim out, and 'these God forgets'—an expression of extraordinary depth and force. And so Our Lady, shocked and weeping, falls before the throne of God and begs for mercy for all in Hell—for all she has seen there, and indiscriminately. Her conversation with God is most interesting. She begs Him, she will not stop. And when God points to the hands and feet of her Son, nailed to the Cross, and asks: 'How can I forgive His tormentors?' she bids all the saints, all the martyrs, all the angels and archangels to fall down with her and pray for mercy for all without discrimination. It ends by her winning from God a respite of suffering every year from Good Friday till Trinity day. And the sinners at once raise a cry of thankfulness from Hell, chanting: 'Thou art just, O Lord, in this judgment.'

"Well, my poem would have been of that kind if it had appeared at that time. He comes on the scene in my poem, but He says nothing, only appears and passes on. Fifteen centuries have passed since He promised to come in His glory, fifteen centuries since His prophet wrote: 'Behold, I come quickly'; 'Of that day and that hour knoweth no man, neither the Son, but the Father,' as He Himself predicted on earth. But humanity awaits Him with the same faith and with the same love. Oh, with greater faith, for it is fifteen centuries since man has ceased to see signs from Heaven.

> *No signs from Heaven come today*
> *To add to what the heart doth say.*

There was nothing left but faith in what the heart did say. It is true there were many miracles in those days. There were saints who performed miraculous cures; some holy people, according to their biographies, were visited by the Queen of Heaven herself. But the devil did not sleep and doubts were already arising among men about the truth of these miracles. And just then there appeared in the north of Germany a terrible new heresy. 'A huge star like to a torch' (that is, to a church) 'fell on the sources of the waters and they became bitter.' These heretics began blasphemously denying miracles. But those who remained faithful were all the more ardent in their faith. The tears of humanity rose up to Him as before, awaiting His coming, loved Him, hoped for Him, yearned to suffer and die for Him as before. And for so many ages had mankind prayed with faith and fervor: 'O Lord our God, hasten Thy coming,' for so many ages had mankind called upon Him, that in His infinite mercy He at last deigned to come down to His servants.

"It is true that before that day He had come down, He had visited some holy men, martyrs and hermits, as is written in their 'Lives.' Among us, Tyutchev, with absolute faith in the truth of his words, bore witness that

> *Bearing the Cross, in slavish dress*
> *Weary and worn, the Heavenly King*
> *Our mother, Russia, came to bless,*
> *And through our land went wandering.*

And that certainly was so, I assure you.

"And behold, He deigned to appear for a moment to the people, to the tortured, suffering people, sunk in iniquity, but loving Him like children. My story is laid in Spain, in Seville, in the most terrible time of the Inquisition, when fires were lighted every day to the glory of God, and 'in the splendid act of faith the wicked heretics were burnt.' Oh, of course, this was not the coming in which He will appear according to His promise at the end of time in all His heavenly glory, and which will be sudden 'as lightning flashing from east to west.' No, He visited His children only for a moment, and there where the flames were crackling round the heretics. In His infinite mercy He came among men in that human shape in which He walked among men for three years fifteen centuries ago. He came down to the 'hot pavement' of the southern town in which on the day before almost a hundred heretics had, 'for the greater glory of God,' been burned by the cardinal, the Grand Inquisitor, in a magnificent 'act of faith.' They had been burned in the presence of the king, the court, the knights, the cardinals, the most charming ladies of the court, and the whole population of Seville.

"He came softly, unobserved, and yet, strange to say, everyone recognized Him. . . . This might be one of the best passages in the poem. I mean, why they recognized Him. . . . The people are irresistibly drawn to Him, they surround Him, they flock about Him, follow Him. He moves silently in their midst with a gentle smile of infinite compassion. The sun of love burns in His heart, light and power shine from His eyes, and their radiance, shed on the people, stirs their hearts with responsive love. He holds out His hands to them, blesses them, and a healing virtue comes from contact with Him, even with His garments. An old man in the crowd, blind from childhood, cries out: 'O Lord, heal me and I shall see Thee!' And, as it were, scales fall from his eyes and the blind man sees Him. The crowd weeps and kisses the earth under His feet. Children throw flowers before Him, sing, and cry hosannah. 'It is He. It is He!' all repeat. 'It must be He, it can be no one but Him!' He stops at the steps of the Seville cathedral at the moment when the weeping mourners are bringing in a little open white coffin. In it lies a child of seven, the only daughter of a prominent citizen. The dead child lies hidden in flowers. 'He will raise your child,' the crowd shouts to the weeping mother. The priest, coming to meet the coffin, looks perplexed, and frowns, but the mother of the dead child throws herself at His feet with a wail. 'If it is Thou, raise my child!' she cries, holding out her hands to Him. The procession halts, the coffin is laid on the steps at His feet. He looks with compassion, and His lips once more softly pronounce: 'Maiden, arise!' And the maiden arises. The little girl sits up in the coffin and looks around smiling, with wide-open wondering eyes, holding a bunch of white roses they had put in her hand.

"There are cries, sobs, confusion among the people, and at that moment the cardinal himself, the Grand Inquisitor, passes by the cathedral. He is an old man, almost ninety, tall and erect, with a withered face and sunken eyes, in which there is still a gleam of light. He is not dressed in his brilliant cardinal's robes, as he was the day before, when he was burning the enemies of the Roman Church—at this moment he is wearing his coarse, old, monk's cassock. At a distance behind him come his gloomy assistants and slaves and the 'holy guard.' He stops at the sight of the crowd and watches it from a distance. He sees everything; he sees them set the coffin down at His feet, sees the child rise up. His face darkens. He knits his thick gray brows and his eyes gleam with a sinister fire. He holds out his finger and bids his guards arrest Him. And such is his power, so completely are the people cowed into submission and trembling obedience to him, that the crowd immediately makes way for the guards. And in the midst of deathlike silence the guards lay hands on Him and lead Him away. The crowd instantly bows down to the earth, like one man, before the old inquisitor. He blesses the people in silence and passes on.

"The guards lead their Prisoner to the close, gloomy vaulted prison in the ancient palace of the Holy Inquisition and lock Him in it. The day passes and is followed by the dark, burning 'breathless' night of Seville. The air is 'fragrant with laurel and lemon.' In the pitch darkness the iron door of the prison is suddenly opened and the Grand Inquisitor himself comes in with a light in his hand. He is alone. The door is closed at once behind him. He stands in silence and for a minute or two gazes into His face. At last he goes up slowly, sets the light on the table and speaks.

" 'Is it Thou? Thou?' But receiving no answer, he adds at once, 'Don't answer, be silent. What canst Thou say, indeed? I know too well what Thou wouldst say. And Thou hast no right to add anything to what Thou hadst said of old. Why, then, art Thou come to hinder us? For Thou hast come to hinder us, and Thou knowest that. But dost Thou know what will be tomorrow? I know not who Thou art and care not to know whether it is Thou or only a semblance of Him. But tomorrow I shall condemn Thee and burn Thee at the stake as the worst of heretics. And the very people who have today kissed Thy feet, tomorrow at the faintest sign from me will rush to heap up the embers of Thy fire. Knowest Thou that? Yes, maybe

Thou knowest it,' he added with thoughtful penetration, never for a moment taking his eyes off the Prisoner."

"I don't quite understand, Ivan. What does it mean?" Alyosha, who had been listening in silence, asked with a smile. "Is it simply a fantasy, or a mistake on the part of the old man—some impossible mistaken identity?"

"Take it as the last," said Ivan, laughing, "if you are so corrupted by modern realism that you can't stand fantasy. If you like it to be a case of mistaken identity, let it be so. It is true," he went on, laughing, "the old man was ninety, and he might well have been crazy over his set idea. He might have been struck by the appearance of the Prisoner. It might, in fact, be simply his ravings, the delusion of an old man of ninety, over-excited by the 'act of faith' of a hundred heretics the day before. But does it matter to us after all whether it was a mistake of identity or a wild fantasy? All that matters is that the old man should speak out, should speak openly of what he has thought in silence for ninety years."

"And the Prisoner too is silent? Does He look at him and not say a word?"

"That's inevitable," Ivan laughed again. "The old man has told Him He hasn't the right to add anything to what He has said of old. One may say it is the most fundamental feature of Roman Catholicism, in my opinion at least. 'All has been given by Thee to the Pope,' they say. 'And all, therefore, is still in the Pope's hands, and there is no need for Thee to come now at all. Thou must not meddle for the time, at least.' That's how they speak and write too—the Jesuits, at any rate. I have read it myself in the works of their theologians. 'Hast Thou the right to reveal to us one of the mysteries of that world from which Thou hast come?' my old man asks Him, and answers the question for Him. 'No, Thou hast not; that Thou mayest not add to what has been said of old, and mayest not take from men the freedom which Thou didst exalt when Thou wast on earth. Whatsoever Thou revealest anew will encroach on men's freedom of faith; for it will be manifest as a miracle, and the freedom of their faith was dearer to Thee than anything else in those days fifteen hundred years ago. Didst Thou not often say then: "I will make you free"? But now Thou has seen these "free" men,' the old man adds suddenly, with a pensive smile. 'Yes, we've paid dearly for it,' he goes on, looking sternly at Him, 'but at last we have completed that work in Thy name. For fifteen centuries we have been wrestling with Thy freedom, but now it is ended and over for good. Dost Thou not believe that it's over for good? Thou lookest meekly at me and deignest not even to be angry with me. But let me tell Thee that now, today, people are more persuaded than ever that they have perfect freedom, yet they have brought their freedom to us and laid it humbly at our feet. But that has been our doing. Was this what Thou didst? Was this Thy freedom?' "

231

"I don't understand," Alyosha broke in again. "Is he ironical, is he joking?"

"No. Not at all! He claims it as a merit for himself and his Church that at last they have vanquished freedom and have done so to make men happy. 'For now' (he is speaking of the Inquisition, of course) 'for the first time it has become possible to think of the happiness of men. Man was created a rebel; and how can rebels be happy? Thou wast warned,' he says to Him. 'Thou hast had no lack of warnings, but Thou didst not listen to those warnings. Thou didst reject the only way by which men might be made happy. But, fortunately, departing Thou didst hand on the work to us. Thou hast promised, Thou hast established by Thy word, Thou hast given to us the right to bind and to unbind, and now, of course, Thou canst not think of taking it away. Why, then, hast Thou come to hinder us?' "

"And what's the meaning of 'no lack of warnings'?" asked Alyosha.

"Why, that's the chief part of what the old man must say."

" 'The wise and dread Spirit, the spirit of self-destruction and non-existence,' the old man goes on, 'the great spirit talked with Thee in the wilderness, and we are told in the books that he "tempted" Thee. Is that so? And could anything truer be said than what he revealed to Thee in three questions which Thou didst reject, and which in the books is called "the temptation"? And yet if there has ever been on earth a real miracle, it took place on that day, on the day of the three temptations. The statement of those three questions was itself the miracle. . . . Imagine simply for the sake of argument that those three questions of the dread spirit had perished utterly from the books, and that we had to restore them and to invent them anew. To do so we had gathered together all the wise men of the earth—rulers, chief priests, learned men, philosophers, poets—and had set them the task of inventing three questions, such as would not only fit the occasion but express in three words, three human phrases, the whole future history of the world and of humanity. Dost Thou believe that all the wisdom of the earth united could have invented anything in depth and force equal to the three questions which were actually put to Thee then by the wise and mighty spirit in the wilderness? From those questions alone, from the miracle of their statement, we can see that we have here to do not with the fleeting human intelligence, but with the absolute and eternal. For in those three questions the whole subsequent history of mankind is, as it were, brought together into one whole, and foretold. In them are united all the unsolved historical contradictions of human nature. At the time it could not be so clear, since the future was unknown. But now that fifteen hundred years have passed, we see that everything in those three questions was so justly divined and foretold, and has been so truly fulfilled, that nothing can be added to them or taken from them.

" 'Judge Thyself who was right—Thou or he who questioned Thee then? Remember the first question. Its meaning was this: "Thou wouldst go into the world, and art going with empty hands, with some promise of freedom which men in their simplicity and their natural unruliness cannot even understand, which they fear and dread—for nothing has ever been more insupportable for a man and a human society than freedom. But seest Thou these stones in this parched and barren wilderness? Turn them into bread, and mankind will run after Thee like a flock of sheep, grateful and obedient, though forever trembling, lest Thou withdraw Thy hand and deny them Thy bread." But Thou wouldst not deprive man of freedom and didst reject the offer, thinking, what is that freedom worth, if obedience is bought with bread? Thou didst reply that man lives not by bread alone. But dost Thou know that for the sake of that earthly bread the spirit of the earth will rise up against Thee and will strive with Thee and overcome Thee? And all will follow him, crying: "Who can compare with this beast? He has given us fire from heaven!" Dost Thou know that the ages will pass, and humanity will proclaim by the lips of their sages that there is no crime, and therefore no sin; there is only hunger? "Feed men, and then ask of them virtue!" that's what they'll write on the banner, which they will raise against Thee, and with which they will destroy Thy temple. Where Thy temple stood will rise a new building; the terrible tower of Babel will be built again. And though, like the one of old, it will not be finished, yet Thou mightest have prevented that new tower and have cut short the sufferings of men for a thousand years; for they will come back to us after a thousand years of agony with their tower. They will seek us again, hidden underground in the catacombs, for we shall be again persecuted and tortured. They will find us and cry to us: "Feed us, for those who have promised us fire from heaven haven't given it!" And then we shall finish building their tower, for he finishes the building who feeds them. And we alone shall feed them in Thy name, declaring falsely that it is in Thy name. Oh, never, never can they feed themselves without us! No science will give them bread so long as they remain free. In the end they will lay their freedom at our feet, and say to us: "Make us your slaves, but feed us." They will understand at last, that freedom and bread enough for all are inconceivable together. Never, never will they be able to have both together! They will be convinced, too, that they can never be free, for they are weak, vicious, worthless and rebellious.

" 'Thou didst promise them the bread of Heaven, but, I repeat again, can it compare with earthly bread in the eyes of the weak, ever sinful and ignoble race of man? And if for the sake of the bread of Heaven thousands and tens of thousands shall follow Thee, what is to become of the millions and tens of thousands of millions of creatures who will not have the strength to forego the earthly bread for the sake of the heavenly? Or dost Thou care only for the tens of thousands of the great and strong, while the millions, numerous as the sands of the sea, who are weak but love Thee, must exist only for the sake of the great and strong? No, we care for the weak too. They are sinful and rebellious, but in the end they too will become obedient. They will marvel at us and look on us as gods, because we are ready to endure the freedom which they have found so dreadful and to rule over them—so awful it will seem to them to be free. But we shall tell them that we are Thy servants and rule them in Thy name. We shall deceive them again, for we will not let Thee come to us again. That deception will be our suffering, for we shall be forced to lie.

" 'This is the significance of the first question in the wilderness, and this is what Thou hast rejected for the sake of that freedom which Thou hast exalted above everything. Yet in this question lies hidden the great secret of this world. Choosing "bread," Thou wouldst have satisfied the universal and everlasting craving of humanity—to find someone to worship. So long as man remains free he strives for nothing so incessantly and so painfully as to find someone to worship. But man seeks to worship what is established beyond dispute, so that all men would agree at once to worship it. For these pitiful creatures are concerned not only to find what one or the other can worship, but to find something that all would believe in and worship; what is essential is that all may be *together* in it. This craving for *community* of worship is the chief misery of every man individually and of all humanity from the beginning of time. For the sake of common worship they've slain each other with the sword. They have set up gods and challenged one another: "Put away your gods and come and worship ours, or we will kill you and your gods!" And so it will be to the end of the world, even when gods disappear from the earth; they will fall down before idols just the same. Thou didst know, Thou couldst not but have known, this fundamental secret of human nature. But Thou didst reject the one infallible banner which was offered Thee to make all men bow down to Thee alone—the banner of earthly bread. And Thou hast rejected it for the sake of freedom and the bread of Heaven.

" 'Behold what Thou didst further. And again in the name of freedom! I tell Thee that man is tormented by no greater fear than to find someone quickly to whom he can hand over that gift of freedom with which he is born. But only one who can appease his conscience can take over his freedom. In bread there was offered Thee an invincible banner; give bread, and man will worship Thee, for nothing is more certain than bread. But if someone else gains possession of his conscience—oh! then he will cast away Thy bread and follow after him who has ensnared his conscience. In that Thou wast right. For the secret of man's being is not only to live but to have something to live

234

for. Without a stable conception of the object of life, man would not consent to go on living, and would rather destroy himself than remain on earth, though he had bread in abundance. That is true. But what happened? Instead of taking men's freedom from them, Thou didst make it greater than ever! Didst Thou forget that man prefers peace, and even death, to freedom of choice in the knowledge of good and evil? Nothing is more seductive for man than his freedom of conscience, but nothing is a greater cause of suffering. And behold, instead of giving a firm foundation for setting the conscience of man at rest forever, Thou didst choose all that is exceptional, vague and puzzling. Thou didst choose what was utterly beyond the strength of men, acting as though Thou didst not love them at all—Thou who didst come to give Thy life for them! Instead of taking possession of men's freedom, Thou didst increase it, and burdened the spiritual kingdom of mankind with its sufferings forever. Thou didst desire man's free love, that he should follow Thee freely, enticed and taken captive by Thee. In place of the rigid ancient law, man must hereafter with free heart decide for himself what is good and what is evil, having only Thy image before him as his guide. But didst Thou not know he would at last reject even Thy image and Thy truth, if he is weighed down with the fearful burden of free choice? They will cry aloud at last that the truth is not in Thee, for they could not have been left in greater confusion and suffering than Thou hast caused, laying upon them so many cares and unanswerable problems.

" 'So that, in truth, Thou didst Thyself lay the foundation for the destruction of Thy kingdom, and no one is more to blame for it. Yet what was offered Thee?

" 'There are three powers, three powers alone, able to conquer and to hold captive forever the conscience of these impotent rebels for their happiness—those forces are miracle, mystery and authority. Thou hast rejected all three and hast set the example for doing so. When the wise and dread spirit set Thee on the pinnacle of the temple and said to Thee, "if Thou wouldst know whether Thou art the Son of God then cast Thyself down, for it is written: The angels shall hold him up lest he fall and bruise himself, and Thou shalt know then whether Thou art the Son of God and shalt prove then how great is Thy faith in Thy Father." But Thou didst refuse and wouldst not cast Thyself down. Oh! of course, Thou didst proudly and well like God. But the weak, unruly race of men, are they gods? Oh Thou didst know then that in taking one step, in making one movement to cast Thyself down, Thou wouldst be tempting God and have lost all Thy faith in Him, and wouldst have been dashed to pieces against that earth which Thou didst come to save. And the wise spirit that tempted Thee would have rejoiced. But I ask again, are there many like Thee? And couldst Thou believe for one moment that men, too, could face such a temptation? Is the nature of men such, that they can reject miracles and at the great moments of their life, the moments of their deepest, most agonizing spiritual difficulties, cling only to the free verdict of the heart? Oh, Thou didst know that Thy deed would be recorded in books, would be handed down to remote times and the utmost ends of the earth, and Thou didst hope that man, following Thee, would cling to God and not ask for a miracle. But Thou didst not know that when man rejects miracles he rejects God too; for man seeks not so much God as the miraculous. And as man cannot bear to be without the miraculous, he will create new miracles of his own for himself, and will worship deeds of sorcery and witchcraft, though he might be a hundred times over a rebel, heretic and infidel. Thou didst not come down from the Cross when they shouted to Thee, mocking and reviling Thee: "Come down from the cross and we will believe that Thou art He." Thou didst not come down, for again Thou wouldst not enslave man by a miracle, and didst crave faith given freely, not based on miracles.

" 'Thou didst crave for free love and not the base raptures of the slave before the might that has overawed him forever. But Thou didst think too highly of men therein, for they are slaves, of course, though rebellious by nature. Look round and judge; fifteen centuries have passed, look upon them. Whom hast Thou raised up to Thyself? I swear, man is weaker and baser by nature than Thou hast believed him! Can he, can he do what Thou didst? By showing him so much respect, Thou didst, as it were, cease to feel for him, for Thou didst ask far too much from him—Thou who hast loved him more than Thyself! Respecting him less, Thou wouldst have asked less of him. That would have been more like love, for his burden would have been lighter. He is weak and vile. He is weak and vile though he is everywhere now rebelling against our power, and proud of his rebellion! It is the pride of a child and a schoolboy. They are little children rioting and barring out the teacher at school. But their childish delight will end; it will cost them dearly. They will cast down temples and drench the earth with blood. But they will see at last the foolish children that, though they are rebels, they are impotent rebels, unable to keep up their own rebellion. Bathed in their foolish tears, they will recognize at last that He who created them rebels must have meant to mock at them. They will say this in despair, and their utterance will be a blasphemy which will make them more unhappy still, for man's nature cannot bear blasphemy, and in the end always avenges it on itself. And so unrest, confusion and unhappiness—that is the present lot of man after Thou didst bear so much for his freedom!

" 'Thy great prophet tells in vision and in image, that he saw all those who took part in the first resurrection and that there were of each tribe twelve thousand. But if there were so many

236

of them, they must have been not men but gods. They had borne Thy cross, they had endured scores of years in the barren, hungry wilderness, living upon locusts and roots—and Thou mayest indeed point with pride at those children of freedom, of free love, of free and splendid sacrifice for Thy name. But remember that they were only some thousands; and what of the rest? And how are the other weak ones to blame, because they could not endure what the strong have endured? How is the weak soul to blame that it is unable to receive such terrible gifts? Canst Thou have simply come to the elect and for the elect? If so, it is a mystery and we cannot understand it. And if it is a mystery, we too have a right to preach a mystery, and to teach men that it's not the free judgment of their hearts, not love that matters, but a mystery which they must follow blindly, even against their conscience. So we have done. We have corrected Thy work and have founded it upon *miracle, mystery* and *authority*. And men rejoiced that they were again led like sheep, and that the terrible gift that had brought them such suffering, was, at last, lifted from their hearts. Were we right teaching them this? Speak! Did we not love mankind, so meekly acknowledging their feebleness, lovingly lightening their burden, and permitting their weak nature even sin with our sanction? Why hast Thou come now to hinder us? And why dost Thou look silently and searchingly at me with Thy mild eyes? Be angry. I don't want Thy love, for I love Thee not. And what use is it for me to hide anything from Thee? Don't I know to Whom I am speaking? All that I can say is known to Thee already. And is it for me to conceal from Thee our mystery? Perhaps it is Thy will to hear it from my lips. Listen, then. We are not working with Thee, but with *him*—that is our mystery. It's long—eight centuries—since we have been on *his* side and not on Thine.

" 'Just eight centuries ago, we took from *him,* the wise and mighty spirit in the wilderness, what Thou didst reject with scorn, that last gift *he* offered Thee, showing Thee all the kingdoms of the earth. We took from *him* Rome and the sword of Caesar, and proclaimed ourselves sole rulers of the earth, though we have not yet been able to complete our work. But whose fault is that? Oh, the work is only beginning, but it has begun. It has long to await completion and the earth has yet much to suffer, but we shall triumph and shall be Caesars, and then we shall plan the universal happiness of man. But Thou mightest have taken even then the sword of Caesar. Why didst Thou reject that last gift? Had Thou accepted that last offer of the mighty spirit, Thou wouldst have accomplished all that man seeks on earth—that is, someone to worship, someone to keep his conscience, and some means of uniting all in one unanimous and harmonious ant heap, because the craving for universal unity is the third and last anguish of men. Mankind as a whole has always striven to organize a universal state. There have been many great nations with great histories, but the more highly they were developed the more unhappy they were, for they felt more acutely than other people the craving for world-wide union. The great conquerors, Timours and Genghis-Khans, whirled like hurricanes over the face of the earth striving to subdue its people, and they too were but the unconscious expression of the same craving for universal unity. Hadst Thou taken the world and Caesar's purple, Thou wouldst have founded the universal state and have given universal peace. For who can rule men if not he who holds their conscience and their bread in his hands.

" 'We have taken the sword of Caesar, and in taking it, of course, have rejected Thee and followed *him*. Oh, ages are yet to come of the confusion of free thought, of their science and cannibalism. For having begun to build their tower of Babel without us, they will end, of course with cannibalism. But then the beast will crawl to us and lick our feet and spatter them with tears of blood. And we shall sit upon the beast and raise the cup, and on it will be written: "Mystery." But then, and only then, the reign of peace and happiness will come for men. Thou art proud of Thine elect, but Thou hast only the elect, while we give rest to all. And besides, how many of those elect, those mighty ones who could become elect, have grown weary waiting for Thee, and have transferred and will transfer the powers of their spirit and the warmth of their heart to the other camp, and end by raising their *free* banner against Thee? Thou didst Thyself lift up that banner. But with us all will be happy and will no more rebel nor destroy one another as under Thy freedom. Oh, we shall persuade them that they will only become free when they renounce their freedom to us and submit to us. And shall we be right or shall we be lying? They will be convinced that we are right, for they will remember the horrors of slavery and confusion to which Thy freedom brought them. Freedom, free thought and science, will lead them into such straits and will bring them face to face with such marvels and insoluble mysteries, that some of them, the fierce and rebellious, will destroy themselves. Others, rebellious but weak, will destroy one another. The rest, weak and unhappy, will crawl fawning to our feet and whine to us: "Yes, you were right, you alone possess His mystery, and we come back to you. Save us from ourselves!"

" 'Receiving bread from us, they will see clearly that we take the bread made by their hands from them, to give it to them, without any miracle. They will see that we do not change the stones to bread, but in truth they will be more thankful for taking it from our hands than for the bread itself! For they will remember only too well that in old days, without our help, even the bread they made turned to stones in their hands, while since they have come back to us, the very stones have turned to bread in their hands. Too, too well they know the value of

238

complete submission! And until men know that, they will be unhappy. Who is most to blame for their not knowing it? Speak! Who scattered the flock and sent it astray on unknown paths?

" 'But the flock will come together again and will submit once more, and then it will be once and for all. Then we shall give them the quiet humble happiness of weak creatures such as they are by nature. Oh, we shall persuade them at last not to be proud, for Thou didst lift them up and thereby taught them to be proud. We shall show them that they are weak, that they are only pitiful children, but that childlike happiness is the sweetest of all. They will become timid and will look to us and huddle close to us in fear, as chicks to the hen. They will marvel at us and will be awestricken before us, and will be proud at our being so powerful and clever, that we have been able to subdue such a turbulent flock of thousands of millions. They will tremble impotently before our wrath, their minds will grow fearful, they will be quick to shed tears like women and children, but they will be just as ready at a sign from us to pass to laughter and rejoicing, to happy mirth and childish song. Yes, we shall set them to work, but in their leisure hours we shall make their life like a child's game, with children's songs and innocent dance. Oh, we shall allow them even sin, they are weak and helpless, and they will love us like children because we allow them to sin. We shall tell them that every sin will be atoned, if it is done with our permission. We shall tell them that we allow them to sin because we love them, and the punishment for these sins we take upon ourselves. And we shall take it upon ourselves, and they will adore us as their saviour because we have taken on their sins before God. And they will have no secrets from us. We shall allow or forbid them to live with their wives and mistresses, to have or not to have children—according to whether they have been obedient or disobedient—and they will submit to us gladly and cheerfully. The most painful secrets of their conscience, all, all they will bring to us, and we shall have an answer for all. And they will be glad to believe our answer, for it will save them from the great fear and terrible agony they endure at present in making a free decision for themselves. And all will be happy, all the millions of creatures except the hundred thousand who rule over them. For only we, we who guard the mystery, shall be unhappy. There will be thousands of millions of happy ones and a hundred thousand sufferers who have taken upon themselves the curse of the knowledge of good and evil. Peacefully they will die, peacefully in Thy name, and beyond the grave they will find nothing but death. But we shall keep the secret, and for their happiness we shall allure them with the reward of heaven and eternity. Though if there were anything in the other world, it certainly would not be for such as they.

" 'It is prophesied that Thou wilt come again in victory,
239

Thou wilt come with Thy chosen, the proud and strong. But we will say that they have only saved themselves, but we have saved all. We are told that the harlot who sits upon the beast, and holds in her hands the *mystery,* shall be put to shame, that the weak will rise up again, and will rend her royal purple and will strip naked her loathsome body. But then I will stand up and point out to Thee the thousand millions of happy creatures who have known no sin. And we who have taken their sins upon us for their happiness will stand up before Thee and say: "Judge us if Thou canst and darest." Know that I fear Thee not. Know that I too have been in the wilderness, I too have lived on roots and locusts, I too prized the freedom with which Thou hast blessed men, and I too was striving to stand among Thy elect, among the strong and powerful, thirsting "to make up the number." But I awakened and would not serve madness. I turned back and joined the ranks of those *who have corrected Thy work.* I left the proud and went back to the humble, for the happiness of the humble.

" 'What I say to Thee will come to pass, and our dominion will be built up. I repeat, tomorrow Thou shalt see that obedient flock who at a sign from me will hasten to heap up the hot cinders about the pile on which I shall burn Thee for coming to hinder us. For if anyone has ever deserved our fires, it is Thou. Tomorrow I shall burn Thee. . . . I have spoken' "

Ivan stopped. He had been carried away as he talked and spoke with excitement. Now he suddenly smiled.

Alyosha had listened in silence. Toward the end he was greatly moved and seemed several times on the point of interrupting, but he restrained himself. Now his words came with a rush.

"But . . . that's absurd!" he cried. "Your poem is in praise of Jesus, not in blame of Him—as you meant it to be. And who will believe you about freedom? Is that the way to understand it? That's not the idea of it in the Orthodox Church . . . That's Rome, and not even the whole of Rome, it's false—those are the worst Catholics, the Inquisitors, the Jesuits! . . . And there could not be such a fantastic creature as your Inquisitor. What are these sins of mankind they take on themselves? Who are these keepers of the mystery who have taken some curse upon themselves for the happiness of mankind? When have they been seen? We know the Jesuits. They are spoken ill of, but surely they are not what you describe? They are not that at all, not at all. . . . They are simply the Romish army for the earthly sovereignty of the world in the future, with the Pontiff of Rome for Emperor . . . That's their ideal, but there's no sort of mystery about it. . . . It's simple lust for power, for filthy earthly gain, for domination—something like a universal serfdom with them as masters—that's all they sand for. They don't even believe in God perhaps. Your suffering Grand Inquisitor is a mere fantasy."

"Wait, wait," laughed Ivan. "How upset you are! A fantasy you say, let it be so! Of course it's a fantasy. But let me say: do you really think that the Roman Catholic movement of the last centuries is actually nothing but the lust for power, for filthy earthly gain? Is that Father Paissy's teaching?"

"No, no, on the contrary, Father Paissy did once say something rather the same as you . . . But of course it's not the same, not at all the same," Alyosha quickly corrected himself.

"A precious admission, in spite of your 'not at all the same.' I ask you why your Jesuits and Inquisitors have united simply for vile material gain? Why can there not be among them one martyr oppressed by great sorrow and loving humanity? You see, only suppose that there was one such man among all those who desire nothing but filthy material gain—if there's only one like my old Inquisitor, who had himself eaten roots in the desert and made frenzied efforts to subdue his flesh to make himself free and perfect. But yet all his life he loved humanity, and suddenly his eyes were opened, and he saw that it is no great moral blessedness to attain perfection and freedom, if at the same time one gains the conviction that millions of God's creatures have been created as a mockery, that they will never be capable of using their freedom, that these poor rebels can never turn into giants to complete the tower, that it was not for such geese that the great idealist dreamt his dream of harmony. Seeing all that he turned back and joined—the clever people. Surely that could have happened?"

"Joined whom, what clever people?" cried Alyosha, completely carried away. "They have no such great cleverness and no mysteries and secrets. . . . Perhaps nothing but atheism, that's all their secret. Your Inquisitor does not believe in God, that's his secret!"

"What if he doesn't believe in God! At last you have guessed it. It's perfectly true that that's the whole secret. But isn't that suffering, at least for a man like that, who has wasted his whole life in the desert and yet could not shake off his incurable love of humanity? In his old age he reached the clear conviction that nothing but the advice of the great dread spirit could build up any tolerable sort of life for the feeble, unruly 'incomplete, empirical creatures created in jest.' And so, convinced of this, he sees that he must follow the council of the wise spirit, the dread spirit of death and destruction, and accept lying and deception, and lead men consciously to death and destruction. He sees that he must deceive them all the way so that they may not notice where they are being led, that the poor blind creatures may at least on the way think themselves happy. And note, the deception is in the name of Him in whose ideal the old man had so fervently believed all his life. Is not that tragic? And if only one such stood at the head of the whole army 'filled with the lust for power only for the sake of filthy gain'—would not one such be enough to make a tragedy? More than that, one

241

such standing at the head is enough to create the actual leading idea of the Roman Church with all its armies and Jesuits, its highest idea. I tell you frankly that I firmly believe that there has always been such a man among those who stood at the head of the movement. Who knows, there may have been some such even among the Roman Popes. Who knows, perhaps the spirit of that accursed old man who loves mankind so obstinately in his own way, is to be found even now in a whole multitude of such old men, existing not by chance but by agreement. Perhaps these old men formed a secret league long ago for the guarding of the mystery, to guard it from the weak and the unhappy, so as to make them happy. No doubt it is so and so it must be indeed. I believe that even among the Masons there's something of the same mystery and that that's why the Catholics detest the Masons. They feel that the Masons are breaking up the unity of the idea, while it is so essential that there should be one flock and one shepherd. . . . But from the way I defend my idea you might think that I am angry at your criticism. Enough of it."

"Maybe you are a Mason yourself!" said Alyosha suddenly. "You don't believe in God," he added, speaking this time very sorrowfully. He felt that his brother was looking at him ironically. "How does your poem end?" he asked, suddenly looking down. "Or was that the end?"

"I meant to end it like this. When the Inquisitor stopped speaking he waited some time for his Prisoner to answer him. His silence weighed down upon him. He saw that the Prisoner had listened carefully all the time, looking gently in his face. But evidently he did not want to reply. The old man longed for Him to say something, however bitter and terrible. But He suddenly approached the old man in silence and softly kissed him on the forehead. That was his answer. The old man shuddered. His lips moved. He went to the door, opened it and said to Him: 'Go, and come no more. . . . Come not at all, never, never!' And he let Him out into the dark alleys of the town. The Prisoner went away."

"And the old man?"

"The kiss glows in his heart, but the old man holds to his idea."

"And you with him, you too?" cried Alyosha sadly.

Ivan laughed.

"Why, it's all nonsense, Alyosha. It's only a senseless poem of a senseless student, who could never write two lines of verse. Why do you take it so seriously? Surely you don't think I am going straight off to the Jesuits, to join the men who are correcting His work? Good Lord, it's no business of mine. I told you, all I want is to live on to thirty, and then . . . dash the cup to the ground!"

"But the little sticky leaves, and the precious tombs, and the blue sky, and the woman you love! How will you live, how

242

will you love them?" Alyosha asked sorrowfully. "With such a hell in your heart and your head, how can you? No, that's just what you are going away for, to join them . . . if not, you will kill yourself, you can't endure it!"

"There is a strength to endure everything," Ivan said with a cold smile.

"What strength?"

"The strength of the Karamazovs—the strength of the Karamazov baseness."

"To sink into debauchery? To stifle your soul with corruption?"

"Possibly even that . . . only perhaps till I am thirty I will escape it, and then."

"How will you escape it? By what will you escape it? That's impossible with your ideas."

"In the Karamazov way."

" 'Everything is lawful,' you mean? Everything is lawful, is that it?"

Ivan scowled, and all at once turned strangely pale. "Ah, you're repeating yesterday's phrase, which so offended Miusov —and which Dmitri pounced upon so naively and paraphrased!" He smiled queerly. "Yes, if you like, 'everything is lawful' since the word has been said. I won't deny it. And Dmitri's version isn't bad."

Alyosha looked at him in silence.

"I thought that in going away from here I would at least have you," Ivan said suddenly with unexpected feeling. "But now I see that there is no place for me even in your heart, my dear hermit. The formula, 'all is lawful,' I won't renounce. Will you renounce me for that?"

Alyosha got up, went to him and softly kissed him on the forehead.

"That's plagiarism," cried Ivan, highly delighted. "You stole that from my poem. But thank you. Come, Alyosha, it's time we were going, both of us."

They went out, but stopped when they reached the street.

"Listen, Alyosha," Ivan began with determination. "If I am really able to care for the sticky little leaves I will only love them, remembering you. It's enough for me that you are somewhere here, and I won't lose my desire for life yet. Is that enough for you? Take it as a declaration of love if you like. And now you go to the right and I to the left. And it's enough, do you hear, enough. I mean even if I don't go away tomorrow (I think I certainly will go) and we meet again, don't say another word on these subjects. I ask that of you particularly. And about Dmitri too, I ask you specially never to speak to me again," he added, with sudden irritation. "It's all been said—exhausted. It has all been said over and over again, hasn't it? And I'll make you one promise in return. When at thirty, I want to 'dash the cup to the ground,' wherever I may be I'll come to have one more talk with you, even though I have to come from America. You may be sure of that. I'll come. It will be very interesting to have a look at you, to see what you'll be by that time. It's rather a solemn promise. We may be parting now for seven years or ten. Come, go now to your Pater Seraphicus, he is dying. If he dies without you, you will be angry at me for having kept you. Good-by, kiss me once more. That's right. Now go."

Ivan turned suddenly and went his way without looking back. It was just as Dmitri had left Alyosha the day before, though the parting had been very different. The strange resemblance flashed like an arrow through Alyosha's mind in the distress and dejection of that moment. He waited a little, looking after his brother. He noticed that Ivan swayed as he walked and that his right shoulder was lower than his left. He had never noticed it before. Then all at once he turned too, and almost ran to the monastery. It was nearly dark, and he felt almost frightened; something new was growing up in him for which he could not account.

The wind had risen again as on the previous evening, and the ancient pines murmured gloomily about him when he entered the grove close by the hermitage. "Pater Seraphicus—he got that name from somewhere—from where?" Alyosha wondered. "Ivan, poor Ivan. And when will I see you again? . . . Here is the hermitage. Yes, yes, that he is, Pater Seraphicus. He will save me—from him and forever!"

Several times afterwards Alyosha wondered how he could on leaving Ivan so completely forget his brother Dmitri. He had that morning, only a few hours before, so firmly resolved to find him and not to give up doing so, even should he be unable to return to the monastery that night.

6. For a While a Very Obscure One

IVAN, ON LEAVING ALYOSHA, started toward his father's house. He was suddenly depressed. There was nothing strange in his being depressed; what was strange was that Ivan could not have said what was the cause of it. He had often been depressed before, and there was nothing surprising at his feeling so at such a moment. He had broken off with everything that had brought him here, and was preparing to make a new start and enter upon a new, unknown future. He would again be as solitary as ever. And although he had great hopes and great—too great—expectations he could not give any definite account of his hopes, his expectations, or his desires.

Yet at that moment, though the fear of the new and unknown certainly found a place in his heart, what was worrying him was something quite different. "Is it loathing for my father's house?" he wondered. "I am so sick of it. And although it's the last time I will cross its hateful threshold, still I loathe it. . . . No, it's not that either. Is it the parting with Alyosha and the conversation I had with him? For so many years I've been silent with the whole world and have not deigned to speak, and all of a sudden I reel off a rigmarole like that." It might have been the vexation of youthful inexperience and vanity—vexation at having failed to express himself, especially with such a person as Alyosha, on whose understanding he had been counting. No doubt that came in, that vexation. It must have. But yet that was not it. That was not it either. "I feel sick I am so depressed and yet I can't tell what I want. I had better try not to think."

Ivan tried "not to think," but that, too, was of no use. What made his depression so irritating was that it had a kind of casual, external character—he felt that. Someone or something seemed to be standing out somewhere, just as something will occasionally obtrude. And though one may be busy with work or conversation so that for a long time one does not notice it, yet it irritates and almost torments one till at last one realizes what it is, and removes the offending object. It is often quite trifling and ridiculous—some article left in the wrong place, a handkerchief on the floor or a book not replaced on the shelf.

At last, feeling very ill-humored, Ivan arrived home. And suddenly, about fifteen yards from the garden gate, he guessed what was irritating and worrying him. On a bench in the gateway Smerdyakov was sitting, enjoying the coolness of the evening. And at the first glance at him Ivan knew that it was Smerdyakov who was on his mind, and that it was this man that he loathed. It all dawned upon him suddenly.

He remembered that before, when Alyosha had been telling him of his meeting with Smerdyakov, he had felt a sudden twinge of gloom and loathing, which immediately stirred anger in his heart. Afterwards, as he talked, Smerdyakov had been forgotten for the time; but still he had been in his mind, and as soon as Ivan parted from Alyosha and was walking home, the forgotten sensation began to obtrude itself again. "Is it possible that a miserable, contemptible creature like that can worry me so much?" Ivan wondered.

It was true that Ivan had lately come to feel an intense dislike for Smerdyakov, especially during the last few days. He had even begun to notice in himself a growing feeling that was almost hatred for the man. Perhaps this hatred was heightened by the fact that when Ivan first came to his father's house he had felt quite differently. Then he had taken a marked interest in Smerdyakov, and had even thought him very original. He had encouraged him to talk, although he had always wondered at a certain incoherence, or rather restlessness, in his mind, and could not understand what it was that continually and insistently worked upon the brain of "the contemplative." They discussed philosophical questions and even how there could have been light on the first day when the sun, moon, and stars were only created on the fourth day, and how that was to be interpreted. But Ivan soon saw that, though the sun, moon, and stars was an interesting subject, yet for Smerdyakov it was of secondary interest. He seemed to be looking for something altogether different. In one way and another, he began to betray a boundless vanity, and a wounded vanity, too, and that Ivan disliked. This was the first thing that made him dislike Smerdyakov.

Later on, there had been trouble in the house. Grushenka had come on the scene, and there had been the scenes with his brother Dmitri—they discussed that, too. But although Smerdyakov always talked of these things with great excitement, it was impossible to discover what his true feelings were. There was, in fact, something surprising in the incoherence of some of his desires, accidentally betrayed and always vaguely expressed. Smerdyakov was always inquiring, asking certain indirect but obviously premeditated questions. But what his object was he never explained. Usually at the most important moment he would break off and relapse into silence or turn to another subject. But what irritated Ivan most and confirmed his dislike for Smerdyakov was the familiarity which Smerdyakov began to assume. Not that he forgot himself and was rude: on the contrary, he always spoke very respectfully, yet he had obviously begun to consider—goodness knows why—that there was some sort of understanding between them. He always spoke in a tone that suggested that they had some kind of compact, some secret between them, that had at some time been expressed on both sides, only known to them and beyond the comprehension of those around them. But for a long while Ivan did not recognize the real cause of his growing dislike and he had only lately realized what was at the root of it.

With a feeling of disgust and irritation Ivan tried to go through the gate without speaking or looking at Smerdyakov. But Smerdyakov got up from the bench, and from that alone, Ivan knew instantly that he wanted to talk to him. Ivan looked at him and stopped. And the fact that he did stop, instead of passing by, as he meant to, infuriated him. With anger and repulsion he looked at Smerdyakov's emasculate, sickly face, with the little curls combed forward on his forehead.

Smerdyakov winked and grinned as though to say: "Where are you going? You won't pass by; you see that we two clever people have something to say to each other."

"Get away, miserable idiot. What have I to do with you?" was on the tip of Ivan's tongue. But to his surprise he heard himself say instead: "Is my father still asleep, or is he up?"

He asked the question softly and meekly, and at once,

again to his own surprise, sat down on the bench. For a moment he felt almost frightened; he remembered this afterwards. Smerdyakov stood facing him, his hands behind his back, looking at him with assurance and almost severity.

"His honor is still asleep," he said deliberately. ("You were the first to speak, not I," he seemed to say.) "I am surprised at you, sir," he added, after a pause, dropping his eyes affectedly, setting his right foot forward, and playing with the tip of his polished boot.

"Why are you surprised at me?" Ivan asked abruptly and sullenly, doing his best to restrain himself. But he suddenly realized, with disgust, that he was intensely curious and would not, on any account, have gone away.

"Why don't you go to Tchermashnya, sir?" Smerdyakov suddenly raised his eyes and smiled. "Why I smile you must understand, if you are a clever man," he seemed to say.

"Why should I go to Tchermashnya?" Ivan asked in surprise. Smerdyakov was silent.

"Your father has begged you to," he said at last, slowly and apparently attaching no significance to his answer. "I put you off with a secondary reason," he seemed to suggest, "simply to say something."

"Damn you! Speak out!" Ivan cried angrily at last, passing from meekness to violence.

Smerdyakov drew his right foot up to his left, pulled himself up, but still looked at Ivan with the same serenity and the same little smile.

"Substantially nothing—but just by way of conversation."

Another silence followed. They did not speak for nearly a minute. Ivan knew that he ought to get up and be angry. And Smerdyakov stood before him as though waiting to see whether he would be angry or not. Or at least so it seemed to Ivan.

At last Ivan moved to get up. Smerdyakov seized the moment.

"I'm in an awful position, Ivan. I don't know how to help myself," he said firmly and distinctly. Ivan sat down again.

"They are both utterly crazy, they are no better than little children," Smerdyakov went on. "I am speaking of your father and your brother Dmitri. . . . Your father will get up directly and begin worrying: 'Has she come? Why hasn't she come?' and so on up till midnight and even after midnight. And if Grushenka doesn't come (she probably does not mean to come at all) then he will be at me again tomorrow morning: 'Why hasn't she come? When will she come?'—as though I were to blame for it. On the other side it's no better. As soon as it gets dark, or even before, Dmitri will appear with his gun in his hands: 'Look out, you fool, you soup maker. If you miss her and don't let me know she's come—I'll kill you.' When the night's over, in the morning, he, too, like your father, begins worrying me to death. 'Why hasn't she come? Will she come soon?' And he, too, thinks I'm to blame because she hasn't come. And every day and every hour they get angrier and angrier, so that I sometimes think I'll kill myself to escape. I can't stand it, sir."

"Then why did you interfere? Why did you begin to spy for Dmitri?" said Ivan irritably.

"How could I help it? Though I haven't interfered at all, if you want to know the truth. I kept quiet from the very beginning, not daring to answer; but he pitched on me to be his spy. He has had only one thing to say since: 'I'll kill you, you scoundrel, if you miss her.' I feel certain, sir, that I'll have a long fit tomorrow."

"What do you mean by 'a long fit'?"

"A long fit, lasting a long time—several hours, or perhaps a day or two. Once it went on for three days. I fell from the attic that time. The struggling ceased and then began again, and for three days I couldn't come back to my senses. Your father sent for Herzenstube, the doctor, and he put ice on my head and tried something else too. . . . I might have died."

"But they say one can't tell with epilepsy when a fit is coming. What makes you say you will have one tomorrow?" Ivan asked with a peculiar, irritable curiosity.

"That's true. You can't tell beforehand."

"Besides, you fell from the attic then."

"I climb up to the attic every day. I might fall from the attic again tomorrow. Or I might fall down the cellar steps. I have to go into the cellar every day, too."

Ivan took a long look at him.

"You are talking nonsense. I don't quite understand you," he said softly. "Are you planning to pretend to be ill tomorrow and three days after that too?"

Smerdyakov, who was looking at the ground again and playing with the toe of his right foot, grinned and said: "If I were able to play such a trick, that is, pretend to have a fit—and it would not be difficult for a man accustomed to them—I would have a perfect right to do so to save myself from death. For even if Grushenka comes to see your father while I am ill, Dmitri could not blame a sick man for not telling him. He'd be ashamed to."

"Damn it all!" Ivan cried in anger. "Why are you always in such fear for your life? All my brother Dmitri's threats are only wild words and mean nothing. He won't kill you; it's not you he'll kill!"

"He'd kill me first of all, like a fly. But even more than that, I am afraid I'll be taken for an accomplice of his when he does something crazy to your father."

"Why should you be taken for an accomplice?"

"They'll think I am an accomplice, because I let him know the signals as a great secret."

248

"What signals? Whom did you tell? Damn you, speak more plainly."

"I have to admit," Smerdyakov drawled with pedantic composure, "that I have a secret with your father. As you know yourself he has for several days past locked himself in as soon as night or evening comes on. Of late you've been going upstairs to your room early every evening, and yesterday you did not come down at all, so perhaps you don't know how carefully he locks himself in at night. Even if Gregory comes to the door he won't open to him till he hears his voice. But Gregory does not come, because I wait upon him alone in his room now. That's the arrangement he made himself ever since this trouble with Grushenka began. But at night, at his orders, I go away to the lodge. But I don't get to sleep till midnight because I am on the watch, getting up and walking about the yard, waiting for Grushenka to come. For the last few days your father has been perfectly frantic expecting her. What he says is that she is afraid of Dmitri 'and so,' he says, 'she'll come the back way, late at night, to me. You look out for her,' he says, 'till midnight and later; and if she does come, you run up and knock at my door or at the window from the garden. Knock at first twice, rather gently, and then three times more quickly, then,' he says, 'I'll understand at once that she has come, and will open the door to you quietly.' He also gave me another signal in case anything unexpected happens. At first, two knocks, and then, after an interval, another much louder. This will mean that something has happened suddenly and that I must see him. And he will open the door to me so that I can go in and speak to him. That's all in case Grushenka can't come herself, but sends a message. Besides, Dmitri might come, too, so I must let him know he is near. His honor is awfully afraid of Dmitri, so that even if Grushenka had come and were locked in with him, and Dmitri were to turn up, I would have to let him know at once, knocking three times. So that the first signal of five knocks means Grushenka has come, while the second signal of three knocks means 'something important to tell you.' His honor has shown them to me several times and explained them. No one knows of these signals but me and his honor, so he'd open the door without the slightest hesitation and without calling out. He is awfully afraid of calling out aloud. . . . Well, those signals are known to Dmitri too, now."

"How does he know? Did you tell him? How dared you tell him?"

"It was through fear I did it. How could I keep it from him? Dmitri kept at me every day: 'You are deceiving me, you are hiding something from me! I'll break both your legs.' I told him the secret signals so that he would see my devotion. I wanted him to be satisfied that I was not deceiving him, but was telling him all I could."

"If you think that he'll make use of those signals and try to get in, don't let him in."

"But if I am laid up with a fit, how can I prevent him? Even if I dared prevent him, you know how desperate he is."

"Damn it! How can you be so sure you are going to have a fit? How? Are you laughing at me?"

"How could I dare laugh at you? I am in no laughing humor. I'm afraid. I feel I am going to have a fit. I have a presentiment. Fright alone will bring it on."

"Damn it! If you are laid up, Gregory will be on the watch. Let Gregory know beforehand. He will be sure not to let Dmitri in."

"I would never dare to tell Gregory about the signals without orders from my master. And as for Gregory hearing him and not admitting him, he has been ill ever since yesterday, and Marfa intends to give him medicine tomorrow. They've just arranged it. It's a very strange remedy of hers. Marfa knows of a preparation and always has it on hand. It's a strong thing made from some herb. She knows the secret of it, and she always gives it to Gregory three times a year when his lumbago's so bad he is almost paralyzed by it. She takes a towel, wets it with the stuff, and rubs his whole back for half an hour till it's red and swollen, and what's left in the bottle she gives him to drink with a special prayer; but not quite all, for she leaves some for herself, and drinks it. And as they never take strong drink, I assure you they both go to sleep at once and sleep sound a long time. And when Gregory wakes up he is perfectly well, but Marfa always has a headache. So, if Marfa carries out her plan tomorrow, they won't hear anything and they won't stop Dmitri if he comes. They'll be asleep."

"What a story! And it all seems to happen at once, as though it were planned. You'll have a fit and they'll both be unconscious," cried Ivan. "But maybe you are trying to arrange it like that!" Ivan said, suddenly frowning.

"How could I? . . . And why should I, when it all depends on Dmitri and his plans? . . . If he means to do anything he'll do it; but if not, I won't be thrusting him upon your father."

"And why should he go to father, especially if, as you say yourself Grushenka won't come at all?" Ivan went on, turning white with anger. "You said that yourself. And all the time I've been here, I've felt sure it was all the old man's fancy, and that Grushenka won't come to him. Why should Dmitri break in on him if she doesn't come? Tell me. I want to know what you are thinking!"

"You know yourself why he'll come. What's the use of what I think? Dmitri will come simply because he is in a rage or suspicious of my illness perhaps. He'll dash in, as he did yesterday to search the rooms, to see whether she hasn't escaped him. He is perfectly well aware, too, that your father has a big envelope with three thousand roubles in it, tied with a pink rib-

250

bon and sealed with three seals. On it is written in his own hand: 'To my angel Grushenka, when she will come to me.' To which he added three days later, 'for my little chicken.' There's no knowing what that might do."

"Nonsense!" cried Ivan, almost beside himself. "Dmitri won't come to steal money and kill my father to do it. He might have killed him yesterday on account of Grushenka, like the savage fool he is, but he won't steal."

"He is in very great need of money now—the greatest need. You don't know in what need he is," Smerdyakov explained, with perfect composure and remarkable distinctness. "Besides he looks on that three thousand as his own. He said so to me himself. 'My father still owes me just three thousand,' he said. And besides that, Ivan, there is something else. It's as good as certain that Grushenka will force him, if only she cares to, to marry her—the master himself, I mean your father, Fyodor Karamazov—if only she cares to, and of course she may care to. All I've said is that she won't come, but maybe she's looking for more than that—I mean to be mistress here. I know myself that Samsonov, her merchant, was laughing with her about it, telling her quite frankly that it would not be a stupid thing to do. And she's got plenty of sense. She wouldn't marry a beggar like Dmitri. So, taking that into consideration, Ivan, remember that neither Dmitri nor yourself nor your brother, Alyosha, would have anything after the master's death. Not a rouble. Grushenka would marry him simply to get hold of all the money there is. But if your father were to die now, there'd be forty thousand for sure. There would be some even for Dmitri whom he hates so because he's made no will. . . . Dmitri knows all that very well."

A sort of shudder passed over Ivan's face. He flushed.

"Then why on earth," he suddenly interrupted Smerdyakov, "do you advise me to go to Tchermashnya? What did you mean by that? If I go away, you see what will happen here." Ivan drew his breath with difficulty.

"Precisely so," said Smerdyakov, softly and reasonably, watching Ivan intently.

"What do you mean by 'precisely so'?" Ivan questioned him, restraining himself with difficulty.

"I spoke because I felt sorry for you. If I were in your place I would simply give it all up . . . rather than stay on in such a position," answered Smerdyakov, with the most candid air looking at Ivan. They were both silent.

"You seem to be a perfect idiot, and what's more . . . an awful scoundrel." Ivan got up suddenly from the bench. He was about to pass through the gate but he stopped short and turned to Smerdyakov. He bit his lip, clenched his fists, and, in another minute, would have flung himself on him. But Smerdyakov shrank back. The moment passed without harm to Smerdyakov, and Ivan turned in silence toward the gate.

251

"I am going to Moscow tomorrow, if you care to know—early tomorrow morning. That's all!" he suddenly said aloud in anger. He wondered afterwards what need there had been to say this to Smerdyakov.

"That's the best thing you can do," Smerdyakov replied as though he had expected to hear it. "Except that you can always be reached by telegraph in Moscow, if anything should happen here."

Ivan stopped again and turned quickly to Smerdyakov. But a change had passed over him, too. All Smerdyakov's familiarity and carelessness had completely disappeared. His face expressed attention and expectation, intent but timid and cringing. "Haven't you something more to say—something to add?" could be read in the intent gaze he fixed on Ivan.

"And couldn't I be reached in Tchermashnya, too—in case anything happened?" Ivan shouted suddenly raising his voice.

"From Tchermashnya, too . . . you could be sent for," Smerdyakov muttered, almost in a whisper, looking disconcerted, but gazing intently into Ivan's eyes.

"Only Moscow is further and Tchermashnya is nearer. Is it to save my spending money on the fare, or to save my going so far out of my way, that you insist on Tchermashnya?"

"Precisely so . . ." muttered Smerdyakov, with a breaking voice. He looked at Ivan with a revolting smile, and again started to draw back. But to his astonishment Ivan broke into a laugh, and went through the gate still laughing.

Anyone looking at Ivan's face at that moment would have known that he was not laughing from lightness of heart. But he could not have explained what he was feeling at that moment. He moved and walked as though in a frenzy.

7. *"It's Always Worth While Speaking to a Clever Man"*

AND IN THE SAME FRENZY, TOO, Ivan spoke. Meeting his father in the drawing room he shouted to him, waving his hand: "I am going upstairs to my room. Good-by!" and he passed by, trying not even to look at the old man. Very possibly the old man was too hateful to him at that moment; but such display of hostility was a surprise even to Fyodor Karamazov. And the old man evidently wanted to tell Ivan something and had come to meet him in the drawing room on purpose. Receiving this strange greeting, he stood in silence and watched his son going upstairs, till he passed out of sight.

"What's the matter with him?" he promptly asked Smerdyakov, who had followed Ivan into the house.

"Angry about something. Who can tell?" the valet muttered evasively.

"Confound him! Let him be angry then. Bring in the samovar, and hurry. Look sharp! No news?"

Then followed a series of questions such as Smerdyakov had just complained of to Ivan, all relating to his expected visitor. Half an hour later the house was locked and the crazy old man was wandering alone through the rooms in expectation of hearing every minute the five knocks agreed upon. Now and then he peered out into the darkness, seeing nothing.

It was very late, but Ivan was still awake and thinking. He sat up late that night, until two o'clock. But we will not give an account of his thoughts, and this is not the place to look into that soul—its turn will come. And even if one tried, it would be very hard to give a true account, for there were no thoughts in Ivan's mind but something very vague. He felt that he had lost his bearings. He was worried, too, by all sorts of strange and almost surprising desires. For instance, after midnight he suddenly had an intense irresistible inclination to go down, open the door, go to the lodge and beat Smerdyakov. But if he had been asked why, he could not have given any exact reason, except perhaps that he loathed the valet as one who had insulted him more seriously than anyone else in the world. On the other hand, he was more than once that night overcome by a sort of humiliating terror, which he felt paralyzed him. His head ached and he was dizzy. A feeling of hatred was rankling in his heart, as though he meant to avenge himself on someone. He even hated Alyosha, recalling the conversation he had just had with him. At moments he hated himself. Of Katerina he almost forgot to think, and he wondered at this afterwards, especially as he remembered perfectly that when he had protested so valiantly to Katerina that he would go away next day to Moscow, something had whispered in his heart: "That's nonsense, you are not going, and it won't be so easy to tear yourself away as you are saying now."

Remembering that night long afterwards, Ivan recalled with peculiar repulsion how he had suddenly got up and stealthily, as though he were afraid of being watched, had opened the door, gone out on the staircase and listened to his father stirring down below. He had listened a long while—some five minutes—with a sort of strange curiosity, holding his breath while his heart throbbed. And why he had done all this, why he was listening, he could not have said. That "action" all his life afterwards he called "infamous," and at the bottom of his heart, he thought of it as the basest action of his life. He felt no hatred for his father at that moment but was simply curious to know why he was walking around down there below and what he was doing. He imagined how the old man must be looking out of the dark windows and stopping in the middle of the room, listening, listening—for someone to knock. Ivan went out onto the stairs twice to listen like this.

About two o'clock when everything was quiet and his father had gone to bed, Ivan finally got into bed. He was determined to fall asleep at once. And he did fall asleep at once, and slept soundly without dreams.

He woke early, at seven o'clock. It was broad daylight. Opening his eyes, he was surprised to feel so rested. He jumped up and dressed quickly; then dragged out his trunk and began packing. His linen had come back from the laundress the previous morning; he smiled at the thought that everything was helping his sudden departure. And his departure certainly was sudden. Though Ivan had said the day before (to Katerina, Alyosha, and Smerdyakov) that he was leaving next day, yet he remembered that he had no thought of leaving when he went to bed or at least, had not dreamed that his first act in the morning would be to pack his trunk.

At last his trunk and bag were ready. And it was about nine o'clock when Marfa came in with her usual question: "Where will your honor take your tea, in your own room or downstairs?" He looked almost cheerful, but there was about him, about his words and gestures, something hurried and scattered. A few minutes later greeting his father warmly and inquiring specially after his health, though he did not wait to hear his answer to the end, he announced that he was starting off in an hour to return to Moscow for good. And he begged his father to send for the horses.

His father heard this announcement with no sign of surprise, and forgot in an unmannerly way to show regret at losing him. Instead of doing so, he went into a great state at the recollection of some important business of his own.

"What a son you are! Not to tell me yesterday! Never mind. We'll manage all the same. Do me a great service, my dear boy. Go to Tchermashnya on the way. It's only a turn to the left from the station at Volovya, only another twelve miles and you come to Tchermashnya."

"I'm sorry, I can't. It's eighty miles to the railroad and the train starts for Moscow at seven o'clock tonight. I can only just make it."

"You'll make it tomorrow or the day after, but today turn off and go to Tchermashnya. It won't hold you up much to humor your father! If I hadn't had something to keep me here, I would have run over myself long ago because I've some business there. But here I . . . it's not the time for me to go now . . . You see, I've two pieces of woodland there. The Maslovs, an old merchant and his son, will give eight thousand for the timber. Last year I just missed a buyer who would have given twelve. There's no one around here who'll buy it. The Maslovs have it all their own way. One has to take what they'll give because no one around here dares bid against them. The priest at

Ilyinskoe wrote to me last Thursday that a merchant called Gorstkin, a man I know, had turned up. What makes him valuable is that he is not from these parts, so he is not afraid of the Maslovs. He says he will give me eleven thousand for the timber. Do you hear? But he'll only be there, the priest writes, for a week altogether, so you must go at once and make a deal with him."

"Well, you write to the priest. He'll make the deal."

"He can't do it. He has no eye for business. He is a wonderful man. I'd give him twenty thousand to take care of me without a receipt. But he has no eye for business. He is a perfect child, a crow could deceive him. And yet he is a learned man, would you believe it? This Gorstkin looks like a peasant, he wears a blue kaftan, but he is a regular thief. That's the common complaint. He is a liar. Sometimes he tells such lies that you wonder why he is doing it. He told me the year before last that his wife was dead and that he had married another woman. And would you believe it, there was not a word of truth in it? His wife has never died at all, she is alive to this day and gives him a beating twice a week. So what you have to find out is whether he is lying or speaking the truth, when he says he wants to buy it and would give eleven thousand."

"I can't help you in such a business. I have no eye either."

"Wait. Wait a minute! You will be of use because I will tell you the signs by which you can judge Gorstkin. I've done business with him a long time. You see, you must watch his beard; he has a nasty, thin, red beard. If his beard shakes when he talks and he gets cross, it's all right, he is saying what he means, he wants to do business. But if he strokes his beard with his left hand and grins—he is trying to cheat you. Don't watch his eyes, you won't find out anything from his eyes. He is a deep one, a rogue—but watch his beard! I'll give you a note and you show it to him. He's called Gorstkin, though his real name is Lyagavy (Setter-dog). But don't call him that, he will be offended. If you come to an understanding with him, and see it's all right, write at once. You need only write: 'He's not lying.' Stand out for eleven thousand; one thousand you can knock off, but not more. Just think! There's a difference between eight thousand and eleven thousand. It's as good as picking up three thousand. It's not so easy to find a buyer and I'm in desperate need of money. Only let me know that he's serious, and I'll run over and fix it up. I'll find the time somehow. But what's the good of my galloping there if it's not a real offer? Come, will you go?"

"Oh, I can't spare the time. You must excuse me."

"You might oblige your father. I won't forget it. You've no heart, any of you—that's what it is! What's a day or two to you? Where are you going now—to Venice? Your Venice will keep another two days. I would have sent Alyosha, but what use is Alyosha in a thing like this? I send you because you are a clever fellow. Do you think I don't see that? You know nothing about timber, but you've got an eye. All that is wanted is to see whether the man is in earnest. I tell you, watch his beard —if his beard shakes you know he is in earnest."

"You force me to go to that damned Tchermashnya!" cried Ivan, with a malignant smile.

His father did not catch, or would not catch, the malignancy, but he caught the smile.

"Then you'll go, you'll go? I'll scribble the note for you at once."

"I don't know whether I'll go. I don't know. I'll decide on the way."

"Nonsense! Decide now. My dear fellow, decide! If you settle the matter, write me a line; give it to the priest and he'll send it on to me at once. And I won't delay you more than that. You can go to Venice. The priest will give you horses back to the Volovya station."

The old man was delighted. He wrote the note, and sent for the horses. A light lunch was brought in with brandy. When Fyodor Karamazov was pleased, he usually became expansive, but today he seemed to restrain himself. Of Dmitri, for instance, he did not say a word. He was quite unmoved by the parting, and seemed, in fact, at a loss for something to say. Ivan noticed this particularly. "He must be bored with me," he thought. Only when accompanying his son out onto the steps did the old man begin to fuss. He wanted to kiss him, but Ivan held out his hand, obviously avoiding the kiss. His father saw this at once and drew back.

"Well, good luck to you. Good luck to you!" he repeated from the steps. "You'll come again some time or other? Be sure to come. I shall always be glad to see you. Well, Christ be with you!"

Ivan got into the carriage.

"Good-by, Ivan! Don't be too hard on me!" the father called for the last time.

The whole household came out to say good-by—Smerdyakov, Marfa and Gregory. Ivan gave them ten roubles each. And when he had seated himself in the carriage, Smerdyakov jumped up to arrange the rug.

"You see . . . I am going to Tchermashnya after all," said Ivan suddenly. Again, as the day before, the words seemed to drop of themselves. And he laughed a peculiar nervous laugh. He remembered it long after.

"It's a true saying then, that 'it's always worth while speaking to a clever man,'" answered Smerdyakov firmly, looking significantly at Ivan.

The carriage rolled away.

Nothing was clear in Ivan's soul, but he looked eagerly around him at the fields, at the hills, at the trees, at a flock of geese flying high overhead in the bright sky. And all of a sudden he felt very happy. He tried to talk to the driver, and he felt intensely interested in an answer the peasant gave him. But a minute later he realized that he was not catching anything, and that he had not really even taken in the peasant's answer. He was silent, and it was pleasant even so. The air was fresh, pure and cool, the sky bright. Images of Alyosha and Katerina floated into his mind. But he smiled, blew softly on the friendly phantoms, and they flew away. "There's plenty of time for them," he thought.

His carriage reached the station quickly. They changed horses, and galloped to Volovya. "Why is it worth while speaking to a clever man? What did Smerdyakov mean by that?" The thought seemed suddenly to clutch at his breathing. "And why did I tell him I was going to Tchermashnya?" They reached Volovya Station. Ivan got out of the carriage. The local drivers stood around him bargaining over the journey of twelve miles to Tchermashnya. He told them to harness the horses. He went into the station house, looked around, glanced at the station master's wife, and suddenly went outside again.

"I won't go to Tchermashnya. Am I too late to reach the train by seven?"

"We can just make it. Shall we get the carriage out?"

"At once. Will any one of you be going to the town tomorrow?"

"To be sure. I will," said one of the drivers.

"Can you do me a service? Go to my father's, to Fyodor Karamazov, and tell him I haven't gone to Tchermashnya. Can you?"

"Of course I can. I've known Fyodor Karamazov a long time."

"And here's something for you, for I'm sure he won't give you anything," said Ivan, laughing.

"You may depend on it he won't." The driver laughed too. "Thank you, sir, I'll be sure to do it."

At seven o'clock Ivan got into the train and set off for Moscow. "Away with the past. I'm through with the old world forever, and I hope I have no news, no echo, from it. To a new life, new places, and no looking back!" But instead of delight his soul was filled with such gloom, and his heart ached with such anguish, as he had never known in his life before. He was thinking all night. The train flew on. And only at daybreak, when he was approaching Moscow, did he suddenly rouse himself from his meditation.

"I am base," he whispered to himself.

Fyodor Karamazov remained well satisfied at having seen his son off. For two hours afterwards he felt almost happy, and sat drinking brandy. But suddenly something happened which was very annoying and unpleasant for everyone in the house, and completely upset the old man. Smerdyakov went to the cellar for something and fell down from the top of the steps. Fortunately, Marfa was in the yard and heard him. She did not see the fall, but heard his scream—the strange, peculiar scream, long familiar to her—the scream of the epileptic falling in a fit.

They could not tell whether the fit had come upon him at the moment he was descending the steps, so that he must have fallen unconscious, or whether it was the fall and the shock that had caused the fit. They found him at the bottom of the cellar steps writhing in convulsions and foaming at the mouth. It was thought at first that he must have broken something—an arm or a leg—and hurt himself, but "God had preserved him," as Marfa expressed it—nothing of the kind had happened. But it was difficult to get him out of the cellar. They asked the neighbors to help and managed it somehow. Fyodor Karamazov himself was present the whole time. He helped, evidently alarmed and upset.

Smerdyakov did not regain consciousness. The convulsions stopped for a time, but then began again. And everyone concluded that the same thing would happen, as had happened a year before, when he accidentally fell from the attic. They remembered that ice had been put on his head then. There was still ice in the cellar, and Marfa brought some up.

In the evening the old Karamazov sent for Doctor Herzenstube. After careful examination, he concluded that the fit was a very violent one and might have serious consequences; that meanwhile he, Herzenstube, did not fully understand it, but that by the following morning, if the remedies were not working, he would venture to try something else. Smerdyakov was then taken to the lodge, to a room next to Gregory's and Marfa's.

After this Fyodor Karamazov had one misfortune after another to put up with that day. Marfa cooked the dinner, and the soup, compared with Smerdyakov's, was no "better than dish water," and the chicken was so dried up that it was impossible to chew it. To her master's bitter though deserved, reproaches, Marfa replied that the chicken was a very old one to begin with, and that she had never been trained as a cook. In the evening there was another trouble in store for Fyodor Karamazov; he was informed that Gregory, who had not been well for the last three days, was completely laid up with lumbago.

Fyodor Karamazov finished his tea as early as possible and locked himself up alone in the house. He was in a state of high excitement and suspense. That evening he counted on Grushenka's coming almost as a certainty. Smerdyakov had told him that morning "that she had promised to come without fail." The old man's heart throbbed with excitement; he paced up and down his rooms listening. He had to be on the alert. Dmitri might be on the watch for her somewhere, and when she knocked on the window (Smerdyakov had told him two days before that he had told her where and how to knock) the door must be opened at once. She must not be a second in the passage, for fear—God forbid!—that she should be frightened and run away.

Fyodor Karamazov had much to think of that night, but never had his heart been steeped in such voluptuous hopes. This time he could say almost certainly that Grushenka would come!

BOOK VI: THE RUSSIAN MONK

1. Father Zossima and His Visitors

WITH AN ANXIOUS AND ACHING HEART Alyosha went into Father Zossima's cell. He had feared to find his elder dying, perhaps unconscious, and he was surprised to see him sitting up in his chair instead. Though weak and exhausted, his face was bright and cheerful. He was surrounded by visitors and engaged in a quiet and pleasant conversation.

He had gotten up from his bed a quarter of an hour before Alyosha's return. His visitors had gathered together in his cell earlier, waiting for him to wake, having received assurance from Father Paissy that "the teacher would get up, and as he had himself promised in the morning, converse once more with those dear to his heart." Father Paissy put implicit trust in this promise as he did in every word of the dying elder. If he had seen him unconscious, if he had seen him breathe his last, and yet had his promise that he would rise up and say good-by to him, he would not have believed perhaps even in death, but would still have expected the dead man to recover and fulfill his promise. In the morning as he lay down to sleep, Father Zossima had told him: "I shall not die without the pleasure of another conversation with all of you, beloved of my heart. I shall look once more on your dear faces and pour out my heart to you once again."

The monks, who had gathered for this last conversation with Father Zossima, had all been his devoted friends for many years. There were four of them; Father Joseph and Father Paissy, Father Michael, the warden of the hermitage, a man not very old and far from being learned. He was of humble origin, of strong will and steadfast faith, of austere appearance, but of deep tenderness, though he concealed it as though he were almost ashamed of it. The fourth, Father Anfim, was a very old and humble little monk of the poorest peasant class. He was almost illiterate, and very quiet, scarcely speaking to anyone. He was the humblest of the humble, and looked as though he had been frightened by something great and awful beyond the scope of his intelligence. Father Zossima had a great affection for this timid man and always treated him with marked respect, though there was no one to whom he had said less, in spite of the fact that he had spent years wandering about holy Russia with him. That was very long ago, forty years before, when Father Zossima first began his life as a monk in a poor and little monastery at Kostroma. He and Father Anfim had gone on a pilgrimage to collect alms for their poor monastery.

These four monks were in the bedroom which was very small. There was scarcely room for them (in addition to Porfiry, the novice, who stood) to sit round Father Zossima on chairs brought from the sitting room. It was already beginning to get dark. The room was lighted up by the lamps and the candles before the ikons.

Seeing Alyosha standing embarrassed in the doorway, Father Zossima smiled at him and held out his hand.

"Welcome, my quiet one. Welcome, my dear. Here you are too. I knew you would come."

Alyosha went up to him, bowed down before him to the ground and wept. Something surged up from his heart, his soul was quivering, he wanted to sob.

"Come, don't weep over me yet," Father Zossima said laying his right hand on Alyosha's head. "You see I am sitting up talking; maybe I shall live another twenty years, as that dear good woman from Vishegorye, with her little girl in her arms, wished me yesterday. God bless the mother and the little girl." He crossed himself. "Porfiry, did you take her offering where I told you?"

Father Zossima meant the sixty pennies brought him the day before by the good-humored woman to be given "to someone poorer than me." Such offerings, always of money gained by personal toil, are made by way of penance voluntarily undertaken. The elder had sent Porfiry the evening before to a widow, whose house had been burned down and who after the fire had gone with her children begging alms. Porfiry replied that he had given the money, as he had been instructed, from an unknown benefactress.

"Get up, my dear boy," the elder went on to Alyosha. "Let me look at you. Have you been home and seen your brother?" It seemed strange to Alyosha that his elder should ask so confidently and precisely about one of his brothers only—but which one? Perhaps he had sent him out both yesterday and today for the sake of that brother?

"I have seen one of my brothers," answered Alyosha.

"I mean the elder one, to whom I bowed down."

"I saw him yesterday but could not find him today," said Alyosha.

"Make haste to find him, go again tomorrow and make haste,

leave everything and make haste. Perhaps you may still have time to prevent something terrible. I bowed down yesterday to the great suffering in store for him."

He was suddenly silent. His words were strange. Father Joseph, who had witnessed the scene yesterday, exchanged glances with Father Paissy.

Alyosha could not help asking: "Father and teacher, your words are obscure. . . . What is this suffering in store for him?" His voice trembled with emotion.

"Do not inquire. I seemed to see something terrible yesterday . . . as though his whole future were expressed in his eyes. A look came into his eyes—so that I was instantly horror-stricken at what that man is preparing for himself. Once or twice in my life I've seen such a look in a man's face . . . reflecting as it were his future fate, and that fate, alas, came to pass. I sent you to him, Alyosha, for I thought you could help him. But everything and all our fates are from the Lord. 'Except a grain of wheat fall into the ground and die, it abideth alone; but if it die, it bringeth forth much fruit.' Remember that. You, Alyosha, I've many times silently blessed, know that," added the elder with a gentle smile. "This is what I think of you: you will go forth from these walls, but will live like a monk in the world. You will have many enemies, but even your foes will love you. Life will bring you many misfortunes, but you will find your happiness in them, and will bless life and will make others bless it—which is what matters most. Well, that is your character. . . . Fathers and teachers," he addressed those gathered about him with a tender smile: "I have never till today told even him why the face of this youth is so dear to me. Now I will tell you. His face has been as it were a remembrance and a prophecy for me. At the dawn of my life when I was a child I had an elder brother who died before my eyes at seventeen. And later on in the course of my life I gradually became convinced that that brother had been for a guidance and a sign from on high for me. For had he not come into my life, I should never perhaps, so I believe at least, have become a monk and entered on this precious path. He appeared first to me in my childhood and here at the end of my pilgrimage, he seems to have come to me again. It is marvelous, fathers and teachers, that Alyosha, who has some, though not a great, resemblance in face, seems to me so like him spiritually, that many times I have taken him for that young man, my brother, mysteriously come back to me as a reminder and an inspiration. I wondered at so strange a dream in myself. Do you hear this, Porfiry?" He turned to the novice who waited on him. "Many times I've seen in your face as it were a look of mortification that I love Alyosha more than you. Now you know why that was so. But I love you too. Know that. And many times I grieved at your mortification. . . . I should like to tell you, dear friends, of that youth, my brother, for there has been no presence in my life more precious, more significant and touching. My heart is full of tenderness, and I look at my whole life at this moment as though living through it again."

Here I must observe that this last conversation of Father Zossima with the friends who visited him on the last day of his life has been partly preserved in writing. Alyosha wrote it down from memory, some time after his elder's death. But whether he recorded only the conversation that took place that evening, or whether he added parts of former conversations with his teacher, I cannot say. In his account, Father Zossima's talk goes on without interruption, as though he told his life to his friends in the form of a story, though there is no doubt, from other accounts of it, that the conversation that evening was general. Though the guests did not interrupt Father Zossima often, yet they too talked. Besides, Father Zossima could not have carried on an uninterrupted narrative, for he was sometimes gasping for breath, his voice failed him, and he even lay down to rest on his bed, though he did not fall asleep and his visitors did not leave their seats. Once or twice the conversation was interrupted by Father Paissy's reading the Gospel. It is worthy of note, too, that not one of those present believed that Father Zossima would die that night, for on that evening of his life after his deep sleep in the day he seemed suddenly to have found new strength. It was like a last effort of love which gave him energy; only for a little time, however, for his life was cut short immediately. . . . But of that later. I will only add now that I have preferred to confine myself to the account given by Alyosha. It will be shorter and not so tiring. I must, of course, repeat that Alyosha probably took a great deal from previous conversations and added them to it.

NOTES OF THE LIFE OF THE DECEASED PRIEST AND MONK, THE ELDER ZOSSIMA, TAKEN FROM HIS OWN WORDS BY ALEXEY KARAMAZOV.

BIOGRAPHICAL NOTES

(a) *Father Zossima's Brother*

Beloved fathers and teachers, I was born in a distant province in the north, in the town of V. My father was a gentleman by birth, but of no great consequence or position. He died when I was only two years old, and I don't remember him at all. He left my mother a small house built of wood, and a fortune, not large, but sufficient to keep her and her children in comfort. There were two of us, my elder brother Markel and I. He was eight years older than I was, of irritable temperament, but kind-hearted and never ironical. He was remarkably silent, especially at home with me, our mother, and the servants. He did well at school, but did not get on with his school-fellows, though he never quarreled, at least so my mother told me. Six months before his death, when he was seventeen, he made friends with a political exile who had been banished from Moscow to our town for freethinking, and led a solitary existence there. This man was a scholar who had gained distinction in philosophy. Something attracted him to Markel and he used to come to see him. He spent whole evenings with my brother during that winter, until he was summoned to Petersburg to take up his post again. He had powerful friends.

It was the beginning of Lent, and Markel would not fast, he was rude and laughed at it. "That's all silly and there is no God," he said, horrifying my mother, the servants, and me too. For though I was only nine, I was aghast at hearing such words. We had four servants, all serfs. I remember my mother selling one of the four, the cook, who was lame and elderly, for sixty paper roubles, and hiring a free servant to take her place.

In the sixth week in Lent, my brother, who was never strong and had a tendency to consumption, was taken ill. He was tall, thin and delicate looking, but of very pleasing countenance. I suppose he caught cold. Anyway the doctor, who came, whispered to my mother that it was galloping consumption and that he would not live through the spring. My mother began weeping, and careful not to alarm my brother she entreated him to go to church, to confess and take the sacrament, as he was still able to move about. This made him angry, and he said something profane about the church. He grew thoughtful, however; he guessed at once that he was seriously ill, and that that was why mother was begging him to confess and take the sacrament. He had been aware, indeed, for a long time past, that he was far from well, and had a year before coolly observed at dinner to our mother and me: "My life won't be long among you, I may not live another year," which seemed now like a prophecy.

Three days passed and Holy Week came. And on Tuesday morning my brother began going to church. "I am doing this simply for your sake, mother, to please and comfort you," he said. My mother wept with joy and grief. "His end must be near," she thought, "if there's such a change in him." But he was not able to go to church long. He took to his bed. After that he had to confess and take the sacrament at home.

It was a late Easter, and the days were bright, fine, and full of fragrance. I remember he used to cough all night and sleep badly, but in the morning he dressed and tried to sit up in an arm chair. That's how I remember him sitting, sweet and gentle, smiling, his face bright and joyous, in spite of his illness. A marvelous change passed over him, his spirit seemed transformed. The old nurse would come in and say: "Let me light the lamp before the holy image, my dear." Before this he would not have allowed it and would have blown it out.

"Light it, light it, dear nurse. I was a wretch to have prevented you doing so before. You pray when you light the lamp, and I pray when I see you. So we are praying to the same God."

Those words seemed strange to us, and mother went to her room and wept. But when she returned to him she wiped her eyes and looked cheerful. "Mother, don't weep, darling," he said. "I've long to live yet, long to rejoice with you, and life is glad and joyful."

"Ah, dear boy, how can you talk of joy when you lie feverish at night, coughing as though you would tear yourself to pieces."

"Don't cry, mother," he answered. "Life is paradise, and we are all in paradise, but we refuse to see it. If we would, we should have heaven on earth the next day."

Everyone wondered at his words, he spoke so strangely. We were all touched and wept.

Friends came to see us. "Dear ones," he would say to them, "what have I done that you should love me so. How can you love anyone like me, and how was it I did not know, I did not appreciate it before?"

When the servants came in to him he would say continually: "Dear, kind people, why are you doing so much for me, do I deserve to be waited on? If it were God's will for me to live, I would wait on you, for all men should wait on one another."

Mother shook her head as she listened. "My darling, it's your illness that makes you talk like that."

"Mother darling," he would say, "there must be servants and masters, but if so I will be the servant of my servants. And another thing, mother, every one of us has sinned against all men, and I more than any."

Mother smiled at that, smiled through her tears. "Why, how could you have sinned against all men, more than all? Robbers and murderers have done that, but what sin have you committed, that you hold yourself more guilty than all?"

"Mother, little heart of mine," he said (he had begun using such strange caressing words at that time), "little heart of mine, my joy, believe me, every one is really responsible to all men for all men and for everything. I don't know how to explain it to you, but I feel it is so. And how is it then that we went on living, getting angry and not knowing?"

In this mood he would get up every day, more and more sweet and joyous and full of love. When the doctor, an old German called Eisenschmidt, came he would ask, joking: "Well, doctor, have I another day in this world?"

"You'll live many days yet," the doctor would answer. "And months and years too."

"Months and years!" my brother would exclaim. "One day is enough for a man to know all happiness. My dear ones, why do we quarrel, try to outshine each other and keep grudges against each other? Let's go straight into the garden, walk and play there, love, appreciate each other and glorify life."

"Your son cannot last long," the doctor told my mother, as she accompanied him to the door. "The disease is affecting his brain."

The windows of my brother's room looked out into the garden. Our garden was a shady one, with old trees in it which were coming into bud. The first birds of spring were chirping and singing in the branches. And looking at them and admiring them, my brother began suddenly begging their forgiveness too. "Birds of heaven, happy birds, forgive me, for I have also sinned against you." None of us could understand these words at the time, but he shed tears of joy. "Yes," he said, "there was always such a glory of God about me: birds, trees, meadows, sky, only I lived in shame and dishonored it all and did not notice the beauty and glory."

"You take too many sins on yourself," mother used to say, weeping.

"Mother, darling, it's for joy, not for grief I am crying. Though I can't explain it to you, I like to humble myself, for I don't know how to love enough. If I have sinned against everyone, yet all forgive me, too, and that's heaven. Am I not in heaven now?"

And there was a great deal more I don't remember. I remember I went once into his room when there was no one else there. It was a bright evening, the sun was setting, and the whole room was lighted up. He beckoned me, and I went up to him. He put his hands on my shoulders and looked into my face tenderly, lovingly. He said nothing for a minute, only looked at me like that. "Well," he said finally, "run and play now, enjoy life for me too."

I went out then to play. And many times in my life afterwards I remembered even with tears how he had told me to enjoy life for him too. There were many other marvelous and beautiful sayings of his, though we did not understand them at the time.

He died the third week after Easter. He was fully conscious though he could not talk; up to his last hour he did not change. He looked happy, his eyes beamed and sought us, he smiled at us, beckoned us. There was a great deal of talk even in the town about his death. I was impressed by all this at the time, but not too much so, though I cried a great deal at his funeral. I was young then, a child, but a lasting impression, a hidden feeling of it all, remained in my heart, ready to rise up and respond when the time came. So indeed it happened.

(b) *Of the Holy Scriptures in the Life of Father Zossima*

I was left alone with my mother. Her friends began advising her to send me to Petersburg as other parents did. "You have only one son now," they said, "and have a fair income, and you will be depriving him of a brilliant career if you keep him here." They suggested I should be sent to Petersburg to the Cadet Corps, that I might afterwards enter the Imperial Guard. My mother hesitated for a long time. It was awful to part with her only child, but she made up her mind to do it at last, though not without many tears, believing she was acting for my happiness. She brought me to Petersburg and put me into the Cadet Corps, and I never saw her again. For she too died three years afterwards. She spent those three years mourning and grieving for both of us.

From the house of my childhood I have brought nothing but precious memories, for there are no memories more precious than those of early childhood in one's first home. And that is almost always so if there is any love and harmony in the family at all. Indeed, precious memories may remain even of a bad home, if only the heart knows how to find what is precious.

With my memories of home I count, too, my memories of the Bible, which, child as I was, I was very eager to read. I also had a book of Scripture history with excellent pictures called, *A Hundred and Four Stories from the Old and New Testament,* and I learned to read from it. I have it lying on my shelf now, I keep it as a precious relic of the past.

I remember first being moved to devotional feeling at eight years of age. My mother took me alone to mass (I don't remember where my brother was at the time) on the Monday before Easter. It was a fine day, and I remember today, as though I saw it now, how the incense rose from the censer and softly floated upwards and, overhead in the cupola, mingled in rising waves with the sunlight that streamed in at the little window. I was stirred by the sight, and for the first time in my life I consciously received the seed of God's word in my heart. A youth came out into the middle of the church carrying a big book, so large that at the time I felt he could scarcely carry it. He laid it on the reading desk, opened it, and began reading, and suddenly I understood something read in the church of God. In the land of Uz, there lived a man, righteous and God-fearing, and he had great wealth, so many camels, so many sheep and asses, and his children feasted, and he loved them very much and prayed for them. "It may be that my sons have sinned in their feasting." Now the devil came before the Lord together with the sons of God, and said to the Lord that he had gone up and down the earth and under the earth. "And hast thou considered my servant Job?" God asked of him. And God boasted to the devil, pointing to his great and holy servant. And the devil laughed at God's words. "Give him over to me and Thou wilt see that Thy servant will murmur against Thee and curse Thy name." And God gave up the just man He loved so, to the devil. And the devil smote his children and his cattle and scattered his wealth, all of a sudden like a thunderbolt from heaven. And Job rent his mantle and fell down upon the ground and cried aloud: "Naked came I out of my mother's womb, and naked shall I return into the earth; the Lord gave and the Lord has taken away. Blessed be the name of the Lord for ever and ever."

Fathers and teachers, forgive my tears, for all my childhood rises up again before me. I breathe now as I breathed then, with the breast of a little child of eight, and I feel as I did then, awe and wonder and gladness. The camels caught my imagination, and Satan, who talked like that with God, and God who gave His servant up to destruction, and His servant crying out: "Blessed be Thy name although Thou dost punish me." All these things caught my imagination as well as the soft and sweet singing in the church: "Let my prayer rise up before Thee," and the incense from the priest's censer and the kneeling and the prayer. Ever since then—only yesterday I took it up—I've never been able to read that sacred tale without tears. And how much that is great, mysterious and unfathomable there is in it!

Afterwards I heard the words of mockery and blame, proud words: "How could God give up the most loved of His saints for the diversion of the devil, take from him his children, smite him with sore boils so that he cleansed the corruption from his sores with a potsherd—and for no other object except to boast to the devil! 'See what My saint can suffer for My sake.' " But the greatness of it lies in the very fact that it is a mystery—that the passing earthly show and the eternal verity are brought together in it. In the face of the earthly truth, the eternal truth is accomplished. The Creator, as on the first days of creation He ended each day with praise: "that is good that I have created," looks upon Job and again praises His creation. And Job praising the Lord, serves not only Him but all his creation for generations and generations, and forever and ever, since for that he was ordained. What a book it is, and what lessons there are in it! What a book the Bible is, what a miracle, what strength is given with it to man! It is like a mold cast of the world and man and human nature. Everything is there, and a law for everything for all the ages. And what mysteries are solved and revealed; God raises Job again, gives him wealth again. Many years pass by, and he has other children and loves them. But how could he love those new ones when those first children are no more, when he has lost them? Remembering them, how could he be fully happy with those new ones, however dear the new ones might be? But he could, he could. It's the great mystery of

267

human life that old grief passes gradually into quiet tender joy. The mild serenity of age takes the place of the riotous blood of youth. I bless the rising sun each day, and, as before, my heart sings to meet it. But now I love even more its setting, its long slanting rays and the soft tender gentle memories that come with them, the dear images from the whole of my long happy life—and over all the Divine Truth, softening, reconciling, forgiving! My life is ending. I know that well. But every day that is left me I feel how my earthly life is in touch with a new infinite, unknown, but approaching life, the nearness of which sets my soul quivering with rapture, my mind glowing and my heart weeping with joy.

Friends and teachers, I have heard more than once, and of late one may hear it more often, that the priests, and above all the village priests, are complaining on all sides of their miserable income and their humiliating lot. They plainly state, even in print—I've read it myself—that they are unable to teach the Scriptures to the people because of the smallness of their means, and if Lutherans and heretics come and lead the flock astray, they let them because they have so little to live on. May the Lord increase the sustenance that is so precious to them, for their complaint is just, too. But of a truth I say, if anyone is to blame in the matter, half the fault is ours.

The priest may be short of time, he may say truly that he is overwhelmed with work and services, but still he must surely have an hour a week to remember God. He does not work the whole year round. Let him gather around him once a week, some hour in the evening, if only the children at first —the fathers will hear of it and they too will begin to come. There's no need to build halls for this, let him take them into his cottage. They won't spoil his cottage, they will only be there one hour. Let him open that book and begin reading it without grand words or superciliousness, without condescension, but gently and kindly, being glad that he is reading to them and that they are listening with attention. Let him read loving the words himself, and only stopping from time to time to explain words that are not understood by the peasants. Don't be anxious, they will understand everything. The faithful heart will understand all!

Let the priest read to them about Abraham and Sarah, about Isaac and Rebecca, of how Jacob went to Laban and wrestled with the Lord in his dream and said: "This place is holy"—and he will impress the devout mind of the peasant. Let him read, especially to the children, how the brothers sold Joseph, the tender boy, the dreamer and prophet, into bondage, and told their father that a wild beast had devoured him, and showed him his blood-stained clothes. Let him read to them how the brothers afterwards journeyed into Egypt for corn, and Joseph, now a greater ruler, unrecognized by them, tormented them, accused them, kept his brother Benjamin, and all through love: "I love you, and loving you I torment you." For he remembered all his life how they had sold him to the merchants in the burning desert by the well, and how, wringing his hands, he had wept and besought his brothers not to sell him as a slave in a strange land. Now, seeing them again after many years, he loved them beyond measure, but he harassed and tormented them in love. Leaving them at last, not able to bear the suffering of his heart he flung himself on his bed and wept. Then, wiping his tears away he went out to them joyful and told them: "Brothers, I am your brother Joseph!" Let the priest read to them further how happy old Jacob was on learning that his boy was still alive, and how he went to Egypt leaving his own country. Let him read to them how Jacob died in a foreign land, bequeathing the great prophecy that had lain mysteriously hidden in his meek and timid heart, that from his offspring, from Judah, would come the great hope of the world, the Messiah and Saviour.

Fathers and teachers, forgive me and don't be angry. Like a little child I've been babbling of what you know long ago, and can teach me a hundred times more skillfully. I only speak from rapture. And forgive my tears, for I love the Bible. Let him weep too, the priest of God, and be sure that the hearts of his listeners will throb in response. Only a tiny seed is needed—drop it into the heart of the peasant and it won't die. It will live in his soul all his life. It will be hidden in the midst of his darkness and sin, like a bright spot, like a great reminder. And there's no need of much teaching or explanation, he will understand it all simply. Do you believe that peasants don't understand? Try reading to them the touching story of the fair Esther and the haughty Vashti; or the miraculous story of Jonah and the whale. Don't forget either the parables of Our Lord, choose especially from the Gospel of St. Luke (that is what I did) and then from the Acts of the Apostles the conversion of St. Paul (that you mustn't leave out on any account), and from the Lives of the Saints, for instance, the life of Alexey, the man of God and, greatest of all, the happy martyr and the seer of God, Mary of Egypt—and you will penetrate their hearts with these simple tales. Give one hour a week to it in spite of your poverty, only one short hour. And you will see for yourself that our people are gracious and grateful, and will repay you a hundredfold. Mindful of the kindness of their priest and the moving words they have heard from him, they will of their own accord help him in his fields and in his house, and will treat him with more respect than before—so that it will even increase his worldly well-being. The thing is so simple that sometimes one is even afraid to put it into words, for fear of being laughed at, and yet how true it is! One who does not believe in God will not

269

believe in God's people. He who believes in God's people will see God's holiness too, even though he has not believed in it till then. Only the people and their future spiritual power will convert our atheists, who have torn themselves away from their native soil.

And what is the use of Christ's words, unless we set an example? The people are lost without the word of God, for their souls thirst for the Word and for all that is good.

In my youth, long ago, nearly forty years ago, I traveled all over Russia with Father Anfim, collecting funds for our monastery. We stayed one night with some fishermen on the bank of a great river. A good-looking peasant youth about eighteen, joined us; he had to hurry back next morning to pull a merchant's barge along the bank. I noticed him looking straight before him with clear and tender eyes. It was a bright, warm, still, July night. A cool mist rose from the broad river. We could hear the splash of fish. The birds were still. All was hushed and beautiful, everything praying to God. Only we two were not sleeping, the lad and I, and we talked of the beauty of this world of God's and of the great mystery of it. Every blade of grass, every insect, ant, and golden bee, all so marvelously know their path, though they have not intelligence, they bear witness to the mystery of God and continually accomplish it themselves. I saw the youth's heart was moved. He told me that he loved the forest and the forest birds. He was a bird-catcher, knew the note of each of them, could call each bird. "I know nothing better than to be in the forest," said he, "though all things are good."

"Truly," I answered him, "all things are good and fair, because all is truth. Look," said I, "at the horse, that great beast that is so near to man; or the lowly, pensive ox, which feeds him and works for him. Look at them. What meekness, what devotion to man, who often beats them mercilessly. What gentleness, what confidence and what beauty! It's touching to know that there's no sin in them, for all, all except man, is sinless. Christ has been with them before us."

"Is Christ with them too?" asked the youth.

"It cannot but be so," said I, "since the Word is for all. All creation and all creatures, every leaf is striving to the Word, singing glory to God, weeping to Christ, unconsciously accomplishing this by the mystery of their sinless life. Yonder," said I, "in the forest wanders the bear, fierce and menacing, and yet innocent."

And I told him how once a bear came to a great saint who had taken refuge in a tiny cell in the woods. And the great saint pitied him, went up to him without fear and gave him a piece of bread. "Go along," said he, "Christ be with you." And the savage beast walked away meekly and obediently, doing no harm. The youth was delighted that the bear had walked

270

away without hurting the saint, and that Christ was with him too. "Ah," said he, "how good that is, how good and beautiful is all God's work!" He sat musing softly and sweetly. I saw he understood. And he slept beside me a light and sinless sleep. May God bless youth! And I prayed for him as I went to sleep. Lord, send peace and light to Thy people!

(c) *Recollections of Father Zossima's Youth Before He Became a Monk. The Duel.*

I spent a long time, almost eight years, in the military school at Petersburg. In these new surroundings many of my childish impressions grew dimmer, though I forgot nothing. I picked up so many new habits and opinions that I was transformed into a cruel, absurd, almost savage creature. But a surface polish of courtesy and society manners I did acquire together with the French language.

But we all, myself included, looked upon the soldiers in our service as cattle. I was perhaps worse than the rest in that respect, for I was so much more impressionable than my companions. By the time we left the school as officers, we were ready to lay down our lives for the honor of the regiment, but none of us had any knowledge of the real meaning of honor, and if anyone had known it, he would have been the first to ridicule it. Drunkenness, debauchery and deviltry were what we prided ourselves on. I don't say that we were bad by nature, all these young men were good fellows, but they behaved badly, and I worst of all. What made it worse for me was that I had come into my own money, and so I flung myself into a life of pleasure, and plunged headlong into all the recklessness of youth.

I was fond of reading, yet strange to say, the Bible was the one book I never opened at that time, though I always carried it about with me. In truth I was keeping that book "for the day and the hour, for the month and the year," though I knew it not.

After four years of this life, I chanced to be in the town of K. where our regiment was stationed at the time. We found the people of the town hospitable, rich and fond of entertaining. I met with a cordial reception everywhere, as I was lively and was known to be well off, which always goes a long way in the world. And then a circumstance happened which was the beginning of it all.

I formed an attachment for a beautiful and intelligent young girl of noble and lofty character, the daughter of people much respected. They were well-to-do people of influence and position. They always gave me a friendly reception. I believed that the young lady looked on me with favor and my

271

heart was aflame at such an idea. Later on I saw and fully realized that I perhaps was not so passionately in love with her at all, but only recognized the elevation of her mind and character, which I could not indeed have helped doing. I was prevented, however, from making her an offer at the time by my selfishness. I was loth to part with the allurements of my free and licentious bachelor life especially as my pockets were full of money. I did drop some hint as to my feelings however, though I put off taking any decisive step for a time. Then, all of a sudden, we were ordered off for two months to another district.

On my return, I found the young lady already married to a rich neighboring landowner, a very amiable man, still young though older than I was, connected with the best Petersburg society, which I was not, and of excellent education, which I also was not. I was so overwhelmed at this unexpected circumstance that my mind was positively clouded. The worst of it all was that, as I learned then, the young landowner had been a long while engaged to her, and I had met him many times in her house. Blinded by my conceit I had noticed nothing. And this particularly mortified me; almost everybody had known all about it, while I knew nothing. I was filled with sudden irrepressible fury. With flushed face I began recalling how often I had been on the point of declaring my love to her, and as she had not attempted to stop me or to warn me, she must, I concluded, have been laughing at me all the time. Later on, of course, I reflected and remembered that she had been very far from laughing at me. On the contrary, she used to turn off any love-making on my part with a joke and begin talking of other subjects. But at that moment I was incapable of reflecting and was all eagerness for revenge. I am surprised to remember that my wrath and revengeful feelings were extremely repugnant to my own nature. Being of an easy temper, I found it difficult to be angry with anyone for long, and so I had to work myself up artificially and I thus became revolting and absurd.

I waited for an opportunity and succeeded in insulting my "rival" in the presence of a large company. I insulted him on a perfectly extraneous pretext, jeering at his opinion upon an important public event—it concerned the revolt of 1826—and my jeer was, so people said, clever and effective. Then I forced him to ask for an explanation, and behaved so rudely that he accepted my challenge in spite of the vast inequality between us, as I was younger, a person of no consequence, and of inferior rank. I learned afterwards for a fact that it was from a jealous feeling on his side also that my challenge was accepted. He had been rather jealous of me on his wife's account before their marriage. He felt now that if he allowed himself to be insulted by me and refused to accept my challenge, and if she heard of it, she might begin to despise him and waver in her love for him. I soon found a second in a comrade, an ensign of our regiment. In those days though duels were severely punished, yet dueling was a kind of fashion among the officers—so strong and deeply rooted will a brutal custom sometimes be.

It was the end of June, and our meeting was to take place at seven o'clock the next day on the outskirts of the town—and then something happened that in truth was the turning point of my life. In the evening, returning home in a savage and brutal humor, I flew into a rage with my orderly and gave him two blows in the face with all my might, so that it was covered with blood. He had not long been in my service and I had struck him before, but never with such ferocious cruelty. And, believe me, though it's forty years ago, I recall it now with shame and pain. I went to bed and slept for about three hours; when I waked up the day was breaking. I got up—I did not want to sleep any more—I went to the window—opened it, it looked out upon the garden. I saw the sun rising. It was warm and beautiful, the birds were singing.

What's the meaning of it, I wondered. I feel in my heart as it were something vile and shameful. Is it because I am going to shed blood? No, it's not that. Can it be that I am afraid of death, afraid of being killed? No, that's not it, that's not it at all. . . . And all at once I knew what it was: it was because I had beaten my orderly the evening before! It all rose before my mind, as it were repeated over again; he stood before me and I was beating him straight on the face and he was holding his arms stiffly down, his head erect, his eyes fixed upon me as though on parade. He staggered at every blow and did not even dare to raise his hands to protect himself. That is what a man has been brought to, and that was a man beating a fellow creature! What a crime! It was as though a sharp dagger had pierced me. I stood as in a trance, while the sun was shining, the leaves were rejoicing and the birds were trilling the praise of God. . . . I hid my face in my hands, fell on my bed and broke into a storm of tears. And then I remembered my brother Markel and what he said on his deathbed to his servants: "My dear ones, why do you wait on me, why do you love me? Am I worth your waiting on me?"

"Yes, am I worth it?" flashed through my mind. After all what am I worth, that another man, a fellow creature, made in the likeness and image of God, should serve me? For the first time in my life this question forced itself upon me. My brother had said: "Mother, my little heart, in truth we are each responsible to all for all, it's only that men don't know this. If they knew it, the world would be a paradise at once."

"God, can that too be false?" I thought as I wept. "In truth perhaps, I am more than all others responsible for all, a greater sinner than all men in the world." And all at once the

273

whole truth in its full light appeared to me. What was I going to do? I was going to kill a good, clever, noble man, who had done me no wrong, and by depriving his wife of happiness for the rest of her life, I should be torturing and killing her too. I lay thus in my bed with my face in the pillow, heedless how the time was passing. Suddenly my second, the ensign, came in with the pistols to call me.

"Ah," said he, "it's a good thing you are up already, it's time we were off, come along!"

I did not know what to do and hurried about undecided; we went out to the carriage, however.

"Wait here a minute," I said to him. "I'll be back directly, I have forgotten my purse."

And I ran back alone, straight to my orderly's little room.

"Friend," I said, "I gave you two blows on the face yesterday, forgive me."

He started as though he were frightened, and looked at me. And I saw that it was not enough, and on the spot, in my officer's uniform, I dropped at his feet and bowed my head to the ground.

"Forgive me," I said.

He was completely aghast.

"Your honor . . . sir, what are you doing? Am I worth it?"

And he burst out crying as I had done before, hid his face in his hands, turned to the window and shook all over with his sobs. I flew out to my comrade and jumped into the carriage.

"Ready," I cried. "Have you ever seen a conqueror?" I asked. "Here is one before you."

I was in ecstasy, laughing and talking all the way, I don't remember what about.

He looked at me. "Well, brother, you are a brave fellow, you'll keep up the honor of the uniform, I can see."

So we reached the place and found them there awaiting us. We were placed twelve paces apart. He had the first shot. I stood looking him full in the face. I did not twitch an eyelash. I looked lovingly at him, for I knew what I would do. His shot just grazed my cheek and ear.

"Thank God," I cried. "No man has been killed." And I seized my pistol, turned back and flung it far away into the woods. "That's the place for you," I cried.

I turned to my adversary.

"Forgive me, young fool that I am, sir," I said, "for my unprovoked insult to you and for forcing you to fire at me. I am ten times worse than you and more, perhaps. Tell that to the person whom you hold dearest in the world."

I had no sooner said this than they all three shouted at me.

"Why," cried my adversary, annoyed, "if you did not want to fight, why did you not let me alone?"

"Yesterday I was a fool, today I know better," I answered.

"As to yesterday, I believe you, but as for today, it is difficult to agree with your opinion," he said.

"Bravo," I cried, clapping my hands. "I agree with you there too, I have deserved it!"

"Will you shoot, sir, or not?"

"No, I won't," I said. "If you like, fire at me again, but it would be better for you not to fire."

The seconds, especially mine, were shouting too: "Can you disgrace the regiment like this, facing your antagonist and begging his forgiveness! If I'd only known!"

I stood facing them all. I was serious.

"Gentlemen," I said, "is it really so wonderful in these days to find a man who can repent of his stupidity and publicly confess that he was wrong?"

"But not in a duel," cried my second again.

"That's what's so strange," I said. "For I should have admitted my fault as soon as I got here, before he fired a shot, before leading him into a great and deadly sin. But we have made our life so grotesque, that to act in that way would have been almost impossible. Only after I faced his shot at the distance of twelve paces could my words have any significance for him. If I had spoken before, he would have said: 'He is a coward. The sight of the pistols frightened him. No use to listen to him.' Gentlemen," I cried suddenly, speaking straight from my heart, "look around you at the gifts of God, the clear sky, the pure air, the tender grass, the birds. Nature is beautiful and sinless. And we, only we, are sinful and foolish, and we don't understand that life is heaven. We have only to understand that and it will at once be fulfilled in all its beauty, we shall embrace each other and weep."

I would have said more but I could not. My voice broke with the sweetness and youthful gladness of it. And there was such bliss in my heart as I had never known before in my life.

"All this is rational and edifying," said my antagonist. "In any case you are an original person."

"You may laugh," I said to him, laughing too. "But afterwards you will approve of me."

"Oh, I am ready to approve of you now," said he. "Will you shake hands, for I believe you are genuinely sincere."

"No," I said, "not now. Later on when I have grown worthier and deserve your esteem, then we will shake hands."

We went home, my second upbraiding me all the way. All my comrades heard of the affair at once and gathered together to pass judgment on me.

"He has disgraced the uniform," they said. "Let him resign his commission."

Some stood up for me. "He faced the shot," they said.

"Yes, but he was afraid of the next shot and begged for forgiveness."

"If he had been afraid of being shot, he would have shot his

275

own pistol first before asking forgiveness. But he threw it away loaded into the woods. No, there's something else in this, something original."

I enjoyed listening and looking at them. "My dear friends and comrades," said I, "don't worry about my resigning my commission, for I have done so already. I have sent in my papers and as soon as I get my discharge I shall go into a monastery—it's with that object I am leaving our regiment."

When I said this they all burst out laughing.

"You should have told us of that first. That explains everything. We can't judge a monk."

They laughed and could not stop. Their laughter was not scornful, but kindly and happy. They all felt friendly to me at once, even those who had been sternest in their censure, and all the following month, before my discharge came, they could not make enough of me. "Ah, you monk," they would say. And every one said something kind to me. They began trying to dissuade me, even to pity me: "What are you doing to yourself?"

"No," they would say, "he is a brave fellow, he faced fire and could have fired his own pistol too, but he had a dream the night before that he should become a monk, that's why he did it."

It was the same thing with the society of the town. Till then I had been kindly received, but had not been the object of special attention, and now all came to know me at once and invited me. They laughed at me, but they loved me. I may mention that although everybody talked openly of our duel, the authorities took no notice of it, because my antagonist was a near relation of our general, and because there had been no bloodshed and no serious consequences. And as I had resigned my commission, they took it all as a joke. And I began then to speak aloud and fearlessly, regardless of their laughter, for it was always kindly and not spiteful laughter. These conversations mostly took place in the evenings, in the company of ladies; women particularly liked listening to me then and they made the men listen.

"But how can I possibly be responsible for all?" everyone would laugh in my face. "Can I, for instance, be responsible for you?"

"You may well not know it," I would answer, "since the whole world has long been going on a different line, since we consider the veriest lies as truth and demand the same lies from others. Here I have for once in my life acted sincerely and, well, you all look upon me as a madman. Though you are friendly to me, yet, you see, you all laugh at me."

"But how can we help being friendly to you?" said my hostess, laughing. The room was full of people. All of a sudden the young lady rose, on whose account the duel had been fought and whom I had intended to marry. I had not noticed her coming into the room. She got up, came to me and held out her hand.

"Let me tell you," she said, "that I am the first not to laugh at you. On the contrary I thank you with tears and express my respect to you for your action."

Her husband too came up and then they all approached me and almost kissed me. My heart was filled with joy, but my attention was especially caught by a middle-aged man who came up to me with the others. I knew him by name already, but had never made his acquaintance nor exchanged a word with him until that evening.

(d) The Mysterious Visitor

He had long been an official in the town; he was in a prominent position, respected by all, rich and had a reputation for benevolence. He subscribed considerable sums to the almshouse and the orphan asylum. He was very charitable, too, in secret, a fact which only became known after his death. He was a man of about fifty, almost stern in appearance, and not much given to conversation. He had been married about ten years and his wife, who was still young, had borne him three children. Well, I was sitting alone in my room the following evening, when my door suddenly opened and this gentleman walked in.

I must mention, by the way, that I was no longer living in my former quarters. As soon as I resigned my commission, I took rooms with an old lady, the widow of a government clerk. My landlady's servant waited upon me, for I had moved into her rooms simply because on my return from the duel I had sent my orderly back to the regiment, as I felt ashamed to look him in the face after my last interview with him. So prone is the man of the world to be ashamed of his righteous action.

"I have," said my visitor, "with great interest listened to you speaking in different houses the last few days and I wanted at last to make your acquaintance, so as to talk to you more intimately. Can you, dear sir, grant me this favor?"

"I can, with the greatest pleasure and I shall look upon it as an honor." I said this, though I felt almost dismayed, so greatly was I impressed from the first moment by the appearance of this man. For though other people had listened to me with interest and attention, no one had come to me before with such a serious, stern and concentrated expression. And now he had come to see me in my rooms. He sat down.

"You are, I see, a man of great strength of character," he said. "You have dared to serve the truth, even when by doing so you risked incurring the contempt of all."

"Your praise is, perhaps, excessive," I replied.

"No, it's not excessive," he answered. "Such a course of

277

action is far more difficult than you think. It is that which has impressed me, and that is why I have come to you," he continued. "Tell me, please, that is if you are not annoyed by my curiosity, what were your sensations at the moment when you made up your mind to ask forgiveness at the duel. Do not think my question unimportant. I have a definite reason for asking it. I will perhaps explain later on, if it is God's will that we should become more intimately acquainted."

All the while he was speaking, I was looking at his face and I felt complete trust in him and great curiosity also. I felt that there was some strange secret in his soul.

"You ask what were my exact sensations at the moment when I asked my opponent's forgiveness," I answered. "But I had better tell you from the beginning what I have not yet told anyone else." And I described all that had passed between my orderly and me, and how I had bowed down to the ground at his feet. "From that you can see for yourself," I concluded, "that at the time of the duel it was easier for me, for I had made a beginning already at home. When once I had started on the road, to go further along it was far from being difficult, but became a source of joy and happiness."

I liked the way he looked at me as he listened. "All that," he said, "is exceedingly interesting. I will come to see you again and again."

And from that time on he came to see me nearly every evening. And we would have become close friends, if he had ever talked of himself. But about himself he scarcely ever said a word, yet he continually asked me about myself. In spite of that I became very fond of him and spoke with perfect frankness to him. I thought, what need have I to know his secrets, since I can see without that that he is a good man. Moreover, though he is such a serious man and older than I, he comes to see me and treats me as his equal. And I learned a great deal that was profitable from him, for he was a man of lofty mind.

"That life is heaven," he said to me suddenly, "that I have long been thinking about." And all at once he added, "In fact, I think of nothing else." He looked at me and smiled. "I am more convinced of it than you are, I will tell you why later on."

I listened to him and thought that he had something that he wanted to tell me.

"Heaven," he went on, "lies hidden within all of us—it lies hidden in me now, and if I will it, it will be revealed to me tomorrow and for all time."

I looked at him. He was speaking with great emotion and looking mysteriously at me, as if he were questioning me.

"And we are all responsible to all for all, apart from our own sins. You were quite right in thinking that. And it is wonderful how you could comprehend it in all its significance at

278

once. And in truth, so soon as men understand that, the Kingdom of Heaven will be for them not a dream, but a living reality."

"And when?" I cried out to him bitterly. "When will that come to pass? Will it ever come to pass? Is it not simply a dream?"

"Then you don't believe it?" he said. "You preach it and don't believe it yourself. Believe me, this dream, as you call it, will come to pass without doubt. It will come, but not now, for every process has its law. It's a spiritual, psychological process. To transform the world, to recreate it afresh, men must turn into another path psychologically. Until you have become really, in actual fact, a brother to everyone, brotherhood will not come to pass. No sort of scientific teaching, no kind of common interest, will ever teach men to share property and privileges with equal consideration for all. Every one will think his share too small and they will be always envying, complaining and attacking one another. You ask when it will come to pass; it will come to pass, but first we have to go through a period of isolation."

"What do you mean by isolation?" I asked him.

"Why, the isolation that prevails everywhere, above all in our age—it has not fully developed, it has not reached its limit yet. For everyone strives to keep his individuality, everyone wants to secure the greatest possible fullness of life for himself. But meantime all his efforts result not in attaining fullness of life but self-destruction, for instead of self-realization he ends by arriving at complete solitude. All mankind in our age is split up into units. Man keeps apart, each in his own groove; each one holds aloof, hides himself and hides what he has, from the rest. He ends by being repelled by others and repelling them. He heaps up riches by himself and thinks, 'How strong I am now and how secure.' And in his madness he does not understand that the more he heaps up, the more he sinks into self-destructive impotence. For he is accustomed to rely upon himself alone and to cut himself off from the whole; he has trained himself not to believe in the help of others, in men and in humanity, and only trembles for fear he should lose his money and the privileges that he has won for himself. Everywhere in these days men have ceased to understand that the true security is to be found in social solidarity rather than in isolated individual effort. But this terrible individualism must inevitably have an end, and all will suddenly understand how unnaturally they are separated from one another. It will be the spirit of the time, and people will marvel that they have sat so long in darkness without seeing the light. And then the sign of the Son of Man will be seen in the heavens. . . . But, until then, we must keep the banner flying. Sometimes even if he has to do it alone, and his conduct seems to be crazy, a man must set an example, and so draw

279

men's souls out of their solitude, and spur them to some act of brotherly love, that the great idea may not die."

Our evenings, one after another, were spent in such talk. I gave up society and visited my neighbors much less frequently. Besides, my vogue was somewhat over. I say this, not as blame, for they still loved me and treated me kindly, but there's no denying that fashion is a great power in society. I began to look upon my mysterious visitor with admiration, for besides enjoying his intelligence, I began to see that he was brooding over some plan in his heart, and was preparing himself perhaps for a great deed. Perhaps he liked my not showing curiosity about his secret, not seeking to discover it by direct question nor by insinuation. . . . I noticed at last, that he showed signs of wanting to tell me something. This had become quite evident, indeed, about a month after he first began to visit me.

"Do you know," he said to me once, "that people are very curious about us in town and wonder why I come to see you so often. But let them wonder, for *soon all will be explained*."

Sometimes he became very agitated and almost always on such occasions he would get up and go away. Sometimes he would fix a long piercing look upon me, and I thought "he will say something now." But he would suddenly begin talking of something ordinary and familiar. He often complained of headaches.

One day, quite unexpectedly indeed, after he had been talking a long time, I saw him suddenly turn pale. His face worked convulsively. He stared at me.

"What's the matter?" I said. "Do you feel ill?" He had just been complaining of a headache.

"I . . . do you know . . . I murdered someone."

He said this and smiled with a face as white as chalk. "Why is it he is smiling?" The thought flashed through my mind before I realized anything else. I too turned pale.

"What are you saying?" I cried.

"You see," he said, with a smile, "how much it has cost me to say the first word. But now that I have said it, I feel I've taken the first step and shall go on."

For a long while I could not believe him, and I did not believe him at that time, but only after he had been to see me three days running and told me all about it. I thought he was mad but ended by being convinced of his crime. It was a great and terrible one.

Fourteen years before, he had murdered the widow of a landowner, a wealthy and handsome young woman who had a house in his town. He fell passionately in love with her, declared his feeling and tried to persuade her to marry him. But she had already given her heart to another man, an officer of noble birth and high rank in the service, who was at that time away at the front, though she was expecting him soon to return. She refused his offer and begged him not to come to see her. After he had stopped visiting her, he took advantage of his knowledge of the house to enter at night through the garden at great risk of being discovered. But as often happens, a crime committed with extraordinary audacity is more successful than others.

Entering the garret through the skylight, he went down the ladder, knowing that the door at the bottom of it was sometimes, through the negligence of the servants, left unlocked. He hoped to find it so, and so it was. He made his way in the dark to her bedroom where a light was burning. As though on purpose, both her maids had gone off to a birthday party without asking leave. The other servants slept in the servants' quarters or in the kitchen on the ground floor. His passion flamed up at the sight of her asleep, and then vindictive, jealous anger took possession of his heart, and like a drunken man, beside himself, he thrust a knife into her heart, so that she did not even cry out. Then with devilish and criminal cunning he contrived that suspicion should fall on the servants. He was so base as to take her purse, to open her chest with keys from under her pillow, and to take some things from it, doing it all as it might have been done by an ignorant servant, leaving valuable papers and taking only money. He took some of the larger gold things, but left smaller articles that were ten times as valuable. He took with him, too, some things for himself as remembrances, but of that later. Having done this awful deed, he returned by the way he had come.

Neither the next day, when the alarm was raised, nor at any time after in his life, did anyone dream of suspecting that he was the criminal. No one knew of his love for her, for he was always reserved and silent and had no friend to whom he would have opened his heart. He was looked upon simply as an acquaintance, and not a very intimate one, of the murdered woman. A serf of hers was at once suspected, and every circumstance confirmed the suspicion. The man knew—indeed his mistress did not conceal the fact—that having to send one of her serfs as a recruit she had decided to send him, as he had no relations and his conduct was unsatisfactory. People had heard him angrily threatening to murder her when he was drunk in a tavern. Two days before her death, he had run away, staying no one knew where in the town. The day after the murder, he was found on the road leading out of the town, dead drunk, with a knife in his pocket and his right hand stained with blood. He said that his nose had been bleeding, but no one believed him. The maids confessed that they had gone to a party and that the street door had been left open till they returned. And a number of similar details came to light, throwing suspicion on the innocent servant.

They arrested him, and he was tried for murder. But a week

281

after the arrest he fell sick of fever and died unconscious in the hospital. There the matter ended and the judges and the authorities and everyone in the town remained convinced that the crime had been committed by no one but the servant who had died in the hospital.

After that the punishment began. My mysterious visitor, now my friend, told me that at first he was not in the least troubled by pangs of conscience. He was miserable a long time, but not for that reason; only from regret that he had killed the woman he loved, that she was no more, that in killing her he had killed his love, while the fire of passion was still in his veins. But of the innocent blood he had shed, of the murder of a fellow creature, he scarcely thought. The thought that his victim might have become the wife of another man was insupportable to him, and so, for a long time, he was convinced in his conscience that he could not have acted otherwise.

At first he was worried at the arrest of the servant, but his illness and death soon set his mind at rest, for the man's death was apparently (so he reasoned at the time) not due to his arrest or his fright, but due to a chill he had taken on the day he ran away, when he had lain all night dead drunk on the damp ground. The theft of the money and other things troubled him little, for he argued that the theft had not been committed for gain but to avert suspicion. The sum stolen was small, and he shortly afterwards subscribed the whole of it, and much more, toward the funds for maintaining an alms-house in the town. He did this on purpose to set his conscience at rest about the theft, and it's a remarkable fact that for a long time he really was at peace—he told me this himself. He entered then upon a career in the service, volunteered for a difficult and laborious duty, which occupied him two years. Being a man of strong will he almost forgot the past. Whenever he recalled it, he tried not to think of it at all. He became active in philanthropy too, founded and helped to maintain many institutions in the town, did a good deal in the two capitals, and in both Moscow and Petersburg was elected a member of philanthropic societies.

At last, however, he began brooding over the past, and the strain of it was too much for him. Then he was attracted by a fine and intelligent girl and soon after married her, hoping that marriage would dispel his lonely depression, and that by entering on a new life and scrupulously doing his duty to his wife and children, he would escape from old memories altogether. But the very opposite of what he expected happened. He began, even in the first month of his marriage, to be continually worried by the thought: "My wife loves me—but what if she knew?" When she first told him that she would soon bear him a child, he was troubled. "I am giving life, but I have taken life." Children came. "How dare I love them, teach

282

and educate them? How can I talk to them of virtue? I have shed blood." They were fine children, he longed to caress them but: "I can't look at their innocent faces. I am unworthy."

At last he began to be bitterly and ominously haunted by the blood of his murdered victim, by the young life he had destroyed, by the blood that cried out for vengeance. He began to have awful dreams. But, being a man of strength, he bore his suffering a long time, thinking: "I shall atone for everything by this secret agony." But that hope, too, was in vain. As time went on, the more intense was his suffering.

He was respected in society for his active benevolence, though every one was overawed by his stern and gloomy character. But the more he was respected, the more intolerable it was for him. He confessed to me that he had thoughts of killing himself. But he began to be haunted by another idea—an idea which he had at first regarded as impossible and unthinkable, though at last it got such a hold on his heart that he could not shake it off. He dreamed of rising up, going out and confessing before all men that he had committed murder. For three years this dream pursued him, haunting him in different forms. At last he believed with his whole heart that if he confessed his crime, he would heal his soul and would be at peace forever. But this belief filled his heart with terror, for how could he carry it out? And then came what happened at my duel.

"Looking at you, I made up my mind."

I looked at him.

"Is it possible," I cried, "that such an incident could give rise to such a decision?"

"My determination has been growing for the last three years," he answered. "Your story only gave the last touch to it. Looking at you, I reproached myself and envied you." He said this to me almost sullenly.

"But you won't be believed," I observed. "It's fourteen years ago."

"I have proof. Unmistakable proof. I shall show them."

Then I wept and embraced him.

"Tell me one thing, one thing," he said (as though it all depended upon me), "my wife, my children! My wife may die of grief, and though my children won't lose their rank and property, they will be a convict's children—and forever! And what a memory, what a memory of me I shall leave in their hearts!"

I said nothing.

"And to part from them, to leave them forever? It's forever, you know, forever!"

I sat still and repeated a silent prayer. I got up at last. I was afraid.

"Well?" He looked at me.

"Go!" said I. "Confess. Everything passes, only truth remains. When they grow up your children will understand the nobility of your resolution."

He left me that time as though he had made up his mind. Yet for more than two weeks afterwards, he came to me every evening, still preparing himself, still unable to bring himself to the point. He made my heart ache. One day he would come determined and say: "I know it will be heaven for me, heaven, the moment I confess. Fourteen years I've been in hell. I want to suffer. I will take my punishment and begin to live. You can pass through the world doing wrong, but there's no turning back. Now I dare not love my neighbor nor even my own children. My children will understand, perhaps, what my punishment has cost me and will not condemn me! God is not in strength but in truth."

"All will understand your sacrifice," I said to him. "If they do not understand at once, they will understand later; because you will have served truth, the higher truth, not of the earth."

And he would go away seeming comforted, but next day he would come again, bitter, pale, sarcastic.

"Every time I come to you, you look at me as though to say: 'He has still not confessed!' But wait, don't despise me too much. It's not such an easy thing to do as you may think. Perhaps I will not do it at all. You won't go and inform against me then, will you?"

And far from looking at him with curiosity, I was afraid to look at him at all. I was ill from anxiety, and my heart was full of tears. I could not sleep at night.

"I have just come from my wife," he went on. "Do you understand what the word 'wife' means? When I went out, the children called to me: 'Good-by, father, hurry back to read *The Children's Magazine* with us.' No, you don't understand that! No one is wise from another man's woe."

His eyes were glittering, his lips were twitching. Suddenly he struck the table with his fist so that everything on it danced —it was the first time he had done such a thing, he was such a mild man.

"But need I?" he exclaimed. "Must I? No one had been condemned, no one has been sent to Siberia in my place; the man died of fever. And I've already been punished by my sufferings for the blood I shed. And I won't be believed, they won't believe my proofs. Need I confess, need I? I am ready to go on suffering all my life for the blood I have shed, if only my wife and children can be spared. Is it right to ruin them with me? Aren't we making a mistake? What is right in this case? And will people recognize it, will they appreciate it, will they respect it?"

"Good Lord!" I thought to myself, "He is thinking of other people's respect at such a moment!" And I felt so sorry for him then, that I believe I would have shared his fate if it could have comforted him. I saw he was beside himself. I was aghast, realizing with my heart as well as my mind what such a resolution meant.

"Decide my fate!" he exclaimed again.

"Go and confess," I whispered to him. My voice failed me, but I whispered it firmly. I took up the New Testament from the table and showed him the Gospel of St. John, 12: 24, which says:

"Verily, verily, I say unto you, except a corn of wheat fall into the ground and die, it abideth alone: but if it die, it bringeth forth much fruit."

I had just been reading that verse when he came in. He read it.

"That's true," he said, but he smiled bitterly. "It's terrible the things you find in those books," he said, after a pause. "It's easy enough to thrust them upon one. And who wrote them? Can they have been written by men?"

"The Holy Spirit wrote them," I answered.

"It's easy for you to talk this way." He smiled again, this time almost with hatred.

I took the book again, opened it in another place and showed him the Epistle to the Hebrews, 10:31. He read: "It is a fearful thing to fall into the hands of the living God."

He read it and flung down the book. He was trembling all over.

"An awful text," he said. "There's no denying you've picked out fitting ones." He got up from his chair. "Well!" he said. "Good-by. I may not come again . . . We shall meet in heaven. So I have been for fourteen years 'in the hands of the living God,' that's how one must think of those fourteen years. Tomorrow I will beseech those hands to let me go."

I wanted to take him in my arms and kiss him, but I did not dare—his face was contorted and sombre. He went away.

"Good God," I thought, "what has he gone to face!" I fell on my knees before the ikon and wept for him before the Holy Mother of God, our swift defender and helper. I was half an hour praying in tears, and it was late, about midnight. Suddenly I saw the door open and he came in again. I was surprised.

"Where have you been?" I asked him.

"I think," he said, "I've forgotten something . . . my handkerchief, I think. . . . Well, even if I've not forgotten anything, let me stay a little."

He sat down. I stood over him.

"You sit down, too," said he.

I sat down. We sat still for two minutes. He looked intently at me and suddenly smiled—I remembered that—then he got up, embraced me warmly and kissed me.

"Remember," he said, "how I came to you a second time. Do you hear, remember it!"

And he went out.

"Tomorrow," I thought.

And so it was. I did not know that evening that the next day was his birthday. I had not been out for the last few days so I had no chance of hearing it from anyone. On that day he always had a party, everyone in the town went to it. It was the same this time. After dinner he walked into the middle of the room, with a paper in his hand—a formal declaration to the chief of his department who was present. This declaration he read aloud to the whole assembly. It contained a full account of the crime, in every detail.

"I cut myself off from men as a monster. God has visited me," he said in conclusion. "I want to suffer for my sin!"

Then he brought out and laid on the table all the things he had been keeping for fourteen years, that he thought would prove his crime. He brought out the jewels belonging to the murdered woman which he had stolen to divert suspicion, a cross and a locket taken from her neck with a portrait of her fiancée in the locket, her notebook and two letters; one from her fiancée telling her that he would soon be with her, and her unfinished answer left on the table to be sent off next day. He carried off these two letters—what for? Why had he kept them for fourteen years instead of destroying them as evidence against him?

And this is what happened: everyone was amazed and horrified, everyone refused to believe it and thought that he was deranged, though all listened with intense curiosity.

A few days later it was fully decided and agreed in every house that the unhappy man was mad. The authorities could not refuse to take the case up, but they too dropped it. Though the trinkets and letters made them wonder, they decided that even if they did turn out to be authentic, no charge could be based on those alone. Besides, the murdered woman might have given him those things as a friend, or asked him to take care of them for her. I heard afterwards, however, that the genuineness of the things was proved by the friends and relations of the murdered woman, and that there was no doubt about them. Yet nothing was destined to come of it, after all.

Five days later, all had heard that he was ill and that his life was in danger. The nature of his illness I can't explain. They said it was an ailment of the heart. But it became known that the doctors had been induced by his wife to look into his mental condition also, and had come to the conclusion that it was a case of insanity. I betrayed nothing, though people ran to question me. But when I wanted to visit him, I was for a long while forbidden to do so, above all by his wife.

"It's you who have caused his illness," she said to me. "He was always gloomy, but for the last year people noticed that he was peculiarly excited and did strange things, and now you have been the ruin of him. Your preaching has brought him to this. For the last month he was always with you."

Indeed, not only his wife but the whole town blamed me. "It's all your doing," they said. I was silent and rejoiced at heart, for I saw plainly God's mercy to the man who had turned against himself and punished himself. I could not believe in his insanity.

They let me see him at last. He insisted upon saying goodby to me. I went in to him and saw at once, that not only his days, but his hours were numbered. He was weak, yellow, his hands trembled, he gasped for breath, but his face was full of tender and happy feeling.

"It is done!" he said. "I've long been yearning to see you. Why didn't you come?"

I did not tell him that they would not let me see him.

"God has had pity on me and is calling me to Him. I know I am dying, but I feel joy and peace for the first time after so many years. There has been heaven in my heart from the moment I did what I had to do. Now I dare to love my children and to kiss them. Neither my wife nor the judges, nor anyone has believed it. My children will never believe it either. I see in that God's mercy to them. I shall die, and my name will be without a stain for them. And now I feel God near, my heart rejoices as in Heaven . . . I have done my duty."

He could not speak any longer. He gasped for breath, he pressed my hand warmly, looking fervently at me. We did not talk for long, his wife kept looking in at us. But he had time to whisper to me: "Do you remember how I came back to you that second time, at midnight? I told you to remember it. You know what I came back for? I came to kill you!"

I stared at him.

"I went out from you then into the darkness, I wandered about the streets, struggling with myself. And suddenly I hated you so that I could hardly bear it. I thought, he is all that binds me, and he is my judge. I can't refuse to face my punishment tomorrow, for he knows all. It was not that I was afraid you would betray me but I thought, 'How can I look him in the face if I don't confess?' And if you had been at the other end of the earth, but alive, it would have been the same. The thought was unendurable that you were alive knowing everything and condemning me. I hated you as though you were the cause, as though you were to blame for everything. I came back to you then, remembering that you had a dagger lying on your table. I sat down and asked you to sit down, and for a whole minute I reasoned with myself. If I had killed you, I would have been ruined by that murder even if I had not confessed the other. But I didn't think about that at all, and I didn't want to think of it at that moment. I only hated you and longed to revenge myself on you for everything. The

287

Lord vanquished the devil in my heart. But let me tell you, you were never nearer death."

A week later he died. The whole town followed him to the grave. The chief priest made a speech full of feeling. All lamented the terrible illness that had cut short his days.

All the town was up in arms against me after the funeral, and people even refused to see me. But then some, at first a few and afterwards more, began to believe in the truth of his story, and they visited me and questioned me with great interest and eagerness, for man loves to see the downfall and disgrace of the righteous. But I held my tongue, and very shortly after, I left the town. And five months later by God's grace I entered upon the safe and blessed path, following the unseen finger which had guided me so clearly to it. But I remember in my prayer to this day, the servant of God, Michael, who suffered so greatly.

2. Conversations and Exhortations of Father Zossima

(e) The Russian Monk and His Possible Significance

FATHERS AND TEACHERS, what is the monk? In the cultivated world the word is nowadays pronounced by some people with a jeer, and by others it is used as a term of abuse. This contempt for the monk is growing. It is true, alas, it is true, that there are many sluggards, gluttons and insolent beggars among the monks. Educated people point to these; "You are idlers, useless members of society, you live on the labor of others, you are shameless beggars." And yet how many meek and humble monks there are, yearning for solitude and fervent prayer in peace. These are less noticed, or passed over in silence. And how surprised men would be if I were to say that from these meek monks, who yearn for solitary prayer, the salvation of Russia will perhaps come. For they are in truth made ready in peace and quiet "for the day and the hour, the month and the year." Meanwhile, in their solitude, they keep the image of Christ fair and undefiled, in the purity of God's truth, from the times of the Fathers of old, the Apostles and the martyrs. And when the time comes they will show it to the tottering creeds of the world. That is a great thought. That star will rise out of the East.

That is my view of the monk, and is it false? Is it too proud? Look at the worldly and all who set themselves up above the people of God. Has not God's image and His truth been distorted in them? They have science; but in science there is nothing but what is the object of sense. The spiritual world, the higher part of man's being is rejected altogether, dismissed with a sort of triumph, even with hatred.

The world has proclaimed the reign of freedom, especially of late, but what do we see in this freedom? Nothing but slavery and self-destruction! For the world says: "You have desires and so satisfy them, for you have the same rights as the most rich and powerful. Don't be afraid of satisfying them and even multiply your desires." That is the modern doctrine of the world. In that they see freedom. And what follows from this right of multiplication of desires? In the rich, isolation and spiritual suicide: in the poor, envy and murder. For they all have been given rights, but have not been shown the means of satisfying their wants. They maintain that the world is getting more and more united, more and more bound together in brotherly community, as it overcomes distance and sets thoughts flying through the air.

Alas, put no faith in such a bond of union. Interpreting freedom as the multiplication and rapid satisfaction of desires, men distort their own nature, for many senseless and foolish desires and habits and ridiculous beliefs are thus fostered. They live only for mutual envy, for luxury and ostentation. To have dinners, carriages, rank and slaves to wait on one is looked upon as a necessity, for which life, honor and human feeling are sacrificed. Men even commit suicide if they are unable to satisfy these desires. We see the same thing among those who are not rich for the poor drown their unsatisfied need and their envy in drunkenness. But soon they will drink blood instead of wine. They are being led on to it. I ask you is such a man free? I knew one "champion of freedom" who told me himself that, when he was deprived of tobacco in prison, he was so wretched that he almost went and betrayed his cause for the sake of getting tobacco again! And such a man says: "I am fighting for the cause of humanity."

How can such a one fight, what is he fit for? He is capable perhaps of some action quickly over, but he cannot hold out long. And it's no wonder that instead of gaining freedom men have sunk into slavery. Instead of serving the cause of brotherly love and the union of humanity, men have fallen, on the contrary, into dissension and isolation, as my mysterious visitor and teacher said to me in my youth. And therefore the idea of the service of humanity, of brotherly love and the solidarity of mankind, is more and more dying out in the world. Indeed this idea is sometimes treated with derision. For how can a man shake off his habits, what can become of him if he is in such bondage to the habit of satisfying the innumerable desires he has created for himself? He is isolated, and what concern has he for the rest of humanity? Men have succeeded in accumulating a greater mass of objects, but the joy in the world has grown less.

The monastic way is very different. Obedience, fasting and

prayer are laughed at, yet only through them lies the way to real, true freedom. I cut off my superfluous and unnecessary desires, I subdue my proud and wanton will and chastise it with obedience, and with God's help I attain freedom of spirit and with it spiritual joy. Which is most capable of conceiving a great idea and serving it—the rich man in his isolation or the man who has freed himself from the tyranny of material things and habits?

The monk is reproached for his solitude: "You have secluded yourself within the walls of the monastery for your own salvation, and have forgotten the brotherly service of humanity!" But we shall see which will be most zealous in the cause of brotherly love. For it is not we, but they, who are in isolation, though they don't see that. Of old, leaders of the people came from among us, and why should they not again? The same meek and humble ascetics will rise up and go out to work for the great cause. The salvation of Russia comes from the people. And the Russian monk has always been on the side of the people. We are isolated only if the people are isolated. The people believe as we do, and an unbelieving reformer will never do anything in Russia, even if he is sincere in heart and a genius. Remember that! The people will meet the atheist and overcome him, and Russia will be one and orthodox. Take care of the peasant and guard his heart. Go on educating him quietly. That's your duty as monks, for the peasant has God in his heart.

(f) *Of Masters and Servants, and of Whether It Is Possible for Them to Be Brothers in the Spirit.*

Of course, I don't deny that there is sin in the peasants too. The fire of corruption is spreading visibly, hourly, working from above downwards. The spirit of isolation is coming upon the people too. Moneylenders and devourers of society are rising up. The merchant grows more and more eager for rank and strives to show himself cultured though he has not a trace of culture. He despises his old traditions, and is even ashamed of the faith of his fathers. He visits princes, though he is only a peasant corrupted. The peasants are rotting in drunkenness and cannot shake off the habit. And what cruelty to their wives, to their children even! All from drunkenness! I've seen in the factories children nine years old, frail, rickety, bent and already depraved. The stuffy workshop, the din of machinery, work all day long, the vile language and the drink, the drink – is that what a little child's heart needs? He needs sunshine, childish play, good examples all about him, and love. There must be no more of this, monks, no more torturing of children. Rise up and preach that. Make haste, make haste!

But God will save Russia, for though the peasants are corrupt and cannot renounce their filthy sin, yet they know it is cursed by God and that they do wrong in sinning. Our people still believe in righteousness, have faith in God and weep tears of devotion.

It is different with the upper classes. They, following science, want to base justice on reason alone, not with Christ as before. They have already proclaimed that there is no crime, that there is no sin. And that's consistent, for if you have no God what is the meaning of crime? In Europe the people are already rising up against the rich, and the leaders of the people are everywhere leading them to bloodshed and teaching them that their wrath is righteous. But their "wrath is accursed, for it is cruel." But God will save Russia as He has saved her many times. Salvation will come from the people, from their faith and their meekness.

Fathers and teachers, watch over the people's faith and this will not be a dream. I've been struck all my life by the dignity of our people, by their true and seemly dignity. I've seen it myself. I can testify to it for I've seen it and marveled at it. I've seen it in spite of the degraded sins and poverty-stricken appearance of our peasantry. They are not servile, and even after two centuries of serfdom, they are free in manner and bearing, yet without insolence, and not revengeful and not envious. "You are rich and noble, you are clever and talented, well be so. God bless you. I respect you, but I know that I too am a man. By the very fact that I respect you without envy I prove my dignity as a man."

In truth if they don't say this (for they don't know how to say this yet) that is how they act. I have seen it myself, I have known it myself. And would you believe it, the poorer our Russian peasant is, the more noticeable is that serene goodness for the rich among them are for the most part corrupt already. Much of this is due to our carelessness and indifference. But God will save His people, for Russia is great in her humility. I dream of seeing, and seem to see clearly already, our future. It will come to pass, that even the most corrupt of our rich will end by being ashamed of his riches before the poor, and the poor, seeing his humility, will understand and give way before him, will respond joyfully and kindly to his honorable shame. Believe me that it will end in that; things are moving to that. Equality is to be found only in the spiritual dignity of man, and that will be understood among us. If we were brothers, there would be fraternity. But man will never agree about the division of wealth. . . . We preserve the image of Christ, and it will shine forth like a precious diamond to the whole world. So may it be, so may it be!

Fathers and teachers, a touching incident befell me once. In my wanderings I met in the town of K. my old orderly whom I had once beaten. It was eight years since I had parted from him. He chanced to see me in the market place, recognized me, ran up to me, and how delighted he was. He simply

291

pounced on me: "Master dear, is it you? Is it really you I see?" He took me home with him.

He was no longer in the army. He was married and already had two little children. He and his wife earned their living by working in the market place. His room was poor, but bright and clean. He made me sit down, set the samovar, sent for his wife, as though my appearance were a festival, for them. He brought me his children: "Bless them, father."

"Is it for me to bless them, I am only a humble monk. I will pray for them as I have prayed for you every day since that day. It all came from you," I said. And I explained it to him as well as I could. And what do you think? The man kept gazing at me and could not believe that I, his former master, an officer, was now before him, a simple monk. It made him shed tears.

"Why are you weeping?" I said. "Better rejoice over me, dear friend, whom I can never forget, for my path is a glad and joyful one."

He did not say much, but kept sighing and shaking his head over me tenderly.

"What has become of your fortune?" he asked.

"I gave it to the monastery," I answered. "We live in common."

After tea I began saying good-by, and suddenly he brought out half a rouble as an offering to the monastery, and another half-rouble he thrust hurriedly into my hand: "That's for you in your wanderings, it may be of use to you, father."

I took his half-rouble, bowed to him and his wife, and went out rejoicing. And on my way I thought: "Here we are both now, he at home and I on the road, sighing and shaking our heads, no doubt, and yet smiling joyfully in the gladness of our hearts, remembering how God brought about our meeting."

I have never seen him again since then. I had been his master and he my servant, but now when we exchanged a loving kiss with softened hearts, there was a great human bond between us. I have thought a great deal about that, and now what I think is this: is it so inconceivable that that grand and simple-hearted unity might in due time become universal among the Russian people? I believe that it will come to pass and that the time is at hand.

And of servants I will add this, in old days when I was young I was often angry with servants: "the cook had served something too hot, the orderly had not brushed my clothes." But what taught me better then was a thought of my dear brother's, which I had heard from him in childhood: "Am I worth it, that another should serve me and be ordered about by me in his poverty and ignorance?" And I wondered at the time that such simple and self-evident ideas should be so slow to occur to our minds.

292

It is impossible that there should be no servants in the world, but act so that your servant may be freer in spirit than if he were not a servant. And why cannot I be a servant to my servant and even let him see it, and that without any pride on my part or any mistrust on his? Why should not my servant be like my own kindred, so that I may take him into my family and rejoice in doing so? Even now this can be done. It will lead to the grand unity of men in the future, when a man will not seek servants for himself, or desire to turn his fellow creatures into servants as he does now, but on the contrary, will long with his whole heart to be the servant of all, as the Gospel teaches.

And can it be a dream, that in the end man will find his joy only in deeds of light and mercy, and not in cruel pleasures as now, in gluttony, fornication, ostentation, boasting and envious rivalry of one with the other? I firmly believe that it is not a dream and that the time is at hand. People laugh and ask: "When will that time come and does it look as though it is coming?" I believe that with Christ's help we shall accomplish this great thing. How many ideas have there been in the history of man which were unthinkable ten years before they appeared? Yet when their destined hour had come, they came forth and spread over the whole earth. So it will be with us, and our people will shine forth in the world, and all men will say: "The stone which the builders rejected has become the cornerstone of the building."

And we may ask the scornful: if our hope is a dream, when will you build your edifice and order things justly by your intellect alone, without Christ? If they declare that it is they who are advancing toward unity, only the most simple-hearted among them believe it, so that one may positively marvel at such simplicity. In truth, they have more fantastic dreams than we. They aim at justice, but, denying Christ, they will end by flooding the earth with blood, for blood cries out for blood, and he that taketh up the sword shall perish by the sword. And if it were not for Christ's covenant, they would slaughter one another down to the last two men on earth. And those two last men would not be able to restrain each other in their pride, and the one would slay the other and then himself. That would come to pass, were it not for the promise of Christ that for the sake of the humble and meek the days shall be shortened.

While I was still wearing an officer's uniform after my duel, I talked about servants in general society, and I remember everyone was amazed at me. "What!" they asked, "are we to make our servants sit down on the sofa and offer them tea?" And I answered them: "Why not, sometimes at least." Everyone laughed. Their question was frivolous and my answer was not clear; but the thought in it was to some extent right.

Young man, be not forgetful of prayer. Every time you pray, if your prayer is sincere, there will be new feeling and new meaning in it, which will give you fresh courage, and you will understand that prayer is an education. Remember too every day, and whenever you can, repeat to yourself: "Lord have mercy on all who appear before Thee today." For every hour and every moment thousands of men leave life on this earth, and their souls appear before God. And how many of them depart in solitude, unknown, sad, dejected; no one mourns for them or even knows whether they have lived or not. And behold, from the other end of the earth perhaps your prayer for their rest will rise up to God though you knew them not nor they you. How touching it must be to a soul standing in dread before the Lord to feel at that instant that, for him too, there is one to pray, that there is a fellow creature left on earth to love him. And God will look on you both more graciously, for if you have had so much pity on him, how much more will He have pity Who is infinitely more loving and merciful than you. And He will forgive him for your sake.

Brothers, have no fear of men's sin. Love a man even in his sin, for that is the semblance of Divine Love and is the highest love on earth. Love all God's creation, the whole and every grain of sand of it. Love every leaf, every ray of God's light. Love the animals, love the plants, love everything. If you love everything, you will perceive the divine mystery in things. Once you perceive it, you will begin to comprehend it better every day. And you will come at last to love the whole world with an all-embracing love. Love animals: God has given them the rudiments of thought and joy untroubled. Do not trouble their joy, don't harass them, don't deprive them of their happiness, don't work against God's intent. Man, do not pride yourself on superiority to animals; they are without sin, and you, with your greatness, defile the earth by your appearance on it, and leave the traces of your foulness after you—alas, it is true of almost everyone of us! Love children especially, for they too are sinless like the angels; they live to soften and purify our hearts and as it were to guide us. Woe to him who offends a child! Father Anfim taught me to love children. This kind, silent man used often on our wanderings to spend the farthings given us on sweets and cakes for the children. He could not pass by a child without emotion, that is the nature of the man.

At some thoughts one stands perplexed, especially at the sight of men's sin, and wonders whether one should use force or humble love. Always decide to use humble love. If you resolve on that once and for all, you may subdue the whole world. Loving humility is marvelously strong, the strongest of all things. There is nothing else like it.

Every day and every hour, every minute, walk around yourself and watch yourself, and see that your image is a seemly one. You pass by a little child, you pass by, spiteful, with ugly words, with angry heart; you may not have noticed the child, but he has seen you, and your image, unseemly and ignoble, may remain in his defenseless heart. You don't know it, but you may have sown an evil seed in him and it may grow, and all because you were not careful before the child, because you did not foster in yourself a careful, actively benevolent love. Brothers, love is a teacher; but one must know how to acquire it, for it is hard to acquire, it is dearly bought, it is won slowly by long labor. For we must love not only occasionally, for a moment, but forever. Everyone can love occasionally, even the wicked can.

My brother asked the birds to forgive him. That sounds senseless, but it was right for all is like an ocean, all is flowing and blending; a touch in one place sets up movement at the other end of the earth. It may be senseless to beg forgiveness of the birds, but birds would be happier at your side—a little happier, anyway—and children and all animals, if you yourself were nobler than you are now. It's all like an ocean, I tell you. Then you would pray to the birds too, consumed by an all-embracing love, in a sort of transport, you would pray that they too would forgive you your sin. Treasure this ecstasy, however senseless it may seem to men.

My friends, pray to God for gladness. Be glad as children, as the birds of heaven. And let not the sin of men confound you in your doings. Fear not that it will wear away your work and hinder its being accomplished. Do not say: "Sin is mighty, wickedness is mighty, evil environment is mighty, and we are lonely and helpless. Evil environment is wearing us away and hindering our good work from being done." Fly from that dejection! There is only one means of salvation. Make yourself responsible for all men's sins. As soon as you sincerely make yourself responsible for everything and for all men, you will see at once that you have found salvation. On the other hand by throwing your indolence and impotence on others you will end by sharing the pride of Satan and murmuring against God.

Of the pride of Satan what I think is this: it is hard for us on earth to comprehend it, and therefore it is so easy to fall into error and to share it, even imagining that we are doing something good and fine. Indeed many of the strongest feelings and movements of our nature we cannot comprehend on earth. Let not that be a stumbling block, and think not that it may serve as a justification to you for anything. For the Eternal Judge asks of you only what you can understand. You will know that yourself hereafter, for you will behold all things truly then and will not dispute them. On earth, indeed, we are as it were astray, and if it were not for the precious image of Christ before us, we should be undone and altogether lost, as was the human race before the flood. Much on earth is hidden from us, but to make up for that we have been given a precious mystic sense of our living bond with the other world, with the higher heavenly world, and the roots of our thoughts and feelings are not here but in other worlds. That is why the philosophers say that we cannot understand the reality of things on earth.

God took seeds from different worlds and sowed them on this earth, and His garden grew up and everything came up that could come up. But what grows lives and is alive only through the feeling of its contact with other mysterious worlds. If that feeling grows weak or is destroyed in you, the heavenly growth will die away in you. Then you will be indifferent to life and even grow to hate it. That's what I think.

(h) *Can a Man Judge His Fellow Creatures? Faith to the End.*

Remember particularly that you cannot be a judge of anyone. For no one can judge a criminal, until he recognizes that he is just such a criminal as the man standing before him, and that he perhaps is more than all men to blame for that crime. When he understands that, he will be able to be a judge. Though that sounds absurd, it is true. If I had been righteous myself, perhaps there would have been no criminal standing before me. If you can take upon yourself the crime of the criminal your heart is judging, take it at once, suffer for him yourself, and let him go without reproach. And even if the law itself makes you his judge, act in the same spirit so far as possible, for he will go away and condemn himself more bitterly than you have done. If, after your kiss, he goes away untouched, mocking at you, do not let that be a stumbling block to you. It shows his time has not yet come. But remember it will come in due course. And if it come not, no matter; if not he, then another in his place will understand and suffer, and judge and condemn himself, and the truth will be fulfilled. Believe that. Believe it without doubt for in that lies all the hope and faith of the saints.

Work without ceasing. If you remember in the night as you go to sleep: "I have not done what I ought to have done," rise up at once and do it. If the people around you are spiteful and callous and will not hear you, fall down before them and beg their forgiveness; for in truth you are to blame for their not wanting to hear you. And if you cannot speak to them in their bitterness, serve them in silence, and in humility, never losing hope. If all men abandon you and drive you away by force, then when you are left alone fall on the earth and kiss it. Water it with your tears and it will bring forth fruit even though no one has seen or heard you in your solitude. Believe to the end, even if all men go astray and you are left the only one faithful; bring your offering even then and praise God in your loneliness. And if two of you are gathered together—then there is a whole world, a world of living love. Embrace each other tenderly and praise God, for if only in you two His truth has been fulfilled.

If you sin and grieve even unto death for your sins or for your sudden sin, then rejoice for others, rejoice for the righteous man. Rejoice that if you have sinned, he is righteous and has not sinned.

If the evil doings of men move you to indignation and overwhelming distress, even to a desire for vengeance on the evildoers, shun above all things that feeling. Go at once and seek suffering for yourself, as though you were yourself guilty of that wrong. Accept that suffering and bear it and your heart will find comfort, and you will understand that you too are guilty, for you might have been a light to the evil-doers and were not a light to them. If you had been a light, you would have lightened the path for others too, and the evil-doer might perhaps have been saved by your light. And even though your light was shining and you see men were not saved by it, hold firm and doubt not the power of the heavenly light. Believe that if they were not saved, they will be saved hereafter. And if they are not saved hereafter, then their sons will be saved, for your light will not die even when you are dead. The righteous man departs but his light remains. Men are always saved after the death of the deliverer. Men reject their prophets and slay them, but they love their martyrs and honor those whom they have slain. You are working for the whole, you are acting for the future. Seek no reward, for great is your reward on this earth: the spiritual joy which is only vouchsafed to the righteous man. Fear not the great nor the mighty, but be wise and ever serene. Know the measure, know the times, study that. When you are left alone, pray. Love to throw yourself on the earth and kiss it. Kiss the earth and love it with an unceasing, consuming love. Love all men, love everything. Seek that rapture and ecstasy. Water the earth with the tears of your joy and love those tears. Don't be ashamed of that ecstasy, prize it, for it is a gift of God and a great one; it is not given to many but only to the elect.

(i) *Of Hell and Hell Fire. A Mystic Reflection.*

Fathers and teachers, I ask: "What is hell?" I maintain that it is the suffering of being unable to love. Once in infinite existence, immeasurable in time and space, a spiritual creature was given on his coming to earth, the power of saying: "I am and I love." Once, only once, there was given him a moment of

297

active *living* love and for that was earthly life given him, and with it times and seasons. And that happy creature rejected the priceless gift, prized it and loved it not, scorned it and remained callous. Such a one, having left the earth, sees Abraham's bosom and talks with Abraham as we are told in the parable of the rich man of Lazarus, and beholds heaven and can go up to the Lord. But that is just his torment, to rise up to the Lord without ever having loved, to be brought close to those who have loved when he has despised their love. For he sees clearly and says to himself: "Now I have understanding and though I now thirst to love, there will be nothing great, no sacrifice in my love, for my earthly life is over, and Abraham will not come even with a drop of living water (that is the gift of earthly, active life) to cool the fiery thirst of a spiritual love which burns in me now, though I despised it on earth. There is no more life for me and there will be no more time! Even though I would gladly give my life for others, it can never be, for that life is passed which can be sacrificed for love, and now there is a gulf fixed between that life and this existence."

They talk of hell fire in the material sense. I don't go into that mystery and I shun it. But I think if there were fire in the material sense, they would be glad of it, for, I imagine, that in material agony, their still greater spiritual agony would be forgotten for a moment. Moreover, that spiritual agony cannot be taken from them, for that suffering is not external but within them. And if it could be taken from them, I think it would be more bitter still for the unhappy creatures. For even if the righteous in Paradise forgave them, beholding their torments, and called them up to heaven in their infinite love, they would only multiply their torments, for they would arouse in them still more keenly a flaming thirst for responsive, active and grateful love which is now impossible. In the timidity of my heart I imagine, however, that the very recognition of this impossibility would serve at last to console them. For accepting the love of the righteous together with the impossibility of repaying it, by this submissiveness and the effect of this humility, they will attain at last a certain semblance of that active love which they scorned in life. . . . I am sorry, friends and brothers, that I cannot express this clearly. But woe to those who have slain themselves on earth, woe to the suicides! I believe that there can be none more miserable than they. We are told that it is a sin to pray for them and outwardly the Church renounces them, but in my secret heart I believe that we may pray even for them. Love can never be an offense to Christ. For such as those I have prayed inwardly all my life, I confess it, fathers and teachers, and even now I pray for them every day.

Oh, there are some who remain proud and fierce even in
298

hell, in spite of their certain knowledge and contemplation of the absolute truth; there are some fearful ones who have given themselves over entirely to Satan and his proud spirit. For such, hell is voluntary and ever consuming; they are tortured by their own choice. For they have cursed themselves, cursing God and life. They live upon their vindictive pride like a starving man in the desert sucking blood out of his own body. But they are never satisfied, and they refuse forgiveness, they curse God Who calls them. They cannot behold the living God without hatred, and they cry out that the God of life should be annihilated, that God should destroy Himself and His own creation. And they will burn in the fire of their own wrath forever and yearn for death and annihilation. But they will not attain to death. . . .

Here Alexey Karamazov's manuscript ends. I repeat, it is incomplete and fragmentary. Biographical details, for instance, cover only Father Zossima's earliest youth. Of his teaching and opinions we find brought together sayings evidently spoken on very different occasions. His words during the last few hours have not been kept separate from the rest, but their general character can be gathered from what we have in Alyosha's manuscript.

The elder's death came in the end quite unexpectedly. For although those who were gathered about him that last evening realized that his death was approaching, yet it was difficult to imagine that it would come so suddenly. On the contrary, his friends, as I observed already, seeing him that night apparently so cheerful and talkative, were convinced that there was at least a temporary change for the better in his condition. Even five minutes before his death, they said afterwards, it was impossible to foresee it. He seemed suddenly to feel an acute pain in his chest, he turned pale and pressed his hands to his heart. All got up from their seats and went to him. But though suffering, he still looked at them with a smile, sank slowly from his chair onto his knees, then bowed his face to the ground, stretched out his arms and as though in joyful ecstasy, praying and kissing the ground, quietly and joyfully gave up his soul to God.

The news of Father Zossima's death spread at once through the hermitage and reached the monastery. His nearest friends and those whose duty it was, began to lay out the corpse according to ancient ritual, and all the monks gathered together in the church.

Before dawn the news of his death reached the town. By morning all the town was talking about it and crowds were flocking to the monastery. But this subject will be treated in the next book; I will only add here that before a day had passed something happened so unexpected, so strange, up-setting, and bewildering in its effect on the monks and the townspeople, that after all these years, that day is still vividly remembered in our town.

PART THREE

BOOK VII: ALYOSHA

1. The Breath of Corruption

THE BODY OF FATHER ZOSSIMA was prepared for burial according to the established ritual. As is well known, the bodies of dead monks and hermits are not washed. In the words of the Church Ritual: "If any one of the monks departs in the Lord, the monk designated (that is, whose office it is) shall wipe the body with warm water, making first the sign of the cross with a sponge on the forehead of the deceased, on the breast, on the hands and feet and on the knees, and that is enough."

All this was done by Father Paissy, who then clothed the elder in his monastic garb and wrapped him in his cloak, which was, according to custom, slit to allow for its being folded about him in the form of a cross. On his head Father Paissy put a hood with an eight-cornered cross. The hood was left open and the dead elder's face was covered with black gauze. In his hands was put an ikon of the Saviour.

Toward morning he was put in a coffin which had been made ready long before. It was decided to leave the coffin all day in the cell, in the larger room in which the elder used to receive his visitors and fellow monks. And as Father Zossima had been a priest and monk of the strictest rule, the Gospel, not the Psalter, was read over his body by monks in holy orders. The reading was begun by Father Joseph immediately after the requiem service. Faither Paissy wanted later on to read the Gospel all day and night over his dead friend, but for the present he, as well as the Father Superintendent of the hermitage, was very busy and occupied, for something extraordinary, and unheard of happened. An "unseemly" excitement and impatient expectation became apparent in the monks, the visitors from the monastery hotel, and the crowds of people flocking from the town. And as time went on, this grew more and more marked. Both the Superintendent and Father Paissy did their best to calm this excitement.

When it was fully daylight, some people began bringing their sick, in most cases children, with them from the town—as though they had been waiting for this moment, evidently persuaded that the dead elder's remains had a power of healing, which would be immediately made manifest in accordance with their faith. It was only then apparent how unquestionably everyone in our town had accepted Father Zossima during his lifetime as a great saint. And those who came were far from being of the humbler classes.

This expectation on the part of believers displayed with such haste, such openness, even with impatience and insistence, impressed Father Paissy as unseemly. Though he had long foreseen something of the sort, the actual manifestation of the feeling was beyond anything he had looked for. When he came across monks who displayed this excitement, Father Paissy reproved them. "Such expectation of something extraordinary," he said, "shows a levity, possible to worldly people but unseemly in us."

But little attention was paid to Father Paissy and he noticed it uneasily. Yet he himself, if the whole truth must be told, secretly cherished the same hopes. Nevertheless, it was unpleasant for him to meet certain people, whose presence aroused in him great misgivings. In the crowd in the dead elder's cell he noticed with inward aversion (for which he immediately reproached himself) the divinity student Rakitin and the monk from Obdorsk, who was still staying at the monastery. Father Paissy felt suddenly suspicious of both of them—though he might well have felt the same about others.

The monk from Obdorsk was conspicuous as the most fussy in the excited crowd. He was to be seen everywhere; everywhere he was asking questions, everywhere he was listening, on all sides he was whispering with a peculiar, mysterious air. His expression showed the greatest impatience and even a sort of irritation.

As for Rakitin, he, it appeared later, had come early to the hermitage at the special request of Madame Hohlakov. As soon as that good-hearted but weak-minded woman, who could not have been admitted to the hermitage, woke up and heard of the death of Father Zossima, she was overtaken with such curiosity that she promptly sent Rakitin to the hermitage, to keep careful lookout and report to her by letter every half hour or so *"everything that takes place."* She regarded Rakitin as a most religious and devout young man. He was particularly clever in getting around people and assuming whatever part he thought most to their taste, if he sensed the slightest advantage for himself from doing so.

It was a bright, clear day and many of the visitors were thronging about the tombs, which were particularly numerous round the church and scattered here and there about the hermitage. As he walked around the hermitage, Father Paissy remembered Alyosha and that he had not seen him for some time, not since the night. He had no sooner thought of him than he noticed him in the furthest corner of the hermitage garden, sitting on the tombstone of a monk who had been famous long ago for his saintliness. He sat with his back to the hermitage and his face to the wall. Going up to him, Father Paissy saw that he was weeping quietly but bitterly, with his face hidden in his hands. Father Paissy stood over him.

"Enough, dear son, enough," he said with feeling. "Why do you weep? Rejoice and weep not. Don't you know that this is the greatest of his days? Think only where he is now, at this moment!"

Alyosha glanced at him, uncovering his face, which was swollen with crying like a child's. But he turned away at once without saying a word and hid his face in his hands again.

"Maybe it is well," said Father Paissy thoughtfully. "Weep if you must, Christ has sent you those tears."

Walking away from Alyosha and thinking lovingly of him, he added to himself: "His touching tears are but a relief to his spirit and will serve to gladden his heart." He walked away quickly, for he felt that he too might weep looking at him.

Meanwhile time was passing. The monastery services and the requiems for the dead followed in their due course. Father Paissy again took Father Joseph's place by the coffin and began reading the Gospel. But before three o'clock in the afternoon something took place, something so unexpected by all of us and so contrary to the general hope, that, I repeat, this trivial incident has been minutely remembered to this day in our town and all the surrounding countryside. I may add here that I personally feel it almost repulsive to recall that event which caused such excitement and was such a stumbling block to so many, though in reality it was the most natural thing. I would, of course, have omitted all mention of it in my story, if it had not exerted a very strong influence on the heart and soul of the chief, *though future*, hero of my story, Alyosha. It brought a crisis and turning point to his spiritual development, giving a shock to his intellect, which finally strengthened it for the rest of his life and gave it a definite aim.

And so, to return to our story. When before dawn they laid Father Zossima's body in the coffin and brought it into the front room, the question of opening the windows was raised among those who were around the coffin. But this suggestion was unanswered and went almost unnoticed. Some may have noticed it, only to reflect that the thought of decay and corruption from the body of such a saint was an absurdity, calling for compassion for the lack of faith it implied. They expected something quite different.

And, behold, soon after noon there were signs of something, at first observed in silence by those who came in and out. But by three o'clock those signs had become so clear and unmistakable, that the news swiftly reached all the monks and visitors in the hermitage, promptly penetrated to the monastery, throwing all the monks into amazement, and finally spread to the town, exciting everyone in it, believers and unbelievers alike. The unbelievers rejoiced. As for the believers some of them rejoiced even more than the unbelievers, for "men love the downfall and disgrace of the righteous," as the deceased elder had said in one of his exhortations.

The fact is that a smell of decomposition began to come from the coffin, growing gradually more marked until by three o'clock it was quite unmistakable. In all the past history of our monastery, no such thing could be recalled. Its immediate effect was to cause a scandalous disorder among the monks. Afterwards, even many years afterwards, some sensible monks were amazed and horrified when they recalled that day, that the scandal could have reached such proportions. For in the past, monks of very holy life had died, God-fearing old men, whose saintliness was acknowledged by all, yet from their humble coffins, too, the breath of corruption had come, naturally, as from all dead bodies, but it had caused not the slightest excitement. Of course there had been, in former times, saints in the monastery whose memory was carefully preserved and whose relics, according to tradition, showed no signs of corruption. This fact was regarded by the monks as mysterious, and the tradition of it was cherished as something blessed and miraculous, and as a promise, by God's grace, of still greater glory from their tombs in the future.

One such saint, whose memory was particularly cherished, was an old monk, Job, who had died seventy years before at the age of a hundred and five. He had been a famous ascetic, rigid in fasting and silence, and his tomb was pointed out to all visitors on their arrival with respect and mysterious hints of great hopes connected with it. (That was the very tomb on which Father Paissy had found Alyosha sitting in the morning.) Another memory cherished in the monastery was that of the famous Father Varsonofy, who had only recently died and had preceded Father Zossima in the eldership. He was reverenced during his lifetime as a crazy saint by all the pilgrims to the monastery. There was a tradition that both of these, the monk Job and Father Varsonofy, had lain in their coffins as though alive, that they had shown no signs of decomposition when they were buried and that there had been a holy light in their faces. And some people even insisted that a sweet fragrance came from their bodies.

Yet, in spite of these memories, it would be difficult to explain the absurdity and malice that were displayed beside the coffin of Father Zossima. It is my private opinion that several different causes were at work, one of which was the deeply rooted hostility to the institution of elders as an evil innovation, a hostility hidden deep in the hearts of many of the monks. Even more powerful was jealousy of the dead man's saintliness, so firmly established during his lifetime that it was almost a forbidden thing to question it. For though the late elder had won over many hearts, more by love than by miracles, and had gathered around him a mass of loving disciples, none the less he had awakened jealousy and so had come to have bitter enemies, secret and open, not only in the monastery but in the world outside. He did no one any harm, but: "Why do they think him so saintly?" And that question alone gradually repeated gave rise at last to an intense, insatiable hatred of him. That, I believe, was the reason why many people were pleased at the smell of decomposition which came so quickly, for not a day had passed since his death. At the same time there were some among those who had been devoted to the elder, who were mortified and personally affronted by this incident. This was how the thing happened.

As soon as signs of decomposition began to appear, the monks betrayed their secret motives in entering the cell. They went in, stayed a little while and hurried out to confirm the news to the other monks waiting outside. Some of these shook their heads mournfully, but others did not conceal the malicious pleasure which gleamed unmistakably in their eyes. And now no one reproached them for it, no one raised his voice in protest, which was strange, for the majority of the monks had been devoted to the dead elder. But it seemed as though God had in this case let the minority get the upper hand for a time.

Visitors from outside, particularly of the educated class, soon went into the cell, too, with the same spying intent. Of the peasantry few went into the cell, though there were crowds of them at the gates of the hermitage. After three o'clock the rush of worldly visitors increased. This was no doubt due to the shocking news. People were attracted to the hermitage who would not otherwise have come on that day and had not intended to come. Among them were some of high standing. But external propriety was still preserved and Father Paissy, with a stern face, continued firmly and distinctly reading aloud the Gospel. He appeared not to notice what was taking place around him, though he had, in fact, observed something unusual long before.

But at last the murmurs, first subdued but gradually louder and more confident, reached even him. "It shows God's judgment is not as man's," Father Paissy heard suddenly. The first to give utterance to this sentiment was a layman, an elderly official from the town, known to be a pious man. But he only repeated aloud what the monks had long been whispering. They had long before formulated this damning conclusion, and the worst of it was that a sort of triumphant satisfaction at that conclusion became more and more apparent every moment. Soon they began to lay aside even external propriety. They seemed to feel they had a right to discard it.

"And for what reason can *this* have happened?" some of the monks asked, at first with a show of regret. "He had a small

305

frame and his flesh was dried up on his bones. What was there to decay?"

"It must be a sign from heaven," others hastened to add, and their opinion was adopted at once without protest. For it was pointed out, too, that if the decomposition had been natural, as in the case of every dead sinner, it would have been apparent later, after a lapse of at least twenty-four hours. But this premature corruption "was in excess of nature," and so the finger of God was evident. It was meant for a sign. This conclusion seemed irresistible.

Gentle Father Joseph, the librarian, a great favorite of the dead elder, tried to answer some of the evil speakers that "this is not held everywhere alike," and that the incorruptibility of the bodies of the just was not a dogma of the Orthodox Church, but only an opinion. He said that even in the most Orthodox regions, at Athos for instance, they were not greatly confounded by the smell of corruption, and there the chief sign of the glorification of the saved was not bodily incorruptibility, but the color of the bones when the bodies have lain many years in the earth and have decayed in it. "And if the bones are yellow as wax, that is the great sign that the Lord has glorified the dead saint. If they are not yellow but black, it shows that God has not deemed him worthy of such glory—that is the belief in Athos, a great place, where the Orthodox doctrine has been preserved from of old, unbroken and in its greatest purity," said Father Joseph in conclusion.

But the meek Father's words had little effect and even brought a mocking reply. "That's all pedantry and innovation, no use listening to it," the monks decided. "We stick to the old doctrine. There are all sorts of innovations nowadays, are we to follow them all?" added others.

"We have had as many holy fathers as they had in Athos. There they are among the Turks, they have forgotten everything. Their doctrine has long been impure and they have no bells even," the most sneering added.

Father Joseph walked away grieving. He was also sad because he had put forward his own opinion with little confidence as though scarcely believing in it himself. He foresaw with distress that something very unseemly was beginning and that there were signs of disobedience. Little by little, all the sensible monks were reduced to silence like Father Joseph. And so it came to pass that all who loved the elder and had accepted with devout obedience the institution of the eldership were terribly let down and glanced timidly at one another's faces. Those who were hostile to the institution of elders held up their heads proudly. "There was no smell of corruption from the late elder Varsonofy, but a sweet fragrance," they recalled with spite. "But he gained that glory not because he was an elder, but because he was a holy man."

And this was followed by a shower of criticism and blame

of Father Zossima. "His teaching was false; he taught that life is a great joy and not a vale of tears," said some of the more unreasonable. "He followed the fashionable belief, he did not recognize material fire in hell," others, still more unreasonable, added. "He was not strict in fasting, allowed himself sweet things, ate cherry jam with his tea. Ladies used to send it to him. Is it for a monk of strict rule to drink tea?" could be heard among some of the envious. "He sat in pride," the most malicious declared vindictively. "He considered himself a saint and he took it as his due when people knelt before him." "He abused the sacrament of confession," the fiercest opponents of the institution of elders added in a whisper. And among these were some of the oldest monks, strictest in their devotion, genuine ascetics, who had kept silent during the life of the deceased elder, but now suddenly unsealed their lips. And this was terrible, for their words had great influence on young monks who were not yet firm in their convictions.

The monk from Obdorsk heard all this, heaving deep sighs and nodding his head. He reasoned: "Yes, clearly Father Ferapont was right in his judgment yesterday," and at that moment the mad Father Ferapont appeared, as though on purpose to increase the confusion.

I have mentioned already that this strange monk rarely left his cell by the apiary. He was seldom even seen at church. They overlooked this neglect because of his craziness, and did not keep him to the rules binding on all the rest. But if the whole truth is to be told, they hardly had a choice about it. For it would have been discreditable to insist on burdening with the common regulations so great an ascetic, who prayed day and night (he even dropped asleep on his knees). If they had insisted, the monks would have said: "He is holier than all of us and he follows a rule higher than ours. And if he does not go to church it's because he knows when he ought to. He has his own rule." It was to avoid the chance of these sinful murmurs that Father Ferapont was left in peace.

As everyone was aware, Father Ferapont particularly disliked Father Zossima. And now the news had reached him in his hut that "God's judgment is not the same as man's," and that something had happened which was "in excess of nature." It may well be supposed that among the first to run to him with the news was the monk from Obdorsk, who had visited him the evening before and left his cell terror-stricken.

I have mentioned above, that though Father Paissy, standing firm and immovable reading the Gospel over the coffin, could not hear nor see what was happening outside the cell, he gauged most of it correctly in his heart for he knew the men surrounding him. He was not shaken by it, but awaited what would come next without fear, watching with penetration and insight for the outcome.

Suddenly an extraordinary uproar in the passage burst upon

his ears. The door was flung open and Father Ferapont appeared in the doorway. Behind him stood a crowd of monks together with many people from the town. They stood at the bottom of the steps, waiting to see what Father Ferapont would say or do. For they felt with a certain awe that he had not come for nothing.

Standing in the doorway, Father Ferapont raised his arms. Under his right arm could be seen the inquisitive little eyes of the monk from Obdorsk. He alone, in his curiosity, could not resist running up the steps after Father Ferapont. The others, on the contrary, pressed further back in sudden alarm when the door was noisily flung open.

Father Ferapont suddenly roared: "Casting out I cast out!" And, turning in all directions, he began making the sign of the cross at each of the four walls and four corners of the cell. All who were present understood his action. For they knew he always did this wherever he went, and that he would not sit down or say a word, till he had driven out the evil spirits.

"Satan, go hence! Satan, go hence!" he repeated at each sign of the cross. "Casting out I cast out," he roared again.

He was wearing his coarse robe girt with a rope. His bare chest, covered with gray hair, could be seen under his hempen shirt. His feet were bare. As soon as he began waving his arms, the cruel irons he wore under his robe could be heard clanking.

Father Paissy paused in his reading, stepped forward and stood before him waiting.

"What have you come for, worthy Father? Why do you offend against good order? Why do you disturb the peace of the flock?" he said at last, looking sternly at him.

"What have I come for? You ask why? What is your faith?" shouted Father Ferapont crazily. "I've come here to drive out your visitors, the unclean devils. I've come to see how many have gathered here while I have been away. I want to sweep them out with a birch broom."

"You cast out the evil spirit, but perhaps you are serving him yourself," Father Paissy went on fearlessly. "And who can say of himself 'I am holy.' Can you, Father?"

"I am unclean not holy. I would not sit in an arm chair and would not have them bow down to me as an idol," thundered Father Ferapont. "Nowadays there are some who destroy the true faith. The dead man, your saint," he turned to the crowd, pointing with his finger to the coffin, "did not believe in devils. He gave medicine to keep off the devils. And so they have become as common as spiders in the corners. And now he has begun to stink himself. In that we see a great sign from God."

The incident he referred to was this. One of the monks was haunted in his dreams and, later on, in waking moments, by visions of evil spirits. When in the greatest terror he confided this to Father Zossima, the elder advised continual prayer and rigid fasting. But when this proved of no use, the elder advised him that while persisting in prayer and fasting, he should take a special medicine. Many in the monastery were shocked at the time and shook their heads as they talked about it—and most of all Father Ferapont, to whom some had reported this "extraordinary" counsel on the part of the elder.

"Go away, Father!" said Father Paissy in a commanding voice. "It's not for man to judge but for God. Perhaps we see here a 'sign' which neither you, nor I, nor any one of us is able to comprehend. Go, Father, and do not trouble the flock!" he repeated impressively.

"He did not keep the fasts according to the rule and therefore the sign has come. That is clear and it's a sin to hide it," cried Father Ferapont. He was carried away by a zeal that outstripped his reason and could not be quieted. "He was seduced by sweets. Ladies brought them to him in their pockets. He sipped tea, he worshiped his belly, filling it with sweet things and his mind with haughty thought. . . . And for this he is put to shame. . . ."

"You speak lightly, Father." Father Paissy too raised his voice. "I admire your fasting and severities, but you speak lightly like some frivolous youth, fickle and childish. Go away, Father, I command you!" Father Paissy thundered in conclusion.

"I will go," said Father Ferapont, seeming somewhat taken aback, but still bitter. "Your learned men! You are so clever you look down upon my humbleness. I came here with little learning and here I have forgotten what I did know. God himself has preserved me in my weakness from your confusions."

Father Paissy stood waiting.

Father Ferapont paused and, suddenly leaning his cheek on his hand despondently, pronounced in a singsong voice, looking at the coffin of the dead elder: "Tomorrow they will sing over him 'Our Helper and Defender'—a splendid anthem—and over me when I die all they'll sing will be 'What Earthly Joy'—a little canticle," he added with tearful regret. "You are proud and puffed up. This is a vain place!" he shouted suddenly like a madman. And with a wave of his hand he turned quickly and quickly went down the steps.

The crowd awaiting him below wavered; some followed him at once and some lingered, for the cell was still open, and Father Paissy, following Father Ferapont onto the steps, stood watching him. But the excited old mad monk was not completely silenced. Walking twenty steps away, he suddenly turned toward the setting sun, raised both his arms and, as though someone had cut him down, fell to the ground with a loud scream.

"My God has conquered! Christ has conquered the setting sun!" he shouted frantically, again stretching up his hands to the sun, and again falling face downwards. He sobbed like a little child, shaken by his tears and spreading out his arms on the ground. All rushed up to him; there were exclamations and sympathetic sobs . . . a kind of frenzy seemed to take possession of everyone.

"This is the one who is a saint! This is the one who is a holy man!" some cried aloud, losing their fear. "This is the one who should be an elder," others added.

"He wouldn't be an elder . . . He would refuse . . . He wouldn't serve a cursed innovation . . . He wouldn't imitate their foolery," other voices chimed in at once. And it is hard to say how far they might have gone, but at that moment the bell rang summoning them to service. All began crossing themselves at once. Father Ferapont, too, got up and crossing himself went back to his cell without looking around, still uttering exclamations which were incoherent. A few followed him, but the greater number hurried off to attend the service.

Father Paissy let Father Joseph read in his place and went down. The frantic outcries of bigots could not shake him, but his heart was suddenly filled with melancholy. He stood still and suddenly wondered: "Why am I sad even to dejection?" And immediately he grasped with surprise that his sudden sadness was due to a very small and special cause. In the crowd thronging at the entrance to the cell, he had noticed Alyosha and he remembered that he had felt at once a pang in heart on seeing him. "Can that boy mean so much to my heart?" he asked himself, wondering.

At that moment Alyosha passed him, hurrying along, but not in the direction of the church. Their eyes met. Then Alyosha quickly cast his eyes to the ground. From this alone, Father Paissy guessed that a great change was taking place in him.

"Have you, too, fallen into temptation?" cried Father Paissy. "Can you be with those of little faith," he added mournfully.

Alyosha stood still and gazed vaguely at Father Paissy, but quickly turned his eyes away again and again looked at the ground. He stood sideways and did not turn his face to Father Paissy, who watched him attentively.

"Where are you going? The bell calls to service," he said.

Alyosha did not answer.

"Are you leaving the hermitage? Leaving without asking permission, without asking a blessing?"

Alyosha smiled weakly, cast a strange, very strange look at Father Paissy to whom his former guide, the former sovereign of his heart and mind, his beloved elder, had entrusted him as he lay dying. And suddenly, still without speaking, he waved his hand, as though not caring even to be respectful, and walked toward the gates away from the hermitage.

"You will come back again!" murmured Father Paissy, looking after him with sorrow.

2. A Critical Moment

FATHER PAISSY WAS NOT WRONG when he decided that Alyosha would come back again. Perhaps he penetrated with insight into the true meaning of Alyosha's spiritual condition. Yet I must frankly say that it would be very difficult for me to give a clear account of that strange, vague moment in the life of the young hero I love so much. To Father Paissy's sorrowful question: "Are you too with those of little faith?" I could of course confidently answer for Alyosha "No." He was not with those of little faith. Quite the contrary. All his troubles came from the fact that he was of great faith. But still the trouble was there and was so agonizing that even long afterwards Alyosha thought of that sorrowful day as one of the most bitter and most fatal days of his life. If the question is asked: "Could all his grief and disturbance have been due only to the fact that his elder's body had shown signs of premature decomposition instead of at once performing miracles?" I must answer: "Yes, it certainly was." I only beg the reader not to be in too great a hurry to laugh at my young hero's pure heart. I am far from trying to apologize for him or to justify his innocent faith on the ground of his youth, or the little progress he had made in his studies, or any such reason. I must say, on the contrary, that I have genuine respect for the qualities of his heart. No doubt a youth who received impressions cautiously, whose love was lukewarm, and whose mind was too wise for his age and so of little value, such a young man might, I admit, have avoided what happened to my hero. But in some cases it is really more to one's credit to be carried away by an emotion, however unreasonable, which springs from a great love, than to be unmoved. And this is even truer in youth, because a young man who is always sensible is to be suspected and is of little worth—that's my opinion!

"But," reasonable people will perhaps say, "every young man cannot believe in such a superstition and your hero is no model for others."

To this I reply again, yes! My hero had faith, a faith holy and steadfast, but still I am not going to apologize for him.

Though I said above, and perhaps too quickly that I would not explain or justify my hero, I see that some explanation is necessary for the understanding of the rest of my story. Let me say then, it was not a question of miracles. There was no frivolous and impatient expectation of miracles in Alyosha's mind. And he needed no miracles at the time, for the triumph of some preconceived idea—oh no, not at all—what he saw before all was one figure—the figure of his beloved elder, the figure of

311

that holy man whom he revered with such adoration. The fact is that all the love that lay concealed in his pure young heart for everyone and everything had, for the past year, been concentrated—and perhaps wrongly so—on one being, his beloved elder. It is true that his elder had for so long been accepted by him as his ideal, that all his young strength and energy could not but turn toward that ideal, even to the forgetting at the moment "of everyone and everything." He remembered afterwards how, on that terrible day, he had entirely forgotten his brother Dmitri, about whom he had been so worried and troubled the day before. He had also forgotten to take the two hundred roubles to Captain Snegiryov, Ilusha's father, though he had intended to do so. But again it was not miracles he needed but only "the higher justice" which had been in his belief outraged by the blow that had so suddenly and cruelly wounded his heart. And what does it signify that this "justice" looked for by Alyosha inevitably took the shape of miracles to be wrought immediately by the ashes of his adored elder? Why, everyone in the monastery cherished the same thought and the same hope, even those Alyosha revered, Father Paissy for instance. And so Alyosha, untroubled by doubts, clothed his dreams too in the same form as all the rest. And a whole year of life in the monastery had formed the habit of this expectation in his heart. But it was justice, justice, he thirsted for, not simply miracles.

And now the man who should, he believed, have been exalted above everyone in the whole world, that man, instead of receiving the glory that was his due, was suddenly degraded and dishonored! What for? Who had judged him? Who could have decreed this? Those were the questions that tore at Alyosha's inexperienced and innocent heart. He could not endure without mortification, without resentment even, that the holiest of holy men should have been exposed to the jeering and spiteful mockery of the frivolous crowd so inferior to him. Even had there been no miracles, had there been nothing marvelous to justify his hopes, why this indignity, why this humiliation, why this premature decay, "in excess of nature," as the spiteful monks said? Why this "sign from heaven," which they so triumphantly acclaimed in company with mad Father Ferapont? And why did they believe they had gained the right to acclaim it? Where is the finger of Providence? Why did Providence hide its face "at the most critical moment" as though voluntarily submitting to the blind, dumb, pitiless laws of nature?

That was why Alyosha's heart was bleeding, and, as I have said already, the sting of it came from the fact that the man he loved above everything on earth should be put to shame and humiliated! This murmuring may have been shallow and unreasonable in my hero, but I repeat again for the third time— and am prepared to admit that it might be difficult to defend my feeling—that I am glad that my hero showed himself not too reasonable at that moment. Any man of sense will always come back to reason in time, but, if love does not gain the upper hand in a youth's heart at such an exceptional moment, when will it? I will not, however, forget to mention something strange which came for a time to the surface of Alyosha's mind at this fatal moment. This new something was the harassing impression left by the conversation with Ivan, which now persistently haunted Alyosha. At this moment it haunted him. Oh, it was not that something of the fundamental, elemental, so to speak, faith of his soul had been shaken; he loved his God and believed firmly in Him though he was suddenly murmuring against Him. Yet a vague but tormenting and evil impression left by his conversation with Ivan the day before, suddenly revived again now in his soul and seemed forcing its way to the surface of his consciousness.

It was dusk when Rakitin, crossing the pine grove from the hermitage to the monastery, suddenly noticed Alyosha, lying face downwards on the ground under a tree, not moving and apparently asleep. He went up and called him.

"You here, Alyosha? Can you have . . ." he began wondering but broke off. He had meant to say: "Can you have come to this?"

Alyosha did not look at him, but from a slight movement Rakitin at once saw that he heard and understood him.

"What's the matter?" Rakitin went on. But the surprise in his face gradually passed into a smile that became more and more ironical. "I've been looking for you for the last two hours. You suddenly disappeared. What are you doing? What is this? You might look at me . . ."

Alyosha raised his head, sat up and leaned against a tree. He was not crying, but there was a look of suffering and irritability in his face. He did not look at Rakitin, however, but looked away to one side of him.

"Do you know your face is changed? There's none of your famous mildness to be seen in it. Are you angry with someone? Have they been ill-treating you?"

"Let me alone," said Alyosha suddenly, with a weary gesture of his hand, still looking away from him.

"Oh! So that's how we are feeling! So you can shout at people like other mortals. That is a comedown from the angels. Alyosha, you do surprise me, do you hear? I mean it. It's long since I've been surprised at anything here. I always took you for an educated man . . ."

Alyosha at last looked at him, but vaguely, as though scarcely understanding what he said.

"Can you really be so upset simply because your old man has begun to stink? You don't mean to say you seriously believed that he was going to work miracles?" exclaimed Rakitin.

313

"I believed. I believe, I want to believe, and I will believe. What more do you want?" cried Alyosha.

"Nothing at all. Damn it all, why no schoolboy of thirteen believes in that now. But there . . . So now you are angry with your God, you are rebelling against Him; He hasn't given promotion, He hasn't bestowed the order of merit! You're angry!"

Alyosha gazed a long while at Rakitin with his eyes half closed. There was a sudden gleam in his eyes . . . but not of anger with Rakitin.

"I am not rebelling against my God. I simply 'don't accept His world.' " Alyosha suddenly smiled a forced smile.

"What do you mean, you don't accept the world?" Rakitin thought a moment over his answer. "What foolishness is this?"

Alyosha did not answer.

"Come, that's enough nonsense. Have you had anything to eat today?"

"I don't remember . . . I think I have."

"You need food to judge by your face. It makes one sorry to look at you. You didn't sleep all night either, I hear. You had a meeting in there. And then all this nonsense afterwards. Most likely you've had nothing to eat but a mouthful of holy bread. I've got some sausage in my pocket. I've brought it from the town in case of need, only you won't eat sausage. . . ."

"Give me some."

"What! You're going to eat it! Why, it's a regular mutiny, with barricades! Well, we must make the most of it. Come to my place . . . I wouldn't mind a drop of vodka myself, I am dead tired. Vodka is going too far for you, I suppose . . . or would you like some?"

"Give me some vodka too."

"You surprise me, Alyosha!" Rakitin looked at him in amazement. "Well, one way or another, vodka or sausage, that is a fine chance and mustn't be missed. Come."

Alyosha got up in silence and followed Rakitin.

"If your brother Ivan could see this—wouldn't he be surprised! By the way, your brother Ivan set off to Moscow this morning, did you know?"

"Yes," answered Alyosha listlessly, and suddenly the image of his brother Dmitri rose before his mind. But only for a minute, and though it reminded him of something that must not be put off for a moment, some duty, some terrible obligation, even that reminder made no impression on him, did not reach his heart and instantly faded out of his mind and was forgotten. But, a long while afterwards, Alyosha remembered this.

"Your brother Ivan declared once that I was a 'liberal fool with no talents whatever.' Once you, too, could not resist letting me know I was 'dishonorable.' Well! I would like to see what your talents and sense of honor will do for you now." These words Rakitin finished to himself in a whisper. Then he said aloud: "Let's go by the path beyond the monastery straight into town. H'm! I ought to go to Madame Hohlakov's by the way. I've written to tell her everything that happened, and would you believe it, she answered me instantly in pencil, she has a passion for writing notes, that 'she would never have expected *such conduct* from a man of such a reverend character as Father Zossima.' That was her very word: 'conduct.' She is angry too. What people you are! Wait!" He suddenly stopped and taking Alyosha by the shoulder made him stop too. "Do you know, Alyosha," he looked into his eyes, absorbed in a sudden new thought which had dawned on him. Although he was laughing outwardly he was afraid to utter that new idea aloud, because he still found it so difficult to believe in the strange and unexpected mood in which he now saw Alyosha. "Alyosha, do you know where we had better go?" he said at last timidly and insinuatingly.

"I don't care . . . Where you like."

"Let's go to Grushenka, eh? Will you come?" asked Rakitin at last.

"Let's go to Grushenka," Alyosha answered calmly. And this prompt and calm agreement was such a surprise to Rakitin that he almost started back.

"Well!" he cried in amazement. And taking Alyosha firmly by the arm he led him along the path still fearing that he might change his mind.

They walked along in silence. Rakitin was afraid to talk.

"And how glad she will be, how delighted," he murmured, but he lapsed into silence again. And indeed it was not to please Grushenka that he was taking Alyosha to her. He was a practical person and never undertook anything without a prospect of gain for himself. His object in this case was twofold: first a revengeful desire to see "the downfall of the righteous," and Alyosha's fall "from saint to sinner," and in the second place he had in view a certain material gain for himself of which more will be said later.

"So the critical moment has come," he thought to himself with spite, "and we shall catch it on the hop, for it's just what we want."

3. An Onion

GRUSHENKA LIVED in the busiest part of the town, near the cathedral square, in a small wooden lodge in the courtyard belonging to the house of the widow Morozov. The house was a large stone building of two stories high, old and very ugly. The widow led a secluded life with her two unmarried nieces, who were also elderly women. She did not need to rent her lodge and everyone knew that she had rented to Grushenka,

315

four years before, solely to please her relative, the merchant Kuzma Samsonov, who was known to be the girl's protector.

It was said that the jealous old man's object in placing his "favorite" with the widow Morozov was that the old woman would keep a sharp eye on her conduct. But this sharp eye proved to be unnecessary, and in the end the widow Morozov seldom met Grushenka and did not worry her by looking after her in any way. It is true that four years had passed since the old man had brought the slim, delicate, shy, timid, dreamy, and sad girl of eighteen from the main town of the province, and that much had happened since then.

Little was known of the girl's history in our town and that little was vague. Nothing more had been learned during the last four years, even after many people had become interested in the beautiful young woman into whom Grushenka had meanwhile developed. There were rumors that she had been at seventeen betrayed by someone, some sort of officer, and immediately afterwards abandoned by him. This officer had gone away and married, while Grushenka had been left in poverty and disgrace. It was said, however, that though Grushenka had been rescued from destitution by the old man, Samsonov, she came of a respectable family belonging to the clerical class, and that she was the daughter of a deacon or something of the sort.

Now after four years the sensitive, injured and pathetic girl was a plump, rosy beauty, a woman of bold and determined character, proud and insolent. She had a good head for business, was saving and careful, and by fair means or foul had succeeded, it was said, in amassing a fair sum of money. There was only one point on which all were agreed. Grushenka was not easily to be approached and except for her aged protector there had not been one man who could boast of her favors during those four years. This was a fact, for there had been a good many, especially during the last two years, who had tried to obtain her favors. But all their efforts had been in vain and some of these men had been forced to beat an undignified and even comic retreat, owing to the firm and ironical resistance they met from the strong-willed young woman. It was also known that Grushenka had, especially of late, been given to what is called "speculation," and that she had shown marked abilities in that direction, so that many people began to say that she was no better than a Jew. It was not that she lent money on interest, but it was known, for instance, that she had for some time past, in partnership with old Karamazov, actually invested in the purchase of bad debts for a trifle, a tenth of their nominal value, and afterwards sold them for ten times their value.

The old widower Samsonov, a man of large fortune, was stingy and merciless. He tyrannized over his grown-up sons, but, for the last year during which he had been ill and lost the use of his swollen legs, he had fallen greatly under the influence of his protégée, whom he had at first kept strictly and in humble surroundings, "on Lenten fare" as the wits said at the time. But Grushenka had succeeded in emancipating herself, while she established in him a boundless belief in her fidelity. The old man had had a large business in his day and was miserly and hard as flint. Though Grushenka's hold upon him was so strong that he could not live without her (it had been so especially for the last two years), he did not settle any fortune on her as it turned out after he died, and he would not have done so even if she had threatened to leave him. But he had once presented her with a small sum, and even that was a surprise to everyone when it became known.

"You are a wench with brains," he said to her, when he gave her eight thousand roubles. "And you must look after yourself. But let me tell you that except for your yearly allowance you'll get nothing more from me to the day of my death, and I'll leave you nothing in my will either."

And he kept his word. When he died he left everything to his sons, whom, with their wives and children, he had treated all his life as servants. Grushenka was not even mentioned in his will. All this became known afterwards. But before his death he helped Grushenka with his advice to increase her capital and put business in her way.

When Fyodor Karamazov, who first met Grushenka over a piece of speculation, ended to his own surprise by falling madly in love with her, old Samsonov, gravely ill as he was, was very amused. It is remarkable that throughout their whole acquaintance Grushenka was absolutely and spontaneously open with the old man Samsonov. He seems to have been the only person in the world with whom she was frank. But of late, when Dmitri too had come on the scene with his love, the old man left off laughing. On the contrary, he once gave Grushenka a stern and earnest piece of advice.

"If you have to choose between the two, father or son, you'd better choose the old man. But be sure the old scoundrel will marry you and settle some fortune on you beforehand. And don't keep on with the son, you'll get no good out of that."

These were the words of old Samsonov, who already felt that his death was not far off and who actually died five months later.

I will note, too, in passing that although many in our town knew of the grotesque and monstrous rivalry of the Karamazovs, father and son, the object of which was Grushenka, scarcely anyone understood what really underlay her attitude to both of them. Even Grushenka's two servants (after the disaster of which we will speak later) testified in court that she received Dmitri Karamazov simply from fear because "he threatened to murder her." These servants were an old invalid cook, almost deaf, who came from Grushenka's old home, and her granddaughter, Fenya, a young girl of twenty who served as a maid. Grushenka lived very economically and her place was anything but luxurious. It consisted of three rooms furnished with mahogany furniture in the fashion of 1820, belonging to her landlady.

It was quite dark when Rakitin and Alyosha entered Grushenka's rooms, yet they were not lighted up. Grushenka was lying down in her drawing room on the big, hard, clumsy sofa, with a mahogany back. The sofa was covered with shabby and ragged leather. Under her head she had two white down pillows taken from her bed. She was lying stretched out on her back with her hands behind her head. She was dressed as though expecting someone, in a black silk dress, with a dainty lace scarf on her head, which was very becoming. Over her shoulders was thrown a lace shawl pinned with a massive gold brooch. She certainly was expecting someone. She lay as though impatient and weary, her face rather pale and her lips and eyes hot, restlessly tapping the arm of the sofa with the tip of her right foot.

The arrival of Rakitin and Alyosha caused a slight commotion. They heard Grushenka leap up from the sofa and cry out in a frightened voice: "Who's there?"

But the maid at once called back to her mistress, "It's not he, it's nothing, only other visitors."

"What can be the matter?" muttered Rakitin, leading Alyosha into the drawing room.

Grushenka was standing by the sofa still frightened. A thick coil of her dark brown hair had escaped from its lace covering and lay on her right shoulder. But she did not notice it and did not put it back till she had looked at her visitors and recognized them.

"Ah, it's you, Rakitin? You frightened me. Whom have you brought? Who is this with you? Good heavens, you have brought him!" she exclaimed, recognizing Alyosha.

"Send for candles!" said Rakitin, with the free-and-easy air of a most intimate friend, one who is privileged to give orders in the house.

"Candles . . . of course, candles . . . Fenya, fetch him a candle. . . . Well, you have chosen a good time to bring him!" she exclaimed again, nodding toward Alyosha. Then turning to the looking glass she began quickly fastening up her hair with both hands. She seemed displeased.

"Haven't I managed to please you?" asked Rakitin, almost offended.

"You frightened me, Rakitin, that's what it is." Grushenka turned with a smile to Alyosha. "Don't be afraid of me, my dear Alyosha, you can't think how glad I am to see you, my unexpected visitor. But you frightened me, Rakitin, I thought it was Dmitri breaking in. You see, I fooled him just now; I made him promise to believe me and I told him a lie. I told him that I was going to spend the evening with my old man, Samsonov, and that I would be there till late counting up his money. I always spend one whole evening a week with him making up his accounts. We lock ourselves in and he counts on the abacus while I sit and put things down in the book. I am the only person he trusts. Dmitri believes that I am there, but I came back and have been sitting locked in here, expecting some news. How was it Fenya let you in? Fenya, Fenya, run out to the gate and see whether the captain is anywhere around! Dmitri may be hiding and spying, I am dreadfully frightened."

"There's no one there, mistress. I've just looked out. I keep running and look through the crack. I am afraid and trembling too."

"Are the shutters locked, Fenya? And we must draw the curtains—that's better!" She drew the heavy curtains herself. "He'd rush in at once if he saw a light. I am afraid of your brother Dmitri today, Alyosha."

Grushenka spoke aloud and, though she was alarmed, she seemed very happy about something.

"Why are you so afraid of Dmitri today?" inquired Rakitin. "I thought you were not timid with him, that you twisted him round your little finger."

"I tell you, I am expecting news, priceless news, so I don't want Dmitri at all. And he didn't believe, I feel he didn't, that I would stay at Kuzma Samsonov's. He must be in his ambush now, behind Fyodor Karamazov's, in the garden, watching for me. And if he's there, he won't come here, so that's good! But I really have been to Samsonov's. Dmitri took me there. I told him I would stay there till midnight, and I asked him to be sure to come at midnight to take me home. He went away and I sat ten minutes with Samsonov and then came back here again. I was afraid, I ran for fear of meeting him."

"And why are you so dressed up? What a curious cap you've got on!"

"How curious you are yourself, Rakitin! I tell you, I am expecting a message. If the message comes, I shall fly. I shall gallop away and you will see no more of me. That's why I am dressed up, so as to be ready."

"And where are you flying to?"

"If you know too much, you'll get old too soon."

"Goodness! You seem very happy . . . I've never seen you like this before. You are dressed up as if you were going to a ball." Rakitin looked her up and down.

"What do you know about balls!"

"And do you know much about them?"

"I have seen a ball. The year before last, Samsonov's son was married and I looked on from the gallery. Do you think I want to be talking to you, Rakitin, while a prince like this is standing here. Such a visitor! Alyosha, my dear boy, I look at you and can't believe my eyes. Good heavens, can you have come here to see me! To tell you the truth I never had a thought of seeing you and I didn't think that you would ever come and see me. Though this is not the moment now, I am awfully glad to see you. Sit down on the sofa, here, that's right. I really can't take it in even now . . . Ah, Rakitin, if only you had brought him yesterday or the day before! But I'm glad anyway! Perhaps it's better he has come now, at such a moment, and not the day before yesterday."

She sat down beside Alyosha on the sofa, looking at him with positive delight. And she really was glad, she was not lying when she said so. Her eyes glowed, her lips laughed, but it was a good-natured happy laugh. Alyosha had not expected to see such a friendly expression on her face. . . . He had never met her till two days before, he had formed a bad impression of her, and had been horribly upset by the treacherous trick she had played on Katerina. He was greatly surprised to find her now altogether different. And, crushed as he was by his own sorrow, his eyes rested on her with attention. Her whole manner seemed changed for the better since yesterday, there was scarcely any trace of that mawkish sweetness in her speech, of that voluptuous softness in her movements. Everything was simple and good-natured, her gestures were rapid, direct, confiding. But she was very excited.

"Dear me, how everything comes together today," she chattered on again. "And why I am so glad to see you, Alyosha, I couldn't say myself! If you ask me, I couldn't tell you."

"Really, don't you know why you're glad?" said Rakitin, grinning. "You used to be always pestering me to bring him. You had some plan, I suppose."

"I had a different object once, but now that's over. This is not the moment. I want you to have something nice. I am so happy now. You sit down, too, Rakitin, why are you standing? You've sat down already? There's no fear of Rakitin's forgetting to look after himself. Look, Alyosha, he's sitting there opposite us, so offended that I didn't ask him to sit down before you. Oh, Rakitin takes offense so easily!" laughed Grushenka. "Don't be angry, Rakitin, I'm kind today. Why are you so depressed, Alyosha, are you afraid of me?" She looked into his eyes with a teasing expression.

"He's sad. The promotion has not been given," boomed Rakitin.

"What promotion?"

"His elder stinks."

"What? You are talking nonsense. You want to say something nasty. Be quiet, you're stupid! . . . Let me sit on your knee, Alyosha, like this." She suddenly got up and laughing, nestled like a kitten on his knee, with her right arm about his neck. "I'll cheer you up, my pious boy. You'll let me sit on your knee, you won't be angry? If you tell me, I'll get off?"

Alyosha did not speak. He sat afraid to move. He heard her words, "If you tell me, I'll get off," but he did not answer. But there was nothing in his heart such as Rakitin, for instance, watching him might have expected or thought. The grief in his heart swallowed up every sensation that might have been aroused, and, if only he could have thought clearly at that moment, he would have realized that he had now the strongest armor to protect him from every lust and temptation. Yet in spite of the vague irresponsiveness of his spiritual condition and the sorrow that overwhelmed him, he could not help wondering at a new and strange sensation in his heart. This woman, this "dreadful" woman, had no terror for him now, none of that terror that had stirred in him at any passing thought of women. On the contrary, this woman, dreaded above all women, sitting now on his knee, holding him in her arms, aroused in him now a quite different, unexpected, peculiar feeling, a feeling of the intensest and purest interest without a trace of fear. That was what surprised him.

"You've talked nonsense enough," cried Rakitin. "You'd much better give us some champagne. You owe it to me, you know you do!"

"Yes, I really do. Do you know, Alyosha, I promised him champagne on the top of everything, if he'd bring you? I'll have some too! Fenya, Fenya, bring us the bottle Dmitri left! Though I'm stingy, I'll open a bottle, not for you, Rakitin, you're a toadstool, but for Alyosha, he is a falcon! And though my heart is full of something very different, I'll drink with you. I long for some distraction."

"But what's the matter with you? And what is this message may I ask, or is it a secret?" Rakitin asked, doing his best not to notice the snubs that were being continually aimed at him.

"Oh, it's not a secret, and you know it, too," Grushenka said, in a voice suddenly anxious. She turned her head toward Rakitin, and drew a little away from Alyosha, though she still sat on his knee with her arm around his neck. "My officer is coming, Rakitin, my officer is coming."

"I heard he was coming, but is he so near?"

"He is at Mokroe right now. He'll send a messenger from there, so he wrote. I got a letter from him today. I am expecting the messenger any minute."

"You don't say so! Why at Mokroe?"

"That's a long story. I've told you enough."

"Dmitri will be up to something now—I bet! Does he know or doesn't he?"

"He know! Of course he doesn't. If he knew, there would be murder. But I am not afraid of that now, I am not afraid of his knife. Be quiet, Rakitin, don't remind me of Dmitri. And I don't want to think of him at this moment. I can think of Alyosha here, I can look at Alyosha . . . Smile at me, dear, cheer up, smile at my foolishness, at my pleasure. . . . Ah, he's smiling, he's smiling! How kindly he looks at me! And you know, Alyosha, I've been thinking all this time you were angry with me, because of yesterday, because of that young lady. I was mean, that's the truth. . . . But it's a good thing it happened. It was a horrid thing, but a good thing too." Grushenka smiled dreamily, and a little cruel line showed in her smile. "Dmitri told me that she screamed out that I 'ought to be flogged.' I did insult her terribly. She sent for me, she wanted to make a conquest of me, to win me over with her chocolates. . . . No, it's a good thing it ended like that." She smiled again. "But I am still afraid of your being angry."

"Yes, that's really true," Rakitin added suddenly with genuine surprise. "Alyosha, she is really afraid of a chicken like you."

"He is a chicken to you, Rakitin . . . because you've no conscience, that's what it is! You see, I love him with all my soul, that's how it is! Alyosha, do you believe I love you with all my soul?"

"Oh, you're shameless! She is making advances to you, Alyosha!"

"Well, what of it, I love him!"

"And what about your officer? And the priceless message from Mokroe?"

"That is quite different."

"That's a woman's way of looking at it!"

"Don't make me angry, Rakitin," Grushenka said quickly. "This is different. I love Alyosha in a different way. It's true, Alyosha, I had designs on you before because I am a horrid, violent creature. But at other times I've looked upon you, Alyosha, as my conscience. I've kept thinking 'how anyone like that must despise a nasty thing like me.' I thought that the day before yesterday, as I ran home from the young lady's. I have thought of you a long time in that way, Alyosha, and Dmitri knows it. I've talked to him about it. Dmitri understands. Would you believe it, I sometimes look at you and feel ashamed, ashamed of myself. . . . And how, and since when, I began to think about you like that, I can't say, I don't remember . . ."

Fenya came in and put a tray with an uncorked bottle and three glasses of champagne on the table.

"Here's the champagne!" cried Rakitin. "You're excited, Grushenka, and not yourself. When you've had a glass of champagne, you'll be ready to dance. Eh, they can't even do that properly," he added, looking at the bottle. "The old woman's poured it out in the kitchen, and the bottle's been brought in warm and without a cork. Well, let me have some, anyway."

He went up to the table, took a glass, emptied it at one gulp and poured himself another.

"One doesn't often stumble upon champagne," he said, licking his lips. "Now, Alyosha, take a glass, show what you can do! What shall we drink to? The gates of paradise? Take a glass, Grushenka. Drink to the gates of paradise, too."

"What gates of paradise?"

She took a glass. Alyosha took his, tasted it and put it back.

"No, I'd better not," he smiled gently.

"And you bragged!" cried Rakitin.

"Well, if Alyosha won't drink, I won't either," chimed in Grushenka, "I really don't want any. You can drink the whole bottle alone, Rakitin. If Alyosha has some, I will."

"How touching!" said Rakitin. "And she's sitting on his knee, too! He's got something to grieve over, but what's the matter with you? He is rebelling against his God and ready to eat sausage . . ."

"Why?"

"His elder died today, Father Zossima, the saint."

"So Father Zossima is dead!" cried Grushenka. "Good God, I did not know!" She crossed herself devoutly. "Goodness, what have I been doing, sitting on his knee like this at such a moment!" She instantly slipped off his knee and sat on the sofa.

Alyosha bent a long wondering look upon her and a light seemed to dawn in his face.

"Rakitin," he said suddenly, in a firm and loud voice. "Don't taunt me with having rebelled against God. I don't want to feel angry with you, so you must be kinder, too. I've lost a treasure such as you have never had, and so you cannot judge me. You had much better look at her—do you see how she has pity on me? I came here to find a wicked soul—I felt drawn to evil because I was base and evil myself, and I've found a true sister, I have found a treasure—a loving heart. She had pity on me just now. . . . Grushenka, I am speaking of you. You've raised my soul from the depths."

Alyosha's lips were quivering and he caught his breath.

"She has saved you, it seems," laughed Rakitin spitefully. "And she meant to get you in her clutches, do you realize that?"

"Wait, Rakitin." Grushenka jumped up. "Keep quiet, both of you. Now I'll tell you all about it. Keep quiet, Alyosha, your words make me feel ashamed, because I am bad and not good—that's what I am. And you keep quiet, Rakitin, because you are telling lies. I had the idea of trying to get him in my clutches, but now you are lying, now it's all different. And don't let me hear anything more from you, Rakitin."

All this Grushenka said with extreme emotion.

"They are both crazy," said Rakitin looking at them with amazement. "I feel as though I were in a madhouse. They're both getting so feeble they'll begin crying in a minute."

"I will begin to cry, I will," repeated Grushenka. "He called me his sister and I shall never forget that. Only let me tell you, Rakitin, though I am bad, I did give away an onion."

"An onion? Damn it all, you really are crazy."

Rakitin wondered at them. He was annoyed, though he should have recognized that each of them was just passing through a spiritual crisis such as does not come often in a lifetime. But though Rakitin was very sensitive about everything that concerned himself, he was very stupid about the feelings and sensations of others—partly from his youth and inexperience, partly from his intense egoism.

"You see, Alyosha," Grushenka turned to him with a nervous laugh. "I was boasting when I told Rakitin I had given away an onion, but it's not to boast that I tell you about it. It's only a story, but it's a nice story. I used to hear it when I was a child from our cook, who is still with me. It's like this. 'Once upon a time there was a peasant woman and a very wicked woman she was. And she died and did not leave a single good deed behind. The devils caught her and plunged her into a lake of fire. So her guardian angel stood and wondered what good deed of hers he could remember to tell to God. "She once pulled up an onion in her garden," said he, "and gave it to a beggar woman." And God answered: "You take that onion then, hold it out to her in the lake, and let her take hold of it and be pulled out. And if you can pull her out of the lake, let her come to Paradise, but if the onion breaks, then the woman must stay where she is." The angel ran to the woman and held out the onion to her. "Come," said he, "catch hold and I'll pull you out." And he began cautiously pulling her out. He had just about pulled her out, when the other sinners in the lake, seeing how she was being drawn out, caught hold of her so as to be pulled out with her. But she was a very wicked woman and she began kicking them off. "I'm to be pulled out, not you. It's my onion, not yours." As soon as she said that, the onion broke. And she fell back into the lake and she is burning there to this day. So her guardian angel wept and went away.' So that's the story, Alyosha. I know it by heart, because I am that wicked woman myself. I boasted to Rakitin that I had given away an onion, but to you I'll say: 'I've done nothing but give away one onion all my life, that's the only good deed I've done.' So don't praise me, Alyosha, don't think me good. I am bad. I am wicked and you make me ashamed if you praise me. . . . I must confess everything. Listen, Alyosha, I was so anxious to get hold of you that I promised Rakitin twenty-five roubles if he would bring you to me. Wait, Rakitin, wait!"

She went quickly to the table, opened a drawer, pulled out a purse and took from it a twenty-five rouble note.

"What nonsense! What nonsense!" cried Rakitin, disconcerted.

"Take it, Rakitin, I owe it to you. There's no fear of your refusing it because you asked for it yourself." And she threw the note at him.

"Perhaps I should refuse it," boomed Rakitin, obviously

abashed, but carrying off his confusion with a swagger. "It will come in very handy; fools are made for wise men's profit."

"And now hold your tongue, Rakitin. What I am going to say now is not for your ears. Sit down in that corner and keep quiet. You don't like us, so hold your tongue."

"Why should I like you?" Rakitin snarled, not concealing his ill-humor. He put the twenty-five rouble note in his pocket. He felt ashamed at Alyosha's seeing him do so. He had planned on receiving his payment later, without Alyosha's knowing of it, and now, feeling ashamed, he lost his temper. Till that moment he had thought it best not to contradict Grushenka too flatly in spite of her snubbing him, since he had something to get out of her. But now he, too, was angry.

"One loves people for some reason, but what have either of you done for me?" he asked.

"You should love people without a reason, as Alyosha does."

"How does he love you? How has he shown it, that you make such a fuss about it?"

Grushenka was standing in the middle of the room. She spoke with emotion and there were hysterical notes in her voice.

"Hush, Rakitin, you know nothing about us! And don't you dare to speak to me like that again. How dare you be so familiar? Sit in that corner and be quiet, as though you were my footman. And now, Alyosha, I'll tell you the whole truth, that you may see what a wretch I am! I am not talking to Rakitin, but to you. I wanted to ruin you, Alyosha, that's the holy truth. I quite meant to. I wanted to so much, that I bribed Rakitin to bring you. And why did I want to do such a thing? You knew nothing about it, Alyosha, you turned away from me; if you passed me on the street, you dropped your eyes. And I've looked at you a hundred times before today. I began asking everyone about you. Your face haunted my heart. 'He despises me,' I thought. 'He won't even look at me.' And I felt it so much at last that I wondered at myself for being so frightened of you. I'll get him in my clutches and laugh at him. I was full of spite and anger. Would you believe it, nobody here dares talk or think of coming to Grushenka with any evil purpose. Old Kuzma Samsonov is the only man I have anything to do with here. I was bound and sold to him. Satan brought us together. But there has been no one else. But looking at you, I thought, I'll get him in my clutches and laugh at him. You see what a spiteful creature I am, and you called me your sister! And now that man who wronged me has come; I sit here waiting for a message from him. And do you know what that man has been to me? Five years ago, when Samsonov brought me here, I used to shut myself up so that no one might see or hear of me. I was a silly slip of a girl; I used to sit here sobbing, I used to lie awake all night, thinking: 'Where is he now, the man who wronged me? He is laughing at me with another woman, most likely. If only I could see him, if I could meet him again, I'd get even with him, I'd get even with him!' At night I used to lie sobbing in the dark, and I used to brood over it. I used to tear my heart on purpose and gloat over my anger. 'I'll get even with him, I'll get even with him!' That's what I used to cry out in the dark. And when I suddenly realized that I would really do nothing to him, and that he was laughing at me then or perhaps had utterly forgotten me, I would fling myself on the floor and melt into helpless tears, and lie there shaking till dawn. In the morning I would get up more spiteful than a dog, ready to tear the whole world to pieces. And then what do you think? I began saving money, I became hardhearted, grew plump—grew wiser, would you say? No, no one in the whole world sees it, no one knows it, but when night comes on, I sometimes lie as I did five years ago, when I was a silly girl, clenching my teeth and crying all night, thinking: 'I'll get even with him, I'll get even with him!' Do you hear? Well then, now you understand me. A month ago a letter came to me—he is coming, he is a widower, he wants to see me. It took my breath away, then I suddenly thought: 'If he comes and whistles to me, I will creep back to him like a beaten dog.' I couldn't believe myself. Am I so low? Will I run to him or not? And I've been in such a rage with myself all month that I am worse than I was five years ago. Do you see now, Alyosha, what a violent, vindictive creature I am? I have shown you the whole truth! I played with Dmitri to keep from running to that other. Hush, Rakitin, it's not for you to judge me, I am not speaking to you. Before you came in, I was lying here waiting, brooding, deciding my whole future life and you can never know what was in my heart. Yes, Alyosha, tell your young lady not to be angry with me for what happened the day before yesterday. . . . Nobody in the whole world knows what I am going through now, and no one ever can know. . . . Perhaps I will take a knife with me today. I can't make up my mind . . ."

And at this "tragic" phrase Grushenka broke down, hid her face in her hands, flung herself on the sofa pillows, and sobbed like a little child.

Alyosha got up and went to Rakitin.

"Don't be angry," he said. "She insulted you, but don't be angry. You heard what she said just now? You mustn't ask too much of human endurance. One must be merciful."

Alyosha said this at the prompting of his heart. He felt obliged to speak and he turned to Rakitin. If Rakitin had not been there, he would have spoken to the air. But Rakitin looked at him ironically and Alyosha stopped short.

"You are so primed up with your elder's teaching last

night that now you have to let it off on me, Alyosha, man of God!" said Rakitin with a smile of hatred.

"Don't laugh, Rakitin, don't smile, don't talk of the dead—he was better than anyone in the world!" cried Alyosha with tears in his voice. "I didn't speak to you as a judge but as the lowest of the judged. What am I beside her? I came here looking for my ruin, and said to myself: 'What does it matter?' But she, after five years of torment, as soon as anyone says a word from the heart to her—it makes her forget everything, forgive everything! The man who wronged her has come back, he sends for her and she forgives him everything, and hurries to meet him. And she won't take a knife with her. She won't! No, I am not like that. I don't know whether you are, Rakitin, but I am not like that. It's a lesson to me . . . She is more loving than we. . . . Have you heard her speak before of what she has just told us? No, you haven't. If you had, you'd have understood her long ago . . . And the person insulted the day before yesterday must forgive her, too! She will, when she knows . . . And she will know . . . This soul is not yet at peace with itself, one must be tender with it . . . There may be a treasure in this soul . . ."

Alyosha stopped to catch his breath. Rakitin looked at him with astonishment. He had never expected such a lecture from the gentle Alyosha.

"She's found someone to plead her cause! Why, are you in love with her? Grushenka, our monk's really in love with you. You've made a conquest!" he cried, with a coarse laugh.

Grushenka lifted her head from the pillow and looked at Alyosha with a tender smile shining on her tear-stained face.

"Let him alone, Alyosha. You see what he is. He is not a person for you to speak to." She turned to Rakitin, "I meant to beg your pardon for being rude to you, but now I don't want to. Alyosha, come to me, sit down here," she said to him with a happy smile. "That's right, sit here. Tell me," she took Alyosha's hand and looked into his face, smiling. "Tell me, do I love that man or not? The man who wronged me, do I love him or not? Before you came, I lay here in the dark, asking my heart whether I loved him. Decide for me, Alyosha. The time has come, it shall be as you say. Am I to forgive him or not?"

"But you have forgiven him already," said Alyosha, smiling.

"Yes, I really have forgiven him," Grushenka murmured thoughtfully. "What a low heart! To my low heart!" She snatched up a glass from the table, emptied it at a gulp, lifted it in the air and flung it on the floor. The glass broke with a crash. A little cruel line came into her smile.

"Perhaps I haven't forgiven him, though," she said, with a slight threat in her voice, and she lowered her eyes to the ground as though she were talking to herself. "Perhaps my heart is only getting ready to forgive. I shall struggle with my

327

heart. You see, Alyosha, I've grown to love my tears in these five years. . . . Perhaps I only love my resentment, not him . . ."

"Well, I wouldn't care to be in his shoes," observed Rakitin.

"Well, you won't be, Rakitin, you'll never be in his shoes. You will shine my shoes, Rakitin, that's what you are fit for. You'll never get a woman like me . . . And he won't either, perhaps . . ."

"Won't he? Then why are you dressed up like that?" asked Rakitin with a sneer.

"Don't irritate me, Rakitin. You don't know everything that is in my heart! If I choose to tear off my finery, I'll tear it off at once, this minute," she cried. "You don't know what this finery is for, Rakitin! Perhaps I shall see him and say: 'Have you ever seen me look like this before?' He left me a thin, consumptive cry-baby of seventeen. I'll sit by him, fascinate him and work him up. 'Do you see what I am like now?' I'll say to him. 'Well, and that's enough for you, my dear sir, there's many a slip twixt the cup and the lip!' That may be what the finery is for, Rakitin." Grushenka finished with a malicious laugh. "I'm violent and resentful, Alyosha. I'll tear off my finery, I'll destroy my beauty, I'll scorch my face, slash it with a knife, and turn beggar. If I choose, I won't go anywhere now to see anyone. If I choose, I'll send Kuzma Samsonov back all he has ever given me, tomorrow—and all his money. And I'll go out as a scrub woman for the rest of my life. You think I wouldn't do it, Rakitin, that I wouldn't dare to do it? I would, I would. I could do it right now, only don't exasperate me . . . And I'll send him about his business. I'll snap my fingers in his face. He will never see me again!"

She uttered the last words in an hysterical scream, broke down again, hid her face in her hands, buried it in the pillow and shook with sobs.

Rakitin got up.

"It's time we left," he said. "It's late, we shall be shut out of the monastery."

Grushenka jumped up.

"You don't want to go, Alyosha!" she cried in mournful surprise. "What are you doing to me? You've stirred up my feelings, tortured me, and now you're going to leave me to face this night alone!"

"He can hardly spend the night with you! Though if he wants to, let him! I'll go alone," Rakitin scoffed.

"Keep quiet!" Grushenka cried angrily at him. "You never said such words to me as he has come to say."

"What has he said to you that's so special?" asked Rakitin.

"I can't say, I don't know. I don't know what he said to me but it went straight to my heart. . . . He is the first, the only one who has pitied me, that's what it is. Why did you not come before, you angel?" She fell on her knees before Alyosha. "I've been waiting all my life for someone like you. I knew that someone like you would come and forgive me. I believed that, nasty as I am, someone would really love me, not only with a lustful love!"

"What have I done to you?" answered Alyosha bending over her and gently taking her by the hands. "I only gave you an onion, nothing but a tiny little onion, that was all!"

At that moment there was a sudden noise in the passage. Someone came into the hall. Grushenka jumped up frightened. Fenya ran into the room, crying:

"Mistress, mistress darling, a messenger has galloped up," she cried, breathless and happy. "A carriage from Mokroe for you! Timofey the driver, with three horses! They are just putting in fresh horses! . . . A letter, here's the letter, mistress." The letter was in her hand and she waved it in the air all the while she talked.

Grushenka snatched the letter from her and carried it to the candle. It was only a note, a few lines. She read it quickly.

"He has sent for me," she cried, her face white and distorted with a wan smile. "He whistles! Crawl back, little dog!"

But she stood as though hesitating only for one instant. Suddenly the blood rushed to her head and sent a glow to her cheeks.

"I will go," she cried. "Five years of my life! Good-by! Good-by, Alyosha, my fate is sealed. Go, go, leave me. Don't let me see either of you again! Grushenka is flying to a new life. . . . Don't remember evil against me either, Rakitin. I may be going to my death! Ugh! I feel as though I were drunk!"

She suddenly left them and ran into her bedroom.

"Well, she has no thoughts for us now!" grumbled Rakitin. "Let's go, or we may hear that feminine shriek again. I am sick of all these tears and cries."

Alyosha let himself be led out. In the yard stood a covered cart. Horses were being taken out of the shafts, men were running to and fro with a lantern. Three fresh horses were being led in at the open gate.

When Alyosha and Rakitin reached the bottom of the steps, Grushenka's bedroom window suddenly opened and she called in a ringing voice after Alyosha: "Alyosha, give my greetings to your brother Dmitri and tell him not to remember evil against me even though I've made him unhappy. And tell him: 'Grushenka has fallen to a scoundrel, and not to you, noble heart.' And add, too, that Grushenka loved him only one hour, only one short hour she loved him—so let him remember that hour all his life—say: 'Grushenka tells you to!' "

She ended in a voice full of tears. The window was shut with a slam.

"Hm, hm!" said Rakitin, laughing. "She murders your brother Dmitri and then tells him to remember it all his life! What viciousness!"

Alyosha did not reply. He seemed not to have heard. He walked fast beside Rakitin as though in a terrible hurry. He was lost in thought and moved mechanically. Rakitin felt a sudden twinge as though he had been touched on an open wound. He had expected something quite different by bringing Grushenka and Alyosha together. Something very different from what he had hoped for had happened.

"He is a Pole, that officer of hers," he began again, restraining himself. "And he is not an officer at all now. He served in the customs in Siberia, somewhere on the Chinese frontier—some puny little beggar of a Pole. Lost his job, they say. He's heard now that Grushenka's saved a little money, so he's turned up again—that's the explanation of the mystery."

Again Alyosha seemed not to hear. Rakitin could not control himself.

"Well, so you've saved the sinner?" he laughed spitefully. "Have you turned the Magdalene into the true path? Driven out the seven devils, eh? So you see the miracles you were looking for just now have come to pass!"

"Hush, Rakitin," Alyosha answered.

"So you despise me now for those twenty-five roubles? I've sold my friend, you think. But you are not Christ, you know, and I am not Judas."

"Oh, Rakitin, I assure you I'd forgotten about it," cried Alyosha. "You remind me of it yourself . . ."

But this was the last straw for Rakitin.

"Damnation take you all and each of you!" he cried suddenly. "Why the devil did I take you up to Grushenka? I don't want to see you any more, ever. Go alone, there's your road!" And he turned abruptly into another street, leaving Alyosha alone in the dark.

Alyosha came out of the town and walked across the fields to the monastery.

4. Cana of Galilee

IT WAS VERY LATE, according to the monastery rules, when Alyosha returned to the hermitage. The doorkeeper let him in by a special entrance. It had struck nine o'clock—the hour of rest and repose.

Alyosha timidly opened the door and went into the elder's cell where his coffin was now resting. There was no one in the cell but Father Paissy, reading the Gospel in solitude over the coffin. The young novice Porfiry, exhausted by the previous night's conversation and the disturbing events of that day, was sleeping the deep sound sleep of youth on the floor of the other room. Though Father Paissy heard Alyosha come in, he did not look in his direction. Alyosha turned to the right from the door to the corner, fell on his knees and began to pray.

His soul was overflowing but with mingled feelings. No single sensation stood out distinctly, on the contrary, one drove out another in a slow, continual rotation. But there was a sweetness in his heart and, strange to say, Alyosha was not surprised at it. Again he saw that coffin before him, the hidden dead figure so precious to him, but the weeping and grief of the morning was no longer aching in his soul.

The one window of the cell was open, the air was fresh and cool. "So the smell must have become stronger, if they opened the window," thought Alyosha. But even this thought of the smell of corruption, which had seemed to him so awful and humiliating a few hours before, no longer made him feel miserable. He continued quietly praying, but he soon felt that he was praying almost mechanically. Fragments of thought floated through his soul, flashed like stars and went out again at once, to be succeeded by others. But yet there was reigning in his soul a sense of the wholeness of things—something steadfast and comforting—and he was aware of it himself. He began praying ardently, he longed to pour out his thankfulness and love. . . .

But then his prayers were interrupted and he passed suddenly to something else, and sank into thought, forgetting both the prayer and what had interrupted it. He began listening to what Father Paissy was reading. And worn out he began to doze.

"And the third day there was a marriage in Cana of Galilee;" read Father Paissy. *"And the mother of Jesus was there. And both Jesus was called, and his disciples, to the marriage."*

"Marriage? What's that. . . . A marriage!" floated through Alyosha's mind. "There is happiness for her, too . . . She has gone to the feast. . . . No, she has not taken the knife. . . . That was only a tragic phrase. . . . Well . . . tragic phrases should be forgiven, they must be. Tragic phrases comfort the heart . . . Without them, sorrow would be too heavy for men to bear. Rakitin has gone off to the back alley. As long as Rakitin broods over his wrongs, he will always go off to the back alley. . . . But the high road. . . . The road is wide and straight and bright as crystal, and the sun is at the end of it. . . . Ah! . . . What's being read?" . . .

"And when they wanted wine, the mother of Jesus saith unto him; 'They have no wine'" . . . Alyosha heard.

"Ah, yes, I was missing that, and I didn't want to miss it, I love that passage: it's Cana of Galilee, the first miracle. . . . Ah, that miracle! Ah, that sweet miracle! It was not men's grief, but their joy Christ visited. He worked His first miracle to help men's gladness. . . . 'He who loves men loves their gladness, too' . . . Dmitri was always repeating that, it was one of his leading ideas. . . . 'There's no living without joy,' Dmitri says. . . . Yes, Dmitri . . . 'Everything that is true and good is always full of forgiveness,' he used to say that, too" . . .

"Jesus saith unto her, Woman, what has it to do with thee? Mine hour is not yet come.

"His mother saith unto the servants: Whatsoever he saith unto you, do it" . . .

"Do it. . . . Gladness, the gladness of some poor, very poor, people. . . . Of course they were poor, since they hadn't wine enough even at a wedding. . . . The historians write that, in those days, the people living about the Sea of Galilee were the poorest that can possibly be imagined . . . And another great heart, that other great being, His Mother, knew that He had come not only to make His great sacrifice. She knew that His heart was open even to the simple, artless merry-making of some obscure and unlearned people, who had warmly bidden Him to their poor wedding. 'Mine hour is not yet come,' He said, with a soft smile (He must have smiled gently to her). And indeed was it to make wine abundant at poor weddings that He had come down to earth? And yet He went and did as she asked Him. . . . Ah, he is reading again" . . .

"Jesus saith unto them. Fill the waterpots with water. And they filled them up to the brim.

And he saith unto them, Draw out now and bear unto the Governor of the feast. And they bare it.

When the ruler of the feast had tasted the water that was made wine, and knew not whence it was; [but the servants which drew the water knew] the Governor of the feast called the bridegroom,

And saith unto him: Every man at the beginning doth set forth good wine; and when men have well drunk, then that which is worse; but thou hast kept the good wine until now."

"But what's this, what's this? Why is the room growing wider? . . . Ah, yes . . . It's the marriage, the wedding . . . Yes, of course. Here are the guests, here is the young couple and the merry crowd and . . . Where is the wise governor of the feast? But who is this? Who? Again the walls are receding . . . Who is getting up there from the great table? What! . . . He here, too? But he's in the coffin . . . But he's here, too. He has stood up, he sees me, he is coming. . . . God!"

Yes, he came up to him, to him, he, the little, thin old man, with tiny wrinkles on his face, joyful and laughing softly. There was no coffin now, and he was in the same robe he had worn yesterday sitting with them, when the visitors had gathered about him. His face was uncovered, his eyes were shining. How was this then, he, too, had been called to the feast. He, too, at the marriage of Cana in Galilee. . . .

"Yes, my son, I am called, too, called and bidden," he heard a soft voice saying over him. "Why have you hidden yourself here, out of sight? Come and join us too."

332

It was his voice, the voice of Father Zossima. And it must be he, since he called him.

The elder took Alyosha by the hand and raised him from his knees.

"We are rejoicing," the little, thin old man went on. "We are drinking the new wine, the wine of new, great gladness. Do you see how many guests are tasting the new wine? Here are the bride and bridegroom, here is the wise governor of the feast, he is tasting the new wine. Why do you wonder at me? I gave an onion to a beggar, so I, too, am here. And many here have given only an onion each—only one little onion. . . . What are all our deeds? And you, my gentle one, you, my kind boy, you too have known how to give a famished woman an onion today. Begin your work, dear one, begin it, gentle one! . . . Do you see our Son, do you see Him?"

"I am afraid . . . I dare not look," whispered Alyosha.

"Do not fear Him. He is terrible in His greatness, awful in His sublimity, but infinitely merciful. He has made Himself like unto us from love and rejoices with us. He is changing the water into wine that the gladness of the guests may not be cut short. He is expecting new guests, He is calling new ones unceasingly forever and ever. . . . There they are bringing new wine. Do you see they are bringing the vessels . . ."

Something glowed in Alyosha's heart. Something filled it until it ached. Tears of rapture rose from his soul. . . . He stretched out his hands, uttered a cry and waked up.

Again the coffin, the open window, and the soft, solemn, distinct reading of the Gospel. But Alyosha did not listen to the reading. It was strange, he had fallen asleep on his knees, but now he was on his feet, and suddenly, as though thrown forward, with three firm steps he went right up to the coffin. His shoulder brushed against Father Paissy without his noticing it. Father Paissy raised his eyes for an instant from his book, but looked away again at once, seeing that something strange was happening.

Alyosha gazed for half a minute at the coffin, at the covered, motionless dead man that lay in the coffin, with the ikon on his breast and the peaked cap with the octangular cross, on his head. He had only just been hearing his voice, and that voice was still ringing in his ears. He was listening, still expecting other words, but suddenly he turned sharply and went out of the cell.

He did not stop on the steps either, but went quickly down; his soul, overflowing with rapture, yearned for freedom, space, openness. The vault of heaven, full of soft, shining stars, stretched vast and fathomless above him. The Milky Way ran in two pale streams from the zenith to the horizon. The fresh, motionless, still night enfolded the earth. The white towers and golden domes of the church gleamed out against the sapphire sky. The autumn flowers, in the garden, were slumbering. The

333

silence of earth seemed to melt into the silence of the heavens. The mystery of earth was one with the mystery of the stars. . . .

Alyosha stood, gazed out before him and then suddenly threw himself down on the earth. He did not know why he embraced it. He could not have told why he longed so irresistibly to kiss it, to kiss it. But he kissed it weeping and watering it with his tears, and vowed passionately to love it, to love it forever and ever. "Water the earth with the tears of your joy and love those tears." His elder's words echoed in his soul.

Why was he weeping?

Oh! In his rapture he was weeping even over those stars, which were shining to him from the abyss of space, and "he was not ashamed of that ecstasy." There seemed to be threads from all those innumerable worlds of God, linking his soul to them, and his soul was trembling all over "in contact with other worlds." He longed to forgive everyone and for everything, and to beg forgiveness. Oh, not for himself, but for all men, for all and for everything. "And others are praying for me too," echoed again in his soul. But with every instant he felt clearly and, as it were, tangibly, that something firm and unshakable as that vault of heaven had entered into his soul. It was as though some idea had seized the sovereignty of his mind—and it was for all his life and forever and ever. He had fallen on the earth a weak soul, but he rose up in strength, and he knew and felt it suddenly at the very moment of his ecstasy. And never, never, all his life, did Alyosha forget that minute.

"Someone visited my soul in that hour," he used to say afterwards with implicit faith.

Within three days he left the monastery in accordance with the words of his elder, who had bidden him to "go forth into the world."

BOOK VIII: DMITRI

1. Kuzma Samsonov

GRUSHENKA, FLYING AWAY TO A NEW LIFE, had left her last greetings to Dmitri, bidding him to remember the hour of her love forever. Dmitri, however, knew nothing of what had happened and was in a highly nervous condition. For the last two days he had been in such a state of mind that he might easily have fallen ill with brain fever. Alyosha had not been able to find him the morning before, and Ivan had not succeeded in meeting him at the tavern on the same day. The people at his lodgings, by his orders, concealed his whereabouts.

He had spent those two days, literally rushing in all directions, "struggling with his destiny and trying to save himself," as he expressed it himself afterwards. And for some hours he even made a dash out of the town on urgent business, terrible as it was to him to lose sight of Grushenka for a moment. All this was explained afterwards in detail, and confirmed by documentary evidence. But for the present we will only note the most essential incidents of those two horrible days immediately preceding the awful catastrophe, that broke so suddenly upon him.

Though Grushenka had, it is true, loved him for an hour, genuinely and sincerely, yet at times she tortured him cruelly and mercilessly. The worst part of it was that he could never tell what she meant to do. To prevail upon her by force or kindness was impossible; she would yield to nothing. She would only become angry and turn away from him altogether. He knew this. He suspected, quite correctly, that she, too, was going through an emotional crisis and was in a state of indecision, that she was trying to make up her mind about something and was unable to do so. And so he felt, with a sinking heart, that at moments she must hate him and his passion. But what was worrying Grushenka he did not understand. For him the whole tormenting question lay between him and his father.

Here we must note one fact: Dmitri was firmly convinced that his father would offer, or perhaps had offered, marriage to Grushenka. And he did not for a moment believe, as Smerdyakov had told him, that the old wretch hoped to gain his object for three thousand roubles. Dmitri had reached this conclusion from his knowledge of Grushenka and her character. That was how it was that he could believe at times that all Grushenka's uneasiness arose from not knowing which of them to choose, which was most to her advantage.

Strange to say, during those days it never occurred to him to think of the return of the "officer," that is, of the man who had been such an unfortunate influence in Grushenka's life, and whose arrival she was expecting with such emotion and dread. It is true that of late Grushenka had been very silent about it. Yet he knew of a letter she had received a month ago from her "officer." He had heard of it from her own lips. He knew, too, what the letter contained. In a moment of spite Grushenka had shown him that letter, but to her astonishment he attached hardly any importance to it. It would be hard to say why this was. Perhaps, weighed down by all the hideous horror of his struggle with his own father for this woman, he was incapable of imagining any danger more terrible. At any rate he simply did not believe in a suitor who would suddenly turn up again after five years. Moreover, in the "officer's" first letter which he had seen, the possibility of his new rival's visit was very vaguely suggested. The letter was indefinite, high-flown, and full of sentimentality. It must be noted that Grushenka had concealed from him the last lines of the letter, in which the "officer's" return was alluded to more definitely. He had, besides, noticed at that time a certain proud contempt for this letter from Siberia on Grushenka's part. Grushenka told him nothing of what had passed later between her and this rival; so that by degrees he had completely forgotten the officer's existence.

Dmitri felt that whatever might come later, whatever turn things might take, his final conflict with his father was close at hand, and must be decided before anything else. With a sinking heart he expected every moment Grushenka's decision, always believing that it would come suddenly, on the impulse of the moment. All of a sudden she would say to him: "Take me, I'm yours forever." And it would all be over. He would seize her and carry her away at once to the ends of the earth. Oh, then he would carry her away at once, as far, far away as possible; to the furthest end of Russia, if not of the earth. Then he would marry her, and settle down with her incognito, so that no one would know anything about them, there, here, or anywhere. Then, oh then, a new life would begin.

Of this different, reformed and "virtuous" life ("it must, it must be virtuous") he dreamed at every moment. He thirsted for that reformation and renewal. The filthy morass, in which he had sunk of his own free will, was too revolting to him, and, like many men in such cases, he put faith above all in change of place. If only it were not for these people, if only it were not for these circumstances, if only he could get away from this accursed place—he would be altogether different, would begin on a new path. That was what he believed in, and for what he was yearning.

But all this could only be on condition of the first, the *happy* solution. There was another possibility, a different and awful ending. Grushenka might suddenly say to him: "Go away. I have just come to terms with your father. I am going to marry him and don't want you"—and then . . . But then. . . . But Dmitri did not know what would happen then. Up to the very last he didn't know. That must be said to his credit. He had no definite intentions, had planned no crime. He was simply watching and spying in agony, while he prepared himself for the first, the happy solution of his destiny. He drove away any other idea, in fact. But before that ending, that happy solution, could be reached, a new, incidental, but yet fatal and insoluble difficulty presented itself.

If she were to say to him: "I'm yours; take me away," how could he take her away? How had he the means, the money to do it? It was just at this time that all his revenue from his father, doles which had gone on without interruption for so many years, suddenly stopped. Grushenka had money, of course, but Dmitri was proud; he wanted to carry her away and begin the new life with her at his own expense, not at hers. He could not conceive of taking her money, the very idea caused him intense repulsion. I won't enlarge on this fact or analyze it here, but confine myself to remarking that this was his attitude. All this may have arisen indirectly and unconsciously from the secret stings of his conscience about Katerina's money which he had dishonestly appropriated. "I've been a scoundrel to one of them, and if I did this I would be a scoundrel again to the other," was his feeling. As he explained after: "When Grushenka knows, she won't care for such a scoundrel."

Where then was he to get the means, where was he to get the fateful money? Without it, all would be lost and nothing could be done, "and only because I don't have the money!"

To anticipate things; he did, perhaps, know where to get the money, knew, perhaps, where it lay at that moment. I will say no more of this here, as it will all be clear later. But his chief trouble, I must explain however, lay in the fact that to have the sum he knew of, to *have the right* to take it, he must first restore Katerina's three thousand—if not: "I'm a common pickpocket, I'm a scoundrel, and I don't want to begin a new life as a scoundrel." And so he made up his mind to move heaven and earth to return to Katerina that three thousand, and that *first of all*. The final stage of this decision, so to say, had been reached only during the last hours, that is after his last interview with Alyosha two days before, at the crossroads on the evening when Grushenka had insulted Katerina. Dmitri, after hearing Alyosha's account of it, had admitted that he was a scoundrel, and had told his brother to tell Katerina so, if it would be any comfort to her. After parting from his brother on that night, he had felt in his frenzy that it would be better "to murder and rob someone than fail to pay my debt to Katerina. I'd rather everyone thought me a robber and a murderer, I'd rather go to Siberia than have Katerina say that I deceived her and stole her money, and used her money to run away with Grushenka and begin a new life! That I can't do!" So Dmitri decided. But meanwhile he went on struggling. . . .

Strange to say, though one would have thought there was nothing left for him but despair—for what chance had he to raise such a sum—yet to the very end he persisted in hoping that he would get that three thousand, that the money would somehow come to him, of itself, as though it might drop from heaven. That is just how it is with people who, like Dmitri, have never had anything to do with money, except to squander what has come to them by inheritance without any effort of their own. A whirl of the most fantastic notions took possession of him immediately after he parted from Alyosha two days before, and threw his thoughts into a tangle of confusion. This is how it was he plunged first into a perfectly wild scheme. And perhaps to men of that kind in such circumstances the most impossible, fantastic schemes occur first, and seem most practical.

He suddenly determined to go to Samsonov, the old merchant who was Grushenka's protector, and to propose a "scheme" to him, and by this means get from him at once the whole of the sum required. Of the value of his scheme he had no doubt, not the slightest, and he was only uncertain about how Samsonov would look upon his plan, if he were to consider it from any but the commercial point of view. Though Dmitri knew the merchant by sight, he had not met him and had never spoken a word to him. But for some unknown reason he had long entertained the idea that the old man, who was lying at death's door, would perhaps now not at all object to Grushenka becoming respectable and marrying a man "to be depended upon." And he believed not only that Samsonov would not object, but that this was what he wanted, and, if opportunity arose, that he would be ready to help. From some rumor, or perhaps from some stray words of Grushenka's, he had gathered further that the old man would perhaps prefer him to his father as a husband for Grushenka.

It is possible that many of my readers will feel that in counting on such assistance, and being ready to take his bride, so to speak, from the hands of her protector, Dmitri showed great coarseness. I will only say that Dmitri looked upon Grushenka's past as something completely over. He looked on that past with infinite pity and resolved with all the fervor of his passion that when once Grushenka told him she loved him and would marry him, it would mean the beginning of a new Grushenka and a new Dmitri, free from every vice. They would forgive one another and would begin their lives afresh. As for Kuzma Samsonov, Dmitri looked upon him as a man who had had a fateful influence on Grushenka's remote past, though she had never loved him, and who was now himself a thing of the past, completely done with, and, so to say, non-existent. Besides, Dmitri hardly looked upon him as a man at all, for it was known to everyone in town that he was only a shattered wreck and that his relations with Grushenka were now simply paternal.

In any case there was much simplicity on Dmitri's part in all this, for in spite of all his shortcomings he was very simple-hearted. It is proof of this simplicity that Dmitri seriously felt that the dying Samsonov must sincerely repent of his past relations with Grushenka, and that she had no more devoted friend and protector in the world than this, now harmless, old man.

After his conversation with Alyosha, at the crossroads, Dmitri hardly slept all night, and at ten o'clock the next morning, he was at the house of Samsonov asking the servant to announce him. It was a very large and gloomy old house with a lodge and outhouses. On the ground floor lived Samsonov's two married sons with their families, his old sister, and his unmarried daughter. In the lodge lived two of his clerks, one of whom also had a large family. Both the lodge and the lower floor were overcrowded, but the old man kept the upper floor to himself, and would not even let his daughter live there with him, although she took care of him, and in spite of her asthma was obliged at certain fixed hours, and at any time he might call her, to run upstairs to him.

This upper floor contained a number of large rooms kept purely for show, furnished in the old-fashioned merchant style, with long, monotonous rows of clumsy mahogany chairs along the walls, with glass chandeliers under shades, and gloomy mirrors. All these rooms were unused, for the old man kept to one room, a small bedroom, where he was waited upon by an old servant with a kerchief on her head, and by a boy who used to sit on a chest in the passage. Because of his swollen legs, the old man could hardly walk, and was only rarely lifted from his leather arm chair. The old woman, supporting him, occasionally led him up and down the room once or twice. He was morose and disagreeable even with this old woman.

When old Samsonov was informed of the arrival of Dmitri Karamazov he refused to see him. But Dmitri persisted and sent his name up again. Samsonov questioned the servant minutely: What he looked like? Whether he was drunk? Was he going to make a row? The answer he received was that Dmitri was sober, but wouldn't go away. The old man again refused to see him. Then Dmitri, who had foreseen this, and purposely brought pencil and paper with him, wrote the words: "On most important business closely concerning Agrafena Svyetlov." He sent this note up to the old man.

After thinking a little Samsonov told the servant to show the visitor to the drawing room, and he sent the old woman downstairs with a summons to his younger son to come upstairs to him at once. This younger son, a man over six foot and of exceptional physical strength, who was closely shaven and dressed in the European style, though his father still wore a kaftan and a beard, came at once, without a comment. The whole family trembled before the father. The old man had sent for this giant, not because he was afraid of Dmitri but in order to have a witness in case of any emergency. Supported by his son and the servant he waddled at last into the drawing room where Dmitri was awaiting him. It was a vast, dreary room that laid a weight of depression on the heart. It had a double row of windows, a gallery, marbled walls, and three immense chandeliers.

Dmitri was sitting on a little chair at the entrance, awaiting his fate with nervous impatience. When the old man appeared at the opposite door, seventy feet away, Dmitri jumped up at once, and with his long, military stride walked to meet him. Dmitri was well dressed, in a frock coat, buttoned up, with a round hat and black gloves in his hands, just as he had been three days before at Father Zossima's, at the family meeting with his father and brothers. The old man waited for him, standing dignified and unbending, and Dmitri felt at once that he had looked him through and through as he advanced. Dmitri was impressed with Samsonov's immensely swollen face. His lower lip, which had always been thick, hung down now, looking like a bun. He bowed to his guest in dignified silence, motioned him to a low chair by the sofa, and, leaning on his son's arm began lowering himself onto the sofa, groaning painfully, so that Dmitri immediately felt remorseful and conscious of his insignificance.

"What is it you want of me, sir?" said the old man, deliberately, distinctly, severely, but courteously, when he was at last seated.

Dmitri jumped up but sat down again. Then he began speaking in a loud nervous voice and waving his arms. He was unmistakably a man driven into a corner, on the brink of ruin, catching at the last straw, ready to sink if he failed. Old Samsonov grasped all this in an instant, though his face remained cold and immovable as a statue's.

"Most honored sir, you have no doubt heard, more than once, of my disagreements with my father, Fyodor Karamazov, who robbed me of my inheritance from my mother . . . The whole town is talking about it . . . For here everyone's gossiping of what they shouldn't . . . And besides, it might have reached you through Grushenka . . . I beg your pardon, through Agrafena Svyetlov . . . Agrafena Svyetlov, the lady for whom I have the highest respect and esteem . . ."

So Dmitri began, and broke down at the first sentence. I will not reproduce his speech word for word, but will only summarize it. Three months ago, he said, he had of express intention (Dmitri purposely used these words instead of "intentionally") consulted a lawyer in the chief town of the province, "a distinguished lawyer, Pavel Korneplodov. You have perhaps heard of him? A man of vast intellect, the mind of a statesman . . . He knows you, too . . . Spoke of you in the highest terms . . ." Dmitri broke down again. But these breaks did not stop him. He leapt instantly over the gaps, and struggled on and on.

This Korneplodov, after questioning him minutely and inspecting the documents he was able to bring (Dmitri referred somewhat vaguely to these documents, and slurred over the subject), reported that they certainly might take proceedings concerning the village of Tchermashnya, which should, he said, have come to him, Dmitri, from his mother, and so check the old villain, his father . . . "Because every door was not closed and justice might still find a loophole." In fact, he might count on an additional sum of six or even seven thousand roubles from his father, as Tchermashnya was worth at least twenty-five thousand, he might say twenty-eight thousand, in fact, "thirty, thirty, sir, and would you believe it, I didn't get seventeen from that heartless man?" So he, Dmitri, had given the business up, for the time, knowing nothing about the law, but on coming home was struck dumb by a cross-claim made upon him (here Dmitri went adrift again, and again took a flying leap forward), "so will you, excellent and honored sir, be willing to take over all my claims against that unnatural monster, my father, and pay me a sum of only three thousand? . . . You see, you cannot lose. On my honor, my honor, I swear to that. Quite the contrary, you may make six or seven thousand instead of three" . . . Above all, Dmitri wanted this business concluded that very day.

"I'll do the business with you at a notary's, or whatever it is . . . In fact, I'm ready to do anything. . . . I'll hand over all the deeds . . . Whatever you want, sign anything . . . And we could draw up the agreement at once . . . And if it were possible, if it were only possible, this very morning. . . . You could pay me that three thousand and so save me from . . . Save me, in fact . . . for a good, I might say an honorable, deed . . . For I cherish the most honorable feelings for a certain person, whom you know and care for as a father. I would not have come, indeed, if it had been otherwise. And it's a struggle of three in this business, for it's fate—that's a fearful thing, sir! A tragedy, sir, a tragedy! And as you've dropped out long ago, it's a tug of war between two. I'm expressing it awkwardly, perhaps, but I'm not a literary man. You see, I'm on the one side, and that monster, my father, is on the other. So you must choose. It's either I or the monster. It all lies in your hands—the fate of three lives, and the happiness of two. . . . Excuse me, I'm making a mess of it, but you understand . . . I see from your eyes that you understand . . . And if you don't understand, I'm done for . . . So you see!"

Dmitri broke off his clumsy speech with that "so you see!" and jumping up from his chair awaited the answer to his impossible proposal. At the last phrase he had suddenly become hopelessly aware that it had all fallen flat and that he had been talking utter nonsense. "How strange it is! On the way here it seemed all right, and now it's nothing but nonsense." The idea suddenly came to him in his despair.

All the while he had been talking, the old man Samsonov sat motionless, watching him with an icy expression. After keeping him for a moment in suspense he pronounced in the most positive and chilling tone: "Excuse me, we don't undertake such business."

Dmitri suddenly felt his legs growing weak under him.

"What am I to do now, sir?" he muttered, with a pale smile. "I suppose it's all up with me—what do you think?"

"Excuse me . . ."

Dmitri remained standing, staring motionless. He suddenly noticed a movement in the old man's face. He started.

"You see, sir, business of that sort's not in our line," said the old man slowly. "There are courts and lawyers—it's a perfect misery. But if you like, there is a man you might see."

"Who is he? You're my salvation, sir," faltered Dmitri.

"He doesn't live here, and he's not here just now. He is a peasant, he does business in timber. His name is Lyagavy. He's been haggling with your father for the last year, over your woodland at Tchermashnya. They can't agree on the price, maybe you've heard? Now he's come back again and is staying with the priest at Ilyinskoe, about twelve miles from the Volovya station. He wrote to me about the business of the woodland, asking my advice. Your father means to go and see him himself. So if you were to get there before your father and to make Lyagavy the offer you've made me, he might possibly . . ."

"An excellent idea!" Dmitri interrupted. "He's the very man, it would just suit him. He's haggling for it, being asked too much, and here he would have all the documents entitling him to the property itself. Ha-ha-ha!"

And Dmitri suddenly went off into his short, wooden laugh, startling Samsonov.

"How can I thank you, sir?" cried Dmitri effusively.

"Don't mention it," said Samsonov, inclining his head.

"But you don't know, you've saved me. Oh, it was a premonition that brought me to you. . . . So now to this priest!"

"No need of thanks."

"I'll hurry there. I'm afraid I've overtaxed your strength. I shall never forget it. It's a Russian says that, Kuzma Samsonov, a R-r-russian!"

"To be sure!"

Dmitri seized his hand to press it, but there was a mean gleam in the old man's eye. Dmitri drew back his hand, but at once blamed himself for his mistrust.

"It's because he's tired," he thought.

"For her sake! For her sake, sir! You understand that it's for her," he cried, his voice ringing through the room. He bowed, turned sharply round, and with his long stride walked to the door without looking back. He was trembling with expectation.

"Everything was on the verge of ruin and my guardian angel saved me," was the thought in his mind. And if such a businessman as Samsonov (a most worthy old man, and what dignity!) had suggested this course, then . . . Then success was assured. He would go to Ilyinskoe immediately. "I will be back before night, I will be back at night and the thing will be settled. . . . Could the old man have been laughing at me?" Dmitri suddenly asked as he walked toward his lodging. He could, of course, imagine nothing but that the advice was practical "from such a businessman" with an understanding of the business, with an understanding of this Lyagavy (Setter-dog, what a strange surname!). Or—the old man was laughing at him.

Alas! the second alternative was the correct one. Long afterwards, when the disaster had happened, old Samonov himself confessed, laughing, that he had made a fool of Dmitri. He was a cold, spiteful and sarcastic man, given to violent dislikes. Whether it was Dmitri's face or his foolish conviction that he, Samsonov, could be taken in by such a scheme, or jealousy over Grushenka, in whose name this "fool" had rushed in on him to get money—which worked on the old man I can't tell. But, at the moment when Dmitri stood before him, feeling his legs grow weak and frantically exclaiming that he was ruined, at that moment the old man looked at him with intense spite, and decided to make a laughingstock of him.

When Dmitri had gone, Samsonov, white with rage, turned to his son and told him to see to it that that beggar should never be seen again, and should never be admitted even into the yard, or else he'd . . .

He did not utter his threat. But even his son, who often saw him enraged, trembled with fear. For a whole hour afterwards, the old man was shaking with anger, and by evening he was worse, and sent for the doctor.

2. Lyagavy

HE MUST DRIVE AT FULL SPEED, and he did not have the money for horses. He had forty cents and that was all, all that was left after so many years of living on an income. But he had an old silver watch which had long ago stopped running. He took it to a Jewish watchmaker who had a shop in the market place. He got six roubles for it.

"And I didn't expect that," cried Dmitri. (He was still in a state of excitement.) He seized his six roubles and ran home. At home he borrowed three roubles from the people of the house, who loved him so much that they were pleased to give it to him, though it was all they had, Dmitri in his excitement told them that his fate would be decided that day, and he described in desperation the whole scheme he had put before Samsonov, the old man's decision, his own hopes for the future, and so on. These people had been told many of their lodger's secrets before, and so they looked upon him as a gentleman who was not at all proud, and almost one of themselves. Having thus collected nine roubles, Dmitri sent for horses to take him to the Volovya station. This was how the fact came to be remembered and established that "at noon, on the day before the disaster, Dmitri did not have a penny, and that he had sold his watch to get money and had borrowed three roubles, all in the presence of witnesses."

I note this fact, later on it will be clear why I do so.

Though he was buoyed up with anticipation that he would at last solve all his difficulties, yet, as he drew near Volovya station, he grew tense at the thought of what Grushenka might be doing in his absence. What if she made up her mind to go to his father? This was why he had gone off without telling her and why he left orders with his landlady not to say where he had gone, if anyone came to inquire for him.

"I must, I must get back tonight," he repeated, as he was jolted along in the cart. "And I daresay I shall have to bring this Lyagavy back with me . . . to draw up the deed." So Dmitri reasoned, with a throbbing heart. But his dreams were not fated to be carried out.

To begin with, he was late, having taken a short cut from Volovya station which turned out to be eighteen miles instead of twelve. Secondly, he did not find the priest at home at Ily-inskoe; he had gone off to a neighboring village. Dmitri set off to look for him. In the meantime it grew dark.

The priest, a shy and amiable-looking little man, informed Dmitri at once that, though Lyagavy had been staying with him at first, he was now at Suhoy Possyolok. He was staying the night in the forester's cottage, as he was buying timber there too. At Dmitri's urgent request that he should take him to Lyagavy at once and "save him, so to speak," the priest agreed, after some demur, to go with him to Suhoy Possyo-lok. His curiosity was aroused. But, unluckily, he advised their going on foot, as it would not be "much over" a mile. Dmitri, of course, agreed, and marched off with his yard-long strides, so that the poor priest almost ran after him. He·was a very cautious man, though not old.

Dmitri at once began talking to him of his plans and asking advice in regard to Lyagavy. He talked all the way.

The priest replied to Dmitri's questions with: "I don't know. Ah, I can't say. How can I tell?" and so on. But when Dmitri began to speak of his quarrel with his father over his inherit-ance, the priest was alarmed, as he was in some way depend-ent on Fyodor Karamazov.

Dmitri asked with surprise why the priest called the peasant trader Gorstkin when his name was Lyagavy. The priest explained that, though the man's name really was Lya-gavy (Setter-dog), he was never called that as he would be of-fended at the name, and that he must be sure to call him Gorstkin, "or you'll do nothing with him; he won't even listen to you."

Dmitri was surprised, and explained that that was what

Samsonov had called him. On hearing this, the priest dropped the subject, though he would have done well to ask whether, if Samsonov had sent Dmitri to that peasant, calling him Lyagavy, he was setting a trap for him. But Dmitri had no time to waste over such trifles. He hurried, striding along, and only when they reached Suhoy Possyolok did he realize that they had come not one mile, nor one and a half, but at least three. This annoyed him, but he controlled himself.

They went into the forester's hut. The forester lived in one half of the hut, and Gorstkin was staying in the other, the better room on the other side of the passage. They went into that room and lighted a tallow candle. The room was overheated. On the table there was a samovar that had gone out, a tray with cups, an empty rum bottle, a bottle of vodka partly full, and some half-eaten crusts of bread. Gorstkin himself lay stretched at full length on the bench, with his coat crushed up under his head for a pillow, snoring heavily. Dmitri stood puzzled.

"Of course I must wake him. My business is important. I'm in a hurry to get back today," he said in great agitation. But the priest and the forester stood in silence, not giving their opinion. Dmitri went up and began trying to wake him. He shook him. But it did no good.

"He's drunk," Dmitri decided. "What am I to do? What am I to do?" And, terribly impatient, he began pulling Gorstkin by the arms, by the legs, shaking his head, lifting him up and making him sit on the bench. Yet he could only succeed in getting the drunken man to utter absurd grunts and violent but inarticulate oaths.

"No, you'd better wait a little," the priest said at last. "He's obviously not in a good state."

"He's been drinking the whole day," the forester added.

"Good Heavens!" cried Dmitri. "If only you knew how important it is to me and how desperate I am!"

"No, you'd better wait till morning," the priest repeated.

"Till morning! That's impossible!"

And in his despair he was on the point of attacking the sleeping man again, but he stopped short, realizing the uselessness of his efforts. The priest said nothing. The sleepy forester looked gloomy.

"What terrible tragedies real life contrives for people," said Dmitri in complete despair. The perspiration was streaming down his face.

The priest seized the moment to put before him, very reasonably, that even if he succeeded in awakening Gorstkin, he would still be drunk and incapable of conversation. "And your business is important," he said. "So you'd certainly better put it off till morning." With a gesture of despair Dmitri agreed.

"I will stay here with a light, and wait. As soon as he wakes I'll begin. I'll pay you for the light," he said to the forester.

"And for the night's lodging, too; you'll remember Dmitri Karamazov." Then turning to the priest he added, "Only, father, I don't know what to do with you. Where will you sleep?"

"No, I'm going home. I'll take his horse and go home," he said, indicating the forester. "And now I'll say good-by. I wish you all success."

So it was settled. The priest rode off on the forester's horse, delighted to escape, though he shook his head uneasily, wondering, whether he should not next day inform his benefactor Fyodor Karamazov of this curious incident, "or he may in an unlucky hour hear of it, be angry, and withdraw his favor."

The forester, scratching himself, went back to his room without a word, and Dmitri sat on the bench to wait. Dejection clung about his soul like a heavy mist. A profound, intense dejection! He sat thinking, but could reach no conclusion. The candle burned dimly, a cricket chirped; it became insufferably close in the overheated room. He suddenly pictured the garden, the path behind the garden, the door of his father's house mysteriously opening and Grushenka running in. He jumped up from the bench.

"It's a tragedy!" he said clenching his teeth. Mechanically he went up to the sleeping man and looked in his face. He was a lean, middle-aged peasant, with a very long face, flaxen curls, and a long, thin, reddish beard. He was wearing a blue cotton shirt with a black waistcoat, with a chain and silver watch. Dmitri looked at his face with hatred. For some unknown reason his curly hair particularly irritated him.

What was insufferably humiliating was, that, after leaving things of such importance and making such sacrifices, he, Dmitri, completely worn out, and with business of such importance should be standing over this drunkard upon whom his whole fate depended, while he snored as though there were nothing the matter, as though he'd dropped from another planet.

"Oh, the irony of fate!" cried Dmitri, and losing his head, he tried again to rouse the peasant. He pulled him, pushed him, even beat him; but after five minutes he returned to his bench in helpless despair, and sat down.

"Stupid! Stupid!" cried Dmitri. "And how dishonorable it all is!" something made him add. His head began to ache horribly. Should he give up and go away? he wondered. "No, I'll wait till tomorrow. I'll stay. What else did I come for? Besides, I've no means of going. How am I to get away from here now? Oh, the stupidity of it!"

His head ached more and more. He sat without moving and fell asleep. He slept two hours or more. He woke up with his head aching so unbearably that he could have screamed. There was a hammering in his temples, and the top of his

346

head ached. It was a long time before he could wake up fully and understand what had happened to him.

At last he realized that the room was full of charcoal fumes from the stove, and that he might die of suffocation. And the drunken peasant still lay snoring. The candle flickered and was about to go out. Dmitri cried out, and staggered across the passage into the forester's room. The forester woke up at once. Dmitri told him about the fumes and to his surprise the forester accepted the fact with strange unconcern, though he did go to see about it.

"But he's dead, he's dead! And . . . what am I to do now?" cried Dmitri frantically.

They threw open the doors, opened a window and the chimney damper. Dmitri brought a pail of water from the passage. First he wetted his own head, then, finding a rag, dipped it into the water, and put it on Gorstkin's head. The forester still treated the matter lightly, and when he opened the window said: "It'll be all right, now."

He went back to his room leaving Dmitri a lighted lantern. Dmitri fussed with the drunken peasant for half an hour, wetting his head. He resolved not to sleep all night. But he was so worn out that when he sat down for a moment to take a breath, he closed his eyes, unconsciously stretched himself full length on the bench and slept like the dead.

It was dreadfully late when he woke up. It was about nine o'clock. The sun was shining brightly. The curly-headed peasant was sitting on the bench and had his coat on. He had another samovar and another bottle in front of him. Yesterday's bottle had already been finished and the new one was more than half empty. Dmitri jumped up and saw at once that the cursed peasant was drunk again, hopelessly and incurably. He stared at him for a moment with wide opened eyes. The peasant was silent. Dmitri rushed up to him.

"Excuse me, you see. . . . I . . . You've most likely heard from the forester here in the hut. I'm Lieutenant Dmitri Karamazov, the son of the old Karamazov whose timber you are buying."

"That's a lie!" said the peasant, calmly and confidently.

"A lie? You know Fyodor Karamazov?"

"I don't know any of your Fyodor Karamazovs," said the peasant thickly.

"You're bargaining with him for the woodland, for the timber. Wake up. The priest at Ilyinskoe brought me here. You wrote to Samsonov, and he has sent me to you," Dmitri said breathlessly.

"You're l-lying!" Gorstkin blurted out again. Dmitri's legs went cold.

"For God's sake! It isn't a joke! You're drunk. Yet you can speak and understand . . . Or else . . . I understand nothing!"

"You're a painter!"

"For God's sake! I'm Karamazov, Dmitri Karamazov. I have an offer to make you, a good offer . . . A very good offer, concerning the woodland!"

The peasant stroked his beard.

"No, you've contracted for the job and haven't done it. You're a scoundrel!"

"I assure you you're mistaken," cried Dmitri.

The peasant stroked his beard and screwed up his eyes.

"No, you show me this: you tell me the law that allows dishonesty. D'you hear? You're a scoundrel! Do you understand that?"

Dmitri stepped back gloomily, and suddenly "something seemed to hit him on the head," as he said afterward. A light seemed to dawn in his mind, "a light was kindled and I grasped it all." He stood stupefied wondering how he, a man of intelligence, could have given in to such foolishness, have been led into such an adventure, and have kept it up for almost twenty-four hours, fussing around this drunken peasant, wetting his head.

"Why, the man's drunk, dead drunk, and he'll go on drinking now for a week. What's the use of waiting here? And what of it if Samsonov sent me here on purpose? What if she . . . Oh God, what have I done?"

The peasant sat watching him and grinning. Another time Dmitri might have killed the fool in a fury, but now he felt as weak as a child. He went quietly to the bench, took up his overcoat, put it on without a word. He did not find the forester in the next room; there was no one there. He took fifty cents in small change out of his pocket and put them on the table for his night's lodging, the candle, and the trouble he had given. Coming out of the hut he saw nothing but forest all around.

He walked not knowing which way to turn, to the right or to the left. Hurrying there the evening before with the priest, he had not noticed the road. He had no revengeful feeling in his heart for anybody, even for Samsonov. He strode along a narrow forest path, aimless, dazed, without knowing where he was going. A child could have knocked him down, so weak was he in body and soul. He got out of the forest somehow, however, and a view of fields, bare after the harvest, stretched as far as the eye could see.

"What despair! What death all around!" he repeated striding on and on.

He was saved by meeting an old merchant who was being driven across country in a hired rig. Dmitri asked the way, and it turned out that the old merchant was also going to Volovya. After some discussion Dmitri got into the rig.

Three hours later they arrived at Volovya. Dmitri at once ordered horses to drive to town, and suddenly realized that he was terribly hungry. While the horses were being harnessed, an omelette was prepared for him. He ate it all quickly, ate a huge hunk of bread, ate a sausage, and swallowed three glasses of vodka. After eating, his heart grew lighter.

Urging on the driver he flew toward town. He suddenly made a new and "unalterable" plan to procure that "accursed money" before evening. "And to think, only to think that a man's life should be ruined for the sake of that miserable three thousand!" he cried. "I'll settle it today." And if it had not been for the thought of Grushenka and of what might have happened to her, which never left him, he would perhaps have become quite cheerful again. . . . But the thought of her was stabbing him in the heart every moment, like a sharp knife.

At last they arrived. And Dmitri at once ran to Grushenka.

3. Gold Mines

THIS WAS THE VISIT of which Grushenka had spoken to Rakitin with such horror. She was just then expecting the "message," and was much relieved that Dmitri had not been to see her that day or the day before. She hoped that "please God he won't come till I've gone away," and he suddenly burst in on her. The rest we know already. To get him off her hands she suggested that he walk with her to Samsonov's, where she said she absolutely must go "to work on his accounts." She said good-by to Dmitri at the gate, making him promise to come at twelve o'clock to take her home again. Dmitri was delighted at this arrangement. If she was sitting at Samsonov's she could not be going to his father's. "If only she's not lying," he added. But he believed she was not lying.

He was that sort of jealous man who, in the absence of the loved woman, at once invents all sorts of awful ideas of what may be happening to her, and how she may be betraying him. But at the first glance at her face, her gay, laughing, affectionate face, he lays aside all suspicion, and with joyful shame abuses himself for his jealousy.

After leaving Grushenka at the gate he rushed home. Oh, he had so much still to do that day! But a load had been lifted from his heart, anyway.

"Now I must hurry and find out from Smerdyakov whether anything happened last night, whether, by any chance, she went to my father!" This thought again entered his mind. And before he had time to reach his lodging jealousy had surged up again in his restless heart.

Jealousy! "Othello was not jealous, he was trustful," observed the poet Pushkin. And that remark alone is enough to show his deep insight. Othello's soul was shattered and his whole outlook clouded because *his ideal was destroyed*. But

349

Othello did not begin hiding and spying. He was trustful. On the contrary, he had to be led up, pushed on, before he could entertain the idea of deceit. The truly jealous man is not like that. It is impossible to picture to oneself the shame and moral degradation to which a jealous man can descend without a qualm of conscience. And yet it's not as though jealous people were all vulgar and base. On the contrary, a man of lofty feelings, whose love is pure and full of self-sacrifice, may yet hide under tables, bribe the vilest people, and be familiar with spying and eavesdropping.

Othello was incapable of making up his mind to faithlessness —not incapable of forgiving it, but of making up his mind to it—though his soul was as innocent and free from malice as a child's. It is not so with the really jealous man. It is hard to imagine what some jealous men can make up their mind to and overlook, and what they can forgive! The jealous are the readiest of all to forgive, and all women know this. This jealous man can forgive quickly (though, of course, after a violent scene), and he is able to forgive infidelity almost conclusively proved, the very kisses and embraces he has seen. He can forgive everything if only he can somehow be convinced that it has all been "for the last time," and that his rival will vanish, will depart to the ends of the earth, or that he himself will carry his loved one away somewhere, where that dreaded rival will not get near her. Of course the reconciliation is only for an hour. For, even if the rival did disappear next day, the jealous man would invent another one.

One might wonder what there is in a love that has to be so watched over, what a love can be worth that needs such strenuous guarding. But this the jealous will never understand. And yet among them are men of noble hearts. It is remarkable, too, that those very men of noble hearts, standing hidden in some closet listening and spying, never feel the stings of conscience at that moment, anyway, though they understand clearly enough with their "noble hearts" the shameful depths to which they have voluntarily sunk.

At the sight of Grushenka, Dmitri's jealousy vanished, and for an instant he became trustful and generous and positively despised himself for his evil feelings. But that only proved that, in his love for her, there was an element of something far higher than he himself imagined, that it was not only a sensual passion, not only the "curve of her body," of which he had talked to Alyosha. But, as soon as Grushenka had gone, Dmitri began to suspect her of low cunning and faithlessness. And he felt no sting of conscience about this.

And so jealousy surged up in him again. He had to hurry. The first thing he had to do was to get hold of at least a small, temporary loan of money. The nine roubles had almost all gone on his trip. And, as we all know, one can't take a step without money. But driving back to town he had decided where he would get a loan. He had a pair of fine dueling pistols in a case, which he had not pawned till then because he prized them above all his possessions.

In the "Metropolis" tavern he had made the acquaintance of a young official named Peter Perhotin and he had learned that this very wealthy bachelor was passionately fond of guns. He used to buy pistols, revolvers, rifles, hang them on his wall and show them to his friends. He prided himself on them, and was quite a specialist on the mechanism of the revolver. Dmitri, without stopping to think, went straight to him, and offered to pawn his pistols with him for ten roubles. The official, delighted, began trying to persuade him to sell them outright. But Dmitri would not consent, so the young man gave him ten roubles, protesting that nothing would induce him to take interest. They parted friends.

Dmitri was in a hurry. He rushed toward his father's house by the back way, to his arbor, to get hold of Smerdyakov as soon as possible. In this way the fact was established that three or four hours before the tragedy, of which I shall speak later on, Dmitri did not have a penny and pawned a possession he valued for ten roubles, though, three hours later, he was in possession of thousands. . . . But I am anticipating.

From Maria, the young woman living next door to Fyodor Karamazov, Dmitri learned the very disturbing news of Smerdyakov's illness. He heard the story of his fall down the cellar stairs, his fit, the doctor's visit. Fyodor Karamazov's anxiety. He heard with interest, too, that his brother Ivan had set off that morning for Moscow.

"Then he must have driven through Volovya before me," thought Dmitri lightly. But he was terribly distressed about Smerdyakov. "What will happen now? Who'll keep watch for me? Who'll bring me word?" he thought. He began questioning Maria and her mother whether they had seen anything the evening before. They understood what he was trying to find out, and completely reassured him. No one had been there. Ivan had been there during the night; everything had been just as usual. Dmitri grew thoughtful. He would himself have to keep watch today, but where? Here or at Samsonov's gate? He decided that he must be on the lookout at both places, and meanwhile . . . Meanwhile . . . The difficulty was that he had to carry out the new plan that he had made on the journey back. He was sure of its success, and so he must not delay acting upon it. Dmitri decided to sacrifice an hour to it: "in an hour I shall know everything, I shall settle everything, and then, then, first of all to Samsonov's. I'll inquire whether Grushenka's there and come back here again, stay till eleven, and then to Samsonov's again to bring her home." This was what he decided.

He ran home, washed, combed his hair, brushed his clothes, dressed, and went to Madame Hohlakov's. Alas! he had built his hopes on her. He planned to borrow three thousand from her. And what was more, he felt convinced that she would not refuse to lend it to him. It may be wondered why, if he felt so certain, he had not gone to her at first, one of his own sort, so to speak, instead of to Samsonov, a man he did not know, who was not of his own class, and to whom he hardly knew how to speak.

But the fact was that he had never known Madame Hohlakov well, and had seen nothing of her for the last month, and that he knew she could not endure him. She detested him from the first because he was engaged to Katerina, while she had, for some reason, suddenly conceived the idea that Katerina should throw him over, and marry the "charming, chivalrously refined Ivan, who had such excellent manners." Dmitri's manners she detested. Dmitri laughed at her, and had once said that she was just as lively and at her ease as she was uncultivated. But that morning driving back from Volovya a brilliant idea had struck him: "If she is so anxious that I should not marry Katerina (and he knew she was hysterical upon the subject) why should she refuse me now the three thousand, which would enable me to leave Katerina forever? These spoilt ladies, if they set their hearts on anything will spare no expense to satisfy their desires. Besides, she's so rich," Dmitri argued.

As for his "plan" it was just the same as before; it consisted of the offer of his rights to Tchermashnya—but not with a commercial object, as it had been with Samsonov, not trying to win Madame Hohlakov with the possibility of making a profit of six or seven thousand—but simply as a security for the loan. As he worked out this new idea, Dmitri was pleased with it, but so it always was with him in all his undertakings, in all his sudden decisions. He gave himself up to every new idea with passionate enthusiasm. Yet, when he mounted the steps of Madame Hohlakov's house he felt a shiver of fear run down his spine. At that moment he saw fully, as a mathematical certainty, that this was his last hope, that if this broke down, nothing else was left to him in the world but to "rob and murder someone for the three thousand." It was half-past seven when he rang the bell.

At first fortune seemed to smile upon him. He was received without delay. "As though she were waiting for me," thought Dmitri. And as soon as he had been led to the drawing room, Madame Hohlakov ran in and declared that she was expecting him.

"I was expecting you! I was expecting you! Though I'd no reason to suppose you would come to see me, as you will admit yourself. Yet, I did expect you. You may marvel at my instinct, Dmitri, but I was convinced all the morning that you would come."

"That is certainly strange," observed Dmitri sitting down limply. "I have come to you on a matter of great importance. . . . On a matter of supreme importance for me that is . . . For me alone . . . And I . . ."

"I know you've come on important business, Dmitri. It's not a case of presentiment, no old-fashioned harking back to the miraculous. Have you heard about Father Zossima? This is a case of mathematics: you couldn't help coming, after all that has happened with Katerina. You couldn't, you couldn't. That's a mathematical certainty."

"The realism of actual life, that's what it is. But let me explain . . ."

"Realism indeed, Dmitri. I'm all for realism. I've seen too much of miracles. You've heard that Father Zossima is dead?"

"No. It's the first time I've heard of it." Dmitri was a little surprised. The image of Alyosha rose to his mind.

"Last night, and only imagine . . ."

"Madame Hohlakov," said Dmitri, "I can imagine nothing except that I'm in a desperate position, and that if you don't help me everything will collapse. I'm in a fever . . ."

"I know, I know that you're in a fever. You could hardly fail to be, and whatever you may say to me, I know beforehand. I have long been thinking over your destiny, Dmitri, I am watching over it and studying it. . . . Oh, believe me, I'm an experienced doctor of the soul, Dmitri."

"If you are an experienced doctor, I'm certainly an experienced patient," said Dmitri with an effort to be polite. "And I feel that if you are watching over my destiny in this way, you will come to my rescue. And so let me at least explain my plan. . . . And what I am hoping for. . . . I have come, Madame . . ."

"Don't explain it. It's of secondary importance. But as for help, you're not the first I have helped, Dmitri. You have most likely heard of my cousin, Madame Belmesov. Her husband was ruined. I recommended that he take up horse breeding, and now he's doing well. Do you know anything about horse breeding, Dmitri?"

"No. Nothing, nothing!" cried Dmitri impatiently starting from his seat. "I implore you, Madame Hohlakov, to listen to me. Only give me two minutes so that I may explain to you everything, my whole plan. Besides I am short of time. I'm in a hurry," Dmitri cried hysterically, feeling that she was going to begin talking again, and hoping to cut her short. "I have come in despair . . . In the last gasp of despair, to beg you to lend me three thousand roubles, a loan, but on safe, most safe security, with guarantees! Only let me explain . . ."

"You must tell me all that afterwards, afterwards!" Madame Hohlakov with a gesture demanded silence. "And whatever you may tell me, I know it all beforehand; I've told you so already. You ask for a certain sum, for three thousand, but I can give you more, immeasurably more! I will save you, Dmitri, but you must listen to me."

Dmitri started from his chair again.

"Will you really be so good!" he cried. "Good God, you've saved me! You have saved a man from a violent death, from a bullet. . . . My eternal gratitude . . ."

"I will give you more, infinitely more than three thousand roubles!" cried Madame Hohlakov, looking with a radiant smile at Dmitri.

"Infinitely? But I don't need more. I only need three thousand, and I can give security for that sum with infinite gratitude, and I have a plan which . . ."

"Enough, Dmitri, it's said and done." Madame Hohlakov cut him short with triumph. "I have promised to save you, and I will save you. I will save you as I saved Belmesov. What do you think of the gold mines, Dmitri?"

"Of the gold mines? I have never thought anything about them."

"But I have thought of them for you. Thought of them over and over again. I have been watching you for the last month. I've watched you a hundred times as you've walked past, saying to myself; that's a man who ought to be at the gold mines. I've studied your walk and come to the conclusion; that's a man who would find gold."

"From my walk?"

"Yes, from your walk. You surely don't deny that character can be told from a person's walk, Dmitri? Science supports the idea. I'm all for science and realism now. After all this business with Father Zossima, which has so upset me, from this day on I'm a realist and I want to devote myself to practical usefulness. I'm cured. Enough!"

"But the three thousand you so generously promised to lend me . . ."

"It is yours, Dmitri," Madame Hohlakov cut in at once. "The money is as good as in your pocket, not three thousand, but three million, Dmitri, in less than no time. I'll make you a present of the idea. You will find gold mines, make millions, return and become a leader, and wake us up and lead us to better things. Are we to leave it all to the Jews? You will found institutions and enterprises of all sorts. You will help the poor, and they will bless you. This is the age of railways, Dmitri. You'll become famous and indispensable to the Department of Finance, which is so badly off at present. The depreciation of the rouble keeps me awake at night, Dmitri; people don't know that side of me . . ."

"Madame Hohlakov!" Dmitri interrupted with an uneasy presentiment. "I shall perhaps follow your advice, your wise advice. . . . I shall perhaps set off . . . To the gold mines. . . . I'll come and see you again about it . . . Many times, indeed . . . But now, that three thousand you so generously . . . Oh, that would set me free, and if you could today . . . You see, I haven't a minute, a minute to lose today . . ."

"Enough, Dmitri, enough!" Madame Hohlakov interrupted emphatically. "The question is, will you go to the gold mines or not. Have you made up your mind? Answer yes or no."

"I will go, afterwards. . . . I'll go where you like . . . But now . . ."

"Wait!" cried Madame Hohlakov. And jumping up and running to a handsome bureau with numerous little drawers, she began pulling out one drawer after another, looking for something.

"The three thousand," thought Dmitri, his heart almost stopping. "And without any papers or formalities . . . That's doing things in style! She's a splendid woman, if only she didn't talk so much!"

"Here!" cried Madame Hohlakov, running back joyfully to Dmitri. "Here is what I was looking for!"

It was a tiny silver ikon on a cord, such as is sometimes worn next to the skin with a cross.

"This is from Kiev, Dmitri," she went on reverently, "from the relics of the Holy Martyr, Varvara. Let me put it on your neck myself, and with it dedicate you to a new life, to a new career."

And she actually put the cord around Dmitri's neck, and began arranging it. In extreme embarrassment he bent down and helped her. At last he got it under his necktie and collar through his shirt to his chest.

"Now you can set off," Madame Hohlakov pronounced, sitting down triumphantly in her place again.

"I am so touched. I don't know how to thank you, indeed . . . for such kindness, but . . . If only you knew how precious time is to me. . . . That money, for which I shall be indebted to you. . . . Oh, since you are so kind, so touchingly generous to me (Dmitri exclaimed impulsively) then let me tell you . . . Though, of course, you've known it a long time . . . that I love somebody here. . . . I have been false to Katerina. . . . Oh, I've behaved inhumanly, dishonorably to her, but I fell in love here with another woman . . . A woman whom you, Madame Hohlakov, perhaps despise for you know everything already, but whom I cannot leave on any account, and therefore that three thousand . . ."

"Leave everything, Dmitri," Madame Hohlakov interrupted in the most decisive tone. "Leave everything, especially women. Gold mines are your goal, and there's no place for women there. Afterwards, when you come back rich and famous, you will find the girl of your heart in the highest society. She will be a modern girl, a girl of education and advanced ideas. By that time the dawning woman question will have gained ground, and the new woman will have appeared."

"But that's not the point, not at all. . . ." Dmitri pleaded.

"Yes, it is, Dmitri, just what you need; the very thing you're yearning for, though you don't realize it yourself. I am not

355

at all opposed to the present woman movement, Dmitri. The development of woman, and even the political emancipation of woman in the near future—that's my ideal. I've a daughter myself, Dmitri, people don't know that side of me. I wrote a letter to the author, Shtchedrin, on that subject. He has taught me so much, so much about the vocation of woman. So last year I sent him an anonymous letter of two lines: 'I kiss and embrace you, my teacher, for the modern woman. Persevere.' And I signed myself, 'a Mother.' I thought of signing myself 'a contemporary Mother,' and hesitated, but I stuck to the simple 'Mother'; there's more moral beauty in that, Dmitri. And the word 'contemporary' might have reminded him of the magazine, *The Contemporary*—a painful memory because of censorship. . . . Good Heavens, what is the matter!"

"Madame Hohlakov!" cried Dmitri jumping up at last in desperation. "You will make me weep if you delay what you have so generously . . ."

"Oh, do weep, Dmitri, do weep! That's a noble feeling . . . such a path lies open before you! Tears will ease your heart, and later on you will return rejoicing. You will hurry back to me from Siberia on purpose to share your happiness with me . . ."

"But allow me!" Dmitri cried suddenly. "For the last time I beg you, tell me, can I have the money you promised me today, if not, when may I come for it?"

"What money, Dmitri?"

"The three thousand roubles you promised me . . . That you so generously . . ."

"Three thousand? Roubles? Oh, no, I haven't got three thousand," Madame Hohlakov announced with amazement. Dmitri was stupefied.

"Why, you said just now . . . You said . . . You said it was as good as in my hands. . . ."

"Oh, no, you misunderstood me, Dmitri. In that case you misunderstood me. I was talking of the gold mines. It's true I promised you more, infinitely more than three thousand, I remember it all now, but I was referring to the gold mines."

"But the money? The three thousand?" Dmitri said awkwardly.

"Oh, if you meant money, I haven't any. I haven't a penny, Dmitri. I'm quarreling with my steward about it, and I've just borrowed five hundred roubles from Miusov, myself. No, no, I've no money. And, do you know, Dmitri, if I had, I wouldn't give it to you. In the first place I never lend money. Lending money means losing friends. And I wouldn't give it to you particularly. I wouldn't give it to you, because I like you and want to save you, for all you need is the gold mines, the gold mines, the gold mines!"

"Oh, the devil!" roared Dmitri. And with all his might he brought his fist down on the table.

"Oh! Oh!" cried Madame Hohlakov, and she ran to the other end of the drawing room.

Dmitri spat on the floor and strode out of the room, out of the house, into the street, into the darkness! He walked like one possessed, beating himself on the breast, on the very spot where he had struck himself two days previously, in front of Alyosha, the last time he saw him in the dark at the cross-roads. What those blows upon his breast signified, *on that spot,* and what he meant by it—that was, for the time, a secret which was known to no one in the world, and had not been told even to Alyosha. But that secret meant for him more than disgrace; it meant ruin, suicide. This is what it meant, if he did not get hold of the three thousand that would pay his debt to Katerina, and thus remove from his breast, from *that spot on his breast,* the shame he carried upon it, the shame that weighed on his conscience. All this will be fully explained to the reader later on, but now that his last hope had vanished, this man, so strong in appearance, burst out crying like a little child a few steps from the Hohlakovs' house. He walked on, and not knowing what he was doing, wiped away his tears with his fist. In this way he reached the square, and suddenly he became aware that he had stumbled against something. He heard a piercing wail from an old woman whom he had almost knocked down.

"Good Lord, you've nearly killed me! Why don't you look where you're going, you fool?"

"Why, it's you!" cried Dmitri, recognizing the old woman in the dark. It was the old servant who waited on Samsonov, whom Dmitri had seen the day before.

"And who are you, my good sir?" said the old woman in quite a different voice. "I don't know you in the dark."

"You live at Kuzma Samsonov's. You're the servant there?"

"Just so, sir, I was only running out to . . . But I don't know you."

"Tell me, my good woman, is Agrafena Svyetlov still with your master?" asked Dmitri. "I saw her to his house some time ago."

"She has been there, sir. She stayed a little while and went off again."

"What? Went away?" cried Dmitri. "When did she go?"

"Why, as soon as she came. She only stayed a minute. She only told my old master a story that made him laugh, and then she ran away."

"You're lying, damn you!" roared Dmitri.

"Aie! Aie!" shrieked the old woman, but Dmitri had vanished.

He ran with all his might to the house where Grushenka lived. At the moment he reached it, Grushenka was on her way to Mokroe. It was not more than a quarter of an hour after her departure.

Fenya was sitting with her grandmother, the old cook in the kitchen when Dmitri ran in. Fenya uttered a piercing shriek on seeing him.

"You scream?" roared Dmitri. "Where is she?"

But without giving the terror-stricken Fenya time to utter a word he fell at her feet.

"Fenya, for Christ's sake, tell me. Where is she?"

"I don't know. My dear sir, I don't know. You may kill me but I can't tell you." Fenya swore and protested. "You went out with her yourself not long ago . . ."

"She came back!"

"No she didn't. I swear by God, she didn't come back."

"You're lying!" shouted Dmitri. "From your terror I know where she is."

He rushed away. Fenya in her fright was glad she had gotten off so easily; she knew very well that it was only because he was in such a hurry. But as he ran out, he surprised both Fenya and the old cook by doing something unexpected. On the table stood a brass mortar with a pestle in it, a small brass pestle, not much more than six inches long. Dmitri had already opened the door with one hand when, with the other, he snatched up the pestle and shoved it into his pocket.

"Oh Lord! He's going to murder someone!" cried Fenya, throwing up her hands.

4. In the Dark

WHERE WAS HE RUNNING? "Where could she be except at his father's? She must have run straight to him from Samsonov's, that was now clear. The whole intrigue, the whole deceit was evident." . . . It all rushed whirling through his mind. He did not run to Maria, the young woman next door. "There was no need to go there . . . Not the slightest . . . He must raise no alarm . . . They would run and tell immediately. . . . Maria was clearly in the plot. Smerdyakov too, he too, all had been bought over!"

He formed another plan: he ran a long way around his father's house, crossing the lane, running down Dmitrovsky Street, then over a little bridge and to the deserted alley at the back, which was empty and uninhabited, with, on one side the low fence of a neighbor's kitchen garden, and on the other, the strong high fence that ran all around his father's garden. Here he chose a spot, the very spot where he had heard that Lizaveta had once climbed this high fence. "If she could climb over it," the thought, God knows why, occurred to him, "surely I can." He did in fact jump up and catch hold of the top of the fence. Then he pulled himself up and sat astride it. Close by, in the garden stood the bath-house. And he could see a lighted window in the house.

"Yes, the old wretch's bedroom is lighted up. She's there!" and he jumped from the fence into the garden. Though he knew Gregory was ill and Smerdyakov, too, and that there was no one to hear him, he instinctively hid himself, stood still, and began to listen. But there was dead silence on all sides and, as though planned, complete stillness, not the slightest breath of wind.

"And naught but the whispering silence." This line of poetry for some reason came to his mind. "If only no one heard me! I don't think anyone did." Standing still for a minute, he then walked softly over the grass in the garden, avoiding the trees and shrubs. He walked slowly, creeping stealthily, listening to his own footsteps. It took him five minutes to reach the lighted window. He remembered that just under the window there were several large bushes of elder and white beam. The door from the house into the garden, on the left-hand side, was shut; he had looked purposely to see. At last he reached the bushes and hid behind them. He held his breath. "I must wait now," he thought, "to reassure them in case they heard my footsteps and are listening . . . If only I don't cough or sneeze."

He waited two minutes. His heart was beating violently and at moments, he could scarcely breathe. "No, this throbbing of my heart won't stop," he thought. "I can't wait any longer." He was standing behind a bush in the shadow. The light of the window fell on the front part of the bush.

"How red the white beam berries are!" he murmured, not knowing why. Softly and noiselessly, step by step, he approached the window and stood on tiptoe. All his father's bedroom lay open before him. It was not a large room and was divided into two parts by a red screen, "Chinese," as the old man used to call it. The word "Chinese" flashed into Dmitri's mind. "And behind the screen, is Grushenka," he thought.

He began watching his father who was wearing a new striped-silk dressing gown, which Dmitri had never seen. It had a silk cord with tassels round the waist. A clean shirt of fine linen with gold studs showed under the collar of the dressing gown. On his head Fyodor Karamazov had the same red bandage which Alyosha had seen.

"He has gotten himself all dressed up," thought Dmitri.

His father was standing near the window, apparently lost in thought. Suddenly he jerked up his head, listened a moment, and hearing nothing, went up to the table, poured out half a glass of brandy from a decanter, and drank it. Then he sighed deeply, again stood still a moment, walked carelessly up to the looking glass on the wall, with his right hand raised the red bandage on his forehead a little, and began examining his bruises and scars, which had not yet disappeared.

"He's alone," thought Dmitri. "It seems as though he's alone."

The old man moved away from the looking glass, turned suddenly to the window and looked out. Dmitri quickly slipped away into the shadow.

"She may be there behind the screen. Perhaps she's asleep by now," he thought, with a pang in his heart. His father moved away from the window. "He's looking for her out of the window, so she's not there. Why should he stare out into the dark? He's wild with impatience" . . . Dmitri came back to the window and looked in again. The old man was sitting down at the table, apparently disappointed. He put his elbow on the table, and laid his right cheek against his hand. Dmitri watched him.

"He's alone, he's alone!" he repeated again. "If she were here, his face would be different."

Strange to say, a queer, irrational vexation rose up in his heart that she was not there. "It's not that she's not here," he explained to himself immediately, "but that I can't tell for certain whether she is or not." Dmitri remembered afterwards that his mind was, at that moment, exceptionally clear, that he took in everything to the slightest detail, and missed nothing. But a feeling of misery, the misery of uncertainty and indecision was growing in his heart. "Is she here or not?" The angry doubt filled his heart, and suddenly, making up his mind, he put out his hand and softly knocked on the window frame. He knocked the signal the old man had agreed upon with Smerdyakov, twice slowly and then three times more quickly, the signal that meant: "Grushenka is here!"

The old man started, jerked up his head and jumping up quickly, ran to the window. Dmitri slipped away into the shadow. Fyodor Karamazov opened the window and thrust his whole head out.

"Grushenka, is it you? Is it you?" he said, in a sort of trembling half-whisper. "Where are you, my angel, where are you?" He was fearfully agitated and breathless.

"He's alone," Dmitri decided.

"Where are you?" cried the old man again. And he thrust his head out further, thrust it out to the shoulders, looking in all directions, right and left. "Come here, I've a little present for you. Come, I'll show you . . ."

"He means the three thousand," thought Dmitri.

"But where are you? Are you at the door? I'll open it at once."

And the old man almost climbed out of the window, peering out to the right where there was a door into the garden, trying to see into the darkness. In another second he would certainly have run out to open the door without waiting for Grushenka's answer.

Dmitri looked at him without stirring. The old man's profile that he loathed so, his pendant Adam's apple, his hooked nose, his lips that smiled in greedy expectation, were all brightly lighted up by the lamplight from the room. A horrible fury of hatred suddenly surged up in Dmitri's heart. "There he was, his rival, the man who had tormented him, had ruined his life!" It was a rush of that sudden, furious, revengeful anger of which he had spoken, as though foreseeing it, to Alyosha, four days ago in the arbor in answer to Alyosha's question: "How can you say you'll kill father?" "I don't know, I don't know," he had said then. "Perhaps I shall not kill him, perhaps I shall. I'm afraid he'll suddenly be so loathsome to me at that moment. I hate his double chin, his nose, his eyes, his shameless grin. I feel a repulsion. That's what I'm afraid of, that's what may be too much for me" . . . This repulsion was now growing unendurable. Dmitri suddenly pulled the brass pestle out of his pocket.

"God was watching over me then," Dmitri said afterwards. At that very moment Gregory woke up on his bed of sickness. Earlier in the evening he had undergone the treatment which Smerdyakov had described to Ivan. He had rubbed himself all over with vodka mixed with a very strong secret extract of herbs, had drunk what was left of the mixture while his wife repeated a "certain prayer" over him, after which he had gone to bed. Marfa had tasted the stuff, too, and being unaccustomed to strong drink, slept like the dead beside her husband.

But Gregory woke up in the night quite suddenly and after a moment's reflection, though he felt a sharp pain in his back, sat up in bed. Then he deliberated again, got up and dressed hurriedly. Perhaps he was uneasy at the thought of sleeping while the house was unguarded "in such uneasy times." Smerdyakov, exhausted by his fit, lay motionless in the next room. Marfa did not stir. "The stuff's been too much for the woman," Gregory thought, glancing at her and groaning he went out on the steps. He only meant to look out from the steps for he was hardly able to walk, the pain in his back and his right leg was intolerable. But he suddenly remembered that he had not locked the little gate into the garden that evening. He was the most punctual and precise of men, a man who adhered to an unchangeable routine and habits that lasted for years. Limping and writhing with pain he went down the steps and toward the garden. Yes, the gate stood wide open. He stepped into the garden. Perhaps he imagined something, perhaps caught some sound, and glancing to the left he saw his master's window open. No one was looking out of it then.

"What's it open for? It's not summer now," thought Gregory, and suddenly, at that very instant he caught a glimpse of something in the garden. A man seemed to be running in the dark, a sort of shadow was moving very fast.

"Good Lord!" cried Gregory beside himself, and forgetting the pain in his back, he hurried after the running figure. The man went toward the bathhouse, ran behind it and rushed to the garden fence. Gregory followed, not losing sight of him, and ran forgetting everything. He reached the fence at the very moment the man was climbing over it. Gregory cried out, pounced on him, and clutched his leg with his two hands.

Yes, his foreboding had not deceived him. He recognized him, it was he, the "monster," the "parricide."

"Parricide!" the old man shouted so that the whole neighborhood could hear. But he had not time to shout more, he fell as though struck by lightning.

Dmitri jumped back into the garden and bent over Gregory. In Dmitri's hand was the brass pestle, and he flung it away. It fell close to Gregory, not in the grass but on the path, in a most conspicuous place. For some seconds Dmitri examined Gregory. The old man's head was covered with blood. Dmitri put out his hand and began feeling it. He remembered afterwards clearly, that he had been awfully anxious to make sure whether he had broken the old man's skull, or simply stunned him with the pestle. But the blood was flowing horribly; and in a moment Dmitri's fingers were drenched with the hot stream. He remembered taking out of his pocket a clean white handkerchief with which he had provided himself for his visit to Madame Hohlakov and putting it to the old man's head, senselessly trying to wipe the blood from his face and temples. The handkerchief was instantly soaked with blood.

"Good heavens! What am I doing it for?" thought Dmitri suddenly pulling himself together. "If I have broken his skull, how can I find out now? And what difference does it make now?" he added hopelessly. "If I've killed him, I've killed him . . . You've come to grief, old man, so there you must lie!" he said aloud. And suddenly, turning to the fence, he climbed over it into the lane and began running—he had the handkerchief soaked with blood crushed up in his right fist, and as he ran, he thrust it into the back pocket of his coat. He ran headlong, and the few people who met him in the dark, in the streets, remembered afterwards that they had met a man running that night. He ran straight back to Grushenka's house.

Immediately after he had left Grushenka's that evening, Fenya had rushed to the porter and begged him, for Christ's sake, "not to let Dmitri Karamazov in again today or tomorrow." The porter promised, but went upstairs to his mistress who had suddenly sent for him, and meeting his nephew, a young man of twenty, who had recently come from the country, on the way up told him to take his place, but forgot to mention Dmitri.

Dmitri now running up to the gate, knocked. The young man instantly recognized him, for Dmitri had more than once

362

tipped him. Opening the gate he let him in and told him with a good-humored smile that "Agrafena Svyetlov is not at home now, you know."

"Where is she then?" asked Dmitri, stopping short.

"She set off this evening, some two hours ago with Timofey to Mokroe."

"What for?" cried Dmitri.

"That I can't say. To see some officer. Someone invited her and horses were sent to fetch her."

Dmitri left him. He ran into the house like a madman seeking Fenya.

5. A Sudden Resolution

FENYA WAS SITTING IN THE KITCHEN with her grandmother; they were about to go to bed. Relying on the porter they had not locked themselves in. Dmitri ran in and grabbed Fenya by the throat.

"Speak! Where is she? With whom is she now, at Mokroe?" he roared furiously.

Both the women squealed.

"Aie! I'll tell you. Aie, sir, I'll tell you everything. I won't hide anything," gabbed Fenya, frightened to death. "She's gone to Mokroe, to her officer."

"What officer?" roared Dmitri.

"To her officer, the same one she used to know, the one who threw her over five years ago," cackled Fenya as fast as she could speak.

Dmitri withdrew his hands from her throat. He stood facing her, pale as death, unable to utter a word, but his eyes showed that he understood it all, all, from the first word. Poor Fenya was not in a condition at that moment to observe whether he understood or not. She remained sitting on the trunk as she had been when he ran into the room, trembling all over, holding her hands out before her as though trying to defend herself. She seemed to have grown rigid in that position. Her wide-opened, scared eyes were fixed upon him. And to make matters worse both his hands were smeared with blood. On the way, as he ran, he must have touched his forehead with them, wiping off the perspiration, so that on his forehead and his right cheek there were also blood-stained patches. Fenya was on the verge of hysterics. The old cook had jumped up and was staring at him like a mad woman, almost unconscious with terror.

Dmitri stood for a moment, then sank onto a chair next to Fenya. He sat, not thinking but terror-stricken, benumbed. Yet everything was clear as day; that officer, he knew about

him, he knew everything perfectly, he had known it from Grushenka herself, had known that a letter had come from him a
month before. So that for a month, for a whole month this
had been going on and he had never thought of him! But how
could he, how could he not have thought of him? Why was it
he had forgotten this officer, forgotten him as soon as he had
heard of him? That was the question that faced him like some
monstrous thing. And he looked at this monstrous thing with
horror, growing cold with horror.

But suddenly, as gently and mildly as an affectionate child,
he began speaking to Fenya. He spoke as though he had completely forgotten how he had just scared and hurt her. He
questioned Fenya with a preciseness astonishing in his condition, and though the girl looked wildly at his blood-stained
hands, she answered every question as though eager to put
the whole truth and nothing but the truth before him. Little
by little, even with a sort of pleasure she began explaining
every detail, not wanting to torment him, but eager to be of
service to him. She described the whole of that day, in great
detail, the visit of Rakitin and Alyosha, how she, Fenya, had
stood on the watch, how her mistress had set off, and how she
had called out of the window to Alyosha to give him, Dmitri,
her greetings, and to tell him "to remember forever how she
had loved him for an hour."

Hearing this message, Dmitri suddenly smiled, and there
was a flush of color in his pale cheeks. At the same moment
Fenya said to him, not a bit afraid now to be inquisitive:
"Look at your hands, sir. They're all over blood!"

"Yes," answered Dmitri mechanically. He looked carelessly
at his hands and at once forgot them and Fenya's question.

He sank into silence again. Twenty minutes had passed
since he had run in. His first horror was over, but some new
determination had taken possession of him. He suddenly stood
up, smiling dreamily.

"What has happened to you, sir?" said Fenya, pointing to
his hands again. She spoke compassionately, as though she
felt very near to him now in his grief. Dmitri looked at his
hands again.

"That's blood, Fenya," he said, looking at her with a strange
expression. "That's human blood, and, my God! Why was it
shed? But . . . Fenya . . . There's a fence." (He looked at her
as though asking her a riddle.) "A high fence, and terrible to
look at. But at dawn tomorrow, when the sun rises, Dmitri
will leap over that fence. . . . You don't understand what
fence, Fenya, and, never mind. . . . You'll hear tomorrow and
understand . . . And now, good-by. I won't stand in her way.
I'll step aside. I know how to step aside. Live, my joy. . . .
You loved me for an hour, remember Dmitri Karamazov so
forever."

And with those words he suddenly left the kitchen. Fenya

was almost more frightened at this sudden departure than she had been when he ran in and attacked her.

Just ten minutes later Dmitri went to see Peter Perhotin, the young official with whom he had pawned his pistols. It was by now half-past eight, and Perhotin had finished his evening tea and had just put his coat on to go to the "Metropolis" Tavern to play billiards.

Seeing Dmitri with his face all smeared with blood, Perhotin uttered a cry of surprise. "Good Heavens! What is the matter?"

"I've come for my pistols," said Dmitri. "I've brought you the money. And thanks very much. I'm in a hurry. Please get them for me quickly."

Perhotin grew more and more surprised; he suddenly caught sight of a bundle of banknotes in Dmitri's hand. He had walked in holding the notes as no one walks in and no one carries money; he had them in his right hand, and held them outstretched as if to show them. Perhotin's servant boy, who met Dmitri in the passage, said afterwards that he walked into the passage in the same way, with the money outstretched in his hand, so he must have been carrying them like that even in the street. They were all rainbow-colored hundred-rouble notes, and the fingers holding them were covered with blood.

When Peter Perhotin was questioned later on as to the sum of money, he said that it was difficult to judge at a glance, but that it might have been two thousand, or perhaps three, but that at any rate it was a big, "fat" bundle. "Dmitri Karamazov," so he testified afterwards, "seemed unlike himself, too; not drunk, but, as it were, exalted, lost to everything, but at the same time absorbed as though pondering and searching for something and unable to come to a decision. He was in a great hurry, answered abruptly and very strangely, and at moments seemed not at all dejected but quite cheerful."

"But what *is* the matter with you? What's wrong?" asked Perhotin looking at his guest. "How is it that you're all covered with blood? Have you fallen? Look at yourself!"

He took Dmitri by the elbow and led him to a mirror.

Seeing his blood-stained face, Dmitri scowled.

"Damn it! That's the last straw," he muttered angrily. Then quickly changing the notes from his right hand to his left, he impulsively jerked his handkerchief out of his pocket. The handkerchief was soaked with blood. It was the handkerchief he had used to wipe Gregory's face. There was scarcely a white spot on it and the blood had begun to dry and had stiffened it into a crumpled ball. Dmitri threw it angrily on the floor.

"Oh, damn it!" he said. "Haven't you a rag of some sort . . . to wipe my face?"

"So you're only stained, not wounded? You'd better wash,"

said Perhotin. "Here's a washstand. I'll pour out some water."

"A washstand? That's all right . . . But where am I to put this?"

With the strangest perplexity he indicated his bundle of hundred-rouble notes, looking inquiringly at Perhotin as though it were for him to decide what he, Dmitri, was to do with his own money.

"Put it in your pocket, or on the table here. They won't be lost."

"In my pocket? Yes, in my pocket. All right. . . . But really it's all nonsense," he cried, as though suddenly coming out of his daze. "Look, let's first settle that business of the pistols. Give them back to me. Here's your money . . . Because I need them . . . And I haven't a minute, a minute to spare."

And taking the top note from the bundle he held it out to Perhotin.

"But I haven't change enough. Haven't you less?"

"No," said Dmitri, looking again at the bundle. And then as though not trusting his own words, he turned over two or three of the top notes. "No, they're all alike," he added, and again he looked inquiringly at Perhotin.

"How have you grown so rich?" Perhotin asked. "Wait, I'll send my boy to Plotnikov's, they close late—to see if they won't change it. Here, Misha!" he called into the passage.

"To Plotnikov's shop—good!" cried Dmitri as though struck by an idea. "Misha," he turned to the boy as he came in, "look here, run to Plotnikov's and tell them that Dmitri Karamazov sends his greetings, and will be there at once. . . . But listen, listen, tell them to have champagne, three dozen bottles ready before I come, and packed as before to take to Mokroe. I took four dozen with me then," he added suddenly addressing Perhotin. "They know all about it, Misha," he turned again to the boy. "Listen. Tell them to pack cheese, Strasburg pies, smoked fish, ham, caviar, and everything, everything they've got, up to a hundred roubles, or a hundred and twenty as before. . . . But wait. Don't let them forget dessert, sweets, pears, watermelons, two or three or four—no, one melon's enough, and chocolate, candy, toffee, fondants; in fact, everything I took to Mokroe before, three hundred roubles' worth with the champagne . . . Let it be just the same again. And remember, Misha, if you are called Misha. . . . His name is Misha, isn't it?" He turned to Perhotin again.

"Wait a minute," Perhotin intervened, listening and watching him uneasily. "You'd better go yourself and tell them. He'll get it all mixed up."

"He will. I guess he will! Eh, Misha! If you don't make a mistake, I'll give you ten roubles, run along, hurry. . . . Champagne's the chief thing, let them bring up champagne. And brandy, too, and red and white wine, and all I had the last time. . . . They know what I had then."

"But listen!" Perhotin interrupted with some impatience. "Let him simply run and change the money and tell them not to close, and you go and tell them. . . . Give him your note. Go, Misha! Put your best leg forward!"

Perhotin seemed to want to hurry Misha off because the boy was standing with his mouth and eyes wide open, apparently understanding little of Dmitri's orders and gazing up with amazement and terror at Dmitri's blood-stained face and trembling blood-stained fingers that held the notes.

"Well, now come and wash," said Perhotin sternly. "Put the money on the table or else in your pocket. . . . That's right, come along. But take off your coat."

And beginning to help him off with his coat, he cried out again: "Look, your coat's covered with blood, too!"

"That . . . it's not the coat. It's only a little here on the sleeve. . . . And that's only where the handkerchief was. It must have soaked through. I must have sat on the handkerchief at Fenya's, and the blood's come through," Dmitri explained with a childlike unconsciousness that was astounding. Perhotin listened, frowning.

"Well, you must have been up to something; you must have been fighting with someone," he muttered.

Dmitri began to wash. Perhotin held the jug and poured out the water.

Dmitri in desperate haste scarcely soaped his hands (they were trembling, and Perhotin remembered it afterward). But Perhotin insisted on his soaping them thoroughly and rubbing them more. He seemed to exercise more and more sway over Dmitri as time went on. It may be noted in passing that he was a young man of strong character.

"Look, you haven't got your nails clean. Now rub your face. Here, on your temples, by your ear. . . . Will you go in that shirt? Where are you going? Look, the cuff of your right sleeve is covered with blood."

"Yes, it's all bloody," observed Dmitri looking at the cuff.

"Then change your shirt."

"I haven't time. You see I'll . . ." Dmitri went on with the same confiding simplicity, drying his face and hands on the towel, and putting on his coat. "I'll turn it up at the wrist. It won't show under the coat. . . . You see!"

"Tell me now, what have you been up to? Have you been fighting with someone? In the tavern again, as before? Have you been beating that poor captain again?" Perhotin asked him. "Whom have you been beating now . . . or killing, perhaps?"

"Nonsense!" said Dmitri.

"Why 'nonsense'?"

"Don't worry," said Dmitri, and he suddenly laughed. "I smashed an old woman in the market place just now."

"Smashed? An old woman?"

"An old man!" cried Dmitri, looking Perhotin straight in the face and laughing and shouting at him as though he were deaf.

"Damn it! An old woman, an old man. . . . Have you killed someone?"

"We made up. We had a fight—and made up. In a place I know of. We parted friends. A fool. . . . He's forgiven me. . . . He's sure to have forgiven me by now . . . If he had got up, he wouldn't have forgiven me"—Dmitri suddenly winked—"Only, damn him, you know, Perhotin, damn him! Don't worry about him! I don't want to just now!"

"Why do you want to go picking fights with everyone? . . . Just as you did with that poor captain over some nonsense. . . . You've been fighting and now you're rushing off on a spree—that's you all over! Three dozen bottles of champagne —what do you want all that for?"

"All right! Now give me the pistols. On my honor, I've no time now. I would like to talk with you, but I haven't the time. And there's no need, it's too late for talking. Where's my money? Where have I put it?" he cried, thrusting his hands into his pockets.

"You put it on the table . . . yourself. . . . Here it is. Had you forgotten? Money's like dirt or water to you, it seems. Here are your pistols. It's an odd thing, at six o'clock you pledged them for ten roubles, and now you've got thousands. Two or three I should say."

"Three," laughed Dmitri, stuffing the notes into the side pocket of his trousers.

"You'll lose it like that. Have you found a gold mine?"

"The mines? The gold mines?" Dmitri shouted at the top of his voice and then he roared with laughter. "Would you like to go to the mines, Perhotin? There's a lady here who'll give three thousand if only you'll go. She did it for me, she's so awfully fond of gold mines. Do you know Madame Hohlakov?"

"I don't know her, but I've heard of her and seen her. Did she really give you three thousand? Did she really?" asked Perhotin, eyeing him.

"As soon as the sun rises tomorrow, as soon as Phoebus, ever young, flees upwards, praising and glorifying God, you go to her, this Madame Hohlakov and ask her whether she gave me three thousand or not. Try and find out."

"I don't know on what terms you are . . . Since you say it so positively, I suppose she did give it to you. You've got the money in your hand, but instead of going to Siberia you're spending it all. . . . Where are you really going to now?"

"To Mokroe."

"To Mokroe? But it's night!"

"Once the lad had all, now the lad has naught," cried Dmitri suddenly.

"How 'naught'? You say that with all those thousands!"

"I'm not talking about thousands. Dawn thousands! I'm talking of the female character.

> *Fickle is the heart of woman*
> *Treacherous and full of vices,*

I agree with Ulysses. That's what he says."

"I don't understand you!"

"Am I drunk?"

"Not drunk, but worse."

"I'm drunk in spirit, Perhotin, drunk in spirit! But that's enough!"

"What are you doing, loading the pistol?"

"I'm loading the pistol."

Unfastening the pistol case, Dmitri actually opened the powder horn, and carefully sprinkled and rammed in the charge. Then he took the bullet and before inserting it, held it in two fingers in front of the candle.

"Why are you looking at the bullet?" asked Perhotin watching him uneasily.

"Oh just an idea I have. Why, if you meant to put that bullet in your brain, would you look at it or not?"

"Why look at it?"

"It's going into my brain, so it's interesting to look and see what it's like. But that's all foolishness. Foolishness. Now that's done," he added, putting in the bullet and driving it home with the ramrod. "Perhotin, it's nonsense, all nonsense, and if only you knew what nonsense! Give me a little piece of paper."

"Here's some paper."

"No, a clean new piece, writing paper. That's right."

And taking a pen from the table, Dmitri quickly wrote two lines, folded the paper in four, and put it in his waistcoat pocket. He then put the pistols in the case, locked it and held it in his hand. Then he looked at Perhotin with a slow, thoughtful smile.

"Now, let's go," he said.

"Where are we going? No, wait a minute. . . . Are you thinking of putting that bullet in your brain, perhaps?" Perhotin asked uneasily.

"I was fooling about the bullet! I want to live. I love life! You may be sure of that. I love golden-haired Phoebus and his warm light. . . . Perhotin, do you know how to step aside?"

"What do you mean by 'step aside'?"

"Making way. Making way for a dear creature, and for one I hate. And to let the one I hate become dear—that's what 'step aside' means. And to say to them: God bless you, go your way, pass on, while I . . ."

"While you?"

"That's enough, let's go."

"Really I'll tell someone to stop you from going there,"

said Perhotin looking at him. "What are you going to Mokroe for anyway?"

"There's a woman there, a woman. That's enough for you. You shut up."

"Listen, though you're such a savage I've always liked you. . . . I'm worried."

"Thank you. I'm a savage you say. Savages, savages! That's what I'm always saying. Savages! Why, here's Misha! I had forgotten him."

Misha ran in with a handful of notes in change, and cried out that everyone was in a bustle at Plotnikovs'. "They're carrying down the bottles, and the fish, and the tea; it will all be ready at once." Dmitri grabbed ten roubles and handed it to Perhotin, then tossed another ten-rouble note to Misha.

"Don't do such a thing!" cried Perhotin. "I won't have it in my house. It's bad, demoralizing. Put your money away. Here, put it here, why waste it? It will come in handy to-morrow and I bet you'll be coming to me to borrow ten roubles again. Why do you keep putting the notes in your side pocket? You'll lose them!"

"How about it, let's go to Mokroe together."

"What should I go for?"

"Wait, let's open a bottle at once, and drink to life! I want to drink, and especially to drink with you. I've never drunk with you, have I?"

"All right let's go to the Metropolis. I was just going there."

"I haven't time for that. Let's drink at the Plotnikovs', in the back room. Shall I ask you a riddle?"

"Fire away."

Dmitri took the piece of paper out of his waistcoat pocket, unfolded it and showed it to Perhotin. In a large, distinct hand was written: "I punish myself for my whole life, my whole life I punish!"

"I certainly will speak to someone. I'll go at once," said Perhotin after reading the paper.

"You won't have time. Come and have a drink. Come!"

Plotnikovs' was at the corner of the street not far from Perhotin's. It was the largest grocery store in our town, and by no means a bad one, belonging to some rich merchants. They kept everything that could be obtained in a Petersburg shop, groceries of all sorts, wines "bottled by the brothers Eliseyev," fruits, cigars, tea, coffee, sugar, and so on. There were three clerks and two errand boys always employed. Though our part of the country had grown poorer, the landowners had gone away, and trade had become worse, yet the grocery stores flourished as before. There were plenty of customers.

They were awaiting Dmitri with impatience in the shop. They had vivid recollections of how he had bought, three or four weeks ago, wine and goods of all sorts to the value of several hundred roubles, paid for in cash (they would never have let him have anything on credit, of course). They remembered that then, as now, he had had a bundle of hundred-rouble notes in his hand, and had scattered them at random, without bargaining, without reflecting, or caring to reflect what use so much wine and provisions would be to him. The story was told all over town that, driving off then with Grushenka to Mokroe he had "spent three thousand in one night and the following day, and had come back from the spree without a penny." He had picked up a whole troop of gypsies (encamped in our neighborhood at the time), who for two days got money out of him while he was drunk, and drank expensive wine which he bought. People used to tell, laughing at Dmitri, how he had given champagne to grimy-handed peasants and feasted the village women and girls on candies and Strasburg pies. Though to laugh at Dmitri to his face was rather risky, there was much laughter behind his back, especially in the tavern, at his public avowal that all he had got out of Grushenka by this "escapade" was "permission to kiss her foot, and that was the utmost she had allowed him."

By the time Dmitri and Perhotin reached the shop, they found a small open carriage with three horses harnessed abreast with bells, and with Andrey, the driver, already waiting at the entrance. In the shop they had almost entirely finished packing one box of provisions, and were only waiting for Dmitri's arrival to nail it down and put it in the cart. Perhotin was astounded.

"Where did this carriage come from in such a hurry?" he asked Dmitri.

"I met Andrey as I ran to your house and told him to drive straight here to the shop. There's no time to lose. Last time I drove with Timofey, but Timofey now has gone on before me with the witch. Will we be very late, Andrey?"

"They'll only get there an hour at the most before us, not even that maybe. I helped Timofey to start. I know how he'll go. Their pace won't be ours, sir. How could it be? They won't get there an hour earlier!" Andrey replied. He was a lanky, red-haired, middle-aged driver, wearing a full-skirted coat.

"Fifty roubles for vodka if we're only an hour behind them."

"I warrant the time, sir. They won't be half an hour before us, let alone an hour."

Dmitri tried to see after things. But he gave his orders strangely, as it were disconnectedly, and inconsecutively. He began a sentence and forgot the end of it. Perhotin had to come to the rescue.

"Four hundred roubles' worth, not less than four hundred roubles' worth, just as it was then," commanded Dmitri. "Four dozen bottles of champagne, not a bottle less."

"What do you want with so much? What's it for? Wait!"

cried Perhotin. "What's this box? What's in it? Surely there isn't four hundred roubles' worth here?"

The officious clerks began explaining with oily politeness that the first box contained only half a dozen bottles of champagne, and only "the most indispensable articles" such as pies, cakes, toffee, etc. The main part of the order would be packed and sent off, as on the previous occasion, in a special cart, also with three horses, traveling at full speed, so that it would arrive not more than an hour later than Dmitri Karamazov himself.

"Not more than an hour! Not more than an hour! And put in more toffee and fondants. The girls there are so fond of them," Dmitri insisted.

"The fondants are all right. But what do you want with four dozen bottles of champagne? One would be enough," said Perhotin almost angry. He began bargaining, asking for a bill and refused to be satisfied. But he only succeeded in saving a hundred roubles. In the end it was agreed that only three hundred roubles' worth should be sent.

"Well, go to the devil!" cried Perhotin on second thought. "What's it to do with me? Throw away your money, since it's cost you nothing."

"This way, my economist, this way, don't be angry." Dmitri drew him into a room at the back of the shop. "They'll give us a bottle here. We'll taste it. Come along with me. You're a nice fellow, the sort I like."

Dmitri sat down on a wicker chair, before a little table, covered with a dirty tablecloth. Perhotin sat down opposite him and the champagne soon appeared. Oysters were suggested to the gentlemen. "First-class oysters, the last lot in."

"Hang the oysters. I don't eat them. And we don't need anything," cried Perhotin almost angrily.

"There's no time for oysters," said Dmitri. "And I'm not hungry. Do you know, friend," he said suddenly, with feeling, "I never have liked all this disorder."

"Who does like it? Three dozen bottles of champagne for peasants! That's enough to make anyone angry!"

"That's not what I mean. I'm talking of a higher order. There's no order in me, no higher order. But . . . that's all over. There's no use grieving about it. It's too late, damn it! My whole life has been disorder, and one must set it in order. Is that a joke?"

"You're raving, not joking!"

> *Glory be to God in Heaven,*
> *Glory be to God in me . . .*

"That verse," said Dmitri, "came from my heart once, it's not a verse but a tear. . . . I composed it myself . . . Not while I was pulling the poor captain's beard, though."

"Why do you bring him in all of a sudden?"

"Why do I bring him in? Foolishness! All things come to an end; all things are made equal. That's the long and short of it."

"You know, I keep thinking of your pistols."

"That's all foolishness, too! Drink, and don't invent things. I love life, I've loved life too much, shamefully much. Enough! Let's drink to life. I propose a toast. Why am I pleased with myself? I'm a scoundrel, but I'm satisfied with myself. And yet I'm tortured by the thought that I'm a scoundrel, but satisfied with myself. I bless creation. I'm ready to bless God and His creation but . . . I must kill one poisonous insect for fear it will crawl and spoil life for others. . . . Let us drink to life. What can be more precious than life? Nothing! To life, and to the queen of queens."

"Let's drink to life and to your queen, too, if you like."

They drank a glass each. Although Dmitri was excited and expansive, yet he was depressed too. It was as though some heavy, overwhelming trouble were weighing upon him.

"Misha . . . here's your Misha come! Misha, come here, my boy, drink this glass to Phoebus, the golden-haired, of tomorrow morn . . ."

"What are you giving it to him for?" cried Perhotin irritably.

"Yes, yes, yes, let me! I want to!"

"E-ech!"

Misha emptied the glass, bowed, and ran out.

"He'll remember it afterwards," Dmitri remarked. "Woman. I love woman! What is woman? The queen of creation! My heart is sad, my heart is sad, Perhotin. Do you remember Hamlet? 'I am very sorry, good Horatio! Alas, poor Yorick!' Perhaps that's me, Yorick? Yes, I'm Yorick now, and a skull afterwards."

Perhotin listened in silence. Dmitri, too, was silent for a while.

"What dog's that you've got here?" he asked a clerk, noticing a little lapdog with dark eyes, sitting in the corner.

"It belongs to the mistress," answered the clerk. "She brought it and forgot it here. It must be taken back to her."

"I saw one like it . . . In the regiment . . ." murmured Dmitri dreamily. "Only that one had its hind leg broken. . . . By the way, Perhotin, I wanted to ask you; have you ever stolen anything?"

"What a question!"

"Oh, I didn't mean anything. From somebody's pocket, you know. I don't mean government money, everyone steals that, and you probably do too."

"Go to the devil."

"I'm talking of other peoples' money. Stealing straight out of somebody's pocket? Out of a wallet?"

"I stole twenty cents from my mother when I was nine years

373

old," said Perhotin. "I took it off the table and held it tight in my hand."

"Well, and what happened?"

"Oh, nothing. I kept it three days, then I felt ashamed, confessed and gave it back."

"And what then?"

"Naturally I was whipped. But why do you ask? Have you stolen something?"

"I have," said Dmitri smiling.

"What have you stolen?" asked Perhotin curiously.

"I stole twenty cents from my mother when I was nine years old, and gave it back three days later." As he said this, Dmitri suddenly got up.

"Sir, won't you come now?" called Andrey, the driver, from the door of the shop.

"Are you ready? We'll come!" Dmitri started. "A few more words and . . . Andrey, a glass of vodka before starting. Give him some brandy as well! That box" (the one with the pistols) "put it under my seat. Good-by, Perhotin, don't remember evil against me."

"But you're coming back tomorrow?"

"Of course."

"Will you settle the little bill now?" cried the clerk coming forward.

"Oh yes, the bill. Of course."

Dmitri pulled the bundle of notes out of his pocket, again, picked out three hundred roubles, threw him on the counter, and ran out of the shop. Everyone followed him out, bowing and wishing him good luck. Andrey, coughing from the brandy he had just swallowed, jumped up on the box. But Dmitri was only just taking his seat when suddenly, to his surprise, he saw Fenya. She ran up panting, clasped her hands before him with a cry and fell down at his feet.

"Oh, sir, dear good sir, don't harm my mistress. And it was I told you all about it. . . . And don't murder him, he came first, he's hers! He'll marry my mistress now. That's why he's come back from Siberia. Sir, dear sir, don't take a fellow creature's life!"

"Oh! That's it, is it? So you're off there to make trouble!" muttered Perhotin. "Now it's all clear, as clear as daylight. Dmitri Karamazov, give me your pistols at once. . . . Do you hear, Dmitri?"

"The pistols? Wait a minute, I'll throw them into the pool on the road," answered Dmitri. "Fenya, get up, don't kneel before me. Dmitri Karamazov won't hurt anyone, the silly fool won't hurt anyone again. But, Fenya," he shouted, after having taken his seat, "I hurt you before, so forgive me and have pity on me, forgive a scoundrel. . . . But it doesn't matter if you don't. It's all the same now. Now, Andrey, look alive, fly along at full speed!"

Andrey whipped up the horses, and the bells began ringing. "Good-by, Perhotin! My last tear is for you! . . ."

"He's not drunk, but he keeps babbling like a lunatic," Perhotin thought as he watched him go. He had half a mind to stay and see the cart packed with the rest of the wines and provisions, knowing that the shopkeeper would be dishonest. But, suddenly feeling angry with himself, he turned away with a curse and went to the Metropolis to play billiards.

"He's a fool, though he's a good fellow," he muttered as he went. "I've heard of that officer, Grushenka's former flame. Well, if he has turned up. . . . Oh, those pistols! Damn it all! I'm not his nurse! Let them do what they like! Besides, it'll all come to nothing. They're a bunch of brawlers, that's all. They'll drink and fight, fight and make friends again. They are not men who do anything real. What does he mean by 'I'm stepping aside, I'm punishing myself'? It'll come to nothing! He's shouted such phrases a thousand times, drunk, in the taverns. But now he's not drunk. 'Drunk in spirit'—they're fond of fine phrases, the bastards. Am I his nurse? He must have been fighting, his face was all covered with blood. With whom? I'll find out at the Metropolis. And his handkerchief was soaked with blood. . . . It's still lying on my floor. . . . Damn it!"

He reached the tavern in a bad humor and at once made up a game. The game cheered him. He played a second game, and suddenly began telling one of his partners that Dmitri Karamazov had come in for some cash again—something like three thousand roubles, and had gone to Mokroe again to spend it with Grushenka. . . . This news roused interest in his listeners. They all spoke of it, not laughing, but with a strange seriousness. They stopped playing.

"Three thousand? But where can he have gotten three thousand?"

Questions were asked. The story of Madame Hohlakov's present was heard with skepticism.

"Has he robbed his old father, that's the question?"

"Three thousand! There's something odd about it."

"He boasted that he would kill his father; we all heard him, here. And it was three thousand he talked about . . ."

Perhotin listened. All at once he became short and dry in his answers. He said not a word about the blood on Dmitri's face and hands, although he had meant to speak of it at first.

They began a third game, and the talk about Dmitri died away. But by the end of the game, Perhotin had had enough. He laid down the cue, and without having supper as he had planned, he walked out of the tavern. When he reached the market place he stood still, wondering at himself. He realized that what he wanted to do was to go to Fyodor Karamazov's and find out if anything had happened there. "On account of some stupid nonsense—as it's sure to turn out—am I going to wake up the household and make a scandal? Fooh! damn it, is it my business to look after them?"

And so in a very bad humor he started for home. Then suddenly remembering Fenya he said to himself: "Damn it all! I should have questioned her. I should have heard everything." And the desire to speak to her, and find out, became so pressing and importunate that when he was halfway home he turned abruptly and went toward the house where Grushenka lived. Going up to the gate he knocked. The sound of the knock in the silence of the night sobered him and made him feel annoyed. And no one answered him; everyone in the house was asleep.

"And I shall be causing a disturbance!" he thought, with discomfort. But instead of going away he knocked again with all his might, filling the street with clamor.

"Not coming? Well, I will wake them up. I will!" he muttered at each knock, fuming at himself, but at the same time he redoubled his knocks on the gate.

6. "I Am Coming, Too!"

IT WAS A LITTLE MORE THAN TWENTY MILES to Mokroe, and Andrey drove his three horses at a gallop. The swift motion revived Dmitri. The air was fresh and cool, there were big stars shining in the sky. It was the very night, the very hour, when Alyosha fell on the earth, and rapturously swore to love it forever and ever.

All was confusion, confusion in Dmitri's soul but although many things were goading his heart, at that moment his whole being was yearning for her, his queen. He was flying to her, to look on her for the last time. One thing I can say for certain; his heart did not waver for one moment. I shall perhaps not be believed when I say that this jealous lover felt not the slightest jealousy of this new rival, who seemed to have sprung out of the earth. If any other rival had appeared, he would have been jealous at once, and would probably have stained his hands with blood again. But as he dashed through the night, he felt no envy, no hostility, for the man who had been her first lover. . . . It is true he had not yet seen him.

"Here there was no room for argument, it was her right. This was her first love which, after five years, she had not forgotten; she had loved him for those five years. And I, how do I come in? What right have I? Step aside, Dmitri, and make way! What am I now? Now everything is over. Even if her officer had not appeared, everything would be over . . ."

These words would have expressed his feelings, if he had been capable of reasoning. But he could not reason at that moment. His present plan had arisen without reasoning. At Fenya's first words, it had sprung from feeling, and been adopted in a flash, with all its consequences. And yet, in spite of his decision there was confusion in his soul, an agonizing confusion; his decision did not give him peace. There was so much in the background that tortured him. And it seemed strange to him, at moments, to think that he had written his own sentence of death with pen and paper: "I punish myself." And the paper was there in his pocket, ready; the pistol was loaded. He had already decided how, next morning, he would meet the first warm ray of "golden-haired Phoebus."

And yet he could not be free of the past, of all that he had left behind and all that tortured him. He felt this keenly, and the thought of it sank into his heart with despair. There was one moment when he felt an impulse to stop Andrey, to jump out of the cart, to pull out his loaded pistol, and to make an end of everything without waiting for the dawn. But that moment flew by like a spark. The horses galloped on, "devouring space," and as he drew near his goal, the thought of her, of her alone, took more and more possession of his soul, chasing away the fearful images that had been haunting it. Oh, how he longed to look upon her, if only for a moment, if only from a distance!

"She's now with *him*," he thought. "Now I shall see what she looks like with him, her first love. That's all I want." Never had this woman, who was such a fateful influence in his life, aroused such love in him, such a new and unknown feeling, a feeling tender to devoutness, to self-effacement! "I will efface myself!" he said in a rush of almost hysterical ecstasy.

They had been galloping nearly an hour. Dmitri was silent and though Andrey was, as a rule, a talkative peasant, he did not utter a word, either. He seemed afraid to talk, he only whipped up his three lean bay horses.

Suddenly Dmitri cried out in anxiety: "Andrey! What if they're asleep?"

This thought fell upon him like a blow. It had not occurred to him before.

"It may well be that they have gone to bed, by now, sir."

Dmitri frowned as though in pain. Yes . . . He was rushing there . . . with such feelings . . . while they were asleep . . . She was asleep, perhaps, there too. . . . Anger surged up in his heart.

"Drive on, Andrey! Whip them up! Hurry!" he cried.

"But maybe they're not in bed!" Andrey went on after a pause. "Timofey said there were a lot of them there . . ."

"At the station?"

"Not at the posting-station, but at Plastunovs', at the inn, where they also rent out horses."

"I know. So you say there are a lot of them? How's that?

Who are they?" cried Dmitri, dismayed at this unexpected news.

"Well, Timofey was saying they're all gentlefolk. Two from our town—who they are I don't know—and there are two others, strangers. Maybe more besides. I didn't ask. They've started playing cards, so Timofey said."

"Cards?"

"So, maybe they're not in bed if they're playing cards. It's most likely not more than eleven."

"Faster, Andrey! Faster!" Dmitri cried again.

"May I ask you something, sir?" said Andrey, after a pause. "Only I'm afraid of making you angry, sir."

"What is it?"

"Well, Fenya threw herself at your feet just now, and begged you not to harm her mistress, and someone else, too . . . So you see, sir . . . I am taking you there . . . Forgive me, sir, it's my conscience . . . Maybe it's stupid of me to speak of it . . ."

Dmitri suddenly grabbed him by the shoulders from behind.

"Are you a driver?" he asked frantically.

"Yes, sir . . ."

"Then you know that one has to make way for people. What would you say about a driver who wouldn't make way for anyone, but would just drive on and crush people? No, a driver mustn't run over people. One can't run over a man. One can't spoil peoples' lives. And if you have spoiled a life—punish yourself . . . If you've spoiled, if you've ruined anyone's life— punish yourself and go away."

These words burst from Dmitri almost hysterically. Though Andrey was surprised, he kept up the conversation.

"That's right, sir, you're quite right, one mustn't crush or torment a man, or any kind of creature, for every creature is created by God. Take a horse, for instance, some folks even among us drivers mistreat them. Nothing will stop them, they just force their horses."

"To hell?" Dmitri interrupted, and went off into his abrupt, short laugh. "Andrey, simple soul," he grabbed him by the shoulders again. "Tell me, will Dmitri Karamazov go to hell, or not. What do you think?"

"I don't know, sir, it depends on you, for you are . . . you see, sir, when the Son of God was nailed on the Cross and died, He went straight down to hell from the Cross, and set free all sinners that were in agony. And the devil groaned, be- cause he thought that he would get no more sinners in hell. And God said to him, then: 'Don't groan, for you shall have all the mighty of the earth, the rulers, the chief judges, and the rich men, and shall be filled up as you have been in all the ages till I come again.' Those were His very words . . ."

"A peasant's legend! . . . Whip up the left, Andrey!"

"So you see, sir, who it is hell's for," said Andrey, whipping up the left horse. "But you're like a little child . . . That's how we look on you . . . And though you're quick tempered, sir, yet God will forgive you for your kind heart."

"And you, do you forgive me, Andrey?"

"What should I forgive you for, sir? You've never done me any harm."

"No, for everyone, for everyone. You here alone, on the road, will you forgive me for everyone? Speak, simple peasant heart!"

"Oh, sir! I'm afraid. Your talk is so strange."

But Dmitri did not hear. He was frantically praying and muttering to himself.

"Lord, receive me, with all my lawlessness, and do not condemn me. Let me pass by Thy judgment . . . Do not condemn me, for I have condemned myself. Do not condemn me, for I love Thee O Lord. I am a wretch, but I love Thee. If Thou sendest me to hell, I shall love Thee there, and from there I shall cry out that I love Thee forever and ever. . . . But let me love to the end. . . . Here and now for just five hours . . . Till the first light of Thy day . . . For I love the queen of my soul . . . I love her and I can not help loving her. Thou seest my whole heart. . . . I shall gallop up, I shall fall before her and say: 'You are right to pass on and leave me. Farewell and forget your victim . . . Never torment yourself about me!' "

"Mokroe!" cried Andrey, pointing ahead with his whip.

Through the pale darkness of the night loomed a solid black mass of buildings, flung down, as it were, in the vast plain. The village of Mokroe numbered two thousand inhabitants, but at that hour all were asleep, and only here and there a few lights still twinkled.

"Drive on, Andrey!" Dmitri exclaimed.

"They're not asleep," said Andrey again, pointing with his whip to the Plastunovs' inn, which was at the entrance to the village. The six windows, looking on the street, were all brightly lighted up.

"They're not asleep," Dmitri repeated happily. "Quicker, Andrey! Gallop! Drive up with a dash! Set the bells ringing! Let everyone know that I have arrived. I'm coming! I'm coming, too!"

Andrey lashed his steaming, panting horses into a gallop. He drove with a dash and pulled up at the high flight of steps.

Dmitri jumped out just as the innkeeper, on his way to bed, looked out to see who had arrived.

"Trifon Plastunov, is that you?"

The innkeeper bent down, looked intently, ran down the steps, and rushed up to the guest with delight.

"Dmitri Karamazov, your honor! Do I see you again?"

Trifon Plastunov was a thick-set, healthy peasant, of middle height, with a rather fat face. His expression was severe and uncompromising, especially with the peasants of Mokroe, but he had the power of assuming the most pleasant countenance, when he had an inkling that it was to his interest. He dressed in Russian style, with a shirt buttoning down on one side, and a full-skirted coat. He had saved a good sum of money but was forever dreaming of improving his position. More than half the local peasants were in his clutches, everyone in the neighborhood was in debt to him. From the neighboring landowners he bought and rented lands which were worked by the peasants, in payment of debts which they could never shake off. He was a widower, with four grown-up daughters. One of them was already a widow and lived in the inn with her two children, his grandchildren, and worked for him like a charwoman. Another of his daughters was married to a petty official and in one of the rooms of the inn, on the wall could be seen, among the family photographs, a miniature photograph of this official in uniform and official epaulettes. The two younger daughters used to wear fashionable blue or green dresses, fitting tight at the back, and with trains a yard long, on Church holidays or when they went to pay visits. But next morning they would get up at dawn, as usual, sweep out the rooms with birch brooms, empty the slops, and clean up after guests.

In spite of the thousands of roubles he had saved, Trifon Plastunov was very fond of emptying the pockets of a drunken guest. And now remembering that not a month before he had, in twenty-four hours, made two if not three hundred roubles out of Dmitri when he had come on his escapade with Grushenka, he met him with eager welcome. He scented his prey the moment Dmitri drove up to the steps.

"Dmitri Karamazov, dear sir, we see you once more!"

"Wait, Trifon Plastunov," began Dmitri. "First and foremost, where is she?"

"Agrafena Svyetlov?" The innkeeper understood at once, looking sharply into Dmitri's face. "She's here, too . . ."

"With whom? With whom?"

"Some strangers. One is an official gentleman, a Pole, to judge from his speech. He sent horses for her from here. And there's another with him, a friend of his, or a fellow traveler, there's no telling. They're dressed like civilians."

"Well, are they celebrating? Have they money?"

"Poor sort of a feast! Nothing to boast of, sir."

"Nothing to boast of? And who are the others?"

"They're two gentlemen from the town. . . . They've come back from a trip, and are staying here. One's quite young, a relative of Mr. Miusov, he must be, but I've forgotten his name . . . and I think you know the other, too, a gentleman called Maximov. He's been on a pilgrimage, so he says, to the monastery in the town. He's traveling with this young relative of Mr. Miusov."

"Is that all?"

"Yes."

"Wait, listen, Trifon Plastunov. Tell me the main thing: What of her? How is she?"

"Oh, she's only just arrived. She's sitting with them."

"Is she cheerful? Is she laughing?"

"No, I don't think she's laughing much. She's sitting quietly. She's combing the young gentleman's hair."

"The Pole—the officer?"

"He's not young, and he's not an officer, either. Not him, sir. It's the young gentleman that's Mr. Miusov's relative . . . I've forgotten his name."

"Kalganov?"

"That's it, Kalganov!"

"All right. I'll see for myself. Are they playing cards?"

"They have been playing, but they've stopped. They've been drinking tea. The official gentleman asked for liqueurs."

"Wait, I'll see for myself. Now answer one more question: are the gypsies here?"

"You can't have gypsies now, sir. The authorities have sent them away. But we've Jews that play the zither and the fiddle in the village, so one might send for them. They'd come."

"Send for them. Certainly send for them!" cried Dmitri. "And you can get the girls together as you did last time. Mary especially, Stepanida, too, and Arina. Two hundred roubles for a chorus!"

"Oh, for a sum like that I can get the whole village together, though by now they're all asleep. Are the peasants here worth such kindness, sir, or the girls either? To spend a sum like that on such coarseness and rudeness! What's the good of giving a peasant a cigar to smoke, the stinking ruffian! And the girls are all lousy. Besides, I'll get my daughters up for nothing, let alone a sum like that. They've only just gone to bed. I'll give them a kick and set them singing for you. You gave the peasants champagne to drink the last time, e-ech!"

For all his pretended compassion for Dmitri, Trifon Plastunov had hidden half a dozen bottles of champagne on the last occasion, and he had picked up a hundred-rouble note from under the table. And it had remained in his clutches.

"Trifon Plastunov, I sent more than one thousand roubles flying last time I was here. Do you remember?"

"You did send them flying. I well remember. You must have left three thousand behind you."

"Well, I've come to do the same again, do you understand?"

And he pulled out his bundle of notes and held them up before the innkeeper's nose.

"Now, listen and remember. In an hour's time the wine will arrive, fruit, pies, and candies—bring them all up at once. That box Andrey has got is to be brought up at once, too. Open it, and serve champagne immediately. And the girls, we must have girls, Mary especially."

He turned and pulled out the box of pistols from under the seat.

"Here, Andrey, let's settle up. Here's fifteen roubles for the drive, and fifty for vodka . . . For your readiness, for your love. . . . Remember Dmitri Karamazov!"

"I'm afraid, sir," faltered Andrey. "Give me five roubles extra, but more I won't take. Trifon Plastunov, bear witness. Forgive my foolish words . . ."

"What are you afraid of?" asked Dmitri looking at him. "Well, go to the devil, if that's it!" he cried, flinging him five roubles. "Now, Trifon Plastunov, take me up quietly and let me first get a look at them, so that they don't see me. Where are they? In the blue room?"

The innkeeper looked suspiciously at Dmitri, but obediently did his bidding. Leading him into the passage, he went himself into the first large room, adjoining that in which the visitors were sitting, and took the light away. Then he quietly led Dmitri in, and put him in a corner in the dark, from where he could watch without being seen. But Dmitri did not look long. He could not see them; he saw only her. His heart throbbed violently, and all was dark before his eyes.

She was sitting sideways to the table in a low chair, and beside her, on the sofa, was the young man, Kalganov. She was holding his hand and laughing, while he, irritated and not looking at her, was saying something in a loud voice to Maximov, who sat the other side of the table, facing Grushenka. Maximov was laughing violently at something. On the sofa sat *he,* and on a chair by the sofa there was another stranger. The one on the sofa was lolling backwards, smoking a pipe, and Dmitri got the impression of a stoutish broad-faced short little man, who was apparently angry about something. His friend, the other stranger, struck Dmitri as extraordinarily tall, but he could make out nothing more. He caught his breath. He could bear it no longer. He put the pistol case on a chest, and with a throbbing heart he walked, feeling cold all over, straight into the blue room to face the company.

"Oh!" shrieked Grushenka, the first to notice him.

7. *The First and Rightful Lover*

WITH HIS LONG STRIDES, Dmitri walked straight up to the table.

"Gentlemen," he said in a loud voice, almost shouting, yet stammering at every word, "I . . . I'm all right! Don't be afraid! I—there's nothing the matter." He turned suddenly to Grushenka, who had shrunk back in her chair toward Kalganov. "I . . . I'm coming, too. I'm here till morning. Gentlemen, may I stay with you till morning? Only till morning, for the last time, in this same room?"

With these words he finished, turning to the fat little man with the pipe, sitting on the sofa. The man removed his pipe from his lips with dignity and observed severely: "Sir, we're here in private. There are other rooms."

"Why, it's you, Dmitri! What do you mean?" answered Kalganov suddenly. "Sit down with us. How are you?"

"Delighted to see you . . . I always thought a lot of you," Dmitri answered, eagerly holding out his hand across the table.

"Oh! How tight you squeeze! You've almost broken my fingers," laughed Kalganov.

"He always squeezes like that, always," Grushenka put in gaily, with a timid smile, seeming suddenly convinced from Dmitri's face that he was not going to make a scene. She was watching him with curiosity and some uneasiness. She was struck by something about him, and it was the last thing she expected of him that he would come in and speak like this at such a moment.

"Good evening," Maximov ventured blandly. Dmitri rushed up to him, too.

"Good evening. You're here, too! How glad I am to find you here, too! Gentlemen, gentlemen, I . . ." (He addressed the Polish gentleman with the pipe again, evidently taking him for the most important person present.) "I flew here. . . . I wanted to spend my last day, my last hour in this room, in this very room . . . where I, too, adored . . . my queen. . . . Forgive me, gentlemen," he cried wildly. "I flew here and vowed. . . . Oh, don't be afraid, it's my last night! Let's drink to our good understanding. They'll bring the champagne at once. . . . I brought it with me." (Something made him pull out his bundle of notes.) "Allow me, gentlemen! I want to have music, singing, like we had last time. But the worm, the unnecessary worm, will crawl away, and there'll be no more of him. I will commemorate my day of joy and my last night."

He was almost choking. There was so much, so much he wanted to say, but strange exclamations were all that came from his lips. The Pole stared at him, at the bundle of notes in his hand. He looked at Grushenka. He was puzzled.

"If my suverin lady permits . . ." Dmitri began.

"What does 'suverin' mean? 'Sovereign,' I suppose?" interrupted Grushenka. "I can't help laughing at you, the way you talk. Sit down, Dmitri, what are you talking about? Don't frighten us, please. You won't frighten us, will you? If you don't, I am glad to see you . . ."

"Me, me frighten you?" cried Dmitri, throwing up his hands. "Oh, pass me by, go your way, I won't hinder you!"

And suddenly he surprised them all, and no doubt himself as well, by flinging himself on a chair and bursting into tears.

He turned his head away to the opposite wall, while his arms clasped the back of the chair tight, as though embracing it.

"Come, come, what a man you are!" cried Grushenka reproachfully. "That's just how he comes to see me—he begins talking, and I can't make out what he means. He cried like that once before, and now he's crying again! It's shameful! Why are you crying? *As though you had anything to cry for!*" she added, emphasizing each word with some irritability.

". . . I'm not crying. . . . Well, good evening!" He turned around in his chair and suddenly laughed, not his abrupt, wooden laugh, but a long, quivering nervous laugh.

"Well, there you are again. . . Come, cheer up, cheer up!" Grushenka said to him persuasively. "I'm very glad you've come, very glad. Dmitri, do you hear, I'm very glad? I want him to stay here with us," she said peremptorily, addressing the whole company, though her words were obviously meant for the man sitting on the sofa. "I want it, I want it! And if he goes away I will go, too!" she added with flashing eyes.

"What my queen commands is law!" pronounced the Pole, gallantly kissing Grushenka's hand. "I beg you, sir, to join our company," he added politely, addressing Dmitri.

Dmitri jumped up with the obvious intention of speaking, but the words did not come.

"Let's drink, gentlemen," he blurted out instead of making a speech. Everyone laughed.

"Good Heavens! I thought he was going to begin again!" Grushenka exclaimed nervously. "Do you hear, Dmitri," she went on insistently. "Don't jump around, but it's nice that you've brought champagne. I want some. I can't bear liqueurs. And best of all, you've come yourself. We were fearfully dull here. . . . You've come for a good time again, I suppose? But put your money in your pocket. Where did you get such a lot of money?"

All this time Dmitri had been holding in his hand the crumpled bundle of notes on which the eyes of all, especially of the Poles, were fixed. In confusion he thrust them hurriedly into his pocket. He flushed. At that moment the innkeeper brought in an uncorked bottle of champagne and glasses on a tray. Dmitri snatched up the bottle but he was so bewildered that he did not know what to do with it. Kalganov took it from him and poured out the champagne.

"Another! Another bottle!" Dmitri cried to the innkeeper, and, forgetting to clink glasses with the Pole whom he had so solemnly invited to drink to their good understanding, he drank off his glass without waiting for anyone else. His whole manner suddenly changed. The solemn and tragic expression with which he had entered vanished completely, and a look of something childlike came into his face. He seemed to have become suddenly gentle and subdued. He looked shyly and happily at everyone, with a continual nervous little laugh, and

384

the blissful expression of a dog who had done wrong, been punished, and forgiven. He seemed to have forgotten everything, and was looking around at everyone with a childlike smile of delight. He looked at Grushenka, laughing continually, and bringing his chair close up to her. By degrees he had gained some idea of the two Poles, though he had formed no definite opinion of them yet.

The Pole on the sofa struck him by his dignified manner and his Polish accent; and, above all, by his pipe. "Well, what of it? It's a good thing he's smoking a pipe," he reflected. The Pole's puffy, middle-aged face, with its tiny nose and two very thin, pointed, dyed and impudent-looking mustaches, had not so far roused the faintest doubts in Dmitri. He was not even particularly struck by the Pole's absurd wig made in Siberia, with lovelocks combed forward over the temples. "I suppose it's all right since he wears a wig," he went on to himself. The other, younger Pole, who was staring defiantly at the company and listening to the conversation with contempt, still only impressed Dmitri by his great height, which was in striking contrast to the Pole on the sofa. "If he stood up he'd be six foot three." The thought passed through Dmitri's mind. It occurred to him, too, that this Pole must be the friend of the other, as it were, a "bodyguard." But this all seemed to Dmitri perfectly right and not to be questioned. In his mood of submissiveness all feeling of rivalry had died away.

Grushenka's mood and the puzzling tone of some of her words he completely failed to grasp. All he understood was that she was kind to him, that she had forgiven him, and made him sit by her. He was beside himself with delight, watching her sip her glass of champagne. The silence of the company seemed somehow to strike him, however, and he looked around at everyone with expectant eyes.

"Why are we sitting here, gentlemen? Why don't you do something?" his smiling eyes seemed to ask.

"He keeps talking nonsense, and we were all laughing," Kalganov began suddenly, as though guessing his thoughts, and pointing to Maximov.

Dmitri stared at Kalganov and then at Maximov. "He's talking nonsense?" He laughed his short, wooden laugh, as though suddenly delighted at something.

"Yes, would you believe it, he insists that all our cavalry officers in the 'twenties married Polish women. That's nonsense, isn't it?"

"Polish women?" repeated Dmitri.

Kalganov was well aware of Dmitri's attitude to Grushenka, and he guessed about the Pole, too, but that did not interest him so much, perhaps it did not interest him at all. What he was interested in, was Maximov. He had come here with Maximov by chance, and he met the Poles here at the inn for the first time in his life. He had known Grushenka before and had once gone with someone to see her; but she had not taken to him. But now she looked at him very affectionately. Before Dmitri's arrival, she had been making much of him, but he seemed somehow to be unmoved by it. He was young, not over twenty, dressed like a dandy, with a very charming fair-skinned face and thick, fair hair. He had beautiful pale blue eyes, with an intelligent and sometimes even deep expression, although he sometimes looked and talked like a child. He was not ashamed of this even when he was aware of it himself. As a rule he was very wilful, though always friendly. Sometimes there was something fixed and obstinate in his expression. He would look at you and listen, seeming all the while to be dreaming of something else. He was often listless and lazy. At other times he would grow excited over the most trivial matters.

"Imagine, I've been taking Maximov around with me for the last four days," Kalganov went on indolently drawling his words, quite naturally though, without the slighest affectation. "Ever since your brother Ivan, do you remember, shoved him off the carriage and sent him flying. That made me take an interest in him at the time, and I took him into the country. But he keeps talking such nonsense I'm ashamed to be with him. I'm taking him back."

"The gentleman has not seen Polish ladies, and says what is impossible," the Pole with the pipe observed to Maximov.

He spoke Russian fairly well, much better, anyway, than he pretended. If he used Russian words, he always distorted them into a Polish form.

"But I was married to a Polish lady myself," confessed Maximov.

"But did you serve in the cavalry? You were talking about the cavalry. Were you a cavalry officer?" asked Kalganov at once.

"Was he a cavalry officer? Ha, ha!" cried Dmitri. He looked at each as he spoke, as though there was no knowing what he might hear.

"No, you see," Maximov turned to him. "What I mean is that those pretty Polish ladies . . . When they danced the mazurka with our Uhlans . . . When one of them dances a mazurka with a Uhlan she jumps on his knee like a kitten . . . A little white one . . . And her father and mother look on and allow it. . . . They allow it . . . And next day the Uhlan comes and offers her his hand. . . . That's how it is . . . Offers her his hand, he-he!" Maximov ended giggling.

"The gentleman is a good-for-nothing!" The tall Pole on the chair growled suddenly and crossed one leg over the other. Dmitri's eye caught his huge greased boot, with its thick, dirty sole. The clothing of both the Poles looked rather greasy.

"Well, now it's a *good-for-nothing!* What's he irritated about?" said Grushenka suddenly vexed.

"My dear, what the gentleman saw in Poland were servant

girls and not ladies of good birth," the Pole with the pipe observed to Grushenka.

"You can count on that," the tall Pole snapped contemptuously.

"What next! Let him talk! People talk, why stop them? It makes it cheerful," Grushenka said crossly.

"I'm not hindering them," said the Pole with the pipe taking a long look at Grushenka. Then relapsing into silence he sucked his pipe again.

"No, no. The Polish gentleman spoke the truth." Kalganov got excited as though it were a question of great importance.

"He's never been in Poland, so how can he talk about it? I don't suppose you were married in Poland, were you?"

"No, in the Province of Smolensk. Only, a Uhlan had brought her to Russia before that, my future wife, with her mother and her aunt, and another female relation with a grown-up son. He brought her straight from Poland and gave her to me. He was a lieutenant in our regiment, a very nice young man. At first he meant to marry her himself. But he didn't marry her, because she turned out to be lame."

"So you married a lame woman?" cried Kalganov.

"Yes. They both deceived me a little bit at the time, and concealed it. I thought she was hopping; she kept hopping . . . I thought it was for fun."

"So pleased she was going to marry you!" yelled Kalganov, in a ringing, childish voice.

"Yes, so pleased. But it turned out to be quite a different cause. Afterwards, when we were married, after the wedding, that very evening, she confessed, and very touchingly asked forgiveness. 'I once jumped over a puddle when I was a child,' she said, 'and injured my leg.' He-he!"

Kalganov went off into the most childish laughter, almost falling on the sofa. Grushenka, too, laughed. Dmitri was at the pinnacle of happiness.

"You know, that's the truth. He's not lying now," exclaimed Kalganov, turning to Dmitri. "And do you know, he's been married twice. It's his first wife he's talking about. But his second wife, do you know, ran away, and is still living."

"Is it possible?" said Dmitri, turning quickly to Maximov with an expression of astonishment.

"Yes. She did run away. I've had that unpleasant experience," Maximov modestly assented. "With a gentleman. And what was worse, she'd had all my property transferred to her beforehand. 'You're an educated man,' she said to me. 'You can always make your living.' She settled my business with that. A bishop once said to me: 'One of your wives was lame, but the other was too light-footed.' He-he!"

"Listen, listen!" cried Kalganov, bubbling over. "If he's telling lies—and he often is—he's only doing it to amuse us. There's no harm in that, is there? You know, I sometimes like him. He's awfully low, but it's natural to him, eh? Don't you think so? Some people are low from self-interest, but he's simply that way by nature. Only would you believe it he claims (he was arguing about it all day yesterday) that Gogol wrote *Dead Souls* about him. Do you remember, there's a landowner called Maximov in it, whom Nozdryov beat up. He was charged, do you remember, 'for inflicting bodily injury with rods on the landowner Maximov in a drunken condition.' Would you believe it, he claims that he was that Maximov and that he was beaten! Now can that be true? Tchitchikov made his journey, at the very latest, at the beginning of the twenties, so that the dates don't fit. He couldn't have been beaten up then, he couldn't, could he?"

It was difficult to imagine what Kalganov was excited about, but his excitement was genuine. Dmitri followed his lead without protest.

"Well, but if they did beat him up!" he cried, laughing.

"It's not that they beat me exactly, but what I mean is . . ." put in Maximov.

"What do you mean? Either they beat you or they didn't."

"What o'clock is it?" the Pole, with the pipe, asked his tall friend, with a bored expression. The other shrugged his shoulders in reply. Neither of them had a watch.

"Why not talk? Let other people talk. Mustn't other people talk because you're bored?" Grushenka flew at him with the obvious intention of finding fault. Something seemed for the first time to flash upon Dmitri's mind. This time the Pole answered with unmistakable irritability.

"My dear, I didn't oppose it. I didn't say anything."

"All right then. Come, tell us your story," Grushenka cried to Maximov. "Why are you all silent?"

"There's nothing to tell, it's all so foolish," answered Maximov at once. "Besides, all that's all allegorical in Gogol. All his names have a meaning. Nozdryov was really called Nosov, and Kuvshinikov had quite a different name, he was called Shkvornev. Fenardi really was called Fenardi, only he wasn't an Italian but a Russian, and Mamsel Fenardi was a pretty girl with her pretty little legs in tights, and she had a short skirt with spangles, and she kept turning round and round, only not for four hours but for four minutes only, and she bewitched everyone . . ."

"But what were you beaten for?" cried Kalganov.

"For Piron!" answered Maximov.

"What Piron?" cried Dmitri.

"The famous French writer, Piron. We were all drinking then, a big party of us, in a tavern at that very fair. They'd invited me, and first of all I began quoting epigrams. 'Is that you, Boileau? What a funny get-up!' And Boileau answers that he's going to a masquerade, that is to the baths, he-he! And they took it personally. I quickly quoted another, very sarcastic, well known to all educated people:

> *Yes, Sappho and Phaon are we!*
> *But one grief is weighing on me.*
> *You don't know your way to the sea!*

They were still more offended and began abusing me. And as luck would have it, to set things right, I began telling another anecdote about Piron, how he was not accepted into the French Academy, and to revenge himself wrote his own epitaph:

> *Here lies Piron who is nothing*
> *Not even an academician.*

They grabbed me and beat me up."

"But what for? What for?"

"For my education. People can beat up a man for anything," Maximov concluded.

"That's enough! That's all stupid. I don't want to listen. I thought it would be amusing," Grushenka cut them short.

Dmitri at once stopped laughing. The tall Pole stood up and with the haughty air of a man bored and out of his element, began pacing from corner to corner of the room, his hands behind his back.

"Oh, he can't sit still," said Grushenka, looking at him contemptuously. Dmitri began to feel uncomfortable. He noticed besides, that the Pole on the sofa was looking at him with an irritable expression.

"Gentlemen!" cried Dmitri. "Let's drink! And the other gentleman, also! Let us drink."

He had pulled three glasses toward him, and filled them with champagne.

"To Poland, gentlemen. I drink to your Poland!" cried Dmitri.

"I shall be delighted, sir," said the Pole on the sofa, with dignity and condescension. He took a glass.

"And the other gentleman, what's his name? Drink. Take your glass!" Dmitri urged.

"Mr. Vrublevsky," put in the Pole on the sofa.

Mr. Vrublevsky came up to the table, swaying as he walked.

"To Poland, gentlemen!" cried Dmitri raising his glass. "Hurrah!"

All three drank. Dmitri grabbed the bottle and again poured out three glasses.

"Now to Russia, gentlemen, and let us be brothers!"

"Pour out some for us," said Grushenka. "I'll drink to Russia, too!"

"So will I," said Kalganov.

"And I will too. . . . To Russia, the old grandmother!" tittered Maximov.

"All! All!" cried Dmitri. "Plastunov, some more bottles!"

The other three bottles Dmitri had brought with him were put on the table. Dmitri filled the glasses.

"To Russia! Hurrah!" he shouted again. All drank the toast except the Poles. Grushenka tossed off her whole glass at once. The Poles did not touch theirs.

"What's wrong, gentlemen?" cried Dmitri. "Won't you drink?"

Vrublevsky took the glass, raised it, and said in a resonant voice: "To Russia as she was before 1772."

"Come, that's better!" cried the other Pole, and they both emptied their glasses at once.

"You're fools, you gentlemen," broke suddenly from Dmitri.

"Gentleman!" shouted both the Poles, attacking Dmitri like two fighting cocks. Vrublevsky was specially furious.

"Can one help loving one's own country?" he shouted.

"Be silent! Don't quarrel! I won't have any quarreling!" cried Grushenka, and she stamped her foot on the floor. Her face glowed, her eyes were shining. The effect of the champagne she had just drunk was apparent. Dmitri was alarmed.

"Gentlemen, forgive me! It was my fault, I'm sorry. Vrublevsky, I'm sorry."

"Hold your tongue, you, anyway! Sit down, you're stupid!" Grushenka was annoyed.

Everyone sat down. All were silent, looking at one another.

"Gentlemen, I was the cause of it all," Dmitri began again, unable to make anything of Grushenka's words. "Come, why are we sitting here? What shall we do . . . to amuse ourselves?"

"Oh, it's anything but amusing!" Kalganov mumbled.

"Let's play faro again, as we did just now," Maximov suggested.

"Faro? Good!" cried Dmitri. "If only the gentlemen . . ."

"It's lite," the Pole on the sofa said as it were unwillingly.

"That's true," agreed Vrublevsky.

"Lite? What do you mean by 'lite'?" asked Grushenka.

"Late, my dear! 'A late hour' I mean," the Pole on the sofa explained.

"It's always late with them. They can never do anything!" Grushenka almost shrieked in anger. "They're dull themselves, so they want others to be dull. Before you came, Dmitri, they were just as silent and kept turning up their noses at me."

"My goddess!" cried the Pole on the sofa. "You're not friendly to me, that's why I'm gloomy. I'm ready, gentlemen," he added, addressing Dmitri.

"Begin," Dmitri agreed pulling his money out of his pocket, and laying two hundred-rouble notes on the table. "I want to lose a lot to you. Take your cards. Make the bank."

"We'll have cards from the innkeeper, gentlemen," said the little Pole gravely and emphatically.

"That's the best way," chimed in Vrublevsky.

"From the innkeeper? All right, I understand, let's get them from him. Cards!" Dmitri shouted to the innkeeper.

The innkeeper brought in a new unopened pack, and told Dmitri that the girls were getting ready, and that the Jews with the cymbals would most likely come soon; but the cart with the provisions had not yet arrived. Dmitri jumped up from the table and ran into the next room to give orders, but only three girls had arrived, and Mary was not among them. And he did not know exactly what orders to give and why he had run out. He only told them to take out of the box the presents he had brought, the cakes, the toffee and the fondants. "And vodka for Andrey, vodka for Andrey!" he cried suddenly. "I was rude to Andrey!"

Maximov, who had followed him out, touched him on the shoulder. "Give me five roubles," he whispered to Dmitri. "I'll stake something at faro, too, he-he!"

"Good! Take ten. Here!"

Again he took all the notes out of his pocket and picked out one for ten roubles. "And if you lose that, come again, come again."

"All right," Maximov whispered and he ran back again. Dmitri also returned, apologizing for having kept them waiting. The Poles had already sat down and opened the pack. They looked much more amiable, almost cordial. The Pole on the sofa had lighted another pipe and was preparing to deal. He looked very serious.

"Take your places, gentlemen," cried Vrublevsky.

"No, I'm not going to play any more," observed Kalganov. "I lost fifty roubles to them before."

"The gentleman had no luck, perhaps he'll be lucky this time," the Pole on the sofa observed.

"How much in the bank? To correspond?" asked Dmitri.

"That's according, maybe a hundred, maybe two hundred, as much as you want to stake."

"A million!" laughed Dmitri.

"Have you heard of Podvysotsky, perhaps?"

"Podvysotsky?"

"In Warsaw there was a bank and anyone could come and stake against it. Podvysotsky comes, sees a thousand gold pieces, stakes against the bank. The banker says, 'Mr. Podvysotsky, are you laying down the gold, or must we trust to your honor?' 'To my honor, sir,' says Podvysotsky. 'So much the better.' The banker throws the dice. Podvysotsky wins. 'Take it,' says the banker, and pulling out the drawer he gives him a million. 'Take it, sir, it's yours.' There was a million in the bank. 'I didn't know that,' says Podvysotsky. 'Mr. Podvysotsky,' said the banker, 'you pledged your honor and we pledged ours.' Podvysotsky took the million."

"That's not true," said Kalganov.

"Mr. Kalganov, in gentlemanly society one doesn't say such things."

"As if a Polish gambler would give away a million!" cried Dmitri, but he checked himself at once. "Forgive me, it's my fault again. He would, he would give away a million, for honor, for Polish honor. You see how I talk Polish, ha-ha! Here, I stake ten roubles, the jack leads."

"And I put a rouble on the queen, the queen of hearts, the pretty little woman, he-he!" laughed Maximov, pulling out his queen. Then as though trying to conceal it from everyone, he moved right up and crossed himself hurriedly under the table. Dmitri won. The rouble won, too.

"A corner!" cried Dmitri.

"I'll bet another rouble, a 'single' stake," Maximov muttered, hugely delighted at having won a rouble.

"Lost!" shouted Dmitri. "A 'double' on the seven!"

The seven too was trumped.

"Stop!" cried Kalganov suddenly.

"Double! Double!" Dmitri doubled his stakes, and each time he doubled the stake, the card he doubled was trumped by the Poles. The rouble stakes kept winning.

"On the double!" shouted Dmitri furiously.

"You've lost two hundred, sir. Will you stake another hundred?" the Pole on the sofa inquired.

"What? Lost two hundred already? Then another two hundred! All doubles!"

And pulling his money out of his pocket. Dmitri was about to fling two hundred roubles on the queen, but Kalganov covered it with his hand.

"That's enough!" he shouted.

"What's the matter?" Dmitri stared at him.

"That's enough! I don't want you to play any more. Don't!"

"Why?"

"Because I don't. Damn it, come away. That's why. I won't let you go on playing."

Dmitri gazed at him in astonishment.

"Give up, Dmitri. He may be right. You've lost a lot as it is," said Grushenka, with a curious note in her voice. Both the Poles got up from their seats with a deeply offended air.

"Are you joking, sir?" said the one with the pipe looking severely at Kalganov.

"How dare you!" Vrublevsky growled at Kalganov.

"Don't you dare to shout like that," cried Grushenka. "You turkey-cocks!"

Dmitri looked at each of them in turn. But something in Grushenka's face suddenly struck him, and at the same moment something new flashed into his mind—a strange new thought!

"My dear," the little Pole crimson with anger addressed

Grushenka. But just then Dmitri went up to him and slapped him on the shoulder.

"Sir, two words with you."

"What do you want?"

"In the next room, I've two words to say to you, something pleasant, very pleasant. You'll be glad to hear it."

The little Pole was taken aback and looked apprehensively at Dmitri. He agreed at once, however, on condition that Vrublevsky went with him.

"Your bodyguard? Let him come. I want him, too. I must have him!" cried Dmitri. "March, gentlemen!"

"Where are you going?" asked Grushenka anxiously.

"We'll be back in one moment," answered Dmitri.

There was a sort of boldness, a sudden confidence shining in his eyes. His face had looked very different when he entered the room an hour before.

He led the Poles, not into the large room where the chorus of girls was gathering and the table was being laid, but into the bedroom on the right, where the trunks and packages were kept. There was a lighted candle on a small table in the corner. The little Pole and Dmitri sat down at this table, facing each other, while the huge Vrublevsky stood beside them, his hands behind his back. The Poles looked serious but curious.

"What can I do for you, sir?" lisped the little Pole.

"Well, look here, I won't keep you long. There's money for you." Dmitri pulled out his money. "Would you like three thousand? Take it and go your way."

The Pole gazed, open-eyed at Dmitri with a searching look.

"Three thousand, sir?" He exchanged glances with Vrublevsky.

"Three, sir, three! Listen, my friend, you're a sensible man. Take three thousand and go to the devil, and Vrublevsky with you—d'you hear? But, at once, this very minute, and forever. You understand that, forever. Here's the door; you go out of it. What have you got there, an overcoat, a fur coat? I'll bring it out to you. They'll get the horses at once, and then—good-by, my friend!"

Dmitri waited for an answer with assurance. He had no doubts.

There was an expression of acceptance on the Pole's face. "And the money, sir?"

"The money? I'll give you five hundred roubles this moment for the trip, and as a first installment, and two thousand five hundred tomorrow, in town—I swear on my honor, I'll get it, I'll get it at any cost!" cried Dmitri.

The Poles exchanged glances again. The short man's face looked more forbidding.

"Seven hundred, seven hundred, not five hundred, at once, this minute, cash down!" Dmitri added, feeling there was something wrong. "What's the matter? Don't you trust me? I

393

can't give you the whole three thousand straight off. If I give it to you, you may come back to her tomorrow. . . . Besides, I haven't the three thousand with me. I've got it at home in town," faltered Dmitri, his spirit sinking at every word he uttered. "On my word, the money's, there, hidden."

An extraordinary sense of personal dignity suddenly showed on the little Pole's face "What next?" he asked ironically. "Shame!" And he spat on the floor. Vrublevsky spat too.

"You do that, sir," said Dmitri, recognizing with despair that all was over, "because you hope to make more out of Grushenka? You're a couple of capons, that's what you are!"

"This is a mortal insult!" The little Pole turned as red as a crab, and he went out of the room as though unwilling to hear another word. Vrublevsky swung out after him, and Dmitri followed, confused and crestfallen. He was afraid of Grushenka, afraid that the Pole would tell her. And he did. The Pole walked into the room and threw himself in a theatrical attitude before Grushenka.

"My dear, I have received a mortal insult," he exclaimed. But Grushenka suddenly lost all patience.

"Speak Russian! Speak Russian!" she cried. "Not another word of Polish! You used to talk Russian. You can't have forgotten it in five years."

She was red with anger.

"My dear . . ."

"My name's Agrafena, Grushenka, speak Russian or I won't listen!"

The Pole gasped with offended dignity, and quickly and pompously began in broken Russian: "My dear, I came here to forget the past and forgive it, to forget all that has happened till today . . ."

"Forgive? Came here to forgive me?" Grushenka cut him short, jumping up.

"Yes, my dear. I'm magnanimous. But I was astonished when I saw your lovers. Your Dmitri offered me three thousand, in the other room, to leave. I spat in his face."

"What? He offered you money for me?" cried Grushenka hysterically. "Is it true, Dmitri? How dare you? Am I for sale?"

"Sir, sir!" yelled Dmitri. "She's pure and shining, and I have never been her lover! That's a lie . . ."

"How dare you defend me to him?" shrieked Grushenka. "It wasn't virtue kept me pure, and it wasn't that I was afraid of Kuzma Samsonov, but that I might hold up my head when I met him, and tell him he's a cad. And did he actually refuse the money?"

"He took it! He took it!" cried Dmitri. "Only he wanted to get the whole three thousand at once, and I could only give him seven hundred now."

"I see. He heard I had money, and came here to marry me!"

"My dear!" cried the little Pole. "I'm—a gentleman, I'm—a nobleman, and not a good-for-nothing. I came here to make you my wife and I find you a different woman, perverse and shameless."

"Oh, go back where you came from! I'll tell the innkeeper to turn you out and you'll be turned out," cried Grushenka, furious. "I've been a fool, a fool, to have been miserable these five years! But it wasn't for his sake, it was my anger that made me miserable. And this isn't he at all! Was he like this? It might be his father! Where did you get that wig from? He was a falcon, but this is a gander. He used to laugh and sing to me. . . . And I've been crying for five years, I was a damned fool!"

She sank back in her low chair and hid her face in her hands. At that moment the chorus of Mokroe girls began singing in the room on the left—a rollicking dance song.

"A regular Sodom!" Vrublevsky roared suddenly. "Innkeeper, send the hussies away!"

The innkeeper who had been listening and watching from a crack in the door, hearing shouts and guessing that his guests were quarreling, now entered the room.

"What are you shouting for? D'you want to split your throat?" he said, addressing Vrublevsky with surprising rudeness.

"Animal!" bellowed Vrublevsky.

"Animal? And what sort of cards were you playing with just now? I gave you a pack and you hid it. You played with marked cards! I could send you to Siberia for playing with marked cards, d'you know that? It's just the same as passing counterfeit money . . ."

And going up to the sofa he reached between the sofa back and the cushion, and pulled out an unopened pack of cards.

"Here's my pack unopened!"

He held it up and showed it to all in the room. "From where I stood I saw him slip my pack away, and put his in place of it—you're a cheat and not a gentleman!"

"And I saw him substitute two cards!" cried Kalganov.

"How shameful! How shameful!" exclaimed Grushenka, clasping her hands, and blushing for shame. "Good Lord, he's come to that!"

"I thought so, too!" said Dmitri. But before he had finished these words, Vrublevsky shook his fist at Grushenka, shouting: "You harlot!"

Dmitri flew at him, grabbed him, lifted him in the air, and carried him into the room on the right.

"I've laid him on the floor, there," he announced from the doorway, gasping with excitement. "He's struggling! But he won't come back, no fear of that!"

He closed one half of the folding doors, and holding the other ajar called out to the little Pole: "Most illustrious sir, will you be pleased to retire as well?"

"My dear Dmitri Karamazov," said the innkeeper, Plastunov, "make them give you back the money you lost. It's as good as stolen from you."

"I don't want my fifty roubles back," Kalganov declared suddenly.

"I don't want my two hundred, either," cried Dmitri. "I wouldn't take it for anything! Let him keep it as a consolation."

"Dmitri! You're wonderful!" cried Grushenka.

The little Pole, crimson with fury but still conscious of his dignity, was going toward the folding doors, but he suddenly stopped short and said, addressing Grushenka: "My dear, if you want to come with me, come. If not, it's good-by."

And swelling with indignation and importance he went to the door. This was a man of character. He had so good an opinion of himself that after all that had happened, he still expected that Grushenka would marry him. Dmitri slammed the door after him.

"Lock it," said Kalganov. But the key clicked on the other side. The Poles had locked it from within.

"That's good!" exclaimed Grushenka. "Serves them right!"

8. Delirium

WHAT FOLLOWED WAS ALMOST AN ORGY, a feast to which all were welcomed. Grushenka was the first to call for wine.

"I want to drink. I want to be drunk, like we were last time. Do you remember, Dmitri, do you remember how we became friends here last time!"

Dmitri was almost delirious, feeling that his happiness was at hand. But Grushenka was continually sending him away from her.

"Go and enjoy yourself. Tell them to dance, to be gay, 'let the stove and cottage dance'; as they did last time," she kept exclaiming. She was excited. And Dmitri obeyed her. The girls were in the next room. The room in which they had been sitting till that moment was too small, and was divided in two by cotton curtains, behind which was a huge bed with a puffy feather mattress and a pyramid of cotton pillows. In the four rooms for visitors there were beds. Grushenka sat at the door. Dmitri had brought an easy chair for her. She had sat in the same place to watch the dancing and singing "the time before." All the girls were the same as had been there then. The Jewish band with fiddles and zithers came. And at last the long expected cart arrived with the wines and provisions.

Dmitri hurried about. All sorts of people began coming into the room to look on, peasants and their women, who had been roused from sleep and attracted by the hopes of another marvelous party such as they had enjoyed a month before. Dmitri remembered their faces. He greeted and embraced everyone he knew. He uncorked bottles and poured out wine for everyone. The girls wanted champagne. The men preferred rum, brandy, and hot punch. Dmitri had chocolate made for all the girls, and ordered that three samovars should be kept boiling all night to provide tea and punch for everyone.

An absurd confusion followed, but Dmitri was in his element and the more foolish it became the more his spirits rose. If the peasants had asked him for money at that moment, he would have pulled out his notes and given them away right and left. This was probably why the innkeeper, Trifon Plastunov, kept hovering about Dmitri to protect him. He seemed to have given up all idea of going to bed that night, though he drank little, only one glass of punch, and kept a sharp lookout on Dmitri's interests after his own fashion. Several times he intervened in the nick of time persuading Dmitri not to give away "cigars and Rhine wine," and, above all, money to the peasants as he had done before. He was very indignant, too, at the peasant girls drinking liqueur, and eating candy.

"They're a lousy lot, sir," he said. "I'd give them a kick, every one of them, and they'd take it as an honor—that's all they're worth!"

Dmitri suddenly remembered Andrey again, and ordered punch to be sent out to him. "I was rude to him," he repeated with a sinking, softened voice.

Kalganov did not want to drink, and at first he did not care for the girls' singing. But after he had drunk a couple of glasses of champagne he became extraordinarily lively, strolling about the room, laughing and praising the music and the songs, admiring everyone and everything. Maximov, blissfully drunk, never left his side. Grushenka, too, was beginning to get drunk. Pointing to Kalganov, she said to Dmitri: "What a charming person he is!"

And Dmitri, delighted, embraced Kalganov and Maximov. Oh, great were his hopes! She had said nothing yet, and seemed, indeed, purposely to refrain from speaking. But she looked at him from time to time with caressing and passionate eyes. At last she gripped his hand and drew him to her. She was sitting at the moment in the low chair by the door.

"How was it you happened to come here? How you walked in! . . . I *was* frightened. So you wanted to give me up to him, did you? Did you really want to?"

"I didn't want to spoil your happiness!" Dmitri faltered. But she did not need his answer.

'Well, go and enjoy yourself . . ." she sent him away once more. "Don't cry, I'll call you back again."

He went away, and she listened to the singing and watched the dancing, though her eyes followed him wherever he went. But in another quarter of an hour she called him once more and again he ran back to her.

"Come, sit beside me. Tell me, how did you hear about me, and my coming here yesterday? Who told you?"

And Dmitri began telling her all about it, disconnectedly, incoherently, feverishly. He spoke strangely, often frowning, and stopping abruptly.

"What are you frowning at?" she asked.

"Nothing. . . . I left a man ill there. I'd give ten years of my life for him to get well, to know he was all right!"

"Well, never mind, if he's ill. So you meant to shoot yourself tomorrow! What a silly boy! What for? I like reckless men like you," she said. "So you would go to any length for me? Did you really mean to shoot yourself tomorrow, you stupid thing? No, wait a little. Tomorrow I may have something to say to you. . . . I won't say it today, but tomorrow. You'd like it to be today? No, I don't want to today. Come, go along now, go and amuse yourself."

Once, however, she called him, as it were, puzzled and uneasy.

"Why are you sad? I see you're sad. . . . Yes, I see it," she added, looking intently into his eyes. "Though you keep kissing the peasants and shouting, I see something. No, be happy. I'm happy. You must be happy too. . . . I love somebody here. Guess who it is. Ah, look, my boy has fallen asleep. He's drunk."

She meant Kalganov. He was, in fact, drunk, and had dropped asleep for a moment, sitting on the sofa. But he was not merely drowsy from drink; he felt suddenly dejected, or, as he said, "bored." He was depressed by the girls' songs, which, as the drinking went on, gradually became coarse and more reckless. And the dances were as bad. Two girls dressed up as bears, and a lively girl, called Stepanida, with a stick in her hand, acted the part of keeper, and began to "show them."

"Look alive, Mary, or you'll get the stick!"

The bears rolled on the ground at last in the most unseemly fashion, amid roars of laughter from the closely packed crowd of men and women.

"Well, let them! Let them!" said Grushenka. "When they get a day to enjoy themselves, why shouldn't people be happy?"

Kalganov looked as though he had been besmirched with dirt.

"It's swinish, all this peasant foolery," he murmured, moving away. "These are the games they play when it's light all night in summer."

He particularly disliked one "new" song which was sung to a jaunty dance tune. It described how a gentleman came and tried his luck with the girls, to see whether they would love him.

> *The master came to try the girls;*
> *Would they love him, would they not?*

But the girls could not love the master:

> *He would beat me cruelly*
> *And such love won't do for me.*

Then a gypsy comes along and he, too, tries:

> *The gypsy came to try the girls:*
> *Would they love him, would they not?*

But they couldn't love the gypsy either:

> *He would be a thief, I fear,*
> *And would cause me many a tear.*

And many more men came to try their luck, among them a soldier:

> *The soldier came to try the girls:*
> *Would they love him, would they not?*

But the soldier is rejected with contempt, in two indecent lines, sung with absolute frankness and producing coarse laughter. The song ends with a merchant:

> *The merchant came to try the girls:*
> *Would they love him; would they not?*

And it appears that he wins their love because:

> *The merchant will make gold for me*
> *And his queen I'll gladly be.*

Kalganov was irritated.

"Who writes such things for them?" he said aloud. "They might just as well have had a railway man or a Jew come to try his luck with the girls. They'd have carried all before them."

And, almost as though it were a personal affront he declared that he was bored, sat down on the sofa and immediately fell asleep. His face looked rather pale as it fell back on the sofa cushion.

"Look how attractive he is," said Grushenka, taking Dmitri up to him. "I was combing his hair before. His hair's like flax, and so thick . . ."

And, bending over him, she kissed his forehead. Kalganov opened his eyes, looked at her, stood up, and asked where Maximov was.

"So that's who it is you want." Grushenka laughed. "Stay with me a minute. Dmitri, run and find Maximov."

Maximov, it appeared, could not tear himself away from

the girls, only running away from time to time to pour himself a glass of liqueur. He had drunk two cups of chocolate. His face was red, and his nose was crimson; his eyes were moist, and mawkishly sweet. He ran up and announced that he was going to dance the "sabotière."

"They taught me all those well-bred, aristocratic dances when I was little . . ."

"Go, go with him, Dmitri, and I'll watch from here how he dances," said Grushenka.

"No, no, I'm coming to look on, too," exclaimed Kalganov, brushing aside in the most naive way Grushenka's offer to sit with him. They all went to look on, Maximov danced his dance. But it roused no great admiration in anyone but Dmitri. It consisted of nothing but skipping and hopping. At every skip Maximov slapped the upturned sole of his foot. Kalganov did not like it at all, but Dmitri loved it.

"Thanks. You're tired? What are you looking for? Would you like some cake? A cigar, perhaps?" Dmitri asked.

"A cigarette."

"Don't you want a drink?"

"I'll just have a liqueur. . . . Have you any chocolates?"

"Yes, there's lots of them on the table there."

"I like one with vanilla . . . for old people. He-he!"

"No, Maximov, we've none of that kind."

Maximov bent down to whisper in Dmitri's ear. "That girl there, little Mary, he-he! How would it be if you were to help me to make friends with her?"

"So that's what you're after! No, brother, that won't do!"

"I'd do no harm to anyone," Maximov muttered.

"Oh, all right, all right. They only come here to dance and sing, you know. But damn it all, wait a minute! . . . Eat and drink and be merry, meanwhile. Don't you want money?"

"Later on perhaps," smiled Maximov.

"All right, all right . . ."

Dmitri's head was burning. He went outside, on a wooden balcony which ran around the whole building, overlooking an inner courtyard. The fresh air revived him. He stood alone in a dark corner, and suddenly clutched his head in both hands. His scattered thoughts came together; his sensations blended into a whole and threw a sudden light into his mind. A fearful and terrible light! "If I'm to shoot myself, why not now?" passed through his mind. "Why not go for the pistols, bring them here, and here, in this dark, dirty corner, make an end of it all?" He stood undecided. A few hours earlier, dashing here, he was pursued by disgrace, by the theft he had committed, and that blood, that blood! . . . But yet it was easier for him then. Then everything was over; he had lost her, given her up. She was lost—oh, then his death sentence was easier. Then it had seemed necessary, inevitable, for what had he to stay on earth for?

But now? Was it the same as then? Now one phantom, one terror at least was at an end; that first, rightful lover, that fateful figure had vanished, leaving no trace. The terrible phantom had turned into something so small, so comic; it had been driven into the bedroom and locked in. It would never return. She was ashamed and from her eyes he could see now whom she loved. Now he had everything to make life happy . . . But he could not go on living. He could not. Oh, damnation! "Oh, God! restore to life the man I knocked down at the fence! Let this fearful cup pass from me! Lord, Thou hast wrought miracles for such sinners as me! But what, what if the old man's alive? Oh, then the shame of the other disgrace I would wipe away. I would restore the stolen money. I'd give it back; I'd get it somehow. . . . No trace of that shame will remain except in my heart—forever! But no, no. Oh, impossible cowardly dreams! Oh, damnation!"

Yet there was a ray of light and hope in his darkness. He ran back into the room—to her, to her, his queen forever! Was not one moment of her love worth all the rest of life, even in the agonies of disgrace? This wild question clutched at his heart. "To her, to her alone. To see her, to hear her, to think of nothing, to forget everything. If only for that night, for an hour, for a moment!" Just as he turned from the balcony into the passage, he came upon the innkeeper. He thought he looked gloomy and worried, and he felt that he had come to find him.

"What is it, Plastunov? Are you looking for me?"

"No, sir." The innkeeper seemed disconcerted. "Why should I be looking for you? Where have you been?"

"Why do you look so gloomy? You're not angry, are you? Wait a minute, you'll soon get to bed. . . . What time is it?"

"It'll be three o'clock. Past three, it must be."

"We'll stop soon. We'll leave off."

"Don't mention it. It doesn't matter. Keep it up as long as you like . . ."

"What's the matter with him?" Dmitri wondered for an instant, and then he ran back to the room where the girls were dancing. But she was not there. She was not in the blue room either; there was no one but Kalganov asleep on the sofa. Dmitri looked behind the curtain—she was there. She was sitting in the corner, on a trunk. Bent forward, with her head and arms on the bed she was crying bitterly, doing her best to stifle her sobs so that she might not be heard. Seeing Dmitri, she beckoned to him and when he ran to her, she grasped his hand tightly.

"Dmitri, Dmitri. I loved him, you know. How I have loved him these five years, all that time? Did I love him or only my own anger? No, him, him! It's a lie that it was my anger I loved and not him. Dmitri, I was only seventeen then. He was so kind to me, so gay. He used to sing to me. . . . Or so it

401

seemed to a silly girl like me. . . . And now, O Lord, he's not the same man. Even his face is not the same; he's different altogether. I wouldn't have known him. I drove here with Timofey, and all the way I was thinking how I would meet him, what I would say to him, how we would look at one another. My soul was faint and all of a sudden it was just as though he had emptied a pail of dirty water over me. He talked to me like a schoolmaster, all so grave and learned; he met me so solemnly that I was struck dumb. I couldn't get a word in. At first I thought he was ashamed to talk before his great big Pole. I sat staring at him and wondering why I couldn't speak to him any more. His wife must have ruined him; you know he threw me over to get married. She must have changed him like that. Dmitri, how shameful it is! Oh, Dmitri, I'm ashamed, I'm ashamed for all my life. Curse it, curse it, curse those five years!"

And again she burst into tears. But she clung to Dmitri's hand and did not let it go.

"Dmitri darling, stay, don't go away. I want to say one word to you," she whispered, and suddenly raised her face to him. "Listen, tell me who it is I love? I love one man here. Who is that man? That's what you must tell me."

A smile lighted up her face that was swollen with weeping and her eyes shone in the half darkness.

"A falcon flew in, and my heart sank. 'Fool! that's the man you love!' That was what my heart whispered to me. You came in and all grew bright. What's he afraid of? I wondered. For you were frightened; you couldn't speak. It's not them he's afraid of—could you be frightened of anyone? It's me he's afraid of, I thought, only me. So Fenya told you how I called to Alyosha out of the window that I'd loved Dmitri for one hour, and that I was going now to love . . . another. Dmitri, Dmitri, how could I be such a fool as to think I could love anyone after you? Do you forgive me, Dmitri? Do you forgive me or not? Do you love me? Do you love me?" She jumped up and put both hands on his shoulders. Dmitri, numb with rapture, gazed into her eyes, at her face, at her smile, and then suddenly clasped her tightly in his arms and kissed her passionately.

"You will forgive me for having tormented you? It was through spite I tormented you all. It was for spite I drove your old father out of his mind. . . . Do you remember how you drank at my house one day and broke the wine-glass? I remembered that and I broke a glass today and drank 'to my vile heart.' Dmitri my falcon, why don't you kiss me? He kissed me once, and now he draws back and looks and listens. Why listen to me? Kiss me hard, that's right. If you love, well then love! I'll be your slave now, your slave for the rest of my life. It's sweet to be a slave. Kiss me! Beat me, ill-treat me, do what you will with me. . . . I deserve to suffer.

402

. . . Wait! Wait, afterwards! I won't have that . . ." She suddenly pushed him away. "Go away, Dmitri. I'll come and have some wine, I want to be drunk. I'm going to get drunk and dance. I must, I must!" She tore herself away from him and disappeared behind the curtain. Dmitri followed like a drunken man.

"Yes, come what may—whatever may happen now, for one minute I'd give the whole world," he thought. Grushenka tossed off a whole glass of champagne at one gulp, and became very tipsy. She sat down in the same chair as before, with a blissful smile on her face. Her cheeks were glowing, her lips were burning, her flashing eyes were moist; there was passion in her eyes. Even Kalganov felt it and went up to her.

"Did you feel how I kissed you when you were asleep before?" she said thickly. "I'm drunk now, that's what it is. . . . And aren't you drunk? And why isn't Dmitri drinking? Why don't you drink, Dmitri? I'm drunk, and you don't drink . . ."

"I am drunk! I'm drunk as it is . . . drunk with you . . . And now I'll be drunk with wine, too."

He drank another glass, and—he thought it strange himself —that last glass made him completely drunk. He was suddenly drunk, although till that moment he had been quite sober, he remembered that. From that moment everything whirled about him, as though he were delirious. He walked, laughed, talked to everybody, without knowing what he was doing. Only one persistent burning sensation continually made itself felt "like a red-hot coal in his heart," he said afterward. He went up to her, sat beside her, gazed at her, listened to her. . . . She became very talkative, kept calling everyone to her, and beckoned to different girls in the chorus. When the girls came up, she either kissed them or made the sign of the cross over them. In another minute she might have cried. She was amused by the "little old man," as she called Maximov. He ran up every minute to kiss her hands, "each little finger," and finally he danced another dance to an old song, which he sang himself. He danced with special vigor to the refrain:

> *The little pig says—umph! umph! umph!*
> *The little calf says—moo, moo, moo,*
> *The little duck says—quack, quack, quack,*
> *The little goose says—ga, ga, ga.*
> *The hen goes strutting through the porch*
> *Troo-roo-roo-roo-roo, she'll say*
> *Troo-roo-roo-roo-roo, she'll say!*

"Give him something, Dmitri," said Grushenka. "Give him a present, he's poor, you know. Ah, the poor, the insulted. . . . Do you know, Dmitri, I shall go into a nunnery. No, I really shall one day. Alyosha said something to me today that I shall remember all my life. . . . Yes. . . . But today let us dance. Tomorrow to the nunnery, but today we'll dance. I want to play today and what of it? God will forgive us. If I were God, I'd forgive everyone: 'My dear sinners, from this day forth I forgive you.' I'm going to beg forgiveness: 'Forgive me, a silly wench.' I'm a beast, that's what I am. But I want to pray. I gave a little onion. Wicked as I've been, I want to pray. Dmitri, let them dance, don't stop them. Everyone in the world is good. Everyone—even the worst of them. The world's a nice place. Though we're bad the world's all right. We're good and bad, good and bad. . . . Come tell me, I've something to ask you; come here everyone, and I'll ask you: Why am I so good? You know I am good. I'm very good. . . . Come, why am I so good?"

Grushenka babbled on getting more and more drunk. At last she announced that she was going to dance, too. She got up from her chair, staggering. "Dmitri, don't give me any more wine—if I ask you, don't give it to me. Wine doesn't give peace. Everything's going around, the stove, and everything. I want to dance. Let everyone see how I dance . . . Let them see how beautifully I dance . . ."

She really meant it. She pulled a white cambric handkerchief out of her pocket to wave it in the dance. Dmitri ran back and forth. The girls were quiet, and got ready to break into a dancing song at the first signal. Maximov, hearing that Grushenka wanted to dance, squealed with delight, and ran skipping about in front of her, humming:

> With legs so slim and sides so trim
> And its little tail curled tight.

But Grushenka waved her handkerchief at him and drove him away.

"Sh-h! Dmitri, why don't they come? Let everyone come . . . to look at me. Call them in, too, those who were locked in. . . . Why did you lock them in? Tell them I'm going to dance. Let them look on, too . . ."

Dmitri walked with a drunken swagger to the locked door, and began knocking to the Poles with his fist.

"Hi, you . . . Come, she's going to dance. She's calling you."

"Good-for-nothing!" one of the Poles shouted in reply.

"You're a good-for-nothing yourself! You're a cad, that's what you are."

"Stop laughing at Poland," said Kalganov. He too was drunk.

"Be quiet! If I call him a cad, it doesn't mean that I called all Poland that. One good-for-nothing doesn't make a Poland. Be quiet."

"Oh, what fellows! As though they were not men. Why aren't they friendly?" said Grushenka, and she went forward to dance. The chorus broke into "Ah, my porch, my new porch!" Grushenka flung back her head, half opened her lips, smiled, waved her handkerchief, and suddenly, with a violent lurch, stood still in the middle of the room, looking bewildered.

"I'm weak . . ." she said in an exhausted voice. "Forgive me. . . . I'm weak, I can't. . . . I'm sorry."

She bowed to the chorus and then began bowing in all directions.

"I'm sorry. . . . Forgive me . . ."

"The lady's been drinking. The pretty lady has been drinking," voices were heard saying.

"The lady's drunk too much," Maximov explained to the girls, giggling.

"Dmitri, take me away . . . Take me," said Grushenka helplessly. Dmitri snatched her up in his arms and carried the precious burden through the curtains.

"Well, now I'll go," thought Kalganov, and walking out of the blue room, he closed the two halves of the door after him. But the orgy in the larger room went on and grew louder and louder.

Dmitri laid Grushenka on the bed and kissed her on the lips.

"Don't touch me . . ." she begged in an imploring voice. "Don't touch me, till I'm yours. . . . I've told you I'm yours, but don't touch me . . . Spare me. . . . With them here, with them close, you mustn't. He's here. It's nasty here . . ."

"I'll obey you! I won't think of it . . . I worship you!" muttered Dmitri. "Yes, it's nasty here, it's abominable."

And still holding her in his arms, he sank on his knees by the bedside.

"I know, though you're a brute, you're generous," Grushenka said with difficulty. "It must be honorable . . . It shall be honorable for the future . . . And let us be honest, let us be good, not brutes, but good . . . Take me away, take me far away, do you hear? I don't want it to be here, but far, far away . . ."

"Oh, yes, yes, it must be!" said Dmitri pressing her in his arms. "I'll take you away. . . . Oh, I'd give my whole life for one year only to know about that blood!"

"What blood?" asked Grushenka, bewildered.

"Nothing," muttered Dmitri. "Grushenka, you want to be honest, but I'm a thief. But I've stolen money from Katerina. . . . Disgrace, a disgrace!"

"From Katerina? No, you didn't steal it. Give it back to her, take it from me. . . . Why make a fuss? Now everything of mine is yours. What does money matter? We shall waste it anyway. . . . People like us are bound to waste money. We'd better go and work the land. I want to dig the earth with my own hands. We must work, do you hear? Alyosha said so. I won't be your mistress. I'll be faithful to you, I'll be your slave, I'll work for you. We'll go to Katerina and bow down to her together, so that she may forgive us, and then we'll go away.

And if she won't forgive us, we'll go, anyway. Take her her money and love me. . . . Don't love her. . . . Don't love her any more. If you love her, I'll strangle her. . . . I'll put out both her eyes with a needle . . ."

"I love you. I love only you. I'll love you in Siberia . . ."

"Why Siberia? Never mind, Siberia if you like. I don't care . . . We'll work . . . There's snow in Siberia. . . . I love driving in the snow . . . And must have bells. . . . Do you hear, there's a bell ringing? Where is that bell ringing? There are people coming. . . . Now it's stopped."

She closed her eyes, exhausted, and suddenly fell asleep. There had certainly been the sound of a bell in the distance, but the ringing had now stopped. Dmitri let his head sink on her breast. He did not notice that the bell had stopped ringing, nor did he notice that the songs had stopped and that instead of singing and drunken clamor there was absolute stillness in the house. Grushenka opened her eyes.

"What's the matter? Was I asleep? Yes . . . a bell . . . I've been asleep and dreamt I was driving over the snow with bells, and I dozed. I was with someone I loved, with you. And far, far away. I was holding you and kissing you, nestling close to you. I was cold, and the snow glistened. . . . You know how the snow glistens at night when the moon shines. It was as though I was not on earth. I woke up, and you are close to me. How sweet it is . . ."

"Close to you," murmured Dmitri, kissing her dress, her bosom, her hands. And suddenly he had a strange feeling; it seemed to him that she was looking straight before her, not at him, not into his face, but over his head, with an intent, almost uncanny stare. An expression of wonder, almost of alarm, came into her face.

"Dmitri, who is that looking at us?" she whispered.

Dmitri turned, and saw that someone had parted the curtains and was watching them. And not one person alone, it seemed.

He jumped up and walked forward.

"Here, come to us, come here," said a voice, speaking not loudly, but firmly.

Dmitri passed to the other side of the curtain and stood stock still. The room was filled with people, but not those who had been there before. He shuddered. He recognized everyone instantly. That tall, stout old man in the overcoat and cap with a cockade—was the police captain, Michael Makarov. And that "consumptive-looking" trim dandy, "who always has such polished boots"—that was the deputy prosecutor. "He has a chronometer worth four hundred roubles; he showed it to me." And that small young man in spectacles. . . . Dmitri forgot his surname though he knew him, had seen him: he was the "investigating lawyer," from the "law school," who had only lately come to the town. And this man

—the inspector of police, Mavriky Schmertsov, a man he knew well. And those fellows wearing the brass plates, why are they here? And those other two . . . peasants. . . . And there at the door Kalganov with the innkeeper Trifon Plastunov. . . .

"Gentlemen! What's this for, gentlemen?" began Dmitri. But suddenly, as though beside himself, not knowing what he was doing, he cried aloud, at the top of his voice: "I un—der—stand!"

The young man wearing spectacles moved forward and stepping up to Dmitri, began with dignity, though hurriedly: "We have to make . . . in brief, I beg you to come this way, this way to the sofa. . . . It is absolutely imperative that you should give an explanation."

"The old man!" cried Dmitri frantically. "The old man and his blood! . . . I understand."

And he sank, almost fell, on a chair close by, as though he had been mown down by a scythe.

"You understand? He understands it! Monster and parricide! Your father's blood cries out against you!" the old captain of police roared suddenly, stepping up to Dmitri. He was beside himself, crimson in the face and quivering all over.

"This is impossible!" cried the small young man. "Michael Makarov, Michael Makarov, this won't do! . . . I beg you, allow me to speak. I never expected such behavior from you . . ."

"This is delirium, gentlemen, raving delirium," cried the captain of police. "Look at him. Drunk, at this time of night, in the company of a disreputable woman, with his father's blood on his hands. . . . It's delirium! . . ."

"I beg you, dear Michael Makarov, to restrain your feelings," the prosecutor said in a rapid whisper to the old police captain. "Or I shall be forced to . . ."

But the little lawyer did not allow him to finish. He turned to Dmitri and spoke in a loud, firm voice:

"Ex-Lieutenant Karamazov, it is my duty to inform you that you are charged with the murder of your father, Fyodor Karamazov, perpetrated this night . . ."

He said something more, and the prosecutor, too, put in something. But though Dmitri heard them he did not understand them. He stared at them all with wild eyes.

BOOK IX:
THE PRELIMINARY INVESTIGATION

1. The Beginning of Perhotin's Official Career

PETER PERHOTIN, whom we left knocking at the strong locked gates where Grushenka lived, ended of course, by making himself heard. Fenya, who was still excited by the fright she had had two hours before, and too much "upset" to go to bed, was almost hysterical on hearing the furious knocking. Though she had seen him drive away, she thought that it must be Dmitri knocking again, no one else could knock so savagely. She ran to the porter, who had already waked up and gone out to the gate, and began imploring him not to open it. But having questioned Perhotin and learned that he wanted to see Fenya on very "important business," the porter at last opened the gate.

Perhotin was admitted into Fenya's kitchen but the girl begged him to allow the porter to be present, "because of her misgivings." He began questioning her and at once learned the most vital fact, that is, that when Dmitri had run out to look for Grushenka, he had snatched up a pestle from the mortar, and that when he returned, the pestle was not with him and his hands were smeared with blood.

"And the blood was simply flowing, dripping from him, dripping!" Fenya kept saying. This horrible detail was simply the product of her imagination. But although not "dripping," Perhotin had himself seen those hands stained with blood, and had helped to wash them. Moreover, the question he had to decide was not how soon the blood had dried, but where Dmitri had run with the pestle, whether it really was to Fyodor Karamazov's, and how he could find out about this. Perhotin persisted in returning to this point, and though he found out nothing conclusive, yet he carried away a conviction that Dmitri could have gone nowhere but to his father's house and that something must have happened there.

"And when he came back," Fenya added with excitement, "I told him the whole story. And then I began asking him: 'Why have you got blood on your hands, sir?' And he answered that it was human blood, and that he had just killed someone. He confessed it all to me, and suddenly ran off like a madman! I sat down and began thinking, where's he run off to now? He'll go to Mokroe, I thought, and kill my mistress. I ran out to beg him not to kill her. I was running to his lodgings, but I looked in at Plotinkov's shop, and saw him just starting out. . . . And there was no blood on his hands then." (Fenya had noticed this and remembered it.) Fenya's old grandmother confirmed her evidence as far as she was capable. After asking some more questions, Perhotin left, even more upset and uneasy than he had been when he arrived.

The most direct and easiest thing for him to do would have been to go straight to Fyodor Karamazov's, to find out whether anything had happened there, and if so, what; and only to go to the police captain, as he firmly intended doing, when he had satisfied himself of the fact. But the night was dark, Fyodor Karamazov's gates were strong, and he would have to knock again. His acquaintance with old Karamazov was of the slightest, and what if, after he had been knocking, they opened to him, and nothing had happened. Fyodor Karamazov in his jeering way would then go telling the story all over town. He would tell how a stranger, called Perhotin, had broken in upon him at midnight to ask if anyone had killed him. It would create a scandal. And scandal was what Perhotin dreaded more than anything in the world.

Yet the feeling that possessed him was so strong, that though he swore at himself, he set off, not to Fyodor Karamazov's but to Madame Hohlakov's. He decided that if she denied having just given Dmitri three thousand roubles, he would go straight to the police captain, but if she admitted having given him the money, he would go home and let the matter rest till morning.

It is, of course, perfectly clear that there was more likelihood of causing scandal by going at eleven o'clock at night to a fashionable lady, a complete stranger, and perhaps waking her up to ask her an odd question, than by going to Fyodor Karamazov. But that is just how it is, sometimes, especially in cases like the present one, with the decisions of the most precise and phlegmatic people. Peter Perhotin was by no means phlegmatic at that moment. He remembered all his life how a haunting uneasiness gradually gained possession of him, growing more and more painful and driving him on, against his will. He kept cursing himself all the way for going to Madame Hohlakov's, but "I will get to the bottom of it, I will!" he kept repeating. And he carried out his intention.

It was exactly eleven o'clock when he entered Madame Hohlakov's house. He was admitted into the yard quickly, but, in answer to his inquiry whether the lady was still up, the porter could give no reply, except that she was usually in bed at that time.

"Ask at the top of the stairs. If Madame wants to receive you, she'll receive you. If she won't, she won't."

Perhotin went up, but did not find things so easy there. The footman was unwilling to take in his name, but finally called a maid. Perhotin politely but insistently begged her to inform her lady that an official, living in the town, called Perhotin, was calling on particular business, and that, if it were not of the greatest importance he would not have ventured to come. "Tell her in those words, in those words exactly," he instructed the girl.

She went away. He waited in the entry.

Madame Hohlakov was in her bedroom, though not yet asleep. She had been upset ever since Dmitri's visit, and had a presentiment that she would not get through the night without the sick headache which always, with her, followed such excitement. She was surprised on hearing the announcement from the maid. She irritably declined to see him, although the unexpected visit at such an hour, of an "official living in the town," who was a total stranger, aroused her curiosity. But this time Perhotin was as obstinate as a mule. He begged the maid to take another message in these very words.

"That he had come on business of the greatest importance, and that Madame Hohlakov might have cause to regret it later, if she refused to see him now."

"I plunged headlong," he described it afterwards.

The maid gazed at him in amazement. She then took his message. Madame Hohlakov was impressed. She thought a little, asked what he looked like, and learned that he was "very well dressed, young and so polite." We may note that Perhotin was a rather good-looking young man, and well aware of the fact. Madame Hohlakov decided to see him. She was in her dressing gown and slippers, but she flung a black shawl over her shoulders. "The official" was asked to walk into the drawing room, the very room in which Dmitri had been received shortly before.

She came to meet her visitor with a sternly inquiring countenance and, without asking him to sit down, began at once with the question: "What do you want?"

"I have ventured to disturb you, Madame, on a matter concerning our common acquaintance, Dmitri Karamazov," Perhotin began.

But he had hardly spoken the name, when Madame Hohlakov showed signs of acute irritation. She almost shrieked, and interrupted him in a fury: "How much longer am I to be worried by that awful man?" she cried hysterically. "How dare you, sir, how could you venture to disturb a lady who is a stranger to you, in her own house at such an hour! . . . And to force yourself upon her to talk of a man who came here, to this very drawing room, only three hours ago, to murder me. Then he went stamping out of the room, as no one would go out of a decent house. Let me tell you, sir, that I shall bring a

410

complaint against you, that I will not let it pass. Kindly leave at once . . . I am a mother. . . . I . . . I . . ."

"Murder! Then he tried to murder you, too?"

"Why, has he killed somebody?" Madame Hohlakov asked.

"If you would kindly listen, Madame, for half a moment, I'll explain it all," answered Perhotin firmly. "At five o'clock this afternoon Dmitri Karamazov borrowed ten roubles from me, and I know for a fact he had no money. Yet at nine o'clock, he came to see me with a bundle of hundred-rouble notes in his hand, about two or three thousand roubles. His hands and face were all covered with blood, and he looked like a madman. When I asked him where he had gotten so much money, he answered that he had just received it from you, that you had given him three thousand to go to the gold mines . . ."

Madame Hohlakov's face revealed intense and painful excitement.

"Good God! He must have killed his old father!" she cried, clasping her hands. "I have never given him money, never! Oh, run, run! . . . Don't say another word! Save the old man . . . Run to his father . . . run!"

"Then you did not give him money? You remember for a fact that you did not give him any money?"

"No, I didn't, I didn't! I refused to give it to him because he could not appreciate it. He ran out in a fury, stamping. He rushed at me, but I slipped away . . . And let me tell you, as I wish to hide nothing from you now, that he positively spat at me. Can you believe that! But why are we standing? Please sit down. . . . Excuse me, I . . . or better run, run, you must run and save the poor old man from an awful death!"

"But if he has killed him already?"

"Oh, good heavens, yes! What are we to do now? What do you think we should do now?"

She made Perhotin sit down and sat down herself, facing him. Briefly, but fairly clearly, Perhotin told her everything he knew. He described, too, his visit to Fenya, and told her about the pestle. All these details overwhelmed Madame Hohlakov, who kept shrieking and covering her face with her hands.

"Would you believe it, I foresaw all this! I have that special faculty, whatever I imagine comes to pass. And how often I've looked at that awful man and always thought, that man will end by murdering me. And now it's happened . . . That is, if he hasn't murdered me, but only his own father, it's only because the finger of God preserved me, and what's more, he was ashamed to murder me because, on this very place, I put the holy ikon from the relics of the holy martyr, Saint Varvara, on his neck. . . . And to think how near I was to death at that minute! I went close up to him and he stretched out his neck to me! . . . Do you know, I don't believe in miracles,

but that ikon and this unmistakable miracle with me now—
That shakes me, and I'm ready to believe in anything you like.
Have you heard about Father Zossima? . . . But I don't know
what I'm saying . . . And would you believe it, with the ikon
on his neck he spat at me. . . . He only spat, it's true, he didn't
murder me and . . . he dashed away! But what shall we do? But
What should we do now? What do you think?"

Perhotin got up, and announced that he was going straight
to the police captain, to tell him all about it. He would leave
him to do what he thought fit.

"Oh, he's an excellent man, excellent! Michael Makarov, I
know him. Of course, he's the person to go to. How practical
you are! How well you've thought of everything! I should never
have thought of it in your place!"

"Especially as I know the police captain very well, too,"
observed Perhotin, who continued to stand and was now obviously anxious to escape as quickly as possible. But Madame
Hohlakov would not let him say good-by and go away.

"And be sure, be sure," she prattled on, "to come back and
tell me what you see there, and what you find out . . . What
comes to light . . . How they'll try him . . . and what he's condemned to . . . Tell me, we have no capital punishment, have
we? But be sure to come, even if it's at three o'clock at night,
at four, at half-past four. . . . Tell them to wake me, to wake
me, to shake me, if I don't get up. . . . But, good heavens, I
won't sleep! But wait, hadn't I better come with you?"

"N—no. But if you would write three lines with your own
hand, stating that you did not give Dmitri Karamazov any
money, it might, perhaps, be of use . . . In case it's needed . . ."

"Of course!" Madame Hohlakov ran delighted to her desk.
"And you know I'm simply struck, amazed at your foresight,
your good sense. Are you in the service here? I'm delighted to
think that you're in the service here!"

And still speaking, she scribbled on half a sheet of note-
paper the following lines:

I've never in my life lent to that unhappy man, Dmitri Karamazov (for, in spite of all, he is unhappy) three thousand roubles
today. I've never given him money, never! That I swear by all
that's holy!

K. Hohlakov.

"Here's the note!" She turned quickly to Perhotin. "Go,
save him. It's a noble deed on your part!"

And she made the sign of the cross three times over him.
She ran out to accompany him to the passage.

"How grateful I am to you! You can't think how grateful
I am to you for having come to me, first. How is it I haven't
met you before? I shall feel flattered at seeing you at my
house in the future. How delightful it is that you are living
here! . . . Such precision! Such ability! . . . They must appreciate you, they must understand you. If there's anything I can

do, believe me . . . Oh, I love young people! I'm in love with young people! The younger generation is the one prop of our suffering country. Her one hope. . . . Oh, go, go!"

But Perhotin had already run away or she would not have let him go. Yet Madame Hohlakov had made a rather agreeable impression on him, which had somewhat softened his anxiety at being drawn into such an unpleasant affair. Tastes differ, as we all know. "She's by no means so elderly," he thought. "On the contrary I should have taken her for her daughter."

As for Madame Hohlakov she was simply enchanted by the young man. "Such sense! Such exactness! In so young a man! In our day! And all that with such manners and appearance! People say the young people of today are no good for anything, but here's an example!" etc., etc., etc. So she simply forgot the "dreadful affair." It was only as she was getting into bed that, suddenly recalling "how near death she had been," she exclaimed: "Oh, it is awful, awful!"

But she fell at once into a sound, sweet sleep.

I would not have dwelt on such trivial and irrelevant details, if this meeting between the young official and the by no means elderly widow, had not later turned out to be the beginning of the career of that "practical" and "precise" young man. His story is remembered to this day with amazement in our town, and I shall perhaps have something to say about it.

2. The Alarm

OUR POLICE CAPTAIN, Michael Makarov, a retired lieutenant-colonel, was a widower and an excellent man. He had only come to us three years before, but had won general esteem, chiefly because he "knew how to keep society together." He was never without visitors, and could not have gotten on without them. Some one or other was always dining with him; he never sat down to table without guests. He gave regular dinners, too, on all sorts of occasions, sometimes most surprising ones. Though the food was not too good, it was abundant. The fish pies were excellent, and the wine made up in quantity for what it lacked in quality.

The first room his guests entered was a well-appointed billiard room, with pictures of English race horses in black frames on the walls, an essential decoration for a bachelor's billiard room. There was card-playing every evening at his house, if only at one table. But at frequent intervals, all the society of our town, with the mothers and young ladies, assembled at his house to dance.

Although Michael Makarov was a widower, he did not live

413

alone. His widowed daughter lived with him, with her two unmarried daughters, grown-up girls, who had finished their education. They were attractive and lively and though everyone knew they would have no dowry, they attracted all the young men to their grandfather's house.

Michael Makarov was by no means efficient in his work, although he performed his duties no worse than many others. To speak plainly, he was a man of rather narrow education. His understanding of the limits of his administrative power could not always be relied upon. It was not so much that he failed to grasp certain reforms enacted during the present reign, as that he made conspicuous blunders in his interpretation of them. This was not from any special lack of intelligence, but from carelessness, for he was always in too great a hurry to go into the subject.

"I have the heart of a soldier rather than of a civilian," he used to say of himself. He had not even formed a definite idea of the fundamental principles of the reforms connected with the emancipation of the serfs, and only picked it up, so to speak, from year to year, involuntarily increasing his knowledge by practice. And yet he was himself a landowner.

Perhotin knew for certain that he would meet some of Michael Makarov's visitors there that evening, but he didn't know which. As it happened, at that moment the prosecutor, and Varvinsky, our district doctor, a young man who had only just come to us from Petersburg after graduating from the Academy of Medicine, were playing whist. Ippolit Kirillovitch, the prosecutor (he was really the deputy prosecutor, but we always called him the prosecutor) was rather a peculiar man, of about thirty-five, inclined to be consumptive, and married to a fat and childless woman. He was vain and irritable, though he had a good intellect, and even a kind heart. It seemed that all that was wrong with him was that he had a better opinion of himself than his ability warranted. And that made him seem constantly uneasy. He had, moreover, certain higher even artistic leanings toward psychology, for instance, a study of the human emotions, a knowledge of the criminal and his crime. He cherished a grievance on this ground. He felt that he had been passed over in the service, and being firmly persuaded that in higher places he had not been properly appreciated, he was certain he had enemies. In gloomy moments he even threatened to give up his post, and practice criminal law. The unexpected Karamazov case interested him at once: "It was a case that might well be talked about all over Russia." But I am anticipating.

Nicholas Nelyudov, the young investigating lawyer, who had only come from Petersburg two months before, was sitting in the next room with the young ladies. People talked about it afterwards and wondered that all these gentlemen should, as though intentionally, on the evening of "the crime" have been gathered together at the police captain's house. Yet it was perfectly simple and happened quite naturally.

Ippolit Kirillovitch's wife had had toothache for the last two days, and he had to go out to escape from her groans. The doctor, Varvinsky, from his very nature, could not spend an evening except at cards. Nicholas Nelyudov had been intending for three days past to drop in casually that evening at Michael Makarov's, so as to startle the eldest granddaughter, Olga, by showing that he knew her secret, that he knew it was her birthday. He wanted to tease her by saying that she was trying to conceal it so as not to be obliged to give a dance. He anticipated a great deal of fun, many jokes about her age, and her being afraid to reveal it, about his knowing her secret and telling everybody, and so on. This charming young man was very good at such teasing; the ladies had christened him "the naughty man," and he was delighted at the name. He was extremely well bred, however, of good family, education and, though leading a life of pleasure, his humor was always innocent and in good taste. He was short and delicate looking. On his white, slender, little fingers he always wore a number of big, glittering rings. When he was busy with his official duties, he always became extraordinarily serious, as though realizing his position and the sanctity of the obligations laid upon him. He had a special gift for mystifying murderers and other criminals of the peasant class during questioning, and if he did not win their respect, he certainly succeeded in arousing their wonder.

Perhotin was dumbfounded when he went into the police captain's. He saw instantly that everyone knew that something had happened. They had thrown down their cards and were all standing up and talking. Even Nicholas Nelyudov had left the young ladies and come in. Perhotin was met with the astounding news that old Fyodor Karamazov really had been murdered that evening in his own house, murdered and robbed. The news had only just reached them in the following manner.

Marfa, the wife of old Gregory, whom Dmitri struck on the head with the pestle, was sleeping soundly in her bed and might well have slept till morning after the draught she had taken. But, all of a sudden she woke up, roused by a fearful epileptic scream from Smerdyakov, who was lying in the next room unconscious. That scream always preceded his fits, and always terrified and upset Marfa. She could never get accustomed to it. She jumped up and ran half-awake to Smerdyakov's room. But it was dark there, and she could only hear the invalid beginning to gasp and struggle. Then Marfa herself screamed out and was going to call her husband, but suddenly realized that when she had gotten up, he was not beside her in bed. She ran back to the bed and began groping with her hands, but the bed was really empty. Then he must have

415

gone out—where? She ran to the steps and timidly called him. She got no answer but she caught the sound of groans far away in the garden in the darkness. She listened. The groans were repeated.

"Good Lord! Just as it was with Lizaveta, Smerdyakov's mother!" she thought distractedly. She went timidly down the steps and saw that the gate into the garden was open.

"He must be out there, poor dear," she thought. She went up to the gate and all at once she distinctly heard Gregory calling her by name: "Marfa! Marfa!" His voice was weak, moaning, dreadful.

"Lord, preserve us from harm!" Marfa murmured. She ran toward the voice, and that was how she found Gregory. But she found him not by the fence where he had been knocked down, but about twenty yards away. It appeared later, that he had crawled away on coming to himself, and had been a long time getting so far, losing consciousness several times. She noticed at once that he was covered with blood, and screamed at the top of her voice.

Gregory was muttering incoherently: "He has murdered . . . his father murdered. . . . Why scream, silly . . . Run . . . Fetch someone . . ."

But Marfa continued screaming, and seeing that her master's window was open and that there was a lighted candle in the window, she ran there and began calling Fyodor Karamazov. But looking in at the window she saw a fearful sight. Her master was lying on his back, motionless, on the floor. His light colored dressing gown and white shirt were soaked with blood. The candle on the table lighted up the blood and his motionless dead face. Terror-stricken, Marfa rushed away from the window, ran out of the garden, drew the bolt of the big gate, and ran headlong by the back way to the neighbors. Both the old bedridden mother and Maria, the daughter, were asleep, but they woke up at Marfa's desperate and persistent screaming and knocking at the shutter. Marfa, shrieking and screaming incoherently, managed to tell them what she had seen and to beg for help. It happened that Foma, their lodger, had come back from his wanderings and was staying there that night. Maria got him up immediately and all three ran to the scene of the crime. On the way, Maria remembered that at about eight o'clock she heard a dreadful scream. This was no doubt Gregory's scream, "Parricide!" when he caught hold of Dmitri's leg.

"Someone screamed and then was silent," Maria explained. Running to the place where Gregory lay, Marfa and Maria with the help of Foma carried him to the lodge. They lighted a candle and saw that Smerdyakov was no better, that he was writhing in convulsions, his eyes fixed in a squint, and that foam was on his lips. They moistened Gregory's forehead with water mixed with vinegar. It revived him at once. He immediately asked: "Is the master murdered?"

Then Foma and both the women ran to the house and saw this time that not only the window, but also the door of the house leading into the garden was wide open, though Fyodor Karamazov had for the last week locked himself in every night and did not allow even Gregory to come in on any pretext. Seeing this door open, they were afraid to go in to Fyodor Karamazov "for fear anything should happen afterwards." And when they returned to Gregory, the old man told him to go straight to the police captain. Maria ran there at once. She had arrived only five minutes before Perhotin, so that his story came, not as his own surmise and theory, but as the direct confirmation, by a witness, of the theory held by all, as to the identity of the criminal (a theory he had in the bottom of his heart refused to believe till that moment).

It was decided to act at once. The deputy police inspector, Mavriky Schmertsov, was commissioned to take four witnesses, to enter Fyodor Karamazov's house and open an inquiry on the spot, according to the regular forms. The district doctor, Varvinsky, new to his work, almost insisted on going with the police captain, the prosecutor, and the investigating lawyer.

I will note briefly that Fyodor Karamazov was found to be quite dead, with his skull battered in. But with what? Most likely with the same weapon with which Gregory had been attacked later. Gregory, to whom all possible medical assistance had at once been given, described in a weak and breaking voice how he had been knocked down. They began looking with a lantern by the fence and found the brass pestle on the garden path. There were no signs of disturbance in the room where Fyodor Karamazov was lying. But by the bed, behind the screen, they picked up from the floor a big thick envelope with the inscription: "A present of three thousand roubles for my angel Grushenka, if she is willing to come." And below had been added by Fyodor Karamazov "For my little chicken." There were three seals of red sealing wax on the envelope, but it had been torn open and was empty; the money had been removed. They found also on the floor a piece of narrow pink ribbon, with which the envelope had been tied.

One piece of Perhotin's evidence made a great impression on the prosecutor and the investigating magistrate, namely, his idea that Dmitri would shoot himself before daybreak, that he had determined to do so, had spoken of it, had taken the pistols, and loaded one of them, written a note, put it in his pocket, etc. When Perhotin, though still unwilling to believe in it, threatened to tell someone so as to prevent the suicide, Dmitri had answered grinning: "You'll be too late." So they must make haste to Mokroe to find him before he really did shoot himself.

"That's clear, that's clear!" repeated the prosecutor in great excitement. "That's just the way with mad fellows like that: 'I shall kill myself tomorrow, so I'll make merry till I die'!"

The story of how Dmitri had bought the champagne and other things excited the prosecutor more than ever.

"Do you remember the fellow that murdered a merchant called Olsufyev, gentlemen? He stole fifteen hundred, went at once to have his hair curled, and then, without even hiding the money, carrying it almost in his hand in the same way, he went off to the girls."

All were delayed, however, by the inquiry, the search, and the formalities, etc., in the house of Fyodor Karamazov. It all took time and so, two hours before starting, they sent on ahead to Mokroe the officer of the rural police, Mavriky Schmertsov, who had arrived in the town the morning before to get his pay. He was instructed to avoid raising an alarm when he reached Mokroe, but to keep constant watch over the "criminal" till the arrival of the proper authorities. He was also to procure witnesses for the arrest, police constables, and so on. Mavriky Schmertsov did as he was told, preserving his incognito, and giving no one but his old acquaintance, the innkeeper Trifon Plastunov, the slightest hint of his secret business. He had spoken to him just before Dmitri met the innkeeper on the balcony, looking for him in the dark. So neither Dmitri nor anyone else knew that he was being watched. The box with the pistols had been put away by the innkeeper. It was only after four o'clock, almost at sunrise, that all the officials, the police captain, the prosecutor, the investigating lawyer, drove up in two carriages, each drawn by three horses. The doctor remained at Fyodor Karamazov's to perform an autopsy. But he was particularly interested in the condition of Smerdyakov.

"Such violent and protracted epileptic fits, recurring continually for twenty-four hours, are rarely to be met with, and are of interest to science," he declared to his friends just before they left. They laughingly congratulated him on his find. And later the prosecutor and the investigating lawyer distinctly remembered the doctor's saying that Smerdyakov could not outlive the night.

3. The Sufferings of a Soul. The First Ordeal

IN THE INN AT MOKROE, DMITRI sat looking wildly at the people around him, not understanding what was said to him. Suddenly he got up, flung up his hands and shouted aloud:

"I'm not guilty! I'm not guilty of that blood! I'm not guilty of my father's blood. . . . I meant to kill him. But I'm not guilty. Not I."

He had hardly said this, before Grushenka rushed from behind the curtain and flung herself at the police captain's feet.

"It was my fault! Mine! My wickedness!" she cried in a heart-rending voice, bathed in tears, stretching out her clasped hands toward them. "He did it through me. I tortured him and drove him to it. I tortured that poor old man that's dead, too, in my wickedness, and brought him to this! It's my fault, mine first, mine most, my fault!"

"Yes, it's your fault! You're the chief criminal! You fury! You harlot! You're the most to blame," shouted the police captain, threatening her with his hand. But he was quickly stopped. The prosecutor grabbed hold of him.

"This is absolutely irregular, Michael Makarov!" he cried. "You are interfering with the inquiry. . . . You're ruining the case."

"Follow the regular course! Follow the regular course!" cried Nicholas Nelyudov, excited too. "Otherwise, it's absolutely impossible!"

"Judge us together!" Grushenka cried, still kneeling. "Punish us together. I will go with him now, even if it's to death!"

"Grushenka, my life, my blood, my holy one!" Dmitri fell on his knees beside her and held her in his arms. "Don't believe her," he cried. "She's not guilty of anything, of any blood, of anything!"

He remembered afterward that he was forcibly dragged away from her by several men, and that she was led out, and that when he recovered himself he was sitting at the table. Beside him and behind him stood the men with metal plates. Facing him on the other side of the table sat Nicholas Nelyudov, the investigating lawyer. He kept persuading him to drink a little water out of a glass that stood on the table.

"It will refresh you, it will calm you. Be calm, don't be frightened," he added, extremely politely. Dmitri (he remembered it afterward) became suddenly interested in his big rings, one with an amethyst, and another with a transparent bright yellow stone. And long afterward he remembered with wonder how those rings had riveted his attention through all those terrible hours of questioning, so that he was unable to tear himself away from them and dismiss them, as things that had nothing to do with what was happening at the moment.

On Dmitri's left, in the place where Maximov had been sitting at the beginning of the evening, the prosecutor was now seated and on Dmitri's right, where Grushenka had been, was a young man in a sort of shabby hunting jacket, with ink and paper before him. This was the secretary of the investigating lawyer. The police captain was now standing by the window

419

at the other end of the room, beside Kalganov, who was sitting there.

"Drink some water," said the investigating lawyer softly, for the tenth time.

"I have drunk it, gentlemen, I have . . . but . . . Come, gentlemen, crush me, punish me, decide my fate!" cried Dmitri, staring with fixed wide-open eyes at the investigating lawyer.

"So you say, absolutely, that you are not guilty of the death of your father, Fyodor Karamazov?" asked the investigating lawyer, softly but insistently.

"I am not guilty. I am guilty of the blood of another old man, but not of my father's. And I weep for it! I killed, I killed the old man and knocked him down. . . . But it's hard to have to answer for that murder with another, a terrible murder of which I am not guilty. . . . It's a terrible accusation, gentlemen. But who has killed my father, who has killed him? Who can have killed him if I didn't? It's extraordinary, impossible."

"Yes, who can have killed him?" the investigating lawyer was beginning, but Ippolit Kirillovitch, the prosecutor, glancing at him, addressed Dmitri.

"You need not worry about the old servant, Gregory. He is alive. He has recovered, and in spite of the terrible blows inflicted by you, according to his own and your evidence, there seems no doubt that he will live. So the doctor says, at least."

"Alive? He's alive?" cried Dmitri throwing up his hands. His face beamed. "Lord, I thank Thee for the miracle Thou has wrought for me, a sinner and evildoer. That's an answer to my prayer. I've been praying all night." And he crossed himself three times. He was almost breathless.

"But from this Gregory we have received such important evidence concerning you, that . . ." The prosecutor would have continued, but Dmitri suddenly jumped up from his chair.

"One minute, gentlemen, for God's sake, one minute; I will run to her . . ."

"Excuse me, at this moment it's quite impossible," Nicholas Nelyudov almost shrieked. He, too, leaped to his feet. Dmitri was grabbed by the men with the metal plates, but he sat down of his own accord.

"Gentlemen, what a pity! I wanted to see her for one minute only. I wanted to tell her that it has been washed away, it has gone, that blood that was weighing on my heart all night, and that I am not a murderer now! Gentlemen, she is my fiancée!" he said ecstatically and reverently, looking around at them all. "Oh, thank you, gentlemen! Oh, in one minute you have given me new life, new heart! . . . That old man used to carry me in his arms, gentlemen. He used to wash

420

me in a tub when I was three years old, abandoned by every-one. He was like a father to me!"

"And so you . . ." the investigating lawyer began.

"Allow me, gentlemen, allow me one minute more," said Dmitri, putting his elbows on the table and covering his face with his hands. "Let me have a moment to think, let me breathe, gentlemen. All this is horribly upsetting, horribly. A man is not a drum, gentlemen!"

"Drink a little more water," murmured Nelyudov. Dmitri took his hands from his face and laughed. His eyes were con-fident. He seemed completely transformed in a moment. His whole bearing was changed; he was once more the equal of these men, with all of whom he was acquainted. We may note in passing that, on his arrival in our town Dmitri had been made very welcome at the police captain's, but later, during the last month especially, he had hardly called at all, and when the police captain met him, in the street, for instance, Dmitri noticed that he frowned and only bowed out of politeness. His acquaintance with the prosecutor was less intimate, although he sometimes paid his wife, a nervous and fanciful lady, so-cial visits, without quite knowing why. She always received him graciously and had, for some reason, taken an interest in him. He had not had time to get to know the investigating lawyer, though he had met him and talked to him twice, each time about women.

"You're a most skillful lawyer, I see, Nicholas Nelyudov," cried Dmitri laughing. "I can help you now. Oh, gentlemen, I feel like a new man, and don't be offended at my addressing you so simply and directly. I'm rather drunk, I'll tell you that frankly. I believe I've had the honor and pleasure of meeting you, Nicholas Nelyudov, at my relative Miusov's. Gentlemen, gentlemen, I don't pretend to be on equal terms with you. I understand, of course, in what position I am sitting before you. Oh, of course, there's a horrible suspicion . . . hanging over me . . . If Gregory has given evidence. . . . A horrible suspicion! It's awful, awful, I understand that! But to business, gentlemen, I am ready. And we will be finished in one moment; for, listen, listen, gentlemen! Since I know I'm innocent, we can put an end to it in a minute. Can't we? Can't we?"

Dmitri spoke quickly, nervously and effusively, as though he took his listeners to be his best friends.

"So, for the present, we will write that you absolutely deny the charge brought against you," said Nicholas Nelyudov. And bending down to the secretary he dictated to him in an under-tone what to write.

"Write it down? You want to write that down? Well, write it. I consent, I give my full consent, gentlemen, only . . . Do you see. . . . Wait, wait, write this. Of disorderly conduct I am guilty, of violence on a poor old man I am guilty. And there is something else at the bottom of my heart, of which I am guilty, too—but that you need not write down." He turned suddenly to the secretary. "That's my personal life, gentlemen, that doesn't concern you, the bottom of my heart, that's to say. . . . But of the murder of my old father I'm not guilty. That's a wild idea. It's a wild idea! . . . I will prove it and you'll be convinced. . . . You will laugh, gentlemen. You'll laugh yourself at your own suspicion! . . ."

"Be calm, sir," said the investigating lawyer, evidently trying to quiet Dmitri's excitement by his own composure. "Before we go on with our inquiry, I should like, if you will consent to answer, to hear you confirm the statement that you disliked your father, Fyodor Karamazov; that you were involved in continual arguments with him. Here at least, a quarter of an hour ago, you exclaimed that you wanted to kill him: 'I didn't kill him,' you said, 'but I wanted to kill him'."

"Did I say that? Oh, that may be so, gentlemen! Yes, unhappily, I did want to kill him . . . Many times I wanted to . . . Unhappily, unhappily!"

"You wanted to. Would you explain what motives precisely led you to such a feeling of hatred for your father?"

"What is there to explain, gentlemen?" Dmitri shrugged his shoulders sullenly, looking down. "I have never concealed my feelings. The whole town knows about it—everyone knows in the tavern. Only lately I declared my feelings in Father Zossima's cell. . . . And the very same day, in the evening I beat my father. I nearly killed him, and I swore I'd come again and kill him, before witnesses. . . . Oh, a thousand witnesses! I've been shouting it aloud for the last month, anyone can tell you that! . . . The fact stares you in the face, it speaks for itself, it cries aloud, but . . . feelings, gentlemen, feelings are another matter. You see, gentlemen," (Dmitri frowned) "it seems to me that about feelings you've no right to question me. I know that you are bound by your office, I understand that, but my feelings are my affair, my private, intimate affair, yet . . . since I haven't concealed my feelings in the past . . . in the tavern, for instance, I've talked to everyone, so . . . so I won't make a secret of them now. You see, I understand, gentlemen, that there are terrible facts against me in this business. I told everyone that I'd kill my father, and now, all of a sudden, he's been killed. So it must have been me! Ha, ha! I can make allowances for you, gentlemen, I can make allowances. I'm puzzled myself, for who can have murdered him, if not I? That's what it comes to, isn't it? If not I, who can it be, who? Gentlemen, I want to know, I insist on knowing!" he exclaimed suddenly. "Where was he murdered? How was he murdered? How, and with what? Tell me," he asked quickly, looking at the two lawyers.

"We found him in his study, lying on his back on the floor, with his head battered in," said the prosecutor.

"That's horrible!" Dmitri shuddered and, putting his elbows on the table, hid his face in his right hand.

"We will continue," said Nicholas Nelyudov. "So what was it that impelled you to this feeling of hatred? You have said in public, I believe, that it was based upon jealousy?"

"Well, yes, jealousy. And not only jealousy."

"Disagreements about money?"

"Yes, about money, too."

"There was an argument about three thousand roubles, I think, which you claimed as part of your inheritance?"

"Three thousand! More, more," cried Dmitri. "More than six thousand, more than ten, perhaps. I told everyone so, shouted it at them. But I made up my mind to let it go at three thousand. I was desperately in need of that three thousand . . . So the bundle of notes for three thousand that I knew he kept under his pillow, ready for Grushenka, I considered as simply stolen from me. Yes, gentlemen, I looked upon it as mine, as my own property."

The prosecutor looked significantly at the investigating lawyer.

"We will return to that subject later," said the lawyer promptly. "You will allow us to note that point and write it down; that you looked upon that money as your own property?"

"Write it down, by all means. I know that's another fact that tells against me, but I'm not afraid of facts and I tell them against myself. Do you hear? Do you know, gentlemen, you take me for a different sort of man from what I am," he added, suddenly, gloomy and dejected. "You have to deal with a man of honor, a man of the highest honor; above all—don't lose sight of it—a man who's done a lot of nasty things, but has always been, and still is, honorable in his inner being. I don't know how to express it. That's just what's made me wretched all my life, that I yearned to be honorable, that I was, so to say, a martyr to a sense of honor, seeking for it with a lantern, with the lantern of Diogenes and yet, all my life I've been doing filthy things like all of us, gentlemen . . . that is like me alone. That was a mistake, like me alone, me alone! . . . Gentlemen, my head aches . . ." He frowned with pain. "You see, gentlemen, I couldn't bear the look of him. There was something about him that was ignoble, impudent, trampling on everything sacred, something sneering and irreverent, loathsome, loathsome. But now that he's dead, I feel differently."

"How do you mean?"

"I don't feel differently, but I wish I hadn't hated him so."

"You feel sorry?"

"No, not sorry, don't write that. I'm not much good myself, I'm not very beautiful, so I had no right to consider him repulsive. That's what I mean. Write that down, if you like."

Saying this Dmitri became very depressed. He had grown more and more gloomy as the inquiry continued.

At that moment an unexpected thing happened. Althoug Grushenka had been removed, she had not been taken fa. away, only into the next room. It was a little room with one window, beyond the large room in which they had danced and feasted so lavishly. She was sitting there alone with Maximov, who was terribly depressed, terribly scared, and clung to her side, as though for security. At the door stood one of the peasants with a metal plate on his breast. Grushenka was crying, and suddenly her grief was too much for her. She jumped up, flung up her arms, and with a loud wail of sorrow, rushed out of the room to him, to her Dmitri. It all happened so unexpectedly that they had not time to stop her. Dmitri hearing her cry jumped up and with a yell rushed to meet her, not knowing what he was doing. But they were not allowed to come together, though they saw one another. He was grabbed by the arms. He struggled, and tried to tear himself away. It took three or four men to hold him. She was held too, and he saw her stretching out her arms to him, crying aloud as they carried her away.

When the scene was over, Dmitri came to himself again, sitting in the same place as before, opposite the investigating lawyer, and crying out: "What do you want with her? Why do you torment her? She's done nothing, nothing!"

The lawyers tried to calm him. About ten minutes passed. At last Michael Makarov, who had been absent, came hurriedly into the room, and said in a loud and excited voice to the prosecutor: "She's been removed, she's downstairs. Will you allow me to say one word to this unhappy man, gentlemen? In your presence, gentlemen, in your presence."

"By all means," answered the investigating lawyer. "We have nothing against it."

"Listen, Dmitri, my dear fellow," began the police captain, and there was a look of warm, almost fatherly, feeling on his excited face. "I took your friend, Agrafena Svyetlov, downstairs myself, and entrusted her to the care of the innkeeper's daughters. And that old fellow Maximov is with her too. And I soothed her, do you hear? I soothed and calmed her. I impressed on her that you have to clear yourself, so she mustn't interfere, must not depress you, or you may lose your head and say the wrong thing. In fact, I talked to her and she understood. She's a sensible girl, a good-hearted girl. She would have kissed my old hands, begging help for you. She sent me herself to tell you not to worry about her. And I must go, my dear fellow, I must go and tell her that you are calm and comforted about her. And so you must be calm, do you understand? I was unfair to her; she is a Christian soul, gentlemen. Yes, I tell you, she's a gentle soul, and not to blame for anything. So what am I to tell her, Dmitri, will you sit quietly or not?"

The good-natured police captain said a great deal that was irregular, but Grushenka's suffering, a fellow creature's suffering, touched his good-natured heart. There were tears in his eyes. Dmitri jumped up and rushed toward him.

"Forgive me, gentlemen, oh, allow me, allow me!" he cried. "You've the heart of an angel, an angel, Michael Makarov, I thank you for her. I will, I will be calm, cheerful, in fact. Tell her, in the kindness of your heart, that I am cheerful, cheerful, that I shall be laughing in a minute, knowing that she has a guardian angel like you. I will be finished with all this very soon, and as soon as I'm free, I'll be with her, she'll see, let her wait. . . . Gentlemen," he said, turning to the two lawyers, "now I'll open my whole soul to you; I'll pour out everything. We'll finish quickly, finish happily. We'll laugh at it in the end, won't we? But, gentlemen, that woman is the queen of my heart. Oh, let me tell you that. That one thing I'll tell you now. . . . I see I'm with honorable men. She is my light, she is my holy one, and if only you knew! Did you hear her cry: 'I'll go with him even if it's to death'? And what have I, a penniless beggar, done for her? Why such love for me? How can a clumsy, ugly brute like me, with my ugly face, deserve such love, that she is ready to go into exile with me? And how she fell down at your feet for my sake, just now! . . . And she's proud and has done nothing! How can I help adoring her? How can I help crying out and rushing to her as I did just now? Gentlemen, forgive me! But now, now I am comforted."

And he sank back in his chair and covering his face with his hands, burst into tears. But they were happy tears. He recovered himself instantly. The old police captain seemed pleased, and the lawyers also. They felt that the examination was passing into a new phase. When the police captain went out, Dmitri was in a much happier mood.

"Now, gentlemen, I am at your disposal, entirely at your disposal. And if it were not for all these trivial details, we would understand one another in a minute. I'm ready for those details again. I'm at your disposal, gentlemen, but I feel that we must have mutual confidence, you in me and I in you, or it will go on forever. I speak in your interests. . . . But don't rummage in my soul; don't irritate me with trifles. Only ask me about facts and what matters, and I will answer you at once. And damn the details!"

The questioning began again.

4. The Second Ordeal

"You don't know how you encourage us by your readiness to answer," said Nicholas Nelyudov to Dmitri. There was obvious satisfaction in his very prominent, short-sighted, light gray eyes, from which he had just removed his spectacles. "And you have made a very good remark about mutual confidence, without which it is impossible to get on. If the suspected party really hopes to defend himself and is in a position to do so then mutual confidence is essential. We, on our side, will do everything in our power, and you can see for yourself how we are conducting the case. You approve, Ippolit Kirillovitch?" He turned to the prosecutor.

"Oh, absolutely," replied the prosecutor. His tone was somewhat cold, compared with Nicholas Nelyudov's impulsiveness.

I will note once and for all that Nicholas Nelyudov, who had but lately arrived among us, had from the first felt marked respect for Ippolit Kirillovitch, our prosecutor, and had become almost his bosom friend. He was almost the only person who put implicit faith in Ippolit Kirillovitch's extraordinary talents as a psychologist and orator. He had heard of him in Petersburg. On the other hand, young Nicholas Nelyudov was the only person in the whole world whom our "unappreciated" prosecutor really liked. On their way to Mokroe they had time to come to an understanding about the present case. And now as they sat at the table, the sharp-witted junior caught and interpreted every indication on his senior colleague's face, at half a word, at a glance, or at a wink.

"Gentlemen, only let me tell my own story and don't interrupt me with trivial questions and I'll tell you everything," said Dmitri.

"Good! Thank you. But before we proceed will you let me inquire as to another fact of great interest to us. I mean the ten roubles you borrowed yesterday at about five o'clock on the security of your pistols, from your friend, Peter Perhotin."

"I pledged them, gentlemen. I pledged my pistols for ten roubles. What else is there to say? That's all. As soon as I got back to town I pledged them."

"You got back to town? Then had you been out of town?"

"Yes, I went a trip of forty miles into the country. Didn't you know?"

The prosecutor and Nicholas Nelyudov exchanged glances.

"Well, how would it be if you began your story with a systematic description of all you did yesterday, from the morning onwards? Allow us, for instance, to inquire why you were absent from the town, and just when you left and when you came back—all those facts."

"You should have asked me this from the beginning," cried Dmitri laughing. "And, if you like, we won't begin from yesterday, but from the morning of the day before; then you'll understand how, why, and where I went. I went the day before yesterday, gentlemen, to a merchant in town, called Samsonov, to borrow three thousand roubles from him on security. It was a pressing matter, gentlemen, it was a necessity."

"Let me interrupt you," the prosecutor put in politely. "Why were you in such pressing need for just that sum, three thousand?"

"Oh, gentlemen, you needn't go into details, how, when and why, and why just so much money, and not so much, and all that rigmarole. Why, it'll run to three volumes, and then you'll want an epilogue!"

Dmitri said all this with the good-natured but impatient familiarity of a man who is anxious to tell the whole truth and is full of the best intentions.

"Gentlemen!" he corrected himself hurriedly, "don't be irritated with me for my digressions, I beg you again. Believe me, I feel the greatest respect for you and understand the situation. Don't think I'm drunk. I'm quite sober now. And, besides, being drunk would be no hindrance. It's with me, you know, like the saying: 'When he is sober, he is a fool; when he is drunk, he is a wise man.' Ha, ha! But I see, gentlemen, it's not the proper thing to make jokes at this moment. And I've my own dignity to keep up, too. I fully understand the difference for the moment. I am, after all, in the position of a criminal, and so, far from being on equal terms with you. And it's your business to watch me. I can't expect you to pat me on the head for what I did to Gregory, for one can't go around breaking old men's heads. I suppose you'll put me away for six months, or a year perhaps, in a house of correction. I don't know what the punishment is—but it will be without loss of the rights of my rank, without loss of my rank, won't it? So you see, gentlemen, I understand the distinction between us. . . . But you must see that you could puzzle God Himself with such questions. 'How did you step? Where did you step? When did you step? And on what did you step?' I'll get mixed up, if you go on like this, and you will put it all down against me. And what will that lead to? To nothing! And even if it's nonsense I'm talking now, let me finish, and you, gentlemen, being men of honor and refinement, will forgive me! I'll finish by asking you, gentlemen, to drop your conventional method of questioning. I mean, beginning from some miserable trifle; how I got up, what I had for breakfast, how I spat, and where I spat, and so distracting my attention, then suddenly stunning me with an overwhelming question: 'Whom did you murder? Whom did you rob?' Ha, ha! That's your method, that's where all your cunning comes in. You can put peasants off their guard like that, but not me. I know the tricks. I've been in the service, too. Ha, ha, ha! You're angry, gentlemen? You forgive my impertinence?" he cried, looking at them with a good-nature that was almost surprising. "It's only Dmitri Karamazov, you know, so you can overlook it. It would be

427

inexcusable in a sensible man; but you can forgive it in Dmitri. Ha, ha!"

Nicholas Nelyudov listened and laughed too. But the prosecutor did not laugh. He kept his eyes fixed on Dmitri as though anxious not to miss the least syllable, the slightest movement, the smallest twitch of any feature of his face.

"That's how we have treated you from the beginning," said Nicholas Nelyudov, still laughing. "We haven't tried to confuse you by asking how you got up in the morning and what you had for breakfast. We began with questions of the greatest importance."

"I understand. I saw it and appreciated it. And I appreciate still more your present kindness to me, an unprecedented kindness. We three here are gentlemen, and so let everything be on the footing of mutual confidence between us. We are educated, well-bred people, who have the common bond of noble birth and honor. In any case, allow me to look upon you as my best friends at this moment of my life, at this moment when my honor is at stake. That's no offense to you gentlemen, is it?"

"On the contrary. You've expressed all that so well," Nicholas Nelyudov answered.

"And enough of those trivial questions, gentlemen, all those tricky questions!" cried Dmitri enthusiastically. "Or there's no knowing where we will end! Is there?"

"I will follow your advice entirely," the prosecutor said, addressing Dmitri. "But I don't withdraw my question. It is now vitally important for us to know exactly why you needed that sum, I mean precisely three thousand roubles."

"Why I needed it? . . . Oh, for one thing and another. . . . Well, it was to pay a debt."

"A debt to whom?"

"That I absolutely refuse to answer, gentlemen. Not because I couldn't or because I wouldn't dare, or because it would be damaging, for it's all trifling, but . . . I won't, because it's a matter of principle. That's my private life, and I won't allow any intrusion into my private life. That's my principle. Your question has no bearing on the case, and whatever has nothing to do with the case is my private affair. I wanted to pay a debt. I wanted to pay a debt of honor, but to whom I won't say."

"Let me make a note of that," said the prosecutor.

"By all means. Write down that I won't say, that I won't. Write that I would think it dishonorable to say. Yes! You can write it down. You've nothing else to do with your time."

"Allow me to warn you, sir, and to remind you once more, if you are unaware of it," the prosecutor began, with a peculiar and stern impressiveness, "that you have a perfect right not to answer the questions put to you now. And we on our side, have no right to demand an answer from you, if you decline

428

to give it for one reason or another. That is entirely a matter for your personal decision. But it is our duty, on the other hand, to explain to you the injury you will be doing yourself by refusing to give this or that piece of evidence. After which I will beg you to continue."

"Gentlemen, I'm not angry . . . I . . ." Dmitri muttered in a rather disconcerted tone. "Well, gentlemen, you see, that Samsonov to whom I went then . . ."

It is not necessary to record his account of what is known to the reader already. Dmitri was anxious not to omit the slightest detail. At the same time he was in a hurry to get it over. But as he gave his evidence it was written down, and therefore they had continually to interrupt him. Dmitri disliked this, but submitted; got angry, but controlled himself. He did, it is true, exclaim from time to time: "Gentlemen, that's enough to make an angel lose patience!" Or: "Gentlemen, it's no good your irritating me."

But even though he said these things he still preserved for a time his genially expansive mood. He told them how Samsonov had made a fool of him two days before. (He had completely realized by now that he had been fooled.) The sale of his watch for six roubles to obtain money for the journey was something new to the lawyers. They were greatly interested, and even, to Dmitri's indignation, thought it necessary to write down the fact as a secondary confirmation of the circumstance that he had hardly a penny in his pocket at the time. Little by little Dmitri began to grow surly. Then, after describing his journey to see Lyagavy, the night spent in the stifling hut, and so on, he came to his return to the town. Here he began, without being particularly urged, to give a minute account of the agonies of jealousy he endured on Grushenka's account.

He was heard with silent attention. They asked particularly about his having a place of ambush next door in Maria's house at the back of Fyodor Karamazov's garden to keep watch on Grushenka, and of Smerdyakov's bringing him information. They laid particular stress on this, and noted it down. Of his jealousy he spoke freely, and though inwardly ashamed at exposing his most intimate feelings, so to speak, to "public disgrace," he evidently overcame his shame in order to tell the truth. The frigid severity with which the investigating lawyer, and still more the prosecutor, stared intently at him as he told his story, disconcerted him.

"That young fellow Nicholas Nelyudov, to whom I was talking nonsense about women only a few days ago, and that sickly prosecutor are not worth my telling this to," he reflected. "It's a disgrace. 'Be patient, humble, hold thy peace.'" He concluded with that line. And he pulled himself together to go on again. When he came to telling of his vitit to Madam Hohlakov, he regained his spirits and even wanted to tell an anecdote of that lady which had nothing to do with the case. But the investigating lawyer stopped him, and suggested that he should pass on to "more essential matters." At last, when he described his despair and told them how, when he left Madame Hohlakov's he thought that he'd "get three thousand if he had to murder someone to do it," they stopped him again and noted down that he had "meant to murder someone." Dmitri let them write it without protest. At last he reached the point in his story when he learned that Grushenka had deceived him and had returned from Samsonov's as soon as he left her there, though she had said that she would stay there till midnight.

"If I didn't kill Fenya then, gentlemen, it was only because I didn't have time," he said suddenly at that point in his story. That, too, was carefully written down. Dmitri waited gloomily, and was beginning to tell how he ran into his father's garden when the investigating lawyer suddenly stopped him, and opening a big portfolio that lay on the sofa beside him he brought out the brass pestle.

"Do you recognize this object?" he asked, showing it to Dmitri.

"Oh, yes," Dmitri laughed gloomily. "Of course I recognize it. Let me have a look at it. . . . Damn it, never mind!"

"You have forgotten to mention it," observed the investigating lawyer.

"Damn it all, I shouldn't have concealed it from you. Do you think that I could have managed without it? It simply escaped my memory."

"Be so good as to tell us precisely how you came to arm yourself with it."

"Certainly I will, gentlemen."

And Dmitri described how he took the pestle and ran.

"But why did you arm yourself with such a weapon?"

"Why? I just picked it up and ran off."

"What for, if you had no reason?"

Dmitri flared up. He looked intently at "the young fellow" and smiled. He was feeling more and more ashamed at having told "such people" the story of his jealousy so sincerely and spontaneously.

"The hell with the pestle!" he said suddenly.

"But still . . ."

"Oh, to keep off dogs. . . . Oh, because it was dark. . . . In case anything turned up."

"But have you ever on previous occasions taken a weapon with you when you went out, since you're afraid of the dark?"

"Damn it all, gentlemen! There's positively no talking to you!" cried Dmitri, exasperated beyond endurance. And turning to the secretary he said quickly, with a note of fury in his voice: "Write down at once . . . at once . . . 'that I snatched up the pestle to go and kill my father . . . Fyodor Karamazov . . . by hitting him on the head with it!' Well, now are you satisfied, gentlemen? Are your minds relieved?" he said, glaring defiantly at the lawyers.

"We quite understand that you made that statement just now through exasperation with us and the questions we put to you, which you consider trivial, though they are, in fact, essential," the prosecutor remarked drily in reply.

"Well, gentlemen! Yes, I took the pestle. . . . What does one pick things up for at such moments? I don't know what for. I snatched it up and ran—that's all. Gentlemen, let's get on or I won't tell you any more."

He sat with his elbows on the table and his head in his hand. He sat sideways to them and gazed at the wall, struggling against a feeling of nausea. He had, in fact, an awful desire to get up and declare that he wouldn't say another word, "not if you hang me for it."

"You see, gentlemen," he said at last, controlling himself with difficulty. "You see, I listen to you and am haunted by a dream. . . . It's a dream I have sometimes, you know. . . . I often dream it—it's always the same. . . . That someone is hunting me, someone I'm awfully afraid of . . . that he's hunting me in the dark, in the night . . . tracking me, and I hide from him, behind a door or cupboard, hide in a degrading way. And the worst of it is, he always knows where I am, but he pretends not to know where I am on purpose, to prolong my agony, to enjoy my terror. . . . That's just what you're doing now. It's just like my dream!"

"Is that the sort of thing you dream about?" asked the prosecutor.

"Yes, it is. Don't you want to write it down?" suggested Dmitri with a distorted smile.

"No. There's no need to write it down. But still you do have curious dreams."

"It's not a question of dreams now, gentlemen—this is realism, this is real life! I'm a wolf and you're the hunters. Well, hunt him down!"

"You are wrong to make such comparisons . . ." began Nicholas Nelyudov, with extraordinary softness.

"No, I'm not wrong, not at all!" Dmitri flared up again. His outburst of wrath obviously relieved his heart. He grew more good-humored at every word. "You may not trust a criminal or a man on trial tortured by your questions, but an honorable man, the honorable impulses of the heart (I say that boldly!)—no! That you must believe. You have no right . . . But . . .

> Be silent, heart,
> Be patient, humble, hold thy peace.

Well, shall I go on?" he asked gloomily.

"If you'll be so kind," answered Nicholas Nelyudov.

5. The Third Ordeal

THOUGH DMITRI SPOKE SULLENLY, it was clear that he was trying more than ever not to forget or miss a single detail of his story. He told them how he had climbed over the fence into his father's garden; how he had gone up to the window; told them all that had passed under the window. Clearly, precisely, distinctly, he described the feelings that troubled him during those moments in the garden when he longed so terribly to know whether Grushenka was with his father or not. But, strange to say, both the lawyers listened now with a sort of awful reserve, looked coldly at him, asked few questions. Dmitri could gather nothing from their faces.

"They're angry and offended," he thought. "Well, to hell with them!"

When he described how he made up his mind at last to give the secret "signal" to his father that Grushenka had come, so that he would open the window, the lawyers paid no attention to the word "signal," as though they failed to grasp the meaning of the word in this connection. Coming at last to the moment when, seeing his father peering out of the window, his hatred flared up and he pulled the pestle out of his pocket, he suddenly stopped short. He sat gazing at the wall and was aware that their eyes were fixed upon him.

"Well?" said the investigating lawyer. "You pulled out the weapon and . . . And what happened then?"

"Then? Why, then I murdered him . . . Hit him on the head and cracked his skull. . . . I suppose that's your story. That's it!"

His eyes suddenly flashed. All his smothered anger suddenly flamed up with violence in his soul.

"Our story?" repeated Nicholas Nelyudov. "Well—and yours?"

Dmitri lowered his eyes and was silent for a long time.

"My story, gentlemen? Well, it was like this," he began softly. "Whether it was someone's tears, or my mother prayed to God, or a good angel kissed me at that moment, I don't know. But the devil was conquered. I rushed from the window and ran to the fence. My father was frightened and ho saw me then, cried out and sprang back from the window. I remember that very well. I ran across the garden to the fence . . . and there Gregory caught me, when I was sitting on the fence."

At that point he raised his eyes at last and looked at his listeners. They seemed to be staring at him with perfectly unruffled attention.

"Why, you're laughing at me, gentlemen!" he said suddenly.

"What makes you think that?" observed Nicholas Nelyudov.

"You don't believe one word—that's why! I understand, of course, that I have come to the vital point. My father is lying there now with his skull broken, while I—after describing how I wanted to kill him, and how I snatched up the pestle—I suddenly ran away from the window. Invented! Fiction! As though one could believe such a thing. Ha, ha! You are laughing at me, gentlemen!"

And he swung round so hard on his chair that it creaked.

"And did you notice," asked the prosecutor suddenly, as though not observing Dmitri's excitement, "did you notice when you ran away from the window, whether the door from the house into the garden was open?"

"No, it was not open."

"It was not?"

"It was shut. And who could open it? The door? Wait a minute!" He suddenly seemed to think of something and he said, almost with a start: "Why, did you find the door open?"

"Yes, it was open."

"Why, who could have opened it if you did not open it yourselves?" cried Dmitri, greatly astonished.

"The door stood open, and your father's murderer undoubtedly went in at that door, and, having accomplished the crime, went out again by the same door," the prosecutor pronounced deliberately, as though chiseling out each word separately. "That is perfectly clear. The murder was committed in the room and *not through the window;* that is absolutely certain from the examination that has been made, from the position of the body, and everything. There can be no doubt of that circumstance."

Dmitri was absolutely dumbfounded.

"But that's impossible!" he cried, completely at a loss. "I . . . I didn't go in. . . . I tell you positively, definitely, that the door was shut the whole time I was in the garden, and it was shut when I ran out of the garden. I only stood at the window and saw him through the window. That's all, that's all. . . . I remember to the last minute. And if I didn't remember, it would be just the same. I know it, for no one knew the signals except Smerdyakov, and me, and my father. And he wouldn't have opened the door to anyone in the world without the signals."

"Signals? What signals?" asked the prosecutor with curiosity. He lost all trace of his reserve and dignity. He asked the question with a sort of cringing timidity. He scented an important fact of which he had known nothing, and was already filled with dread that Dmitri might be unwilling to disclose it.

"So you didn't know!" Dmitri winked at him with a smile. "What if I won't tell you? From whom could you find out? No one knew about the signals except my father, Smerdyakov, and me; that was all. Heaven knew, too, but it won't tell you. But it's an interesting fact. There's no knowing what you

433

might build on it. Ha, ha! Take comfort, gentlemen, I'll reveal it. You've some foolish idea in your hearts. You don't know the man you have to deal with! You have to do with a Dmitri Karamazov, a man who gives evidence against himself, to his own damage! Yes, for I'm a man of honor and you—are not."

The prosecutor swallowed this without a murmur. He was impatient to hear about the new fact. Minutely and diffusely Dmitri told them everything about the signals invented by his father for Smerdyakov. He told them exactly what every tap on the window meant, tapped the signals on the table. And when Nicholas Nelyudov said that he supposed he, Dmitri, had tapped the signal "Grushenka has come," when he tapped on the window, he answered that he had tapped precisely that signal, that "Grushenka had come."

"So now you can build up your tower," Dmitri broke off. And again he turned away from them contemptuously.

"So no one knew of the signals but your dead father, you, and the valet Smerdyakov? No one else?" Nicholas Nelyudov asked once more.

"Yes. The valet Smerdyakov, and heaven. Write down about heaven. That may be of use. Besides, you will need God yourselves."

And they had already, of course, begun writing it down. But while they wrote, the prosecutor said suddenly, as though hooking into a new idea: "But if Smerdyakov also knew about these signals and you absolutely deny all responsibility for the death of your father, was it not he, perhaps, who knocked the signal agreed upon, induced your father to open the door, and then . . . committed the murder?"

Dmitri turned upon him a look of profound irony and intense hatred. His silent stare lasted so long that it made the prosecutor uneasy.

"You've caught the fox again," commented Dmitri at last. "You've got him by the tail. Ha, ha! I see through you, Mr. Prosecutor. You thought, of course, that I would jump at that, catch at your prompting, and shout with all my might: 'It's Smerdyakov! He's the murderer!' Confess that's what you thought. Confess, and I'll go on."

But the prosecutor did not confess. He held his tongue and waited.

"You're mistaken. I'm not going to shout: 'It's Smerdyakov!' " said Dmitri.

"And you don't even suspect him?"

"Why, do you suspect him?"

"He is suspected, too."

Dmitri fixed his eyes on the floor.

"Joking apart," he finally said gloomily. "Listen. From the very beginning, almost from the moment when I came out to you from behind the curtain, I've had Smerdyakov in my mind. I've been sitting here, shouting that I'm innocent and thinking

434

all the time 'Smerdyakov!' I can't get Smerdyakov out of my head. In fact, I, too, thought of Smerdyakov just now; but only for a second. Almost at once I thought: 'No, it's not Smerdyakov.' It's not his doing, gentlemen."

"In that case is there anybody else you suspect?" Nicholas Nelyudov inquired cautiously.

"I don't know anyone it could be, whether it's the hand of Heaven or of Satan, but . . . not Smerdyakov," Dmitri said with decision.

"But what makes you so confident that it's not Smerdyakov?"

"From my conviction—my impression. Because Smerdyakov is a man of the lowest character and a coward. He's not a coward, he's the epitome of all the cowardice in the world walking on two legs. He has the heart of a chicken. When he talked to me, he was always trembling for fear I would kill him, though I never raised my hand against him. He fell at my feet and blubbered. He has kissed these very boots, literally, beseeching me 'not to frighten him.' Do you hear? 'Not to frighten him.' What a thing to say! Why, I offered him money. He's a puling chicken—sickly, epileptic, weak-minded—a child of eight could beat him up. He has no character. It's not Smerdyakov, gentlemen. He doesn't care for money; he wouldn't take my presents. Besides, what motive had he for murdering the old man? Why, he's probably his son, you know—his illegitimate son. Did you know that story?"

"We have heard that story. But you are your father's son, too, you know; yet you yourself told everyone you meant to murder him."

"That's not fair! Oh, gentlemen, isn't it base of you to say that to my face? It's base, because I told you that myself. I not only wanted to murder him, but I might have done it. And, what's more, I went out of my way to tell you of my own accord that I nearly murdered him. But, you see, I didn't murder him. You see, my guardian angel saved me—that's what you've not taken into account. And that's why it's so base of you. For I didn't kill him, I didn't kill him! Do you hear, I did not kill him."

He was almost choking. He had not been upset before during the whole questioning.

"And what has he told you, gentlemen—Smerdyakov, I mean?" he added suddenly, after a pause. "May I ask that question?"

"You may ask any question," the prosecutor replied with frigid severity, "any question relating to the facts of the case, and we are, I repeat, bound to answer every question you ask. We found the servant Smerdyakov lying unconscious in his bed, in an epileptic fit of extreme severity, that had recurred, possibly, ten times. The doctor who was with us told us, after seeing him, that he may possibly not live through the night."

"Well, if that's so, then the devil must have killed him," Dmitri said suddenly, as though until that moment he had been asking himself: "Was it Smerdyakov or not?"

"We will come back to this later," Nicholas Nelyudov decided. "Now, wouldn't you like to continue your statement?"

Dmitri asked for a rest. His request was courteously granted. After resting, he went on with his story. But he was depressed. He was exhausted, mortified and morally shaken. To make things worse the prosecutor exasperated him, as though intentionally, with interruptions about "trifling points." Scarcely had Dmitri described how, sitting on the wall, he had struck Gregory on the head with the pestle, while the old man had hold of his left leg, and how he had then jumped down to look at him, when the prosecutor stopped him to ask him to describe exactly how he was sitting on the wall. Dmitri was surprised.

"Oh, I was sitting like this, astride, one leg on one side of the wall and one on the other."

"And the pestle?"

"The pestle was in my hand."

"Not in your pocket? Do you remember that precisely? Was it a violent blow you gave him?"

"It must have been a violent one. But why do you ask?"

"Would you mind sitting on the chair just as you sat on the wall then and showing us just how you moved your arm, and in what direction?"

"You're making fun of me, aren't you?" asked Dmitri, looking haughtily at the speaker. But the prosecutor did not flinch.

Dmitri turned abruptly, sat astride on his chair, and swung his arm.

"This was how I struck him! That's how I knocked him down! What more do you want?"

"Thank you. May I trouble you now to explain why you jumped down, with what object, and what you had in view?"

"Oh, damn it! . . . I jumped down to look at the man I'd hurt . . . I don't know what for!"

"Though you were so excited and were running away?"

"Yes, though I was excited and running away."

"You wanted to help him?"

"Help! . . . Yes, perhaps I did want to help him. . . . I don't remember."

"You don't remember? Then you didn't quite know what you were doing?"

"No. I remember everything—every detail. I jumped down to look at him, and wiped his face with my handkerchief."

"We have seen your handkerchief. Did you hope to restore him to consciousness?"

"I don't know whether I hoped it. I simply wanted to make sure whether he was alive or not."

"Oh! You wanted to be sure? Well, what then?"

"I'm not a doctor. I couldn't decide. I ran away thinking I'd killed him. And now he has recovered."

"Good," commented the prosecutor. "Thank you. That's all I wanted. Kindly proceed."

Alas! It never entered Dmitri's head to tell them, though he remembered it, that he had jumped down from pity, and standing over Gregory had even said some words of regret: "You've come to grief, old man, so there you must lie."

The prosecutor could only draw one conclusion: that Dmitri had jumped down "at such a moment simply with the object of ascertaining whether the *only* witness to his crime were dead; that he must therefore be a man of great strength, coolness, decision and foresight even at such a moment," . . . and so on. The prosecutor was satisfied: "I've provoked him by 'trifles' and he has said more than he meant to."

With painful effort Dmitri went on. But this time he was pulled up immediately by Nicholas Nelyudov.

"How was it that you ran to the servant, Fenya, with your hands so covered with blood, and, as it appears, your face too?"

"Why, I didn't notice the blood at all at the time," answered Dmitri.

"That's quite likely. It does happen sometimes." The prosecutor exchanged glances with Nicholas Nelyudov.

"I simply didn't notice. You're quite right, sir," Dmitri agreed.

Next came the account of Dmitri's sudden decision to "step aside" and make way for Grushenka's happiness. But he could not make up his mind to open his heart to them as before, and tell them about "the queen of his soul." He disliked speaking of her before these people "who were fastening on him like bugs." And so in answer to their questions he replied briefly and abruptly: "Well, I made up my mind to kill myself. What had I left to live for? That question stared me in the face. Her first rightful lover had come back, the man who wronged her but who'd hurried back to offer his love, after five years, and atone for the wrong with marriage. . . . So I knew it was all over for me. . . . And behind me disgrace, and that blood—Gregory's. . . . What had I to live for? So I went to redeem the pistols I had pledged, to load them and put a bullet in my brain the next morning."

"And a feast the night before?"

"Yes, a feast the night before. Damn it all, gentlemen! Do hurry and finish. I meant to shoot myself not far from here, beyond the village. I'd planned to do it at five o'clock in the morning. And I had a note in my pocket. I wrote it at Perhotin's when I loaded my pistol. Here's the note. Read it! It's not for you I wrote it," he added contemptuously. He took it from his waistcoat pocket and flung it on the table. The law-

437

yers read it with curiosity and, as is usual, added it to the papers connected with the case.

"And you didn't even think of washing your hands at Perhotin's? You were not afraid then of arousing suspicion?"

"What suspicion? Suspicion or not, I would have galloped here just the same, and shot myself at five o'clock. And you wouldn't have been in time to do anything. If it hadn't been for what's happened to my father, you would have known nothing about it, and wouldn't have come here. Oh, it's the devil's doing. It was the devil murdered my father. It was through the devil that you found it out so soon. How did you manage to get here so quickly? It's marvelous, a dream!"

"Mr. Perhotin informed us that when you came to him, you held in your hands . . . your blood-stained hands . . . Money . . . A lot of money . . . A bundle of hundred-rouble notes, and that his servant boy saw it too."

"That's true, gentlemen. I remember it."

"Now, there's one point presents itself. Can you tell us," Nicholas Nelyudov began, with extreme gentleness, "where you got so much money all of a sudden, when it appears from the facts, from the lapse of time, that you had not been home?"

The prosecutor's brows contracted at the question being asked so plainly, but he did not interrupt.

"No, I didn't go home," answered Dmitri, perfectly composed, but looking at the floor.

"Allow me then to repeat my question," Nicholas Nelyudov went on as though creeping up to the subject. "Where were you able to procure such a sum all at once, when, by your own confession, at five o'clock the same day you . . ."

"I was in want of ten roubles and pledged my pistols with Perhotin, and then went to Madame Hohlakov to borrow three thousand which she wouldn't give me, and so on, and all the rest of it," Dmitri interrupted sharply. "Yes, gentlemen, I was in want of money and suddenly thousands turned up, eh? Do you know, gentlemen, you're both afraid now 'what if he won't tell us where he got it?' That's just how it is. I'm not going to tell you, gentlemen. You've guessed right. You'll never know," said Dmitri, chipping out each word with extraordinary determination. The lawyers were silent for a moment.

"You must understand, Mr. Karamazov, that it is of vital importance for us to know," said Nicholas Nelyudov softly and suavely.

"I understand. But still I won't tell you."

The prosecutor intervened, and again reminded Nicholas Nelyudov that Dmitri was at liberty to refuse to answer questions, if he thought it to his interest, and so on. But in view of the damage he might do himself by his silence, especially in a case of such importance as . . .

"And so on, gentlemen, and so on. Enough! I've heard that rigmarole before," Dmitri interrupted again. "I can see for myself how important it is, and that this is the vital point, and still I won't tell you where I got the money."

"What is it to us? It's not our business but yours. You are doing yourself harm," observed Nicholas Nelyudov nervously.

"You see, gentlemen, joking apart," Dmitri said, raising his eyes and looking firmly at them both, "I had an inkling from the first that we would come to loggerheads at this point. But at first when I began to give my evidence, it was all still far away and misty; it was all floating, and I was so simple that I began with the supposition of mutual confidence existing between us. Now I can see for myself that such confidence is out of the question, for in any case we were bound to come to this cursed stumbling-block. And now we've come to it! It's impossible! But I don't blame you. You can't believe it all simply on my word. I understand that, of course."

He relapsed into gloomy silence.

"Couldn't you, without abandoning your decision to be silent about this point . . . Could you not give us some slight hint as to the nature of the motives which are strong enough to induce you to refuse to answer?"

Dmitri smiled almost dreamily.

"I'm much more good-natured than you think, gentlemen. I'll tell you the reason why and give you that hint, though you don't deserve it. I won't speak about where I got the money, gentlemen, because it would be a stain on my honor. The answer to the question where I got the money would expose me to far greater disgrace than the murder and robbing of my father, if I had murdered and robbed him. That's why I can't tell you. I can't for fear of disgrace. What, gentlemen, are you going to write that down!"

"Yes, we'll write it down," lisped Nicholas Nelyudov.

"You ought not to write that down about 'disgrace.' I only told you that from the goodness of my heart. I didn't have to tell you. I made you a present of it, so to speak, and you pounce upon it at once. Oh, well, write—write what you like," he concluded with disgust. "I'm not afraid of you and I can still hold up my head."

"And can't you tell us the nature of that disgrace?" Nicholas Nelyudov ventured.

The prosecutor frowned.

"No, no, I'm through. Don't trouble yourselves. It's not worth while soiling one's hands. I have soiled myself enough through you as it is. You're not worth it—no one is . . . Enough, gentlemen. I'm not going on."

This was said emphatically. Nicholas Nelyudov did not insist further, but from the prosecutor's eyes he saw that he had not given up hope.

"Can you not, at least, tell us what sum you had in your hands when you went into Mr. Perhotin's—how many roubles exactly?"

"I can't tell you that."

"You spoke to Mr. Perhotin, I believe, of having received three thousand from Madame Hohlakov."

"Perhaps I did. Enough, gentlemen. I won't say how much I had."

"Will you be so good then as to tell us how you came here and what you have done since you arrived?"

"Oh! You might ask the people here about that. But I'll tell you if you like."

He proceeded to do so, but it is not necessary to repeat his story. He told it drily and curtly. Of the passion of his love he said nothing, but he told them that he abandoned his decision to shoot himself because of "new factors in the case." He told the story without going into motives or details. And this time the lawyers did not worry him much. It was obvious that there was no essential point of interest to them here.

"We shall verify all that. We will come back to it during the examination of the witnesses, which will, of course, take place in your presence," said Nicholas Nelyudov in conclusion. "And now let me ask you to lay on the table everything in your possession, especially all the money you still have with you."

"My money, gentlemen? Certainly. I understand that that is necessary. I'm surprised, in fact, that you haven't asked about it before. It's true I couldn't hide it anywhere. I'm sitting here where I can be seen. But here's my money—count it—take it. That's all, I think."

He turned it all out of his pockets; even the small change—forty cents—he pulled out of his waistcoat pocket. They counted the money, which amounted to eight hundred and thirty-six roubles, and the small change.

"And is that all?" asked the investigating lawyer.

"Yes."

"You stated just now in your evidence that you spent three hundred roubles at Plotnikovs'. You gave Perhotin ten, your driver twenty, here you lost two hundred, then . . ."

Nicholas Nelyudov figured it all up. Dmitri helped him. He accounted for every penny. Nicholas Nelyudov added up the total.

"With this eight hundred you must have had about fifteen hundred at first?"

"I suppose so," said Dmitri sharply.

"How is it they all say there was much more?"

"Let them say it."

"But you said it yourself."

"Yes, I did, too."

"We will compare all this with the evidence of other persons not yet examined. Don't worry about your money. It will be properly taken care of and be returned to you at the conclusion of . . . what is now beginning . . . if it appears, or, so to speak, is proved that you have undisputed right to it. Well, and now . . ."

Nicholas Nelyudov suddenly got up, and told Dmitri that it was his duty and obligation to conduct a minute and thorough search "of your clothes and everything else . . ."

"By all means, gentlemen. I'll turn out all my pockets, if you like."

And he did, in fact, begin turning out his pockets.

"It will be necessary to take off your clothes, too."

"What! Undress! Damn it! Won't you search me as I am? Can't you?"

"It's impossible. You must take off your clothes."

"Well if you must," Dmitri submitted gloomily. "Only, please not here, but behind the curtains. Who will search them?"

"Behind the curtains, of course."

Nicholas Nelyudov bent his head in agreement. His small face wore an expression of peculiar seriousness.

6. *The Prosecutor Catches Dmitri*

SOMETHING COMPLETELY UNEXPECTED and amazing to Dmitri followed. He could never, even a minute before, have conceived that anyone could behave like that to him, Dmitri Karamazov. What was the worst of all was that there was something humiliating in it, and on their side something "supercilious and scornful." It was nothing to take off his coat, but he was asked to undress further, or rather not asked but "commanded." From pride and contempt he submitted without a word. Several peasants accompanied the lawyers and remained on the same side of the curtain. "To be ready if force is required," thought Dmitri. "And perhaps for some other reason, too."

"Well, must I take off my shirt, too?" he asked sharply, but Nicholas Nelyudov did not answer. He was busy with the prosecutor examining the coat, the trousers, the waistcoat and the cap. And it was evident that they were both much interested in what they were doing. "They make no bones about it," thought Dmitri. "They don't pretend even the most elementary politeness."

"I ask you for the second time—need I take off my shirt or not?" he said, still more sharply and irritably.

"Don't trouble yourself. We will tell you what to do," Nicholas Nelyudov said, and his voice was commanding or so it seemed to Dmitri.

Meanwhile a consultation was going on in undertones between the lawyers. There turned out to be on the coat, especially on the left side at the back, a huge patch of blood, dry and stiff. There were bloodstains on the trousers, too. Nicholas Nelyudov, moreover, in the presence of the peasant witnesses, passed his fingers along the collar, the cuffs, and all the seams of the coat and trousers, obviously looking for something—money, of course. He didn't even hide from Dmitri his suspicion that he was capable of sewing money up in his clothes.

"He treats me not as a gentleman but as a thief," Dmitri muttered to himself. They exchanged their ideas with one another with amazing frankness. The secretary, for instance, who was also behind the curtain, fussing about and listening, called Nicholas Nelyudov's attention to the cap.

"You remember that copying clerk last summer," observed the secretary. "He was entrusted with the wages of the whole office, and pretended to have lost the money when he was drunk. And where was it found? Why, in just such pipings in his cap. The hundred-rouble notes were screwed up in little rolls and sewed into the piping."

Both the lawyers remembered the case perfectly, and so laid aside Dmitri's cap, and decided that all his clothes must be more thoroughly examined later.

"Excuse me," cried Nicholas Nelyudov suddenly noticing that the right cuff of Dmitri's shirt was turned in, and covered with blood. "Excuse me, what's that, blood?"

"Yes," Dmitri said.

"That is, what blood . . . And why is the cuff turned in?"

Dmitri told him how he had gotten the sleeve stained with blood looking after Gregory, and had turned it in when he was washing his hands at Perhotin's.

"You must take off your shirt, too. That's very important as material evidence."

Dmitri flushed red and flew into a rage.

"What, am I to be stripped naked?" he shouted.

"Don't disturb yourself. We will arrange something. And meanwhile take off your socks."

"You're not joking? Is that really necessary?" Dmitri's eyes flashed.

"We are in no mood for joking," answered Nicholas Nelyudov.

"Well, if I must . . ." muttered Dmitri and sitting down on the bed, he took off his socks. He felt unbearably awkward. Everyone else in the room was clothed, while he was naked, and strange to say, when he was undressed he felt somehow guilty. He was almost ready to believe that he was inferior to them, and that now they had a perfect right to despise him.

"When all are undressed, one is somehow not ashamed, but when you are the only one undressed and everybody is looking, it's degrading," he kept repeating to himself, again and again. "It's like a dream, I've sometimes dreamed of being degraded like this." It was a misery to him to take off his socks. They

442

were dirty, and so were his underclothes, and now everyone could see it. And what was worse, he disliked his feet. All his life he had thought both his big toes hideous. He particularly loathed the coarse, flat, crooked nail on the right one, and now they would all see it, too. Feeling ashamed made him intentionally rougher. He pulled off his shirt, himself.

"Would you like to look anywhere else if you're not ashamed to?"

"No, there's no need to, at present."

"Well, am I to stay naked like this?" he added savagely.

"Yes, that can't be helped for the time . . . Kindly sit down here for a while. You can wrap yourself in a quilt from the bed, and I . . . I'll see to all this."

All his clothing was shown to the witnesses. The report of the search was drawn up, and at last Nicholas Nelyudov went out. The clothes were carried out after him. Ippolit Kirillovitch, the prosecutor, went out too. Dmitri was left alone with the peasants, who stood in silence, never taking their eyes off him. Dmitri wrapped himself up in a quilt. He felt cold. His bare feet stuck out, and he couldn't pull the quilt over so as to cover them. Nicholas Nelyudov seemed to be gone a long time, "an insufferable time." "He thinks of me as a puppy," thought Dmitri. "That rotten prosecutor has gone, too. Contemptuous no doubt. It disgusts him to see me naked!"

Dmitri imagined that his clothes would be examined and returned to him. But Nicholas Nelyudov came back with quite different clothes.

"Here are clothes for you," he observed, seeming well satisfied with the success of his mission. "Mr. Kalganov has kindly provided these for this emergency, as well as a clean shirt. Luckily he had them all in his trunk. You can keep your own socks and underclothes."

Dmitri flew into a rage.

"I won't have other people's clothes!" he shouted. "Give me my own!"

"It's impossible!"

"Give me my own. Damn Kalganov and his clothes too!"

It was a long time before they could persuade him. But they succeeded somehow in quieting him down. They impressed upon him that, his clothes being stained with blood, must be "included with the other material evidence," and that they "had not even the right to let him have them now . . . taking into consideration the possible outcome of the case." Dmitri at last understood this. He subsided into gloomy silence and hurriedly dressed himself. He merely observed, as he put them on, that the clothes were much better than his old ones, and that he disliked "gaining by the change." But the clothes were "ridiculously tight. And I to be dressed up like a fool . . . for your amusement?"

They told him that he was exaggerating, that Kalganov was

only a little taller, so that only the trousers might be a little too long. But the coat turned out to be really tight in the shoulders.

"Damn it all! I can hardly button it," Dmitri grumbled. "Be good enough to tell Kalganov from me that I didn't ask for his clothes, and it's not my doing that they've dressed me up like a clown."

"He quite understands that, and is sorry . . . I mean, not sorry to lend you his clothes, but sorry about all this business," mumbled Nicholas Nelyudov.

"Damn him! Well, where now, or am I to go on sitting here?"

He was asked to go back to the "other room." Dmitri went in, scowling with anger, and trying to avoid looking at anyone. Dressed in another man's clothes he felt himself disgraced, even in the eyes of the peasants and of the innkeeper, whose face appeared for some reason in the doorway and vanished immediately. "He's come to look at me dressed up," thought Dmitri. He sat down on the same chair as before. He had a strange nightmarish feeling, as though he were out of his mind.

"Well, what now? Are you going to flog me? That's all that's left for you," he said, clenching his teeth and addressing the prosecutor. He would not look at Nicholas Nelyudov, as though he disdained to speak to him.

"He looked too closely at my socks, and turned them inside out on purpose to show everyone how dirty they were!"

"Well, now we must proceed to the examination of witnesses," observed Nicholas Nelyudov, as though in reply to Dmitri's question.

"Yes," said the prosecutor thoughtfully, as though reflecting on something.

"We've done what we could in your interest," Nicholas Nelyudov went on. "But having received from you an uncompromising refusal to explain to us where you got the money, we are, at the present moment . . ."

"What is the stone in your ring?" Dmitri interrupted suddenly as though waking from a dream. He pointed to one of the three large rings on Nicholas Nelyudov's right hand.

"Ring?" repeated Nicholas Nelyudov with surprise.

"Yes, that one . . . On your middle finger, with the little veins in it, what stone is that?" Dmitri persisted, like a peevish child.

"That's a smoky topaz," said Nicholas Nelyudov, smiling. "Would you like to look at it? I'll take it off. . . ."

"No, don't take it off," cried Dmitri furiously, suddenly waking up, and angry with himself. "Don't take it off . . . There's no need. . . . Damn it. . . . Gentlemen, you've sullied my heart! Can you imagine that I would conceal it from you, if I really had killed my father, that I would shuffle, lie, and hide myself? No, that's not like Dmitri Karamazov, that he

444

couldn't do. And if I were guilty, I swear I wouldn't have waited for you to come, or for the sunrise as I meant at first, but would have killed myself before this, without waiting for the dawn! I know that about myself now. I couldn't have learned so much in twenty years as I've found out in this accursed night! . . . And would I have been like this on this night, and at this moment, sitting with you . . . Could I have talked like this, could I have moved like this, could I have looked at you and at the world like this, if I had really been the murderer of my father, when the very thought of having accidentally killed Gregory gave me no peace all night—not from fear— oh, not simply from fear of your punishment! The disgrace of it! And you expect me to be open with such people as you, who see nothing and believe in nothing, blind moles and scoffers, and you expect me to tell you another evil thing I've done, another disgrace, even if that would save me from your accusation! No, better Siberia! The man who opened the door to my father and went in at that door, he killed him, he robbed him. Who was he—I'm racking my brains and can't think who. But I can tell you it was not Dmitri Karamazov, and that's all I can tell you, and that's enough, enough! Leave me alone. . . . Exile me, punish me, but don't bother me any more. I'll say no more. Call your witnesses!"

Dmitri spoke as though he were determined to be absolutely silent for the future. The prosecutor watched him the whole time and only when he had stopped speaking, observed, as though it were the most ordinary thing, with the most frigid and composed air: "Oh, about the open door of which you spoke just now . . . We may as well inform you of a very important piece of evidence that has been given us by Gregory, the old man you wounded. On his recovery, he clearly and emphatically stated, in reply to our questions, that on coming out to the steps and hearing a noise in the garden, he made up his mind to go through the little gate which stood open. This was before he noticed you running, as you have told us already, in the dark from the open window where you saw your father. He, Gregory, then glanced to the left, and, while noticing the open window, observed at the same time, much nearer to him, the door, standing wide open—that door which you have stated was shut the whole time you were in the garden. I will not conceal from you that Gregory himself swears and bears witness that you must have run from that door, though, of course, he did not see you do so with his own eyes, since he only noticed you first some distance away in the garden, running toward the fence."

Dmitri had jumped up from his chair halfway through this speech.

"Nonsense!" he yelled, in a sudden frenzy. "It's a lie. He couldn't have seen the door open because it was shut. He's lying!"

"I consider it my duty to repeat that he is firm in his statement. He does not waver. He adheres to it. We've cross-examined him several times."

"Precisely. I have cross-examined him several times," Nicholas Nelyudov confirmed warmly.

"It's false, false! It's either an attempt to accuse me, or the hallucination of a madman," Dmitri shouted. "He's simply raving, from loss of blood, from the wound. He must have imagined it when he came to. . . . He's raving."

"Yes, but he noticed the open door, not when he came to after his injuries, but before, as soon as he went into the garden from his cottage."

"But it's false, it's false! It can't be so! He's accusing me from spite. . . . He couldn't have seen it . . . I didn't come from the door," gasped Dmitri.

The prosecutor turned to Nicholas Nelyudov and said: "Confront him with it."

"Do you recognize this object?"

Nicholas Nelyudov laid upon the table a large, thick official envelope, on which three seals still remained intact. The envelope was empty, and slit open at one end. Dmitri stared at it.

"It . . . it must be that envelope of my father's, the envelope that contained the three thousand roubles . . . And if there's inscribed on it, allow me 'for my little chicken' . . . Yes—three thousand!" he shouted. "Do you see, three thousand, do you see?"

"Of course we see. But we didn't find the money. It was empty and lying on the floor by the bed, behind the screen."

For some seconds Dmitri stood as though thunderstruck.

"Gentlemen, it's Smerdyakov!" he shouted suddenly at the top of his voice. "It's he who murdered my father! He robbed him! No one else knew where my father hid the envelope. It's Smerdyakov, that's clear, now!"

"But you, too, knew of the envelope and that it was under the pillow."

"I never knew it. I've never seen it. This is the first time I've looked at it. I'd only heard of it from Smerdyakov. . . . He was the only one who knew where my father kept it hidden, I didn't know . . ." Dmitri was breathless.

"But you told us yourself that the envelope was under your father's pillow. You stated that it was under the pillow, so you must have known it."

"We've got it written down," confirmed Nicholas Nelyudov.

"Nonsense! It's absurd! I'd no idea it was under the pillow. And perhaps it wasn't under the pillow at all. . . . It was just a chance guess that it was under the pillow. What does Smerdyakov say? Have you asked him where it was? What does Smerdyakov say? That's the main point. . . . And I went out of my way to tell lies against myself. . . . I told you without thinking that it was under the pillow, and now you . . . Oh, you know how one says the wrong thing, without meaning it. No one knew but Smerdyakov, only Smerdyakov, and no one else. . . . He didn't even tell me where it was! But it's his doing, his doing. There's no doubt about it, he murdered him, that's as clear as daylight now," Dmitri spoke more and more frantically, repeating himself incoherently, and growing more and more exasperated and excited. "You must understand that, and arrest him at once. . . . He must have killed him while I was running away and while Gregory was unconscious, that's clear now. . . . He gave the signal and my father opened the door to him . . . For no one but he knew the signal, and without the signal my father would never have opened the door. . . ."

"But you're again forgetting the circumstances," the prosecutor observed, still speaking with the same restraint, though with a note of triumph. "You forget that there was no need to give the signal if the door already stood open when you were there, while you were in the garden . . ."

"The door, the door," muttered Dmitri and he stared at the prosecutor. He sank back helpless in his chair. All were silent.

"Yes, the door! . . . It's a nightmare! God is against me!" he exclaimed, staring before him completely stupefied.

"Come, you see," the prosecutor went on with dignity. "You can judge for yourself. On the one hand we have the evidence of the open door from which you ran out, a fact which overwhelms you and us. On the other side your incomprehensible, persistent silence with regard to the source from which you obtained the money which was so suddenly seen in your hands, when only three hours earlier you pledged your pistols for the sake of ten roubles! In view of all these facts, judge for yourself. What are we to believe, and what can we depend upon? And don't accuse us of being 'frigid, cynical, scoffing people,' who are incapable of believing in the generous impulses of your heart. . . . Try to enter into our position . . ."

Dmitri was agitated. He turned pale.

"All right!" he exclaimed suddenly. "I will tell you my secret. I'll tell you where I got the money! . . . I'll reveal my shame, that I won't have to blame myself on you later on."

"And believe me," put in Nicholas Nelyudov in a voice of almost pathetic delight, "that every sincere and complete confession on your part at this moment may, later on, have an immense influence in your favor, and may, indeed, moreover . . ."

But the prosecutor gave him a slight shove under the table and he checked himself in time. Dmitri, it is true, had not heard him.

7. Dmitri's Great Secret Received with Hisses

"GENTLEMEN," HE BEGAN, still agitated. "I want to make a full confession; that money was *my own*."

The lawyers' faces lengthened. That was not at all what they expected.

"How do you mean?" faltered Nicholas Nelyudov. "At five o'clock on the same day, from your own confession . . ."

"Damn five o'clock on the same day and my own confession. That has nothing to do with it now! That money was my own, my own, that is, stolen by me . . . Not mine, I mean, but stolen by me, and it was fifteen hundred roubles, and I had it on me all the time, all the time . . ."

"But where did you get it?"

"I took it off my neck, gentlemen, off this very neck . . . It was here, round my neck, sewn up in a rag, and I'd had it around my neck a long time. It's a month since I put it around my neck . . . To my shame and disgrace!"

"And from whom did you . . . obtain it?"

"You mean, 'steal it'? Speak out plainly. Yes, I consider that I practically stole it, but, if you prefer, I 'obtained it.' I consider I stole it. And last night I stole it finally."

"Last night? But you said that it's a month since you . . . obtained it?"

"Yes. But not from my father. Not from my father, don't be uneasy. I didn't steal it from my father, but from her. Let me tell you without being interrupted. It's hard to do, you know. You see, a month ago, Katerina, my former fiancée, sent for me. Do you know her?"

"Yes, of course."

"I know you know her. She's noble, the noblest of the noble. But she has hated me ever so long, oh, ever so long . . . and hated me with good reason, good reason!"

"Katerina!" Nicholas Nelyudov exclaimed with wonder. The prosecutor, too, stared.

"Oh, don't take her name in vain! I'm a scoundrel to bring her into it. Yes, I've seen that she hated me . . . a long while. . . . From the very first, even that evening at my lodging . . . But enough, enough. You're unworthy even to know of that. No need of that at all. . . . I need only tell you that she sent for me a month ago, gave me three thousand roubles to send to her sister and another relative in Moscow (as though she couldn't have sent it off herself!), and I . . . It was just at that fatal moment in my life when I . . . Well, in fact, when I'd just fallen in love with another, *her*, she's sitting down below

448

now, Grushenka. I brought her here to Mokroe then, and in two days squandered half of that damned three thousand. But the other half I kept on me. Well, I kept that other half, that fifteen hundred like a locket around my neck. But yesterday I undid it, and spent it. What's left of it, eight hundred roubles, is now in your hands. That's what is left out of the fifteen hundred I had yesterday."

"Excuse me. How's that? Why, when you were here a month ago you spent three thousand, not fifteen hundred. Everybody knows that."

"Who knows it? Who counted the money? Did I let anyone count it?"

"Why, you told everyone yourself that you'd spent exactly three thousand."

"It's true, I did. I told the whole town that and the whole town said so. And here, at Mokroe, too, everyone thought it was three thousand. But I didn't spend three thousand, only fifteen hundred. And the other fifteen hundred I sewed into a little bag. That's how it was, gentlemen. That's where I got that money yesterday . . ."

"This is almost unbelievable," murmured Nicholas Nelyudov.

"Let me ask," observed the prosecutor at last. "Have you informed anyone of this circumstance before. I mean that you had fifteen hundred left a month ago?"

"I told no one."

"That's strange. Do you mean absolutely no one?"

"Absolutely no one. No one and nobody."

"What was your reason for this? What was your motive for making such a secret of it? To be more precise: You have at last told us your secret, which you consider so 'disgraceful,' though in my view at least, it's only a reckless act and not so disgraceful, when one takes into consideration your character. . . . Even admitting that it was a discreditable act, still, discreditable is not "disgraceful" . . . Many people have already guessed, during this last month, about the three thousand of Katerina's that you have spent. I had heard about it myself, apart from your confession. . . . Michael Makarov heard it, too, so that it was scarcely a secret, but the gossip of the whole town. There are indications, too, if I am not mistaken, that you confessed this yourself to someone, I mean that the money was Katerina's and so, it's extremely surprising to me that up to the present moment, you have made such an extraordinary secret of the fifteen hundred you say you put away, apparently connecting a feeling of positive horror with that secret. . . . It's not easy to believe that it could cause you such agony to confess such a secret. . . . You cried out, just now, that Siberia would be better than confessing it."

The prosecutor stopped speaking. He was provoked. He did not conceal his irritation, which was almost anger, and he gave vent to all his accumulated spleen, without choosing words, disconnectedly and incoherently.

"It's not the fifteen hundred that's the disgrace, but that I put it apart from the rest of the three thousand," said Dmitri firmly.

"Why," smiled the prosecutor irritably. "What is there disgraceful, to your thinking, in your having set aside half of the three thousand you had discreditably, if you prefer, 'disgracefully,' appropriated? Your taking the three thousand is more important than what you did with it. And by the way, why did you do that—why did you put that half away, for what purpose, for what object did you do it? Can you explain that to us?"

"Oh, gentlemen, the purpose is the whole point!" cried Dmitri. "I put it aside because I was base, that is, because I was calculating, and to be calculating in such a case is base . . . and that baseness has been going on a whole month."

"It's not understandable."

"I wonder at you. But I'll make it clearer. Perhaps it really is incomprehensible. You see, listen to what I say. I take three thousand entrusted to my honor, I spend it on a spree, say I spend it all, and next morning I go to her and say, 'Katerina, I've done wrong, I've squandered your three thousand,' well, is that right? No, it's not right—it's dishonest and cowardly, I'm a beast, with no more self-control than a beast, that's so, isn't it? But still I'm not a thief? Not a downright thief, you'll admit! I squandered it, but I didn't steal it. Now a second, rather more favorable alternative: follow me carefully, or I may get confused again—my head's going around—and so, for the second alternative: I spend here only fifteen hundred out of the three thousand, that is, only half. Next day I go and take that half to her: 'Katerina, take this fifteen hundred from me, I'm a beast, and an untrustworthy scoundrel, for I've wasted half the money, and I will waste this, too, so keep me from temptation!' Well, what of that alternative? I would be a beast and a scoundrel, and whatever you like but not a thief, not altogether a thief, or I would not have brought back what was left. I would have kept that, too. She would see at once that since I brought back half, I would in time pay back what I'd spent, that I would never give up trying to, that I would work to get it and pay it back. So in that case, I would be a scoundrel, but not a thief. Not a thief!"

"I admit that there is a certain distinction," said the prosecutor, with a cold smile. "But it's strange that you see such a vital difference."

"Yes, I see a vital difference! Every man may be a scoundrel, and perhaps every man is a scoundrel, but not everyone can be a thief, it takes an arch-scoundrel to be that. Oh, of course I don't know how to make these fine distinctions . . . But a thief is lower than a scoundrel, that's my conviction.

Listen, I carry the money about me a whole month. I may make up my mind to give it back tomorrow, and I'm a scoundrel no longer. But I cannot make up my mind, you see, though I'm making up my mind every day, and every day spurring myself on to do it, and yet for a whole month I can't bring myself to it, you see. Is that right to your thinking, is that right?"

"Certainly, that's right. That I can quite understand, and that I don't dispute," answered the prosecutor with reserve. "But let us give up all discussions of these subtleties and distinctions and get back to the point. And the point is, that you have still not told us, although we've asked you, why, in the first place, you halved the money, squandering one half and hiding the other? For exactly what purpose did you hide it? What did you mean to do with that fifteen hundred? I insist upon that question."

"Yes, of course!" cried Dmitri, striking himself on the forehead. "Forgive me, I'm worrying you, and am not explaining the main point, or you'd understand in a minute, because it's just the motive of it that's the disgrace! You see, it had to do with my father. He was always pestering Grushenka, and I was jealous. I thought then that she was hesitating between me and him. So I kept thinking every day, suppose she were to make up her mind all of a sudden, suppose she were to stop tormenting me, and were suddenly to say to me: 'I love you, not him. Take me to the other end of the world.' Suppose she were to say that and I had only forty cents? How could I take her away, what could I do? Why, I'd be lost. You see, I didn't know her then, I didn't understand her. I thought she wanted money, and that she wouldn't forgive my poverty. And so I set aside half of that three thousand, sewed it up, counting on it. I sewed it up before I was drunk, and after I had sewn it up, I went off to get drunk on the rest. Yes, that was base. Do you understand now?"

Both the lawyers laughed.

"I should have called it sensible and moral on your part not to have squandered it all," chuckled Nicholas Nelyudov. "For after all what does it amount to?"

"Why, that I stole it, that's what it amounts to! Oh, God, you shock me by not understanding! Every day that I had that fifteen hundred sewn up round my neck, every day and every hour I said to myself: 'You're a thief! You're a thief!' Yes, that's why I've been so savage all this month, that's why I fought in the tavern, that's why I attacked my father. It was because I felt I was a thief. I couldn't make up my mind, I didn't dare even to tell Alyosha, my brother, about the fifteen hundred. I felt I was such a scoundrel and such a pickpocket. But, do you know, while I carried it I said to myself at the same time every hour: 'No, Dmitri, you are not yet a thief.' Why? Because I could go next day and pay back that fifteen hundred to Katerina. And only yesterday I made up my mind to tear this money off my neck, on my way from Fenya's to Perhotin. I hadn't been able till that moment to bring myself to do it. And it was only when I tore it off that I became a thief, a thief and a dishonest man for the rest of my life. Why? Because, with that I destroyed my dream of going to Katerina and saying: 'I'm a scoundrel, but not a thief!' Do you understand now? Do you understand?"

"What made you decide to do it yesterday?" Nicholas Nelyudov interrupted.

"Why? It's silly to ask. Because I had condemned myself to die at five o'clock this morning, here, at dawn. I thought it made no difference whether I died a thief or a man of honor. But I see it's not so, it turns out that it does make a difference. Believe me, gentlemen, what has tortured me most during this night has not been the thought that I'd killed old Gregory, and that I was in danger of Siberia just when my love was being rewarded, and Heaven was open to me again. Oh, that did torture me, but not in the same way; not so much as the damned consciousness that I had torn that damned money off my breast and spent it, and had become a thief! Oh, gentlemen, I tell you again, with a bleeding heart, I have learned a great deal this night. I have learned that it's not only impossible to live a scoundrel, but impossible to die a scoundrel. . . . No, gentlemen, one must die honest . . ."

Dmitri was pale. His face was haggard and exhausted, in spite of his being intensely excited.

"I am beginning to understand you," the prosecutor said slowly, in a soft and almost compassionate tone. "But all this, if you'll excuse my saying so, is a matter of nerves, in my opinion . . . You're overwrought, that's what it is. Why, for instance, should you not have saved yourself such misery for almost a month, by going and returning that fifteen hundred to the lady who had entrusted it to you? And why could you not have explained things to her, and in view of your position, which you describe as being so awful, why could you not have had recourse to the plan which would so naturally have occurred to one's mind, that is, after honorably confessing your errors to her, why could you not have asked her to lend you the sum you needed? She would certainly not have refused you, especially if it had been with some guarantee, or even on the security you offered to the merchant Samsonov, and to Madame Hohlakov. I suppose you still regard that security as of value?"

Dmitri suddenly crimsoned.

"Certainly you don't think I'm such an out and out scoundrel as that? You can't be in earnest?" he said, looking at the prosecutor straight in the face and seeming unable to believe his ears.

"I assure you I'm in earnest. . . . Why do you imagine I'm

452

not serious?" It was the prosecutor's turn to be surprised.

"Oh, how base that would have been! Gentlemen, do you know, you are torturing me! Let me tell you everything. I'll confess all if only to put you to shame, and you'll be surprised yourself at the depth to which human passions can sink. You must know that I already had that plan myself, that plan you spoke of, just now, prosecutor! Yes, gentlemen, I, too, have had that thought in my mind all this month, so that I was on the point of deciding to go to Katerina—I was low enough for that. But to go to her, to tell her of my treachery, and for that very treachery, to carry it out, for the expenses of that treachery, to beg for money from her, Katerina (to beg, do you hear, to beg), and to go straight from her and run away with Grushenka, who hated and insulted her—to think of it! You must be mad!"

"Mad I am not, but I did speak without thinking . . . of feminine jealousy . . . if there could be jealousy in this case, as you suggest . . . Yes, perhaps there is something of the kind," said the prosecutor, smiling.

"But that would have been infamous!" Dmitri brought his fist down on the table. "That would have been filthy! Yes, do you know that she might have given me that money. Yes she would have given it. She'd have given it to satisfy her vengeance, to show her contempt for me, for hers is an infernal nature. She's a woman of wrath. I'd have taken the money, too. Oh, I would have taken it. I would have taken it, and then, for the rest of my life . . . Oh, God! Forgive me, gentlemen, I'm making such an outcry because I've had that thought in my mind so much lately . . . Only the day before yesterday, that night when I was having all that trouble with Lyagavy, I mean Gorstkin . . . And afterwards yesterday, all day yesterday, I remember, till that happened . . ."

"Till what happened?" asked Nicholas Nelyudov. But Dmitri did not hear it.

"I have made an awful confession," Dmitri said gloomily in conclusion. "You must appreciate it, and what's more, you must respect it, for if not, if it leaves your souls untouched, then you've simply no respect for me, gentlemen. I tell you that. And I shall die of shame at having confessed to men like you! Oh, I shall kill myself! Yes, I see, I see already that you don't believe me. . . . What, you want to write that down, too?" he cried in dismay.

"Yes, what you said just now," said Nicholas Nelyudov, looking at him in surprise. "We want to record that up to the last hour you were still contemplating going to Katerina to beg that sum from her. . . . I assure you, that's a very important piece of evidence for us, I mean for the whole case . . . And particularly for you, particularly important for you."

"Have mercy, gentlemen!" Dmitri threw up his hands. "Don't write that down. Have some shame. Here I've torn my

453

heart apart before you, and you seize the opportunity and are fingering the wounds in both halves. . . . Oh, my God!"

In despair he hid his face in his hands.

"Don't worry so," said the prosecutor. "Everything that is written down will be read over to you afterwards, and what you don't agree to we'll alter as you like. But now I'll ask you one question for the second time. Has no one, absolutely no one, heard from you of that money you sewed up? That, I must tell you, is almost impossible to believe."

"No one. No one. I told you so before, or you've not understood anything! Let me alone!"

"All right, it's bound to be explained, and there's plenty of time for it. But meantime, consider; we have perhaps a dozen witnesses that say that you yourself spread it abroad and shouted everywhere about the three thousand you'd spent here. Three thousand, not fifteen hundred. And now, too, when you got hold of the money you had yesterday, you gave many people to understand that you had brought three thousand with you."

"You've got not dozens, but hundreds of witnesses. Two hundred witnesses. Two hundred have heard it, thousands have heard it!" cried Dmitri.

"Well, you see, all bear witness to it. And the word *all* means something."

"It means nothing. I talked rot, and everyone began repeating it."

"But what need had you to 'talk rot,' as you call it?"

"The devil knows. From bravado perhaps . . . at having wasted so much money. . . . To try and forget that money I had sewn up, perhaps . . . Yes, that was why . . . Damn it . . . How often are you going to ask me that question? Well, I told a lie, and that was the end of it. Once I'd said it, I didn't care to correct it. What does a man tell lies for sometimes?"

"It's very difficult to decide what makes a man tell lies," observed the prosecutor impressively.

"Tell me, though, was that 'little bag' as you call it, on your neck, a big thing?"

"No, not big."

"How big for instance?"

"If you fold a hundred rouble note in half, that would be the size."

"You'd better show it to us. You must have it somewhere."

"Damnation, what nonsense! I don't have it."

"But where and when did you take it off your neck? According to your own evidence you didn't go home."

"When I was going from Fenya's to Perhotin's, on the way I tore it off my neck and took out the money."

"In the dark?"

"What should I want a light for? I did it with my fingers in one minute."

454

"Without scissors, in the street?"

"In the market place I think it was. Why scissors? It was an old rag. It was torn in a minute."

"Where did you put it afterwards?"

"I dropped it there."

"Where exactly?"

"In the market place, in the market place! The devil knows where. What do you want to know for?"

"It's extremely important. It would be material evidence in your favor. How is it you don't understand that? Who helped you to sew it up a month ago?"

"No one helped me. I did it myself."

"Can you sew?"

"A soldier has to know how to sew. No great knowledge was needed to do that."

"Where did you get the material, that is, the rag in which you sewed the money?"

"Are you laughing at me?"

"Not at all. We are in no mood for laughing."

"I don't know where I got the rag from—somewhere I suppose."

"I should have thought you couldn't have forgotten it."

"I swear I don't remember. I might have torn a bit off my linen."

"That's very interesting. We might find in your lodgings tomorrow the shirt or whatever it is from which you tore the rag. What sort of rag was it, cotton or linen?"

"God only knows what it was. Wait a minute. . . . I believe I didn't tear it off anything. It was a piece of calico. . . . I believe I sewed it up in a cap of my landlady's."

"In your landlady's cap?"

"Yes, I took it from her."

"How did you get it?"

"You see, I remember once taking a cap for a rag, perhaps to wipe my pen on. I took it without asking, because it was a rag. I tore it up, and I took the money and sewed it up in it. I believe it was in that very rag I sewed it. An old piece of calico, washed a thousand times."

"And you remember that for certain now?"

"I don't know whether for certain. I think it was in the cap. But damn it, what does it matter?"

"In that case your landlady will remember that her cap was lost?"

"No, she won't. She didn't miss it. It was an old rag, I tell you, an old rag not worth anything."

"And where did you get the needle and thread?"

"I'll stop now. I won't say any more. Enough!" said Dmitri losing his temper.

"It's strange that you should have so completely forgotten where you threw the pieces in the market place."

455

"Give orders for the market place to be swept tomorrow, and perhaps you'll find it," said Dmitri, sneering. "Enough, gentlemen, enough!" he decided, in an exhausted voice. "I see you don't believe me! Not for a moment! It's my fault, not yours. I should not have been so willing. Why, why did I degrade myself by confessing my secret to you? It's a joke to you. I see that from your eyes. You led me on! Sing a hymn of triumph if you can. . . . Damn you, you torturers!"

He bent his head and hid his face in his hands. The lawyers were silent. A minute later he raised his head and looked at them almost vacantly. His face now expressed complete and hopeless despair. He sat mute and passive as though hardly conscious of what was happening.

In the meantime the lawyers had to finish the investigation. They had to begin examining the witnesses. It was now eight o'clock in the morning. The lights had been put out long ago. Michael Makarov and Kalganov, who had been in and out of the room all the time Dmitri was being questioned, had now both gone out again. The lawyers, too, looked very tired. It was a wretched morning, the whole sky was overcast, and rain streamed down in bucketfuls. Dmitri gazed blankly out of the window.

"May I look out of the window?" he asked Nicholas Nelyudov suddenly.

"Oh, certainly."

Dmitri got up and went to the window. The rain lashed against the little greenish panes. He could see the muddy road just below and further away, in the rainy mist, a row of poor, black, dismal huts, looking even blacker and poorer in the rain. Dmitri thought of "Phoebus the golden-haired," and how he had meant to shoot himself at his first ray. "Perhaps it would be even better on a morning like this," he thought with a smile, and suddenly he turned to his "torturers."

"Gentlemen," he cried, "I see that I am lost! But she? Tell me about her, I beg you. Surely she need not be ruined with me? She's innocent, you know. She was out of her mind when she cried last night 'It's all my fault!' She's done nothing, nothing! I've been worrying over her all night as I sat with you. . . . Can't you, won't you tell me what you are going to do with her now?"

"You can set your mind at rest," the prosecutor answered at once. "We have, so far, no grounds for interfering with the lady in whom you are so interested. I trust that it may be the same in the later development of the case. . . . On the contrary, we'll do everything that lies in our power in that matter. Set your mind completely at rest."

"Gentlemen, I thank you. I knew that you were honest, straightforward people in spite of everything. You've taken a load off my heart. . . . Well, what are we to do now? I'm ready."

"Well, we ought to hurry. We must examine the witnesses without delay. That must be done in your presence and therefore . . ."

"Shouldn't we have some tea first?" asked Nicholas Nelyudov. "I think we deserve it!"

They decided that if tea were ready downstairs they would have a glass and then "go on and on," putting off their breakfast until later. Tea was ready below, and was soon brought up. Dmitri at first refused the glass that Nicholas Nelyudov politely offered him, but afterwards he asked for it himself and drank it greedily. He looked exhausted. It might have been supposed from his herculean strength that one night of carousing, even accompanied by the most violent emotions, could have had little effect on him. But he could hardly hold his head up, and from time to time everything heaved and danced before his eyes. "A little more and I will begin raving," he said to himself.

8. The Evidence of the Witnesses. The Babe

THE EXAMINATION OF THE WITNESSES BEGAN. But it is not necessary to continue our story in such detail as before. And so I will not dwell on how Nicholas Nelyudov impressed on every witness that he must give his evidence in accordance with truth and conscience, and that he would afterwards have to repeat his evidence on oath, how every witness was called upon to sign the protocol of his evidence, and so on. I will only note that the principal point of the examination was the question of the three thousand roubles, that is, was the sum spent earlier, at Mokroe, by Dmitri on the first occasion, a month earlier, three thousand or fifteen hundred? And again had he spent three thousand or fifteen hundred yesterday? Alas, the evidence given by everyone turned against Dmitri. There was not one in his favor, and some witnesses introduced new, almost crushing facts, in contradiction of Dmitri's story.

The first witness examined was the innkeeper, Trifon Plastunov. He was not in the least abashed as he stood before the lawyers. He displayed, on the contrary, an air of stern and severe indignation toward the accused, which gave him an appearance of truthfulness and personal dignity. He spoke little, and with reserve, waited to be questioned, answered precisely and deliberately. Firmly and unhesitatingly he bore witness that the sum spent a month before could not have been less than three thousand, and that all the peasants about would testify that they had heard the sum of three thousand mentioned by Dmitri Karamazov himself. "What a lot of money he flung away on the gypsy girls alone. He wasted a thousand, I daresay, on them alone."

"I don't believe I gave them five hundred," was Dmitri's gloomy comment on this. "It's a pity I didn't count the money at the time, but I was drunk . . ."

Dmitri was sitting sideways with his back to the curtains. He listened with a melancholy and exhausted air, as though to say: "Oh, say what you like. It makes no difference now."

"More than a thousand went on them," repeated the innkeeper firmly, looking at Dmitri. "You flung it about at random and they picked it up. They were a thievish lot, horse-stealers. They've been driven away from here, or maybe they'd bear witness themselves as to how much they got from you. I saw the money in your hands, myself—count it I didn't, you didn't let me, that's true enough—but by the look of it I should say it was far more than fifteen hundred . . . fifteen hundred, indeed! We've seen money too. We can judge amounts . . ."

As for the sum spent yesterday he said that Dmitri had told him, as soon as he arrived, that he had brought three thousand with him.

"Is that really true, Trifon Plastunov?" asked Dmitri. "Surely I didn't say so definitely that I'd brought three thousand?"

"You did say so. You said it before Andrey. Andrey himself is still here. Send for him. And in the hall, when you were treating the chorus, you shouted straight out that you would leave your sixth thousand here—that is what you spent before, we must understand. Stephen and Simon heard it, and Peter Kalganov, too, was standing beside you at the time. Maybe he'd remember it . . ."

The evidence as to the "sixth" thousand made a deep impression on the two lawyers. They were pleased with this new way of counting, three and three made six, three thousand then and three now made six, that was clear.

They questioned all the peasants suggested by the innkeeper, Stephen and Simon and the driver Andrey. And they questioned Kalganov, too. The peasants and the driver confirmed Trifon Plastunov's evidence. They noted down, with particular care, Andrey's account of the conversation he had had with Dmitri on the road: " 'Where,' says he, 'am I, Dmitri Karamazov, going, to Heaven or to Hell, and shall I be forgiven in the next world or not?' "

The psychological Ippolit Kirillovitch heard this with a subtle smile, and ended by recommending that these remarks as to where Dmitri would go should be "included in the case."

Kalganov, when called, came in reluctantly, frowning and ill-humored, and he spoke to the lawyers as though he had never met them before in his life, although they were men whom he had been meeting every day for a long time past. He began by saying that "he knew nothing about it and didn't want to." But it appeared that he had heard of the "sixth" thousand, and he admitted that he had been standing close by at the moment. As far as he could see he "didn't know" how much money Dmitri had in his hands. He agreed that the Poles had cheated at cards. In reply to repeated questions he stated that, after the Poles had been turned out, Dmitri's position with Grushenka had improved, and that she had said that she loved him. He spoke of Grushenka with reserve and respect, as though she had been a lady of the best society. In spite of the young man's obvious dislike at giving evidence, Ippolit Kirillovitch examined him at great length, and learned from him all the details of what made up Dmitri's "romance," so to say, on that night. Dmitri did not once contradict Kalganov. At last they let the young man go, and he left the room with indignation.

The Poles, too, were examined. Though they had gone to bed in their room, they had not slept all night, and on the arrival of the police they dressed and got ready, realizing that they would certainly be sent for. They gave their evidence with dignity, though not without some uneasiness. The little Pole turned out to be a retired official of the twelfth class, who had served in Siberia as a veterinary surgeon. His name was Mussyalovitch. Vrublevsky turned out to be an unlicensed dentist. Although Nicholas Nelyudov asked them questions they both addressed their answers to Michael Makarov, who was standing on one side, taking him in their ignorance for the most important person and in command. They addressed him at every word as "Mr. Colonel." Only after several reproofs from Michael Makarov himself, did they grasp that they had to address their answers only to Nicholas Nelyudov. It turned out that they could speak Russian quite correctly except for their accent. Of his relations with Grushenka, past and present, Mussyalovitch spoke proudly and warmly, so that Dmitri was roused at once and declared that he would not allow the "scoundrel" to speak like that in his presence! Mussyalovitch called attention to the word "scoundrel," and begged that it should be put down in the record. Dmitri fumed with rage.

"He's a scoundrel! A scoundrel! You can put that down. And put down, too, that, in spite of everything I still declare that he's a scoundrel!" he cried.

Though Nicholas Nelyudov did insert this in the record, he showed the greatest tact. After reprimanding Dmitri, he cut short all further inquiry into the romantic aspect of the case, and passed to what was essential. One piece of evidence given by the Poles aroused special interest in the lawyers; that was how, in that very room, Dmitri had tried to buy off Mussyalovitch, and had offered him three thousand roubles, seven hundred roubles down, and the remaining two thousand three hundred "to be paid next day in town." Dmitri had sworn at the time that he did not have the whole sum with him at Mokroe, but that his money was in town. Dmitri said angrily that he had not said that he would be sure to pay the remainder next day in town. But Vrublevsky confirmed the statement and Dmitri, after thinking for a moment admitted, frowning, that it must have been as the Poles stated, that he had been excited at the time, and might have said so.

The prosecutor pounced on this piece of evidence. It seemed to establish for the prosecution (and they did, in fact, base this deduction on it) that half, or a part of, the three thousand that had come into Dmitri's hands might have been left hidden somewhere in the town, or even perhaps in Mokroe. This would explain the circumstance, so baffling for the prosecution, that only eight hundred roubles were found in Dmitri's hands. This circumstance had been the one piece of evidence which had hitherto been in Dmitri's favor. Now this one piece of evidence in his favor had broken down. In answer to the prosecutor's inquiry, where he would have gotten the remaining two thousand three hundred roubles, since he himself had denied having more than fifteen hundred, Dmitri confidently replied that he had meant to offer the "little man," not money, but a deed of conveyance of his rights to the village of Tchermashnya, the rights which he had already offered to Samsonov and Madame Hohlakov. The prosecutor smiled at the "innocence of this subterfuge."

"And you imagine that he would have accepted such a deed as a substitute for two thousand three hundred roubles in cash?"

"He certainly would have accepted it," Dmitri declared. "Why, he might have realized not two thousand, but four or six, for it. He would have put his lawyers, Poles and Jews, onto the job, and he might have gotten not three thousand but the whole property out of my father."

The evidence of Mussyalovitch was, of course, entered into the record in the fullest detail. Then they let the Poles go. The incident of the cheating at cards was hardly touched upon. Nicholas Nelyudov was well pleased with them and did not want to worry them with trifles. Moreover, it was nothing but a foolish, drunken quarrel over cards. There had been drinking and disorder enough, that night. . . . So the two hundred roubles remained in the pockets of the Poles.

Then old Maximov was summoned. He came in timidly, approached with little steps, looking very dishevelled and depressed. He had, all this time, taken refuge below with Grushenka, sitting dumbly beside her, and "now and then he'd begin blubbering over her and wiping his eyes with a handkerchief," as Michael Makarov described afterwards. Grushenka had tried to comfort him. Maximov at once confessed that he had done wrong, that he had borrowed "ten roubles in my poverty," from Dmitri, and that he was ready to pay it back. To Nicholas Nelyudov's direct question, had he noticed how much money Dmitri Karamazov held in his hand as he must have been able to see the sum better than anyone else when he took the money from him, Maximov, in the most positive manner, declared that there was twenty thousand.

"Have you ever seen as much as twenty thousand before?" inquired Nicholas Nelyudov with a smile.

"Yes I have. Not twenty, but seven, when my wife mortgaged my property. She'd only let me look at it from a distance. It was a very thick bundle, all rainbow-colored notes. And Dmitri's notes were all rainbow-colored . . ."

He was not kept long. At last it was Grushenka's turn. Nicholas Nelyudov was obviously nervous about the effect her appearance might have on Dmitri, and he muttered a few words of warning to him. Dmitri bowed his head in silence, giving him to understand "that he would not make a scene." Michael Makarov, himself, led Grushenka in. She entered with a stern and gloomy face that looked almost composed, and sat down quietly on the chair offered her by Nicholas Nelyudov. She was very pale, she seemed to be cold, and wrapped herself closely in her magnificent black shawl. She was suffering from a slight feverish chill—the first symptom of a long illness which followed that night. Her seriousness, her direct earnest look and quiet manner made a very favorable impression on everyone. Nicholas Nelyudov was even a little bit "fascinated." He admitted, when talking about it afterward, that only then had he seen "how handsome the woman was," for, though he had seen her several times before, he had always looked upon her as something of a "provincial hetaira." "She has the manners of our best society," he said later, gossiping about her in a circle of ladies. But this was received with indignation by the ladies, who immediately called him a "naughty man," to his great satisfaction.

As she entered the room, Grushenka only glanced at Dmitri, who looked at her uneasily. But her face reassured him at once. After the first inevitable inquiries and warnings, Nicholas Nelyudov asked her, hesitating a little but preserving the most courteous manner, on what terms she was with the retired lieutenant, Dmitri Karamazov.

To this Grushenka firmly and quietly replied: "He was an acquaintance. He came to see me as an acquaintance during the last month." To further questions she answered plainly and with complete frankness, that though "at times" she had thought him attractive, she had not loved him, but had won his heart as well as his old father's "in my nasty spite." She had seen that Dmitri was very jealous of his father and everyone else; but that had only amused her. She had never meant to go to Fyodor Karamazov, she had simply been laughing at him.

"I had no thoughts for either of them all this last month. I was expecting another man who had wronged me. But I think," she said in conclusion, "that there's no need for you to inquire

461

about that, nor for me to answer you, for that's my own affair."

Nicholas Nelyudov immediately acted upon this hint. He again dismissed the "romantic" aspect of the case and passed to the serious one, that is, to the question of most importance, concerning the three thousand roubles. Grushenka confirmed the statement that three thousand roubles had certainly been spent on the first party at Mokroe, and though she had not counted the money herself, she had heard that it was three thousand from Dmitri's own lips.

"Did he tell you that alone, or before someone else, or did you only hear him speak of it to others in your presence?" the prosecutor asked immediately.

Grushenka replied that she had heard him say so before other people, and had also heard him say so when they were alone.

"Did he say it to you alone once, or several times?" inquired the prosecutor, and learned that he had told Grushenka so several times.

Ippolit Kirillovitch was very well satisfied with this evidence. Further examination brought out the fact that Grushenka also knew where the money had come from, and that Dmitri had received it from Katerina.

"And did you ever hear that the money spent a month ago was not three thousand, but less, and that Dmitri Karamazov had saved half that sum for his own use?"

"No, I never heard that," answered Grushenka.

She explained further that Dmitri had, on the contrary, often told her that he didn't have a penny.

"He was always expecting to get some money from his father," said Grushenka in conclusion.

"Did he ever say before you . . . casually, or in a moment of irritation," Nicholas Nelyudov put in suddenly, "that he intended to make an attempt on his father's life?"

"Yes, he did say so," sighed Grushenka.

"Once or several times?"

"He mentioned it several times, always in anger."

"And did you believe he would do it?"

"No, I never believed it," she answered firmly. "I had faith in him."

"Gentlemen, allow me," cried Dmitri suddenly. "Allow me to say one word to her in your presence."

"You can speak."

"Grushenka!" Dmitri got up from his chair. "Have faith in God and in me. I am not guilty of my father's murder!"

Having spoken these words Dmitri sat down again. Grushenka stood up and crossed herself devoutly before the ikon.

"Thanks be to Thee, O Lord," she said, in a voice filled with emotion. Then still standing, she turned to Nicholas Nelyudov and added: "As he has spoken now, believe it! I know him. He'll say anything as a joke or from obstinacy, but he'll never deceive you against his conscience. He's telling the whole truth, you may believe it."

"Thank you, Grushenka, you've given me courage," Dmitri said in a quivering voice.

As to the money spent on the previous day, she declared that she did not know what sum it was, but had heard Dmitri tell several people that he had three thousand with him. And to the question where he got the money, she said that he had told her that he had "stolen" it from Katerina. She said that she had replied that he hadn't "stolen" it and that he must pay the money back next day. On the prosecutor's asking her emphatically whether the money he said he had stolen from Katerina was what he had spent yesterday, or what he had squandered a month ago, she declared that he meant the money spent a month ago; that was how she understood him.

Grushenka was at last released, and Nicholas Nelyudov told her impulsively that she might at once return to town and that if he could be of any assistance to her, with horses for example, or if she would care for an escort he ... would be ...

"I thank you sincerely," said Grushenka, bowing to him. "I'm going with this old gentleman. I am driving him back to town with me, and meanwhile, if you'll allow me, I'll wait downstairs to hear what you decide about Dmitri Karamazov."

She went out. Dmitri was calm and even looked more cheerful, but only for a moment. He felt more and more oppressed by a strange physical weakness. His eyes were closing with fatigue. The examination of the witnesses was at last over. They proceeded to a final revision of the record. Dmitri got up, moved from his chair to the corner by the curtain, lay down on a large chest covered with a rug and instantly fell asleep.

He had a strange dream, utterly out of keeping with the place and the time.

He dreamed he was driving somewhere in the steppes, where he had been stationed long ago. A peasant was driving him in a cart with a pair of horses, through snow and sleet. He was cold, it was early in November, and the snow was falling in big wet flakes, melting as soon as it touched the earth. And the peasant drove him smartly, he had a long blond beard. He was not an old man, somewhere around fifty, and he was wearing a gray smock. Not far off was a village. Dmitri could see the black huts. Half the huts were burned down, there were only charred beams left. And as they drove in, there were peasant women along the road, a lot of women, a whole row, all thin and wan, with their faces a sort of brownish color, especially one at the edge, a tall, bony woman, who looked forty, but might have been only twenty. In her arms was a crying baby. And her breasts seemed so dried up that there was not a drop of milk in them. And the child cried and cried, and held out its little bare arms, with its little fists blue from cold.

"Why are they crying? Why are they crying?" Dmitri asked, as they dashed by.

"It's the babe," answered the driver. "The babe is crying."

Dmitri was struck by his saying, in his peasant way, "the babe." He liked the peasant's calling it a "babe." There seemed more pity in it.

"But why is it crying?" Dmitri persisted stupidly. "Why are its little arms bare? Why don't they wrap it up?"

"The babe's cold. Its little clothes are frozen and don't warm it."

"But why is it? Why?" Dmitri still persisted.

"Why, they're poor people, burned out. They've no bread. They're begging because they've been burned out."

"No, no." Dmitri still did not understand. "Tell me why it is those poor mothers stand there? Why are people poor? Why is the babe poor? Why is the steppe barren? Why don't they hug each other and kiss? Why don't they sing songs of joy? Why are they so dark from black misery? Why don't they feed the babe?"

And he felt that, though his questions were unreasonable and senseless, yet he wanted to ask just that, and he had to ask it just in that way. And he felt that a passion of pity, such as he had never known before, was rising in his heart, that he wanted to cry, that he wanted to do something for them all, so that the babe should cry no more, so that the dark-faced, dried-up mother should not weep, that no one should shed tears again from that moment. He wanted to do all this at once, at once, regardless of obstacles, with the recklessness of the Karamazovs.

"And I'm coming with you. I won't leave you now for the rest of my life, I'm coming with you," he heard close beside him Grushenka's tender voice. And his heart glowed, and he struggled forward toward the light, and he longed to live, to live, to go on and on, toward the new, beckoning light, and to hurry, hurry now, at once!

"What! Where?" he exclaimed opening his eyes, and suddenly sitting up on the chest. Nicholas Nelyudov was standing over him, suggesting that he should hear the record read aloud and sign it. Dmitri thought that he had been asleep an hour or more. He did not hear Nicholas Nelyudov. He was suddenly struck by the fact that there had been a pillow under his head, which hadn't been there when he had leaned back, exhausted, on the chest.

"Who put that pillow under my head? Who was so kind?" he cried, with gratitude and tears in his voice, as though some great kindness had been shown him.

He never found out who this kind man was. Perhaps one of the peasant witnesses, or Nicholas Nelyudov's little secretary had compassionately thought to put a pillow under his head, but his whole soul was quivering with tears. He went to the table and said that he would sign whatever they liked.

"I've had a good dream, gentlemen," he said in a strange voice, with a new light, as of joy, in his face.

9. They Take Dmitri Away

When the record had been signed, Nicholas Nelyudov turned to Dmitri and read him the "Committal," setting forth that in such a year, on such a day, in such a place, the investigating lawyer of such-and-such a district court, having examined so-and-so (to wit, Dmitri) accused of this and of that (all the charges were carefully written out) and having considered that the accused, not pleading guilty to the charges made against him had brought forward nothing in his defense, while the witnesses, so-and-so, and so-and-so, and the circumstances such-and-such testify against him, acting in accordance with such-and-such articles of the Statute Book, and so on, has ruled, that, in order to preclude such-and-such (Dmitri) from all means of evading pursuit and judgment he be detained in such-and-such a prison, which he hereby notifies to the accused and communicates a copy of this same "Committal" to the deputy prosecutor, and so on, and so on.

In brief, Dmitri was informed that he was, from that moment, a prisoner, and that he would be driven at once to town, and there shut up in prison. Dmitri listened attentively and only shrugged his shoulders.

"Well, gentlemen, I don't blame you. I'm ready. . . . I understand that there's nothing else for you to do."

Nicholas Nelyudov informed him gently that he would be escorted at once by the rural police officer, Mavriky Schmertsov, who happened to be present. . . .

"Wait," Dmitri interrupted suddenly. Impelled by uncontrollable feeling he pronounced, addressing all in the room: "Gentlemen, we're all cruel, we're all monsters, we all make men weep, and mothers, and babes at the breast, but of all, let it be settled here, now, of all I am the lowest reptile! I've sworn to reform and every day I've done the same filthy things. I understand now that such men as I need a blow, a blow of destiny to catch them as with a noose, and bind them by a force from without. Never, never should I have risen of myself! But the thunderbolt has fallen. I accept the torture of accusation, and my public shame. I want to suffer because by suffering I shall be purified. Perhaps I shall be purified, gentlemen? But listen, for the last time, I am not guilty of my father's blood. I accept my punishment, not because I killed him, but because I meant to kill him, and perhaps I really might have

465

killed him. Still I mean to fight it out with you, I warn you of that. I'll fight it out with you to the end, and then God will decide. Good-by, gentlemen. Don't be angry with me for having shouted at you during the examination. Oh, I was still such a fool then. . . . In another minute I shall be a prisoner, but now, for the last time, as a free man, Dmitri Karamazov offers you his hand. Saying good-by to you, I say good-by to all men."

His voice quivered and he stretched out his hand, but Nicholas Nelyudov, who happened to stand nearest to him, with a sudden, almost nervous movement hid his hands behind his back. Dmitri saw this. He let his outstretched hand fall.

"The preliminary inquiry is not yet over," Nicholas Nelyudov faltered, somewhat embarrassed. "We will continue it in town, and I, for my part, of course, am ready to wish you all success . . . in your defense. As a matter of fact, I've always regarded you as more unfortunate than guilty. All of us here, if I may speak for all, are ready to recognize that you are basically a man of honor, but unfortunately one who has been carried away by certain passions."

Nicholas Nelyudov's little figure was positively majestic by the time he had finished speaking. It struck Dmitri that in another minute this "young man" would take his arm, lead him to a corner, and renew their conversation about "women." Many quite irrelevant and inappropriate thoughts occur to a prisoner even when he is being led out to execution.

"Gentlemen, you are good, you are humane. May I see *her* to say 'good-by' for the last time?" asked Dmitri.

"Certainly, but considering . . . In fact, now it's impossible except in the presence of . . ."

"Oh, well, if it must be so, it must!"

Grushenka was brought in, but the farewell was brief and did not at all satisfy Nicholas Nelyudov. Grushenka made a deep bow to Dmitri.

"I have told you I am yours, and I will be yours. I will follow you forever, wherever they may send you. Farewell. You are innocent, though you've been your own undoing."

Her lips quivered, tears flowed from her eyes.

"Forgive me, Grushenka, for my love—for ruining you with my love."

Dmitri wanted to say something more, but he broke off and went out. He was surrounded by men who kept a constant watch on him. At the bottom of the steps to which he had driven up with such a dash the night before, two carts stood waiting. Mavriky Schmertsov, a sturdy, thick-set man with a wrinkled face, was annoyed about something, some sudden irregularity. He was shouting. He asked Dmitri, with excessive surliness, to get into the cart.

"When I stood him drinks in the tavern, the man was quite different," thought Dmitri as he got in. At the gates there was a crowd of people, peasants, women and drivers. The innkeeper came down the steps too. All stared at Dmitri.

"Forgive me, good people!" Dmitri shouted suddenly from the cart.

"Forgive us too!" he heard two or three voices answer.

"Good-by to you, too, Trifon Plastunov!"

But the innkeeper did not even turn around. He was too busy. He was shouting and fussing about something. It appeared that everything was not yet ready in the second cart, in which two constables were to accompany Mavriky Schmertsov. The peasant who had been ordered to drive the second cart was pulling on the innkeeper's smock, stoutly maintaining that it was not his turn to go, but Akim's. But Akim was not to be seen. They ran to look for him. The peasant persisted and begged them to wait.

"You see what our peasants are, Mavriky Schmertsov. They've no shame!" exclaimed the innkeeper. "Akim gave you twenty-five cents the day before yesterday. You've drunk it all and now you cry out. . . . I'm surprised at your good nature with our low peasants, Mavriky Schmertsov, that's all I can say."

"But what do we need a second cart for?" Dmitri asked. "Let's start with one, Mavriky Schmertsov. I won't be unruly, I won't run away from you, old fellow. What do we want an escort for?"

"I'll ask you, sir, to learn how to speak to me. I'm not an 'old fellow' to you, and you can keep your advice for another time!" Mavriky Schmertsov snapped out, as though glad to vent his anger.

Dmitri was reduced to silence. He flushed all over. A moment later he felt suddenly very cold. The rain had stopped, but the dull sky was still overcast with clouds, and a sharp wind was blowing straight in his face.

"I'm chilled," thought Dmitri hunching his shoulders.

At last Mavriky Schmertsov got into the cart, sat down heavily, and as though without noticing it, squeezed Dmitri into the corner. It is true that he was out of humor and disliked the task that had been laid upon him.

"Good-by, Trifon Plastunov!" Dmitri shouted again. He felt himself, that he had not called out this time from good nature, but involuntarily, from resentment.

But the innkeeper stood proudly, with both hands behind his back, and staring straight at Dmitri made no reply.

"Good-by, Dmitri, good-by!" he suddenly heard the voice of Kalganov. Running up to the cart he held out his hand to Dmitri.

Dmitri had time to press his hand.

"Good-by! I won't forget your generosity," he cried warmly.

The cart moved and their hands parted. The bell began ringing and Dmitri was driven off.

Kalganov ran back, sat down in a corner, bent his head, hid his face in his hands and burst out crying. For a long time he sat like that, crying as though he were a little boy instead of a young man of twenty. Oh, he believed almost without doubt in Dmitri's guilt.

"What are these people? What can men be after this?" he asked incoherently, in bitter despondency, almost despair. At that moment he had no desire to live.

"Is it worth it? Is it worth it?" he exclaimed in his grief.

PART FOUR

BOOK X: THE BOYS

1. *Kolya Krassotkin*

IT WAS THE BEGINNING OF NOVEMBER. There had been a hard frost, and a little dry snow had fallen on the frozen ground during the night. A sharp dry wind was lifting and blowing it along the dreary streets, especially about the market place. It was a dull morning.

Not far from the market place, close to Plotnikov's shop, there stood a small house, very clean both without and within. It belonged to Madame Krassotkin, the widow of a former provincial secretary, who had been dead for fourteen years. She, still a nice-looking woman of thirty-two, was living in her neat little house on a small income. She lived in respectable seclusion: She was of a soft but fairly cheerful disposition. She was about eighteen at the time of her husband's death; she had been married only a year and had just borne him a son. From the day of his death she had devoted herself heart and soul to the bringing up of her precious treasure, her boy Kolya. Though she had loved him passionately those fourteen years, he had caused her far more suffering than happiness. She had been trembling and fainting with terror almost every day, afraid he would fall ill, would catch cold, do something naughty, climb on a chair and fall off and so on and so on.

When Kolya began going to school, Madame Krassotkin devoted herself to studying all his lessons so as to help him. She made the acquaintance of his teachers and their wives, even made friends with Kolya's schoolfellows. She cultivated them in the hope of saving Kolya from being teased, laughed at or beaten by them. She went so far that the boys actually began to make fun of Kolya and tease him about being a "mother's darling."

But Kolya could take his own part. He was a determined boy, "tremendously strong," as was rumored in his class. He was agile, strong-willed, and of an audacious and enterprising temper. He was good at his lessons, and there was a rumor in the school that he could beat the teacher, Dardanelov, at

arithmetic and history. Though he looked down upon everyone, he was a good companion and not supercilious. He accepted his schoolfellow's respect as his due, but was friendly
with them. Above all, he knew where to draw the line. He
could restrain himself on occasion and in his relations with
the teachers he never overstepped that last mystic limit beyond which a prank became an unpardonable breach of discipline. But he was as fond of mischief on every possible occasion as the smallest boy in the school, and not so much for
the sake of mischief as for creating a sensation, inventing
something, doing something effective and conspicuous. He was
extremely vain.

He knew how to make even his mother give way to him;
she had given way to him for years. The one thought unendurable to her was that her boy had no great love for her.
She was always thinking that Kolya was "unfeeling" to her,
and at times she dissolved into tears and reproached him for
his coldness. The boy disliked this, and the more demonstra-
tions of feeling that were demanded of him the more he
seemed to avoid them. Yet it was not intentional on his part
but instinctive—it was his character. His mother was mistaken; he was very fond of her. He only disliked "sheepish
sentimentality," as he expressed it in his schoolboy language.

There was a bookcase in the house containing a few books
that had been his father's. Kolya was fond of reading and
had read several of them. His mother did not mind that and
only wondered sometimes at seeing the boy stand for hours
by the bookcase poring over a book instead of going out to
play. And in that way Kolya read some things unsuitable for
his age.

Though the boy, as a rule, knew where to draw the line in
his mischief, he had of late begun to play pranks that caused
his mother serious concern. It is true there was nothing vicious
in what he did, only a wild recklessness.

It happened that July, during the summer holidays, that
Madame Krassotkin and Kolya went to another district, forty-
five miles away, to spend a week with a distant relative, whose
husband was an official at the railway station (the very station, the nearest one to our town, from which in August, a
month later, Ivan Karamazov set off for Moscow). There
Kolya began by carefully investigating every detail connected
with the railway, knowing that he could impress his schoolfellows when he got home with his newly acquired knowledge.
But there happened to be some other boys in the place, with
whom he soon made friends. Some of them were living at the
station, others in the neighborhood; there were six or seven of
them, all between twelve and fifteen, and two of them came
from our town. The boys played together, and on the fourth
or fifth day of Kolya's stay at the station, a bet was made.
Kolya, who was almost the youngest of the boys and looked

down upon, was moved by vanity or by reckless bravado to bet two roubles that he would lie down between the rails at night when the eleven o'clock train was due, and would lie there without moving while the train rolled over him at full speed. It is true they checked to see if it was possible to lie so flat between the rails that a train could pass over without touching, but even so to lie there was no joke! Kolya maintained that he would do this. At first they laughed at him, called him a liar, but that only egged him on. What annoyed him most was that these boys of fifteen turned up their noses at him and treated him like "a small boy," not fit to associate with them. This was an unendurable insult.

And so it was decided to go in the evening, half a mile from the station, so that the train might have time to get up full speed after leaving the station. The boys gathered. It was a pitch dark night without a moon. At the appointed time, Kolya lay down between the rails. The five others who had taken the bet waited among the bushes below the bank, their hearts beating with suspense. At last they heard in the distance the rumble of the train leaving the station. Two red lights gleamed out of the darkness; the monster roared as it approached.

"Run, run away from the rails," the boys cried to Kolya with terror. But it was too late; the train roared up and flew past. The boys rushed to Kolya. He lay without moving. They began pulling at him, lifting him up. He suddenly got up and walked away without a word. Then he explained that he had lain there only to frighten them. But the fact was he had lost consciousness, as he confessed long after to his mother. In this way Kolya's reputation as "a desperate character" was established forever. He returned home to the station as white as a sheet. Next day he had a slight fever, but he was in high spirits and well pleased with himself. The incident did not become known at once, but when he and his mother got back to town it was whispered about in the school and reached the ears of the masters. But Kolya's mother appealed to the masters on her boy's behalf, and in the end Dardanelov, a respected and influential teacher, exerted himself in Kolya's favor, and the incident was ignored.

Dardanelov was a middle-aged bachelor, who had been passionately in love with Madame Krassotkin for many years and had once, about a year before, ventured, trembling with fear and the delicacy of his sentiments, to offer her most respectfully his hand in marriage. But she refused him, feeling that to accept him would be an act of treachery to her son. But Dardanelov had reason for believing that he was not an object of aversion to the charming but too chaste and tenderhearted widow. Kolya's mad adventure seemed to have broken the ice, and Dardanelov was rewarded for his help by a suggestion of hope. The suggestion, it is true, was a faint one, but then Dardanelov was such a paragon of purity and delicacy that it was enough for the time being to make him perfectly happy.

Dardanelov was fond of Kolya, though he would have felt it beneath him to try and win him over, and was strict with him in class, Kolya, too, kept him at a respectful distance. He learned his lessons perfectly; he was second in his class. He was reserved with Dardanelov. And the whole class firmly believed that Kolya was so good at history that he could "beat" even Dardanelov. Kolya did in fact ask him the question: "Who founded Troy?" to which Dardanelov had made a very vague reply, referring to the movements and migrations of races, to the remoteness of the period, to the mythical legends. But the question: "Who had founded Troy?" that is, what individuals, he could not answer, and he seemed for some reason to regard the question as idle and frivolous. But the boys remained convinced that Dardanelov did not know who founded Troy. Kolya had read of the founders of Troy in Smaragdov, whose history was among the books in his father's bookcase. In the end all the boys became interested in the question, who it was that had founded Troy, but Kolya would not tell his secret, and his reputation for knowledge remained unshaken.

After the incident on the railway a certain change came over Kolya's attitude toward his mother. When Madame Krassotkin heard of what her son had done, she almost went out of her mind with horror. She had such terrible attacks of hysterics, lasting with intervals for several days that Kolya, seriously alarmed at last, promised on his honor that he would never do anything like it again. He swore on his knees before the holy image, and swore by the memory of his father. Then the "manly" Kolya burst into tears like a boy of six. And all that day the mother and son were constantly rushing into each other's arms sobbing. Next day Kolya woke up as "unfeeling" as before, but he had become more silent, more modest, sterner, and more thoughtful.

Six weeks later, it is true, he got into more trouble, which even brought his name to the ears of our Justice of the Peace. But this time it was trouble of quite another kind, amusing, foolish, and Kolya did not, as it turned out, take the leading part in it, but was only implicated in it. But of this later. His mother still worried and trembled, but the more uneasy she became, the greater were the hopes of Dardanelov. It must be noted that Kolya understood and guessed what was in Dardanelov's heart and, of course, despised him for his "feelings." Kolya had once been so tactless as to show this contempt before his mother, hinting vaguely that he knew what Dardanelov was after. But from the time of the railway incident his behavior in this respect also was changed. He did not allow himself the slightest allusion to the subject and began to speak more respectfully of Dardanelov before his mother, which the sensitive woman at once appreciated with boundless gratitude. And now at the slightest mention of Dardanelov by a visitor

472

in Kolya's presence, she would flush as pink as a rose. At such moments Kolya would either stare out of the window scowling, or would investigate the state of his boots, or would shout angrily for "Perezvon," a big, shaggy, mangy dog, which he had picked up a month before, brought home, and kept for some reason secretly indoors, not showing him to any of his schoolfellows. Kolya bullied this dog, teaching him all sorts of tricks, so that the poor dog howled for him whenever he was absent at school, and when he came in, whined with delight, rushed about as if he were crazy, begged, lay down on the ground pretending to be dead, and so on. In fact, the dog did all the tricks Kolya had taught him, not at the word of command, but simply from excitement and eagerness.

I have forgotten, by the way, to mention that Kolya Krassotkin was the boy stabbed with a penknife by Ilusha, already known to the reader as the son of Captain Snegiryov. Ilusha had been defending his father when the schoolboys jeered at him, shouting the nickname "wisp of tow."

2. Children

AND SO ON THAT FROSTY, SNOWY, AND WINDY DAY in November, Kolya Krassotkin was sitting at home. It was Sunday and there was no school. It had just struck eleven and he wanted to go out "on very urgent business," but he was alone in charge of the house. It so happened that all the adults were away owing to a sudden event. Madame Krassotkin had rented two little rooms, separated from the rest of the house by a hallway, to a doctor's wife with her two small children. This lady was the same age as Madame Krassotkin and a great friend of hers. Her husband, a doctor, had left her twelve months before, going first to Orenburg and then to Tashkend. For the last six months she had not heard a word from him. Had it not been for her friendship with Madame Krassotkin, which was some consolation to her, she would certainly have completely dissolved away in tears. And now, to add to her misfortunes, her only servant had suddenly announced the evening before that she was going to give birth to a child before morning. It seemed almost miraculous to everyone for no one had noticed the probability of it before. The astounded doctor's wife decided to move her maid while there was still time to an establishment in town kept by a midwife. As she valued her servant, she promptly carried out this plan and remained there looking after her. By morning all Madame Krassotkin's sympathy and energy were called upon to help in the case.

So both the ladies were away from home, the Krassotkins' servant had gone out to the market, and Kolya was thus left for a time to look after "the children," that is, the son and daughter of the doctor's wife. Kolya was not afraid of taking care of the house, besides he had Perezvon, who had been told to lie flat, without moving, under the bench in the hall. Every time Kolya, walking back and forth through the rooms, came into the hall, the dog shook his head and gave two loud taps on the floor with his tail, but the whistle did not sound to release him. Kolya only looked sternly at the dog. The one thing that troubled Kolya was "the children." He looked, of course, with the utmost scorn on the maid's unexpected adventure, but he was very fond of the children, and had already taken them a picture book. Nastya, the elder, a girl of eight, could read and Kostya, the boy, aged seven, was very fond of being read to by her. Kolya could, of course, have provided more diverting entertainment for them. He could have made them stand side by side and played soldiers with them, or he could have played hide-and-seek with them. He had done so before and was not above doing it, so much so that a report once spread at school that he played horses with the children, prancing with his head on one side like a trace-horse. But Kolya defended himself by pointing out that to play horses with boys of one's own age, boys of thirteen, would certainly be disgraceful, but that he did it for the sake of "the children" because he liked them. He said that no one had a right to tease him for his feelings. The two children adored him.

But on this day he was in no mood for games. He had very important business of his own to attend to, something almost mysterious. Meanwhile time was passing and his mother's maid, with whom he could have left the children, did not come back from market. He several times crossed the passage, opened the door of the lodgers' room and looked at the children who were sitting over the book. Every time he opened the door they grinned at him, hoping he would come in and would do something amusing. But Kolya was bothered and did not go in.

At last it struck eleven and he made up his mind, once and for all, that if that "damned" maid did not come back within ten minutes he would go out without waiting for her, making the children promise to be brave when he was away, not to be bad, not to cry. With this idea he put on his wadded winter overcoat with its catskin fur collar, slung his satchel round his shoulder and ignoring his mother's constant entreaties that he would always put on goloshes in cold weather, he crossed the hall and went out with only his boots on. Perezvon, seeing him in his outdoor clothes, began tapping vigorously on the floor with his tail. Twitching all over, he even uttered a plaintive whine. But Kolya, seeing his dog's passionate excitement, decided that it was a breach of discipline, kept him for another minute under the bench, and only when he had opened
474

the door into the passage did he whistle for him. The dog leapt up like a mad creature and rushed before him.

Kolya opened the door to look in at the children. They were both sitting as before, not reading but arguing about something. The children often argued together and Nastya, being the elder, always got the best of it. If Kostya did not agree with her, he almost always appealed to Kolya and his verdict was regarded as infallible by both of them. This time the children's discussion rather interested Kolya and he stood in the hallway listening. The children saw he was listening and that made them argue all the more.

"I shall never, never believe," Nastya said, "that old women find babies among the cabbages in the kitchen garden. It's winter now and there are no cabbages, and so the old woman couldn't have brought our maid a daughter."

Kolya whistled to himself.

"Perhaps they do bring babies from somewhere, but only to those who are married."

Kostya stared at Nastya and listened.

"Nastya, how silly you are," he said at last, firmly and calmly. "How can our maid have a baby when she isn't married?"

Nastya was exasperated.

"You know nothing about it," she snapped irritably. "Perhaps she has a husband, only he is in prison, so now she's got a baby."

"But is her husband in prison?" the matter-of-fact Kostya inquired gravely.

"Or, I tell you what," Nastya interrupted impulsively, completely rejecting and forgetting what she had said before. "She hasn't a husband, you are right, but she wants to be married, and so she's been thinking of getting married, and thinking and thinking of it till now she's got it, that is, not a husband but a baby."

"Well, maybe you're right," Kostya agreed, entirely vanquished. "But you didn't say so before. So how could I tell?"

"Come, children," said Kolya, coming into the room. "You're terrible people, I see."

"And Perezvon is with you!" grinned Kostya. He began snapping his fingers and calling Perezvon.

"I am in trouble," Kolya began solemnly. "You must help me. My mother's maid who went to market must have broken her leg, since she has not turned up. I must go out. Will you let me go?"

The children looked anxiously at one another. Their smiling faces showed signs of uneasiness, but they did not yet fully grasp what was expected of them.

"You won't be naughty while I am gone? You won't climb on the cupboard and fall down? You won't be frightened and cry?"

A look of sadness came into the children's faces.

"I will show you something as a reward, a little copper cannon which can be fired with real gunpowder."

The children's faces brightened. "Show us the cannon," said Kostya, beaming all over.

Kolya put his hand in his satchel, and pulling out a little bronze cannon stood it on the table.

"Look, it's on wheels." He rolled the toy along on the table. "And it can be fired off, too. It can be loaded with shot and fired off."

"And could it kill anyone?"

"It can kill someone. You've only got to aim it at someone." And Kolya explained where the powder had to be put, where the shot should be rolled in, showed a tiny hole like a touch hole, and told them that it kicked when it was fired.

The children listened with interest. What struck their imagination was that the cannon kicked.

"And have you got any powder?" Nastya asked.

"Yes."

"Show us the powder," she said with a smile.

Kolya dived again into his satchel and pulled out a small bottle containing real gunpowder. He had some shot, too, in a screw of paper. He even uncorked the bottle and shook a little powder into the palm of his hand.

"One has to be careful there's no fire around, or it would blow up and kill us all," Kolya warned them.

The children looked at the powder with alarm that only intensified their enjoyment. Kostya also liked the shot.

"And does the shot burn?" he inquired.

"No, it doesn't."

"Give me a little shot," he asked in an imploring voice.

"I'll give you a little shot. Here, take it. But don't show it to your mother till I come back, or she'll be sure to think it's gunpowder, and will die of fright and spank you."

"Mother never spanks us," Nastya observed at once.

"I know, I only said it to finish the sentence. And don't you ever deceive your mother except just this once, until I come back. And so, can I go out? You won't be frightened and cry when I'm gone?"

"We sha-all cry," drawled Kostya, on the verge of tears already.

"We'll cry, we will be sure to cry," Nastya chimed in.

"Oh, children, children, how fraught with peril are your years! There's no help for it, chickens, I will have to stay with you I don't know how long. And time is passing, time is passing!"

"Tell Perezvon to pretend to be dead!" Kostya begged.

"All right. Here, Perezvon." And Kolya began giving orders to the dog, who performed all his tricks.

Perezvon was a rough-haired dog, of medium size, with a

476

coat of a sort of lilac-gray. He was blind in his right eye, and his left ear was torn. He whined and jumped, stood and walked on his hind legs, lay on his back with his paws in the air, rigid as though he were dead. While this last performance was going on, the door was opened and the maid, Madame Krassotkin's servant, a stout woman of forty, marked with smallpox, appeared in the doorway. She had come back from market and had a bag full of provisions in her hand. Holding up the bag of provisions in her left hand she stood still to watch the dog. Though Kolya had been so anxious for her return, he did not cut short the performance, and after keeping Perezvon dead for the usual time, at last whistled to him. The dog jumped up and began bounding about in his joy at having done his duty.

"Only think, a dog!" the maid observed.

"Why are you late, female?" asked Kolya.

"Female, indeed! Go on with you, you brat."

"Brat?"

"Yes, a brat. What is it to you if I'm late? If I'm late, you may be sure I have good reason," muttered the maid, busying herself about the stove, without a trace of anger or displeasure in her voice. She seemed quite pleased, in fact, at the skirmish with her young master.

"Listen, you frivolous old woman," Kolya began, getting up from the sofa, "can you swear by all you hold sacred in the world and something else besides, that you will watch over the children while I'm gone? I am going out."

"And what am I going to swear for?" laughed the maid. "I'll look after them without that."

"No, you must swear on your eternal salvation. Otherwise I won't go."

"Well, don't then. What does it matter to me? It's cold out. Stay at home."

"Children," Kolya turned to the children. "This woman will stay with you till I come back or till your mother comes, for she ought to have been back long ago. She will give you some lunch, too. You'll give them something to eat, won't you?"

"That I can do."

"Good-by, chickens, I go with my heart at rest. And you, granny," he added gravely, in an undertone, as he passed the maid, "I hope you'll spare their tender years and not tell them any of your old woman's nonsense about how babies are born. Here, Perezvon!"

"Get along with you!" answered the maid really angry this time. "Ridiculous boy! You want a whipping for saying such things, that's what you want!"

3. The Schoolboy

But Kolya did not hear her. At last he could go out. As he went out he looked around him, shrugged his shoulders, and saying: "It is freezing," went straight along the street and turned off to the right toward the market place. When he reached the last house but one before the market place he stopped at the gate, pulled a whistle out of his pocket, and whistled with all his might as though giving a signal. He did not wait more than a minute before a boy of about eleven, wearing a warm, neat coat, ran out to meet him. This was Smurov, a boy in the preparatory class (two classes below Kolya Krassotkin), son of a well-to-do official. He was forbidden by his parents to associate with Kolya, who was always getting into trouble, so he was slipping out on the sly. He was—as the reader will remember—one of the group of boys who two months before had thrown stones at Ilusha, the little son of Captain Snegiryov. He was the one who told Alyosha Karamazov about Ilusha.

"I've been waiting for you for the last hour, Kolya," said Smurov as they walked toward the market place.

"I am late," answered Kolya. "I was held up. You won't be beaten for coming with me?"

"I'm never beaten! And you've got Perezvon with you?"

"Yes."

"You're taking him, too?"

"Yes."

"Ah! If it were only Zhutchka!"

"That's impossible. Zhutchka's nonexistent. Zhutchka is lost."

"Ah! couldn't we do this?" Smurov suddenly stood still. "You see Ilusha says that Zhutchka was a shaggy, grayish, smoky-looking dog like Perezvon. Couldn't you tell him this is Zhutchka, and he might believe you?"

"Boy, shun a lie, even with a good object. Above all, I hope you've said nothing about my coming."

"No! I know what I am doing. But you won't comfort him with Perezvon," said Smurov, with a sigh. "You know his father, the captain, 'the wisp of tow,' told us that he was going to bring him a real mastiff pup, with a black nose, today. He thinks that would comfort Ilusha; but I doubt it."

"And how is Ilusha?"

"Oh, he is bad, very bad! I think he has consumption; he is conscious, but his breathing! His breathing's gone wrong. The other day he asked for his boots. He tried to walk, but he couldn't stand. 'Ah, I told you before, father,' he said, 'that those boots are no good. I could never walk properly in them.' He thought it was his boots that made him stagger, but it was really weakness. He won't live another week. Doctor Herzenstube is looking after him. Now they are rich again—they've got heaps of money."

"They are fakes."

"Who are fakes?"

"Doctors and the whole crew of quacks. I don't believe in medicine. It's useless. I mean to go into all that. But what's going on up there? The whole class seems to be at Ilusha's every day."

"Not the whole class: it's only ten of us who go to see him every day. There's nothing in that."

"What I don't understand in all this is the part Alexey Karamazov is taking in it. His brother, Dmitri, is going to be tried tomorrow or next day for murder, and yet he has time to spend with you boys."

"There's nothing to it. You are going yourself now to make up with Ilusha."

"Make up with him? What an idea! I allow no one to question my actions."

"And how pleased Ilusha will be to see you! He has no idea that you are coming. Why was it, why was it you wouldn't come all this time?" Smurov asked.

"That's my business, not yours. I am going because I want to, but you've all been hauled there by Alexey Karamazov—there's a difference, you know. And how do you know? I may not be going to make up with Ilusha at all."

"It's not Karamazov at all; it's not his doing. We boys began going there by ourselves. Of course, we went with Karamazov at first. And there's been nothing of that sort—no silliness. First one went, and then another. His father was awfully pleased to see us. You know he will go out of his mind if Ilusha dies. He sees that Ilusha's dying. And he seems so glad we've made up with Ilusha. Ilusha asked after you, that was all. He just asks and says no more. His father will go out of his mind or hang himself. He behaved like a madman before. You know he is a very nice man. We made a mistake teasing Ilusha. It's all the fault of that murderer, Dmitri Karamazov, who pulled Ilusha's father by the beard that day."

"Alexey Karamazov's a riddle to me all the same. I might have spoken to him long ago, but I have pride. Besides I have a theory about him."

Kolya was then silent. Smurov, too, was silent. Smurov, of course, worshiped Kolya and never dreamed of putting himself on a level with him. Now he was tremendously interested at Kolya's saying that he was "going of himself" to see Ilusha. He felt that there must be some mystery in Kolya's suddenly taking it into his head to go to him that day. They crossed the market place. At that hour there were many loaded wagons from the country and live poultry all about. The market women were selling rolls, cottons and threads, etc., in their booths. These Sunday markets were called "fairs" in our town, and there were many such fairs during the year.

Perezvon ran about in the wildest spirits, sniffling at one side, then the other. When he met other dogs they smelt each other over.

"I like to watch that, Smurov," said Kolya suddenly. "Have you noticed how dogs sniff at one another when they meet? It seems to be their nature."

"Yes; it's a funny habit."

"No, it's not funny; you are wrong there. There's nothing funny in nature, however funny it may seem to man. If dogs could reason and criticize us they'd be sure to find just as much that would be funny to them, if not far more, in the social relations of men, their masters—far more, I think. I am convinced that there is far more foolishness among us. That's Rakitin's idea—you know Rakitin the divinity student. . . . I am a Socialist, Smurov."

"What is a Socialist?" asked Smurov.

"That's when all are equal and all have property in common, there are no marriages, and everyone has any religion and laws he likes best. You are not old enough to understand that yet. . . . It's cold today."

"Yes, it's freezing. Father just looked at the thermometer."

"Have you noticed, Smurov, that in the middle of winter we don't feel so cold even when there are fifteen or eighteen degrees below zero as we do now, in the beginning of winter, when there is a sudden frost, especially when there is not much snow. It's because people are not used to it. Everything is habit with men, everything even in their social and political relations. Habit is the great motive power. . . . What a funny-looking peasant!"

Kolya pointed to a tall peasant, with a good-natured face. He was wearing a long sheepskin coat and was standing by his wagon, clapping together his hands to warm them. His long blond beard was all white with frost.

"That peasant's beard's frozen," Kolya cried in a loud voice as he passed him.

"Lots of people's beards are frozen," the peasant replied calmly.

"Don't provoke him," observed Smurov.

"It's all right; he won't be cross; he's a nice fellow. Good-bye, Matvey."

"Good-bye."

"Is your name Matvey?"

"Yes. Didn't you know?"

"No, I didn't. I guessed it."

"You don't say so! You are a schoolboy, I suppose?"

"Yes."

"You get whipped, I expect?"

"Nothing to speak of—sometimes."

"Does it hurt?"

"Well, yes, it does."

"Ah, what a life!" The peasant heaved a sigh from the bottom of his heart.

"Good-bye, Matvey."

"Good-bye. You are a nice boy, that you are."

The boys went on.

"That was a nice peasant," Kolya observed to Smurov. "I like talking to the peasants."

"Why did you lie, pretending we get whipped?" asked Smurov.

"I had to say that to please him."

"What do you mean?"

"You know, Smurov, I don't like being asked the same thing twice. I like people to understand the first time. Some things can't be explained. According to a peasant's notions, schoolboys are whipped, and must be whipped. What would a schoolboy be, if he were not whipped? And if I were to tell him we are not, he'd be disappointed. But you don't understand that. One has to know how to talk to peasants."

"Only don't tease them, please, or you'll get into trouble as you did about that goose."

"So you're afraid?"

"Don't laugh, Kolya. Of course, I'm afraid. My father would be awfully cross. I am forbidden to go out with you."

"Don't be uneasy, nothing will happen this time. Hullo, Natasha!" he shouted to a market woman in one of the booths.

"Call me Natasha! What next! My name is Mary," the middle-aged market woman shouted at him.

"I am so glad it's Mary. Good-bye!"

"Ah, you young rascal! A brat like you!"

"I'm in a hurry. I can't stay now. You'll have to tell me next Sunday." Kolya waved his hand at her, as though she had attacked him and he were innocent.

"I've nothing to tell you next Sunday. You started this, you ape! I didn't say anything," bawled Mary. "You want a whipping, that's what you want!"

There was a roar of laughter among the other market women. Suddenly a man in a violent rage darted out from the arcade of shops close by. He was a young man, not a native of our town, with dark, curly hair and a long, pale face, marked with smallpox. He wore a long blue coat and a peaked cap, and looked like a merchant's clerk. He brandished his fist at Kolya.

"I know you," he cried angrily. "I know you!"

Kolya stared at him. He could not recall when he could have had a row with the man. But he had been in so many rows in the street that he could hardly remember them all.

"Do you?" he asked sarcastically.

"I know you! I know you!" the man repeated.

"So much the better for you. Well, it's time I was going. Good-bye!"

"You are making trouble again?" cried the man. "You are looking for trouble? I know, you are at it again!"

"It's none of your business, brother, if I am looking for trouble again," said Kolya, standing still and looking boldly at him.

"Not my business?"

"No. It's not your business."

"Whose then? Whose then? Whose then?"

"It's Nikititch's business, not yours."

"What Nikititch?" asked the man staring with amazement at Kolya, but still angry as ever.

Kolya stared at him.

"Have you been to the Church of the Ascension?" he suddenly asked him with stern emphasis.

"What Church of Ascension? What for? No, I haven't," said the young man, somewhat taken aback.

"Do you know Sabaneyev?" Kolya went on even more emphatically and even more severely.

"What Sabaneyev? No, I don't know him."

"Well, then you can go to the devil," said Kolya, cutting short the conversation, and turning he strode quickly on his way as though he disdained further conversation with a fool who did not even know Sabaneyev.

"Stop, hey! What Sabaneyev?" The young man recovered from his momentary stupefaction and was as excited as before. "What did he say?" He turned to the market women with a silly stare.

The women laughed.

"You can never tell what he's after," said one of them.

"What Sabaneyev is it he's talking about?" the young man repeated, still furious.

"It must be a Sabaneyev who worked for the Kuzmitchovs, that's who it must be," one of the women suggested.

The young man stared at her.

"For the Kuzmitchovs?" repeated another woman. "No, that's another man."

"His name is not Sabaneyev, it's Tchizhov," put in a third woman, who had been silent, "Tchizhov is his name. Tchizhov."

"Not a doubt about it, it's Tchizhov," a fourth woman emphatically confirmed the statement.

The bewildered young man gazed from one to another.

"But what did he ask for, what did he ask for, good people?" he cried almost in desperation. " 'Do you know Sabaneyev?' says he. And who the devil's to know who is Sabaneyev?"

482

"You're a foolish fellow. I tell you it's not Sabaneyev, but Tchizhov. Tchizhov, that's who it is!" one of the women shouted at him.

"Tchizhov? Who is he? Tell me, if you know."

"That tall, sniveling fellow who used to sit in the market in the summer."

"And what has your Tchizhov to do with me, good people, eh?"

"How can I tell what he has to do with you?" put in another. "You ought to know yourself what you want with him, if you make such a fuss about him. He spoke to you, he didn't speak to us, stupid. Don't you really know him?"

"Know whom?"

"Tchizhov."

"The devil take Tchizhov and you with him. I'll give him a beating, I will. He was laughing at me!"

"Will give Tchizhov a beating? He will give you one! You are a fool, that's what you are!"

"Not Tchizhov, not Tchizhov, you spiteful woman. I'll give that boy a beating. Catch him, catch him, he was laughing at me!"

The women roared with laughter. But Kolya was by now a long way off, marching along with a triumphant air. Smurov walked beside him, looking round at the shouting group far behind. He, too, was in high spirits, though he was still afraid of getting into some trouble in Kolya's company.

"What Sabaneyev did you mean?" he asked Kolya, foreseeing what his answer would be.

"How do I know? Now there'll be a hubbub among them all day. I like to stir up fools. There's another blockhead, that peasant there. You know, they say 'there's no one more stupid than a stupid Frenchman.' But a stupid Russian shows it in his face just as much. Can't you see by his face that he is a fool, that peasant?"

"Let him alone, Kolya. Let's go on."

"Nothing can stop me, now that I've started. Hey, good morning, peasant!"

A sturdy-looking peasant, with a round, simple face, and grizzled beard, who was walking by, raised his head and looked at the boy. He was not quite sober.

"Good morning, if you are not laughing at me," he said deliberately in reply.

"And if I am?" laughed Kolya.

"Well, a joke's a joke. Laugh away. I don't mind. There's no harm in a joke."

"I beg your pardon, brother, it was a joke."

"Well, God forgive you!"

"Do you forgive me, too?"

"I forgive you. Go along."

"You seem a clever peasant."

"More clever than you," the peasant answered unexpectedly with the same seriousness.

"I doubt it," said Kolya, somewhat taken aback.

"It's true though."

"Perhaps it is."

"It is, brother."

"Good-bye, peasant!"

"Good-bye!"

"There are all sorts of peasants," Kolya observed to Smurov, after a brief silence. "How could I tell I had hit on a clever one."

In the distance the cathedral clock struck half-past eleven. The boys hurried on. They walked as far as Captain Snegiryov's place, a considerable distance, quickly and almost in silence. Twenty yards from the house Kolya suddenly stopped. He told Smurov to go on ahead and ask Alexey Karamazov to come out.

"One must sniff around a bit first," he observed to Smurov.

"Why ask him to come out?" Smurov protested. "You go in. They will be awfully glad to see you. What's the sense of making friends in the cold out here?"

"I know why I want to see him out here in the cold," Kolya cut him short in the despotic tone he was fond of adopting with "small boys." Smurov ran to do as he had asked.

4. *The Lost Dog*

KOLYA LEANED AGAINST THE FENCE waiting for Alyosha to appear. Yes, he had long wanted to meet him. He had heard a great deal about him from the boys, but he had always pretended indifference when Alyosha was mentioned, and he had even "criticized" what he heard about Alyosha. But secretly he had a great longing to meet him; there was something attractive in all he had been told about Alyosha. So the coming moment was important; to begin with, he wanted to show himself at his best, to show his independence. "Or, he'll think of me as thirteen and take me for a boy, like the rest of them. And what are these boys to him? I shall ask him when I get to know him. It's a pity I am so short. Tuzikov is younger than I am, yet he is half a head taller. But I have a clever face. I am not good looking. I know I'm hideous, but I've a clever face. I mustn't talk too much; if I am too friendly all at once, he may think . . . How horrible if he should think . . . !"

Such were the thoughts that excited Kolya while he was trying to assume an independent air. What distressed him most was his being so short; he did not mind so much his "hideous" face, as being so short. On the wall in a corner at home he had the year before made a pencil mark to show his height, and every two months since, he measured himself against it to see how much he had gained. But he grew very slowly, and this sometimes reduced him almost to despair.

His face was by no means "hideous"; on the contrary, it was rather attractive, with a fair, freckled, pale skin. His small, lively gray eyes had a fearless look, and often glowed with feeling. He had rather high cheek bones; small, very red, but very thick, lips. His nose was small and unmistakably turned up. "I've a regular pug nose, a regular pug nose," Kolya used to mutter to himself when he looked in the looking glass. "And perhaps I haven't got a clever face?" he sometimes thought, doubtful even of that. But it must not be supposed that his mind was preoccupied with his face and his height. On the contrary, however bitter the moments before the looking glass were to him, he quickly forgot them, and forgot them for a long time, "abandoning himself entirely to ideas and to real life," as he formulated it to himself.

Alyosha came out quickly and went up to Kolya. Kolya could see that he was delighted. "Can he be so glad to see me?" Kolya wondered, feeling pleased. We may note here that Alyosha's appearance had undergone a complete change since we saw him last. He had abandoned his cassock and was now wearing a well-cut coat, a soft round hat, and his hair cropped short. All this was very becoming and he looked quite handsome. His charming face always had a good-humored expression; but there was a gentleness and serenity in his good humor.

To Kolya's surprise, Alyosha came out to him just as he was, without an overcoat. He had evidently come without delay. He held out his hand to Kolya.

"Here you are at last! How anxious I've been to see you!"

"There were reasons why I didn't come. Anyway, I am glad to see you. I've been hoping to see you for a long time. I've heard a great deal about you," Kolya muttered, a little breathless.

"We were bound to meet. I've heard a great deal about you, too. But you've been a long time coming here."

"Tell me, how are things going?"

"Ilusha is very ill. He is dying."

"How awful! You must admit that medicine is a fraud, Karamazov," cried Kolya warmly.

"Ilusha has mentioned you often, very often, even in his sleep, in delirium, you know. One can see that you used to be very, very dear to him . . . before the incident . . . with the knife . . . Then there's another reason. . . . Tell me, is that your dog?"

"Yes, Perezvon."

"Not Zhutchka?" Alyosha looked at Kolya with eyes full of pity. "Is she lost forever?"

"I know you would all like it to be Zhutchka. I've heard all about it." Kolya smiled mysteriously. "Listen, Karamazov, I'll tell you all about it. That's what I came for; that's what I asked you to come out here for, to explain the whole thing to you before I go in. You see, Karamazov, Ilusha came into the preparatory class last spring. Well, you know what our preparatory class is—a lot of small boys. They began teasing Ilusha at once. I am two classes higher up, and, of course, I only look on at them from a distance. I saw the boy was weak and small, but he wouldn't give in to them; he fought with them. I saw he was proud, and his eyes were full of fire. I like boys like that. And they teased him all the more. The worst of it was he was horribly dressed at the time, his suit was too small for him, and there were holes in his boots. They teased him about it; they laughed at him. I can't stand that. I stood up for him and gave it to them. I beat them, but they adore me, do you know, Karamazov?" Kolya boasted impulsively. "But I am fond of children. I've two chickens on my hands at home now—that's what detained me. So they left off beating Ilusha and I took him under my protection. I saw the boy was proud. I tell you that, the boy was proud. In the end he became slavishly devoted to me; he obeyed me as though I were God, tried to copy me. In the intervals between the classes he used to run to me and I'd go about with him. On Sundays, too. They always laugh when an older boy makes friends with a younger one like that; but that's foolish. I am teaching him, developing him. Why shouldn't I develop him if I like him? Here you, Karamazov, have made friends with all these nestlings. I see you want to influence the younger generation—to develop them, to be of use to them, and I assure you this trait in your character, which I knew by hearsay, attracted me more than anything. Let us get to the point, though. I noticed that there was a sort of softness and sentimentality coming over Ilusha and you know I have a hatred of this sort of thing. I have had it from babyhood. There were contradictions in him, too; he was proud, but he was slavishly devoted to me, and yet all at once his eyes would flash and he'd refuse to agree with me; he'd argue, fly into a rage. I sometimes presented certain ideas; I could see that it was not so much that he disagreed with the ideas, but that he was simply rebelling against me, because I was cool toward him. And so, in order to train him properly, the more tender he was, the colder I became. I did it on purpose; that was my idea. My object was to form his character, to lick him into shape, to make a man of him . . . and besides . . . You understand me.

"Suddenly I noticed for three days in succession that Ilusha was downcast and depressed, not because of my coldness, but because of something else, something more important. I wondered what it was. I pumped him and found out that he had somehow gotten to know Smerdyakov, who was cook and valet to your late father—it was before his death, of course—and he taught the little fool a silly trick—that is, a brutal, nasty trick. He told Ilusha to take a piece of bread, to stick a pin in it, and throw it to one of those hungry dogs who snap up anything without biting it, and then to watch and see what would happen. So Ilusha prepared a piece of bread like that and threw it to Zhutchka, that shaggy dog there's been such a fuss about. The people of the house it belonged to never fed it at all, though it barked all day. So it rushed at the bread, swallowed it, and began to squeal. It turned round and round and ran away, squealing as it ran out of sight. That is what Ilusha told me. He confessed it to me, and cried. He hugged me, shaking all over. He kept on repeating: 'He ran away squealing.' The sight of it haunted him. He was tormented by remorse, I could see that. I took it seriously. I decided to give him a lesson for other things as well. So I pretended to be more indignant than I was. 'You've done a nasty thing,' I said. 'You are mean. I won't tell anyone, but I will have nothing more to do with you for a time. I'll think it over and let you know through Smurov (that's the boy who's just come with me; he's always ready to do anything for me) whether I will have anything to do with you in the future or whether I'll give you up for good.' He was terribly upset. I felt I'd gone too far but there was no going back. I did what I thought best at the time. A day or two later, I sent Smurov to tell him to go to 'Coventry,' That's what we call it when two boys refuse to have anything more to do with one another. Secretly I only meant to send him to 'Coventry' for a few days and then, if I saw signs of repentance, to hold out my hand to him again. That was my intention. But what do you think happened? 'Tell Kolya from me,' he cried, 'that I will throw bread with pins to all the dogs—all—all of them!'

He was going in for a little temper. I decided to smoke it out of him. I began to treat him with contempt; whenever I met him I turned away or smiled sarcastically. And just then that incident with his father happened. You remember? You must realize that he was terribly worked up by what had happened already. The boys, seeing I'd given him up, turned on him and teased him, shouting: 'Wisp of tow, wisp of tow!' And he had regular fights with them. They seem to have given him one very bad beating. One day he flew at them all as they were coming out of school. I stood a few yards off, looking on. And, I swear, I don't remember that I laughed; it was quite the other way. I felt awfully sorry for him. In another minute I would have run up to take his part. But he suddenly met my eyes. I don't know what he thought but he pulled out a penknife, rushed at me, and struck at my thigh, here in my right leg. I didn't move. I don't mind saying I am brave sometimes, Karamazov. I simply looked at him contemptuously, as though to say: 'This is how you repay all my kindness! Do it again, if you like.' But he didn't stab me again; he broke down. He was frightened at what he had done. He threw away the knife, burst out crying, and ran away. I did not report him, of course, and I made the other boys all keep quiet, so it wouldn't come to the ears of the masters. I didn't even tell my mother till it had healed up. . . . And then I heard that the same day he'd been throwing stones and had bitten your finger—but you understand now what a state he was in! Well, it can't be helped; it was stupid of me not to come and forgive him—that is, to make up with him—when he was taken ill. I am sorry for it now. But I had a special reason. So now I've told you all about it . . . But I'm afraid it was stupid of me."

"Oh, what a pity," exclaimed Alyosha, with feeling, "that I didn't know before what had happened or I'd have come to you long ago to ask you to go to him. Would you believe it, when he was delirious he talked about you. I didn't know how much you meant to him! And you really haven't found that dog? His father and the boys have been hunting all over town for it. Would you believe it, since he's been ill, I've heard him repeat three times with tears: 'It's because I killed Zhutchka, father, that I am ill now. God is punishing me for it.' He can't get that idea out of his head. And if the dog were found alive, one might almost believe the joy would cure him. We all hoped you might find the dog."

"What made you hope that I should be the one to find him?" Kolya asked, with great curiosity. "Why did you count on me rather than anyone else?"

"There was a rumor that you were looking for the dog, and that you would bring it when you'd found it. Smurov said something of the sort. We've all been trying to persuade Ilusha that the dog is alive, that it's been seen. The boys brought him a little rabbit; he just looked at it with a faint smile, and asked them to set it free in the fields. And so we did. His father has just this moment come back, bringing him a mastiff pup, hoping to comfort him with that. But I think it only makes it worse."

"Tell me, Karamazov, what sort of man is his father? I know him, but what do you make of him, a buffoon?"

"Oh, no. There are people of deep feeling who have been somehow crushed. Buffoonery in them is a form of resentful irony against those to whom they daren't speak the truth, from having been for years humiliated and intimidated by them. Believe me, Kolya, that sort of buffoonery is tragic. . . . His whole life is now centered in Ilusha, and if Ilusha dies, he will either go mad with grief, or kill himself. I feel almost certain of that when I look at him."

"I understand, Karamazov," Kolya said with feeling.

"And as soon as I saw you with a dog, I thought it was Zhutchka you were bringing."

"Wait a minute, Karamazov, maybe we shall find him yet; but this is Perezvon. I'll let him go in now. Perhaps he will amuse Ilusha more than the mastiff pup. Wait, Karamazov, you will know something in a minute. But I am keeping you here!" Kolya cried suddenly. "You've no overcoat on in this bitter cold. You see what an egoist I am. Oh, we are all egoists, Karamazov!"

"Don't worry. It is cold, but I don't often catch cold. Let us go in though, and, by the way, what is your name? I know you are called Kolya, but what else?"

"Krassotkin." Kolya laughed for some reason.

"You are thirteen?" asked Alyosha.

"No, fourteen—that is, I will be fourteen very soon, in two weeks. I'll confess one weakness, Karamazov, just to you, since it's our first meeting, so that you may understand me at once. I hate being asked my age, more than that . . . and in fact . . . There's a story going around about me, that last week I played robbers with the preparatory boys. I did play with them, but it's a lie to say I did it for my own amusement. I have reasons for believing that you've heard the story; but I wasn't playing for my own amusement, it was for the sake of the children, because they couldn't think of anything to do by themselves. But they've always got some silly tale. This is an awful town for gossip."

"But what if you had been playing for your own amusement, what's the harm?"

"For my own amusement! You don't play horses, do you?"

"But you must look at it like this," said Alyosha, smiling. "Grown-up people go to the theatre and there the adventures of all sorts of heroes are represented—sometimes there are robbers and battles, too—and isn't that just the same thing, in a different form? And children's games of soldiers or robbers are also art in its early stage. You know, they spring from the artistic instincts of the young. And sometimes these games are much better than performances in the theatre, the only difference is that people go to the theatre to look at actors, while in these games children are the actors themselves."

"You think so? Is that your idea?" Kolya looked at him. "Oh, you know, that's an interesting idea. When I go home, I'll think it over. I'll admit I thought I might learn something from you. I've come to learn from you, Karamazov," Kolya concluded, in a voice full of feeling.

"And I from you," said Alyosha, smiling and pressing his hand.

Kolya was much pleased with Alyosha. What struck him most was that Alyosha treated him exactly like an equal and that he talked to him just as if he were "grown up."

"I'll show you something, Karamazov; it's a theatrical performance, too," Kolya said, laughing nervously. "That's why I've come."

"Let us go first to the people of the house, on the left. All the boys leave their coats in there, because the room is small and hot."

"Oh, I'm only coming in for a minute. I'll keep my overcoat on. Perezvon will stay here in the hallway and pretend to be dead. Here, Perezvon, lie down and be dead! You see how he's dead. I'll go in first and explore, then I'll whistle to him, and you'll see, he'll dash in like mad. Only Smurov must not forget to open the door at the right moment. I'll arrange it all and you'll see something."

5. By Ilusha's Bedside

THE ROOM, where the retired Captain Snegiryov lived with his family, is already familiar to the reader. It was close and crowded at that moment with visitors. Several boys were sitting with Ilusha and, though all of them like Smurov were ready to deny that it was Alyosha who had brought them and reconciled them with Ilusha, it was really the fact. All he had done was to take them, one by one, to Ilusha, without "sheepish sentimentality," appearing to do so casually and without design. It was a great consolation to Ilusha in his suffering. He was touched by seeing the almost tender affection and sympathy shown him by these boys, who had been his enemies. Kolya was the only one missing and his absence was a heavy load on Ilusha's heart. Perhaps the most bitter of all his bitter memories was his stabbing of Kolya who had been his one true friend and protector. Clever little Smurov, who was the first to make up with Ilusha, sensed this. But when Smurov hinted to Kolya that Alyosha wanted to come to see him about something, Kolya cut him short. He said to tell "Karamazov" that he knew best, that he wanted no one's advice, and that, if he went to see Ilusha, he would choose his own time for he had "his own reasons."

That was two weeks before this Sunday. That was why Alyosha had not been to see him, as he had meant to. But though he waited, he sent Smurov to him twice more. Both times Kolya refused, sending Alyosha a message not to bother him any more and saying that if he came himself, he, Kolya, would not go to Ilusha at all. Up to the very last day, Smurov did not know that Kolya meant to go to Ilusha the following morning. Only the evening before, as he parted from Smurov, did Kolya tell him that he would go with him to Ilusha's the next morning. But he warned him not to say he was coming, as he wanted to drop in casually. Smurov obeyed. Smurov's belief that Kolya would bring back the lost dog was based on the words Kolya had dropped that "they must be asses not to

490

find the dog, if it were alive." When Smurov timidly hinted about the dog, Kolya flew into a rage. "I'm not such an ass as to go hunting about the town for other people's dogs when I've got a dog of my own! And how can you imagine a dog could be alive after swallowing a pin? Sheepish sentimentality, that's what it is!"

For the last two weeks Ilusha had not left his little bed under the ikons in the corner. He had not been to school since the day he met Alyosha and bit his finger. He was taken ill the same day, though for a month afterwards he was sometimes able to get up and walk about the room. But of late he had become so weak that he could not move without help from his father. His father was terribly concerned about him. He even gave up drinking and was almost crazy with terror that his boy would die. And often, especially after leading him around the room on his arm and putting him back to bed, he would run to a dark corner in the hallway and, leaning his head against the wall, he would break into violent weeping, stifling his sobs so that they might not be heard by Ilusha.

Returning to the room, he would usually begin doing something to amuse and comfort his precious boy, he would tell him stories, funny anecdotes, or would mimic comic people he had happened to meet, even imitate the howls and cries of animals. But Ilusha could not bear to see his father fooling and playing the buffoon. Though the boy tried not to show how he disliked it, he saw with an aching heart that his father was an object of contempt, and he was continually haunted by the memory of the "wisp of tow" and that "terrible day."

Nina, Ilusha's gentle, crippled sister, did not like her father's buffoonery either (Varvara had been gone for some time past to Petersburg to study at the University). But the half imbecile mother was greatly amused and laughed when her husband began clowning around. It was the only way she could be amused, all the rest of the time she was grumbling and complaining that now everyone had forgotten her, that no one treated her with respect, that she was slighted and so on. But during the last few days she had completely changed. She began looking constantly at Ilusha's bed in the corner and seemed lost in thought. She was more silent, more quiet, and if she cried, she cried quietly, so as not to be heard. The captain noticed the change in her. The boys' visits at first only angered her, but later on their shouts and stories began to entertain her, and at last she liked them so much that, if the boys had given up coming, she would have felt dreary without them. When the children told a story or played a game, she laughed and clapped her hands. She called some of them to her and kissed them. She was particularly fond of Smurov.

As for the captain, the children who came to cheer up Ilusha filled his heart with joy. He even hoped that Ilusha would now get over his depression, and that that would hurry his recovery. In spite of his worry about Ilusha, he had not, till lately, felt one minute's doubt of his boy's ultimate recovery.

The poor captain met the little visitors, waited upon them, was ready to be their horse and even began letting them ride on his back. But Ilusha did not like the game and it was given up. He began buying little things for them, gingerbread and nuts, gave them tea and sandwiches. It must be noted that all this time he had plenty of money. He had taken the two hundred roubles from Katerina just as Alyosha had predicted he would. And afterwards Katerina, learning more about his circumstances and Ilusha's illness, visited them herself, made the acquaintance of the family and succeeded in fascinating the half imbecile mother. Since then she had been lavish in helping them, and the captain, terror-stricken at the thought that his boy might be dying, forgot his pride and humbly accepted her help.

All this time Doctor Herzenstube, who was paid by Katerina, came punctually every other day, but little was gained by his visits. However, on that Sunday morning a new doctor was expected. He came from Moscow where he had a great reputation. Katerina had sent for him at great expense, not for Ilusha alone but for someone else also. More will be said about this later. The captain had been told to expect the new doctor that day. He hadn't the slightest idea that Kolya was also coming, though he had long wished for a visit from the boy about whom Ilusha was worrying.

When Kolya opened the door and came into the room, the captain and all the boys were around Ilusha's bed, looking at the tiny mastiff pup, which the captain had bought to comfort and amuse Ilusha, who was still fretting over the lost and probably dead Zhutchka. Ilusha, who had heard three days before that he was to be presented with a puppy, not an ordinary puppy, but a pedigree mastiff (a very important point, of course) tried to pretend that he was pleased. But his father and the boys could not help seeing that the puppy only served to recall to his little heart the thought of the unhappy dog he had killed. The puppy lay beside him and he, smiling sadly, stroked it with his thin, pale, wasted hand. He liked the puppy but . . . it wasn't Zhutchka. If he could have had Zhutchka and the puppy, too, then he would have been completely happy.

"Kolya!" cried one of the boys suddenly. He was the first to see him come in.

Kolya's arrival created a great excitement. The boys moved away and stood on each side of the bed, so that he could get a full view of Ilusha.

The captain ran to meet Kolya. "Please come in . . . you are welcome!" he said hurriedly. "Ilusha, Kolya has come to see you!"

But Kolya, hurriedly shaking hands with the captain instantly showed his complete knowledge of the manners of good society. He turned first to the captain's wife, who was very ill-humored at the moment and was grumbling that the boys stood between her and Ilusha's bed so that she could not see the new puppy. With the greatest courtesy he bowed, scraping his foot and then turning to Nina he bowed again. This behavior made an extremely favorable impression on the deranged lady.

"There, you can see at once he is a young man that has been well brought up," she commented aloud, throwing up her hands. "But as for our other visitors they come in one on the top of another."

"How do you mean, mother, one on the top of another?" muttered the captain affectionately.

"That's how they ride in. They get on each other's shoulders in the hall and prance in like that on a respectable family. Strange visitors!"

"But who's come in like that, mother?"

"Why, that boy came in riding on that one's back and this one on that one's."

Kolya was already by Ilusha's bedside. The sick boy turned paler. He raised himself in the bed and looked intently at Kolya. Kolya had not seen his little friend for two months, and he was overwhelmed at the sight of him. He had never imagined that he would see such a wasted, yellow face, such enormous, feverish eyes and such thin little hands. He saw, with surprise, Ilusha's rapid, hard breathing and dry lips. He stepped close to him, held out his hand, and said: "Well, old man . . . how are you?" But his voice failed him, he couldn't achieve an appearance of ease; his face suddenly twitched and the corners of his mouth quivered. Ilusha smiled a pitiful little smile, still unable to utter a word. Something moved Kolya to raise his hand and pass it over Ilusha's hair.

"Never mind!" he murmured softly to him to cheer him up, or perhaps not knowing why he said it. For a minute they were silent again.

"Hullo, so you've got a new puppy?" Kolya said suddenly.

"Ye-es," answered Ilusha in a long whisper, gasping for breath.

"A black nose, that means he'll be fierce, a good house-dog," Kolya observed, as if the only thing he cared about was the puppy and its black nose. But in reality he had to do his utmost not to burst out crying like a child. "When it grows up, you'll have to keep it on the chain, I'm sure."

"He'll be a huge dog!" cried one of the boys.

"Of course he will," "a mastiff," "large," "like this," "as big as a calf," shouted several voices.

"As big as a calf, as a real calf," chimed in the captain. "I got one like that on purpose, one of the fiercest . . . His parents are huge and very fierce, they stand as high as this from the floor. . . . Sit down here, on Ilusha's bed, or here on the bench. We've been hoping to see you a long time . . . You came with Alexey Karamazov?"

Kolya sat on the bed, at Ilusha's feet. Though he had prepared a free-and-easy opening for the conversation on his way, he now lost the thread of it.

"No . . . I came with Perezvon. I've got a dog called Perezvon. A Slavonic name. He's out there . . . If I whistle, he'll run in. I've brought a dog too," he said, addressing Ilusha all at once. "Do you remember Zhutchka?" he suddenly asked Ilusha.

Ilusha's little face quivered. He looked with an agonized expression at Kolya. Alyosha, standing at the door, frowned and signaled to Kolya not to speak of Zhutchka, but Kolya did not or would not notice.

"Where . . . is Zhutchka?" Ilusha asked in a broken voice.

"Oh, your Zhutchka's lost and done for!"

Ilusha did not speak. He fixed an intent gaze once more on Kolya. Alyosha, catching Kolya's eye, signaled to him again, but he turned away his eyes pretending not to have noticed.

"It must have run away and died somewhere. It must have died after a meal like that," Kolya pronounced without pity, though he seemed a little breathless. "But I've got a dog, Perezvon . . . A Slavonic name. . . . I've brought him to show you."

"I don't want him!" said Ilusha suddenly.

"No, no, you really must see him . . . It will amuse you. I brought him on purpose. . . . He's the same sort of shaggy dog. . . . Will you let me call in my dog, Madame?" he suddenly addressed Madame Snegiryov.

"I don't want him, I don't want him!" cried Ilusha, with a mournful break in his voice. There was reproach in his eyes.

"You'd better," the captain started up from the chest by the wall on which he had just sat down, "you'd better . . . another time," he muttered, but Kolya could not be restrained. He shouted to Smurov: "Open the door." And as soon as it was open, he whistled. Perezvon dashed headlong into the room.

"Jump, Perezvon, beg! Beg!" shouted Kolya, jumping up. The dog stood erect on its hind legs by Ilusha's bedside. What followed was a surprise to everyone; Ilusha started, lurched violently forward, bent over Perezvon and gazed at him.

"It's . . . Zhutchka!" he cried suddenly, in a voice breaking with joy and suffering.

"And who did you think it was?" Kolya shouted with all his might in a ringing, happy voice. Bending down he lifted the dog up to Ilusha.

"Look, you see, blind of one eye and the left ear is torn, just the marks you described to me. That's how I found him. I found him right away. He did not belong to anyone!" he explained, turning quickly to the captain, to his wife, to Alyosha and then again to Ilusha. "He used to live in the Fedotovs' back yard. Though he made his home there, they did not feed him. He was a stray dog that had run away from the village . . . I found him. . . . You see, Ilusha, he couldn't have swallowed what you gave him. If he had, he would have died! So he must have spit it out. You did not see him do it. But the pin pricked his tongue, that is why he squealed. He ran away squealing and you thought he'd swallowed it. He might well squeal, because the skin of dogs' mouths is so tender . . . More tender than in men, much more tender!"

Ilusha could not speak. White as a sheet, he gazed open-mouthed at Kolya, with his great eyes almost starting out of his head. And if Kolya, who had no suspicion of it, had known what a disastrous and fatal effect such a moment might have on the sick child's health, nothing would have induced him to play such a trick. But Alyosha was perhaps the only person in the room who realized it. As for the captain he behaved like a small child.

"Zhutchka! It's Zhutchka!" he cried happily. "Ilusha, this is Zhutchka, your Zhutchka! Mother, this is Zhutchka!" He was almost weeping.

"And I never guessed!" cried Smurov regretfully. "I always said Kolya would find the dog and here he's found him."

"Here he's found him!" another boy repeated.

"Kolya's a prince!" cried a third voice.

"He's a prince, he's a prince!" cried the other boys, and they began clapping.

"Wait, wait," Kolya did his best to shout above them all. "I'll tell you how it happened, that's the whole point. I found him, I took him home and hid him. I kept him locked up at home and did not show him to anyone till today. Only Smurov knew, but I assured him this dog was called Perezvon and he did not guess. And meanwhile I taught the dog all sorts of tricks. You should see all the things he can do! I trained him so as to bring you a well-trained dog, in good condition, Ilusha, so as to be able to say to you: 'See, Ilusha, what a fine dog your Zhutchka is now!' Haven't you a bit of meat, he'll show you a trick that will make you die laughing. A piece of meat, haven't you got any?"

The captain ran across the hallway to the landlady, where their cooking was done. But not to lose precious time, Kolya shouted to Perezvon: "Dead!" And the dog immediately turned around and lay on its back with its four paws in the air. The boys laughed. Ilusha looked on with the same suffering smile. The person most delighted with the dog's performance was "mother." She laughed at the dog and began snapping her fingers and calling it: "Perezvon, Perezvon!"

"Nothing will make him get up, nothing!" Kolya cried triumphantly. "He won't move for all the shouting in the world.

But if I call to him, he'll jump up in a minute. Here, Perezvon!" The dog leapt up and bounded about, whining with delight. The captain came back with a piece of cooked beef.

"Is it hot?" Kolya asked with a businesslike air, taking the meat. "Dogs don't like hot things. No, it's all right. Look, everybody, look. Ilusha, look. Why aren't you looking? He does not look at him, now that I've brought him."

The new trick consisted in making the dog stand motionless with his nose out and putting a tempting morsel of meat just on his nose. The dog had to stand without moving, with the meat on his nose, as long as Kolya chose to keep him that way, perhaps for half an hour. But he kept Perezvon only a brief moment.

"Paid for!" cried Kolya, and the meat passed in a flash from the dog's nose to his mouth. Everyone was delighted and surprised.

"Did you really put off coming all this time simply to train the dog?" exclaimed Alyosha, with an involuntary note of reproach in his voice.

"Yes!" answered Kolya with perfect simplicity. "I wanted to show him in all his glory."

"Perezvon! Perezvon," called Ilusha suddenly, snapping his thin fingers and beckoning to the dog.

"What is it? Let him jump up on the bed! Here, Perezvon!" Kolya slapped the bed and Perezvon jumped up by Ilusha. The boy threw both arms around his head and Perezvon licked his cheek. Ilusha crept close to him, stretched himself out in bed and hid his face in the dog's shaggy coat.

"Dear, dear!" the captain kept exclaiming. Kolya sat down again at the foot of the bed.

"Ilusha, I can show you another trick. I've brought you a little cannon. You remember, I told you about it before and you said how much you'd like to see it. Well, here, I've brought it for you."

Kolya quickly pulled out of his satchel the little bronze cannon. He hurried, because he was happy himself. Another time he would have waited till the sensation made by Perezvon had passed off, but now he hurried on regardless. "You are happy now," he felt, "so here's something to make you happier!"

"I've been coveting this thing for a long while; but it's for you, Ilusha, it's for you. It belonged to a boy I know. It was of no use to him. He had it from his brother. I swapped a book from father's bookcase for it, *A Kinsman of Mahomet or Salutary Folly,* a scandalous book published in Moscow a hundred years ago, before they had any censorship. And this boy likes such things. He was grateful to me, too . . ."

Kolya held the cannon in his hand so that all could admire it. Ilusha raised himself, and, with his right arm still around the dog, he gazed enchanted at the toy. The sensation was even greater, when Kolya announced that he had gunpowder too, and that it could be fired off at once "if it won't alarm the ladies." "Mother" immediately asked to look at the toy. She was pleased with the little bronze cannon on wheels and began rolling it to and fro on her lap. She gave permission for the cannon to be fired, without any idea of what she had been asked. Kolya showed everyone the powder and the shot. The captain, as a military man, undertook to load it, putting in a minute quantity of powder. He asked that the shot might be put off till another time. The cannon was put on the floor, aimed toward an empty part of the room, three grains of powder were thrust into the touch hole and a match was put to it. An explosion followed. Mother was startled, but laughed with delight. The boys gazed in speechless triumph. But the captain, looking at Ilusha, was more enchanted than any of them. Kolya picked up the cannon and immediately presented it to Ilusha, together with the powder and the shot.

"I got it for you, for you! I've been keeping it for you a long time," he repeated once more.

"Oh, give it to me! No, give me the cannon!" Mother began begging like a little child. Her face showed a piteous fear that she would not get it. Kolya was disconcerted. The captain fidgeted uneasily.

"Mother, mother," he ran to her. "The cannon's yours, of course, but let Ilusha have it, because it's a present to him. But it's just as good as yours. Ilusha will always let you play with it, it will belong to both of you, both of you."

"No, I don't want it to belong to both of us, I want it to be mine, not Ilusha's," she persisted, on the point of tears.

"Take it, mother. Here, keep it!" Ilusha cried. "Kolya, may I give it to my mother?" He turned to Kolya with an imploring face, as though he were afraid Kolya might be offended at his giving his present to someone else.

"Of course, you may," Kolya agreed, and taking the cannon from Ilusha, he handed it himself to mother with a polite bow. She was so touched that she cried.

"Ilusha, darling. Ilusha's the one who loves his mother!" she said tenderly, and at once began wheeling the cannon to and fro on her lap.

"Mother, let me kiss your hand." The captain ran up to her.

"I never saw such a charming person as this nice boy," said the grateful lady, pointing to Kolya.

"I'll bring you as much powder as you like, Ilusha. We make the powder ourselves. Borovikov found out how it's made—twenty-four parts of saltpetre, ten of sulphur and six of birch-wood charcoal. It's all pounded together, mixed into a paste with water and rubbed through a sieve—that's how it's done."

"Smurov told me about your powder, only father says it's not real gunpowder," answered Ilusha.

"Not real?" Kolya flushed. "It burns. I don't know, of course."

"No, I didn't mean that," said the captain with a guilty face. "I only said that real powder is not made like that, but that's nothing. It can be made that way."

"I don't know, you know best. We lighted some in a pot, it burned very well, it all burned away leaving only a tiny ash. But that was only the paste, and if you rub it through . . . But of course you know best, I don't know. . . . And Bulkin's father punished him on account of our powder, did you hear?" he turned to Ilusha.

"Yes," answered Ilusha. He listened to Kolya with great interest and pleasure.

"We had prepared a whole bottle of it and he used to keep it under his bed. His father saw it. He said it might explode. He was going to complain about me to the masters. Bulkin is not allowed to go with me now, no one is allowed to go with me now. Smurov is not allowed to either, I've got a bad name. They say I'm a 'desperate character.' " Kolya smiled scornfully. "It all began from what happened on the railway."

"Oh, we've heard of that, too," cried the captain. "How could you lie so still? Is it possible you weren't the least afraid, lying there under the train? Weren't you frightened?"

"N-not particularly," answered Kolya carelessly. "But what's blasted my reputation more than anything was that cursed goose," he said, turning again to Ilusha. But though he assumed an unconcerned air as he talked, he still could not control himself and was continually failing in the effect he tried to create.

"Ah! I heard about the goose!" Ilusha laughed, beaming all over. "They told me, but I didn't understand. Did they really take you to court?"

"They made a mountain of a molehill as they always do," Kolya began carelessly. "I was walking through the market place one day, just when they'd driven in the geese. I stopped and looked at them. All at once a fellow who is an errand boy at Plotnikov's, looked at me and said: 'What are you looking at the geese for?' I looked at him. He was a stupid, moon-faced fellow of twenty. I like peasants, you know. I like talking to peasants. . . . We've dropped behind the peasants—that's an axiom. I believe you are laughing, Karamazov?"

"No, I am listening," said Alyosha with a most good-natured air. The sensitive Kolya was immediately reassured.

"My theory, Karamazov, is clear and simple," he hurried on, looking pleased. "I believe in the people and am always glad to give them their due, but I am not for spoiling them. . . . But I was telling you about the goose. So I turned to the fool and answered: 'I am wondering what the goose thinks about.' He looked at me quite stupidly: 'And what does the goose think about?' he asked. 'Do you see that cart full of oats?' I said. 'The oats are dropping out of the sack, and the goose has put its neck right under the wheel to gobble them up—do you see?' 'I see,' he said. 'Well,' I said, 'if that cart were to move a little, would it break the goose's neck or not?' 'It'd be sure to break it,' and he grinned. 'Come on then,' I said. 'Let's try.' 'Let's,' he said. And it did not take us long to arrange; he stood at the bridle without being noticed, and I stood on one side to direct the goose. And the owner wasn't looking, he was talking to someone, so I had nothing to do. The goose put its head in after the oats, under the cart, just under the wheel. I winked at the fellow. He tugged at the bridle, and crack! The goose's neck was broken in half. And, as luck would have it, all the peasants saw us at that moment and they kicked up a terrible row. 'You did that on purpose!' 'No, not on purpose.' 'Yes, you did, on purpose!' They shouted: 'Take him to the justice of the peace!' They took me, too. 'You were there, too,' they said. 'You helped, you're known all over the market!' For some reason, I really am known all over the market," Kolya added with conceit. "We all went off to the justice's. They brought the goose, too. The fellow was crying, blubbering like a woman. And the farmer kept shouting that you could kill any number of geese like that. Well, of course, there were witnesses. The justice of the peace settled it in a minute. He said that the farmer was to be paid a rouble for the goose, and that the fellow was to have the goose. And he was warned not to play such tricks again. And the fellow kept blubbering like a woman: 'It wasn't me,' he said. 'He egged me on.' And he pointed to me. I answered calmly that I hadn't egged him on, that I simply stated the general proposition, had spoken hypothetically. The justice of the peace smiled and was irritated with himself at once for having smiled. 'I'll complain to your masters about you so that in the future you won't waste your time on such general propositions, instead of learning your lessons.' He didn't complain to the masters, that was a joke, but the story did reach the ears of the masters. Their ears are long, you know! The classical master, Kolbasnikov, was particularly shocked; but Dardanelov got me off again. But Kolbasnikov is rough with everyone now like a green ass. Did you know, Ilusha, he is just married, got a dowry of a thousand roubles, and his bride's a regular fright of the first rank and the last degree. The third class fellows wrote an epigram on it.

Astounding news had reached the class
Kolbasnikov has been an ass.

And so on, awfully funny, I'll bring it to you later on. I say nothing against Dardanelov, he is a scholar, there's no doubt about it. I respect men like that and it's not because he stood up for me either."

"But you tripped him up about the founders of Troy!" Smurov put in suddenly, unmistakably proud of Kolya. He was particularly pleased with the story of the goose.

"Did you really trip him up?" the captain asked in a flattering way. "We heard of it. Ilusha told me about it at the time."

"He knows everything, father, he knows more than any of us!" said Ilusha. "He is first in every subject . . ."

Ilusha looked at Kolya with infinite happiness.

"Oh, that's all nonsense about Troy. It's unimportant," said Kolya with haughty humility. He had by now completely recovered his dignity, though he was still a little uneasy. He felt that he was too excited and that he had talked about the goose, for instance, with too little reserve. He had noticed that Alyosha had looked serious and had not said a word all the time. And he began by degrees to have a rankling fear that Alyosha was silent because he despised him and thought he was showing off. If Alyosha dared to think anything like that Kolya would . . .

"I regard the question as a trivial one," he rapped out again proudly.

"I know who founded Troy," a boy, who had not spoken before, said suddenly, to the surprise of everyone. He had been silent and seemed to be shy. He was a nice-looking boy of about eleven, called Kartashov. He was sitting near the door. Kolya looked at him with amazement.

The fact was that the identity of the founders of Troy had become a secret for the whole school, a secret which could only be discovered by reading Smaragdov. And no one had a copy of Smaragdov but Kolya. One day when Kolya's back was turned, Kartashov quickly opened Smaragdov, which lay among Kolya's books, and lighted on the passage relating to the foundation of Troy. This was a good time ago, but he felt uneasy and could not bring himself to announce publicly that he, too, knew who had founded Troy. He was afraid of what might happen, that Kolya might somehow put him to shame. But now he couldn't resist saying it. For weeks he had been longing to.

"Well, who did found it?" asked Kolya, turning to him. He saw from his face that he really did know and at once made up his mind how to take it.

"Troy was founded by Teucer, Dardanus, Ilius and Tros," the boy said clearly. He blushed, blushed so, that it was painful to look at him. But the boys stared at him, stared at him for a whole minute. Then all the staring eyes turned upon Kolya, who was looking at the boy with disdainful composure.

"In what sense did they found it?" he deigned to comment at last. "And what is meant by founding a city or a state? What did they do—did they go and each lay a brick?"

There was laughter. The offending boy turned crimson. He was silent and on the point of tears. Kolya held him so for a minute.

"Before you talk of a historical event like the foundation of a nation, you must first understand what you mean by it," he said to him in stern incisive tones. "I attach no consequence to these old wives' tales and I don't think much of universal history in general," he added carelessly, addressing everyone.

"Universal history?" the captain asked, looking almost scared.

"Yes, universal history! It's the study of the successive follies of mankind and nothing more. The only subjects I respect are mathematics and natural science," said Kolya. He was showing off and he stole a glance at Alyosha; his was the only opinion he was afraid of. But Alyosha was still silent and still as serious as before. If Alyosha had said a word it would have stopped him, but Alyosha was silent. "It might be the silence of contempt," thought Kolya.

"The classical languages, too . . . They are useless, nothing more. You seem to disagree with me, Karamazov?"

"I don't agree," said Alyosha with a faint smile.

"The study of the classics, if you ask my opinion, is simply a police measure, that's why it has been introduced into our schools." By degrees Kolya began to get breathless again. "Latin and Greek were introduced because they are a bore and because they stupefy the intellect. It was dull before, so what could they do to make things duller? It was senseless enough before, so what could they do to make it more senseless? So they thought of Greek and Latin. That's my opinion, I hope I never change it," Kolya finished abruptly. His cheeks were flushed.

"That's true," agreed Smurov suddenly. He had listened attentively.

"And yet he is first in Latin himself," cried one of the boys.

"Yes, father, he says that and yet he is first in Latin," echoed Ilusha.

"What of it?" Kolya thought fit to defend himself, though the praise was very sweet to him. "I am plugging away at Latin because I have to; because I promised my mother to pass my examination, and because I think that whatever you do it's worth doing it well. But I have contempt for the classics and all that fraud. . . . You don't agree, Karamazov?"

"Why 'fraud'?" Alyosha smiled again.

"Well, all the classical authors have been translated into all languages, so it was not for the sake of studying the classics they introduced Latin, but solely as a police measure, to stupefy the intelligence. So what can one call it but a fraud?"

"Why, who taught you all this?" asked Alyosha.

"In the first place I am capable of thinking for myself. Besides, what I said just now about the classics being translated, our teacher Kolbasnikov has said to the whole of the third class."

"The doctor has come!" cried Nina, who had been silent till then.

A carriage belonging to Madame Hohlakov drove up to the gate. The captain, who had been expecting the doctor all the morning, rushed out to meet him. Mother pulled herself together and assumed a dignified air. Alyosha went up to Ilusha and began fixing his pillows. Nina, from her invalid chair, anxiously watched him tidying the bed. The boys hurriedly took leave. Some of them promised to come again in the evening. Kolya called Perezvon and the dog jumped off the bed.

"I won't go away, I won't go away," Kolya said quickly to Ilusha. "I'll wait in the hall and come back when the doctor's gone. I'll come back with Perezvon."

By now the doctor had entered. He was an important looking person with long, dark whiskers and a shiny, shaven chin. He was wearing a bearskin coat. As he crossed the threshold he stopped, taken aback; he probably thought he had come to the wrong place. "What is this? Where am I?" he muttered, not taking off his coat nor his peaked sealskin cap. The crowd, the poverty of the room, the washing hanging on a line in the corner, puzzled him.

The captain, bent double, was bowing low before him. "It's here, sir, here, sir," he muttered cringingly. "It's here. You've come right place. You were coming to us . . ."

"Sne-gi-ryov?" the doctor said loudly and pompously. "Mr. Snegiryov—is that you?"

"That's me, sir!"

"Oh!"

The doctor looked around the room once more and threw off his coat, exposing a decoration at his neck. The captain took his fur coat and cap.

"Where is the patient?" he asked.

6. Precocity

"WHAT DO YOU THINK the doctor will say?" Kolya asked. "What a repulsive mug though, hasn't he? I can't stand medicine!"

"Ilusha is dying. I think that's certain," answered Alyosha mournfully.

"They are fakes! Medicine's a fraud! But I am glad to have met you, Karamazov. I wanted to know you for a long time. I am only sorry we meet at such a sad time."

Kolya wanted to say something even warmer and more demonstrative, but he felt ill at ease. Alyosha noticed this, smiled, and pressed his hand.

"I've long learned to respect you as a rare person," Kolya muttered again, faltering and uncertain. "I have heard you are a mystic and have been in the monastery. I know you are a mystic but . . . Contact with real life will cure you. . . . It's always so with people like you."

"What do you mean by mystic? Cure me of what?" Alyosha was rather astonished.

"Oh, God and all the rest of it."

"What, don't you believe in God?"

"Oh, I've nothing against God. Of course, God is only a hypothesis, but . . . I admit that He is needed . . . for the order of the universe and all that . . . And that if there were no God He would have to be invented," added Kolya beginning to blush. He suddenly felt that Alyosha might think he was trying to show off his knowledge and prove that he was "grown up." "I haven't the slightest desire to display my knowledge to him," Kolya thought indignantly. And all of a sudden he felt annoyed.

"I must confess I can't stand such discussions," he said with a final air. "It's possible for one who doesn't believe in God to love mankind, don't you think so? Voltaire didn't believe in God and loved mankind?" ("I am at it again," he thought to himself.)

"Voltaire believed in God, though not very much, I think, and I don't think he loved mankind very much either," said Alyosha quietly, gently, and quite naturally, as though he were talking to someone of his own age, or even older. Kolya was struck by Alyosha's apparent indifference about his opinion of Voltaire. He seemed to be leaving the question for him, little Kolya, to settle.

"Have you read Voltaire?" Alyosha asked.

"No, not really. . . . But I've read *Candide* in the Russian translation . . . in an old translation . . . (At it again! Again!)"

"And did you understand it?"

"Oh, yes, everything. . . . That is . . . Why do you think I wouldn't understand it? There's a lot of nastiness in it, of course. . . . Of course, I can understand that it's a philosophical novel and written to advocate an idea. . . ." Kolya was getting confused. "I am a Socialist, Karamazov. I am an incurable Socialist," he announced suddenly apropos of nothing.

"A Socialist?" laughed Alyosha. "When have you had time to become one? Why, I thought you were only thirteen?"

Kolya winced.

"In the first place I am not thirteen, but fourteen, fourteen in two weeks." He flushed angrily. "And in the second place I don't understand what my age has to do with it. The question is what are my convictions not what is my age, isn't it?"

"When you are older, you'll understand for yourself the influence of age on convictions. I also believe that you were not expressing your own ideas," Alyosha answered serenely and modestly.

Kolya interrupted him. "Come, you want obedience and

mysticism. You must admit that the Christian religion, for instance, has only been of use to the rich and the powerful to keep the lower classes in slavery. That's so, isn't it?"

"Oh, I know where you read that. I am sure someone told you that!" cried Alyosha.

"What makes you think I read it? And certainly no one told me about it. I can think for myself. . . . I am not opposed to Christ, if you like. He was a most humane person, and if He were alive today, He would be found in the ranks of the revolutionists, and would play a conspicuous part. . . . There's no doubt about that."

"Oh, where, where did you get that from? What fool have you made friends with?" exclaimed Alyosha.

"It happens that I have often talked to Rakitin, the divinity student, but . . . old Byelinsky said that, too, so they say."

"Byelinsky? I don't remember. He hasn't written that anywhere."

"If he didn't write it, they say he said it. I heard that from a . . . But never mind."

"And have you read Byelinsky?"

"Well, no . . . I haven't read all of him, but . . . I read the passage about Tatyana, why she didn't go off with Onyegin."

"Didn't go off with Onyegin? Surely you don't . . . understand that already?"

"Why, you seem to take me for little Smurov," said Kolya with irritation. "But please don't think I'm a revolutionist. I often disagree with Rakitin. Though I mention Tatyana, I am not at all for the emancipation of women. I admit that women are a subject race and must obey. The women do the knitting, as Napoleon said." Kolya, for some reason, smiled. "On that question at least I am quite of one mind with that pseudo-great man. I also think that to leave one's own country and go to America is mean, worse than mean—silly. Why go to America when one can be of great service to humanity here? Now especially. There's so much open to us. That's what I answered."

"What do you mean? Answered whom? Has someone suggested your going to America?"

"I must admit they've been at me to go, but I don't want to. That's between ourselves, of course, Karamazov. Do you hear, not a word to anyone. I say this only to you. I am not at all anxious to fall into the clutches of the secret police and take lessons at the Chain bridge,

> Long will you remember
> The house at the Chain bridge.

Do you remember? Why are you laughing? You don't think I am lying, do you?" ("What if he should find out that I've only that one number of *The Bell* in father's bookcase, and

504

haven't read any more of it?" Kolya thought with a shudder.)

"Oh, no, I am not laughing and I don't think for a moment that you are lying. No, for all this is perfectly true. But tell me, have you read Pushkin, Onyegin, for instance? . . . You spoke just now of Tatyana."

"No, I haven't read it yet, but I want to read it. I have no prejudices, Karamazov. I want to hear both sides. What makes you ask?"

"Oh, nothing."

"Tell me, Karamazov, have you contempt for me?" Kolya asked suddenly. He drew himself up before Alyosha as though he were on drill. "Tell me without beating about the bush."

"I have contempt for you?" Alyosha looked at him wondering. "What for? I am only sad that a charming nature such as yours should be perverted by all this crude nonsense before you have begun life."

"Don't worry about my nature," Kolya interrupted. "But it's true that I am stupidly sensitive, crudely sensitive. You smiled just now, and I thought you seemed to . . ."

"Oh, my smile meant something quite different. I'll tell you why I smiled. Not long ago I read a criticism, made by a German who had lived in Russia, of our students and schoolboys. 'Show a Russian schoolboy,' he writes, 'a map of the stars, which he knows nothing about, and he will return the map next day with corrections on it.' No knowledge and unbounded conceit—that's what the German meant to say about the Russian schoolboy."

"Yes, that's perfectly right." Kolya laughed suddenly. "Exactly right! But this German did not see the good side, what do you think? Conceit maybe, that comes from youth and will be corrected if need be. But, on the other hand, there is an independent spirit almost from childhood, boldness of thought and conviction, and not the spirit of those sausage makers, groveling before authority. . . . But this German was right all the same. Hurray the German! But Germans need strangling all the same. Even though they are so good at science and learning they must be strangled."

"Strangled, what for?" smiled Alyosha.

"Well, perhaps I am talking nonsense. I am awfully childish sometimes, and when I am pleased about anything I can't restrain myself and am ready to say anything. But here we are talking about nothing, and that doctor has been a long time in there. Perhaps he's examining the mother and that poor crippled Nina. I like Nina. She whispered to me suddenly as I was coming away: 'Why didn't you come before?' And in such a voice, so reproachfully! I think she is awfully nice and pathetic."

"Yes, yes! Well, you'll be coming often, you will see what she is like. It would do you a great deal of good to know people like these. You will learn a great deal from knowing these people," Alyosha observed. "That would help you more than anything."

"How I regret not having come sooner!" Kolya exclaimed with bitter feeling.

"Yes, it's a great pity. You saw for yourself how happy poor Ilusha was to see you. And how he longed for you to come!"

"Don't tell me! You make it worse! But it serves me right. What kept me from coming was my conceit, my vanity, and the wilfulness, which I never can get rid of. I see that now. I am mean in lots of things, Karamazov!"

"No, you have a good nature, but it's been distorted. And I understand now why you have had such an influence on this sensitive boy," Alyosha answered warmly.

"You say that to me!" cried Kolya. "Would you believe it, I thought—I've thought several times since I've been here—that you despised me! If only you knew how I prize your opinion!"

"But are you really so sensitive? At your age! Would you believe it, just now, when you were telling your story, I thought, as I watched you, that you must be very sensitive!"

"You thought so? I bet that was when I was talking about the goose. That was just when I thought you had contempt for me for being in such a hurry to show off. For a moment I hated you for it, and began talking like a fool. Then I thought —just now, here—when I said that if there were no God He would have to be invented, that I was in too great a hurry to display my knowledge, especially as I got that phrase out of a book. But I swear I wasn't showing off out of vanity, though I really don't know why, because I was so pleased, yes, I believe it was because I was so pleased . . . Though it's disgraceful for anyone to talk like that because they are pleased, I know that. But I am convinced now that you don't despise me; it was all my imagination. Oh, Karamazov, I am so unhappy. I sometimes think all sorts of things; that everyone is laughing at me, the whole world. And then I want to overturn the whole order of things."

"And you worry everyone," smiled Alyosha.

"Yes, I worry everyone, especially my mother. Karamazov, tell me, am I being very ridiculous now?"

"Don't think about that, don't think of it at all!" cried Alyosha. "And what does ridiculous mean? Isn't everyone constantly being or seeming ridiculous? Besides, nearly all clever people are afraid of being ridiculous, and that makes them unhappy. I am surprised that you should feel ridiculous so early, though nowadays little children have begun to suffer from it. It's almost a sort of insanity. The devil has taken the form of that vanity and entered into the whole generation. It's the devil," added Alyosha, without a trace of the smile that Kolya, staring at him expected to see. "You are like everyone else," said Alyosha, in conclusion. "That is, like very many others. Only you must not be like everybody else, that's all."

"Even if everyone is like that?"

"Yes, even if everyone is like that. You be the only one not like that. You really are not like everyone else; you are not ashamed to confess to something bad and ridiculous. And who today will admit so much? No one. People have even ceased to feel the impulse to self-criticism. Don't be like everyone else, even if you are the only one."

"Good! I was not mistaken in you. You know how to console one. Oh, how I have longed to know you, Karamazov! I've been eager to meet you. Have you thought about me, too? You said just now that you thought of me?"

"Yes, I'd heard of you and had thought of you, too . . . And if it's partly vanity that makes you ask, it doesn't matter."

"Do you know, Karamazov, our talk has been like a declaration of love," said Kolya in a bashful voice. "That's not ridiculous, is it?"

"Not at all ridiculous, and if it were, it wouldn't matter, because it's been a good thing," Alyosha smiled.

"But do you know, Karamazov, you must admit that you are a little ashamed yourself, now. . . . I see it by your eyes." Kolya smiled with a sort of sly happiness.

"Why ashamed?"

"Well, why are you blushing?"

"You make me blush," laughed Alyosha, and he really did blush. "Oh, well, I am a little, goodness knows why, I don't know . . ." he muttered, embarrassed.

"Oh, how I love you and admire you at this moment just because you are ashamed! Because you are just like me," cried Kolya. His cheeks glowed, his eyes beamed.

"You know, Kolya, you will be very unhappy in life," something made Alyosha say suddenly.

"I know, I know. How do you know?" Kolya agreed at once.

"But you will bless life on the whole, all the same."

"Yes! You are a prophet. Oh, we will get on together, Karamazov! Do you know, what I like best is that you treat me like an equal. But we are not equals, no, we are not. You are better! But we will be friends. Do you know, all this last month I've been saying to myself, 'either we shall be friends at once, forever, or we shall be enemies to the grave!' "

"And saying that, of course, you loved me," Alyosha laughed.

"I did. I loved you awfully. I've been loving and dreaming of you. And how did you know it all beforehand? . . . Oh, here's the doctor. What will he tell us? Look at his face!"

7. Ilusha

THE DOCTOR CAME OUT OF THE ROOM muffled in his fur coat and with his cap on his head. His face looked almost angry and disgusted, as though he were afraid of getting dirty. He cast a glance around the hallway, looking at Alyosha and Kolya as he did so. Alyosha waved from the door to the coachman, and the carriage that had brought the doctor drove up. The captain ran out after the doctor and bowing apologetically, stopped him to get a last word. He looked utterly crushed; there was a scared look in his eyes.

"Your Excellency, your Excellency . . . is it possible?" he began. But he could not go on and clasped his hands in despair. Yet he still gazed imploringly at the doctor, as though a word from him might change Ilusha's fate.

"I can't help it, I am not God!" the doctor answered offhand.

"Doctor . . . your Excellency . . . And will it be soon, soon?"

"You must be prepared for anything," said the doctor in emphatic and incisive tones, and dropping his eyes, he was about to step out to the coach.

"Your Excellency, for Christ's sake," the terror-stricken captain stopped him again. "Your Excellency! Can nothing, absolutely nothing save him now?"

"It's not in my hands," said the doctor impatiently. "But h'm . . ." he stopped suddenly. "If you could, for instance . . . send . . . your patient . . . at once, without delay to Syracuse, the change to the new be-ne-fi-cial climatic conditions might possibly affect . . ."

"To Syracuse!" cried the captain, unable to grasp what was said.

"Syracuse is in Sicily," Kolya said suddenly in explanation. The doctor looked at him.

"Sicily! Your Excellency," said the captain. "But you've seen—" he spread out his hands, indicating his surroundings —"my wife and my family?"

"N-no, Sicily is not the place for the family, the family should go to Caucasus in the early spring . . . Your daughter must go to the Caucasus, and your wife . . . after a course of the waters in the Caucasus for her rheumatism . . . must be sent straight to Paris to the mental specialist Lepelletier. I could give you a note to him, and then . . . There might be a change . . ."

"Doctor, doctor! But you see!" The captain flung wide his hands again despairingly, indicating the bare wooden walls of the hallway.

"Well, that's not my business," grinned the doctor. "I have only given you the medical answer to your question. As for the rest, to my regret . . ."

"Don't be afraid, apothecary, my dog won't bite you," Kolya cried out loudly, noticing the doctor's uneasy glance at Perezvon. There was anger in Kolya's voice. He used the word apothecary instead of doctor on purpose, and, as he explained afterwards: "I used it to insult him."

"What's that?" The doctor flung up his head, staring with surprise at Kolya. "Who's this?" he addressed Alyosha, as though asking him to explain.

"It's Perezvon's master, don't worry about me," Kolya replied.

"Perezvon," repeated the doctor, perplexed.

"Good-bye, we shall meet in Syracuse," said Kolya sarcastically.

"Who's this? Who's this?" The doctor flew into a rage.

"He is a schoolboy, doctor, he is a mischievous boy. Take no notice of him," said Alyosha, frowning and speaking quickly. "Kolya, hold your tongue!" he cried. "Take no notice of him, doctor," he repeated, rather impatiently.

"He wants a beating, a good beating!" the doctor cried.

"And you know, apothecary, my Perezvon might bite!" said Kolya, turning pale. "Here, Perezvon!"

"Kolya, if you say another word, I'll have nothing more to do with you," Alyosha cried.

"There is only one man in the world who can command Kolya Krassotkin—this is the man." Kolya pointed to Alyosha. "I obey him, good-bye!"

He stepped forward, opened the door, and quickly went into the inner room. Perezvon ran after him. The doctor stood still for five seconds in amazement, looking at Alyosha. Then, with a curse, he went out to the carriage, repeating aloud: "This is . . . this is . . . I don't know what it is!" The captain ran forward to help him into the carriage. Alyosha followed Kolya into the room. He was already by Ilusha's bedside. The sick boy was holding his hand and calling for his father. A minute later the captain, too, came back.

"Father, father, come . . . we . . .," Ilusha faltered in excitement. Apparently unable to go on, he then flung his wasted arms around his father and Kolya, uniting them in one embrace, and hugging them as tightly as he could. The captain suddenly began to shake with dumb sobs, and Kolya's lips and chin twitched.

"Father, father! How sorry I am for you!" Ilusha moaned.

"Ilusha . . . darling . . . the doctor said . . . You would be all right . . . We shall be happy . . . The doctor . . ." the captain began.

"Oh, father! I know what this new doctor said to you about me. . . . I saw!" cried Ilusha. And again he hugged his father

509

and Kolya with all his strength, hiding his face on his father's shoulder.

"Father, don't cry, and when I die get a good boy, another one . . . Choose one of my friends, a good one, call him Ilusha and love him instead of me . . ."

"Hush, Ilusha, you'll get well," Kolya cried suddenly in a voice that sounded almost angry.

"But don't ever forget me, father," Ilusha went on. "Come to my grave . . . And father, bury me by our big stone, where we used to go for our walk. And come to me there with Kolya in the evening . . . and Perezvon . . . I shall expect you. . . . Father, father!"

His voice broke. They were all three silent, still embracing. Nina was crying quietly in her chair, and at last seeing them all crying, mother, too, burst into tears.

"Ilusha! Ilusha!" she exclaimed.

Kolya suddenly broke free from Ilusha's embrace.

"Good-bye, Ilusha, mother expects me back for dinner," he said quickly. "What a pity I did not tell her! She will be worried. . . . But after dinner I'll come back to you for the whole day, for the whole evening, and I'll tell you all sorts of things, all sorts of things. And I'll bring Perezvon, but now I will take him with me, because he will begin to howl when I am away and bother you. Good-bye!"

And he ran out into the hall. He didn't want to cry, but in the hall he burst into tears. Alyosha found him crying.

"Kolya, you must be sure to keep your word and come, or he will be terribly disappointed," Alyosha said.

"I will! Oh, how I curse myself for not having come before!" muttered Kolya, crying, and no longer ashamed of it.

At that moment the captain came out of the room closing the door behind him. He looked frenzied, his lips were trembling. He stood before Alyosha and Kolya and threw up his arms.

"I don't want a good boy! I don't want another boy!" he muttered in a wild whisper. "If I forget thee, Jerusalem, may my tongue . . ." he broke off with a sob and sank on his knees before the wooden bench. Pressing his fists against his head, he began sobbing with whimpering cries, doing his best so that his cries should not be heard in the room.

Kolya ran out into the street.

"Good-bye, Karamazov! Will you also come?" he cried sharply and angrily to Alyosha.

"I will certainly come this evening."

"What was that he said about Jerusalem? . . . What did he mean by that?"

"It's from the Bible. 'If I forget thee, Jerusalem,' that is, if I forget all that is most precious to me, if I let anything take its place, then may . . ."

"I understand! Be sure to come! Here, Perezvon!" he cried. And he hurried home as fast as he could.

BOOK XI: IVAN

1. At Grushenka's

ALYOSHA WENT TOWARD THE CATHEDRAL SQUARE to the widow Morozov's house to see Grushenka, who had sent Fenya to him early in the morning with a message begging him to come. Questioning Fenya, Alyosha learned that Grushenka had been very distressed since the previous day. During the two months that had passed since Dmitri's arrest, Alyosha had gone quite often to Grushenka's, both from his own inclination and to take messages for Dmitri.

Three days after Dmitri's arrest, Grushenka was taken very ill and was ill for nearly five weeks. For one whole week she was unconscious. She was very much changed—thinner and a little sallow, though she had for the past two weeks been well enough to go out. But to Alyosha her face was even more attractive than before, and he liked to meet her eyes when he visited her. A look of firmness and purpose had developed in her face. There were signs of a spiritual transformation in her; a steadfast, fine and humble determination. There was a small vertical line between her brows which gave her charming face a look of concentrated thought, almost austere at the first glance. There was scarcely a trace of her former frivolity.

It seemed strange to Alyosha, too, that in spite of the misfortune that had overtaken her, engaged to a man who had been arrested for a terrible crime almost at the moment of their engagement, in spite of her illness and in spite of the almost inevitable sentence hanging over Dmitri, Grushenka had not lost her cheerfulness. There was a soft light in the once proud eyes, though at times they gleamed with the old vindictive fire when she was visited by one disturbing thought stronger than ever in her heart. The reason for that uneasiness was the same as ever—Katerina, of whom Grushenka had raved when she was delirious. Alyosha knew that she was very jealous of her. Yet Katerina had not once visited Dmitri in prison, though she might have done so whenever she liked. All this was very difficult for Alyosha, because he was the only person to whom Grushenka spoke freely and from whom she asked advice. Sometimes he was unable to say anything.

He was worried as he entered her rooms. She was at home. She had returned from seeing Dmitri half an hour before, and she had been expecting him with great impatience. A pack of cards dealt for a game of "fools" lay on the table. A bed had been made up on the leather sofa on the other side and Maximov lay, half-reclining, on it. He wore a dressing gown and a cotton nightcap, and was evidently ill and weak, though he was smiling. When the homeless old man returned with Grushenka from Mokroe two months before, he had stayed on and was still staying with her. He arrived with her in rain and sleet, sat down on the sofa, drenched and scared, and gazed at her with a timid, appealing smile. Grushenka, who was in terrible grief and feverish, almost forgot him because of all she had to do the first half hour after her return. Suddenly she chanced to look at him. He laughed a pitiful, helpless little laugh. She called Fenya and told her to give him something to eat. All that day he sat in the same place, almost without stirring. When it got dark and the shutters were closed, Fenya asked her mistress: "Is the gentleman going to stay the night?"

"Yes. Make up a bed for him on the sofa," answered Grushenka.

Questioning Maximov, Grushenka learned that he had literally nowhere to go, and that "Mr. Kalganov told me that he wouldn't receive me again and gave me five roubles."

"Well, God bless you, you'd better stay then," Grushenka decided in her grief, smiling compassionately at him. Her smile wrung the old man's heart and his lips twitched with emotion. And so the destitute wanderer had stayed with her ever since. He did not leave the house even when she was ill. Fenya and her grandmother, the cook, did not turn him out, but went on serving him meals and making up his bed on the sofa. Grushenka had grown used to him, and coming back from seeing Dmitri (whom she had begun to visit in prison before she was really well) she would sit down and begin talking to Maximov about trifling matters, to keep from thinking of her sorrow. The old man turned out to be a good storyteller, so that at last he became necessary to her. Grushenka saw scarcely anyone else except Alyosha, who did not come every day and never stayed long. Her old merchant, Samsonov, lay seriously ill at this time, "at his last gasp," as they said in town. He did, in fact, die a week after Dmitri's trial. Three weeks before his death, feeling the end approaching, he made his sons, their wives and children, come upstairs to him and told them not to leave him again. From that moment on he gave strict orders to his servants not to admit Grushenka and to tell her if she came: "The master wishes you long life and happiness and tells you to forget him." Grushenka did not try to visit him but she sent almost every day to inquire after his health.

"You've come at last!" she cried, flinging down the cards and greeting Alyosha. "Maximov has been trying to scare me saying that perhaps you wouldn't come. Oh, how I need you! Sit down. What will you have—coffee?"

"Yes, please," said Alyosha, sitting down at the table. "I am very hungry."

"That's right, Fenya, Fenya, coffee," cried Grushenka. "It's ready for you. And bring some little pies, and be sure they are hot. Do you know, we've had an argument over those pies today. I took them to prison for him, and would you believe it, he would not eat them. He threw one of them on the floor and stamped on it. So I said to him: 'I will leave them with the guard; if you don't eat them before evening, it will be that your venomous spite is enough for you!' With that I went away. We quarreled again, would you believe it? Whenever I go, we quarrel."

Grushenka said all this in one breath. Maximov, feeling nervous, smiled and looked at the floor.

"What did you quarrel about this time?" asked Alyosha.

"I didn't expect it in the least. Would you believe it, he is jealous of the Pole. 'Why are you keeping him?' he said. 'So you've begun keeping him.' He is jealous, jealous of me all the time, jealous eating and sleeping! He even took it into his head to be jealous of Samsonov last week."

"But he knew about the Pole before?"

"Yes, but that's how it is. He has known about him from the very beginning, but today he suddenly got up and began carrying on about him. I am ashamed to repeat what he said! Rakitin went in as I came out. Perhaps Rakitin is egging him on. What do you think?" she added carelessly.

"He loves you, that's what it is; he loves you so much. And now he is worried."

"I should think he might be, with the trial starting tomorrow. And I went to him to say something about tomorrow, for I dread to think what's going to happen. You say that he is worried, but how worried I am! And he talks about the Pole! He's too silly! He is not jealous of Maximov yet, anyway."

"My wife was dreadfully jealous, too," Maximov put in.

"Jealous of you?" Grushenka laughed in spite of herself. "Of whom could she have been jealous?"

"Of the servant girls."

"Hold your tongue, Maximov. I am in no laughing mood now, I feel angry. Don't look at the pies. I won't give you any; they are not good for you, and I won't give you any vodka either. I have to look after him," she laughed.

"I don't deserve your kindness. I am worthless," said Maximov, with tears in his voice. "You would do better to spend your time on people of more use than me."

"Oh, everyone is of use, Maximov. And besides how can we tell who's of most use. If only that Pole didn't exist, Alyosha. He's taken it into his head to fall ill today. I've been to see him too. And I shall send him some pies, too, on purpose. I hadn't sent him any, but Dmitri accused me of it, so now I will send

513

some! Oh, here's Fenya with a letter! Yes, it's from the Poles —begging again!"

Mussyalovitch had sent an extremely long and characteristically eloquent letter in which he begged her to lend him three roubles. In the letter was enclosed a receipt for the sum, with a promise to repay it within three months, signed by Vrublevsky as well. Grushenka had received many such letters, accompanied by receipts, from her former lover during the two weeks of her convalescence. And the two Poles had come to ask after her health during her illness. The first letter Grushenka got from them was a long one, written on large note paper embossed with a family crest. It was so obscure and rhetorical that Grushenka put it down before she had read half, unable to make head or tail of it. She could not attend to letters then. The first letter was followed next day by another in which Mussyalovitch begged her for a loan of two thousand roubles for a very short period. Grushenka left that letter, too, unanswered. A whole series of letters followed—one every day —all as pompous and rhetorical, but the loan asked for gradually diminished. It dropped to a hundred roubles, then to twenty-five, to ten, and finally Grushenka received a letter in which both the Poles begged her for only one rouble.

Grushenka suddenly felt sorry for them, and at dusk she went herself to their rooms. She found the two Poles in great poverty, almost destitution, without food or fuel, without cigarettes and in debt to their landlady. The two hundred roubles they had won dishonestly from Dmitri at Mokroe had soon disappeared. Grushenka was surprised at their meeting her with arrogant dignity and self-assertion, with pompous speeches. She simply laughed, and gave her former admirer ten roubles. Then later she told Dmitri of it and he was not in the least jealous. But ever since, the Poles had attached themselves to Grushenka and bombarded her daily with requests for money and she had always sent them small sums. And now that day Dmitri had taken it into his head to be fearfully jealous.

"Like a fool, I went around to him just for a minute, on the way to see Dmitri, for he is ill too, my Pole," Grushenka began again. "I was laughing, telling Dmitri about it. 'Would you believe it,' I said, 'my Pole had the happy thought to play the guitar and sing his old songs to me. He thought I would be touched and marry him!' Dmitri jumped up swearing. . . . So, there, I'll send them the pies! Fenya, is it that little girl they've sent? Here, give her three roubles and pack a dozen pies up in a paper and tell her to take them. And you, Alyosha, be sure to tell Dmitri that I sent them pies."

"I wouldn't tell him for anything," said Alyosha smiling.

"Oh! You think he is unhappy about it. Why, he's jealous on purpose. He doesn't care," said Grushenka bitterly.

"On purpose?" asked Alyosha.

"You are silly, Alyosha. You know nothing about it, with

514

all your cleverness. I am not offended that he is jealous of a girl like me. I would be offended if he were not jealous. I am like that. I am not offended at jealousy. I have a fierce heart, too. I can be jealous myself. Only what offends me is that he doesn't love me at all. I tell you he is jealous now on *purpose*. Am I blind? Don't I see? He began talking to me just now of that woman, of Katerina, saying she was this and that, how she had ordered a doctor from Moscow for him, to try to save him; how she had ordered the best lawyer, too. So he loves her! He's treated me badly, so he attacks me, to make out I am at fault in order to throw the blame on me. 'You saw your Pole just now, so I can't be blamed for Katerina,' that's what it amounts to. He wants to throw the whole blame on me. He attacked me on purpose, on purpose, I tell you, but I'll . . ."

Grushenka could not finish saying what she would do. She hid her eyes in her handkerchief and sobbed.

"He doesn't love Katerina," said Alyosha firmly.

"Well, whether he loves her or not, I'll soon find out for myself," said Grushenka, taking the handkerchief from her eyes. Her face was distorted. Alyosha saw that from being mild and serene, it had become sullen and spiteful.

"Enough of this foolishness," she said suddenly. "It's not for this I sent for you. Alyosha, darling, tomorrow—what will happen tomorrow? That's what worries me! And it's only me it worries! I look at everyone and no one is thinking of it. No one cares about it. Are you thinking about it? Tomorrow he'll be tried, you know. Tell me, how will it end? You know it's Smerdyakov, the valet, the valet killed him! Good heavens! Can they condemn him in place of Smerdyakov. Will no one stand up for him? They haven't troubled the valet at all, have they?"

"He's been carefully cross-examined," said Alyosha thoughtfully. "But everyone has come to the conclusion it was not he. Now he is very ill. He has been ill ever since that attack. Really ill," added Alyosha.

"Oh, dear! Couldn't you go to that lawyer and tell him the whole story? He's been brought from Petersburg for three thousand roubles, they say."

"We gave these three thousand together—Ivan, Katerina and I. But Katerina paid two thousand for the doctor from Moscow herself. The lawyer Fetyukovitch would have charged more, but the case has become known all over Russia; it's written up in all the papers and magazines. Fetyukovitch agreed to come more for the glory of the thing, because the case has become so notorious. I saw him yesterday."

"Well? Did you talk to him?" Grushenka asked eagerly.

"He listened and said nothing. He told me that he had already formed his opinion. But he promised to give my words consideration."

"Consideration! Oh, they are swindlers! They'll ruin him. And why did she send for the doctor?"

"As an expert. They want to prove that Dmitri's mad and committed the murder when he didn't know what he was doing," Alyosha smiled gently. "But Dmitri won't agree to that."

"That would be all right if he had killed him!" cried Grushenka. "He was mad then, perfectly mad, and that was my fault, wretch that I am! But, of course, he didn't do it, he didn't do it! And they are all against him, the whole town. Even Fenya's evidence went to prove he had done it. And the people at the shop where he bought the champagne and other things, and that official, Perhotin . . . and at the tavern, too, people had heard him say so! They are all, all against him. All are crying out against him."

"Yes, there's a frightening accumulation of evidence," Alyosha observed.

"And Gregory—Gregory sticks to his story that the door was open, persists that he saw it—there's no shaking him. I went and talked to him myself. He's rude about it, too."

"Yes, that's perhaps the strongest evidence against Dmitri," said Alyosha.

"And as for Dmitri's being mad, he certainly seems like it now," Grushenka began mysteriously. "Do you know, Alyosha, I've been wanting to talk to you about it for a long time. I go to him every day and simply wonder at him. Tell me, now, what do you suppose he's always talking about? He talks and talks and I can make nothing of it. I thought he was talking of something intellectual that I couldn't understand in my ignorance. He suddenly began talking to me about a babe—that is, about some child. 'Why is the babe poor?' he said. 'It's for that babe I am going to Siberia. I am not a murderer, but I must go to Siberia!' What that meant, what babe, I couldn't tell for the life of me. Only I cried when he said it, because he said it so nicely. He cried himself, and I cried, too. He suddenly kissed me and made the sign of the cross over me. What did it mean, Alyosha, tell me? What is this babe?"

"It must be Rakitin, who's been going to see him lately," smiled Alyosha. "Though . . . that's not Rakitin's doing. I didn't see Dmitri yesterday. I'll see him today."

"No, it's not Rakitin. It's Ivan who is upsetting him. It's his going to see him, that's what it is," Grushenka began, and suddenly broke off. Alyosha looked at her in amazement.

"Ivan? Has he been to see him? Dmitri told me himself that Ivan hasn't come once."

"There . . . there! What a girl I am! Blurting things out!" exclaimed Grushenka, confused and suddenly blushing. "Wait, Alyosha, hush! Since I've said so much I'll tell you everything. Ivan's been to see him twice, the first time right after he arrived. He galloped here from Moscow at once, of course, before I was taken ill; and the second time was a week ago. He told Dmitri not to tell you about it, under any circumstances. Not to tell anyone, in fact. He came secretly."

Alyosha sat in thought, considering something. This news evidently impressed him.

"Ivan doesn't talk to me of Dmitri's case," he said slowly. "He's said very little to me these last two months. And whenever I go to see him, he seems annoyed at my coming, so I've not been to him for the last three weeks. Hm! . . . if he was there a week ago . . . There certainly has been a change in Dmitri this week."

"There has been a change," Grushenka agreed quickly. "They have a secret, they have a secret! Dmitri told me himself there was a secret, and such a secret that Dmitri can't rest. Before then, he was cheerful—and as a matter of fact, he is cheerful now—but when he shakes his head like that, you know, and strides about the room and keeps pulling at the hair on his right temple with his right hand, I know there is something worrying him. . . . I know! He was cheerful before . . . Though he is cheerful today."

"But you said he was worried."

"Yes, he is worried and yet cheerful. He keeps on being irritable for a minute and then cheerful and then irritable again. And you know, Alyosha, I am constantly wondering at him— with this awful thing hanging over him, he sometimes laughs at such trifles as though he were a baby himself."

"And did he really tell you not to tell me about Ivan? Did he say 'don't tell him'?"

"Yes, he said: 'Don't tell him.' It's you that Dmitri's most afraid of. Because it's a secret; he said himself it was a secret. Alyosha, darling, go to him and find out what their secret is and come and tell me," Grushenka besought him with sudden eagerness. "Set my mind at rest. Let me know the worst that's in store for me. That's why I sent for you."

"You think it's something to do with you? If it were, he wouldn't have told you there was a secret."

"I don't know. Perhaps he wants to tell me, but doesn't dare to. He warns me. There is a secret, he tells me, but he won't tell me what it is."

"What do you think yourself?"

"What do I think? It's the end for me, that's what I think. They all three have been plotting my end, for Katerina's in it. It's all Katerina, it all comes from her. He tells me beforehand —warns me. He is planning to throw me over, that's the whole secret. They've planned it together, the three of them—Dmitri, Katerina, and Ivan. Alyosha, I've been wanting to ask you a long time. A week ago he suddenly told me that Ivan was in love with Katerina, because he often goes to see her. Did he tell me the truth or not? Tell me, on your word of honor, tell me the worst."

517

"I won't tell you a lie. I don't think that Ivan is in love with Katerina."

"Oh, that's what I thought! Dmitri is lying to me, that's what it is! And he was jealous of me just now, so as to put the blame on me afterwards. He is stupid, he can't disguise what he is doing; he is so open, you know. . . . But I'll get even with him, I'll get even with him! 'You believe I did it,' he said. He said that to me, to me. He reproached me with that! God forgive him! You wait, I'll make it hot for Katerina at the trial! I'll just say a word then . . . I'll tell everything then!"

And again she cried bitterly.

"This I can tell you for certain, Grushenka," Alyosha said, getting up. "First, that he loves you, loves you more than anyone in the world, and you only, believe me. I know. I do know. The second thing is that I don't want to get his secret out of him, but if he tells me, I will tell him straight out that I have promised to tell you. Then I'll come and tell you. Only . . . I believe . . . Katerina has nothing to do with it; the secret is about something else. That's certain. It isn't likely to be about Katerina, it seems to me. Good-bye for now."

Alyosha shook hands with her. Grushenka was still crying. He saw that she put little faith in his consolation, but she was better for having had her sorrow out, for having spoken of it. He was sorry to leave her in such a state of mind, but he was in a hurry. He had a great many things still to do.

2. The Injured Foot

THE FIRST OF THESE THINGS was at the house of Madame Hohlakov, and he hurried there to get it over as quickly as possible and not to be too late for Dmitri. Madame Hohlakov had been ailing for the last three weeks; her foot had for some reason swollen up, and although she was not in bed, she lay all day on the couch in her bedroom, in a beautiful dressing gown. Alyosha had recently noted with innocent amusement that, in spite of her illness, Madame Hohlakov had begun to be rather dressy—ribbons, loose gowns, had made their appearance, and he had an inkling of the reason, though he dismissed such ideas from his mind as frivolous. During the last two months the young official, Perhotin, had become a regular visitor at the house.

Alyosha had not called for four days and he was in a hurry to go straight to Lise, as it was with her that he had to speak. Lise had sent a maid to him the day before, asking him to come to her "about something very important." But while the maid went to take his name in to Lise, Madame Hohlakov heard of his arrival and immediately sent to beg him to come to her "just for one minute." Alyosha thought that it was better to give in to Madame Hohlakov, otherwise she would be sending down to Lise's room every minute that he was there.

Madame Hohlakov was lying on her couch. She was very excited. She greeted Alyosha with cries of rapture.

"It's ages, ages, perfect ages since I've seen you! It's a whole week—only think of it! Ah, but you were here only four days ago, on Wednesday. You have come to see Lise. I'm sure you meant to slip into her room on tiptoe, without my hearing you. My dear, dear Alyosha, if you only knew how worried I am about her! But of that later, though that's the most important thing, of that later. Dear Alyosha, I trust you implicitly with my Lise. Since the death of Father Zossima—God rest his soul! (she crossed herself)—I look upon you as a monk, though you look charming in your new suit. Where did you find such a tailor? No, no, that's not the main thing—of that later. Forgive me for calling you Alyosha; an old woman like me may take liberties and be intimate," she smiled coquettishly. "But that will hold till later, too. The important thing is that I shouldn't forget what is important. Please remind me of it yourself. As soon as my tongue runs away with me, you just say 'the important thing?' Oh! How do I know now what is of most importance? Ever since Lise took back her promise—her childish promise, Alyosha—to marry you, you've realized, of course, that it was only the playful fancy of a sick child who had been so long confined to her chair—thank God, she can walk now! . . . That new doctor Katerina sent for from Moscow for your unhappy brother, who will tomorrow . . . But why speak of tomorrow? I am ready to die at the very thought of tomorrow. Ready to die of curiosity. . . . That doctor was with us yesterday and saw Lise. . . . I paid him fifty roubles for the visit. But that's not the point, that's not the point. You see, I'm mixing everything up. I am in such a hurry. Why am I in a hurry? I don't understand. It's awful how I seem to be unable to understand anything. Everything seems mixed up in a sort of tangle. I am afraid you are so bored you will jump up and run away, and that will be all I shall see of you. Goodness! Why are we sitting here and no coffee? Julia, coffee!"

Alyosha hurried to thank her, and said that he had only just had coffee.

"Where?"

"At Grushenka's."

"At . . . at that woman's? Ah, she has brought ruin on everyone. I know nothing about it though. They say she has become a saint, though it's rather late in the day. It would be better if she had done it before. What use is it now? Hush, hush, Alyosha, I have so much to say to you that I am afraid I shall tell you nothing. This awful trial . . . I shall certainly go, I am making arrangements. I shall be carried there in my chair; besides I can sit up. I shall have people with me. And, you know,

I am a witness. How shall I speak, how shall I speak? I don't know what I shall say. One has to take an oath, doesn't one?"

"Yes. But I don't think you will be able to go."

"I can sit up. Oh, you make me angry. Oh, this trial, this savage act, and then they are all going to Siberia. Some are getting married. And all this so quickly, so quickly, everything's changing, and at last—nothing. All grow old and have death to look forward to. Well, so be it! I am weary. This charming Katerina has disappointed all my hopes. Now she is going to follow one of your brothers to Siberia, and your other brother is going to follow her, and will live in the nearest town, and they will all torment one another. It drives me out of my mind. Worst of all—the publicity. The story has been told a million times over in all the papers in Moscow and Petersburg. Ah! yes, would you believe it, there's a story that I was 'a dear friend' of your brother's—, I can't repeat the horrid word. Just imagine, just imagine!"

"Impossible! Where did this story appear? What did it say?"

"I'll show you. I got the paper and read it yesterday. Here, in the Petersburg paper *Gossip*. The paper began coming out this year. I am awfully fond of gossip, and I subscribe to it, and now it pays me back—this is what gossip comes to! Here it is, here, this passage. Read it."

And she handed Alyosha a newspaper which had been under her pillow.

It was not exactly that she was upset, she seemed overwhelmed, and perhaps everything really was mixed up in a tangle in her head. The paragraph was typical, and must have been a great shock to her. But fortunately perhaps, she was unable to keep her mind fixed on any one subject at that moment, and would soon forget the newspaper.

Alyosha was aware that the story of his father's murder had spread all over Russia. What wild rumors about the Karamazovs he had read in the course of those two months! One paper had even stated that he, Alyosha, had gone into a monastery and become a monk, in horror at his brother's crime. Another contradicted this, and stated that he and his elder, Father Zossima, had broken into the monastery chest and "made tracks from the monastery." The present story in the *Gossip* was under the heading: "The Karamazov Case at Skotoprigonyevsk." (That was the name of our little town. I have till now kept it concealed.) It was brief, and Madame Hohlakov was not directly mentioned in it. No names appeared, in fact. It was merely stated that the criminal, whose approaching trial was making such a sensation—retired army captain, an idle swaggerer, and reactionary bully—was continually involved in love affairs and particularly popular with certain ladies "who were pining in solitude." One such lady, a pining widow, who tried to seem young though she had a grown-up daughter, was so fascinated by him that only two hours before the crime she offered him three thousand roubles, on condition that he would elope with her to the gold mines. But the criminal, counting on escaping punishment, had preferred to murder his father to get the three thousand, rather than go off to Siberia with the middle-aged lady. This playful story finished, of course, with an outburst of indignation at the wickedness of parricide and at the lately abolished institution of serfdom. Reading it with curiosity, Alyosha folded up the paper and handed it back to Madame Hohlakov.

"Well, that must be me," she hurried on again. "Of course I am meant. Scarcely more than an hour before, I suggested gold mines to Dmitri, and here they talk of 'middle-aged charms' as though that were my motive! He writes that out of spite! God Almighty forgive him for the middle-aged charms, as I forgive him! You know it's . . . Do you know who it is? It's your friend Rakitin."

"Perhaps," said Alyosha, "though I've heard nothing about it."

"It's he, it's he! No 'perhaps' about it. You know I turned him out of the house. . . . You know all about that, don't you?"

"I know that you asked him not to visit you again, but why it was, I haven't heard . . . from you, at least."

"Ah, then you've heard it from him! He abuses me, I suppose, abuses me dreadfully?"

"Yes, he does. But then he abuses everyone. But why you are not seeing him, I haven't heard from him either. I meet him very seldom now. We are not friends."

"Well, then, I'll tell you all about it. I'll confess there is one point in which I was perhaps to blame. Only a little, little point, so little that perhaps it doesn't count. You see, my dear boy"—Madame Hohlakov suddenly looked arch and a charming, though mysterious, smile played about her lips—"you see, I suspect . . . You must forgive me, Alyosha. I am like a mother to you. . . . No, no; quite the contrary. I speak to you now, as though you were my father—mother's quite out of place. Well, it's as though I were confessing to Father Zossima, that's just it. I called you a monk just now. Well, that poor young man, your friend, Rakitin (Mercy on us! I can't be angry with him. I feel cross, but not very), that frivolous young man, would you believe it, seems to have taken it into his head to fall in love with me. I only noticed it lately. At first—a month ago—he began to come to see me almost every day; though, of course, we were acquainted before. I knew nothing about it . . . And suddenly it dawned upon me, and I began to notice things. You know, two months ago, that charming young man, Peter Perhotin, who's in the service here, began to be a regular visitor at the house. You met him here ever so many times yourself. And he is an excellent, earnest young man, isn't he? He comes once every three days, not every day (though I should be glad to see him every day), and always so well dressed.

521

Altogether, I love young people, Alyosha, talented, modest, like you. And he has the mind of a statesman, he talks so charmingly. I shall certainly, certainly try and get a promotion for him. He is a future diplomat. . . . On that awful day he almost saved me from death by coming in the night. And your friend Rakitin comes wearing such boots and always stretches them out on the carpet. . . . He began hinting at his feelings, in fact, and one day, as he was going, he squeezed my hand terribly hard. My foot began to swell directly after he pressed my hand like that. He had met Peter Perhotin here before, and would you believe it, he was always gibing at him, growling at him, for some reason. I just looked at the way they went on together and laughed inwardly. So I was sitting here alone—no, I was laid up then. Well, I was lying here alone and suddenly Rakitin comes in, and would you believe it he brought me a poem he had composed—a short poem, on my bad foot. That is, he described my foot in a poem. Wait a minute—how did it go?

A captivating little foot.

It began something like that. I can never remember poetry. I've got it here. I'll show it to you later. But it's a charming thing—charming. And, you know, it's not only about my foot, it had a moral, too, a charming idea, only I've forgotten it. In fact, it was just the thing for an album. So, of course, I thanked him, and he was flattered. But I'd hardly had time to thank him when in comes Peter Perhotin, and Rakitin suddenly looked as black as night. I could see that Peter Perhotin was in the way, for Rakitin certainly wanted to say something after giving me the poem. I had a presentiment of it; but Perhotin came in. I showed Perhotin the poem but didn't say who was the author. But I am convinced that he guessed, though he won't admit it to this day, and says he had no idea. But he says that on purpose. He began to laugh and criticize it at once. 'Doggerel,' he said. 'Some divinity student must have written it.' And with such vehemence, such vehemence! Then, instead of laughing, Rakitin flew into a rage. 'Good gracious!' I thought, 'they'll fly at each other.' 'It was I who wrote it,' he said. 'I wrote it as a joke,' he said, 'for I think it degrading to write verses. . . . But it is good poetry. They want to erect a monument to Pushkin for writing about women's feet, while I wrote with a moral purpose, and you,' he said, 'are an advocate of serfdom. You've no humane ideas,' he said. 'You have no modern, enlightened feelings, you are uninfluenced by progress, you are a mere official,' he said. 'And you take bribes.' Then I began screaming and imploring them. And, you know, Peter Perhotin is anything but a coward. He at once took up the most gentlemanly tone, looked at Rakitin sarcastically, listened, and apologized. 'I'd no idea,' he said. 'I wouldn't have said it if I had known. I would have praised it. Poets are so irritable,' he said. In short,

522

he laughed at him. He explained to me afterward that it was all sarcastic. I thought he was in earnest. Only as I lay there, just as before you now, I thought: 'Would it, or would it not, be the proper thing for me to turn Rakitin out for shouting so rudely at a visitor in my house?' And, would you believe it, I lay here, shut my eyes, and wondered, would it be the proper thing or not. I kept worrying and worrying, and my heart began to pound. I couldn't make up my mind whether to speak out or not. One voice seemed to be telling me, 'speak,' and the other, 'no, don't speak.' And no sooner had the second voice said that than I cried out, and fainted. Of course, there was a terrible fuss. I got up suddenly and said to Rakitin: 'It's painful for me to say it, but I don't wish to see you in my house again.' So I turned him out. Ah! Alyosha, I know I did wrong. I was too impulsive. I wasn't angry with him at all really; but I suddenly felt—that was what did it—that it would make such a fine scene. . . . And yet, believe me, it was quite natural, for I really shed tears and cried for several days afterwards. And then suddenly, one afternoon, I forgot all about it. So it's two weeks since he's been here, and I keep wondering whether he will come again. I wondered even yesterday, then suddenly last night came this *Gossip*. I read it and gasped. Who could have written it? Rakitin must have written it. He went home, sat down, wrote it, sent it, and they put it in. It was two weeks ago, you see. But, Alyosha, it's awful how I keep talking and don't say what I want to say. Ah, the words come of themselves!"

"It's very important for me to be in time to see my brother today," Alyosha faltered.

"To be sure, to be sure! You bring it all back to me. Listen, what is an aberration?"

"What aberration?" asked Alyosha, wondering.

"In the legal sense. An aberration in which everything is pardonable. Whatever you do, you will be acquitted."

"What do you mean?"

"I'll tell you. Katerina . . . Ah, she is a charming, charming creature, only I never can make out who it is she is in love with. She was with me some time ago and I couldn't get anything out of her. Especially as she won't talk to me except on the surface now. She is always talking about my health and nothing else, and she takes up such a tone with me, too. I simply said to myself: 'Well, so be it. I don't care.' . . . Oh, yes. I was talking of aberration. This doctor has come. You know a doctor has come? Of course you know it—the one who discovers madmen. You wrote for him. No, it wasn't you, but Katerina. It's all Katerina's doing. Well, you see, a man may be sitting perfectly sane and suddenly have an aberration. He may be conscious and know what he is doing and yet be in a state of aberration. And there's no doubt that Dmitri was suffering from aberration. They found out about aberration as soon as the law courts were reformed. It's all due to the reformed law courts. The doctor has been here and questioned me about that evening, about the gold mines. 'How did he seem then?' he asked me. He must have been in a state of aberration. He came in shouting: 'Money, money, three thousand! Give me three thousand!' And then he went away and immediately committed the murder. 'I don't want to murder him,' he said, and he suddenly went and murdered him. That's why they'll acquit him, because he struggled against it and yet he murdered him."

"But he didn't murder him," Alyosha interrupted rather sharply. He felt more and more sick with anxiety and impatience.

"Yes, I know it was that old man Gregory murdered him."

"Gregory?" cried Alyosha.

"Yes, yes. It was Gregory. He lay as Dmitri struck him down, and then got up, saw the door open, went in and killed your father."

"But why, why?"

"Suffering from aberration. When he recovered from the blow Dmitri gave him on the head, he was suffering from aberration: he went and committed the murder. As for his saying he didn't, he very likely doesn't remember. Only, you know, it'll be better, ever so much better, if Dmitri murdered him. And that's how it must have been, though I say it was Gregory. It certainly was Dmitri, and that's better, ever so much better! Oh, not better that a son should have killed his father, I don't defend that. Children ought to honor their parents. And yet it would be better if it were Dmitri, as you'd have nothing to cry over then, for he did it when he was unconscious or rather when he was conscious, but did not know what he was doing. Let them acquit him—that's so humane, and would show what a blessing reformed law courts are. I knew nothing about it, but they say the courts have been reformed for a long time. And when I heard it yesterday, I was so struck by it that I wanted to send for you at once. And if Dmitri is acquitted, make him come straight from the law courts to dinner with me, and I'll have a party of friends, and we'll drink to the reformed law courts. I don't believe he'd be dangerous; besides, I'll invite a great many people, so that he could always be led out if he did anything. And then he might be made a justice of the peace or something in another town, for those who have been in trouble themselves make the best judges. And, besides, who isn't suffering from aberration nowadays? You, I, all of us are in a state of aberration. There are ever so many examples of it; a man sits singing a song, suddenly something annoys him, he takes a pistol and shoots the first person he comes across. And no one blames him for it. I read that lately and all the doctors confirm it. The doctors are always confirming; they confirm anything. Why, my Lise is in a state of aberration. She made me cry again yesterday, and the day before, too. And today I suddenly realized that it's all due to aberration. Oh, Lise grieves me so! I believe she's quite mad. Why did she send for you? Did she send for you or did you come of yourself?"

"Yes, she sent for me, and I am going to her now." Alyosha got up with determination.

"Oh, my dear, dear Alyosha, perhaps that's what's most important," Madame Hohlakov cried, suddenly bursting into tears. "God knows I trust Lise to you with all my heart, and it doesn't matter her sending for you secretly, without telling me. But forgive me, I can't trust my daughter so easily to your brother Ivan, though I still consider him the most chivalrous young man. But only think, he's been to see Lise and I knew nothing about it!"

"How? What? When?" Alyosha was surprised.

"I will tell you, that's perhaps why I asked you to come, for I don't know now why I did ask you to come. Well, Ivan has been to see me twice, since he came back from Moscow. The first time he came as a friend to call on me, and the second time Katerina was here and he came because he heard she was here. I didn't, of course, expect him to come often, knowing what a lot he has to do as it is, you understand, on account of your father's terrible death. But I suddenly heard he'd been here again, not to see me but to see Lise. That was six days ago. He came, stayed five minutes, and went away. And I didn't hear of it till three days afterward, from the maid, so it was a great shock to me. I sent for Lise directly. She laughed. 'He thought you were asleep,' she said, 'and came in to me to ask after your health.' Of course, that's how it happened. But Lise, Lise, mercy on us, how she upsets me! Would you believe it, one night, four days ago, just after you saw her last time, she suddenly had a fit, screaming, shrieking, hysterics! Why is it I never have hysterics? Then, next day another fit and the same thing on the third, and yesterday too. And then yesterday that aberration. She suddenly screamed out, 'I hate Ivan Karamazov. Never let him come to the house again.' I was struck dumb at these words, and answered: 'On what grounds could I refuse to see such an excellent young man, a young man of such learning too, and so unfortunate?' For all this business is a misfortune, isn't it? She suddenly burst out laughing at my words, and so rudely, you know. Well, I was pleased. I thought I had amused her and the fits would pass off. Then besides I wanted to refuse to see Ivan anyway on account of his secret visits. I meant to ask him for an explanation. But early this morning Lise woke up and flew into a passion with Julia and, would you believe it, slapped her in the face. That's monstrous, I am always polite to my servants. And an hour later she was hugging Julia's feet and kissing them. She sent a message to me, that she wasn't coming to me at all, and would never come and see me again. And when I dragged myself down to her, she rushed to kiss me, crying, and as she kissed me, she pushed me out of the room without saying a word so that I couldn't find out what was the matter. Now, dear Alyosha, I rest all my hopes on you. My whole life is in your hands. I beg you to go to Lise and find out everything, as you alone can, and come back and tell me—me, her mother. You understand it will be the death of me, simply the death of me, if this goes on, or else I shall run away. I can stand no more. I have patience; but I may lose patience, and then . . . Then something awful will happen. . . . Oh, dear me! At last, Peter Perhotin!" cried Madame Hohlakov, beaming all over as she saw Perhotin enter the room. "You are late, you are late! Well, sit down, speak. What does the lawyer say? Where are you going, Alyosha?"

"To Lise."

"Oh, yes. You won't forget, you won't forget what I asked you? It's a question of life and death!"

"Of course I won't forget, if I can . . . But I am so late," muttered Alyosha leaving the room.

"No, be sure, be sure to come back. Don't say 'if I can.' I shall die if you don't," Madame Hohlakov called after him.

3. A Little Demon

GOING IN TO LISE, Alyosha found her reclining in the invalid chair, in which she had been wheeled when she was unable to walk. She did not move to meet him, but her keen eyes were simply riveted on his face. There was a feverish look in her eyes, her face was pale and yellow. Alyosha was amazed at the change that had taken place in her in three days. She was thinner. She did not hold out her hand to him. He touched the thin, long fingers which lay motionless on her dress, then without a word he sat down facing her.

"I know you are in a hurry to go to the prison," Lise said curtly, "and mother's kept you there for hours. She's been telling you about me and Julia."

"How do you know?" asked Alyosha.

"I've been listening. Why do you stare at me? I want to listen and I do listen, there's no harm in that. I don't apologize."

"You are upset about something?"

"No, I am very happy. I've only just been thinking for the thirtieth time what a good thing it is I refused you and won't be your wife. You are not fit to be a husband. If I were to marry you and give you a note to take to the man I loved, you'd take it and be sure to give it to him and bring an answer back, too. If you were forty, you would still go on delivering my love letters for me."

She suddenly laughed.

"There is something spiteful and yet open-hearted about you," Alyosha smiled to her.

"The open-heartedness consists in my not being ashamed of myself with you. What's more, I don't want to feel ashamed with you, just with you. Alyosha, why is it I don't respect you? I am very fond of you, but I don't respect you. If I respected you, I wouldn't talk to you without shame, would I?"

"No."

"But do you believe that I am not ashamed with you?"

"No, I don't believe it."

Lise laughed nervously again. She spoke quickly.

"I sent your brother Dmitri some candy in prison. Alyosha, you know, you are quite handsome! I love you awfully for having so quickly allowed me not to love you."

"Why did you send for me today, Lise?"

"I wanted to tell you of a longing I have. I would like someone to torture me, marry me and then torture me, deceive me and go away. I don't want to be happy."

"You are in love with disorder?"

"Yes, I want disorder. I keep wanting to set fire to the house. I keep imagining how I'll creep up and set fire to the house secretly, it must be secretly. They'll try to put it out, but it'll go on burning. And I will know and say nothing. Oh, what silliness! And how bored I am!"

She waved her hand with a look of repulsion.

"It's your luxurious life," said Alyosha softly.

"Is it better then to be poor?"

"Yes, it is better."

"That's what your monk taught you. That's not true. Let me be rich and all the rest poor. I'll eat cake and drink cream and I won't give any to anyone else. Oh, don't speak, don't say anything," she shook her hand at him, although Alyosha had not opened his mouth. "You've told me all that before, I know it all by heart. It bores me. If I am ever poor, I will murder somebody, and even if I am rich, I may murder someone, perhaps —why do nothing! But do you know, I would like to reap, cut the rye? I'll marry you, and you will become a peasant, a real peasant; we'll keep a colt, won't we? Do you know Kalganov?"

"Yes."

"He is always wandering about, dreaming. He says, why live in real life, it's better to dream. One can dream the most delightful things, but real life is a bore. But he'll be married soon, he's been making love to me. Can you spin tops?"

"Yes."

"Well, he's just like a top; he wants to be wound up and set spinning and then to be lashed, lashed, lashed with a whip. If I marry him, I'll keep him spinning all his life. You are not ashamed to be with me?"

"No."

"You are awfully cross, because I don't talk about holy things. I don't want to be holy. What will they do to one in the next world for the greatest sin? You must know all about that."

"God will censure you." Alyosha was watching her steadily.

"That's just what I would like. I would go up and they would censure me and I would burst out laughing in their faces. . . . I would like to set fire to the house, Alyosha, to our house. You still don't believe me?"

"Why? There are children twelve years old, who have a longing to set fire to something and they do set things on fire. It's a sort of disease."

"That's not true, that's not true. There may be children, but that's not what I mean."

"You take evil for good. It's a passing crisis. It's the result of your illness, perhaps."

"You do despise me! It's simply that I don't want to do good, I want to do evil, and it has nothing to do with illness."

"Why do evil?"

"So that everything will be destroyed. Oh, how nice it would be if everything were destroyed! You know, Alyosha, I sometimes think of doing a lot of harm. I would do it for a long while secretly and then suddenly everyone would find out. Everyone will stand around and point their fingers at me and I will look at them all. That would be awfully nice. Why would it be so nice, Alyosha?"

"I don't know. It's a craving to destroy something good or, as you say, to set fire to something. It happens sometimes."

"I not only say it, I will do it."

"I believe you."

"Oh, how I love you for saying you believe me. And you are not lying. But perhaps you think that I am saying all this just to annoy you?"

"No, I don't think that . . . Though perhaps there is a desire to do that, too."

"There is a little. I never can tell lies to you," she declared with a strange fire in her eyes.

What struck Alyosha above everything was her earnestness. There was not a trace of joking in her face now, though in the old days fun and gaiety never deserted her even at her most "earnest" moments.

"There are moments when people love crime," said Alyosha thoughtfully.

"Yes, yes! People love crime. Everyone loves crime, they love it always, not at some 'moments.' You know, it's as though people have made an agreement to lie about it and have lied about it ever since. They all say that they hate evil, but secretly they all love it."

"And are you still reading nasty books?"

"Yes, I am. Mother reads them and hides them under her pillow and I steal them."

"Aren't you ashamed? You are destroying yourself."

"I want to destroy myself. There's a boy here who once lay down between the railway tracks when the train was passing. Lucky fellow! Listen, your brother is being tried now for murdering your father and everyone loves his having killed your father."

"Loves his having killed father?"

"Yes, loves it, everyone loves it! Everybody says it's so awful, but secretly they love it. I for one love it."

"There is some truth in what you say," said Alyosha softly.

"Oh, what ideas you have!" Lise shrieked in delight. "And you a monk, too! You wouldn't believe how I respect you, Alyosha, for never telling lies. Oh, I must tell you a funny dream I had. I sometimes dream of devils. It's night, I am in my room with a candle and suddenly there are devils all over the place, in all the corners, under the table. And they open the doors, there's a crowd of them behind the doors and they want to come and grab me. And they are just coming, just grabbing me. But I suddenly cross myself and they all draw back, though they don't go away altogether. They stand at the doors and in the corners, waiting. And suddenly I have a frightful longing to revile God aloud, and so I begin. And then they come crowding back to me, delighted, and grab me again and I cross myself again and they all draw back. It's awful fun, it takes one's breath away."

"I've had the same dream, too," said Alyosha suddenly.

"Really?" cried Lise, surprised. "Alyosha, don't laugh, it's awfully important. Can two different people have the same dream?"

"It seems they can."

"Alyosha, I tell you, it's awfully important," Lise went on, with amazement. "It's not the dream that's important, but your having the same dream as me. You never lie to me. Don't lie now. Is it true? You are not laughing?"

"It's true."

Lise seemed extraordinarily impressed and for half a minute she was silent.

"Alyosha, come and see me, come and see me more often," she said suddenly, pleading.

"I'll always come to see you, all my life," answered Alyosha firmly.

"You are the only person I can talk to, you know," Lise began again. "I talk to no one but myself and you. Only you in the whole world. And to you more easily than to myself. And I am not a bit ashamed with you, not a bit. Alyosha, why am I not ashamed with you, not a bit? Alyosha, is it true that at Easter certain religious sects steal a child and kill it?"

"I don't know."

"There's a book here in which I read about the trial of a man who took a four year old child and cut off the fingers from both hands, and then crucified him on the wall, hammered nails into him, and crucified him. And afterwards, when he was tried, he said that the child died quickly, within four hours. That was 'quickly'! He said the child moaned, kept on moaning and he stood admiring it. That's nice!"

"Nice?"

"Nice. I sometimes imagine that it was I who crucified him. He would hang there moaning and I would sit opposite him eating pineapple jam. I am awfully fond of pineapple jam. Do you like it?"

Alyosha looked at her in silence. Her pale, sallow face was suddenly contorted, her eyes burned.

"You know, when I read about that child, I cried all night. I kept thinking of how the little thing cried and moaned (a child of four understands, you know) and all the while the thought of pineapple jam haunted me. In the morning I wrote a letter to a certain person, begging him to come and see me. He came and I told him all about the child and the pineapple jam. *All* about it, *all*, and said that it was nice. He laughed and said it really was nice. Then he got up and went away. He was only here five minutes. Did he despise me? Did he despise me? Tell me, tell me, Alyosha, did he despise me or not?" She sat up.

"Tell me," Alyosha asked anxiously. "Did you send for that person?"

"Yes, I did."

"Did you send him a letter?"

"Yes."

"Simply to ask about that, about that child?"

"No, not about that at all. But when he came, I asked him about that at once. He answered, laughed, got up and went away."

"That person behaved honorably," Alyosha murmured.

"And did he despise me? Did he laugh at me?"

"No, for perhaps he believes in pineapple jam himself. He is very ill now, Lise."

"Yes, he does believe in it," said Lise, with flashing eyes.

"He doesn't despise anyone," Alyosha went on. "Only he does not believe anyone. If he doesn't believe in people, of course, he does despise them."

"Then he despises me, me?"

"You, too."

"Good. When he went out laughing, I felt that it was nice to be despised. The child with fingers cut off is nice and to be despised is nice . . ."

And she laughed in Alyosha's face, a feverish malicious laugh.

"Do you know, Alyosha, do you know, I would like . . . Alyosha save me!" she suddenly jumped from the invalid chair, rushed to him and grabbed him with both hands. "Save me!" she almost groaned. "Is there anyone in the world I could tell what I've told you? I've told you the truth, the truth. I will kill myself, because I hate everything! I don't want to live, because I hate everything! I hate everything, everything, Alyosha, why don't you love me?" she finished in a frenzy.

"But I do love you!" answered Alyosha warmly.

"And will you weep over me, will you?"

"Yes."

"Not because I won't be your wife, but simply because . . . Thank you! It's only your tears I want. Everyone else may punish me and trample me under foot, everyone, everyone. For I don't love anyone. Do you hear, not anyone! On the contrary, I hate him! Go, Alyosha, it's time you went to your brother." She tore herself away from him suddenly.

"How can I leave you like this?" said Alyosha, almost in alarm.

"Go to your brother. The prison will be closed. Go, here's your hat. Give my love to Dmitri. Go, go!"

And she almost pushed Aloysha out of the door. He looked at her with surprise. He was suddenly aware of a letter in his right hand, a tiny letter folded up and sealed. He glanced at it and instantly read: "To Ivan Karamazov." He looked quickly at Lise. Her face had become almost menacing.

"Give it to him, you must give it to him!" she ordered him, trembling. "Today, at once, or I'll poison myself! That's why I sent for you."

And she slammed the door quickly. The bolt clicked. Alyosha put the note in his pocket and went straight downstairs, without going back to Madame Hohlakov, forgetting her, in fact.

As soon as Alyosha had gone, Lise unbolted the door, opened it a little, put her finger in the crack and slammed the door with all her might, pinching her finger. Ten seconds later, releasing her finger, she walked softly, slowly to her chair. She sat up straight in it and looked intently at her blackened finger and at the blood that oozed from under the nail.

Her lips were quivering and she kept whispering to herself: "I am a wretch, wretch, wretch, wretch!"

4. A Hymn and a Secret

IT WAS QUITE LATE (days are short in November) when Alyosha rang at the prison gate. It was beginning to get dusk. But Alyosha knew that he would be admitted without difficulty. Things were managed in our little town, as everywhere else. At first, of course, on the conclusion of the preliminary inquiry, relatives and a few other persons could only obtain interviews with Dmitri by going through certain formalities. But later, though the formalities were not relaxed, exceptions were made for some of Dmitri's visitors.

These exceptions, however, were few in number: only Grushenka, Alyosha and Rakitin were treated like this. But the captain of the police, Michael Makarov was very well disposed to Grushenka. His abuse of her at Mokroe weighed on his conscience, and when he learned the whole story, he completely changed his view of her. And, strange to say though he was firmly persuaded of Dmitri's guilt, yet after Dmitri was once in prison, the old man took a more and more lenient view of him. "He is a man of good heart, perhaps," he thought, "who has come to grief from drinking and dissipation." His first horror had been succeeded by pity.

As for Alyosha, the police captain was very fond of him and had known him for a long time. And Rakitin, who had of late taken to coming very often to see Dmitri, was one of the most intimate acquaintances of the "police captain's young ladies," as he called them, and was always hanging around their house. He gave lessons in the house of the prison superintendent, too, who, although scrupulous in the performance of his duties, was a kind-hearted old man. Alyosha also had an intimate acquaintance of long standing with the superintendent, who was fond of talking to him on sacred subjects. He respected Ivan Karamazov and stood in awe of his opinions, though he was a great philosopher himself; "self-taught," of course. But Alyosha had an irresistible attraction for him. During the last year the old man had taken to studying the Apocryphal Gospels, and constantly talked over his impressions with his young friend. He used to go to visit Alyosha in the monastery and discuss religion with him and the monks. So even if Alyosha were late at the prison, he had only to go to the superintendent and everything was made easy. Besides, everyone in the prison, down to the humblest warden, had grown used to Alyosha. The sentry, of course, did not trouble him so long as the authorities were satisfied.

As Alyosha entered the room set aside for interviews, he came upon Rakitin, who was just saying good-by to Dmitri. They were both talking loudly. Dmitri was laughing, while Rakitin seemed to be grumbling. Rakitin did not like meeting Alyosha, especially of late. He scarcely spoke to him, and bowed to him stiffly. Seeing Alyosha enter now, he frowned and looked away, as though he were entirely absorbed in buttoning his big, warm, fur-trimmed overcoat. Then he began looking for his umbrella.

"I must not forget my belongings," he muttered, simply to say something.

"Be sure you don't forget other people's belongings," said Dmitri as a joke. Rakitin flared up at once.

"You'd better give that advice to your own family, who've

always been a slave-driving lot, and not to Rakitin," he cried, suddenly trembling with anger.

"What's the matter? I was joking," cried Dmitri. "Damn it all! They are all like that," he turned to Alyosha, nodding toward Rakitin's hurriedly retreating figure. "He was sitting here, laughing and cheerful, and all at once he boils up like that. He didn't even nod to you. Have you broken with him completely? Why are you so late? I've not only been waiting, but thirsting for you all day. But never mind. We'll make up for it now."

"Why does he come here so often? Surely you are not such great friends?" asked Alyosha. He, too, nodded at the door through which Rakitin had disappeared.

"Great friends with Rakitin? No, not as much as that. Is it likely—a pig like that? He thinks I am . . . a blackguard. They can't understand a joke, either, that's the worst of such people. They never understand a joke, and their souls are dry, dry and flat. They remind me of prison walls. But he is a clever fellow, very clever. . . . Well, Alyosha, it's all over with me now."

He sat down on the bench and made Alyosha sit down beside him.

"Yes, the trial's tomorrow. Are you so hopeless, Dmitri?" Alyosha asked with an apprehensive feeling.

"What are you talking about?" said Dmitri, looking at him rather uncertainly. "Oh, you mean the trial! Damn it all! Till now we've been talking of things that don't matter, about this trial, but I haven't said a word to you about the main thing. Yes, the trial is tomorrow; but it wasn't the trial I meant when I said it was all over with me. Why do you look at me so critically?"

"What do you mean, Dmitri?"

"Ideas, ideas, that's all! Ethics! What is ethics?"

"Ethics?" asked Alyosha, wondering.

"Yes. Is it a science?"

"Yes, there is such a science . . . But . . . I can't explain to you what sort of science it is."

"Rakitin knows. Rakitin knows a lot, damn him! He's not going to be a monk. He plans to go to Petersburg. There he'll go in for criticism of a cultural sort. Who knows, he may be of use and make his own career, too. Ough! They are always good, these people, at making a career! Damn ethics. I am done for, Alyosha, I am, you man of God! I love you more than anyone. It makes my heart ache to look at you. Who was Karl Bernard?"

"Karl Bernard?" Alyosha was surprised again.

"No, not Karl. Wait, I made a mistake. Claude Bernard. What was he? A chemist or what?"

"He must be a scholar," answered Alyosha. "But I confess I can't tell you much about him. I've heard of him, but that's all I know."

"Well, damn him, then! I don't know either," swore Dmitri. "A scoundrel of some sort, most likely. They are all scoundrels. And Rakitin will make his way. Rakitin will get ahead anywhere; he is another Bernard. Ugh, these Bernards! They are all over the place."

"But what is the matter?" Alyosha asked.

"He wants to write an article about me, about my case, and in this way begin his career. That's what he comes for; he said so himself. He wants to prove some theory. He wants to say 'he couldn't help murdering his father, he was corrupted by his environment,' and so on. He explained it all to me. He is going to put in a tinge of Socialism, he says. Damn him, he can put in a tinge, if he likes, I don't care. He can't bear Ivan, he hates him. He doesn't like you, either. But I don't refuse to see him because he is a clever fellow. Awfully conceited though. I said to him just now: 'The Karamazovs are not blackguards, but philosophers; for all true Russians are philosophers. And although you've studied, you are not a philosopher—you are low.' He laughed, so maliciously. And I said to him the idea is not debatable." Dmitri laughed suddenly.

"Why is it all over with you? You said so just now," Alyosha asked.

"Why is it all over with me? Mm! . . . . The fact is . . . If you take it as a whole, I am sorry to lose God—that's what it is."

"What do you mean by 'sorry to lose God'?"

"Imagine; inside, in the nerves, in the head—that is, these nerves are there in the brain . . . (damn them!) there are sort of little tails, the little tails of those nerves, and as soon as they begin quivering . . . That is, you see, I look at something with my eyes and then they begin quivering, those little tails . . . And when they quiver, then an image appears . . . It doesn't appear at once, but an instant, a second, passes . . . and then something like a moment appears; that is, not a moment—devil take the moment!—but an image; that is, an object, or an action, damn it! That's why I see and then think, because of those tails, not because I have a soul, and am some sort of image and likeness. All that is nonsense! Rakitin explained it all to me yesterday and it bowled me over. It's wonderful, Alyosha, this science! A new man's arising—that I understand. . . . And yet I am sorry to lose God!"

"Well, that's a good thing, anyway," said Alyosha.

"That I am sorry to lose God! It's chemistry, Alyosha, chemistry! There's no help for it, your reverence, you must make way for chemistry. And Rakitin dislikes God. Oh! Doesn't he dislike Him! That's the sore point with all of them. But they conceal it. They tell lies. They pretend. 'Will you preach this in your reviews?' I asked him. 'Oh, well, if I do it openly, they won't let it through,' he said. He laughed. 'But what will become of men then,' I asked him, 'without God and immortal life? All things are lawful then, they can do what they like?'

'Didn't you know?' he said laughing. 'A clever man can do what he likes,' he said. 'A clever man knows his way around. But you've put your foot in it, committing a murder, and now you are rotting in prison.' He said that to my face! A regular pig! I used to kick such people out, but now I listen to them. He talks a lot of sense, too. Writes well. He began reading me an article last week. I copied out three lines of it. Wait a minute. Here it is."

Dmitri pulled out a piece of paper from his pocket and read: " 'In order to determine this question, it is above all essential to put one's personality in contradiction to one's reality.' Do you understand that?"

"No, I don't," said Alyosha. He looked at Dmitri and listened to him with curiosity.

"I don't understand either. It's dark and obscure, but intellectual. 'Everyone writes like that now,' he says. 'It's the effect of their environment.' They are afraid of environment. He writes poetry, too. He's written a poem in honor of Madame Hohlakov's foot. Ha, ha, ha!"

"I've heard about it," said Alyosha.

"Have you? And have you heard the poem?"

"No."

"I've got it. Here it is. I'll read it to you. You don't know— I haven't told you—there's quite a story about it. He's a bastard! Three weeks ago he began to tease me: 'You've got yourself into a mess, like a fool, for the sake of three thousand, but I'm going to collar a hundred and fifty thousand. I am going to marry a widow and buy a house in Petersburg.' And he told me he was courting Madame Hohlakov. She didn't have much brains when she was young, and now at forty she has lost what she had. 'But she's awfully sentimental,' he said. 'That's how I will get hold of her. When I marry her, I will take her to Petersburg and there I will start a newspaper.' And his mouth was watering, the beast, not for the widow, but for the hundred and fifty thousand. And he made me believe it. He came to see me every day. 'She is coming around,' he declared. He was beaming with delight. And then, all of a sudden, he was turned out of Madame Hohlakov's house. Perhotin's carrying everything before him! I could kiss the silly old female for turning him out of the house. And he had written this doggerel. 'It's the first time I've soiled my hands with writing poetry,' he said. 'It's to win her heart, so it's in a good cause. When I get hold of the silly woman's fortune, I can be of great social help.' They have this social justification for every shady thing they do! 'Anyway it's better than Pushkin's poetry,' he said, 'because I've managed to advocate enlightenment.' I understand what he means about Pushkin, if he really was a man of talent and only wrote about women's feet. But wasn't Rakitin proud about his doggerel! The vanity of these fellows!

'On the convalescence of the swollen foot of the object of my affections'—he thought of that for a title. He's a clown.

> *A captivating little foot,*
> *Though swollen and red and tender!*
> *The doctors come and plasters put,*
> *But still they cannot mend her.*
>
> *Yet, 'tis not for her foot I dread—*
> *A theme for Pushkin's muse more fit—*
> *It's not her foot, it is her head:*
> *I tremble for her loss of wit!*
>
> *For as her foot swells, strange to say,*
> *Her intellect is on the wane—*
> *Oh, for some remedy I pray*
> *That may restore both foot and brain!*

He is a pig, a regular pig, but he's very sharp! And he really has put in a liberal idea. And wasn't he mad when she kicked him out! He was gnashing his teeth!"

"He's taken his revenge already," said Alyosha. "He's written a piece about Madame Hohlakov."

And Alyosha told him briefly about the story in *Gossip*.

"That's his doing, that's his doing!" Dmitri agreed, frowning. "That's him! These pieces . . . I know . . . The insulting things that have been written about Grushenka, for instance! . . . And about Katerina, too. . . . Hm!"

He walked across the room.

"Dmitri, I can't stay long," Alyosha said, after a pause. "Tomorrow will be a great and awful day for you. The judgment of God will be accomplished . . . I am amazed at you, you walk about here, talking of I don't know what . . ."

"No, don't be amazed at me," Dmitri said warmly. "Am I to talk of that stinking dog? Of the murderer? We've talked enough of him. I don't want to say more of the stinking son of Stinking Lizaveta! God will kill him, you will see. Hush!"

He went up to Alyosha and embraced him. His eyes glowed.

"Rakitin wouldn't understand," he began in a sort of exaltation. "But you, you'll understand it all. That's why I was thirsting for you. You see, there's so much I've been wanting to tell you for ever so long, here, within these peeling walls. But I haven't said a word about what matters most; the moment seems never to have come. Now I can't wait any longer. I must pour out my heart to you, Alyosha, these last two months I've found in myself a new man. A new man has risen up in me. He was hidden in me, but would never have come to the surface, if it hadn't been for this blow from heaven. I am afraid! And what do I care if I spend twenty years in the mines, breaking out ore with a hammer? I am not a bit afraid of that—it's something else I am afraid of now: that the new man may leave me. Even there, in the mines, underground, I may find a human heart in another convict or murderer by my side. And I may make friends with him, for even there one may live and love and suffer. One may thaw and revive a frozen heart in that convict, one may wait upon him for years, and at last bring up from the dark depths a lofty soul, a feeling, suffering creature; one may bring forth an angel, create a hero! There are so many of them, hundreds of them, and we are all to blame for them. Why was it I dreamed of that 'babe' at such a moment? 'Why is the babe so poor?' That was a sign to me at that moment. It's for the babe I'm going. Because we are all responsible for all. For all the 'babes,' for there are big children as well as little children. All are 'babes.' I go for all, because someone must go for all. I didn't kill father, but I've got to go. I accept it. It's all come to me here, here, within these peeling walls. There are numbers of them there, hundreds of them underground, with hammers in their hands. Oh, yes, we shall be in chains and there will be no freedom, but then, in our great sorrow, we shall rise again to joy, without which man cannot live nor God exist. For God gives joy; it's His privilege—a grand one. Ah, man should be dissolved in prayer! What should I be underground there without God? Rakitin's laughing! If they drive God from the earth, we shall shelter Him underground. One cannot exist in prison without God; it's even more impossible than out of prison. And then we men underground will sing from the bowels of the earth a glorious hymn to God, with Whom is joy. Hail to God and His joy! I love Him!"

Dmitri was almost gasping for breath as he finished his wild speech. He turned pale, his lips quivered, and tears rolled down his cheeks.

"Yes, life is full, there is life even underground," he began again. "You wouldn't believe, Alyosha, how I want to live now, what a thirst for existence and consciousness has sprung up in me within these peeling walls. Rakitin doesn't understand that; all he cares about is building a house and renting out apartments. But I've been longing for you. And what is suffering? I am not afraid of it, even if it were beyond reckoning. I am not afraid of it now. I was afraid of it before. Do you know, I may not even defend myself at the trial at all. . . . I seem to have such strength now, that I think I could stand anything, any suffering, only to be able to say and to repeat to myself every moment: 'I exist.' In thousands of agonies—I exist. I'm tortured on the rack—but I exist! Although I sit alone—I exist! I see the sun, and if I don't see the sun, I know it's there. And there's a whole life in that, in knowing that the sun is there. Alyosha, my angel, all these philosophies are the death of me. Damn them! Ivan. . . ."

"What about Ivan?" interrupted Alyosha, but Dmitri did not hear.

"You see, I never had any of these doubts before: it was all hidden away inside of me. It was perhaps just because ideas I

537

did not understand were surging up in me, that I used to drink and fight. It was to stifle them in myself, to still them, to smother them. Ivan is not Rakitin, there is an idea in him. Ivan is a sphinx and is silent; he is always silent. . . . It's God that's worrying me. That's the only thing that's worrying me. What if He doesn't exist? What if Rakitin's right—that it's an idea made up by men? Then, if He doesn't exist, man is the king of the earth, of the universe. Magnificent! Only how is he going to be good without God? That's the question. I always come back to that. Who is man going to love then? To whom will he be thankful? To whom will he sing the hymn? Rakitin laughs. Rakitin says that one can love humanity instead of God. Well, only an idiot can maintain that. I can't understand it. Life's easy for Rakitin. 'You'd better think about the extension of civic rights, or of keeping down the price of meat. You will show your love for humanity more simply and directly by that, than by philosophy.' I answered him: 'Well, but you, without a God, are more likely to raise the price of meat, if it suits you, and make a rouble on every penny.' He lost his temper. But after all, what is goodness? Answer that, Alyosha. Goodness is one thing with me and another with a Chinaman, so it's relative. Or isn't it? Is it not relative? A treacherous question! You won't laugh if I tell you it's kept me awake for two nights. I only wonder now how people can live and think nothing about it. Vanity! Ivan has no God. He has an idea. It's beyond me. But he is silent. I believe he is a Freemason. I asked him, but he was silent. I wanted to drink from the springs of his soul—but he was silent. But once he did say something."

"What did he say?" asked Alyosha.

"I said to him, 'Then everything is lawful, if it is so?' He frowned. 'Fyodor Karamazov, our father,' he said, 'was a pig, but his ideas were right.' That was what he said. That was all he said. That was going one better than Rakitin."

"Yes," agreed Alyosha bitterly. "When was he with you?"

"I'll tell you about that later, now I must speak of something else. I have said nothing about Ivan to you before. I left it to the last. When my business here is over and the verdict has been given, then I'll tell you something. I'll tell you everything. We are planning something. . . . And you will judge it. But don't begin about that now; be silent. Talk about tomorrow, about the trial; would you believe it, I know nothing about it."

"Have you talked to your lawyer?"

"What's the use of a lawyer? I told him all about it. He's a soft, city-bred fellow—a Bernard! But he doesn't believe me— not a bit. Imagine, he believes I did it. I see it. 'In that case,' I asked him, 'why have you come to defend me?' Damn them all! They've got a doctor down, too, who wants to prove I'm mad. I won't have that! Katerina wants to do her 'duty' to the end!" Dmitri smiled bitterly. "The cat! Hard-hearted creature! She knows that I said at Mokroe that she is a woman of 'wrath.' They repeated it. Yes, the facts against me have grown numerous as the sands of the sea. Gregory sticks to his point. Gregory's honest, but a fool. Many people are honest because they are fools; that's Rakitin's idea. Gregory's my enemy. And there are some people who are better as enemies than friends. I mean Katerina. I am afraid, oh, I am afraid she will tell how she bowed to the ground before me after I gave her that four thousand. She'll pay it back to the last penny. I don't want her sacrifice. They'll put me to shame at the trial. How can I stand it! Go to her, Alyosha, ask her not to speak of that in the court, can't you? But damn it all, it doesn't matter! I will get through somehow. I don't pity her. It's her own doing. She deserves what she gets. I'll have my own story to tell, Alyosha." He smiled bitterly again. "Only . . . only Grushenka, Grushenka! God! Why should she have to bear such suffering?" he exclaimed suddenly. "Grushenka is killing me; the thought of her is killing me, killing me. She was with me just now . . ."

"She told me you made her very unhappy today."

"I know. Damn my temper! It was jealousy. I was sorry, I kissed her as she was going. But I didn't ask her forgiveness."

"Why didn't you?" exclaimed Alyosha.

Suddenly Dmitri laughed.

"God preserve you, Alyosha, from ever asking forgiveness from a woman you love. From one you love especially, however greatly you may have been at fault. For a woman—devil only knows what to make of a woman; I know something about them, anyway. But try acknowledging you are at fault to a woman. Say: 'I am sorry, forgive me,' and a shower of reproaches will follow! Nothing will make her forgive you simply and directly. She'll humble you to the dust, bring forward things that have never happened, recall everything, forget nothing, add something of her own, and only then forgive you. And even the best, the best of them do it. She'll sweep up all the scrapings and load them on your head. They are ready to flay you alive, I tell you, every one of them, all these angels without whom we cannot live! I tell you plainly and openly, Alyosha, every decent man ought to be under some woman's thumb. That's my conviction—not conviction, but feeling. A man ought to be magnanimous, and it's no disgrace to a man! No disgrace to a hero, not even a Caesar! But don't ever beg her pardon for anything. Remember that rule given you by your brother Dmitri, who's come to ruin through women. No, I'd better make up with Grushenka somehow, without begging for forgiveness. I worship her, Alyosha, worship her. Only she doesn't see it. No, she still thinks I don't love her enough. And she tortures me, tortures me with her love. The past was nothing! In the past it was only that infernal body of hers that tortured me, but now I've taken all her soul into my soul and through her I've become a man. Will they marry us? If they

539

don't I will die of jealousy. I imagine something every day. . . . What did she say to you about me?"

Alyosha repeated everything Grushenka had said to him that day. Dmitri listened, made him repeat things, and seemed pleased.

"Then she is not angry at my being jealous?" he exclaimed. "She is a regular woman! 'I've a fierce heart myself!' Ah, I love such fierce hearts, though I can't bear anyone's being jealous of me. I can't stand it. We'll fight. But I will love her, I will love her infinitely. Will they marry us? Do they let convicts marry? That's the question. Without her I can't exist . . ."

Dmitri walked frowning across the room. It was almost dark. He suddenly seemed terribly worried.

"So there's a secret, she says, a secret? We have a plot against her, and Katerina is mixed up in it, she thinks. No, my good Grushenka, that's not it. You are very wide of the mark, in your foolish feminine way. Alyosha, darling, well here goes! I'll tell you our secret!"

He looked around, went close to Alyosha and whispered to him, although in reality no one could hear them; the old warden was dozing in the corner, and not a word could reach the ears of the soldiers on guard.

"I will tell you our secret," Dmitri whispered hurriedly. "I planned to tell you later, because how could I decide on anything without you? You are everything to me. Though I say that Ivan is superior to us, you are my angel. It's your decision that will count. Perhaps it's you that is superior and not Ivan. You see, it's a question of conscience, question of the higher conscience—the secret is so important that I can't decide it myself. I've put it off until I could speak to you. But anyway it's too early to decide now, for we must wait for the verdict. As soon as the verdict is given, you will decide my fate. Don't decide now. I'll tell you now. You listen, but don't decide. I won't tell you everything. I'll only tell you the idea, without details, and you keep quiet. Don't ask any questions. Don't move. Do you agree? But what shall I do with your eyes? I'm afraid your eyes will tell me your decision, even if you don't speak. I'm afraid! Alyosha, listen! Ivan suggests my *escaping*. I won't tell you the details; it's all been thought out; it can all be arranged. Hush, don't decide. I am to go to America with Grushenka. You know I can't live without Grushenka! What if they won't let her follow me to Siberia? Do they let convicts get married? Ivan doesn't think they do. And without Grushenka what would I do there underground with a hammer? I would only smash my skull with the hammer! But on the other hand, my conscience? I would have run away from suffering. A sign has come, I reject the sign. I have a way of salvation and I turn my back on it. Ivan says that in America, 'with good will,' I can be of more use than underground. But what becomes of our hymn from underground? What's America?

America is vanity again! And there's a lot of swindling in America, too. I should have run away from crucifixion! I tell you, you know, Alyosha, because you are the only person who can understand this. There's no one else. It's foolishness, madness to others, everything I've told you of the hymn. They'll say I'm out of my mind or a fool. I am not out of my mind and I am not a fool. Ivan understands about the hymn, too. He understands, only he doesn't answer—he doesn't speak. He doesn't believe in the hymn. Don't speak don't speak. I see how you look! You have already decided. Don't decide! I can't live without Grushenka. Wait till after the trial!"

Dmitri was beside himself. He held Alyosha by both shoulders, and his yearning, feverish eyes were fixed on Alyosha's eyes.

"They don't let convicts marry, do they?" he repeated for the third time.

Alyosha listened and was deeply moved.

"Tell me one thing," he said, "is Ivan in favor of this plan and whose idea was it?"

"His, his. It's his plan. He didn't come to see me at first, then he suddenly came a week ago and he told me about it. He is very keen about it. He doesn't ask me, but orders me to escape. He doesn't doubt I will obey him, though I showed him all my heart as I have to you, and told him about the hymn, too. He told me he'd arrange it; he's found out about everything. But we'll talk about that later. He's set on it. It's all a matter of money; he'll pay ten thousand for the escape and give me twenty thousand for America. He says we can arrange an escape for ten thousand."

"And he told you not to tell me?" Alyosha asked again.

"To tell no one, and especially not you. On no account to tell you. He is afraid that you'll stand before me as my conscience. Don't tell him I told you. Don't tell him."

"You are right," Alyosha said. "It's impossible to decide anything before the trial is over. After the trial you'll decide for yourself. Then you'll find that new man in yourself and he will decide."

"A new man, or a Bernard who'll decide. I believe I'm a Bernard myself," said Dmitri with bitterness.

"But, Dmitri, have you no hope then of being acquitted?"

Dmitri shrugged his shoulders and shook his head.

"Alyosha, it's time you were going," he said. "There's the superintendent shouting in the yard. He'll be here right away. We are late; it's against the rules. Embrace me quickly! Sign me with the cross, for the cross I have to bear tomorrow."

They embraced.

"Ivan," said Dmitri suddenly, "suggests my escaping; but, of course, he believes I did it."

A mournful smile came to his lips.

"Have you asked him whether he believes it?" asked Alyosha.

"No, I haven't. I wanted to, but I couldn't. I didn't have the courage. But I saw it from his eyes. Well, good-by!"

Once more they embraced. And Alyosha was just going out when Dmitri suddenly called him back.

"Stand facing me! That's right!" And again he seized Alyosha, putting both hands on his shoulders. His face became suddenly pale, so that it was dreadfully apparent, even through the gathering darkness. His lips twitched, his eyes fastened upon Alyosha.

"Alyosha, tell me the whole truth, as you would before God. Do you believe I did it? Do you, do you in yourself, believe it? Don't lie!" he cried desperately.

Everything seemed to heave before Alyosha, and he felt something like a stab at his heart.

"What do you mean?" he faltered helplessly.

"The whole truth, the whole truth. Don't lie!" repeated Dmitri.

"I've never for one instant believed that you were the murderer!" said Alyosha in a shaking voice. He raised his right hand in the air, as though calling God to witness his words.

Dmitri's face lighted up.

"Thank you!" he said slowly. "You have given me new life. . . . Until this moment I've been afraid to ask you, you, even you. . . . Well, go! You've given me strength for tomorrow. God bless you! Go! Love Ivan!" were Dmitri's last words.

Alyosha went out in tears. Such distrust in Dmitri, such lack of confidence even in him, Alyosha—all this suddenly opened before Alyosha an unsuspected depth of hopeless grief and despair in the soul of his unhappy brother. Intense, infinite compassion overwhelmed him. His torn heart ached. "Love Ivan" —he suddenly recalled Dmitri's words. And he was going to Ivan. He had wanted to see Ivan all day. He was as much worried about Ivan as about Dmitri. More so now than before.

5. *Not You, Not You!*

ON THE WAY TO IVAN, Alyosha had to pass Katerina's house. There was light in the windows. He suddenly decided to go in. He had not seen Katerina for more than a week. It struck him that Ivan might be with her, especially on this night before the terrible day. Ringing, and mounting the staircase, which was dimly lighted by a Chinese lantern, he saw a man coming down. As they met, he recognized Ivan. So he was just coming from Katerina.

"Oh, it's only you," said Ivan drily. "Well, good-by! You are going to her?"

"Yes."

"I don't advise you to; she's upset and you'll upset her more."

A door was flung open above, and a voice cried: "No, no! Alyosha, have you come from him?"

"Yes, I have been with him."

"Has he sent me a message? Come up, Alyosha, and you, Ivan, you must come back, you must. Do you hear?"

There was such a demanding note in Katerina's voice that Ivan, after a moment's hesitation, made up his mind to go back with Alyosha.

"She was listening," he murmured angrily to himself, but Alyosha heard it.

"Excuse my keeping my greatcoat on," said Ivan, going into the drawing room. "I won't sit down. I won't stay more than a minute."

"Sit down, Alyosha," said Katerina, although she remained standing. She had changed very little during this time, but there was an ominous gleam in her dark eyes. Alyosha remembered afterwards that she had struck him as particularly handsome at that moment.

"What did he ask you to tell me?"

"Only one thing," said Alyosha, looking her straight in the face. "He said that you should spare yourself and say nothing at the trial of what (he was a little confused) . . . passed between you . . . at your first meeting . . . in that town."

"Oh, that I bowed down to the ground for that money!" She broke into a bitter laugh. "Why, is he afraid for me or for himself? He asks me to spare—whom? Him or myself? Tell me, Alyosha!"

Alyosha watched her intently, trying to understand her.

"Both you and him," he answered softly.

"I am glad to hear it," she snapped out, and she suddenly blushed.

"You don't know me yet, Alyosha," she said threateningly. "And I don't know myself yet. Perhaps you'll want to trample me underfoot after my testimony tomorrow."

"You will give your evidence honorably," said Alyosha. "That's all that's wanted."

"Women are often dishonorable," she answered. "Only an hour ago I was thinking that I would be afraid to touch that monster . . . as though he were a reptile . . . But, no, he is still a human being to me! But did he do it? Is he the murderer?" she cried hysterically, turning quickly to Ivan. Alyosha saw at once that she had asked Ivan that question before, perhaps that very afternoon, and not for the first time, but for the hundredth, and that they had ended by quarreling.

"I've been to see Smerdyakov. . . . It was you, you who persuaded me that Dmitri murdered his father. It's you I believed!"

she continued, still addressing Ivan. He gave her a strained smile. Alyosha started at her tone. He had not suspected such intimacy between them.

"Well, that's enough, anyway," Ivan cut short the conversation. "I am going. I'll come tomorrow." And turning, he walked out of the room and went straight downstairs.

Katerina seized Alyosha by both hands.

"Follow him! Overtake him! Don't leave him alone for a minute!" she said in a hurried whisper. "He's mad! Don't you know that he's mad? He has a fever, nervous fever. The doctor told me so. Go, run after him. . . ."

Alyosha jumped up and ran after Ivan, who was not fifty yards ahead of him.

"What do you want?" Ivan turned quickly on Alyosha, seeing that he was running after him. "She told you to catch up with me because I'm mad. I know it all by heart," he added irritably.

"She is mistaken, of course; but she is right that you are ill," said Alyosha. "I was looking at your face just now. You look very ill, Ivan."

Ivan walked on without stopping. Alyosha followed him.

"And do you know, Alyosha, how people go out of their minds?" Ivan asked in a voice suddenly quiet, without a trace of irritation, with a note of the simplest curiosity.

"No, I don't. I suppose there are all kinds of insanity."

"And can one tell when one's going mad oneself?"

"I imagine one can't see oneself clearly at such a time," Alyosha answered.

Ivan paused for half a minute.

"If you want to talk to me, please change the subject," he said suddenly.

"Oh, while I think of it, I have a letter for you," said Alyosha timidly. He took Lise's note from his pocket and held it out. They were just under a lamp post. Ivan recognized the handwriting at once.

"Oh, from that little demon!" he laughed maliciously and, without opening the envelope, he tore it into bits and threw it in the air. The bits were scattered by the wind.

"She's not sixteen yet and already offering herself," he said, striding along the street again.

"What do you mean, offering herself?" asked Alyosha.

"As wanton women offer themselves."

"How can you, Ivan, how can you?" Alyosha cried. "She is a child; you are insulting a child! She is ill; she is very ill, too. She is on the verge of insanity, too, perhaps . . . I had hoped to hear something from you. . . that would save her."

"You'll hear nothing from me. If she is a child I am not her nurse. Keep quiet, Alyosha. Don't talk about her. I am not even thinking about her."

They were silent again for a moment.

"She will be praying all night now to the Mother of God to show her how to act tomorrow at the trial," he said sharply and angrily again.

"You . . . you mean Katerina?"

"Yes. Whether she's to save Dmitri or ruin him. She'll pray for light from above. She can't make up her mind for herself, you see. She has not had time to decide. She takes me for her nurse, too. She wants me to sing lullabys to her."

"Katerina loves you, Ivan," said Alyosha sadly.

"Perhaps. But I am not very fond of her."

"She is suffering. Why do you . . . sometimes say things to her that give her hope?" Alyosha went on with timid reproach. "I know that you've given her hope. Forgive me for speaking to you like this," he added.

"I can't behave to her as I should—break off altogether and tell her so straight out," said Ivan irritably. "I must wait till sentence is passed on the murderer. If I break off with her now, she will avenge herself on me by ruining that scoundrel tomorrow at the trial, for she hates him and knows she hates him. It's all a lie—lie upon lie! As long as I don't break off with her, she goes on hoping, and she won't ruin that monster, knowing how I want to get him out of trouble. If only that damned verdict would come!"

The words "murderer" and "monster" echoed painfully in Alyosha's heart.

"But how can she ruin Dmitri?" he asked, wondering at Ivan's words. "What evidence can she give that can ruin Dmitri?"

"You don't know that yet. She's got a letter in Dmitri's own writing that proves that he did murder our father."

"That's impossible!" cried Alyosha.

"Why is it impossible? I've read it myself."

"There can't be such a letter!" Alyosha insisted. "There can't be, because he's not the murderer. He didn't murder father, he didn't!"

Ivan suddenly stopped.

"Who is the murderer then?" he asked with coldness. There was even a supercilious note in his voice.

"You know who," Alyosha pronounced in a low, penetrating voice.

"Who? You mean that crazy idiot, the epileptic, Smerdyakov?"

Alyosha suddenly felt himself trembling all over.

"You know who," broke helplessly from him. He could scarcely breathe.

"Who? Who?" Ivan cried almost fiercely. All his restraint suddenly vanished.

"I only know one thing," Alyosha went on, still almost in a whisper, *"it wasn't you* who killed father."

"What do you mean by *'not you'*?" Ivan was thunderstruck.

"It was not you who killed father, not you," Alyosha repeated firmly.

The silence lasted for half a minute.

"I know I didn't. Are you raving?" said Ivan with a pale, distorted smile. His eyes were riveted on Alyosha. They were standing again under a lamp post.

"No, Ivan. You've told yourself several times that you are the murderer."

"When did I say so? I was in Moscow. . . . When did I say so?" Ivan faltered helplessly.

"You've said so to yourself many times, when you've been alone during these two dreadful months," Alyosha went on softly and distinctly as before. Yet he was speaking now, as it were, not of himself, not of his own will, but obeying some irresistible command. "You have accused yourself and have confessed to yourself that you are the murderer and no one else. But you didn't do it. You are mistaken. You are not the murderer. Do you hear? It was not you! God has sent me to tell you so."

They were both silent. The silence lasted a whole long minute. They stood still, gazing into each other's eyes. They were both pale. Suddenly Ivan began trembling all over, and clutched Alyosha's shoulder.

"You've been in my room!" he whispered hoarsely. "You've been there at night, when he came. . . . Confess . . . Have you seen him, have you seen him?"

"Whom do you mean—Dmitri?" Alyosha asked, bewildered.

"Not him, damn the monster!" Ivan shouted in a frenzy. "You know that he visits me! How did you find out? Speak!"

"Who is *he*? I don't know what you are talking about," Alyosha faltered, beginning to be alarmed.

"Yes, you do know . . . Or how could you? . . . It's impossible that you don't know."

Suddenly Ivan checked himself. He seemed to reflect. A strange grin contorted his lips.

"Ivan," Alyosha began again, in a shaking voice. "I said this to you, because you'll believe me, I know that. I tell you once and for all, it's not you. You hear, once and for all! God has put it into my heart to say this to you, even though it may make you hate me."

But by now Ivan had regained his self-control.

"Alyosha," he said with a cold smile, "I can't endure prophets and epileptics—messengers from God especially—and you know that only too well. I don't want to see you again from this moment on. Leave me at this turning. It's the way to your rooms. Don't come to see me tonight! Do you hear?"

He turned and walked away, not looking back.

"Ivan!" Alyosha called after him. "If anything happens to you tonight, call me before anyone else."

But Ivan did not answer.

Alyosha stood under the lamp post at the cross-roads, till Ivan had vanished into the darkness. Then he turned and walked slowly homewards. Both Alyosha and Ivan were living in rented rooms; neither of them was willing to live in their father's empty house. Alyosha had a furnished room in the house of some working people. Ivan lived some distance from him. He had taken a roomy and fairly comfortable lodge attached to a fine house that belonged to a well-to-do lady, the widow of an official. But his only servant was a deaf and rheumatic old woman who went to bed at six o'clock every evening and got up at six in the morning. Ivan had become very indifferent to his comforts of late, and liked being alone. He did everything for himself in the one room he lived in, and rarely entered any of the other rooms in his lodge.

He reached the gate of his house and had his hand on the bell, when he suddenly stopped. He felt that he was trembling all over with anger. He let go of the bell, turned back with a curse, and walked quickly in the opposite direction. He walked a mile and a half to a tiny, slanting, wooden house, almost a hut, where Maria, the neighbor who used to come to Fyodor Karamazov's kitchen for soup and to whom Smerdyakov had once sung his songs and played on the guitar, was now living. She and her invalid mother had sold their house, and were now living here. Smerdyakov, who was ill—almost dying—had been with them ever since Fyodor Karamazov's murder. It was to him Ivan was now going, drawn by an irresistible compulsion.

6. The First Interview with Smerdyakov

THIS WAS THE THIRD TIME that Ivan had been to see Smerdyakov since his return from Moscow. The first time he had seen him and talked to him was on the first day of his arrival. He had visited him once more, two weeks later. His visits had ended with that second one, so that it was now over a month since he had seen him. And he had scarcely heard anything of him.

Ivan had only returned five days after his father's death, so that he was not present at the funeral, which took place the day before he came back. The reason for this was that Alyosha, not knowing his Moscow address, had to ask Katerina, and she, not knowing his address either, telegraphed to her half-sister and aunt, counting on Ivan's having seen them as soon as he arrived in Moscow. But he had not gone to see them till four days after his arrival. When he finally got the telegram, he, of course, set off immediately for our town.

The first to meet him was Alyosha. And Ivan was greatly surprised to find that contrary to general opinion, he refused

547

to entertain any suspicion against Dmitri, and spoke openly of Smerdyakov as the murderer. Later on, after seeing the police captain and the prosecutor, and hearing the details of the charge and the arrest, he was still more surprised at Alyosha. He felt that Alyosha's opinion was due to his exaggerated feeling of love and sympathy for Dmitri.

By the way, let me say a word or two of Ivan's feeling for his brother Dmitri. He disliked him, at most, he sometimes felt compassion for him, but even that was mixed with contempt. Dmitri's personality, even his appearance, was extremely unattractive to him. Ivan looked with indignation on Katerina's love for his brother, yet he went to see Dmitri on the first day of his arrival, and that interview, far from shaking Ivan's belief in Dmitri's guilt, strengthened it. He found his brother agitated, excited. Dmitri was talkative, but very absent-minded and incoherent. He used violent language, accused Smerdyakov and was muddled. He talked principally about the three thousand roubles, which he said had been "stolen" from him by their father.

"The money was mine, it was my money," Dmitri kept repeating. "Even if I had stolen it, I would have had the right."

He hardly contested the evidence against him, and when he tried to turn a fact to his advantage, it was in an absurd and incoherent way. He hardly seemed to want to defend himself to Ivan or anyone else. On the contrary, he was angry and scornful of the charges against him; he was continually flaring up and abusing everyone. He laughed contemptuously at Gregory's evidence about the open door, and declared that it was "the devil that opened it." But he could not present any coherent explanation of the fact. He even succeeded in insulting Ivan during their first interview, telling him that it was not for people who declared that "everything is lawful," to suspect and question him. Altogether he was anything but friendly with Ivan on that occasion. Immediately after the interview with Dmitri, Ivan went for the first time to see Smerdyakov.

On the train on his way from Moscow, Ivan had kept thinking of Smerdyakov and of his last conversation with him on the evening before he went away. Many things seemed to him puzzling and suspicious. But when he gave his evidence to the investigating lawyer, Ivan said nothing of that conversation. He put that off till he had seen Smerdyakov, who was at that time in the hospital.

Doctor Herzenstube and Varvinsky, the district doctor whom he met in the hospital, asserted in reply to Ivan's persistent questions, that Smerdyakov's epileptic attack was unmistakably genuine. They were surprised indeed at Ivan asking whether Smerdyakov might not have been shamming on the day of the murder. They gave him to understand that the attack was an exceptional one, the fits persisting and recurring several times, so that the patient's life was in danger, and that it was only now, after they had applied remedies, that they could say with confidence that the patient would survive. "Though it might well be," added Doctor Herzenstube, "that his reason will be impaired for a considerable period, if not permanently." On Ivan's asking whether that meant that Smerdyakov was now mad, they told him that this was not yet the case, in the full sense of the word, but that certain abnormalities were perceptible. Ivan decided to find out for himself what those abnormalities were.

At the hospital Ivan was allowed to see the patient. Smerdyakov was lying on a bed in a room where there was only one other patient, a tradesman, swollen with dropsy. This man was obviously dying and could therefore not interfere with their conversation. Smerdyakov grinned with uncertainty on seeing Ivan, and for the first moment seemed nervous. So at least Ivan felt. But that was only momentary. The rest of the time he was composed. From the first glance Ivan had no doubt that Smerdyakov was very ill. He was weak; he spoke slowly, moving his tongue with difficulty; he was much thinner and more sallow. Throughout the interview, which lasted twenty minutes, he kept complaining of a headache and of pain in all his limbs. His thin face seemed to have become so tiny; his hair was ruffled, and his crest of curls stood up in a thin tuft. But in his left eye, which was screwed up and seemed to be insinuating something, Smerdyakov showed himself unchanged. "It's always worth while speaking to a clever man." Ivan was reminded of that at once. He sat down on a chair beside the bed. Smerdyakov, with painful effort, shifted his position in bed, but he was not the first to speak. He remained silent and did not even look interested.

"Can you talk to me?" asked Ivan. "I won't tire you much."

"Certainly I can," mumbled Smerdyakov in a faint voice. "Has your honor been back long?" he added patronizingly, as though encouraging a nervous visitor.

"I only arrived today. . . . To see the mess you are in here."

Smerdyakov sighed.

"Why do you sigh, you knew of it all along?" Ivan blurted out.

Smerdyakov was stolidly silent for a while. "How could I help knowing? It was clear beforehand. But how could I tell it would turn out like this?"

"What would turn out? Don't be evasive! You foretold you'd have a fit; on the way down to the cellar, you know. You mentioned the very spot."

"Have you said so at the inquiry?" Smerdyakov asked with composure.

Ivan felt suddenly angry.

"No, I haven't yet, but I certainly will. You must explain a great deal to me! And let me tell you, I am not going to let you play with me!"

"Why should I play with you, when I put my whole trust in you, as in God Almighty?" said Smerdyakov, with the same composure, only for a moment closing his eyes.

"In the first place," began Ivan, "I know that epileptic fits can't be foretold beforehand. I've inquired, don't try to fool me. It's impossible to foretell the day and the hour. How was it you told me the day and the hour beforehand, and about the cellar, too? How could you tell that you would fall down the cellar stairs in a fit, if you didn't sham a fit on purpose?"

"I had to go to the cellar several times a day," Smerdyakov drawled deliberately. "I fell from the attic just in the same way a year ago. It's quite true you can't foretell the day and hour of a fit beforehand, but you always have a presentiment of it."

"But you did foretell the day and the hour!"

"In regard to my epilepsy, sir, you had much better inquire of the doctors here. You can ask them whether it was a real fit or not. It's no use my saying any more about it."

"And the cellar? How could you know beforehand it would happen in the cellar?"

"You don't seem to be able to get over that cellar! As I was going down to the cellar, I was in terrible dread and doubt. What frightened me most was losing you and being left alone. So I went down into the cellar thinking: 'Here, it'll come on directly, it'll strike me down directly. Will I fall?' And it was through this fear that I suddenly felt the spasm that always comes . . . And so I fell. All that you know because of my conversation with you at the gate the evening before, when I told you how frightened I was and spoke of the cellar. I told all that to Doctor Herzenstube and Nicholas Nelyudov, the investigating lawyer, and it's all been written down in the record. And the doctor here, Doctor Varvinsky, says that it was just the thought of it brought it on, the fear that I might fall. It was just then that the fit seized me. And so they've written it down. That is just how it must have happened, from fear."

As he finished, Smerdyakov drew a deep breath, as though exhausted.

"Then you said all that in your testimony?" said Ivan, somewhat taken aback.

He had meant to frighten him with the threat of repeating their conversation, and it now appeared that Smerdyakov had already reported it all himself.

"What have I to be afraid of? Let them write down the whole truth," Smerdyakov said firmly.

"And have you told them every word of our conversation at the gate?"

"No, not every word."

"And did you tell them that you can sham fits, as you boasted to me that night?"

"No, I didn't tell them that either."

550

"Tell me now, why did you want me to go to Tchermash-nya?"

"I was afraid you'd go away to Moscow, Tchermashnya is nearer."

"You are lying, you suggested my going away yourself. You told me that it would be better for me to get out of the way."

"That was out of affection and devotion to you, foreseeing trouble in the house, to spare you. Only I wanted to spare myself even more. That's why I told you to get out of the way, so that you might understand that there would be trouble in the house, and so that you would stay at home to protect your father."

"You might have said it more directly, you fool!" Ivan suddenly flared up.

"How could I have said it more directly? It was simply my fear that made me speak, and you might have gotten angry. I might have been afraid that Dmitri would make a scene and carry away that money, for he considered it as good as his own, but who could tell that it would end in a murder like this? I thought that he would only take the three thousand that lay under the master's mattress in the envelope, but you see, he murdered him. How could you guess it either, sir?"

"But if you say yourself that it couldn't be guessed, how could I have guessed and stayed at home? You contradict yourself!" said Ivan.

"You might have guessed from my asking you to go to Tchermashnya and not to Moscow."

"How could I guess it from that?"

Smerdyakov seemed exhausted, and again he was silent for a minute.

"You might have guessed from my asking you not to go to Moscow, but to Tchermashnya, that I wanted to have you near. Moscow's a long way off, and Dmitri, knowing you were not far off, might not have been so bold. And if anything had happened, you might have come to protect me, too, for I warned you of Gregory's illness, and that I was afraid of having a fit. And when I explained those secret signals to you, and told you that Dmitri knew them all, I thought that you would guess that he would be sure to do something. Because of this I thought you wouldn't go to Tchermashnya, but would stay."

"He talks very coherently," thought Ivan, "though he does mumble." "What are the mental abnormalities that Herzenstube talked of?"

"You are cunning with me, damn you," he exclaimed, getting angry.

"But I thought at the time that you guessed," Smerdyakov answered simply.

"If I'd guessed, I would have stayed," cried Ivan.

"Why, I thought that it was because you guessed that you

went away in such a hurry, only to get out of trouble, only to run away and save yourself."

"You think that everyone is as great a coward as you?"

"Forgive me, I thought you were like me."

"Of course, I should have guessed," Ivan said, disturbed. "And I did guess there was something brewing on your part . . . Only you are lying, you are lying again," he cried suddenly. "Do you remember how you went up to the carriage and said to me, 'It's always worth while speaking to a clever man'? So you were glad I was going away, since you praised me?"

Smerdyakov sighed again and again. A trace of color came into his face.

"If I was pleased," he said rather breathlessly, "it was simply because you agreed not to go to Moscow, but to Tchermash-nya. For it was nearer. Only when I said those words to you, it was not in praise, but in reproach. You didn't understand it."

"What reproach?"

"Why, that foreseeing such a tragedy you deserted your own father, and would not protect us. I might have been arrested for stealing that three thousand."

"Damn you!" Ivan swore. "Wait. Did you tell the prosecutor and the investigating lawyer about those secret signals?"

"I told them everything just as it was."

Ivan wondered inwardly again.

"If I thought of anything then," Ivan began once more, "it was only of evil on your part. Dmitri might kill father . . . But that he would steal—I did not believe that then. . . . But I was prepared for some evil from you. You told me yourself you could sham a fit. What did you say that for?"

"It was just through my simplicity. I never have shammed a fit in my life. And I only said so then to boast to you. It was just foolishness. I liked you so much then, and was open-hearted with you."

"Dmitri accuses you of the murder and theft."

"What else is left for him to do?" said Smerdyakov with a bitter grin. "And who will believe him with all the evidence against him? Gregory saw the door open. What can he say after that? But never mind him! He is just trying to save himself."

He stopped speaking. Then suddenly, as though on reflection, added: "And look here again. He wants to throw the blame on me and make out that it is the work of my hands—I've heard that already. But as to my shamming a fit; would I have told you beforehand that I could sham one, if I really had had such a plan against your father? If I had been planning such a murder could I have been such a fool as to give evidence against myself beforehand? And to his son, too! Is that likely? As if that could be. Such a thing has never happened. No one hears us talking now, except Providence. And if you tell the prosecutor and Nicholas Nelyudov, you may clear me completely. Who would believe that a criminal could be so open-hearted beforehand? Any one can see that."

"Well!" said Ivan. He got up to cut short the conversation, struck by Smerdyakov's last argument. "I don't suspect you at all. I think it's absurd to suspect you. On the contrary, I am grateful to you for setting my mind at rest. Now I am going, but I'll come again. Meanwhile, good-by. Get well. Is there anything you want?"

"I am very thankful for everything. Marfa does not forget me, and brings me anything I want. Good people visit me every day."

"Good-by. I won't say anything of your being able to sham a fit, and I don't advise you to, either," something made Ivan say suddenly.

"I understand. And if you don't speak of that, I will say nothing of that conversation of ours at the gate."

Ivan went out. And when he had gone only a dozen steps down the corridor, he suddenly felt that there was an insulting significance in Smerdyakov's last words. He was almost on the point of turning back, but it was only a passing impulse. Muttering: "Nonsense!" he went out of the hospital.

His feeling was one of relief at the fact that it was not Smerdyakov, but Dmitri who had committed the murder. He did not want to analyze the reason for this feeling, and even felt a repugnance at prying into his sensations. He felt as though he wanted to forget something. In the following days he became convinced of Dmitri's guilt, as he learned of all the evidence against him. There was the testimony of people of no importance, Fenya and her grandmother, for instance, but the effect was overpowering. As to Perhotin, the people at the tavern, and at Plotnikov's shop, as well as the witnesses at Mokroe, their evidence seemed conclusive. It was the details that were so damning. The secret signals impressed the lawyers almost as much as Gregory's evidence about the open door. Gregory's wife, Marfa, in answer to Ivan's questions, declared that Smerdyakov had been lying all night in the next room: "He was not three yards from our bed." Although she was a sound sleeper she woke up several times and heard him moaning: "He was moaning the whole time, moaning continually."

Talking to Doctor Herzenstube, and giving it as his opinion that Smerdyakov was not mad but only rather weak, Ivan only evoked from the old man a subtle smile.

"Do you know how he spends his time now?" he asked. "He is learning lists of French words by heart. He has an exercise book under his pillow with the French words written out in Russian letters!"

Ivan ended by dismissing all doubts. He could not think of Dmitri without repulsion. Only one thing was strange, however: Alyosha persisted that Dmitri was not the murderer, and that "in all probability" Smerdyakov was. Alyosha's opinion always meant a great deal to Ivan, and he was astonished at it now. Another thing that was strange was that Alyosha did not make any attempt to talk about Dmitri with Ivan, he never brought up the subject and only answered his questions. This troubled Ivan.

But Ivan was very much preoccupied at that time with something quite different. On his return from Moscow, he abandoned himself hopelessly to his mad and consuming passion for Katerina. This is not the time to speak of this passion of Ivan's, which left its mark on all the rest of his life; it would furnish the subject for another novel, which I may perhaps never write. But I cannot neglect to mention here that when Ivan, on leaving Katerina with Alyosha, as I've related already, told him: "I am not very fond of her," it was a lie. He loved her madly, though at times he hated her so violently that he might have murdered her. Many things helped to bring about this feeling. Shattered by what had happened with Dmitri, she rushed on Ivan's return to meet him as her one salvation. She was hurt, insulted and humiliated. And here the man had come back to her, who had loved her so ardently before (oh, she knew that very well), and whose heart and intellect she considered so superior to her own. But the sternly virtuous young woman did not abandon herself altogether to the man she loved, in spite of the Karamazov violence of his passions and the great fascination he had for her. She was continually tormented at the same time by remorse for having deserted Dmitri and in moments of anger (and they were numerous) she told Ivan so. This was what he had told Alyosha was: "Lies upon lies." There was, of course, much that was untrue in it, and that angered Ivan more than anything. . . . But of all this later.

Ivan did, in fact, for a time almost forget Smerdyakov's existence, and yet, two weeks after his first visit to him, he began to be haunted by the same strange thoughts as before. It's enough to say that he was continually asking himself, why was it that on that last night in his father's house he had crept out onto the stairs like a thief and listened to what his father was doing below? Why had he recalled this afterwards with repulsion? Why, next morning on the journey, had he been suddenly so depressed? Why, as he reached Moscow, had he said to himself: "I am a scoundrel"? And now he almost believed that these tormenting thoughts would make him even forget Katerina, so completely did they take possession of him again.

It was just after thinking of all this, that he met Alyosha in the street. He stopped him at once and asked: "Do you remember when Dmitri burst in after dinner and beat father? Afterwards I told you in the yard that I reserved 'the right to desire' . . . Tell me, did you think then that I desired Father's death or not?"

"I did think so," answered Alyosha softly.

"You were right. It was so. But didn't you think then what I wished was just that 'one reptile should devour another'; that is, that Dmitri should kill father, and as soon as possible . . . and that I was prepared to help to bring it about?"

Alyosha turned pale, and looked silently into his brother's face.

"Speak!" cried Ivan. "I want above everything to know what you thought then. I want the truth, the truth!"

He drew a deep breath and looked angrily at Alyosha.

"Forgive me, I did think that too, at the time," whispered Alyosha. He did not add one softening phrase.

"Thank you," said Ivan, and leaving Alyosha he went quickly on his way. From that time on Alyosha noticed that Ivan began to avoid him. He seemed to have taken a dislike to him, so much so that Alyosha gave up going to see him.

Immediately after that chance meeting with Alyosha, Ivan had gone again to see Smerdyakov.

7. The Second Visit to Smerdyakov

BY THAT TIME Smerdyakov had been discharged from the hospital. Ivan knew where he was living, the dilapidated little wooden house, divided in two by a passage on one side of which lived Maria with her bedridden mother. No one knew on what terms he lived with them, whether as a friend or as a lodger. It was believed afterwards that he had come to stay with them as Maria's fiancée, and was living there without paying. Both mother and daughter had the greatest respect for him and looked upon him as greatly superior to themselves.

Ivan knocked, and, on the door being opened, went into the passage. At Maria's directions he went straight to the better room on the left, occupied by Smerdyakov. There was a tiled stove in the room and it was extremely hot. The walls were gay with old blue paper. Where the paper was loose, cockroaches swarmed in amazing numbers, so that there was a continual rustling. The furniture was very scanty: two benches against each wall and two chairs by a table. The table of plain wood was covered with a pink cloth. There was a pot of geraniums on each of the two little windows. In the corner there was a case of ikons. On the table stood a copper samovar with many dents in it, and a tray with two cups. But Smerdyakov had finished tea and the samovar was cold. He was sitting at the table looking at an exercise book and writing with a pen. There was a bottle of ink by him and a flat iron candlestick with the stump of a candle.

Ivan saw at once that Smerdyakov had completely recovered from his illness. His face was fresher, fuller, his hair stood up jauntily in front and was plastered down at the sides. He was sitting in a wadded dressing gown, rather dirty and frayed. He was wearing glasses, which Ivan had never seen him wearing before. This trifling thing suddenly redoubled Ivan's anger: "A creature like that wearing glasses!"

Smerdyakov slowly raised his head and looked intently at his visitor through his glasses; then he slowly took them off and rose from his chair, but by no means respectfully, almost lazily, doing the least required by common civility. All this struck Ivan instantly. He took it all in and noted it at once—most of all the look in Smerdyakov's eyes, positively malicious, surly and haughty. "What do you want to intrude for?" it seemed to say. "We have already settled everything. Why have you come again?" Ivan could scarcely control himself.

"It's hot here," he said, still standing, and unbuttoned his overcoat.

"Take off your coat," Smerdyakov conceded.

Ivan took off his coat and threw it on a bench with trembling hands. He took a chair, moved it quickly to the table and sat down. Smerdyakov managed to sit down before him.

"To begin with, are we alone?" Ivan asked sternly and impulsively. "Can they overhear us in there?"

"No one can hear anything. You've seen for yourself that there's a passage."

"Listen, what was that you babbled, as I was leaving the hospital, that if I said nothing about your being able to sham fits, you wouldn't tell the investigating lawyer all about our conversation at the gate? What do you mean by *all*? What could you mean by it? Were you threatening me? Am I in some sort of conspiracy with you? Do you think I am afraid of you?"

Ivan said this in a fury, giving him to understand that he scorned any subterfuge or indirectness and meant to reveal everything. Smerdyakov's eyes gleamed resentfully, his left eye winked and he at once gave his answer, with his habitual composure and deliberation: "You want to have everything revealed; very well, you shall have it," he seemed to say.

"This is what I meant and this is why I said it. Knowing beforehand that your father might be murdered, you left him to his fate. . . . I didn't want people to think evil of you. And there's something else, too—that's what I promised not to tell the authorities."

Though Smerdyakov spoke slowly, obviously controlling himself, yet there was something in his voice, determined and emphatic, resentful and defiant. He stared boldly at Ivan. A mist passed before Ivan's eyes for the first moment.

"How? What? Are you out of your mind?"

"I'm in perfect possession of all my faculties."

"Do you believe I *knew* that my father was going to be murdered?" Ivan cried, bringing his fist down violently on

556

the table. "What do you mean by 'something else, too'? Speak, you wretch!"

Smerdyakov was silent. He continued looking at Ivan with the same insolent stare.

"Speak, you stinking fool, what is that 'something else, too'?"

"The 'something else' was that you too were probably eager for your father's death."

Ivan jumped up and struck Smerdyakov with all his might on the shoulder, so that he fell back against the wall. In an instant his face was bathed in tears. Saying: "It's a shame, sir, to strike a sick man," he dried his eyes with a very dirty blue check handkerchief and sank into quiet weeping. A minute passed.

"That's enough! Stop!" Ivan ordered, sitting down again. "Don't make me lose all patience."

Smerdyakov took the handkerchief from his eyes. Every line of his face reflected the insult he had just received.

"So you thought, you scoundrel, that together with Dmitri I meant to kill my father?"

"I didn't know what thoughts were in your mind," said Smerdyakov resentfully. "And so I stopped you then at the gate to sound you out on that point."

"To sound out what, what?"

"Why, whether you wanted your father to be murdered or not."

What infuriated Ivan more than anything else was Smerdyakov's aggressive, insolent tone.

"It was you who murdered him?" he cried suddenly.

Smerdyakov smiled contemptuously.

"You know, for a fact, that I didn't murder him. And I would have thought that there was no need for a sensible man to speak of it again."

"But why, why did you have such a suspicion about me at the time?"

"As you know, it was from fear. I was in such a position, shaking with fear, that I suspected everyone. I decided to sound you out too, for I thought if you wanted the same as your brother, then the business was as good as settled and I would be crushed like a fly."

"You didn't say that two weeks ago."

"I meant the same when I talked to you in the hospital, only I thought you'd understand without wasting words, and that being such a sensible man you wouldn't care to talk about it openly."

"What! Come answer, answer, I insist. What was it . . . What could I have done to put such a degrading suspicion into your mean mind?"

"As for the murder, you couldn't have done that and didn't want to. . . . But as for wanting someone else to do it, that was just what you did want."

"How coolly, how coolly you speak! But why should I have wanted it, what grounds had I for wanting it?"

"What grounds had you? What about the inheritance?" said Smerdyakov sarcastically and vindictively. "Why, after your father's death there was at least forty thousand to come to each of you, and maybe more. But if your father married that lady, Agrafena Svyetlov, she would have had all his money turned over to her right after the wedding, for she's got plenty of sense. Then your father would not have left two roubles between the three of you. And were they far from a wedding? Not a hairsbreadth. That lady had only to lift her little finger and he would have run after her to church, with his tongue out."

Ivan restrained himself with effort.

"All right," he commented at last. "You see, I haven't jumped up, I haven't knocked you down. I haven't killed you. Speak on. So, according to you, I had fixed on Dmitri to do it, I was counting on him?"

"How could you help counting on him? If he killed your father then he would lose all the rights of a nobleman, his rank and property, and he would be exiled. His share of the inheritance would come to you and your brother Alexey, in equal parts, so you'd each have not forty, but sixty thousand each. There's no doubt you counted on Dmitri."

"Listen, you wretch, if I had counted on anyone then, it would have been on you, not on Dmitri. And I swear I did expect something from you. . . . at the time . . . I remember!"

"I thought, too, at the time, that you were counting on me as well," said Smerdyakov with a sarcastic grin. "It was by that more than by anything else that you showed me what was in your mind. For if you had a foreboding about me and yet went away, you as good as said to me: 'You can murder my father, I won't stop you!' "

"You scoundrel! So that's how you understood it!"

"It was all that going to Tchermashnya. Why! You meant to go to Moscow and wouldn't listen to your father's entreaties to go to Tchermashnya—and at a word from me you consented at once! What reason had you to go to Tchermashnya? Since you went to Tchermashnya with no reason, simply at my word, it shows that you must have expected something from me."

"No. I didn't!" shouted Ivan.

"You didn't? Then you should, as your father's son, have had me taken to jail and flogged for my words . . . Or at least have given me a punch in the face. But you were not angry, and at once in a friendly way acted on my foolish word and went away, which was very wrong, for you should have stayed to save your father's life. How could I help drawing conclusions?"

Ivan sat scowling, both his fists pressed on his knees.

"Yes, I am sorry I didn't punch you in the face," he said with a bitter smile. "I couldn't have taken you to jail just then. Who would have believed me and what charge could I have brought against you? But the punch in the face . . . Oh, I'm sorry I didn't think of it. I should have pounded your ugly face into jelly."

Smerdyakov looked at him almost with pleasure.

"In the ordinary circumstances of life," he said in the same complacent tone in which he had taunted Gregory and argued with him about religion at Fyodor Karamazov's table, "in the ordinary circumstances of life, blows on the face are forbidden nowadays by law and people have given them up. But in exceptional circumstances people still resort to blows, not only among us but all over the world, even in the Republic of France. It is just as in the time of Adam and Eve. And people won't stop, but you, even in an exceptional case, did not dare."

"What are you learning French for?" Ivan nodded toward the exercise book lying on the table.

"Why shouldn't I learn French so as to improve my education. I may chance to go some day to those happy parts of Europe."

"Listen, monster." Ivan's eyes flashed and he trembled all over. "I am not afraid of your accusations. You can say what you like about me. And if I don't beat you to death, it's only because I suspect you of the crime and I'll drag you to justice. I'll unmask you."

"To my thinking, you'd better keep quiet, for what can you accuse me of, considering my innocence. And who would believe you? Only if you begin, I will tell everything, too, for I must defend myself."

"Do you think I am afraid of you now?"

"If the court doesn't believe all I've said to you just now, the public will. And you will be ashamed."

"That's as much as to say, 'It's always worth while speaking to a clever man,' eh?" said Ivan.

"You're right. And you'd better be sensible."

Ivan got up, shaking all over, put on his coat, and without replying further to Smerdyakov, without even looking at him, walked out of the cottage. The cool evening air refreshed him. There was a bright moon in the sky. A nightmare of ideas and sensations filled his soul. "Shall I go at once and report Smerdyakov? But what information can I give? He is not guilty. He'll only accuse me. And in fact why did I set off for Tchermashnya? What for? What for?" Ivan asked himself. "Yes, of course, I was expecting something. He is right . . ." And he remembered for the hundredth time how, on that last night in his father's house, he had listened on the stairs. But he remembered it now with such anguish that he stood still as though he had been stabbed. "Yes, I expected it then, that's true! I wanted the murder, I did want the murder! Did I want the murder?

Did I want it? I must kill Smerdyakov! If I don't dare kill Smerdyakov now, life is not worth living!"

Ivan did not go home, but went straight to Katerina. He alarmed her by his appearance. He was like a madman. He repeated all his conversation with Smerdyakov, every syllable of it. He couldn't be calmed, however much she tried to soothe him. He kept walking about the room, speaking strangely, disconnectedly. At last he sat down, put his elbows on the table, leaned his head on his hands and pronounced this strange sentence: "If it's not Dmitri, but Smerdyakov who's the murderer, I share his guilt, for I put him up to it. Whether I did or not, I don't know yet. But if he is the murderer, and not Dmitri, then I am the murderer, too."

When Katerina heard this, she got up without a word, went to her writing table, opened a box standing on it, took out a sheet of paper and laid it before Ivan. This was the letter of which Ivan spoke to Alyosha later on as "conclusive proof" that Dmitri had killed their father. This was the letter written by Dmitri to Katerina when he was drunk, on the evening he met Alyosha at the crossroads, after the scene at Katerina's when Grushenka had insulted her. That evening, parting from Alyosha, Dmitri had rushed to Grushenka. I don't know whether he saw her, but in the evening he was at the Metropolis tavern, where he got drunk. Then he asked for pen and paper and wrote a letter of weighty consequences to himself. It was a wordy, disconnected, frantic letter, a drunken letter. It was like the talk of a drunken man, who, on his return home, begins with extraordinary heat telling his wife how he had just been insulted, what a rascal has just insulted him, what a fine fellow he is on the other hand, and how he will get revenge; all this at great length, with great excitement and incoherence, with drunken tears and blows on the table. The letter was written on a dirty piece of ordinary paper of the cheapest kind. It had been provided by the tavern and there were numbers scrawled on the back of it. There was evidently not space enough for his drunken verbosity and Dmitri had not only filled the margins but had written the last line right across the rest. The letter ran as follows:

Fatal Katerina! Tomorrow I will get the money and repay your three thousand. Farewell, woman of wrath. Farewell too my love! Let us make an end! Tomorrow I shall try and get it from everyone, and if I can't borrow it, I give you my word of honor I shall go to my father and break his skull and take the money from under the pillow, if only Ivan has gone. If I have to go to Siberia for it, I'll give you back your three thousand. And farewell. I bow down to the ground before you, for I've been a scoundrel to you. Forgive me! No, better not forgive me, you'll be happier and so shall I! Better Siberia than your love. I love another woman; you got to know her too well today, so how can you forgive? I will murder the man who's robbed me!

560

I'll leave you all and go to the East so as to see no one again. Not *her* either, for you are not my only tormentress, she is too. Farewell!

P.S. — I write my curse, but I adore you! I hear it in my heart. One string is left and it vibrates. Better tear my heart in two! I shall kill myself, but first of all that cur. I shall tear three thousand from him and fling it to you. Though I've been a scoundrel to you, I am not a thief! You can expect three thousand. The cur keeps it under his mattress, in pink ribbon. I am not a thief, but I'll murder my thief. Katerina, don't look disdainful. Dmitri is not a thief; but a murderer! He has murdered his father and ruined himself to hold his ground, rather than endure your pride. And he doesn't love you.

P.P.S. — I kiss your feet. Farewell!! P.P.P.S. — Katerina, pray to God that someone will give me the money. Then I shall not be steeped in gore, and if no one does—I shall! Kill me!

Your slave and enemy,
D. Karamazov.

When Ivan read this letter, he was convinced. So then it was Dmitri, not Smerdyakov. And if not Smerdyakov, then not he, Ivan. This letter at once assumed in Ivan's eyes the aspect of logical proof. There could no longer be the slightest doubt of Dmitri's guilt. The suspicion never occurred to Ivan, by the way, that Dmitri might have committed the murder together with Smerdyakov. Such a theory did not fit in with the facts. Ivan was completely reassured. The next morning he only thought of Smerdyakov and his jibes with contempt. A few days later he actually wondered how he could have been so horribly upset at his suspicions. He decided to dismiss him with contempt and to forget him. In this way a month passed. He made no further inquiry about Smerdyakov, but twice he happened to hear that he was very ill and out of his mind.

"He'll end in madness," the young district doctor, Varvinsky, observed about him and Ivan remembered this. During the last week of that month Ivan himself began to feel very ill. He went to consult the Moscow doctor who had been sent for by Katerina just before the trial. And just at that time his relations with Katerina became acutely strained. They were like two enemies in love with one another. Katerina's "returns" to Dmitri, that is, her brief but violent revulsions of feeling in his favor, drove Ivan to frenzy. Strange to say, until that last scene described above, when Alyosha came from Dmitri to Katerina, Ivan had never once, during that month, heard her express a doubt of Dmitri's guilt, in spite of those "returns" that were so hateful to him. It is remarkable, too, that while he felt that he hated Dmitri more and more every day, he realized that it was not on account of Katerina's "returns" that he hated him, but just *because he was the murderer of his father*. He was conscious of this and recognized it fully.

Nevertheless, he went to see Dmitri ten days before the trial and proposed a plan of escape—a plan he had thought over a long time. He was partly impelled to do this by a sense of guilt. He remembered that Smerdyakov had said that it was to his, Ivan's, advantage that Dmitri should be convicted; that would increase his inheritance and Alyosha's from forty to sixty thousand roubles. Because of this feeling of guilt he decided to sacrifice thirty thousand on arranging Dmitri's escape. On his return from seeing him, he was very mournful and dispirited. He suddenly began to feel that he was anxious for Dmitri's escape, not only to heal that sore place by sacrificing thirty thousand, but for another reason. "Is it because I am as much a murderer at heart?" he asked himself. Something very deep down seemed burning and rankling in his soul. His pride above all suffered cruelly that month. But of that later. . . .

When, after his conversation with Alyosha, Ivan suddenly decided with his hand on the bell of his lodging to go to Smerdyakov, he obeyed a sudden and peculiar impulse. He suddenly remembered how Katerina had only just cried out to him in Alyosha's presence: "It was you, you who persuaded me of his (that is, Dmitri's) guilt!" Ivan was thunderstruck when he recalled it. He had never once tried to persuade her that Dmitri was the murderer. On the contrary, he had suspected himself in her presence that time when he came back from Smerdyakov. It was *she*, she, who had produced the letter and proved his brother's guilt. And now she suddenly exclaimed: "I've been at Smerdyakov's myself!" When had she been there? Ivan had known nothing of it. So she was not at all so sure of Dmitri's guilt! And what could Smerdyakov have told her? What, what, had he said to her? His heart burned with anger. He could not understand how he could, half an hour before, have let those words pass and not have cried out at the moment. He let go of the bell and rushed off to Smerdyakov. "I shall kill him perhaps this time," he thought on the way.

8. *The Third and Last Interview with Smerdyakov*

WHEN IVAN WAS HALFWAY THERE, the keen wind that had been blowing early that morning rose again, and a fine dry snow began falling. It did not lie on the ground, but was whirled about by the wind. There were scarcely any lamp posts in the part of the town where Smerdyakov lived. Ivan strode alone in the darkness, unconscious of the snowstorm, instinctively picking out his way. His head ached and there was a painful throbbing in his temples. He felt that his hands were twitching convulsively. Not far from Maria's cottage, Ivan suddenly came upon a drunken peasant. He was wearing a coarse patched coat, and was walking zigzag, grumbling and swearing to himself. Then suddenly he began singing in a husky drunken voice:

*"Ach, Vanka's gone to Petersburg
I won't wait till he comes back."*

He broke off at the second line and began swearing; then he began the same song again. Ivan felt an intense hatred for him before he had thought about him at all. Suddenly he realized his presence and felt an irresistible impulse to knock him down. At that moment they met, and the peasant with a violent lurch fell against Ivan, who pushed him back furiously. The peasant went flying backwards, and fell like a log on the frozen ground. He uttered one plaintive "O-oh!" and then was silent. Ivan stepped up to him. He was lying on his back, unconscious. "He will freeze to death," thought Ivan, and he went on his way to Smerdyakov's.

Maria, who ran to open the door with a candle in her hand, whispered to Ivan that Smerdyakov was very ill. "It's not that he's laid up, but he doesn't seem himself. He even told us to take the tea away; he wouldn't have any."

"Why, does he make a fuss?" asked Ivan coarsely.

"Oh dear, no, quite the contrary, he's very quiet. Only please don't talk to him too long," Maria begged. Ivan opened the door and stepped into the room.

The room was overheated as before, but there were changes. One of the benches at the side had been removed, and in its place had been put a large old mahogany leather sofa, on which a bed had been made up, with fairly clean white pillows. Smerdyakov was sitting on the sofa, wearing the same dressing gown Ivan had seen before. The table had been brought out in front of the sofa, so that there was hardly room to move. On the table lay a thick book in a yellow cover, but Smerdyakov was not reading it. He seemed to be sitting doing nothing. He met Ivan with a slow silent gaze and was apparently not at all surprised at his coming. There was a great change in his face; he was much thinner and more sallow. His eyes were sunken and there were blue marks under them.

"Why, you really are ill!" Ivan stopped short. "I won't keep you long. I won't even take off my coat. Where can I sit down?"

He went to the other end of the table, moved up a chair and sat down on it.

"Why do you look at me without speaking? I've only come with one question, and I swear I won't go without an answer. Has the young lady, Katerina, been to see you?"

Smerdyakov still remained silent, looking calmly at Ivan as before. Suddenly, with a motion of his hand, he turned his face away.

"What's the matter with you?" cried Ivan.

"Nothing."

"What do you mean by 'nothing'?"

"Yes, she has been here. It's none of your business. Let me alone."

"No, I won't let you alone. Tell me, when was she here?"

"Why, I'd forgotten about her," said Smerdyakov, with a scornful smile. And turning his face to Ivan again, he stared at him with a look of hatred, the same look that he had fixed on him at their last interview, a month before.

"You seem very ill yourself, your face is sunken. You don't look like yourself," he said to Ivan.

"Never mind my health. Answer what I ask you."

"But why are your eyes so yellow? The whites are yellow. Are you so worried?" He smiled contemptuously and suddenly laughed outright.

"Listen, I've told you I won't go away without an answer!" Ivan cried, intensely irritated.

"Why do you keep pestering me? Why do you torment me?" said Smerdyakov with a look of suffering.

"Damn it! I've nothing to do with you. Just answer my question and I'll go away."

"I've no answer to give you," said Smerdyakov, looking down.

"You can be sure I'll make you answer!"

"Why are you so disturbed?" Smerdyakov stared at him, not simply with contempt, but almost with repulsion. "Is it because the trial begins tomorrow? Nothing will happen to you. Can't you believe that? Go home, go to bed and sleep in peace. Don't be afraid of anything."

"I don't understand you. . . . What have I to be afraid of tomorrow?" Ivan asked in astonishment, but suddenly a chill breath of fear passed over his soul.

Smerdyakov measured him with his eyes. "You don't understand?" he drawled reproachfully. "It's a strange thing a clever man should care to play such a farce!"

Ivan looked at him speechless. The startling, incredibly supercilious tone of this man who had once been his father's cook and valet, was extraordinary. He had not assumed such a tone even at their last interview.

"I tell you, you've nothing to be afraid of. I won't say anything about you, there's no proof against you. . . . But look how your hands are trembling. Why are your fingers moving like that? Go home, *you* did not murder him."

Ivan started. He remembered Alyosha.

"I know it was not I," he faltered.

"Do you?" Smerdyakov caught him up again.

Ivan jumped up and grabbed him by the shoulder.

"Tell me everything, you wretch! Tell me everything!"

Smerdyakov was not in the least frightened. He riveted his eyes on Ivan with insane hatred. "Well, it was you who murdered him!" he whispered.

Ivan sank back on his chair, as though pondering something. He laughed malignantly.

"You mean my going away? What you talked about last time?"

"You stood before me last time and understood it all, and you understand it now."

"All I understand is that you are mad."

"Aren't you tired of it? Here we are face to face; what's the use of keeping up a farce to each other? Are you still trying to throw the blame on me? *You* murdered him. You are the murderer! I was only your instrument, your faithful servant, and it was following your words I did it."

"Did it? Did you murder him?" Ivan turned cold.

Something seemed to give way in his brain, and he shuddered all over. Smerdyakov looked at him wonderingly; the genuineness of Ivan's horror struck him.

"You don't mean to say you really did not know?" Smerdyakov faltered mistrustfully, looking with a forced smile into Ivan's eyes.

Ivan gazed at him unable to speak.

> *Ach, Vanka's gone to Petersburg*
> *I won't wait till he comes back,*

suddenly echoed in his head.

"Do you know, I am afraid that you are a dream, a phantom sitting before me," Ivan muttered.

"There's no phantom here, but only us two . . . And one other. He is here, that third one, between us."

"Who is he? Who is here? What third person?" Ivan cried, looking about him, his eyes searching in every corner.

"That third is God Himself, Providence. He is the third One beside us now. Only don't look for Him, you won't find Him."

"It's a lie that you killed him!" Ivan cried madly. "You are mad or trying to torture me again!"

Smerdyakov watched him with no sign of fear. He could not get over Ivan's simplicity; he still believed that Ivan knew everything and was only trying to "throw it all on him."

"Wait a minute," he said at last in a weak voice, and suddenly bringing up his left leg from under the table, he began turning up his trouser. He was wearing long white stockings and slippers. Slowly he took off his garter and fumbled in his stocking. Ivan gazed at him, and shuddered in terror.

"He's mad!" he cried and jumping up, he drew back against the wall standing up against it, stiff and straight. He looked with insane terror at Smerdyakov, who, entirely unaffected, continued fumbling in his stocking. He was trying to get hold of something with his fingers. At last he got hold of it and began pulling it out. Ivan saw that it was a piece of paper, or perhaps a roll of papers. Smerdyakov laid it on the table.

"Here," he said quietly.

"What is it?" asked Ivan trembling.

"Kindly look at it," Smerdyakov answered, still in the same low tone.

Ivan stepped up to the table, took up the roll of paper and began unfolding it. But suddenly he drew back his fingers, as though from something loathsome.

"Your hands keep trembling," observed Smerdyakov and he deliberately unfolded the papers himself. Under the wrapper were three packages of hundred-rouble notes.

"They are all here, all the three thousand roubles. You don't need to count them. Take them," Smerdyakov suggested to Ivan, nodding at the notes. Ivan sank back in his chair. He was as white as a handkerchief.

"You frightened me . . . with your stocking," Ivan said with a strange grin.

"Did you really not know till now?" Smerdyakov asked once more.

"No, I did not know. I kept thinking of Dmitri. Dmitri!" He clutched his head in both hands.

"Listen. Did you kill him alone? With my brother's help or without?"

"It was only with you, with your help, I killed him. Dmitri is innocent."

"All right, all right. Talk about me later. Why do I keep on trembling? I can't speak properly."

"You were bold enough then. You said 'everything is lawful.' But how frightened you are now!" Smerdyakov muttered in surprise. "Won't you have some lemonade? I'll ask for some at once. It's very refreshing. Only I must hide this first."

And again he nodded at the notes. He was just going to get up and call to Maria to make some lemonade, but, looking for something to cover up the notes that she might not see them, he took up the big yellow book that Ivan had noticed lying on the table, and put it over the notes. The book was *The Sayings of the Holy Father Isaac the Syrian*. Ivan read it mechanically.

"I won't have any lemonade," he said. "Talk of me later. Sit down now and tell me how you did it. Tell me all about it."

"You'd better take off your overcoat or you'll be too hot." Ivan, as though he'd only just thought of it, took off his coat and, without getting up from his chair, threw it on the bench.

"Speak. Please, speak."

He seemed calmer. He waited, feeling sure that Smerdyakov would tell him *all* about it.

"How it was done?" sighed Smerdyakov. "It was done in the most natural way, following your words."

"Of my words later," Ivan interrupted again with complete self-possession, firmly uttering his words, and not shouting as before. "Only tell me in detail how you did it. Everything, as it happened. Don't forget anything. The details, above everything, the details, I beg you."

"You'd gone away, then I fell into the cellar."

"In a real fit or in a sham fit?"

"A sham one, naturally. I shammed it all. I went quietly down the steps to the very bottom and lay down. And as I lay down I gave a scream, and then I struggled, till they carried me out."

"Wait! And were you shamming all along, afterwards, and in the hospital?"

"No. Next day, in the morning, before they took me to the hospital, I had a real attack, a more violent one than I've had for years. I was unconscious for two whole days. But before that . . ."

"All right, all right. Go on."

"They laid me on the bed. I knew I'd be the other side of the partition, because whenever I was ill, Marfa used to put me there near them. She's always been very kind to me from my birth. All night I moaned, but quietly. I kept expecting Dmitri to come."

"Expecting him? To come to you?"

"Not to me. I expected him to come because, being without me and getting no news, he'd be sure to come and climb over the fence. He'd be sure to come and do something."

"And if he hadn't come?"

"Then nothing would have happened. I would never have brought myself to do it without him."

"All right, all right . . . Speak more clearly, don't hurry. Above all, don't leave anything out!"

"I expected him to kill your father. I thought that was certain, for I had prepared him for it . . . during the last few days. . . . He knew about the secret signals, that was the main thing. With his suspicious nature and the fury which had been growing in him all those days, he was bound to get into the house by means of those signals. That was inevitable, so I was expecting him."

"Wait," Ivan interrupted. "If he had killed him, he would have taken the money and carried it away; you must have thought of that. What would you have gained by it? I don't see."

"But he would never have found the money. That was only what I told him, that the money was under the mattress. But that wasn't true. It was in a box. And one day I suggested to Fyodor Karamazov, as I was the only person he trusted, to hide the envelope with the notes in the corner behind the ikons. No one would have guessed that place, especially if they came in a hurry. So that's where the envelope was, in the corner behind the ikons. It would have been foolish to keep it under the mattress. The box, at least, could be locked. But everyone believes it was under the mattress. A stupid thing to believe. So if Dmitri had committed the murder, finding nothing, he would either have run away in a hurry, afraid of every

567

sound, as always happens with murderers, or he would have been arrested. So I could always have gone to the ikons and have taken away the money next morning or even that night, and Dmitri would have been blamed for it. I could depend on that."

"But what if he did not kill him, but only knocked him down?"

"If he did not kill him, of course, I would not have ventured to take the money, and nothing would have happened. But I calculated that he would beat him senseless, and I would have time to take it. And then I'd tell Fyodor Karamazov that it was Dmitri who had taken the money after beating him."

"Stop . . . I am getting confused. Then it was Dmitri who killed him, you only took the money?"

"No, he didn't kill him. Well, I could tell you that he is the murderer. . . . But I don't want to lie to you now, because . . . Because if you really haven't understood, and are not pretending, so as to throw your guilt on me, you are still responsible for it all, since you suspected murder and wanted me to do it, and went away knowing all about it. And so I want to prove to you that you are the only real murderer and that I am not the murderer, though I did kill him. You are the real murderer."

"Why, why am I the murderer? Oh, God!" Ivan cried, unable to restrain himself and forgetting that he had put off discussing himself till the end of the conversation. "You still refer to Tchermashnya? Wait, tell me, why did you want my consent, if you really took Tchermashnya for consent? How will you explain that?"

"Assured of your consent, I knew that you wouldn't make an outcry over those three thousand being lost, even if I were suspected, instead of Dmitri. I knew you would protect me from others. . . . And when you got your inheritance you would reward me and thank me all the rest of your life. For you'd receive your inheritance through me, seeing that if your father had married Agrafena Svyetlov, you wouldn't get a penny."

"Ah! Then you intended to worry me all my life afterwards," said Ivan. "And what if I hadn't gone away then, but had reported you?"

"What could you have reported? That I persuaded you to go to Tchermashnya? That's all nonsense. Besides, after our conversation you would either have gone away or have stayed. If you had stayed, nothing would have happened. I would have known that you didn't want it done, and would not have attempted it. But as you went away, it meant that you wouldn't testify against me at the trial, and that you'd overlook my having the three thousand. And you couldn't have prosecuted me afterward, because then I would have told it all in the court; that is, not that I had stolen the money or killed him—I would have said that—but that you'd put me up to the theft and the murder. That's why I needed your consent, so that you couldn't corner me afterwards, for what proof could you have had? I could always have cornered you, revealing your eagerness for your father's death. And I tell you the public would believe it, and you would have been disgraced for the rest of your life."

"Was I so eager then, was I?" Ivan cried.

"To be sure you were. By your consent you silently sanctioned my doing it." Smerdyakov looked steadily at Ivan. He was very weak and spoke slowly and wearily, but some inner force urged him on. He evidently had some design. Ivan felt that.

"Go on," he said. "Tell me what happened that night."

"What more is there to tell! I lay there and I thought I heard the master shout. Before that, Gregory had suddenly gotten up and gone out. There was a scream, and then all was silence and darkness. I lay there waiting, my heart beating; I couldn't bear it. I got up at last and went out. I saw the window open on the left into the garden, and I went up to listen whether the master was alive. I heard him moving about, sighing, so I knew he was alive. Ah! I thought. I went to the window and shouted to him: 'It's I.' And he shouted to me: 'He's been, he's been; he's run away.' He meant Dmitri had been. 'He's killed Gregory!' 'Where?' I whispered. 'There, in the corner,' he pointed. He was whispering, too. 'Wait,' I said. I went to the corner of the garden to look, and there I came upon Gregory lying by the wall, covered with blood, senseless. So it's true that Dmitri has been here, was the thought that came into my head, and I right then determined to make an end of it. Gregory would see nothing because he was unconscious. The only risk was that Marfa might wake up. I knew that, but the longing to do it was so strong that I could scarcely breathe. I went back to the window to the master and said: 'She's here, she's come; Agrafena Svyetlov has come. She wants to be let in.' And he started like a baby. 'Where is she?' he gasped. He couldn't believe it. 'She's standing there,' said I, 'open.' He looked out of the window at me, half believing and afraid to open. 'Why he is afraid of me now,' I wondered. And it was funny. I remembered to knock on the window frame those taps we'd agreed upon as a signal that Grushenka had come. I tapped out that signal in his presence, before his very eyes. He didn't seem to believe my words, but as soon as he heard the taps, he ran at once to open the door. He opened it. I wanted to go in, but he stood in the way to prevent my passing. 'Where is she? Where is she?' He looked at me, trembling all over. Well, thought I, if he's so frightened of me as all that, it's bad! And my legs went weak with fear that he wouldn't let me in or would call out, or that Marfa would run up, or something else might happen. I don't remember now but I must have stood facing him. I whispered to him: 'Why, she's there, there, under the window. How is it you don't see her?' He said: 'Bring her then, bring her.' 'She's afraid,' I said. 'She was frightened at the noise. She's hidden in the bushes. Go and call to her yourself from the study.' He ran to the window, put the candle in the window. 'Grushenka,' he cried, 'Grushenka, are you here?' But he didn't want to lean out of the window, he didn't want to move away from me, because he was panic-stricken. He was so frightened he didn't dare to turn his back on me. 'Why, here she is,' I said. I went up to the window and leaned right out of it. 'Here she is, she's in the bush, laughing at you, don't you see her?' He suddenly believed me. He was shaking all over—he was awfully crazy about her—and he leaned right out of the window. I snatched up the iron paper weight from his table; do you remember it, it weighs about three pounds. I swung it and hit him on the top of the skull with the corner of it. He didn't even cry out. He only sank down, and I hit him again and a third time. And the third time I knew I'd broken his skull. He suddenly rolled on his back, face upwards, covered with blood. I looked around. There was no blood on me, not a spot. I wiped the paper weight, put it back, went up to the ikons, took the money out of the envelope, and flung the envelope on the floor and the pink ribbon beside it. I went out into the garden, straight to the apple tree with a hollow in it—you know that hollow. I'd chosen it long before and put a rag and a piece of paper in it. I wrapped all the notes in the rag and stuffed it deep down in the hole. And there it stayed for over two weeks. I took it out later, when I came out of the hospital. I went back to my bed, lay down and thought, 'If Gregory dies it will be bad for me, but if he recovers, it will be all right. He'll bear witness that Dmitri has been here, and so everyone will think that he killed him and took the money.' Then I began groaning so as to wake up Marfa as soon as possible. At last she got up, and she rushed to me, but when she saw Gregory was not there, she ran out, and I heard her scream in the garden. And that set it all going and set my mind at rest."

He stopped. Ivan had listened all the time in dead silence without stirring or taking his eyes off him. As he told his story Smerdyakov glanced at him from time to time, but for the most part kept his eyes averted. When he finished he was agitated and breathing hard. The perspiration stood out on his face. But it was impossible to tell whether it was remorse he was feeling.

"Wait," cried Ivan. "What about the door? If he only opened the door to you, how could Gregory have seen it open before? For Gregory says he saw it open."

It was remarkable that Ivan spoke quite agreeably, in a different tone, not angry as before. If anyone had opened the door at that moment and looked in at them, he would certainly have concluded that they were talking about some ordinary subject.

"As for the door and Gregory having seen it open, that's only his imagination," said Smerdyakov with a twisted smile. "He is not a man, but an obstinate mule. He didn't see it, but thinks he saw it, and there's no shaking him. It's just our luck he took that notion into his head, for they can't fail to convict Dmitri after that."

"Listen . . ." said Ivan, beginning to seem bewildered again and making an effort to grasp something. "Listen. There are a lot of questions I want to ask you, but I forget them . . . I keep forgetting and getting mixed up. Yes. Tell me this at least, why did you open the envelope and leave it there on the floor? Why didn't you take the envelope with you? . . . When you were telling me, I thought you spoke about it as though it were the right thing to do . . . But why, I can't understand . . ."

"I did it for a good reason. If a man had known all about it, as I did for instance, if he'd seen the money before, and had perhaps put those notes in that envelope himself, and had seen the envelope sealed up and addressed, with his own eyes . . . If such a man had done the murder, what would have made him tear open the envelope, especially when he was in such a desperate hurry, since he knew for certain the notes were in the envelope? No, if the man had been someone like me, he'd simply have put the envelope straight in his pocket and run away with it as fast as he could. But it would be quite different with Dmitri. He only knew about the envelope from hearsay; he had never seen it, and if he'd found it, for instance, under the mattress, he'd have torn it open as quickly as possible to make sure the notes were in it. And he'd have thrown the envelope down, without having time to think that it would be evidence against him. Because he was not a thief and had never stolen anything before. He is a gentleman born, and if he did bring himself to steal, it would not be regular stealing, but simply taking what was his own, for he'd told the whole town he meant to, and had even bragged aloud before everyone that he'd go and take his money from his father. I didn't say that openly to the prosecutor when I was being examined, but I suggested it to him by a hint, as though I didn't see it myself. He believed he thought of it himself. His mouth watered at the idea."

"But how could you possibly have thought of all that at the moment?" cried Ivan with astonishment. He looked at Smerdyakov again with alarm.

"Certainly not! No one could think of it all in such a hurry. It was all thought out beforehand."

"Well . . . Well, it was the devil helped you!" Ivan cried

again. "No, you are not a fool, you are far more clever than I thought . . ."

He got up, obviously intending to walk across the room. He was terribly upset. But as the table blocked his way, and there was hardly space to pass between the table and the wall, he only turned around where he stood and sat down again.

Perhaps the restraint irritated him, for he suddenly cried out: "Listen, you miserable creature! Don't you understand that if I haven't killed you, it's simply because I am keeping you to appear tomorrow at the trial." Ivan raised his hand. "As God is my witness, perhaps I too am guilty; perhaps I really had a secret desire for my father's death. But I swear I am not as guilty as you think, and perhaps I didn't urge you on at all. No. No, I didn't urge you on! But it doesn't matter, I will give evidence against myself tomorrow at the trial. I'm determined to! I will tell everything. Everything. But we'll appear together. And whatever you say against me, whatever evidence you give, I'll face it. I am not afraid of you. I'll confirm it all myself! But you must confess, too! You must. You must. We'll go together. That's how it will be!"

Ivan said this solemnly and with determination. From his eyes alone it could be seen that it would be so.

"You are ill, I see, you are quite ill. Your eyes are yellow," Smerdyakov commented, without the least irony, with apparent sympathy in fact.

"We'll go together," Ivan repeated. "And if you don't go it doesn't matter. I'll go alone."

Smerdyakov was silent. He was thinking.

"It won't be like that; you won't go," he concluded.

"You don't understand me," Ivan exclaimed reproachfully.

"You'll be too much ashamed, if you confess it all. And, what's more, it will be no use at all, for I will say straight out that I never said anything of the sort to you. I'll say that you are either ill (and it looks like it, too), or that you're so sorry for your brother that you are sacrificing yourself to save him and have invented it all against me, because you've always thought no more of me than if I'd been a fly. And who will believe you? What proof have you got?"

"Listen, you showed me those notes just now to convince me."

Smerdyakov lifted the book off the notes and laid it to one side.

"Take that money with you," Smerdyakov sighed.

"Of course I will take it. But why do you give it to me, if you committed the murder for the sake of it?" Ivan looked at him with great surprise.

"I don't want it," Smerdyakov said in a shaking voice. "I did have an idea of beginning a new life with that money in Moscow or, better still, abroad. I did dream of it, chiefly because 'all things are lawful.' That was right what you taught me, for you talked a lot to me about that. For if there's no everlasting God, there's no such thing as virtue, and there's no need of it. You were right there. So that's how I looked at it."

"Did you come to that conclusion by yourself?" asked Ivan with a smile.

"With your help."

"And now, I suppose, you believe in God, since you are giving back the money?"

"No, I don't believe in God," whispered Smerdyakov.

"Then why are you giving it back?"

"Stop . . . That's enough!" Smerdyakov waved his hand. "You used to say that 'everything is lawful,' so now why are you so upset? You even want to go and testify against yourself. . . . Only it won't be like that! You won't go to give evidence," Smerdyakov decided with conviction.

"You'll see," said Ivan.

"It isn't possible. You are very clever. You are fond of money, I know that. You like to be respected, too, for you're very proud. You are far too fond of female charms, too, and you value most of all living in undisturbed comfort, without having to depend on anyone—that's what you care most about. You won't want to spoil your life forever by taking such a disgrace on yourself. You are like your father, Fyodor Karamazov. You are more like him than any of his other children. You have the same soul as he had."

"You are not a fool," said Ivan slowly. The blood rushed to his face. "You are serious now!" he observed, looking suddenly at Smerdyakov with a different expression.

"It was your pride made you think I was a fool. Take the money."

Ivan took the three rolls of notes and put them in his pocket without wrapping them in anything.

"I will show them at the court tomorrow," he said.

"Nobody will believe you, because you have plenty of money of your own. They will say that you have taken it out of your cash box and brought it to court."

Ivan got up.

"I repeat," he said, "the only reason I haven't killed you is that I need you for tomorrow. Remember that. Don't forget it!"

"Well, kill me. Kill me now," Smerdyakov said, all at once looking strangely at Ivan. "You won't even dare do that," he added, with a bitter smile. "You won't dare to do anything, you, who used to be so bold!"

"Tomorrow!" cried Ivan and he moved to go out.

"Wait a moment. . . . Show me those notes again."

Ivan took out the notes and showed them to him. Smerdyakov looked at them for ten seconds.

"Well, you can go," he said, with a wave of his hand. "Ivan!" he called after him.

"What do you want?" Ivan turned without stopping.

"Good-by!"

"Tomorrow!" Ivan cried again, and he walked out of the cottage.

The snowstorm was still raging. He walked the first few steps boldly, but suddenly he began staggering. "It's something physical," he thought with a grin. Something like joy was springing up in his heart. He was conscious of unbounded resolution; he would make an end of the wavering that had so tortured him of late. His determination was taken, "and now it will not be changed," he thought with relief. At that moment he stumbled against something and almost fell down. Stopping short, he saw at his feet the peasant he had knocked down, still lying unconscious and motionless. The snow had almost covered his face. Ivan lifted him in his arms.

Seeing a light in a house to the right he went up, knocked at the shutters, and asked the man to whom the house belonged to help him carry the peasant to the police station, promising him three roubles. The man got ready and came out. I won't describe in detail how Ivan succeeded in bringing the peasant to the police station and arranging for a doctor to see him at once, providing with a liberal hand for the expenses. I will only say that this business took a whole hour but Ivan was content with it. His mind wandered and worked incessantly.

"If I had not made so firm a decision for tomorrow," he thought with satisfaction, "I would not have stayed a whole hour to look after the peasant, but would have passed by, without caring about his being frozen. I am fully aware of what I am doing," he thought at the same instant, with still greater satisfaction, "although they have decided that I am going out of my mind!"

Just as he reached his own house he stopped short, asking himself suddenly if he had not better go at once to the prosecutor and tell him everything. He decided the question quickly. "Everything together tomorrow!" he whispered to himself. And strange to say, almost all his gladness and self-satisfaction passed in that instant.

As he entered his room he felt something like a touch of ice on his heart, like a recollection or, more exactly, a reminder of something agonizing and revolting that was in that room now, at that moment, and had been there before. He sank wearily on his sofa.

The old woman brought him a samovar; he made tea, but did not touch it. He sat on the sofa and felt dizzy. He felt that he was ill and helpless. He began to fall asleep, but got up uneasily and walked across the room to shake off his drowsiness. At moments he thought he was delirious, but it was not illness that he thought of most.

Sitting down again, he began looking around as though searching for something. This happened several times. At last his eyes fastened intently on one point. He smiled, but an angry flush came over his face. He sat a long time, his head propped on both arms, though he looked sideways at the same point, at the sofa that stood against the opposite wall. There was evidently something there, some object that irritated him, worried him and tormented him.

9. *The Devil. Ivan's Nightmare*

I AM NOT A DOCTOR, but yet I feel that the moment has come when I must give the reader some account of the nature of Ivan's illness. Anticipating events I can say at least one thing: he was at that moment on the verge of an attack of brain fever. Though his health had long been affected, it had offered a stubborn resistance to the nervous illness which, in the end gained complete mastery over it. Though I know nothing of medicine, I venture to suggest that he had perhaps, by terrific effort of will, succeeded in delaying the attack for a time, hoping, of course, to check it completely. He knew that he was not well, but he loathed the thought of being ill at that critical time, when he needed to have all his faculties to say what he had to say boldly and "to justify himself to himself."

He had however consulted the new doctor, who had been brought from Moscow by a fantastic notion of Katerina's to which I have already referred. After listening to him and examining him the doctor came to the conclusion that he was actually suffering from some disorder of the brain, and was not at all surprised by an admission which Ivan had reluctantly made to him. "Hallucinations are quite common in your condition," the doctor said, "though it would be better to verify them . . . You must do something about this at once, without a moment's delay, or things will go badly with you." But Ivan did not follow this advice. "I am walking about, so I am strong enough. If I drop, it'll be different then, anyone may take care of me who likes," he decided, dismissing the subject.

And so he was sitting almost conscious himself of his delirium and, as I have said already, looking intently at something on the sofa against the opposite wall. Someone appeared to be sitting there, though goodness knows how he had come in, for he had not been in the room when Ivan came into it, on his return from Smerdyakov. This was a person or, more accurately speaking, a Russian gentleman of a particular kind, no longer young, about fifty, with rather long, thick dark hair, slightly streaked with gray and a small pointed beard. He was wearing a brownish jacket, rather shabby, evidently made by a good tailor. His linen and his long scarflike necktie were the kind worn by people who aim at being stylish. But on closer inspection his linen was not over clean and his wide scarf was very threadbare. The visitor's checked trousers were of excellent cut, but were too light in color and too tight for the present fashion. His soft fluffy white hat was out of keeping with the season.

In brief there was every appearance of gentility on straitened means. It looked as though the gentleman belonged to that class of idle landowners who used to flourish in the times of serfdom. He had unmistakably been, at some time, in good and fashionable society, had once had good connections. But after a gay youth, becoming gradually impoverished on the abolition of serfdom, he had sunk into the position of a poor relative, wandering from one good old friend to another. He was received by them for his companionable and accommodating disposition and as being, after all, a gentleman who could be asked to sit down with anyone, though, of course, not in a place of honor. Such gentlemen of accommodating temper and dependent position, who can tell a story, take a hand at cards, and who have a distinct aversion for any duties that may be forced upon them, are usually solitary creatures, either bachelors or widowers. Sometimes they have children, but if so, the children are always being brought up at a distance, at some aunt's, to whom these gentlemen never refer in good society, seeming ashamed of the relationship. They gradually lose sight of their children altogether, though at intervals they receive a birthday or Christmas letter from them and sometimes even answer it.

The countenance of the unexpected visitor was not so much good-natured, as accommodating and ready to assume any amiable expression as the occasion might arise. He had no watch, but he had tortoise-shell pince-nez on a black ribbon. On the middle finger of his right hand was a massive gold ring with a cheap opal in it.

Ivan was angrily silent and would not begin the conversation. The visitor waited and sat exactly like a poor relation who had come down from his room to keep his host company at tea, and was discreetly silent, seeing that his host was frowning and preoccupied. But he was ready for any pleasant conversation as soon as his host should begin it. All at once his face expressed solicitude.

"I say," he began to Ivan, "excuse me, I only mention it to remind you. You went to Smerdyakov's to find out about Katerina but you left without finding out anything about her. You probably forgot . . ."

"Oh, yes," said Ivan and his face grew gloomy with uneasi-

576

ness. "Yes, I'd forgotten . . . But it doesn't matter now. Never mind, till tomorrow," he muttered to himself. "But you," he added, addressing his visitor, "I would have remembered it myself in a minute, for that was just what was tormenting me! But you, why do you interfere? You act as though you prompted me, and that I didn't remember it myself."

"Don't believe it then," said the gentleman, smiling pleasantly. "What's the good of believing against your will? Besides, proof is no help to believing, especially material proof. Thomas believed, not because he saw Christ risen, but because he wanted to believe, before he saw. Look at the spiritualists, for instance. . . . I am very fond of them . . . Only would you believe it, they imagine that they are serving the cause of religion, because the devils show them their horns from the other world. That, they say, is material proof of the existence of another world. The other world and material proof, what next! And if you come to that, does proving there's a devil prove that there's a God? I want to join an idealist society, I'll lead the opposition in it. I'll say I am a realist, but not a materialist, he-he!"

"Listen." Ivan suddenly got up from the table. "I seem to be delirious . . . I am delirious, in fact. Talk any nonsense you like, I don't care! You won't drive me to fury, as you did last time. But I feel somehow ashamed . . . I want to walk around the room . . . I sometimes don't see you and don't even hear your voice as I did last time, but I always guess what you are saying, for it's I, *I myself speaking, not you*. Only I don't know whether I was dreaming last time or whether I really saw you. I'll wet a towel and put it on my head and perhaps you'll vanish into the air."

Ivan went into the corner, took a towel and wet it. With it on his head he began walking up and down the room.

"I am so glad you treat me with such familiarity," the visitor began.

"Fool," laughed Ivan. "Do you think I should stand on ceremony with you? I am in good spirits now, though I've a pain in my forehead . . . and on the top of my head . . . Only please don't talk philosophy, as you did last time. If you must stay, talk of something amusing. Gossip. You are a poor relative, you ought to gossip. What a nightmare to have! But I am not afraid of you. I'll get the better of you. I won't be taken to a madhouse!"

"How charming, 'poor relative.' Yes, I am in my natural shape. For what am I on earth but a poor relative? By the way, I am listening to you and am rather surprised to find you are actually beginning to take me for something real, not simply your imagination, as you persisted in declaring last time . . ."

"Never for one minute have I taken you for reality," Ivan cried with a sort of fury. "You are a lie, you are my illness, you are a phantom. It's only that I don't know how to destroy you and I see I must suffer for a time. You are an hallucination. You are the incarnation of myself, but only of one side of me . . . of my thoughts and feelings, but only the worst and most stupid of them. From that point of view you might be of interest to me, if only I had time to waste on you . . ."

"Excuse me, excuse me, I'll catch you. When you called out to Alyosha under the lamp post this evening: 'You learned it from *him!* How do you know that *he* visits me?' you were thinking of me. So for one brief moment you did believe that I really exist," the gentleman laughed blandly.

"Yes, that was a moment of weakness . . . But I couldn't believe in you. I don't know whether I was asleep or awake last time. Perhaps I was only dreaming then and didn't really see you at all . . ."

"And why were you so surly with Alyosha? He is so good; I've treated him badly over Father Zossima."

"Don't talk of Alyosha! How dare you, you flunkey!" Ivan laughed again.

"You scold me, but you laugh—that's a good sign. But you are ever so much more polite than you were last time and I know why; that great decision of yours . . ."

"Don't speak of my decision," cried Ivan savagely.

"I understand, I understand. It's all very noble and charming. You are going to defend your brother and sacrifice yourself . . . It's chivalrous."

"Keep quiet, I'll kick you!"

"I won't be altogether sorry, for then my object will be attained. If you kick me, you must believe in my reality, for people don't kick ghosts. Joking apart, it doesn't matter to me, scold if you like, though it's better to be a trifle more polite even to me. 'Fool, flunkey!' What words!"

"Scolding you, I scold myself," Ivan laughed again. "You are myself, myself, only with a different face. You just repeat what I am thinking . . . You are incapable of saying anything original!"

"If I am like you in my way of thinking, it's all to my credit," the gentleman declared, with delicacy and dignity.

"You choose only my worst thoughts, and what's more, the stupid ones. You are stupid and vulgar. You are awfully stupid. No, I can't go on with you! What am I to do, what am I to do!" Ivan said.

"My dear friend, above all things I want to behave like a gentleman and to be recognized as such," the visitor began in an access of deprecating and simple-hearted pride, typical of a poor relative. "I am poor, but . . . I won't say very honest, but . . . It's an axiom generally accepted in society that I am a fallen angel. I certainly can't conceive how I can ever have been an angel. If I ever was, it must have been so long ago that there's no harm in forgetting it. Now I only prize the reputation of being a gentlemanly person and live as I can, trying to make myself agreeable. I really love mankind, I've been slandered! Here when I stay with you from time to time, my life gains a kind of reality and that's what I like most of all. You see, like you, I suffer from the fantastic and so I love the realism of earth. Here, with you, everything is circumscribed, here all is formulated and geometrical, while we have nothing but indeterminate equations! I wander about here dreaming. I like dreaming. Besides, on earth I become superstitious. Please don't laugh. That's just what I like, to become superstitious. I adopt all your habits here; I like going to the public baths, would you believe it? I go and steam myself with merchants and priests. What I dream of is becoming incarnate once and for all in the form of some merchant's wife weighing two hundred and fifty pounds, and of believing all she believes. My ideal is to go to church and offer a candle in simplehearted faith, this is the absolute truth. Then there would be an end to my sufferings. I like going to the doctor too; in the spring there was an outbreak of smallpox and I went and was vaccinated in a foundling hospital—if only you knew how I enjoyed myself that day. I donated ten roubles for the Slavs! . . . But you are not listening. Do you know, you are not at all well this evening? I know you went to that doctor yesterday . . . Well, what about your health? What did the doctor say?"

"Fool!" Ivan cried.

"But you are clever, anyway. You are scolding again? I didn't ask out of sympathy. You don't have to answer. Now rheumatism has become fashionable again . . ."

"Fool!" repeated Ivan.

"You keep saying the same thing; but I had such an attack of rheumatism last year that I remember it to this day."

"The devil has rheumatism!"

"Why not, if I sometimes put on fleshly form? I put on fleshly form and I take the consequences. Nothing human is beyond the possibility of Satan."

"What, what? Nothing human is beyond . . . That's not bad for the devil!"

"I am glad I've pleased you at last."

"But you didn't get that from me," Ivan stopped suddenly, seeming struck. "That never entered my head, that's strange."

"It's original, isn't it? This time I'll be honest and explain it to you. Listen, in dreams and especially in nightmares, from indigestion or something else, a man sometimes sees such visions, such complex and real actuality, such events, even a whole world of events, woven into such a plot, with such unexpected details from the most exalted matters to the last button on a cuff, as I swear Leo Tolstoy has never invented. Yet such visions are sometimes seen not by writers, but by the most ordinary people, officials, journalists, priests. . . . The subject

579

of dreams is a complete mystery. A statesman once confessed to me that all his best ideas came to him when he was asleep. Well, that's how it is now, though I am your hallucination, yet just as in a nightmare, I say original things which have not entered your head before. So I don't repeat your ideas, yet I am only your nightmare, nothing more."

"You are lying. You are trying to convince me you exist independently and are not my nightmare. You are trying to convince me that you are a dream."

"My dear fellow, I've adopted a special method today, I'll explain it to you afterwards. Wait, where did I break off? Oh, yes! I caught cold then, only not here but some place else."

"Where? Tell me, will you be here long? Can't you go away?" Ivan exclaimed almost in despair. He stopped walking back and forth, sat down on the sofa, leaned his elbows on the table again and held his head tightly in both hands. He pulled the wet towel off and flung it away. It was of no use.

"Your nerves are on edge," observed the gentleman, with a carelessly easy, though perfectly polite, manner. "You are angry with me for being able to catch cold, though it happened in a most natural way. I was hurrying to a diplomatic party at the house of a lady of high rank in Petersburg, who was aiming at influence in the Ministry. Well, an evening suit, white tie, gloves, though I was God knows where and had to fly through space to reach your earth. . . . Of course, it took only an instant, you know a ray of light from the sun takes eight minutes, and just imagine in an evening suit and open waistcoat. Spirits don't freeze, but when one's in fleshly form, well . . . In brief, I didn't think, and set off, and you know in those ethereal spaces, in the water that is above the firmament, there's such a frost . . . At least one can't call it frost, you can imagine, 150° below zero! You know the game the village girls play—they invite the unwary to lick an ax in zero weather, the tongue instantly freezes to it and the fool tears the skin off, so it bleeds. But that's only at zero, at 150° below I imagine it would be enough to put your finger on the ax and it would be the end of it . . . If only there could be an ax there."

"And can there be an ax there?" Ivan interrupted carelessly. He was exerting himself to the utmost not to believe in the delusion and not to sink into complete insanity.

"An ax?" the guest interrupted in surprise.

"Yes, what would become of an ax there?" Ivan cried suddenly, with a sort of savage and insistent obstinacy.

"What would become of an ax in space? What an idea! If it were to fall any distance, it would begin, I think, flying around the earth without knowing why, like a satellite. The astronomers would calculate the rising and the setting of the ax, *Gatzuk* would put it in his calendar, that's all."

"You are stupid, awfully stupid," said Ivan peevishly. "Lie

580

more cleverly or I won't listen. You want to get the better of me by realism in order to convince me that you exist, but I don't want to believe you exist! I won't believe it!"

"But I am not lying, it's all the truth; the truth is hardly ever amusing. I see you expect something big of me, something fine. That's a great pity, for I only give what I can . . ."

"Don't talk philosophy, you ass!"

"Philosophy, indeed, when all my right side is numb and I am moaning and groaning. I've tried many doctors; they diagnose beautifully, they have the whole of your disease at their fingertips, but they've no idea how to cure you. There was an enthusiastic little student here: 'You may die,' he said, 'but you'll know what disease you are dying of!' And then what a way they have of sending people to specialists. 'We only diagnose,' they say, 'but go to such-and-such a specialist, he'll cure you.' The old doctor who used to cure all sorts of diseases has completely disappeared. I assure you, now there are only specialists and they all advertise in the newspapers. If anything is wrong with your nose, they send you to Paris; there, they say, is a European specialist who cures noses. If you go to Paris, he'll look at your nose. I can only cure your right nostril, he'll tell you, for I don't cure the left nostril, that's not my specialty, but go to Vienna, there there's a specialist who will cure your left nostril. What are you to do? I fell back on popular remedies, a German doctor advised me to rub myself with honey and salt in the bathhouse. Solely to get an extra bath I went, smeared myself all over and it did me no good at all. In despair I wrote to Count Mattei in Milan. He sent me a book and some drops, bless him and would you believe it, Hoff's malt extract cured me! I bought it by accident, drank a bottle and a half of it, and I was ready to dance. I made up my mind to write to the papers to thank him. I was prompted by a feeling of gratitude. But it led to no end of trouble. Not a single paper would take my letter. 'It would be very reactionary,' they said. 'No one would believe it. The devil does not exist. You'd better remain anonymous,' they advised me. What use is a letter of thanks if it's anonymous? I laughed with the men at the newspaper office. 'It's reactionary to believe in God today,' I said, 'but I am the devil, so people can believe in me.' 'We quite understand that,' they said. 'Who doesn't believe in the devil? Yet we won't print your letter, it might injure our reputation. As a joke, if you like.' But I thought as a joke it wouldn't be very witty. So it wasn't printed. And do you know, I am angry about it to this day. My best feelings, gratitude, for instance, are denied me simply because of my social position."

"Philosophical reflections again?" Ivan snarled.

"God preserve me from it, but one can't help complaining sometimes. I am a slandered man. You upbraid me every moment with being stupid. One can see you are young. My dear fellow, intelligence isn't the only thing! I have a kind and happy heart. 'I also write vaudeville skits of all sorts.' You seem to take me for Hlestakov grown old, but my fate is a far more serious one. Before time was, by some decree which I could never make out, I was predestined 'to deny' and yet I am genuinely good-hearted and not at all inclined to negation. 'No, you must go and deny. Without denial there's no criticism and what would a newspaper be without a column of criticism?' Without criticism it would be nothing but one 'hosannah.' But hosannah is not enough for life. The hosannah must be tried in the crucible of doubt and so on, in the same style. But I don't interfere in that, I didn't create it, I am not answerable for it. Well, they've chosen their scapegoat; they've made me write the column of criticism and so life has been made possible. We understand that comedy; I, for instance, simply ask for annihilation. No, live, I am told, for there'd be nothing without you. If everything in the universe were sensible, nothing would happen. There would be no events without you, and there must be events. So against the grain I serve to produce events and do what's irrational because I am commanded to. For all their indisputable intelligence, men take this farce as something serious, and that is their tragedy. They suffer, of course . . . But then they live, they live a real life, not a fantastic one, for suffering is life. Without suffering what would be the pleasure of life? Life would be transformed into an endless church service; it would be holy, but tedious. But what about me? I suffer, but still, I don't live. I am x in an indeterminate equation. I am a sort of phantom in life who has lost all beginning and end, and who has even forgotten his own name. You are laughing—no, you are not laughing, you are angry again. You are always angry. All you care about is intelligence. But I repeat again that I would give away all this superstellar life, all the ranks and honors, simply to be transformed into a merchant's wife weighing two hundred and fifty pounds and set candles at God's altar."

"Then even you don't believe in God?" asked Ivan with a smile of hatred.

"What can I say—that is, if you are in earnest . . ."

"Is there a God or not?" Ivan cried with savage intensity.

"Ah, then you are in earnest! My dear fellow, upon my word I don't know. There! I've said it now!"

"You don't know, but you see God? No, you are not someone apart, you are myself, you are I and nothing more! You are rubbish, you are my fancy!"

"Well, if you like, I have the same philosophy as you. That is true. 'I think, therefore I am,' I know that for a fact. All the rest, all these worlds, God and even Satan—all that is not proved, to my mind. Does all that exist of itself, or is it only an emanation of myself, a logical development of my ego
582

which alone has existed forever? But I must stop talking, otherwise, I think, you will jump up and start beating me."

"You'd better tell me an anecdote!" said Ivan miserably.

"There is an anecdote on our subject, or rather a legend, not an anecdote. You reproach me with unbelief, yet you yourself don't believe. But, my dear fellow, I am not the only one like that. We are all confused over there now and all the result of your science. Once there used to be atoms, five senses, four elements; and everything hung together somehow. There were atoms in the ancient world even, but since we've learned that you've discovered the chemical molecule and protoplasm and everything else, we had to lower our crest. There's complete confusion, and, above all, superstition, scandal; there's as much scandal among us as among you, you know; a little more in fact. And spying, also, for we have our secret police department where private information is received. Well, this legend belongs to our middle ages—not yours, but ours—and no one believes it even among us, except old ladies of two hundred and fifty pounds, not your old ladies I mean, but ours. We have everything you have. I am revealing one of our secrets out of friendship for you, though it's forbidden. This legend is about Paradise. There was, they say, here on earth a thinker and philosopher. He rejected everything, Laws, Conscience, Faith, but above all, the Future Life. He died; he expected to go straight to darkness and death and he found a future life before him. He was astonished and indignant. 'This is against my principles!' he said. And he was punished for that. That is . . . You must excuse me, I am just repeating what I heard, it's only a legend . . . He was sentenced to walk a quadrillion miles in the dark. And when he has finished that quadrillion, the gates of heaven will be opened to him and he'll be forgiven . . ."

"And what tortures have you in the other world besides walking quadrillion miles?" asked Ivan with a strange eagerness.

"What tortures? Ah, don't ask. In the old days we had all sorts, but now they are chiefly moral punishments—'the stings of conscience' and all that nonsense. We got that, too, from you, from the softening of your manners. And who's the better for it? Only those who have no conscience, for how can they be tortured by conscience when they have none? But decent people who have conscience and a sense of honor suffer. Reforms, when the ground has not been prepared for them, especially if they are institutions copied from abroad, cause nothing but trouble! The ancient fire was better. Well, this man, who was condemned to the quadrillion miles, stood still, looked round and lay down across the road. 'I won't go, I refuse on principle!' Take the soul of an enlightened Russian atheist and mix it with the soul of the prophet Jonah, who sulked for three days and nights in the belly of the whale, and

583

you get the character of that thinker who lay across the road."

"What did he lie on there?"

"Well, I suppose there was something to lie on. You are not laughing?"

"Good!" cried Ivan, still with the same strange eagerness. Now he was listening with an unexpected curiosity. "Well, is he lying there now?"

"That's the point, he isn't. He lay there almost a thousand years and then he got up and started walking."

"What a fool!" cried Ivan, laughing nervously. "Does it make any difference whether he lies there forever or walks the quadrillion miles? It would take a billion years to walk it?"

"Much more than that, I haven't got a pencil and paper or I could work it out. But he finished walking long ago and that's where the story begins."

"What, he accomplished it? But where did he get the billion years to do it?"

"Why, you keep thinking of your present earth! But your present earth may have been repeated a billion times. Why, it's become extinct, been frozen; cracked, broken to bits, disintegrated into its elements, again 'the water above the firmament,' then again a comet, again a sun, again from the sun it becomes earth—and the same sequence may have been repeated endlessly and in exactly the same way in every detail, most unseemly and insufferably tedious . . ."

"Well, well, what happened when he finished walking?"

"Why, at that moment the gates of Paradise were opened and he walked in. And before he had been there two seconds, by his watch (though to my thinking his watch must have dissolved into its elements on the way), he cried out that those two seconds were worth walking not a quadrillion miles but a quadrillion of quadrillions, raised to the quadrillionth power! In fact, he sang 'hosannah' and overdid it so, that some people there wouldn't shake hands with him at first—he'd become too rapidly reactionary, they said. The Russian temperament. I repeat, it's a legend. I give it for what it's worth. So that's the sort of ideas we have on such subjects even now."

"I've caught you!" Ivan cried with an almost childish delight, as though he had succeeded in remembering something at last. "That anecdote about the quadrillion years, I made up myself! I was seventeen then, I was at high school. I made up that anecdote and told it to a classmate called Korovkin, it was in Moscow. . . . The anecdote is so characteristic of me that I couldn't have taken it from anywhere. I thought I'd forgotten it . . . But I've recalled it from my subconscious —I recalled it myself—it was not you who told it! Thousands of things are unconsciously remembered like that even when people are being taken to execution . . . It's come back to me

584

in a dream. You are that dream! You are a dream, not a living creature!"

"From the passion with which you deny my existence," laughed the gentleman, "I am convinced that you believe in me."

"Not in the slightest! I haven't a hundredth part of a grain of faith in you!"

"But you have the thousandth of a grain. Homeopathic doses perhaps are the strongest. Confess that you have faith even to the ten-thousandth part of a grain."

"Not for one minute," cried Ivan. "But I would like to believe in you," he added strangely.

"Ah! There's an admission! But I am good-natured. I'll come to your assistance again. Listen, it was I who caught you, not you who caught me. I told you your anecdote you'd forgotten, on purpose, so as to destroy your faith in me completely."

"You are lying. The object of your visit is to convince me of your existence!"

"Yes. But hesitation, suspense, conflict between belief and disbelief—is sometimes such torture to a conscientious man, such as you are, that it's better to hang oneself at once. Knowing that you are inclined to believe in me, I injected some disbelief by telling you that anecdote. I led you to belief and disbelief by turns, and I have my motive in it. It's the new method. As soon as you disbelieve in me completely, you'll begin assuring me to my face that I am not a dream but a reality. I know you. Then I will have attained my object, which is an honorable one. I will sow in you only a tiny grain of faith and it will grow into an oak tree—and such an oak tree that, sitting under it, you will long to enter the ranks of 'the hermits in the wilderness and the saintly women,' for that is what you are secretly longing for. You'll dine on locusts, you'll wander into the wilderness to save your soul!"

"Then it's for the salvation of my soul you are working, is it, you scoundrel?"

"One must do some good work sometimes. How ill-humored you are!"

"Fool! Did you ever tempt those holy men who ate locusts and prayed seventeen years in the wilderness till they were overgrown with moss?"

"My dear fellow, I've done nothing else. One forgets the whole world and all the worlds, and sticks to one such saint, because he is a very precious diamond. One such soul, you know, is sometimes worth a whole constellation. We have our system of reckoning, you know. The conquest is priceless! And some of them, I swear, are not inferior to you in culture, though you won't believe it. They can contemplate such depths of belief and disbelief at the same moment that sometimes it

585

really seems that they are within a hairsbreadth of being turned upside down."

"Well, did you succeed or fail? If you failed then 'you had your nose pulled off your face.' "

"My dear fellow," observed the visitor, "it's better to fail than not to try at all, as an afflicted marquis observed not long ago (he must have been treated by a specialist) in confession to his spiritual father—a Jesuit. I was present, it was simply charming. 'Give me back my nose!' he said, and he beat his breast. 'My son,' said the priest evasively, 'all things are accomplished in accordance with the inscrutable decrees of Providence, and what seems a failure sometimes leads to extraordinary, though unapparent, benefits. If stern destiny has deprived you of your nose, it's to your advantage that no one can ever pull you by your nose.' 'Holy father, that's no comfort,' cried the despairing marquis. 'I'd be delighted to have my nose pulled every day of my life, if it were only back in its proper place.' 'My son,' sighed the priest, 'you can't expect every blessing at once. This is murmuring against Providence, who even in this has not forgotten you, for if you repine as you repined just now, declaring you'd be glad to have your nose pulled for the rest of your life, your desire has already been fulfilled indirectly, for when you lost your nose, you were led by the nose.' "

"Fool, how stupid!" cried Ivan.

"My dear friend, I only wanted to amuse you. But I swear that's the Jesuit quibbling, and I swear that it all happened word for word as I've told you. It happened just recently and gave me a great deal of trouble. The unhappy young man shot himself that very night when he got home. I was by his side till the very last moment. Those Jesuit confessionals are really my most delightful diversion at melancholy moments. Here's another incident that happened only the other day. A little blonde Norman girl of twenty—a buxom, unsophisticated beauty that would make your mouth water—comes to an old priest. She bends down and whispers her sin into the grating. 'Why, my daughter, have you fallen again already?' cried the priest. 'O Sancta Maria, what do I hear! Not the same man this time, how long is this going on? Aren't you ashamed!' 'Oh, Father,' answers the sinner with tears of penitence, 'it makes him so happy, and it costs me so little!' Imagine such an answer! I drew back. It was the cry of nature, better than innocence itself. I absolved her sin on the spot and was turning to go, but I was forced to turn back. I heard the priest at the grating making an appointment with her for the evening—though he was an old man hard as flint, he fell captive! It was nature, the truth of nature asserted its rights! What, are you turning up your nose again? Angry again? I don't know how to please you . . ."

"Leave me alone. You are beating on my brain like a haunt-
586

ing nightmare," Ivan moaned miserably, helpless before his apparition. "I am bored with you, agonizingly and insufferably. I would give anything to be able to shake you off!"

"I repeat, moderate your expectations, don't demand of me 'everything great and noble' and you'll see how well we will get on," said the gentleman. "You are really angry with me for not having appeared to you in a red glow, with thunder and lightning, with scorched wings, but to have shown myself in such a modest form. You are wounded, in the first place, in your aesthetic feelings, and, secondly, in your pride. How could such a vulgar devil visit such a great man as you! Yes, there is that romantic strain in you. I can't help it, young man, as I got ready to come to you I thought as a joke of appearing as a retired general who had served in the Caucasus, with a star of the Lion and the Sun on my coat. But I was afraid of doing it, for you'd have struck me for daring to pin the Lion and the Sun on my coat, instead of the Polar Star or the Sirius. And you keep on saying I am stupid, but . . . I make no claim of being equal to you in intelligence. Mephistopheles declared to Faust that he desired evil, but did only good. Well, he can say what he likes, it's the opposite with me. I am perhaps the one man in all creation who loves the truth and really desires good. I was there when the Word, Who died on the Cross, rose up into Heaven bearing on His bosom the soul of the penitent thief. I heard the glad shrieks of the cherubim singing and shouting hosannah and the thunderous rapture of the seraphim which shook Heaven and all creation. And I swear to you by all that's sacred, I longed to join the choir and shout hosannah with them all. The word had almost escaped me, had almost broken from my lips . . . You know how susceptible and impressionable I am. But common sense—oh, a most unhappy trait in my character—kept me in bounds and I let the moment pass! For what would have happened, I wondered, what would have happened after my hosannah? Everything on earth would have been extinguished at once and no events could have occurred. And so, solely from a sense of duty and my social position, I was forced to suppress the good moment and to stick to my unpleasant task. Somebody takes all the credit of what's good for himself, and nothing but evil is left for me. But I don't envy the honor of a life of idle imposture, I am not ambitious. Why am I, of all creatures in the world, doomed to be cursed and kicked by all decent people? For if I put on mortal form I am bound to be cursed and kicked. I know, of course, there's a secret in it, but they won't tell me the secret because then, perhaps, seeing the meaning of it, I might bawl out hosannah, and the indispensable minus would disappear at once, and good sense would reign supreme throughout the whole world. And that, of course, would mean the end of everything, even of magazines and newspapers, for who would buy them? I know that at the end of all things I will be reconciled. I, too, shall walk my quadrillion miles and learn the secret. But until that happens I am sulking and fulfill my destiny even though it's against the grain—that is, to ruin thousands for the sake of saving one. How many souls have had to be ruined and how many honorable reputations destroyed for the sake of that one righteous man, Job, over whom they made such a fool of me in old days. Yes, until the secret is revealed, there are two sorts of truth for me—one, their truth, which I know nothing about so far and the other my own. And there's no knowing which will turn out to be better. . . . Are you asleep?"

"I might as well be," Ivan groaned angrily. "All my stupid ideas—outgrown, thrashed out long ago, and flung aside like a dead carcass—you present to me now as something new!"

"There's no pleasing you! And I thought I would fascinate you by my literary style. That hosannah in the skies really wasn't bad, was it? And then that ironical tone like Heine, eh?"

"No, I was never a flunkey! How then can my soul beget a flunkey like you?"

"My dear fellow, I know a most charming and attractive young Russian gentleman, a young thinker and a great lover of literature and art, the author of a promising poem entitled *The Grand Inquisitor*. I was only thinking of him!"

"I forbid you to speak of *The Grand Inquisitor!*" cried Ivan, crimson with shame.

"And the *Geological Cataclysm*. Do you remember? That was a poem!"

"Keep quiet, or I'll kill you!"

"You'll kill me? No, excuse me, I will speak. I came to treat myself to that pleasure. Oh, I love the dreams of my ardent young friends, quivering with eagerness for life! 'There are new men,' you decided last spring, when you were planning to come here, 'they propose to destroy everything and begin with cannibalism. Fools! They didn't ask my advice! I maintain that nothing need be destroyed, that we only need to destroy the idea of God in man, that's how we have to set to work. It's that, that we must begin with. Oh, blind race of men who have no understanding! As soon as men have all denied God—and I believe that period, corresponding with geological periods, will come to pass—the old conception of the universe will fall of itself without cannibalism and what's more the old morality, and everything will begin anew. Men will unite to take from life all it can give, but only for joy and happiness in the present world. Man will be lifted up with a spirit of divine Titanic pride and the man-god will appear. Extending his conquest of nature by his will and his science, man will feel such lofty joy from hour to hour that it will make up for all his old dreams of the joys of heaven. Everyone will know that he is mortal and will accept death proudly and serenely like a god. His pride will teach him that it's use-less for him to grieve at life's being a moment, and he will love his brother without need of reward. Love will be suffi-cient only for a moment of life, but this very consciousness will intensify its fire, which now is dissipated in dreams of eternal love beyond the grave' . . . And so on and so on in the same style. Charming!"

Ivan sat with his eyes cast downward and his hands pressed to his ears. He began trembling all over. The voice continued.

"The question now is, my young thinker reflected, is it pos-sible that such a period will ever come? If it does, every-thing is determined and humanity is settled forever. But since, owing to man's stupidity, this cannot come about for at least a thousand years, everyone who recognizes the truth now may legitimately order his life as he pleases, on the new principles. In that sense, 'all things are lawful' for him. What's more, even if this period never comes to pass, since there is anyway no God and no immortality, the new man may well become the man-god, even if he is the only one in the whole world. Promoted to his new position, he may lightheartedly overstep all the barriers of the old morality of the old slave-man, if necessary. There is no law for God. Where God stands, the place is holy. Where I stand will become the foremost place . . . 'All things are lawful' and that's the end of it! That's all very charming; but if you want to swindle why do you want a moral sanction for doing it? But that's our modern Russian all over. He can't bring himself to swindle without moral sanc-tion. He is so in love with truth . . ."

The visitor talked, obviously carried away by his own elo-quence, speaking louder and louder and looking ironically at his host. But he did not succeed in finishing. Ivan suddenly snatched a glass from the table and threw it at him.

"Oh, how stupid of you," cried the gentleman, jumping up from the sofa and shaking off the drops of tea. "He remem-bers Luther's inkstand! He takes me for a dream and throws glasses at a dream! It's like a woman! I suspected you were only pretending to stop up your ears."

A loud, persistent knocking was suddenly heard at the win-dow. Ivan jumped up from his seat.

"Do you hear? You'd better open," cried the gentleman. "It's your brother Alyosha with the most interesting and sur-prising news!"

"Keep quiet. I know it is Alyosha. I felt he was coming. And of course he has not come for nothing; of course he brings 'news,' " Ivan exclaimed frantically.

"Open, open to him. There's a snowstorm and he is your brother. Do you realize what it is like outdoors? It isn't fit for a dog."

The knocking continued. Ivan wanted to rush to the win-dow, but something seemed to hold back his arms and legs.

He strained every effort to break his chains but in vain. The knocking at the window grew louder and louder. At last the chains were broken and Ivan looked round him wildly. Both candles had almost burned out. The glass he had just thrown at his visitor stood before him on the table, and there was no one on the sofa opposite. The knocking went on persistently, but it was by no means so loud as it had seemed in his dream, on the contrary it was quite subdued.

"It was not a dream! No, I swear it was not a dream, it all happened just now!" cried Ivan. He rushed to the window and opened the movable pane.

"Alyosha, I told you not to come," he cried to his brother. "What do you want? Why have you come?"

"Smerdyakov hung himself an hour ago," Alyosha answered from the yard.

"Come around to the steps, I'll open the door at once," said Ivan.

10. "It Was He Who Said That"

COMING IN, Alyosha told Ivan that a little over an hour before Maria had run to his rooms and told him that Smerdyakov had taken his own life. "I went in to clear away the samovar and he was hanging from a nail in the wall." On Alyosha's asking whether she had informed the police, she answered that she had told no one. "I flew straight to you, I've run all the way." She seemed crazed, Alyosha reported, and was shaking like a leaf. When Alyosha ran with her to the cottage, he found Smerdyakov still hanging. On the table lay a note: "I destroy my life of my own will and desire, so as to throw no blame on anyone." Alyosha left the note on the table and went straight to the police captain and told him all about it. "And from him I've come straight to you," said Alyosha, in conclusion, looking intently into Ivan's face. He had not taken his eyes off him while he told his story, as though struck by something in his expression.

"Ivan," he cried suddenly, "you must be terribly ill. You look and you don't seem to understand what I am telling you."

"It's a good thing you came," said Ivan, as though brooding, and not hearing Alyosha's exclamation. "I knew he had hung himself."

"From whom?"

"I don't know. But I knew. Did I know? Yes, he told me. He told me so just now."

Ivan stood in the middle of the room, and still spoke in the same brooding tone, looking at the ground.

"Who is *he?*" asked Alyosha looking around.

"He's slipped away."

Ivan raised his head and smiled softly.

"He was afraid of you, of a dove like you. You are a 'pure cherub.' Dmitri calls you a cherub. Cherub! . . . The thunderous rapture of the seraphim. What are seraphim? Perhaps a whole constellation. But perhaps that constellation is only a chemical molecule. There's a constellation of the Lion and the Sun. Did you know that?"

"Ivan, sit down," said Alyosha in alarm. "Sit down on the sofa! You are delirious. Put your head on the pillow, that's right. Would you like a wet towel on your head? Maybe it will do you good."

"Give me the towel. It's on the chair. I just threw it down there."

"It's not there. Don't worry. I know where it is—here," said Alyosha, finding a clean towel folded up and unused, by Ivan's dressing table. Ivan looked strangely at the towel; something seemed to come back to him for an instant.

"Wait." He got up from the sofa. "An hour ago I took that new towel from there and wet it. I wrapped it around my head and threw it down here . . . How is it it's dry? There was no other."

"You put that towel on your head?" asked Alyosha.

"Yes, and walked up and down the room an hour ago . . . Why have the candles burned down? What's the time?"

"Nearly twelve."

"No, no, no!" Ivan cried suddenly. "It was not a dream. He was here; he was sitting here on that sofa. When you knocked at the window, I threw a glass at him . . . this one. Wait a minute. I was asleep last time, but this dream was not a dream. It has happened before. I have dreams now, Alyosha . . . yet they are not dreams, but reality. I walk about, talk and see . . . though I am asleep. He was sitting on that sofa there. . . . He is frightfully stupid, Alyosha, frightfully stupid." Ivan laughed suddenly and began pacing about the room.

"Who is stupid? Of whom are you talking, Ivan?" Alyosha asked anxiously again.

"The devil! He's taken to visiting me. He's been here twice, almost three times. He taunted me with being angry at his being a simple devil and not Satan, with scorched wings, and thunder and lightning. But he is not Satan; that's a lie. He is an impostor. He is simply a devil—a paltry, trivial devil. He goes to the baths. If you undressed him, you'd be sure to find he had a tail, long and smooth like a Danish dog's, a yard long, dun color. . . . Alyosha, you are cold. You've been in the snow. Would you like some tea? What? Is it cold? Shall I tell her to bring some? It's not fit for a dog outside . . ."

Alyosha ran to the washstand, wet the towel, persuaded Ivan to sit down again, and put the wet towel around his head. He sat down beside him.

"What were you telling me before about Lise?" Ivan began

591

again. He was becoming very talkative. "I like Lise. I said something nasty about her. It was a lie. I like her . . . I am afraid for Katerina tomorrow. I am more afraid of her than of anything. On account of the future. She will cast me off tomorrow and trample me underfoot. She thinks that I am ruining Dmitri because I am jealous! Yes, she thinks that! But it's not true. Tomorrow the cross, but not the gallows. No, I won't hang myself. I could never commit suicide, Alyosha. Is it because I am base? I am not a coward. Is it from love of life? How did I know that Smerdyakov had hung himself? Yes, it was *he* told me so."

"And you are convinced that there has been someone here?" asked Alyosha.

"Yes, on that sofa in the corner. You would have driven him away. You did drive him away; he disappeared when you arrived. I love your face, Alyosha. Did you know that I loved your face? And *he* is myself, Alyosha. All that's base in me, all that's mean and contemptible. Yes, I am a romantic. He guessed it . . . He is terribly stupid; but it's to his advantage. He has cunning, animal cunning—he knew how to infuriate me. He kept taunting me with believing in him, and that was how he made me listen to him. He fooled me like a boy. He told me a great deal that was true about myself, though. I would never have admitted it to myself. Do you know, Alyosha," Ivan added in an intensely earnest and confidential tone, "I would be awfully glad to think that it was *he* and not I."

"He has worn you out," said Alyosha, looking compassionately at his brother.

"He's been teasing me. And you know he does it so cleverly, so cleverly. 'Conscience! What is conscience! I make it up for myself. Why am I tormented by it? From habit. From the universal habit of mankind for seven thousand years. So let us give it up, and we shall be gods.' It was he who said that, it was he who said that!"

"And not you, not you?" Alyosha could not help crying, looking at his brother. "Never mind him, anyway; forget him. And let him take with him all that you curse now and never come back!"

"Yes, but he is spiteful. He laughed at me. He was rude, Alyosha," Ivan said, with a shudder of offense. "But he was unfair to me, unfair to me about lots of things. He told lies about me to my face. 'Oh, you are going to perform an act of virtue; to confess you murdered your father, that the valet murdered him at your instigation.' "

"Ivan!" Alyosha interrupted. "Restrain yourself. It was not you who murdered him. It's not true!"

"That's what he says, he, and he knows. 'You are going to perform an act of virtue, and you don't believe in virtue. That's what tortures you and makes you angry. That's why

592

you are so vindictive.' He said that to me about myself and he knows what he says."

"It's you who say that, not he," exclaimed Alyosha. "And you say it because you are ill and delirious, tormenting yourself."

"No, he knows what he says. 'You are going from pride,' he says. 'You'll stand up and say it was I killed him, and why do you writhe with horror? You are lying! I despise your opinion, I despise your horror!' He said that about me. 'And do you know you are longing for praise—"he is a criminal, a murderer, but what nobility; he wanted to save his brother and he confessed."' That's a lie, Alyosha!" Ivan cried suddenly, with flashing eyes. "I don't want the rabble to praise me; I swear I don't! That's a lie! That's why I threw the glass at him. . . . It broke against his ugly face."

"Ivan, stop!" Alyosha begged.

"Yes, he knows how to torment me. He's cruel," Ivan went on, unheeding. "I had an inkling from the beginning why he came. 'Granting that you go through pride, still you had a hope that Smerdyakov might be convicted and sent to Siberia. You had a hope that Dmitri would be acquitted, while you would only be punished with *moral* condemnation' ('Do you hear?' he laughed then)—'and some people will praise you. But now Smerdyakov's dead, he has hung himself, and who'll believe you without him? But yet you are going, you are going, you'll go all the same, you've decided to go. What are you going for now?' That's awful, Alyosha. I can't stand such questions. Who dare ask me such questions?"

"Ivan," said Alyosha. His heart sank with terror, but he still hoped to bring Ivan back to reason. "How could he have told you of Smerdyakov's death before I came? No one knew of it and there was no time."

"He told me," said Ivan, refusing to admit doubt. "It was all he talked about, if you come to that. 'And it would be all right if you believed in virtue,' he said. 'No matter if they disbelieve you, you are going for the sake of principle. But you are a pig like your father, Fyodor Karamazov, and what do you want with virtue? Why do you want to go if your sacrifice is of no use to anyone? Because you don't know yourself why you want to go! Oh, you'd give a great deal to know why you want to go! And have you made up your mind? No. You'll sit all night deliberating whether to go or not. But you will go; you know you'll go. You know that whichever way you decide, the decision does not depend on you. You'll go because you won't dare not to go. Why won't you dare? You must figure that out for yourself. That's a riddle for you!' He got up and went away. You came and he went. He called me a coward, Alyosha! 'It is not for such eagles to soar above the earth.' He added that—he! And Smerdyakov said the same. He must be killed! Katerina despises me. I've known that for a whole month. Even Lise will begin to despise me! 'You are going in order to be praised.' That's a lie! And you despise me too, Alyosha. Now I am going to hate you again! And I hate the monster, too! I hate the monster! I don't want to save the monster. Let him rot in Siberia! He's begun singing a hymn! Oh, tomorrow I'll go, stand before them, and spit in their faces!"

He jumped up in a frenzy, threw off the towel, and began pacing up and down the room again.

Alyosha recalled what he just said. "I seem to be sleeping awake. . . . I walk, I speak, I see, but I am asleep." It seemed to be just like that now. Alyosha did not leave him. The thought passed through his mind to run for a doctor, but he was afraid to leave his brother alone. There was no one with whom he could leave him.

By degrees Ivan lost consciousness. He still went on talking, talking incessantly, but incoherently. He spoke with difficulty. Suddenly he staggered but Alyosha was in time to support him. He led him to his bed. He undressed him and put him to bed. He sat watching over him for two hours. Ivan slept soundly, without stirring, breathing softly and evenly.

Alyosha took a pillow and lay down on the sofa, without undressing. As he fell asleep he prayed for Dmitri and Ivan. He began to understand Ivan's illness. "The agony of proud determination. Conscience!" God, in whom Ivan disbelieved, and His truth were gaining mastery over his heart, which still refused to submit. "Yes," the thought floated through Alyosha's mind. "Yes, if Smerdyakov is dead, no one will believe Ivan's evidence; but he will go and testify anyway." Alyosha smiled softly. "God will conquer!" he thought. "Ivan will either rise up in the light of truth, or . . . he'll perish in hate, revenging on himself and on everyone his having served a cause he does not believe in," Alyosha added bitterly. And again he prayed for Ivan.

BOOK XII: A JUDICIAL ERROR

1. The Fatal Day

AT TEN O'CLOCK IN THE MORNING of the day following the events I have described, the trial of Dmitri Karamazov began in our district court.

I want to emphasize the fact that I am far from capable of reporting all that took place at the trial in full detail, or even in the actual order of events. To mention everything with a full explanation would fill a volume, a very large one. And so I trust I will not be reproached for confining myself to what struck me. I may have selected as of most interest what was of secondary importance, and may have omitted the most prominent and essential details, but I will do better not to apologize. I will do my best and the reader will see for himself that I have done all I can.

To begin with, before entering the court, I will mention what surprised me most on that day. As it appeared later, everyone was surprised at it, too. We all knew that the case had aroused great interest, that everyone was impatient for the trial to begin, that it had been a subject of talk, conjecture, exclamation and surmise for the last two months in local society. Everyone also knew that the case had become known throughout Russia, but we had not imagined that it had aroused such burning, such intense interest everywhere. This became evident at the trial.

Visitors had arrived not only from the main town of our province, but from several other Russian towns, as well as from Moscow and Petersburg. Among them were lawyers, ladies and distinguished people. Every ticket of admission had been snatched up. A special place behind the table at which the three judges sat was set apart for the most distinguished and important of the men visitors; a row of armchairs had been placed there—something exceptional, which had never been allowed before. A large proportion—not less than half of those present—were ladies. There was such a large number of lawyers from all parts that they did not know where to seat them. I saw at the end of the room, behind the platform, a special partition hurriedly put up, behind which all these lawyers were admitted. They thought themselves lucky to have standing room there, for all chairs had been removed for the sake of space. They stood throughout the case closely packed, shoulder to shoulder.

Some of the ladies, especially those who had come from a distance, made their appearance in the gallery very smartly dressed, but the majority of the ladies were oblivious even of dress. Their faces betrayed hysterical, intense, almost morbid, curiosity. A peculiar fact—established afterwards by many observations—was that almost all the ladies, or at least the vast majority of them, were on Dmitri's side and in favor of his being acquitted. This was perhaps owing to his reputation as a conqueror of female hearts. It was known that two women, rivals for his love, were to appear in the case. One of them—Katerina—was an object of general interest. All sorts of extraordinary tales were told about her, amazing stories of her passion for Dmitri, in spite of his crime. Her pride and "aristocratic connections" were particularly stressed (she had called upon scarcely anyone in the town). People said she intended to petition the Government for permission to accompany the criminal to Siberia and to be married to him somewhere in the mines. The appearance of Grushenka in court was awaited with no less impatience. The public was looking forward to the meeting of the two rivals—the proud aristocratic girl and "the hetaira." But Grushenka was more familiar to the ladies of the district than Katerina. They had already seen "the woman who had ruined Fyodor Karamazov and his unhappy son." And all, almost without exception, wondered how father and son could be so in love with "such a very common, ordinary girl, who was not even pretty."

In brief, there was a great deal of talk. I know for a fact that there were several serious family quarrels on Dmitri's account in our town. Many ladies quarreled with their husbands about the dreadful case, and so it was only natural that these husbands should enter the court bitterly prejudiced against Dmitri. In fact, one may say that the masculine, as distinguished from the feminine part of the audience was biased against the prisoner. There were numbers of severe, frowning, even vindictive, faces. Dmitri himself had managed to offend many people during his stay in town. Some of the visitors were, of course, unconcerned as to Dmitri's fate. But all were interested in the trial, and the majority of the men were certainly hoping for the conviction of the criminal, except perhaps the lawyers, who were more interested in the legal, than in the moral, aspect of the case.

Everybody was excited at the presence of the celebrated lawyer. Fetyukovitch. His ability was well known; this was not the first time he had defended notorious criminals in the provinces. His cases became famous and were long remembered all over Russia. There were stories, too, about our prosecutor and about the President of the Court. It was said that Ippolit Kirillovitch was nervous at meeting Fetyukovitch. They had been enemies from the beginning of their careers in Petersburg. Our sensitive prosecutor, who felt that he had been wronged by someone in Petersburg because his talents had not been properly appreciated, was excited over the Karamazov case, and was dreaming of rebuilding his flagging fortunes by means of it. Fetyukovitch, they said, was his one obstacle. But these rumors were not quite just. Our prosecutor was not one of those men who lose heart in face of danger. On the contrary, his self-confidence increased with the increase of danger. It must be noted that our prosecutor was in general too hasty and morbidly impressionable. He would put his whole soul into some case and work at it as though his whole fate and his whole fortune depended on its result. This was the subject of some ridicule in the legal world, because by this characteristic our prosecutor had gained a wider notoriety than could have been expected from his modest position. People laughed particularly at his passion for psychology. In my opinion, they were wrong. Our prosecutor was, I believe, a man of greater depth than was generally supposed. But because of poor health he had failed to make his mark at the beginning of his career and had never made up for it later.

As for the President of our Court, I can only say that he was a humane and cultured man who had a practical knowledge of his work and progressive views. He was rather ambitious, but did not worry about his career. The aim of his life was to be a man of advanced ideas. He was also a man of influence and property. He felt, as we learned afterwards, rather strongly about the Karamazov case, but from a social, not from a personal viewpoint. He was interested in it as a social phenomenon, in its classification and its character as a product of our social conditions, as typical of the national character, and so on and so on. His attitude toward the personal aspect of the case, toward its tragic significance and the people involved in it, including the prisoner, was rather indifferent and abstract. This was perhaps best.

The court was packed and overflowing long before the judges made their appearance. Our court is the best hall in the town—spacious and with good acoustics. On the right of the judges, who were on a raised platform, a table and two rows of chairs had been put ready for the jury. On the left was the place for the prisoner and the counsel for the defense. In the middle of the court, near the judges, was a table with the "material proofs." On it lay Fyodor Karamazov's white silk dressing gown, stained with blood; the brass pestle with which the murder was believed to have been committed; Dmitri's shirt with the bloodstained sleeve; his coat, stained with blood in patches over the pocket in which he had put his handkerchief; the handkerchief itself, stiff with blood and by now quite yellow; the pistol loaded by Dmitri at Perhotin's with the intention of suicide, and taken from him at Mokroe by the innkeeper, Trifon Plastunov; the envelope in which the three thousand roubles had been put ready for Grushenka, the narrow pink ribbon with which it had been tied, and many other articles I don't remember. In the center of the hall, at some distance, were the seats for the public. And in front of the balustrade a few chairs had been placed for witnesses who wanted to remain in the court after giving their evidence.

At ten o'clock the three judges arrived—the President, one honorary justice of the peace, and one other. The prosecutor, of course, entered immediately after. The President was a short, stout, thickset man of fifty, with a dyspeptic complexion, dark hair turning gray and cut short, and a red ribbon, of what Order I don't remember. The prosecutor struck me and the others, too, as looking particularly pale, almost green. His face seemed to have grown suddenly thinner, perhaps in a single night, for I had seen him looking as usual only two days before. The President began with asking the court whether all the jury were present.

But I can't go on like this, partly because some things I did not hear, others I did not notice, and others I have forgotten, but mainly because, as I have said before, I have literally no time or space to mention everything that was said and done. I only know that neither side objected to many of the jurymen. I remember the twelve jurymen—four were petty officials of the town, two were merchants, and six were peasants and artisans. I remember, long before the trial began, that questions were askèd with some surprise, especially by ladies: "Can such a complex and psychological case be submitted for decision to petty officials and peasants?" and "What can an official, still more a peasant, understand in such an affair?" All the four officials on the jury were, in fact, men of no consequence and of low rank. Except for one who was rather young, they were gray-headed men, little known in society. They had vegetated on pitiful salaries and probably had elderly, unpresentable wives and crowds of children, without shoes and stockings. They probably spent their leisure playing cards and had never read a single book. The two merchants looked respectable, but were strangely silent and stolid. One of them was close-shaven, and was dressed in European style; the other had a small, gray beard, and wore a red ribbon with some sort of a medal on his neck. There is no need to speak of the artisans and the peasants. The artisans of Skotoprigonyevsk are almost peasants, and even work on the land. Two of them also wore European dress, and, perhaps for that reason, were dirtier and more uninviting looking than the others. One might well wonder, as I did as soon as I had looked at them, "what men like these could possibly make of such a case?" Yet their faces made a strangely imposing, almost menacing, impression; they were stern and frowning.

At last the President opened the case of the murder of Fyodor Karamazov. I don't quite remember how he described him. The court usher was told to bring in the prisoner, and Dmitri made his appearance. There was a hush in the court. One could have heard a fly. I don't know how it was with others but Dmitri made a most unfavorable impression on me. He was over-dressed in a brand-new frock coat. I heard afterwards that he had ordered it in Moscow for the occasion from his own tailor, who had his measure. He wore immaculate black kid gloves and fine linen. He walked in with his yard-long strides, looking straight in front of him, and sat down in his place with an unperturbed air.

At the same moment the counsel for defense, the celebrated Fetyukovitch, entered, and a sort of subdued hum passed through the court. He was a tall, spare man, with long thin legs, with extremely long, thin, pale fingers, clean-shaven face, rather short hair, and thin lips that were at times curved into something between a sneer and a smile. He looked about forty. His face would have been pleasant, if it had not been for his eyes, which, small and inexpressive, were set remarkably close together, with only the thin, long nose as a dividing line between them. In fact, there was something strikingly birdlike about his face. He was in evening dress and white tie.

I remember the President's first questions to Dmitri, about his name, his occupation, and so on. Dmitri answered sharply, and his voice was so unexpectedly loud that it made the President start and look at him with surprise. Then followed a list of people who were to take part in the case—that is, of the witnesses and experts. It was a long list. Four of the witnesses were not present; Miusov, who had given evidence at the preliminary inquiry, was now in Paris; Madame Hohlakov and Maximov who were absent through illness; and Smerdyakov, through his sudden death, of which an official statement from the police was presented.

The news of Smerdyakov's death produced a stir and whisper in the court. Many of those present, of course, had not heard of the suicide. But what struck people most was Dmitri's sudden outburst. As soon as the statement of Smerdyakov's death was made, he cried out aloud from his place: "He was a dog and died like a dog!"

I remember how his lawyer rushed to him, and how the President addressed him, threatening to take stern measures, if such an irregularity were repeated.

Dmitri nodded and in a subdued voice repeated abruptly several times, with no show of regret: "I won't again, I won't. It escaped me. I won't do it again."

This episode, of course, did him no good with the jury or the public. His character was displayed, and it spoke for itself. It was under the influence of this incident that the opening statement was read. It was rather short, but circumstantial. It merely stated the reason why he had been arrested, why he must be tried, and so on. Yet it made a great impression on me. The clerk read it loudly and distinctly. The whole tragedy was suddenly unfolded before us, concentrated, in bold relief, in a fatal and pitiless light.

I remember how immediately after it had been read, the President asked Dmitri in a loud impressive voice: "Prisoner, do you plead guilty?"

Dmitri suddenly rose.

"I plead guilty to drunkenness and dissipation," he exclaimed, again in a startling, almost frenzied voice, "to idleness and debauchery. I meant to become an honest man for good, just at the moment when I was struck down by fate. But I am not guilty of the death of that old man, my enemy and my father. No, no, I am not guilty of robbing him! I could not be. Dmitri Karamazov is a scoundrel but not a thief."

He sat down again trembling all over. The President again briefly but impressively admonished him to answer only what was asked, and not to go off into irrelevant matters. Then he ordered the case to proceed. All the witnesses were led up to take the oath. It was then that I saw them all together. The brothers of the prisoner were, however, allowed to give evidence without taking the oath. After an exhortation from the priest and the President, the witnesses were led away and were made to sit as far as possible from one another. They were later called up one by one.

2. *Dangerous Witnesses*

I DO NOT KNOW whether the witnesses for the defense and for the prosecution were separated into groups by the President, and whether it was arranged to call them in a certain order. But no doubt it was. I only know that the witnesses for the prosecution were called first. I repeat I don't intend to describe all the questions step by step. Besides, my account would be to some extent superfluous, because in the speeches for the prosecution and for the defense all the evidence was brought together and set in a strong and significant light. I took down parts of those two remarkable speeches in full, and will quote them in due course, together with one extraordinary and quite unexpected episode, which occurred before the final speeches, and which undoubtedly influenced the outcome of the trial.

I will only say that from the very beginning of the trial one peculiar characteristic of the case was conspicuous and observed by all, that is, the overwhelming strength of the prosecution as compared with the arguments the defense had to rely upon. Everyone realized from the first moment that the facts began to group themselves around a single point, and the whole horrible and bloody crime was gradually revealed. Everyone, perhaps, felt from the first that the case was beyond dispute, that there was no doubt about it, that there could be really no discussion, and that the defense was only a matter of form; the prisoner was guilty, obviously and conclusively guilty. I imagine that even the ladies, who were longing for the acquittal of the prisoner, were at the same time, without exception, convinced of his guilt. What's more, I believe they would have been mortified if his guilt had not been so firmly established, because that would have lessened the effect of the closing scene of the criminal's expected acquittal. That he would be acquitted all the ladies, strange to say, were firmly persuaded up to the very last moment. "He is guilty, but he will be acquitted, from humane motives in accordance with the new ideas, the new sentiments that have come into fashion," and so on, and so on. And that was why they had crowded into the court. The men were more interested in the contest between the prosecutor and the famous Fetyukovitch. All were wondering and asking themselves what Fetyukovitch, with all his talent, could possibly make of such a case; and so they followed his strategy, step by step, with concentrated attention.

But Fetyukovitch remained an enigma to all up to the very end, up to his final speech. People experienced in such matters suspected that he had some design, that he was working toward some object, but it was impossible to guess what it was. His confidence and self-reliance were unmistakable, however. Everyone noticed with pleasure, moreover, that he, after so short a stay, not more than three days among us, had succeeded in mastering the case and "had studied it to perfection." People described afterward how cleverly he had "broken down" all the witnesses for the prosecution; how he had confused them and damaged their reputations thereby depreciating the value of their evidence. But it was thought that he did this rather by way of sport, for professional glory, to show nothing had been omitted of the accepted methods. All were convinced that he could do no real good by such disparagement of the witnesses, and that he must have some idea in the background, some concealed weapon of defense, which he would suddenly reveal when the time came.

So, for instance, when Gregory, Fyodor Karamazov's old servant who had given the most damning evidence about the open door, was examined, the lawyer for the defense fastened upon him when his turn came to question him. It must be noted that Gregory entered the hall with a composed manner, not the least disconcerted by the majesty of the court or the vast audience listening to him. He gave his evidence with as much confidence as though he had been talking with his Marfa, only perhaps more respectfully. It was impossible to make him contradict himself.

The prosecutor questioned him first in detail about the family life of the Karamazovs. The family picture stood out in lurid colors. It was plain to ear and eye that the witness was guileless and impartial. In spite of his profound reverence for the memory of his deceased master, he yet bore witness that he had been unjust to Dmitri and hadn't brought up his children as he should. "He'd have been devoured by lice when he was little, if it hadn't been for me," he added, describing Dmitri's early childhood. "It wasn't fair either of the father to wrong his son over his mother's property, which was by right his."

In reply to the prosecutor's question concerning the grounds he had for asserting that Fyodor Karamazov had wronged his son in their money relations, Gregory, to the surprise of everyone, had no proof at all. But he still persisted that the arrangement with the son was "unfair," and that the father should "have paid him several thousand roubles more." I must note, by the way, that the prosecutor asked this question, whether Fyodor Karamazov had really kept back part of Dmitri's inheritance, with persistence of all the witnesses who could be asked about it, including Alyosha and Ivan. But he obtained no exact information from anyone; all alleged that it was so, but were unable to bring forward any real proof.

Gregory's description of the scene at the dinner table, when Dmitri had burst in and beaten his father, threatening to come back to kill him, made a deep impression on the court. The old servant's composure in telling it, his economy of words and peculiar phraseology were as effective as eloquence. He said that he was not angry with Dmitri for having knocked him down and struck him on the face; he had forgiven him long ago. Of Smerdyakov he observed, crossing himself, that he was a young man of ability, but stupid and afflicted, and, worse still, an infidel. He then added that it was Fyodor Karamazov and his elder son, Dmitri, who had taught him to be so. But he defended Smerdyakov's honesty almost with warmth. He related how Smerdyakov had once found the master's money in the yard and, instead of concealing it, had taken it to his master, who had rewarded him with a "gold piece" and trusted him implicitly from that time forward. He maintained obstinately that the door into the garden had been open. But he was asked so many questions that I can't recall them all.

At last the lawyer for the defense began to cross-examine him, and the first question he asked was about the envelope in which Fyodor Karamazov was supposed to have put three thousand roubles for a "certain person." "Have you ever seen it, you who were for so many years in close attendance on your master?" Gregory answered that he had not seen it and had never heard of the money from anyone "till everybody was talking about it." This question about the envelope Fetyukovitch asked of everyone who could conceivably have known about it. He was as persistent as the prosecutor was about his question concerning Dmitri's inheritance. And he got the same answer from all; no one had seen the envelope, though many had heard of it. From the beginning everyone noticed Fetyukovitch's persistence on this subject.

"Now, with your permission I'll ask you a question," Fetyukovitch said to Gregory suddenly and unexpectedly. "Of what was that balsam or rather, liniment, made which, as we learn from the preliminary inquiry, you used on that evening to rub your lumbago, in the hope of curing it?"

Gregory looked out blankly and after a brief silence muttered, "There was saffron in it."

"Nothing but saffron? Don't you remember any other ingredient?"

"There was milfoil in it, too."

"And pepper perhaps?" Fetyukovitch queried.

"Yes, there was pepper, too."

"Etcetera. And all dissolved in vodka?"

"In spirit."

There was a faint sound of laughter in the court.

602

"You see, in spirit. After rubbing your back, I believe, you drank what was left in the bottle with a certain prayer, only known to your wife?"

"I did."

"Did you drink much? Roughly speaking, a wineglass or two?"

"It might have been a tumblerful."

"A tumblerful, even. Perhaps a tumbler and a half?"

Gregory did not answer. He seemed to see what was meant.

"A glass and a half of neat spirit—is not at all bad! You might see the gates of heaven open, not only the door into the garden?"

Gregory remained silent. There was more laughter in the court. The President raised his hand.

"Do you know for a fact," Fetyukovitch persisted, "whether you were awake or not when you saw the open door?"

"I was on my legs."

"That's not a proof that you were awake." (There was again laughter in the court.) "Could you have answered at that moment, if anyone had asked you a question—for instance, what year is it?"

"I don't know."

"And what year is it, Anno Domini, do you know?"

Gregory stood with a perplexed face, looking straight at his tormentor. Strange to say, it appeared he really did not know what year it was.

"But perhaps you can tell me how many fingers you have on your hands?"

"I am a servant," Gregory said suddenly in a loud and distinct voice. "If my betters think fit to make fun of me, it is my duty to suffer it."

Fetyukovitch was taken aback, and the President intervened, reminding him that he must ask more relevent questions. Fetyukovitch bowed with dignity and said that he had no more questions to ask of the witness. The public and the jury, of course, were left with a grain of doubt in their minds as to the evidence of a man who might, while undergoing a certain cure, have seen "the gates of heaven," and who did not even know what year he was living in. But before Gregory left the box another episode occurred. The President, turning to the prisoner, asked him whether he had any comment to make on the evidence of the last witness.

"Except about the door, all he has said is true," cried Dmitri in a loud voice. "For combing the lice off me, I thank him; for forgiving my blows, I thank him. The old man has been honest all his life and as faithful to my father as seven hundred poodles."

"Prisoner, be careful in your language," the President warned him.

"I am not a poodle," Gregory muttered.

"All right, I am a poodle myself," cried Dmitri. "If it's an insult, I take it to myself and I beg his pardon. I was a beast and cruel to him. I was cruel to Aesop, too."

"What Aesop?" the President asked sternly.

"Oh, Pierrot . . . my father, Fyodor Karamazov."

The President again and again warned Dmitri to be more careful of his language.

"You are injuring yourself in the opinion of your judges."

The counsel for the defense was equally clever in dealing with the evidence of Rakitin. I should say that Rakitin was one of the leading witnesses and one to whom the prosecutor attached great significance. It appeared that he knew everything; his knowledge was amazing. He had been everywhere, seen everything, talked to everybody, knew every detail of the life of Fyodor Karamazov and all the Karamazovs. Of the envelope, it is true, he had only heard from Dmitri himself. But he described in detail Dmitri's exploits in the Metropolis tavern, all his compromising actions and sayings. He also told the story of Captain Snegiryov's "wisp of tow." But even Rakitin could say nothing positive about Dmitri's inheritance. He confined himself to contemptuous generalities.

"Who could tell which of them was to blame, and which was in debt to the other, with their crazy Karamazov way of confusing things so that no one could make head or tail of anything." He blamed the tragic crime on national habits that had become ingrained by ages of serfdom and on the distressed condition of Russia. He was allowed some latitude of speech. This was the first time Rakitin showed what he could do, and he attracted notice. The prosecutor knew that the witness was writing a magazine article on the case, and afterwards in his speech, as we shall see later, he quoted from the article, showing that he had seen it already. The picture drawn by the witness was a gloomy and sinister one, and strenghtened the case for the prosecution. Altogether, Rakitin's discourse fascinated the public by its independence and the extraordinary nobility of its ideas. There were two or three outbreaks of applause when he spoke of serfdom and the distressed condition of Russia.

But Rakitin, in his youthful ardor, made a slight blunder, of which the counsel for the defense at once took advantage. Answering certain questions about Grushenka, and carried away by his own sentiments and his success, he went so far as to speak somewhat contemptuously of Agrafena Svyetlov as "the mistress of Samsonov." He would have given a good deal to take back his words afterward, because Fetyukovitch caught him at once. And it was all because Rakitin had not counted on the lawyer having been able to become so intimately acquainted with every detail of the case in so short a time.

"Allow me to ask," began the counsel for the defense, with a most respectful smile, "you are, of course, the same Mr.

Rakitin whose pamphlet: *The Life of the Deceased Elder, Father Zossima,* published by the diocesan authorities, full of profound and religious reflections and preceded by an excellent and devout dedication for the Bishop, I have just read with such pleasure?"

"I did not write it for publication . . . it was published afterwards," muttered Rakitin, for some reason disconcerted and almost ashamed.

"Oh, that's good! A scholar like you can, and indeed should take the widest view of every social question. Your most instructive pamphlet has been widely circulated through the patronage of the Bishop, and has been of appreciable service. . . . But this is the main thing I would like to learn from you. You stated just now that you were very intimately acquainted with Madame Svyetlov."

"I cannot answer for all my acquaintances. . . . I am a young man . . . And who can be responsible for everyone he meets?" cried Rakitin, flushing all over.

"I understand, I understand," cried Fetyukovitch, as though he, too, were embarrassed and in a hurry to excuse himself. "You, like any other, might well be interested in a young and beautiful woman, but . . . I only wanted to know . . . It has come to my attention that Madame Svyetlov was particularly anxious a few months ago to make the acquaintance of the younger Karamazov, Alexey Karamazov. She promised you twenty-five roubles if you would bring him to her in his monastic dress. And that actually took place on the evening of the day on which the terrible crime was committed. You brought Alexey Karamazov to Madame Svyetlov, and did you receive the twenty-five roubles from Madame Svyetlov as a reward, that's what I want to hear from you?"

"It was a joke. . . . I don't see of what interest that can be to you. . . . I took it as a joke . . . Meaning to give it back later . . ."

"Then you did take . . . But you have not given it back yet . . . Or have you?"

"That's of no importance," muttered Rakitin. "I refuse to answer such question. . . . Of course I shall give it back."

The President intervened, and Fetyukovitch declared he had no more questions to ask of the witness. Rakitin left the witness box with a stain upon his character. The idealism of his speech was somewhat marred, and Fetyukovitch's expression, as he watched him walk away, seemed to suggest to the public "this is a specimen of the high-minded people who accuse my client."

I remember that this incident, too, did not pass off without an outbreak from Dmitri. Enraged by the tone in which Rakitin had referred to Grushenka, he suddenly shouted "Bernard!" And when, after Rakitin's cross-examination, the President asked the prisoner if he had anything to say, Dmitri cried loudly: "Since I've been arrested, he has borrowed money from me! He is a contemptible Bernard and opportunist, and he doesn't believe in God; he fooled the Bishop!"

Dmitri, of course, was warned again for the intemperance of his language, but Rakitin was done for.

Captain Snegiryov's evidence was a failure, too, but for quite a different reason. He appeared in ragged and dirty clothes, muddy boots, and in spite of the vigilance of the police, he turned out to be hopelessly drunk. On being asked about Dmitri's attack upon him, he refused to answer.

"God bless him. Ilusha told me not to. God will reward me later."

"Who told you not to speak? Of whom are you talking?"

"Ilusha, my little son. 'Father, father, how he insulted you!' He said that at the stone. Now he is dying . . ."

The captain suddenly began sobbing, and sank down on his knees before the President. He was hurriedly led away amidst laughter. The effect prepared by the prosecutor did not come off at all.

Fetyukovitch went on making the most of every opportunity, and amazed people more and more by his minute knowledge of the case. For example, the innkeeper, Trifon Plastunov, made a great impression, of course, very prejudicial to Dmitri. He calculated almost on his fingers that on his first visit to Mokroe, Dmitri must have spent three thousand roubles: "or very little less. Just think what he squandered on those gypsy girls alone! And as for our lousy peasants, it wasn't a case of throwing half a rouble in the street, he made them presents of twenty-five roubles each. He didn't give them less. And what a lot of money was stolen from him! And if anyone did steal, he did not leave a receipt. How could one catch the thief when he was flinging his money away all the time? Our peasants are robbers, you know; they have no regard for their souls. And the way he carried on with the girls, our village girls! They're completely out of hand since then, I tell you, they used to be poor." He recalled, in fact, every item of expense and added it all up. So the theory that only fifteen hundred had been spent and the rest had been put aside in a little bag seemed inconceivable.

"I saw three thousand as clear as a penny in his hands. I saw it with my own eyes. I think I ought to know how to count money," cried the innkeeper, doing his best to satisfy "his betters."

When Fetyukovitch had to cross-examine him, he scarcely tried to refute his evidence, but began asking him about an incident which took place on the first night at Mokroe, a month before the arrest. On this night Timofey and another peasant called Akim had picked up on the floor in the passage a hundred roubles dropped by Dmitri, and had given them to the innkeeper and received a rouble each from him for doing so.

"Well," asked the lawyer, "did you give that hundred roubles back to Mr. Karamazov?" Trifon Plastunov shuffled in vain. . . . He was forced, after the peasants had been examined, to admit the finding of the hundred roubles, only adding that he had religiously returned it all to Dmitri Karamazov "in perfect honesty. It's only because his honor was in liquor at the time that he wouldn't remember it." But, since he had denied the incident of the hundred rubles until the peasants had been called to prove it, his evidence as to returning the money to Dmitri was naturally regarded with great suspicion. In this way one of the most dangerous witnesses brought forward by the prosecution was again discredited.

The same thing happened with the Poles. They took an attitude of pride and independence. They declared loudly that they had both been in the service of the Crown, and that Dmitri had offered them three thousand "to buy their honor," and that they had seen a large sum of money in his hands. Mussyalovitch introduced a terrible number of Polish words into his sentences, and seeing that this only increased his consequence in the eyes of the President and the prosecutor, he grew more and more pompous. He ended by talking in Polish altogether. But Fetyukovitch caught them, too, in his snares. The innkeeper was recalled. And he was forced, in spite of his evasions, to admit that Vrublevsky had substituted another pack of cards for the one he had provided, and that Mussyalovitch had cheated during the game. Kalganov confirmed this, and both the Poles left the witness box with damaged reputations, amidst laughter.

Exactly the same thing happened with almost all of the most dangerous witnesses. Fetyukovitch succeeded in casting a slur on all of them, and dismissing them with certain suspicions. The lawyers and experts were lost in admiration. They were only at a loss to understand what purpose could be served by it, for all, I repeat, felt that the case for the prosecution could not be refuted, but was growing more and more tragically overwhelming. But from the confidence of the "great magician" they felt that he had not come from Petersburg for nothing, and that he was not a man to return unsuccessful.

3. The Medical Experts and a Pound of Nuts

THE EVIDENCE OF THE MEDICAL EXPERTS was also of little use to the prisoner. And it appeared later that Fetyukovitch had not counted much upon it. The medical line of defense had only taken up at the insistence of Katerina, who had sent for the celebrated doctor from Moscow. The case for the defense could, of course, lose nothing by it and might, with luck, gain something from it. There was, however, an element of comedy about it, through the difference of opinion of the doctors. The medical experts were the famous doctor from Moscow, our doctor, Herzenstube, and the young doctor, Varvinsky. The two latter appeared also as witnesses for the prosecution.

The first to be called was Doctor Herzenstube. He was a bald old man of seventy, of middle height and sturdy build. He was much esteemed and respected by everyone in town. He was a conscientious doctor and an excellent and pious man, a Herrnhuter or Moravian brother, I am not quite sure which. He had been living amongst us for many years. He was a kind-hearted and humane man. He treated the poor and peasants for nothing, visited them in their slums and huts, and left money for medicine. But he was as obstinate as a mule. If once he had taken an idea into his head, there was no shaking it. Almost everyone in the town was aware, by the way, that the famous doctor from Moscow had within the first two or three days among us, said some extremely offensive things about Doctor Herzenstube's ability. Though the Moscow doctor asked twenty-five roubles for a visit, several people in town rushed to consult him. All these had, of course, been patients of Doctor Herzenstube, and the celebrated Moscow doctor had criticized his treatment with extreme harshness. Finally, he asked all new patients: "Well, who has been cramming you with nostrums? Herzenstube? Ha, ha!" Doctor Herzenstube, of course, heard about this. And now all three doctors made their appearance in court, one after another, to be examined.

Doctor Herzenstube roundly declared that the abnormality of the prisoner's mental faculties was self-evident. Then giving his ground for this opinion, which I omit here, he added that the abnormality was not only evident in many of the prisoner's actions in the past, but was apparent even now at this very moment. When he was asked to explain how it was apparent now at this moment, the old doctor, with simple-hearted directness, pointed out that the prisoner on entering the court had "an extraordinary manner, remarkable in the circumstances." Dmitri had "marched in like a soldier, looking straight before him, though it would have been more natural for him to look to the left where the ladies were sitting, seeing that he was a great admirer of the fair sex and must have been thinking of what the ladies were saying of him," the old man concluded.

I must add that Doctor Herzenstube spoke Russian, but every phrase was formed in German style. This did not, how-ever, trouble him, for it had always been a weakness of his to believe that he spoke Russian perfectly, better indeed than Russians. He was very fond of using Russian proverbs, always declaring that the Russian proverbs were the best and most expressive sayings in the whole world. I may remark, too, that in conversation, through absent-mindedness he often forgot the most ordinary words though he knew them perfectly. The same thing happened when he spoke German, and at such times he always waved his hand before his face as though trying to catch the lost word. No one could induce him to go on speaking till he had found the missing word. His remark that the prisoner ought to have looked at the ladies on entering roused a whisper of amusement in the audience. All our ladies were very fond of our old doctor; they knew, too, that having been all his life a bachelor and a religious man, he looked upon women as lofty creatures. And so his unexpected observation struck everyone as very queer.

The Moscow doctor, being questioned in his turn, definitely and emphatically repeated that he considered the prisoner's mental condition abnormal in the highest degree. He talked at length and with erudition of "aberration" and "mania." He argued that, from all the facts collected, the prisoner had undoubtedly been in a condition of aberration for several days before his arrest, and, if the crime had been committed by him, it must, even if he were conscious of it, have been almost involuntary, as he had not the power to control the morbid impulse that possessed him.

But apart from temporary aberration, the doctor diagnosed mania, which promised, in his words, to lead to complete insanity in the future. (It must be noted that I report this in my own words, the doctor made use of very learned and professional language.) "All his actions are in contravention of common sense and logic," he continued. "Not to refer to what I have not seen, that is, the crime itself, the day before yesterday, while he was talking to me, he had an unaccountably fixed look in his eye. He laughed unexpectedly when there was nothing to laugh at. He showed continual and inexplicable irritability, using strange words: 'Bernard!' 'Ethics!' and others equally inappropriate. But the doctor detected mania, above all, in the fact that the prisoner could not even speak of the three thousand roubles, of which he considered himself to have been cheated, without extreme irritation, though he could speak comparatively lightly of other misfortunes and grievances. According to all accounts, he had even in the past, whenever the subject of the three thousand roubles was touched on, flown into a frenzy, and yet he was reported to be a disinterested and not a grasping man.

"As to the opinion of my learned colleague," the Moscow doctor added ironically in conclusion, "that the prisoner would on entering the court, have naturally looked at the ladies and not straight before him, I will only say that, apart from the playfulness of this theory, it is radically unsound. Though I fully agree that the prisoner, on entering the court where his fate will be decided, would not naturally look straight before him in that fixed way, and that that may really be a sign of his abnormal mental condition, at the same time I maintain that he would naturally not look to the left at the ladies but to the right to find his legal adviser, on whose help all his hopes rest and on whose defense all his future depends." The doctor expressed his opinion emphatically.

But the unexpected pronouncement of Doctor Varvinsky gave the last touch of comedy to the difference of opinion between the experts. In his opinion the prisoner was now, and had been all along, in a perfectly normal condition and, although he certainly must have been in a nervous and exceedingly excited state before his arrest, this might have been due to several perfectly obvious causes, jealousy, anger, continual drunkenness, and so on. But this nervous condition would not involve the mental aberration of which mention had just been made. As to the question whether the prisoner should have looked to the left or to the right on entering the court, "in his modest opinion," the prisoner would naturally look straight before him on entering the court, as he had in fact done, as that was where the judges, on whom his fate depended, were sitting. So that it was just by looking straight before him that he showed his perfectly normal state of mind at the present. The young doctor concluded his "modest" testimony with some heat.

"Hurray, doctor!" cried Dmitri from his seat. "You're right!"

Dmitri, of course, was checked. But the young doctor's opinion had a decisive influence on the judges and on the public, and, as appeared afterward, everyone agreed with him.

Doctor Herzenstube, when called as a witness, was quite unexpectedly of help to Dmitri. As an old resident in town who had known the Karamazov family for years, he furnished some facts of great value for the prosecution, and suddenly, as though recalling something, he added: "But the poor young man might have had a very different life, for he had a good heart both in childhood and after childhood, that I know. But the Russian proverb says: 'If a man has one head, it's good, but if another clever man comes to visit him, it would be better still, for then there will be two heads and not only one.'"

"One head is good, but two are better," the prosecutor said impatiently. He knew the old man's habit of talking slowly and deliberately, regardless of the impression he was making and of the delay he was causing, and highly prizing his flat, dull and always gleefully complacent German wit. The old man was fond of making jokes.

"Oh, yes, that's what I say," he went on stubbornly. "One head is good, but two are much better. But he did not meet another head with wits, and his wits went. Where did they go? I've forgotten the word." He went on, passing his hand before his eyes, "Oh, yes, they took a walk."

"Wandering?"

"Oh, yes, wandering, that's what I mean. Well, his wits went wandering and fell in such a deep hole that he lost himself. And yet he was a grateful and sensitive boy. Oh, I remember him very well, a little chap so high, left neglected by his father in the back yard. He ran about without boots on his feet, and his little breeches hanging by one button."

A note of feeling and tenderness suddenly came into the honest old man's voice. Fetyukovitch started, as though scenting something and caught at it instantly.

"Oh, yes, I was a young man then. . . . I was . . . Well, I was forty-five then, and had only just come here. And I was so sorry for the child then; I asked myself why shouldn't I buy him a pound of . . . a pound of what? I've forgotten what it's called. A pound of what children are very fond of. What is it, what is it?" The doctor began waving his hand again. "It grows on a tree and is gathered and given to everyone . . ."

"Apples?"

"Oh, no no. You sell apples by the dozen not by the pound. . . . No, there are a lot of them, and all little. You put them in the mouth and crack."

"Nuts?"

"Yes, nuts." The doctor repeated this in the calmest way as though he had been at no loss for the word. "I bought him a pound of nuts, for no one had ever bought the boy a pound of nuts before. And I lifted my finger and said to him: 'Boy, *Gott der Vater*.' He laughed and said: '*Gott der Vater*.' . . . '*Gott der Sohn*.' He laughed again and lisped: '*Gott der Sohn*.' '*Gott der heilige Geist*.' Then he laughed and said as best he could: '*Gott der heilige Geist*.' I went away, and two days later I happened to be passing, and he shouted to me: 'Uncle, *Gott der Vater, Gott der Sohn*.' He had only forgotten: '*Gott der heilige Geist*.' But I reminded him of it, and I felt very sorry for him again. Then he was taken away, and I did not see him again. Twenty-three years passed. I am sitting one morning in my study, a bald-headed old man, when there walks into the room a blooming young man, whom I would never have recognized except that he held up his finger and said, laughing: '*Gott der Vater, Gott der Sohn* and *Gott der heilige Geist*. I have just arrived and have come to thank you for that pound of nuts, for no one else ever bought me a pound of nuts; you are the only one who ever did.' And then I remembered the poor child in the yard, without boots on his feet, and my heart was touched and I said: 'You are a grateful young man, for you have remembered all your life the pound of nuts I bought you in your childhood.' And I embraced him and blessed him. And I shed tears. He laughed, but he shed tears, too . . . for the Russian often laughs when he ought to be weeping. But he did weep; I saw it. And now, alas! . . ."

"And I am weeping now, German. I am weeping now, too, you saintly man," Dmitri cried suddenly.

In any case the anecdote made a favorable impression on the public. But the main sensation in Dmitri's favor was created by Katerina's testimony, which I will describe directly. Indeed, when the witnesses called by the defense, began giving evidence, fortune seemed all at once markedly more favorable to Dmitri. This was a surprise even to the counsel for the defense. But before Katerina was called, Alyosha was examined, and he recalled a fact which seemed to furnish positive evidence against one important point made by the prosecution. It came quite as a surprise even to Alyosha himself.

4. *Fortune Smiles on Dmitri*

ALYOSHA WAS NOT REQUIRED TO TAKE THE OATH, and I remember that both sides addressed him very gently and sympathetically. It was evident that his reputation for goodness had preceded him. Alyosha gave his evidence modestly and with restraint, but his warm sympathy for his unhappy brother was unmistakable. In answer to one question, he sketched his brother's character as that of a man, violent-tempered perhaps and carried away by his passion, but at the same time honorable, proud and generous, capable of self-sacrifice, if necessary. He admitted, however, that through his passion for Grushenka and his rivalry with his father, his brother had recently been in an intolerable position. But he rejected completely the suggestion that his brother might have committed a murder for the sake of gain, though he recognized that the three thousand roubles had become almost an obsession with Dmitri. He agreed that Dmitri looked upon them as part of the inheritance he had been cheated of by his father, and that, indifferent as he was to money as a rule, he could not even speak of that three thousand without fury. As for the rivalry of the two "ladies," as the prosecutor expressed it— that is, of Grushenka and Katerina—he answered evasively and was even unwilling to answer one or two questions altogether.

"Did your brother tell you that he intended to kill your father?" asked the prosecutor. "You can refuse to answer," he added.

"He did not tell me so directly," answered Alyosha.

"Did he say so indirectly?"

"He spoke to me once of his hatred for our father and his fear that at an extreme moment . . . at a moment of fury, he might perhaps murder him."

"And you believed him?"

"I am afraid to say that I did. But I never doubted that some higher feeling would always save him at the fatal mo-

612

ment, as it has indeed saved him, for he did not kill my father," Alyosha said firmly, in a loud voice that was heard throughout the court.

The prosecutor started like a warhorse at the sound of a trumpet.

"Let me assure you that I fully believe in the complete sincerity of your conviction and do not explain it by or identify it with your affection for your unhappy brother. Your peculiar view of the whole tragic episode is known to us already from the preliminary investigation. I won't attempt to conceal from you that it is highly individual and contradicts all the other evidence collected by the prosecution. And so I think it essential to press you to tell me what facts have led you to this conviction of your brother's innocence and of the guilt of another person against whom you gave evidence at the preliminary inquiry?"

"I only answered the questions asked me at the preliminary inquiry," replied Alyosha slowly and calmly. "I made no accusation against Smerdyakov, from my own knowledge."

"Yet you gave evidence against him?"

"I did so because of my brother Dmitri's words. I was told what took place at his arrest and how he had indicated Smerdyakov before I was examined. I believe absolutely that my brother is innocent, and if he didn't commit the murder, then . . ."

"Then Smerdyakov? Why Smerdyakov? And why are you so completely persuaded of your brother's innocence?"

"I cannot help believing my brother. I know he wouldn't lie to me. I saw from his face that he wasn't lying."

"Only from his face? Is that all the proof you have?"

"I have no other proof."

"And of Smerdyakov's guilt have you no proof whatever but your brother's word and the expression of his face?"

"No, I have no other proof."

The prosecutor dropped the examination at this point. The impression left by Alyosha's evidence was most disappointing. There had been talk about Smerdyakov before the trial; someone had heard something, someone had pointed out something else, it was said that Alyosha had gathered together some extraordinary proofs of his brother's innocence and Smerdyakov's guilt. And now after all there was nothing, no evidence except certain moral convictions so natural in a brother.

Fetyukovitch began his cross-examination. On his asking Alyosha when it was that the prisoner had told him of his hatred for his father and that he might kill him, and whether he had heard it, for instance, at their last meeting before the murder, Alyosha suddenly started as though only just remembering and understanding something.

"I remember something now which I'd forgotten. It wasn't clear to me at the time, but now . . ."

And he told eagerly how at his meeting with Dmitri that evening at the crossroads, Dmitri had struck himself on the chest, "the upper part of the chest," and had repeated several times that he had a means of regaining his honor, that that means was here, here on his chest. "I thought, when he struck himself on the chest, that he meant that it was in his heart," Alyosha continued, "that he might find in his heart strength to save himself from some awful disgrace which was awaiting him and which he did not dare confess even to me. I must confess I did think at the time that he was speaking of our father, and that the disgrace he was shuddering at was the thought of going to our father and doing some violence to him. Yet it was just then that he pointed to something on his chest, so that I remember the idea struck me at the time that the heart is not in that part of the chest, but below. He struck himself much too high, just below the neck, and kept pointing to that place. My idea seemed silly to me at the time, but he was perhaps pointing then to that little bag in which he had fifteen hundred roubles!"

"That's right," Dmitri cried from his place. "That's right, Alyosha, it was the little bag I struck with my fist."

Fetyukovitch rushed to him entreating him to keep quiet, and then pounced on Alyosha. Alyosha, carried away by his recollection, expressed his opinion that this disgrace was probably that fifteen hundred roubles which he might have returned to Katerina as half of what he owed her, but which he had determined not to repay her but to use for another purpose—to enable him to elope with Grushenka, if she consented.

"It is so, it must be so," exclaimed Alyosha, in excitement. "My brother cried several times that half of the disgrace, half of it (he said half several times) he could free himself from at once, but that he was so unhappy in his weakness of will that he wouldn't do it . . . That he knew beforehand he was incapable of doing it!"

"And you clearly, confidently remember that he struck himself just on this part of the chest?" Fetyukovitch asked eagerly.

"Clearly and confidently. I thought at the time: 'Why does he strike himself up there when the heart is lower down,' and the thought seemed stupid to me at the time . . . I remember its seeming stupid . . . It flashed through my mind. That's what brought it back to me just now. How could I have forgotten it till now! It was that little bag he meant when he said he had the means but wouldn't give back that fifteen hundred. And when he was arrested at Mokroe he cried out—I know, I was told—that he considered it the most disgraceful act of his life that when he had the means of repaying Katerina half (half, note!) what he owed her, he could not bring himself to repay the money and preferred to remain a thief in

614

her eyes rather than part with it. . . . What torture, what torture that debt has been to him!" Alyosha exclaimed in conclusion.

The prosecutor intervened. He asked Alyosha to describe once more how it had all happened, and several times insisted on the question, had the prisoner seemed to point to anything? Perhaps he had simply struck himself with his fist?

"But it was not with his fist," cried Alyosha. "He pointed with his fingers and pointed here, very high up. . . . How could I have completely forgotten it till this moment!"

The President asked Dmitri what he had to say to the last witness's evidence. Dmitri confirmed it, saying that he had been pointing to the fifteen hundred roubles which were on his chest, just below the neck, and that that was, of course, the disgrace. "A disgrace I cannot deny. The most shameful act of my whole life," cried Dmitri. "I might have repaid it and didn't repay it. I preferred to remain a thief in her eyes rather than give it back. And the most shameful part of it was that I knew beforehand I wouldn't give it back! You are right, Alyosha! Thank you, Alyosha!"

So Alyosha's cross-examination ended. What was important and striking about it was that one fact at least had been found. Even though it was only one tiny bit of evidence, a mere hint at evidence, it did go some little way toward proving that the bag had existed and had contained fifteen hundred roubles and that the prisoner had not been lying at the preliminary inquiry, when he alleged at Mokroe that those fifteen hundred roubles were "his own." Alyosha was glad. With a flushed face he moved away to the seat assigned to him. He kept repeating to himself: "How did I forget! How could I have forgotten it! And what made it come back to me now?"

Katerina was then called to the witness box. As she entered something extraordinary happened in the court. The ladies clutched their lorgnettes and opera glasses. There was a stir among the men; some stood up to get a better view. Everybody said afterwards that Dmitri had turned "white as a sheet." All in black, she advanced modestly, almost timidly. It was impossible to tell from her face that she was nervous; there was a determined gleam in her dark and gloomy eyes. I may remark that many people mentioned that she looked particularly handsome at that moment.

She spoke softly but clearly, so that she was heard all over the court. She expressed herself with composure, or at least tried to appear composed. The President began his examination discreetly and very respectfully, as though afraid to touch on "certain chords," and showing consideration for her great unhappiness. But in answer to one of the first questions Katerina replied firmly that she had been engaged to the prisoner "until he left me of his own accord . . ." she added quietly. When she was asked about the three thousand she had entrusted to Dmitri to mail to her relatives, she said firmly: "I didn't give him the money simply to send it off. I felt at the time that he was in great need of money. . . . I gave him the three thousand on the understanding that he would mail it within the month if he cared to. There was no need for him to worry himself about that debt afterwards."

I will not repeat all the questions asked her and all her answers in detail. I will only give the substance of her evidence.

"I was firmly convinced that he would send off that sum as soon as he got money from his father," she went on. "I have never doubted his honesty . . . his scrupulous honesty . . . in money matters. He felt quite certain that he would receive money from his father, and spoke to me several times about it. I knew he had a feud with his father and I have always believed that he was unfairly treated by his father. I don't remember any threat uttered by him against his father. He certainly never uttered any such threat before me. If he had come to me at that time, I would have at once relieved him of worry about that unlucky three thousand roubles. But he had given up coming to see me . . . and I was put in such a position . . . that I could not invite him. . . . And I had no right to be exacting as to that money," she added suddenly, and there was a ring of resolution in her voice. "I was once indebted to him for assistance for more than three thousand, and I took it, although I could not at that time foresee that I would ever be in a position to repay my debt."

There was a note of defiance in her voice. It was then that Fetyukovitch began his cross-examination.

"Did that take place at the beginning of your friendship?" Fetyukovitch suggested cautiously, feeling his way, instantly scenting something favorable. I must mention that, though Fetyukovitch had been brought from Petersburg partly at the instance of Katerina herself, he knew nothing about the five thousand roubles given to her by Dmitri and of her "bowing to the ground to him." She concealed this from him, had said nothing about it, and that was strange. It may be assumed that she herself did not know till the very last minute whether she would mention that episode in court. She may have waited for the inspiration of the moment.

No, I can never forget those moments. She began telling her story. She told everything (the whole episode that Dmitri had told Alyosha) about her bowing to the ground and her reason for doing so. She told about her father and her going to Dmitri and did not in one word, in a single hint, suggest that Dmitri had himself, through her sister, proposed they should "send him Katerina" to get the money. She concealed that and was not ashamed to make it appear as though she had of her own impulse run to the young officer, relying on something . . . to beg him for the money. It was tremendous! I turned cold and trembled as I listened. The court was hushed, trying to catch each word. It was without precedent. Even from such a self-willed and contemptuously proud girl as she was, such an extremely frank avowal, such sacrifice seemed incredible. And for what, for whom? To save the man who had deceived and insulted her? And, indeed, the picture of the young officer who, with a respectful bow to the innocent girl, handed her his last five thousand roubles—all he had in the world—was thrown into a very sympathetic and attractive light, but . . . I had a painful misgiving at heart! I felt that trouble might come of it later (and it did, in fact, it did). It was repeated all over town afterwards with spiteful laughter that the story was perhaps not quite complete—that is, in the statement that the officer had let the young lady depart "with nothing but a respectful bow." It was hinted that something must have been omitted.

"And even if nothing has been omitted, if this is the whole story," the most highly respected of our ladies maintained, "even then it's very doubtful whether it was right for a young girl to behave in that way, even for the sake of saving her father."

Could Katerina, with her intelligence, her morbid sensitiveness, have failed to understand that people would talk like that? She must have understood it, yet she made up her mind to tell everything. Of course, all these suspicions as to the truth of her story only arose afterwards. At first all were deeply impressed by it. As for the judges and the lawyers, they listened in reverent, almost shame-faced silence to Katerina. The prosecutor did not venture upon even one question on the subject. Fetyukovitch made a low bow to her. He was almost triumphant! Much ground had been gained. For a man to give his last five thousand on a generous impulse and then for the same man to murder his father for the sake of robbing him of three thousand—the idea seemed incongruous. Fetyukovitch felt that now the charge of theft, at least, was as good as disproved. "The case" was thrown into quite a different light. There was a wave of sympathy for Dmitri. As for him . . .

Once or twice, while Katerina was testifying, he jumped up from his seat, sank back again, and hid his face in his hands. But when she had finished, he suddenly cried in a sobbing voice: "Katerina, why have you ruined me?" and his sobs were audible all over the court. But he restrained himself, and cried again: "Now I am condemned!"

Then he sat rigid in his place, with his teeth clenched and his arms across his chest. Katerina remained in the court and sat down in her place. She was pale and sat with her eyes cast down. Those who were sitting near her said later that for a long time she shivered all over as though in a fever. Grushenka was now called.

I am approaching the sudden castastrophe which was perhaps the final cause of Dmitri's ruin. I am convinced, so is everyone—all the lawyers said the same afterwards—that if this episode had not occurred, the prisoner would at least have been recommended to mercy. But of that later. A few words first about Grushenka.

She, too, was dressed entirely in black, with her magnificent black shawl on her shoulders. She walked to the witness box with her smooth, noiseless tread, with the slightly swaying gait common to women of full figure. She looked steadily at the President, turning her eyes neither to the right nor to the left. To my thinking she looked very handsome at that moment, and not at all pale, as the ladies said afterwards. They claimed, too, that she had a concentrated and spiteful expression. I believe that she was simply irritated and painfully conscious of the contemptuous and inquisitive eyes of our scandal-loving public. She was proud and could not stand contempt. She was one of those people who flare up, angry and eager to retaliate, at the mere suggestion of contempt. There was an element of timidity, too, of course, and inward shame at her own timidity, so that it was not strange that her tone kept changing. At one moment it was angry, contemptuous and rough, and at another there was a sincere note of self-condemnation. Sometimes she spoke as though she were taking a desperate plunge; as though she felt: "I don't care what happens. I'll say it. . . ." Concerning her acquaintance with Fyodor Karamazov she remarked curtly: "That's all nonsense, and was it my fault that he pestered me?" But a minute later she added: "It was all my fault. I was laughing at them both —at the old man and at him, too—and I brought both of them to this. It was all on account of me that it happened."

Samsonov's name came up somehow. "That's nobody's business," she called out with a sort of insolent defiance. "He was my benefactor; he took me when I hadn't a shoe to my foot, when my family had turned me out." The President reminded her, though very politely, that she must answer the questions directly, without going off into irrelevant details. Grushenka crimsoned and her eyes flashed.

The envelope with the notes in it she had not seen. She had only heard from "that wicked wretch" that Fyodor Karamazov had an envelope with notes for three thousand in it. "But that was all foolishness. I was only laughing. I wouldn't have gone to him for anything."

"To whom are you referring as 'that wicked wretch'?" inquired the prosecutor.

"The lackey, Smerdyakov, who murdered his master and hanged himself last night."

She was, of course, at once asked what ground she had for such a definite accusation. But it appeared that she, too, had no grounds for it.

"Dmitri told me so himself; you can believe him. The woman who came between us has ruined him. She is the cause of it all, let me tell you," Grushenka added. She seemed to be quivering with hatred, and there was a vindictive note in her voice. She was again asked to whom she was referring. "The young lady, Katerina there. She sent for me, offered me chocolate, tried to win me over. There's not much true shame about her, I can tell you that . . ."

At this point the President checked her, telling her sternly to moderate her language. But her jealous woman's heart was burning, and she did not care what she did.

"When the prisoner was arrested at Mokroe," the prosecutor asked, "everyone saw and heard you run out of the next room and cry out: 'It's all my fault. We'll go to Siberia together!' So you already believed him to have murdered his father?"

"I don't remember what I felt at the time," answered Grushenka. "Everyone was crying out that he had killed his father, and I felt that it was my fault, that it was on my account he had murdered him. But when he said he wasn't guilty, I believed him at once, and I believe him now and always shall believe him. He is not the kind of man to tell a lie."

Fetyukovitch began his cross-examination. I remember that among other things he asked about Rakitin and the twenty-five roubles "you paid him for bringing Alexey Karamazov to see you."

"There was nothing strange about his taking the money," sneered Grushenka with contempt. "He was always coming to me for money. He used to get thirty roubles a month at least out of me, chiefly for luxuries. He had enough money to live on without my help."

"What led you to be so liberal to Mr. Rakitin?" Fetyukovitch asked, in spite of an uneasy movement on the part of the President.

"Why, he is my cousin. His mother was my mother's sister. But he's always begged me not to tell anyone here about it, he is so dreadfully ashamed of me."

This fact was a complete surprise to everyone. No one in town nor in the monastery, not even Dmitri, knew of it. I was told that Rakitin turned purple with shame. Grushenka had somehow heard before she came into the court that he had given evidence against Dmitri, and so she was angry. The whole effect of Rakitin's speech, of his noble sentiments, of his attacks upon serfdom and the political disorder of Russia, was this time completely ruined. Fetyukovitch was satisfied; it was another godsend.

Grushenka's cross-examination did not last long and, of course, there could be nothing particularly new in her evidence. She left a very bad impression on the public; hundreds of contemptuous eyes were fixed upon her, as she finished giving her evidence and sat down again in the court, at a good distance from Katerina.

Dmitri was silent throughout her testimony. He sat as though turned to stone, with his eyes fixed on the ground. Ivan was the next witness to be called.

5. A Sudden Catastrophe

I MUST NOTE that Ivan had been called before Alyosha. But the court usher had announced to the President that, owing to an attack of illness or some sort of fit, the witness could not appear at the moment, but was ready to give his evidence as soon as he recovered. No one seemed to have heard of this at the time; it only came out later.

Ivan's entrance was for the first moment almost unnoticed. The principal witnesses, especially Katerina and Grushenka, had already been questioned. Curiosity was satisfied for the time; those present felt almost tired. Several more witnesses were still to be heard; they probably had little information to give after all that had been given. Time was passing. Ivan walked up very slowly, looking at no one, and with his head bowed, as though plunged in gloomy thought. He was irreproachably dressed, but his face made a painful impression, on me at least; there was an earthy look in it, a look like a dying man's. His eyes were lusterless. He raised them and looked slowly around the court. Alyosha jumped up from his seat and moaned "Ah!" I remember that, but it was hardly noticed.

The President began by informing Ivan that he was not under oath, that he might answer or refuse to answer, but that, of course, he must bear witness according to his conscience, and so on and so on. Ivan listened and looked at him blankly. Then his face relaxed into a smile, and as soon as the President finished, he laughed.

"Well, and what else?" he asked in a loud voice.

There was a hush in the court; there was a feeling of something strange. The President showed signs of uneasiness.

"You . . . are perhaps still ill?" he began, looking everywhere for the usher.

"Don't trouble, your excellency, I am well enough and can tell you something interesting," Ivan answered with sudden calmness and respect.

"You have something special to report?" the President went on, still mistrustful.

Ivan looked down, waited a few seconds and, raising his head, answered, almost stammering: "No . . . I haven't. I have nothing in particular."

They began asking him questions. He answered, as it were

620

reluctantly, with extreme brevity, with a sort of disgust which grew more and more marked, though he answered rationally. To many questions he answered that he did not know. He knew nothing of his father's money relations with Dmitri. "I wasn't interested in the subject," he added. Threats to murder his father he had heard from the prisoner. Of the money in the envelope he had heard from Smerdyakov.

"The same thing over and over again," he interrupted suddenly, with a look of weariness. "I have nothing in particular to tell the court."

"I see you are ill and I understand your feelings," the President began.

He turned to the prosecutor and the counsel for the defense to invite them to examine the witness, if necessary.

Ivan suddenly asked in an exhausted voice: "Let me go, your excellency. I feel very ill."

And with these words, without waiting for permission, he turned to walk out of the court. But after taking four steps he stood still, as though he had reached a decision, smiled slowly, and went back.

"I am like the peasant girl, your excellency . . . you know. How does it go? 'I'll stand up if I like, and I won't if I don't.' They were trying to put on her sarafan to take her to church to be married, and she said: 'I'll stand up if I like, and I won't if I don't' . . . It's in some book."

"What do you mean by that?" the President asked severely.

"Why, this." Ivan suddenly pulled out a roll of notes. "Here's the money . . . The notes that were in that envelope" (he nodded toward the table on which lay the material evidence). "This is the money for which our father was murdered. Where shall I put it? Mr. Superintendent, take it."

The court usher took the roll of notes and handed it to the President.

"How could this money have come into your possession if it is the same money?" the President asked.

"I got it from Smerdyakov, from the murderer, yesterday. . . . I was with him just before he hung himself. It was he, not my brother, who killed our father. He murdered him and I led him on to do it. . . . Who doesn't desire his father's death?"

"Are you in your right mind?" broke involuntarily from the President.

"I think I am in my right mind . . . In the same evil mind as all of you . . . as all these . . . ugly faces." He turned suddenly to the crowd. "My father has been murdered and they pretend they are horrified," he snarled. "They keep up the fraud with one another. Liars! They all desire the death of their fathers. One reptile devours another. . . . If there hadn't been a murder, they'd have been angry and gone home disappointed. It's a spectacle they want! Bread and circuses! Though

I am not one to talk! Have you any water? Give me a drink for Christ's sake!" He suddenly clutched his head.

The usher approached him. Alyosha jumped up and cried: "He is ill. Don't believe him: he has brain fever." Katerina rose from her seat and, rigid with horror, gazed at Ivan. Dmitri stood up and looked at his brother and listened to him with a wild, strange smile.

"Don't disturb yourselves. I am not mad, I am only a murderer," Ivan began again. "You can't expect eloquence from a murderer," he added suddenly for some reason and laughed a queer laugh.

The prosecutor bent over to the President obviously troubled. The two other judges spoke to each other in whispers. Fetyukovitch listened. The hall was hushed in expectation. The President seemed suddenly to recollect himself.

"Witness, your words are incomprehensible and not acceptable. Calm yourself, if you can, and tell your story . . . if you really have something to tell. How can you confirm your statement . . . if you are not delirious?"

"That's just it. I have no proof. That cur Smerdyakov won't send you proofs from the other world . . . in an envelope. You think of nothing but envelopes—one is enough. I've not witnesses . . . except one, perhaps," he smiled thoughtfully.

"Who is your witness?"

"He has a tail, your excellency, and that would be irregular! The devil does not exist! Don't pay attention; he is a paltry, pitiful devil," he added suddenly. He stopped laughing and spoke, as it were, confidentially. "He is here somewhere—under that table with the material evidence on it, perhaps. Where should he sit if not there? You see, listen to me. I told him I don't want to keep quiet, and he talked about the geological cataclysm . . . Idiocy! Come, release the monster . . . He's been singing a hymn. That's because his heart is light! It's like a drunken man in the street bawling how 'Vanka went to Petersburg,' and I would give a quadrillion quadrillions for two seconds of joy. You don't know me! Oh, how stupid all this business is! Come, take me instead of him! I didn't come for nothing. . . . Why, why is everything so stupid? . . ."

And he began slowly, and as it were reflectively, looking around him again. The court was all excited by then. Alyosha rushed toward him, but the court usher had already seized Ivan by the arm.

"What are you doing?" he cried, staring into the man's face. Then suddenly grabbing him by the shoulders, he flung him to the floor. But the police were on the spot and he was seized. He screamed furiously. And all the time he was being removed, he yelled and screamed something incoherent.

The whole court was thrown into confusion. I don't remember everything as it happened. I was excited myself and could not follow everything. I only know that afterwards, when everything was quiet again and everyone understood what had happened, the court usher was reprimanded although he very reasonably explained that the witness had been quite well, that the doctor had seen him an hour before when he had a slight attack of dizziness, and that, until he had come into the court, he had talked quite consecutively, so that nothing could have been foreseen—that he had, in fact, insisted on testifying.

But before everyone had completely recovered from this scene, it was followed by another. Katerina became hysterical. She cried, shrieking loudly, but refused to leave the court, struggled, and begged them not to remove her.

Suddenly she cried to the President: "There is more evidence I must give at once . . . at once! Here is a paper, a letter . . . Take it, read it quickly, quickly! It's a letter from that monster . . . that man there, there!" She pointed to Dmitri. "It was he who killed his father, you will see that now. He wrote me how he would kill his father! But the other one is ill, he is ill, he is delirious!" she kept crying out.

The court usher took the letter to the President. And Katerina, dropping into her chair, hiding her face in her hands, began convulsively and noiselessly sobbing, shaking all over, and stifling every sound for fear she would be removed from the court. The letter she had handed up was the one Dmitri had written at the "Metropolis" tavern, which Ivan had spoken of as a "mathematical proof." Alas! Its mathetmatical conclusiveness was recognized. Had it not been for that letter, Dmitri might have escaped his doom or, at least, that doom would have been less terrible. It was, I repeat, difficult to notice every detail. What followed is still confused to my mind. The President must, I suppose, have at once passed on the letter to the judges, the jury, and the lawyers on both sides. I only remember how they began examining the witness.

On being asked by the President whether she had recovered sufficiently, Katerina said impetuously: "I am ready, I am ready! I am equal to answering you," she added, evidently still afraid that she would somehow be prevented from giving evidence. She was asked to explain in detail what the letter was and under what circumstances she had received it.

"I received it the day before the murder was committed, but he wrote it the day before that, at the tavern—that is, two days before he committed the crime. Look, it is written on some sort of bill!" she cried breathlessly. "He hated me at the time, because he had behaved so badly and was running after that creature . . . And because he owed me three thousand. . . . Oh, he was humiliated by that three thousand because of his own meanness! This is how it happened about that three thousand. I beg you, I beseech you, to listen to me. Three weeks before he murdered his father, he came to me one morning. I knew he needed money, and what he wanted it for. Yes, yes—to win over that creature and carry her off. I knew then that he had been false to me and meant to abandon me, and it was I, I, who gave him that money, who offered it to him on the pretext of his sending it to my sister in Moscow. And as I gave it to him, I looked him in the face and said that he could send it when he liked, 'in a month's time would do.' How, how could he have failed to understand that I was practically telling him to his face: 'You want money to be false to me with that creature, so here it is. I give it to you myself. Take it, if you have so little honor as to take it!' I wanted to prove what he was . . . And what happened? He took it, he took it, and squandered it with that creature in one night. . . . But he knew, he knew that I knew all about it. I assure you he understood, too, that I only gave him that money to test him, to see whether he was so devoid of honor as to take it from me. I looked into his eyes and he looked into mine, and he understood it all and he took it—he took my money!"

"That's true, Katerina," Dmitri roared suddenly, "I looked into your eyes and I knew that you were dishonoring me, and yet I took your money. Despise me. Despise me, all of you! I deserve it!"

"Prisoner," cried the President. "Another word and I will order you to be removed."

"That money was a torment to him," Katerina went on hurriedly. "He wanted to repay it. He wanted to, that's true; but he needed money for that creature, too. So he murdered his father. But he didn't repay me. He went off with her to that village where he was arrested. There he squandered the money he had stolen after murdering his father. And a day before the murder he wrote me this letter. He was drunk when he wrote it. I recognized that at once, at the time. He wrote it from spite. He was certain that I would never show it to anyone, even if he did kill him, or else he wouldn't have written it. He knew I wouldn't want to revenge myself and ruin him! But read it, read it, please, and you will see that he described it all in his letter, all beforehand, how he would kill his father and where his money was kept. Look, please, don't overlook that, there's one phrase there: 'I will kill him as soon as Ivan has gone away.' So he thought it all out beforehand how he would kill him," Katerina pointed out to the court with venomous and malignant triumph. Oh, it was clear she had studied every line of that letter and detected every meaning in it. "If he hadn't been drunk, he wouldn't have written to me. But, look, everything was written there beforehand, just as he later committed the murder. A complete program of it!" she exclaimed frantically.

She was heedless now of all consequences to herself. A month ago she had probably foreseen what would happen; she had probably debated whether or not to show Dmitri's letter at the trial. Now she had taken the fatal plunge. I remember that the letter was read aloud by the clerk, directly afterward.

It made an overwhelming impression. They asked Dmitri whether he admitted having written the letter.

"It's mine, mine!" cried Dmitri. "I wouldn't have written it if I hadn't been drunk! . . . We've hated each other for many things, Katerina, but I swear, I swear I loved you even while I hated you, and you didn't love me!"

He sank back on his chair, wringing his hands in despair. The prosecutor and counsel for the defense began cross-examining Katerina to find out why she had concealed such a document and previously given evidence of quite a different tone and spirit.

"Yes, yes. I was telling lies. I was lying against my honor and my conscience, but I wanted to save him, for he has hated and despised me so!" Katerina cried madly. "Oh, he has despised me, he has always despised me. He has despised me from the very moment that I bowed down to him for that money. I know that. . . . I felt it at the time, but for a long while I wouldn't believe it. How often I have read it in his eyes 'you came of yourself, though.' Oh, he didn't understand, he had no idea why I ran to him . . . He can suspect nothing but baseness. He judged me by himself, he thought everyone was like him!" Katerina cried furiously. "And he only wanted to marry me because I inherited a fortune, because of that, because of that! I always suspected it was because of that! Oh, he is a brute! He was convinced that I would tremble with shame all my life because I went to him then. He felt that he had a right to despise me forever for it, and be superior to me—that's why he wanted to marry me! That's true, that's all true! I tried to conquer him with love—a love that knew no bounds. I even tried to forgive his faithlessness. But he understood nothing, nothing! How could he understand? He is a monster! I only received his letter the next evening: it was brought to me from the tavern—and only that morning, only that morning I wanted to forgive him everything, everything—even his treachery!"

The President and the prosecutor tried to calm her. I can't help thinking that they felt ashamed of taking advantage of her hysteria and of listening to such confessions. I remember hearing them say to her: "We understand how hard it is for you; we feel for you," and so on, and so on. And yet piece by piece they dragged the evidence out of her, raving, hysterical as she was. She described at last with extraordinary clearness, which is so often seen, though only for a moment, in such overwrought states, how Ivan had been nearly driven out of his mind during the last two months trying to save "the monster and murderer," his brother.

"He tortured himself," she exclaimed. "He was always trying to minimize his brother's guilt and confessing to me that he, too, had never loved his father, and had perhaps also desired his death. He has a tender, over-tender conscience! He tormented himself with his conscience! He told me everything,

625

everything! He came every day and talked to me as his only friend. I have the honor to be his only friend!" she cried suddenly with a sort of defiance and her eyes flashed. "He went twice to see Smerdyakov. One day he came to me and said: 'If it was not my brother, but Smerdyakov who committed the murder (for the rumor was circulating everywhere that Smerdyakov had done it), perhaps I too am guilty because Smerdyakov knew I didn't like my father and perhaps believed that I desired my father's death.' Then I brought out Dmitri's letter and showed it to him. After that he was convinced that his brother had done it, and he was overwhelmed by it. He couldn't bear the thought that Dmitri was a parricide! Only a week ago I saw that it was making him ill. During the last few days he has talked incoherently. I saw his mind was giving way. He walked about, raving: he was seen muttering in the streets. The doctor from Moscow, at my request, examined him the day before yesterday and told me that he was on the eve of brain fever—and all because of Dmitri, because of that monster! And last night he learned that Smerdyakov was dead! It was such a shock that it drove him out of his mind . . . And all because of this monster, all for the sake of saving the monster!"

Oh, of course, such an outpouring, such a confession is only possible once in a lifetime—at the hour of death, for instance, on the way to the scaffold! But it was in Katerina's character, and it was such a moment in her life. It was the same impetuous Katerina who had thrown herself on the mercy of a young rake to save her father; the same Katerina who had just before, in her pride and chastity, sacrificed herself and her modesty before all these people, telling of Dmitri's generous conduct, in the hope of softening his fate. And now, again, she sacrificed herself; but this time it was for another person. Only now perhaps did she feel and know how dear that other was to her! She had sacrificed herself in terror for him, conceiving all of a sudden that he had ruined himself by his confession that it was he who had committed the murder, not his brother Dmitri. She had sacrificed herself to save him, to save his name, his reputation!

And yet a terrible doubt occurred—was she lying about her former relations with Dmitri?—that was the question. No, she had not intentionally slandered him when she cried out that he despised her for her bowing down to him! She believed it herself. She had been firmly convinced, perhaps ever since that bow, that the simple-hearted Dmitri, who even then adored her, was laughing at her and despising her. She had loved him with an hysterical, "lacerated" love only from pride, from wounded pride, and that love was not like love, but more like revenge. Oh! perhaps that lacerated love would have grown into real love. Perhaps Katerina longed for nothing more than that, but Dmitri's faithlessness had wounded her to the bottom of her heart, and her heart could not forgive him. The moment of revenge had come upon her suddenly, and everything that had been accumulating so long and so painfully in her offended heart burst out unexpectedly. She betrayed Dmitri, but she betrayed herself, too. And no sooner had she given full expression to her feelings than she was overwhelmed with shame. She became hysterical again. She fell on the floor, sobbing and screaming. She was carried out.

At that moment Grushenka rushed toward Dmitri before they had time to prevent her.

"Dmitri," she wailed. "Your serpent has destroyed you!" She turned to the judges and shouted: "There, she has shown you what she is!"

At a signal from the President they seized her and tried to remove her from the court. She wouldn't allow it. She fought and struggled to get back to Dmitri. Dmitri cried out and struggled to get to her. He was overpowered.

Yes, I think the ladies who came to see the spectacle must have been satisfied—the show had been a varied one. Then I remember the Moscow doctor appeared on the scene. I believe the President had sent the court usher to arrange for medical aid for Ivan. The doctor announced to the court that the sick man was suffering from a dangerous attack of brain fever and that he must be removed at once. In answer to questions from the prosecutor and the lawyer for the defense he said that the patient had come to him of his own accord the day before yesterday and that he had warned him that he had such an attack coming on, but he had not consented to treatment. "He was certainly not in a normal state of mind. He told me himself that he saw visions, that he met several persons in the street who were dead, and that the Devil visited him every evening," said the doctor, in conclusion. Having given his evidence, the celebrated doctor withdrew.

The letter produced by Katerina was added to the material proofs. After some deliberation, the judges decided to proceed with the trial and to enter into the record both the unexpected pieces of evidence given by Ivan and Katerina.

I will not detail the evidence of the other witnesses, who only repeated and confirmed what had already been said. I repeat, all was brought together in the prosecutor's speech, which I will quote immediately. Everyone was excited, everyone was electrified by the unexpected developments. And all were awaiting the speeches for the prosecution and the defense with intense impatience. Fetyukovitch was obviously shaken by Katerina's evidence. But the prosecutor was triumphant. When all the evidence had been taken, the court was adjourned for almost an hour. I believe it was just eight o'clock when the President returned to his seat and our prosecutor, Ippolit Kirillovitch, began his speech.

6. *The Prosecutor's Speech.*
Sketches of Character

IPPOLIT KIRILLOVITCH BEGAN HIS SPEECH, trembling with nervousness, with cold sweat on his forehead, feeling hot and cold all over by turns. He described this himself afterwards. He regarded this speech as his masterpiece, the masterpiece of his whole life, as his swan song. He died, as a matter of fact, nine months later of rapid consumption, so that he had the right, as it turned out, to compare himself to a swan singing his last song. He had put his whole heart and ability into that speech. And he unexpectedly revealed that at least some feeling for the public welfare and "the eternal question" lay concealed in him. Where his speech really excelled was in its sincerity. He genuinely believed in the prisoner's guilt; he was accusing him not as an official duty only. And in calling for vengeance he quivered with a genuine passion "for the security of society." Even the ladies in the audience, though they remained hostile to Ippolit Kirillovitch, admitted that he made an extraordinary impression. He began in a breaking voice, but it soon gained strength and filled the court to the end of his speech. But as soon as he had finished, he almost fainted.

"Gentlemen of the jury," he began, "this case has made a stir throughout Russia. But what is there to wonder at, what is there so peculiarly horrifying in it for us? We are accustomed to such crimes! That's what's so horrible, that such dark deeds have ceased to horrify us. What ought to horrify us is that we are so accustomed to it, and not this or that isolated crime. What are the causes of our indifference, our lukewarm attitude to such deeds, to such symptoms of the times, ominous of an unenviable future? Is it our cynicism, is it the premature exhaustion of intellect and imagination in a society that is sinking into decay, in spite of its youth? Is it that our moral principles are shattered to their foundations, or is it, perhaps, a complete lack of such principles among us? I cannot answer such questions; nevertheless they are disturbing, and every citizen not only must, but ought to be harassed by them. Our newborn and still timid press has already done good service to the public, for without it we would never have heard of the horrors of unbridled violence and moral degradation which are continually made known to those who attend the new jury courts established in the present reign. And what do we read almost daily? Of things beside which the present case grows pale, and seems almost commonplace. But what is most important is that the majority of our national crimes of violence bear witness to a widespread evil, now so general among us that it is difficult to contend against it.

"One day we hear of a brilliant young officer, at the very outset of his career, in a cowardly way without a pang of conscience, murdering a servant girl and an official who had once been his benefactor. He does this in order to steal his own IOU and what ready money he could find on the official. 'It will come in handy for my pleasures and for my career in the future.' After murdering them, he puts pillows under the head of each of his victims; he goes away. Next we hear about a young hero 'decorated for bravery' who kills the mother of his chief and benefactor. To urge his companions to join him he says that 'she loves him like a son, and so will follow all his directions and take no precautions.' Granted that he is a monster, yet I dare not say in these days that he is unique. Another man will not commit the murder, but will feel and think like him, and is as dishonorable in soul. In silence, alone with his conscience, he asks himself perhaps: 'What is honor, and isn't the condemnation of bloodshed a prejudice?'

"Perhaps people will cry out against me that I am morbid, hysterical, that it is a monstrous slander, that I am exaggerating. Let them say so! I would be the first to rejoice if it were so! Oh, don't believe me, think of me as morbid, but remember my words; if only a tenth, if only a twentieth part of what I say is true—even so it's awful! Look how our young people commit suicide, without asking themselves Hamlet's question what there is beyond, without a sign of such a question. They act as though all that relates to the soul and to what awaits us beyond the grave had long been erased in their minds and buried under the sands. Look at our vice, at our degenerates. Fyodor Karamazov, the luckless victim in the present case, was almost an innocent babe compared with many of them. And yet we all knew him, 'he lived among us!' . . .

"Yes, one day perhaps the leading intellects of Russia and of Europe will study the psychology of Russian crime, for the subject is worth it. But this study will come later, at leisure, when all the tragic topsy-turvy of today is behind us, so that it will be possible to examine it with more insight and more impartiality than we can do now. Now we are either horrified or pretend to be horrified, though we really gloat over the spectacle, and love strong and eccentric sensations which tickle our cynical, pampered idleness. Or, like little children, we brush the dreadful ghosts away and hide our heads in the pillow so as to return to our sports and pleasures as soon as they have vanished. But we must one day begin life in earnest, we must look at ourselves as a society; it's time we tried to grasp something of our social position, or at least to make a beginning in that direction.

"Gogel, a great writer of the last epoch, comparing Russia to a swift troika galloping to an unknown goal, exclaims: 'Oh, troika, birdlike troika, who invented thee!' And he adds, in proud ecstasy, that all the peoples of the world stand aside respectfully to make way for the recklessly galloping troika. That may be, they may stand aside, respectfully or no, but in my opinion the great writer ended his book in this way either in an access of childish and naive optimism, or simply in fear of the censorship of the day. For if the troika were drawn by his heroes, Sobakevitch, Nozdryov, Tchitchikov, it could reach no rational goal, whoever might be driving it. And those were the heroes of an older generation, ours are worse specimens still . . ."

At this point Ippolit Kirillovitch's speech was interrupted by applause. The liberal significance of this simile was appreciated. The applause was brief, it's true, so that the President did not think it necessary to caution the public, and only looked severely in the direction of the offenders. But Ippolit Kirillovitch was encouraged; he had never been applauded before. He had been all his life unable to get a hearing, and now he suddenly had an opportunity of securing the ear of all Russia.

"What, after all, is this Karamazov family, which has gained such an unenviable notoriety throughout Russia?" he continued. "Perhaps I am exaggerating, but it seems to me that certain fundamental features of the educated class of today are reflected in this family picture—only, of course, in miniature, 'like the sun in a drop of water.' Think of that unhappy, vicious, unbridled old man, who has met with such a tragic end, the head of a family! Beginning life of noble birth, but in a poor dependent position, through an unexpected marriage he came into a small fortune. A low person, a toady and buffoon, of fairly good though undeveloped intelligence, he was above all, a moneylender who grew bolder with growing prosperity. His abject and servile characteristics disappeared, his malicious and sarcastic cynicism was all that remained. On the spiritual side he was undeveloped, while his vitality was excessive. He saw nothing in life but sensual pleasure. He had no feelings for his duties as a father. He ridiculed those duties. He left his little children to the servants, and was glad to be rid of them, forgot about them completely. The old man's maxim was 'after me the deluge.' He was an example of everything that is opposed to civic duty, of the most complete and malignant individualism: 'The world may burn for all I care, so long as I am all right.' And he was all right; he was content, he was eager to go on living in the same way for another twenty or thirty years. He swindled his own son and spent his money, his maternal inheritance, on trying to get his mistress away from him. No, I don't intend to leave the prisoner's defense altogether to my talented colleague from Petersburg. I will speak the truth myself. I can well understand what resentment he had heaped up in his son's heart against him.

"But enough, enough of that unhappy old man; he has paid

630

the penalty. Let us remember, however, that he was a father, and one of the typical fathers of today. Am I unjust in saying that he is typical of many modern fathers? Alas! Many of them only differ in not openly professing such cynicism, for they are better educated, more cultured, but their philosophy is essentially the same as his. Perhaps I am a pessimist, but you have agreed to forgive me. Let us agree beforehand, you need not believe me, but let me speak. Let me say what I have to say, and remember something of my words.

"Now for the children of this father, this head of a family. One of them is the prisoner before us, all the rest of my speech will deal with him. Of the other two I will speak only briefly.

"The elder is one of those modern young men of education and intellect who has lost faith in everything. He has denied and rejected much already, like his father. We have all heard him, he was a welcome guest in local society. He never concealed his opinions, quite the contrary in fact, which justifies me in speaking rather openly of him now, of course, not as an individual, but as a member of the Karamazov family. Another person closely connected with the case died here by his own hand last night. I mean an afflicted idiot, formerly the servant, and possibly the illegitimate son of Fyodor Karamazov, Smerdyakov. At the preliminary inquiry, he told me with hysterical tears how the young Ivan Karamazov had horrified him by his spiritual audacity. 'Everything in the world is lawful according to him, and nothing must be forbidden in the future—that is what he always taught me.' I believe that idiot was driven out of his mind by this theory, though, of course, the epileptic attacks from which he suffered, and this terrible murder helped to unhinge his faculties. But he made one very interesting observation, which would have done credit to a more intelligent observer, and that is why I mention it: 'If there is one of the sons that is like Fyodor Karamazov in character, it is Ivan.'

"With that remark I conclude my sketch of his character, feeling it indelicate to continue. Oh, I don't want to draw any further conclusions and croak like a raven over the young man's future. We've seen today in this court that there are still good impulses in his young heart, that family feeling has not been destroyed in him by lack of faith and cynicism, which has come to him rather by inheritance than by independent thinking.

"Then the third son. Oh, he is a devout and modest youth, who does not share his elder brother's gloomy and destructive theory of life. He has sought to cling to the 'ideas of the people,' or to what goes by that name in some circles of our intellectual classes. He clung to the monastery, and was within an ace of becoming a monk. He seems to me to have betrayed unconsciously that timid despair which leads so many in our unhappy society, who dread cynicism and its corrupting influences and mistakenly attribute all the trouble to European

631

enlightenment, to return to their 'native soil,' to the bosom, so to speak, of their mother earth. Like frightened children, they yearn to fall asleep on the withered bosom of their decrepit mother; to sleep there forever in order to escape the horrors that terrify them.

"For my part I wish the young man every success. I trust that his youthful idealism and impulse toward the ideas of the people may never degenerate, as often happens, on the moral side into gloomy mysticism, and on the political into blind Chauvinism. These two elements are even a greater menace to Russia than the premature decay, due to misunderstanding and gratuitous adoption of European ideas, from which his elder brother is suffering."

Two or three people clapped at the mention of Chauvinism and mysticism. Ippolit Kirillovitch had been, indeed, carried away by his own eloquence. All this had little to do with the case in hand, to say nothing of the fact of its being somewhat vague, but the sickly and consumptive man was overcome by the desire to express himself once in his life. People said afterwards that he was prompted by unworthy motives in his criticism of Ivan, because Ivan had on one or two occasions got the better of him in arguments. They said he was now taking revenge. But I don't know whether it was true. All this was only introductory, however, and the speech passed to more direct consideration of the case.

"But to return to the eldest son," Ippolit Kirillovitch went on. "He is the prisoner before us. We have his life and his actions, too, before us; the fatal day has come and all has been brought to the surface. While his brothers seem to stand for 'Europeanism' and 'the principles of the people,' he seems to represent Russia *as she is*. Oh, not all Russia, not all! God preserve us, if it were! Yet, here we have her, our mother Russia, the very scent and sound of her. Oh, he is spontaneous, he is a marvelous mingling of good and evil, he is a lover of culture and Schiller, yet he brawls in taverns and plucks out the beards of his boon companions. Oh, he, too, can be good and noble, but only when all goes well with him. What is more, he can be carried off his feet, positively carried off his feet by noble ideals, but only if they come of themselves, if they fall from heaven for him, if they need not be paid for. He dislikes paying for anything, but is very fond of receiving, and that's so with him in everything. Oh, give him every possible good in life (he couldn't be content with less), and put no obstacle in his way, and he will show that he, too, can be noble. He is not greedy, no, but he must have money, a great deal of money, and you will see how generously, with what scorn, he will fling it all away in the reckless dissipation of one night. But if he has no money, he will show what he is ready to do to get it when he is in great need of it. But all this later, let us take events in their chronological order.

632

"First, we have before us a poor abandoned child, running about the back yard 'without boots on his feet,' as our worthy and esteemed fellow citizen, of foreign origin, alas, expressed it just now. I repeat it again, I yield to no one the defense of the criminal. I am here to accuse him, but to defend him also. Yes, I too am human. I too can weigh the influence of home and childhood on the character. But the boy grows up and becomes an officer; for a duel and other reckless conduct he is exiled to one of the remote frontier towns of Russia. There he led a wild life. And, of course, he needed money, money above all things. And so after prolonged disputes he came to a settlement with his father, and the last six thousand was sent to him. A letter is in existence in which he practically gives up his claim to the rest and settles his conflict with his father over his inheritance on the payment of this six thousand roubles.

"Then came his meeting with a young girl of fine character and education. Oh, I do not venture to repeat the details; you have only just heard them. Honor, self-sacrifice were shown there, and I will be silent. The figure of the young officer, reckless and dissolute, doing homage to true nobility and a lofty ideal, was shown to us in a very sympathetic light. But the other side of the medal was unexpectedly turned to us immediately after in this very court. Again I will not venture to conjecture why it happened so, but there were causes. The same lady, bathed in tears of long-concealed indignation, alleged that he, he of all men, had despised her for her act, which, though incautious, reckless perhaps, was still dictated by noble and generous motives. He, he, the girl's fiancé, looked at her with that smile of mockery, which was more insufferable from him than from anyone else. And knowing that he had already deceived her (he had deceived her, believing that she was bound to endure everything from him, even treachery), she intentionally offered him three thousand roubles, and clearly, too clearly, let him understand that she was offering him money to deceive her. 'Well, will you take it or not, are you so lost to shame?' was the dumb question in her scrutinizing eyes. He looked at her, saw clearly what was in her mind (he's admitted here before you that he understood it all), appropriated that three thousand unconditionally, and squandered it in two days with the new object of his affections.

"What are we then to believe? The first story of the young officer sacrificing his last cent in a noble impulse of generosity and doing reverence to virtue: or this other revolting picture? As a rule, between two extremes one has to find the mean, but in the present case this is not true. The probability is that in the first case he was genuinely noble, and in the second genuinely base. And why? Because he was of the broad Karamazov character—that's just what I am leading up to—capable of combining the most incongruous contradictions, and capable of the greatest heights and of the greatest depths. Remember the brilliant remark made by a young observer who has seen the Karamazov family at close quarters—Mr. Rakitin: 'The sense of their own degradation is as essential to these reckless, unbridled natures as the sense of their generosity.' And that's true, they need continually this unnatural mixture. Two extremes at the same moment, or they are miserable and dissatisfied and their existence is incomplete. They are wide, wide as mother Russia; they include everything and put up with everything.

"By the way, gentlemen of the jury, we've just touched upon that three thousand roubles, and I will venture to anticipate things a little. Can you conceive that a man like this, on receiving that sum and in such a way, at the price of such shame, such disgrace, such utter degradation, could have been capable that very day of setting apart half that sum, that very day, and sewing it up in a little bag? And can you believe that he would have had the firmness of character to carry it about with him for a whole month afterwards, in spite of every temptation and in spite of his extreme need! Neither drunk in taverns, nor when traveling into the country to get from God knows whom, the money so essential to him to remove the object of his affections from being tempted by his father, did he bring himself to touch that little bag! Why, he would have been certain to have opened that bag! He would have opened it if only to avoid abandoning his mistress to the rival of whom he was so jealous! He would have opened it in order to be able to stay at home to keep watch over her, and to await the moment when she would say to him at last 'I am yours,' and to fly with her far from their fatal surroundings.

"But no, he did not touch the money in the little bag. And what is the reason he gives? The chief reason, as I have just said, was that when she would say 'I am yours, take me where you will,' he might have the wherewithal to take her. But that first reason, in the prisoner's own words, was of little weight beside the second. While I have that money on me, he said, I am a scoundrel, not a thief. I can always go to my insulted fiancée and laying down half the sum I have fraudulently appropriated, I can always say to her: 'You see I've squandered half your money, and shown I am a weak and immoral man, and, if you like, a scoundrel' (I use the prisoner's own expressions), 'but though I am a scoundrel, I am not a thief, for if I were a thief, I wouldn't have brought back this half of the money, but would have taken it as I did the other half!' A marvelous explanation! This frantic but weak man, who could not resist the temptation of accepting the three thousand roubles at the price of such disgrace, this very man suddenly develops the most stoical firmness, and carries about fifteen hundred roubles without daring to touch them. Does that fit in at all with the character we have analyzed? No, and I will venture to tell you how the real Dmitri Karamazov would have behaved

634

in such circumstances, if he really had put away the money.

"At the first temptation—for instance, to entertain the woman with whom he had already squandered half the money —he would have unpicked his little bag and have taken out some hundred roubles. For why should he have taken back precisely half the money, that is, fifteen hundred roubles; why not fourteen hundred? He could just as well have said then that he was not a thief, because he brought back fourteen hundred roubles. Then another time he would have unpicked it again and taken out another hundred, and then a third, and then a fourth. And before the end of the month he would have taken the last note but one, feeling that if he took back only a hundred it would answer the purpose, for a thief would have stolen it all. And then he would have looked at this last note, and have said to himself: 'It's really not worth while to give back one hundred; let's spend that, too!' That's how the real Dmitri Karamazov, as we know him, would have behaved. One cannot imagine anything more incongruous than this story of the little bag. Nothing could be more inconceivable. But we shall return to that later."

After touching upon what had come out in the trial concerning the financial relations of father and son, and arguing again and again that it was utterly impossible, from the facts known, to determine which was in the wrong, Ippolit Kirillovitch passed to the evidence of the medical experts in reference to Dmitri's fixed idea about the three thousand owing him.

7. An Historical Survey

"THE MEDICAL EXPERTS have tried to convince us that the prisoner is out of his mind and, in fact, a maniac. I maintain that he is in his right mind, and that if he had not been, he would have behaved more cleverly. As for his being a maniac, that I would agree with, but only in one point, that is, his fixed idea about the three thousand. Yet I think one might find a much simpler cause than his tendency to insanity. For my part I agree thoroughly with the young doctor who maintained that the prisoner's mental faculties have always been normal, and that he has only been irritable and exasperated. The object of the prisoner's continual and violent anger was not the sum itself; there was a special motive at the bottom of it. That motive was jealousy!"

Here Ippolit Kirillovitch described at length the prisoner's passion for Grushenka. He began from the moment when the prisoner went to the "young person's" lodgings "to beat her." "I use his own expression," the prosecutor explained. "But instead of beating her, he remained there, at her feet. That was the beginning of the passion. At the same time the prisoner's father was captivated by the same young person—a strange and fatal coincidence, for they both lost their hearts to her simultaneously, though both had known her before. And she inspired in both of them the most violent, characteristically Karamazov passion. We have her own confession: 'I was laughing at both of them.' Yes, the sudden desire to make jest of them came over her, and she conquered both of them at once. The old man, who worshiped money, at once set aside three thousand roubles as a reward for one visit from her. But soon after that, he would have been happy to lay his property and his name at her feet, if only she would become his lawful wife. We have proof of this. As for the prisoner, the tragedy of his fate is evident; it is before us. But such was the young person's 'game.' The enchantress gave the unhappy young man no hope until the last moment, when he knelt before her, stretching out hands that were already stained with the blood of his father and rival. It was in that position that he was arrested. 'Send me to Siberia with him. I have brought him to this, I am most to blame,' the woman herself cried, in genuine remorse at the moment of his arrest.

"The talented young man, to whom I have referred already, Mr. Rakitin, characterized this heroine in brief and impressive terms: 'She was disillusioned early in life, deceived and ruined by a man who seduced and abandoned her. She was left in poverty, cursed by her respectable family, and taken under the protection of a wealthy old man, whom she still, however, considers as her benefactor. There was perhaps much that was good in her young heart, but it was embittered too early. She became prudent and saved money. She grew sarcastic and resentful against society.' After this sketch of her character it may well be understood that she might laugh at both of them simply from bitterness, from malice.

"After a month of hopeless love and moral degradation, during which he betrayed his fiancée and appropriated money entrusted to his honor, the prisoner was driven almost to frenzy, almost to madness by continual jealousy—and of whom? His father! And the worst of it was that the crazy old man was alluring and enticing the object of his affection by means of that very three thousand roubles, which the son looked upon as his own property, part of his inheritance from his mother, of which his father was cheating him. Yes, I admit it was hard to bear! It might well drive a man to madness. It was not the money, but the fact that this money was used with such revolting cynicism to ruin his happiness!"

Then the prosecutor went on to describe how the idea of murdering his father had entered the prisoner's head, and illustrated his theory with facts.

"At first he only talked about it in taverns—he was talking about it all that month. Ah, he likes being always surrounded

636

with company, and he likes to tell his companions everything, even his most diabolical and dangerous ideas. He likes to share every thought with others, and expects, for some reason, that those he confides in will meet him with perfect sympathy, enter into all his troubles and anxieties, take his part and not oppose him in anything. If not, he flies into a rage and smashes up everything in the tavern. Then came the incident with Captain Snegiryov. Those who heard the prisoner began to think at last that he might mean more than threats, and that such a frenzy might turn threats into actions."

Here the prosecutor described the meeting of the family at the monastery, the conversations with Alyosha, and the horrible scene when the prisoner had rushed into his father's house just after dinner.

"I cannot positively assert," the prosecutor continued, "that the prisoner fully intended to murder his father before that incident. Yet the idea had several times presented itself to him, and he had deliberated on it—for that we have facts, witnesses, and his own words. I confess, gentlemen of the jury," he added, "that until today I have been uncertain whether to attribute to the prisoner premeditaton of the crime. I was firmly convinced that he had pictured the fatal moment beforehand, but had only pictured it, contemplating it as a possibility. He had not definitely considered when and how he might commit the crime.

"But I was only uncertain until today, until that fatal letter was presented to the court. You yourselves heard that young lady's exclamation: 'it is the plan, the program of the murder!' That is how she defined that miserable, drunken letter written by the unhappy prisoner. And from that letter we see that the whole murder was premeditated. It was written two days before, and so we know now for a fact that, forty-eight hours before the perpetration of his terrible deed, the prisoner swore that, if he could not get money the next day, he would murder his father in order to take the envelope with the notes from under his pillow, as soon as Ivan had left. 'As soon as Ivan had gone away'—you hear that; so he had thought everything out, weighing every circumstance, and he carried it all out just as he had written it. The proof of premeditation is conclusive; the crime must have been committed for the sake of the money, that it stated clearly, that is written and signed. The prisoner does not deny his signature.

"I shall be told that he was drunk when he wrote it. But that does not diminish the value of the letter, quite the contrary; he wrote when drunk what he had planned when sober. Had he not planned it when sober, he would not have written it when drunk. I shall be asked: Then why did he talk about it in taverns? A man who premeditates such a crime is silent and keeps it to himself. Yes, but he talked about it before he had drawn up a plan, when he had only the desire, only the impulse. Afterward he talked less about it. On the evening he wrote that letter at the 'Metropolis' tavern, contrary to his usual manner he was silent, though he had been drinking. He did not play billiards, he sat in a corner, talked to no one. He did turn a workingman out of his seat, but that was done almost unconsciously, because he could never go into a tavern without making a disturbance. It is true that after he had taken the final decision, he must have felt apprehensive that he had talked too much about his plan beforehand, and that this might lead to his arrest and prosecution afterwards. But there was nothing he could do about it; he could not take his words back. But his luck had served him before, it would serve him again. He believed in his lucky star, you know! I must confess, too, that he did a great deal to avoid the crime. 'Tomorrow I will try and borrow the money from everyone,' as he writes in his peculiar language. 'And if they won't give it to me, there will be bloodshed.' "

Here Ippolit Kirillovitch passed to a detailed description of all Dmitri's efforts to borrow the money. He described Dmitri's visit to Samsonov, his journey into the country to see a man about the woodland, a man whose real name was Lyagavy (Setter-dog) but who preferred to be called Gorstkin. "Harassed, jeered at, hungry, after selling his watch to pay for the journey (though he tells us he had fifteen hundred roubles on him!), tortured by jealousy at having left the object of his affections in town, suspecting that she would go to his father, Fyodor Karamazov, in his absence, he returned at last to town to find to his joy that she had not been near his father. He walked with her himself to her protector. (Strange to say, he doesn't seem to have been jealous of Samsonov, which is psychologically interesting.) Then he hurries back to his ambush in the neighbor's garden, and learns that Smerdyakov has had a fit, that the other servant is ill—the coast is clear and he knows the 'signals'—what a temptation! Still he resists it. He goes off to a lady who has for some time been staying in town, and who is highly regarded among us, Madame Hohlakov. That lady, who has long watched him with compassion gives him the most judicious advice, to give up his dissipated life, his unseemly love affair, the waste of his youth and vigor in pot-house debauchery, and to go to Siberia to the gold mines: 'It would provide an outlet for your turbulent energies, your romantic character, your thirst for adventure.' "

After describing the result of this conversation and the moment when the prisoner learned that Grushenka had not stayed at Samsonov's, and after describing the sudden frenzy of the luckless man, worn out with jealousy and nervous exhaustion at the thought that she had deceived him and was now with his father, Ippolit Kirillovitch concluded by dwelling upon the fatal influence of chance. "Had the maid told him that her mistress was at Mokroe with her former lover, nothing would have happened. But she lost her head, she could only swear and protest her ignorance. And if the prisoner did not kill her on the spot, it was only because he flew in pursuit of his unfaithful mistress.

"But note, frantic as he was, he took with him a brass pestle. Why? Why not some other weapon? But since he had been planning and preparing himself for the crime for a whole month, he would snatch up any weapon that caught his eye. He had realized for a month past that any object of the kind would serve as a weapon, so without hesitation, he recognized that the pestle would serve his purpose. So it was by no means unconsciously, by no means involuntarily, that he snatched up that fatal pestle. And then we find him in his father's garden —the coast is clear, there are no witnesses—darkness and jealousy. The suspicion that she was there, with his father, with his rival, in his arms, and perhaps laughing at him at that moment, possessed him. And it was not mere suspicion, the deception was open, obvious. She must be there, in that lighted room, she must be behind the screen! And the prisoner would have us believe that he stole up to the window, peeped in, and discreetly withdrew, for fear something terrible and immoral might happen. And he tries to persuade us of that, us, who understand his character, who know his state of mind at the moment, and that he knew the secret signals by which he could enter the house."

At this point Ippolit Kirillovitch broke off to discuss the suspected connection of Smerdyakov with the murder. He did this very circumstantially, and everyone realized that, although he claimed to despise that suspicion, he thought the subject of great importance.

8. A Treatise on Smerdyakov

"To BEGIN WITH, what was the source of this suspicion?" Ippolit Kirillovitch began. "The first person who cried out that Smerdyakov had committed the murder was the prisoner himself at the moment of his arrest. Yet from that time to this he has not brought forward a single fact to confirm the charge, nor the faintest suggestion of a fact. The charge is confirmed by three people only—the two brothers of the prisoner and Madame Svyetlov. The elder of these brothers expressed his suspicions only today, when he was undoubtedly suffering from brain fever. But we know that for the last two months he has completely shared our conviction of his brother's guilt and did not try to refute that idea. But of that later. The younger brother has admitted that he has not the slightest fact to support his notion of Smerdyakov's guilt, and has only been led to that conclusion from the prisoner's own words and the expression of his face. Yes, that astounding piece of evidence has been brought forward twice today by him. Madame Svyetlov was even more astounding. 'What the prisoner tells you, you must believe; he is not a man to tell a lie.' That is all the evidence against Smerdyakov produced by these three people, who are all deeply concerned in the prisoner's fate. And yet the theory of Smerdyakov's guilt has been noised about, has been and is still maintained. Is it credible? Is it conceivable?"

Here Ippolit Kirillovitch thought it necessary to describe the personality of Smerdyakov, "who had cut short his life in a fit of insanity." He depicted him as a man of weak intellect, with a smattering of education, who had been thrown off his balance by philosophical ideas above his level and certain modern theories of duty, which he learned in practice from the reckless life of his master, who was also perhaps his father —Fyodor Karamazov. He was also influenced by various strange philosophical conversations with his master's second son, Ivan, who indulged in this diversion from boredom or to amuse himself at the valet's expense. "He spoke to me himself of his spiritual condition during the last few days at his father's house," Ippolit Kirillovitch explained. "But others too have borne witness to it—the prisoner himself, his brother, and the servant Gregory—that is, all who knew him well.

"Moreover, Smerdyakov, whose health was shaken by his attacks of epilepsy, had not the courage of a chicken. 'He fell at my feet and kissed them,' the prisoner himself has told us, before he realized how damaging such a statement was to his case. 'He is an epileptic chicken,' he declared about him in his characteristic way. And the prisoner chose him for his confidant (we have his own word for it) and he frightened him into consenting at last to act as a spy for him. In that capacity he deceived his master, revealing to the prisoner the existence of the envelope with the three thousand roubles in it and the secret signals by means of which he could get into the house. How could he help telling him? 'He would have killed me, I could see that he would have killed me,' he said at the inquiry, trembling and shaking even before us, though his tormentor was by that time arrested and could do him no harm. 'He suspected me at every instant. In fear and trembling I told him every secret to pacify him, so that he might see that I had not deceived him and let me off alive.' Those are his own words. I wrote them down and I remember them. 'When he began shouting at me, I would fall on my knees.'

"Smerdyakov was very honest and enjoyed the complete confidence of his master, ever since he had restored to him some money he had lost. So it may be supposed that the poor fellow suffered pangs of remorse at having deceived his master, whom he loved as his benefactor. People severely afflicted with epilepsy are, so the most skillful doctor tells us, always prone to continual and morbid self-reproach. They worry over their 'wickedness,' they are tormented by pangs of conscience, often entirely without cause; they exaggerate and often invent all sorts of faults and crimes. And here we have a man of that type who had really been driven to wrongdoing by terror and intimidation.

"He had, besides, a strong presentiment that something terrible would result from the situation that was developing before his eyes. When Ivan was leaving for Moscow, just before the murder, Smerdyakov begged him to remain, though he was too timid to tell him openly what he feared. He confined himself to hints, but his hints were not understood.

"It must be observed that he looked on Ivan Karamazov as a protector, whose presence in the house was a guarantee that no harm would come to pass. Remember the phrase in Dmitri Karamazov's drunken letter: 'I shall kill the old man, if only Ivan goes away.' So Ivan Karamazov's presence seemed to everyone a guarantee of peace and order in the house.

"But Ivan Karamazov went away, and within an hour of his young master's departure Smerdyakov was taken with an epileptic fit. But that's perfectly understandable. Here I must mention that Smerdyakov, oppressed by terror and despair of a sort, had felt during those last few days that one of the fits from which he had suffered before at moments of strain, might be coming upon him again. The day and hour of such an attack cannot, of course, be foreseen, but every epileptic can feel beforehand that he is likely to have one. So the doctors tell us. And so, as soon as Ivan Karamazov had driven out of the yard, Smerdyakov, depressed by his lonely and unprotected position, went to the cellar. He went down the stairs wondering if he would have a fit or not, and whether it would come upon him suddenly. And that very apprehension, that very fear, brought on the spasm in his throat that always precedes such attacks, and he fell unconscious into the cellar. And in this perfectly natural occurrence people try to detect a suspicion, a hint that he was shamming an attack *on purpose*. But, if it were on purpose, the question arises at once, what was his motive? What was he counting on? What was he aiming at? I say nothing about medicine; science, I am told, may go astray; the doctors were not able to discriminate between the counterfeit and the real. That may be so, but answer one question: what motive had Smerdyakov for such a counterfeit? Would he, had he been plotting the murder, have wanted to attract the attention of the household by having a fit just then?

"You see, gentlemen of the jury, on the night of the murder, there were five people in Fyodor Karamazov's home: Fyodor Karamazov himself (but he did not kill himself, that's evident); then his servant, Gregory, but he was almost killed himself; the third person was Gregory's wife, Marfa, but it would be simply shameful to imagine her murdering her master. Two people are left—the prisoner and Smerdyakov. But, if we are to believe the prisoner's statement that he is not the murderer, then Smerdyakov must be the murderer, for there is no other alternative, no one else can be found. That is what accounts for the astounding accusation against the unhappy idiot who committed suicide yesterday. Had a shadow of suspicion rested on anyone else, had there been a sixth person, I am certain that even the prisoner would have been ashamed to accuse Smerdyakov, and would have accused that sixth person, for to charge Smerdyakov with that murder is perfectly absurd.

"Gentlemen, let us lay aside psychology, let us lay aside medicine, let us even lay aside logic, let us turn only to the facts and see what the facts tell us. If Smerdyakov killed him, how did he do it? Alone or with the assistance of the prisoner? Let us consider the first alternative—that he did it alone. If he killed him it must have been with some object, for some advantage to himself. But not having a shadow of the motive that the prisoner had for the murder—hatred, jealousy, and so on—Smerdyakov could only have murdered his master for the sake of gain, in order to steal the three thousand roubles he had seen his master put in the envelope. And yet he tells another person—and a person very closely interested, that is, the prisoner—everything about the money and the secret signals, where the envelope lay, what was written on it, what it was tied up with, and, above all, how to rap those signals by which he could enter the house. Did he do this simply to betray himself, or to invite to the same enterprise one who would be anxious to get that envelope for himself? 'Yes,' I shall be told, 'but he betrayed it from fear.' But how do you explain this? A man who could conceive such a crime, and carry it out, tells facts which are known to no one else in the world, and which, if he held his tongue, no one would ever have guessed!

"No, however cowardly Smerdyakov might be, if he had plotted such a crime, nothing would have induced him to tell anyone about the envelope and the signals, because that was as good as betraying himself beforehand. He would have invented a story, he would have told some lie if he had been forced to give information, but he would have been silent about the money and the secret signals. For if he had said nothing about the money but had committed the murder and stolen the money, no one in the world could have charged him with murder for the sake of robbery, since no one but he had seen the money, no one but he knew of its existence. If he had been accused of the murder, one would have thought that he committed it from some other motive. But since no one had observed any such motive in him beforehand, and

642

since everyone knew, on the contrary, that his master was fond of him and honored him with his confidence, he would have been the last to be suspected. People would have suspected first the man who had a motive, the man who had himself declared he had such motives, who had made no secret of it; they would, in fact, have suspected Dmitri Karamazov, the son of the murdered man. Had Smerdyakov killed and robbed his master, and had the son been accused of it, that would of course have suited Smerdyakov. Yet are we to believe that, though plotting the murder, he told that son, Dmitri, about the money, the envelope, and the signals! Is that logical? Is that believable?

"When the day of the murder planned by Smerdyakov arrived, we have him falling downstairs in a 'sham' fit—why? In the first place so that Gregory, who had been planning to take his medicine, might put it off and remain on guard seeing there was no one to look after the house, and in the second place, I suppose, so that his master seeing that there was no one to guard him and in terror of a visit from his son, might redouble his vigilance and precaution. And, most of all, I suppose so that he, Smerdyakov, disabled by the fit, might be carried from the kitchen where he always slept and where he could go in and out as he liked to the room next to Gregory and Marfa's. This was the custom established by his master and the kind-hearted Marfa whenever he had a fit. There, lying three yards away from them he would most likely, to keep up the sham, have begun groaning, and so kept them awake all night (as Gregory and his wife testified). And he did all this, we are asked to believe, that he might more conveniently get up and murder his master!

"But I shall be told that he shammed illness on purpose that he might not be suspected and that he told the prisoner of the money and the signals to tempt him to commit the murder. I shall be told that when the prisoner had murdered his father and had gone away with the money making a noise and waking people, Smerdyakov got up and went in! What for? To murder his master a second time and carry off the money that had already been stolen? Gentlemen, are you laughing? I am ashamed to put forward such suggestions, but, incredible as it seems, that's just what the prisoner alleges. When he had left the house, had knocked Gregory down and raised an alarm, he tells us Smerdyakov got up, went in and murdered his master and stole the money! I won't press the point that Smerdyakov could hardly have counted on this beforehand and could hardly have foreseen that the furious and jealous son would simply come to peep in respectfully, though he knew the signals, and then beat a retreat, leaving Smerdyakov his three thousand roubles. Gentlemen of the jury, I put this question to you in earnest; when was the moment when Smerdyakov could have committed the crime? Name that moment, or you can't accuse him.

"But, perhaps, the fit was a real one, the sick man suddenly recovered, heard a shout, and went out. Well—what then? He looked about him and said, 'Why not go and kill the master?' And how did he know what had happened, since he had been lying unconscious till that moment? But there's a limit to these flights of fancy.

" 'Certainly,' some people will say. 'But what if they were in agreement? What if they murdered him together and shared the money—what then?' A good question! And the facts to confirm it are astounding. One commits the murder and takes all the trouble while his accomplice lies on one side shamming a fit, apparently to arouse suspicion in everyone, alarm in his master and alarm in Gregory! It would be interesting to know what motives could have induced the two accomplices to form such an insane plan.

"But perhaps it was not a case of active cooperation on Smerdyakov's part, but only a passive acquiescence. Perhaps Smerdyakov was intimidated and agreed not to prevent the murder; foreseeing that he would be blamed for letting his master be murdered without screaming for help or resisting, he may have obtained permission from Dmitri Karamazov to get out of the way by shamming a fit—'you may murder him as you like; it's nothing to me.' But as this attack of Smerdyakov's was bound to throw the household into confusion, Dmitri Karamazov could never have agreed to such a plan. I will waive that point however. Supposing that he did agree, it would still follow that Dmitri Karamazov is the murderer and the instigator, and Smerdyakov is only a passive accomplice, and not even an accomplice, but merely acquiesced against his will through terror.

"But what do we see? As soon as he is arrested the prisoner instantly throws all the blame on Smerdyakov, not accusing him of being his accomplice, but of being the actual murderer. 'He did it alone,' he says. 'He murdered and robbed him. It was the work of his hands.' Strange sort of accomplices who begin to accuse one another! And think of the risk for Dmitri Karamazov. After committing the murder while his accomplice lay in bed, he throws the blame on the invalid, who might well have resented it and in self-preservation might well have confessed the truth. For Smerdyakov might have seen that the court would at once judge how far he was responsible, and so he might have realized that if he were punished, it would be far less severely than the real murderer. In that case, he would have been certain to make a confession, yet he has not done so. Smerdyakov never hinted at their being accomplices though the prisoner insists in accusing him and declaring that he had committed the crime alone.

"What's more, Smerdyakov at the inquiry volunteered the

statement that it was *he* who told the prisoner about the envelope of money and about the signals. But for him, Dmitri Karamazov would have known nothing about them. If he had really been an accomplice, would he so readily have made this statement at the inquiry? On the contrary, he would have tried to conceal it, to distort the facts or minimize them. But he was far from distorting or minimizing them. No one but an innocent man, who had no fear of being charged with the crime could have acted as he did. And in a state of depression, the result of his illness and this horrible crime, he hanged himself yesterday. He left a note written in his peculiar language: 'I destroy myself of my own will and inclination so as to throw no blame on anyone.' What would it have cost him to add: 'I am the murderer, not Dmitri Karamazov'? But that he did not add. Did his conscience lead him to suicide and not to admitting his guilt?

"And what followed? Notes for three thousand roubles were brought into court today, and we were told that they were the same notes that lay in the envelope now on the table before us, and that the witness had received them from Smerdyakov the day before. But I need not recall the painful scene, though I will make one or two comments, selecting such trivial ones as might not be obvious at first sight to everyone, and so might have been overlooked. In the first place, Smerdyakov must have given back the money and hanged himself yesterday from remorse. Only yesterday he confessed his guilt to Ivan Karamazov, as the latter informs us. If it were not so, indeed, why should Ivan Karamazov have kept silent until now? And so, if he has confessed, then why, I ask again, did he not admit the whole truth in his suicide note, knowing that the innocent prisoner had to face this terrible ordeal today?

"The money alone is no proof. A week ago, by chance, the fact became known to me and two other people in this court that Ivan Karamazov had sent two five per cent coupons of five thousand each—that is, ten thousand in all—to the main town of the province to be changed. I only mention this to point out that anyone may have money, and that it can't be proved that these notes now before you are the same as were in Fyodor Karamazov's envelope.

"Ivan Karamazov, after hearing yesterday a confession of such importance from the real murderer, did not stir. Why didn't he report it at once? Why did he put it off till morning? I think I have a right to suggest why. His health had been giving way for the last week; he had admitted to a doctor and to his most intimate friends that he was suffering from hallucinations and seeing phantoms of the dead; he was on the eve of the attack of brain fever by which he has been stricken down today. In this condition he suddenly heard of Smerdyakov's death and at once thought: 'The man is dead, I can throw the blame on him and save my brother. I have money. I will take a roll of notes and say that Smerdyakov gave them to me before his death.' You will say that is dishonorable; it's dishonorable to slander even the dead, and even to save a brother. True, but what if he slandered him unconsciously? What if, finally unhinged by the sudden news of the valet's death, he imagined it really was so? You saw the scene today; you have seen the witness's condition. He was standing up and was speaking, but where was his mind?

"Then followed the letter, the prisoner's letter written two days before the crime, containing a complete program of the murder. Why, then, are we looking for any other program? The crime was committed precisely according to this program, and by no one else than the writer of this letter. Yes, gentlemen of the jury, it went off without a hitch! He did not run respectfully and timidly away from his father's window, though he was firmly convinced that the object of his affections was with him. No, that is absurd and unlikely! He went in and murdered him. Most likely he killed him in anger, burning with resentment, as soon as he looked on his hated rival. But having killed him, probably with one blow of the brass pestle, and having convinced himself, after careful search, that she was not there, he did not, however, forget to put his hand under the pillow and take out the envelope, the torn cover of which lies now on the table before us.

"I mention this fact that you may note, to my thinking, one very characteristic circumstance. Had he been an experienced murderer and had he committed the murder only for the sake of the money, would he have left the torn envelope on the floor beside the corpse? Had Smerdyakov murdered his master to rob him, he would have carried away the envelope with him, without opening it because he knew for certain that the notes were in the envelope—they had been put in and sealed up in his presence. Had he taken the envelope with him, no one would ever have known of the robbery. I ask you, gentlemen, would Smerdyakov have behaved in such a way? Would he have left the envelope on the floor?

"No, this was the action of a frantic murderer, a murderer who was not a thief and had never stolen before that day, who snatched the notes from under the pillow, not like a thief stealing them, but as though seizing his own property from the thief who had stolen it. For that was the idea which had become an obsession with Dmitri Karamazov in regard to that money. And pouncing upon the envelope, which he had never seen before, he tore it open to make sure that the money was in it. He ran away with the money in his pocket, forgetting that he had left an astounding piece of evidence against himself in that torn envelope on the floor. Because it was Dmitri Karamazov, not Smerdyakov, he didn't think, he didn't reflect! Why should he? He ran away; he heard behind him the

646

servant, Gregory, cry out; the old man caught him, stopped him and was beaten to the ground by the brass pestle.

"The prisoner, moved by pity, jumped down from the fence to look at him. Would you believe it, he tells us that he jumped down out of pity, out of compassion, to see whether he could do anything for Gregory. Was that a moment to show compassion? No. He jumped down simply to make certain whether the only witness to his crime were dead or alive. Any other feeling, any other motive would be unnatural. Note that he took trouble over Gregory, wiped his head with his handkerchief and, convincing himself he was dead, he ran to the house of his mistress, dazed and covered with blood. How was it he never thought that he was covered with blood and that this would be noticed? But the prisoner himself assures us that he did not see that he was covered with blood. That may be, that is very possible, that happens with criminals. On one point they will show diabolical cunning, while another will escape them altogether. He was thinking at that moment of one thing only—where was *she?* He wanted to find out at once where she was, so he ran to her place and learned an unexpected and astounding piece of news—she had gone off to Mokroe to meet her first lover."

9. The Galloping Troika. The End of the Prosecutor's Speech

IPPOLIT KIRILLOVITCH had chosen the historical method of exposition, beloved by all nervous orators, who find in its limitations a check on their own eager rhetoric. At this moment in his speech he went off into a dissertation on Grushenka's "first lover," and brought forward several interesting thoughts on this subject.

"Dmitri Karamazov, who had been frantically jealous of everyone, collapsed, so to speak, and effaced himself at once before this first lover. What makes it all the more strange is that he seems to have hardly thought of this rival. He seems to have looked upon him as a remote danger, and Dmitri Karamazov always lives in the present. He may have regarded him as a fiction. But his wounded heart grasped instantly that the woman had been concealing this new rival and deceiving him, because he was anything but a fiction to her, because he was the one hope of her life. Grasping this instantly, he resigned himself.

"Gentlemen of the jury, I cannot help dwelling on this unexpected trait in the prisoner's character. He suddenly shows an irresistible desire for justice, a respect for woman and a recognition of her right to love. And all this at the very moment when he has stained his hands with his father's blood for her sake! It is true that the blood he shed was already crying out for vengeance, for, after having ruined his soul and his life in this world, he was forced to ask himself what he was and what he could be *now* to her, to that being, dearer to him than his own soul, in comparison with that former lover who had returned penitent, with new love, with honorable offers, with the promise of a reformed and happy life. And he, unhappy man, what could he give her now, what could he offer her?

"Dmitri Karamazov felt all this, knew that all ways were barred to him by his crime and that he was now a criminal, and not a man with a life before him! This thought crushed him. And so he entered into a frantic plan, which appeared the one inevitable way out of his terrible position. That way out was suicide. He ran for the pistols he had pledged with his friend Perhotin and on the way, as he ran, he pulled out of his pocket the money, for the sake of which he had stained his hands with his father's blood. Oh, now he needed money more than ever. Dmitri Karamazov would die! Dmitri Karamazov would shoot himself and it should be remembered! To be sure, he was a poet and had burned the candle at both ends all his life. 'To her, to her! and there, oh, there I will give a feast to the whole world, such as never was before, that will be remembered and talked of long after! In the midst of shouts, reckless gypsy songs and dances I shall raise the glass and drink to the woman I adore and her new-found happiness! And then, on the spot, at her feet, I shall dash out my brains before her and punish myself! She will remember Dmitri Karamazov sometimes, she will see how Dmitri loved her, she will feel for Dmitri!'

"Here we see in excess a love of effect, a romantic despair and sentimentality, and the wild recklessness of the Karamazovs. Yes, but there is something else, gentlemen of the jury, something that cries out in the soul, throbs incessantly in the mind, and poisons the heart unto death—that *something* is conscience, gentlemen of the jury, its judgment, its terrible torments! The pistol will settle everything, the pistol is the only way out! But *beyond*—I don't know whether Dmitri Karamazov wondered at that time 'What lies beyond,' or whether he could, like Hamlet, wonder 'What lies beyond.' No, gentlemen of the jury, they have their Hamlets, but we have our Karamazovs!"

Then Ippolit Kirillovitch drew a detailed picture of Dmitri's preparations, the scene at Perhotin's, at the shop, with the drivers. He quoted conversations and recorded actions confirmed by witnesses, and the picture made a terrible impression on everyone. The guilt of this harassed and desperate man stood out clearly and convincingly when the facts were brought together.

"What need had he of precaution? Two or three times he

almost confessed, hinted at it, all but spoke out. (Then followed the evidence given by witnesses.) He even cried out to the peasant who drove him: 'Do you know, you are driving a murderer!' But it was impossible for him to speak out, he had to get to Mokroe and there to finish his romance.

"But what was awaiting the luckless man? Almost from the first minute at Mokroe he saw that his invincible rival was perhaps not invincible, that the toast to their new-found happiness was not desired and would not be acceptable. But you know the facts, gentlemen of the jury, from the preliminary inquiry. Dmitri Karamazov's triumph over his rival was complete and his soul passed into quite a new phase, perhaps the most terrible phase through which his soul has passed or will pass.

"One may say with certainty, gentlemen of the jury," the prosecutor continued, "that outraged nature and the criminal heart bring their own vengeance more completely than any earthly justice. What's more, justice and punishment on earth alleviate the punishment of nature and are, indeed, essential to the soul of the criminal at such moments, as its salvation from despair. For I cannot imagine the horror and moral suffering of Dmitri Karamazov when he learned that she loved him, that for his sake she had rejected her first lover, that she was calling him, Dmitri, to a new life, that she was promising him happiness—and when? When everything was over for him and nothing was possible!

"By the way, I will mention a point of importance because of the light it throws on the prisoner's position at that moment. This woman, this love of his, had been till the last moment, till the very instant of his arrest, a being unattainable, passionately desired by him but unattainable. Yet why did he not shoot himself then, why did he give up his plan and even forget where his pistol was? It was just that passionate desire for love and the hope of satisfying it that restrained him. Throughout the party that night he kept close to his adored mistress, who was at the banquet with him and was more charming and fascinating to him than ever—he did not leave her side, humbling himself in his homage before her.

"His passion might well, for a moment, stifle not only the fear of arrest, but even the torments of conscience. For a moment, only for a moment! I can picture the state of mind of the criminal hopelessly enslaved by these influences—first, the influence of drink, of noise and excitement, of the thud of the dance and the scream of the song, and of her, flushed with wine, singing and dancing and laughing! Secondly, the hope in the background that the fatal end might still be far off, that not till next morning, at least, they would come and take him. So he had a few hours and that's much, very much! In a few hours one can think of many things. I imagine that he felt something like what criminals feel when they are being taken to the scaffold. They have another long, long street to pass down and at a walking pace, past thousands of people. Then there will be a turning into another street and only at the end of that street the dread place of execution! I imagine that at the beginning of the journey the condemned man, sitting on his shameful cart, must feel that he has infinite life still before him. The houses recede, the cart moves on—oh, that's nothing, it's still far to the turning into the second street and he still looks boldly to the right and to the left at those thousands of callously curious people with their eyes fixed on him, and he still believes that he is just such a man as they. But now the turning comes to the next street. Oh, that's nothing, nothing, there's still a whole street before him, and however many houses have been passed, he will still think there are many left. And so to the very end, to the very scaffold.

"This I imagine is how it was with Dmitri Karamazov during that night. 'They have not had time yet,' he must have thought. 'I may still find some way out. Oh, there's still time to make some plan. And now, now—she is so fascinating!'

"His soul was full of confusion and dread. He managed however, to put aside half his money and hide it somewhere—I cannot otherwise explain the disappearance of half of the three thousand he had just taken from under his father's pillow. He had been in Mokroe more than once. He had caroused there for two days once before. He knew the big inn with all its passages and outbuildings. I believe that part of the money was hidden in the inn, not long before the arrest, in some crevice, under some floor, in some corner, under the roof. 'Why?' I shall be asked. Because the catastrophe may take place at once; he hadn't yet considered how to meet it, he hadn't the time, his head was throbbing and his heart was with *her*, but money—money was indispensable in any case! With money a man is always a man. Perhaps such foresight at such a moment may strike you as unnatural? But the prisoner assures us himself that a month before, at a critical and exciting moment, he had taken half his money and sewn it up in a little bag. And though that is not true, as we shall prove directly, it shows the idea was a familiar one to Dmitri Karamazov, he had contemplated it. What's more, when he said at the inquiry that he had put fifteen hundred roubles in a bag he probably invented that little bag on the inspiration of the moment, because he had two hours before hidden half of it some place in the inn. He did this in case of emergency and not to have it on himself. Two extremes, gentlemen of the jury, remember that Dmitri Karamazov can contemplate two extremes and both at once.

"We have searched the inn but we haven't found the money. It may still be there or it may have disappeared next day. In any case he was at her side, on his knees before her, she was lying on the bed, he had his hands stretched out to her and he had so entirely forgotten everything that he did not even hear the men coming to arrest him. He hadn't time to prepare any line of defense. He was caught unawares and confronted with his judges, the arbiters of his destiny.

"Gentlemen of the jury, there are moments in the execution of our duties when it is terrible for us to face a man, terrible on his account, too! The moments of contemplating that animal fear, when the criminal sees that all is lost, but still struggles, still means to struggle, the moments when every instinct of self-preservation rises up in him at once and he looks at you with questioning and suffering eyes, studies you, your face, your thoughts, uncertain on which side you will strike . . . His distracted mind frames thousands of plans in an instant, but he is still afraid to speak, afraid of giving himself away! This purgatory of the spirit, this animal thirst for self-preservation, these humiliating moments of the human soul, are awful, and sometimes arouse horror and compassion for the criminal even in a lawyer. . . . And this was what we all witnessed that morning at Mokroe.

"At first he was thunderstruck and in his terror some very compromising phrases escaped him. 'Blood! I deserve it!' But he quickly restrained himself. He had not prepared what to say, what answer to make, he had nothing but a bare denial ready. 'I am not guilty of my father's death.' That was his defense for the moment and behind it he hoped to throw up a barricade of some sort. His first compromising exclamations he tried to explain by declaring that he was only responsible for the death of the servant Gregory. 'Of that bloodshed I am guilty, but who has killed my father, gentlemen, who has killed him? Who can have killed him, *if not I?*' Do you hear, he asked us that, us, who had come to ask him that question! Do you hear that phrase uttered with such premature haste—'if not I' —the animal cunning, the naïveté, the Karamazov impatience of it? 'I didn't kill him and you mustn't think I did! I wanted to kill him, gentlemen, I wanted to kill him,' he quickly admits (he was in a hurry, in a terrible hurry). 'But still I am not guilty, I did not murder him.' He concedes that he wanted to murder him, as though to say, you can see for yourselves how truthful I am, so you'll believe that I didn't murder him. Oh, in such cases the criminal is often amazingly shallow and credulous.

"At that point one of the lawyers asked him, as it were incidentally, the most simple question: 'Wasn't it Smerdyakov killed him?' Then, as we expected, he was horribly angry at our having anticipated him and caught him unawares, before he had time to pave the way to choose and snatch the moment when it would be most natural to bring in Smerdyakov's name. He rushed at once to the other extreme, as he always does, and began to assure us that Smerdyakov could not have killed him, was not capable of it. But don't believe him, that was only his cunning. He didn't really give up the idea of Smerdyakov; on the contrary, he meant to accuse him again for, indeed, he had no one else to accuse. But he would do that later, because for the moment that loophole was blocked. He would accuse him again perhaps next day, or even a few days later, choosing an opportunity to cry out to us: 'You know I was more suspicious of Smerdyakov than you, you remember that yourselves, but now I am convinced. He killed him, he must have done it!' And for the present he falls back upon a gloomy and irritable denial. Impatience and anger prompted him, however, to the most inept and incredible explanation of how he looked into his father's window and how he respectfully withdrew. The worst of it was that at the time he was unaware of the evidence given by Gregory.

"We searched him. The search angered, but encouraged him; the whole three thousand was not found on him, only half of it. And it was probably at that moment of angry silence that the story of the little bag first occurred to him. He was undoubtedly conscious of the improbability of the story and he tried to make it sound more likely, to weave it into a romance that would sound plausible. In such cases the first duty, the chief task of the investigating lawyers, is to prevent the criminal from being prepared, to pounce upon him unexpectedly so that he may blurt out his cherished ideas in all their simplicity, improbability and inconsistency. The criminal can only be made to speak by the sudden and apparently incidental introduction of some new fact, of some circumstance of great importance in the case, of which he had no previous idea and which he could not have foreseen. We had such a fact in readiness—that was Gregory's evidence about the open door through which the prisoner had run out. He had completely forgotten about that door and had not even suspected that Gregory could have seen it.

"The effect of it was amazing. He jumped up and shouted to us: 'Then Smerdyakov murdered him, it was Smerdyakov!' Through this he betrayed the basis of his defense. He betrayed it in its most improbable shape, because Smerdyakov could only have committed the murder after the prisoner had knocked Gregory down and run away. When we told him that Gregory saw the door open before he fell down, and that he had heard Smerdyakov in the next room as he came out of his bedroom—Dmitri Karamazov was crushed. My esteemed and witty colleague, Nicholas Nelyudov, told me afterwards that he was almost moved to tears at the sight of him. And to improve matters, the prisoner hurried to tell us about the much-talked-of little bag—so be it, you shall hear this story!

"Gentlemen of the jury, I have told you already why I consider this story not only an absurdity, but the most improbable invention that could have been brought forward under the circumstances. If one tried to invent the most unlikely story, one could hardly find anything more incredible. The worst of such stories is that the triumphant story-teller can always be confused and crushed by the details in which real life is so rich and which these unhappy and involuntary story-tellers neglect as insignificant trifles. Oh, they have no thought to spare for such details, their minds are concentrated on their grand invention as a whole. Imagine anyone tripping them up with a trifling detail! But that's how they are caught. The prisoner was asked the question: 'Where did you get the cloth for your little bag and who made it for you?' 'I made it myself.' 'And where did you get the cloth?' The prisoner was positively offended. He thought it almost insulting to ask him such a trivial question. And would you believe it, his resentment was genuine! But they are all like that. 'I tore it off my shirt.' 'Then we will find that shirt among your linen tomorrow, with a piece torn off.' And only imagine, gentlemen of the jury, if we really had found that torn shirt (and how could we have failed to find it in his chest of drawers or trunks?) that would have been a fact, a material fact in support of his statement! But he was incapable of that kind of reasoning. 'I don't remember, it may not have been my shirt. I sewed it up in one of my landlady's caps.' 'What sort of a cap?' 'It was an old cotton rag of hers lying about.' 'Do you remember that clearly?' 'No, I don't.' And he was angry, very angry, and yet imagine not remembering it! At the most terrible moments of a man's life, for instance when he is being led to execution, he remembers just such trifles. He will forget everything but some green roof that has flashed past him on the road, or a blackbird on a cross—that he will remember. He concealed the making of that little bag from those in the house; he must have remembered his humiliating fear that someone might come in and find him needle in hand and how at the slightest sound he slipped behind the screen (there is a screen in his rooms).

"But, gentlemen of the jury, why do I tell you all this, all these details, trifles?" cried Ippolit Kirillovitch suddenly. "Just because the prisoner still persists in these absurdities to this moment. He has not explained anything since that fatal night two months ago. He has not added one actual fact to his former fantastic statements; all those are trivialities. 'You must believe it in my honor.' Oh, we are eager to believe it, even if only on his word of honor! Are we jackals thirsting for human blood? Show us a single fact in the prisoner's favor and we will be happy. But let it be a substantial, real fact, and not a conclusion drawn by the prisoner's own brother, that, for instance, when he beat himself on the breast he must have meant to point to the little bag—in the darkness, too. We shall be happy to accept any new fact, we shall be the first to repudiate our charge. But now justice cries out and we persist, we cannot repudiate anything."

Ippolit Kirillovitch passed to the concluding remarks of his speech. He looked as though he were in a fever; he spoke of the blood that cried for vengeance, the blood of the father murdered by his son, with the base motive of robbery! He pointed to the tragic and glaring facts.

"And whatever you may hear from the talented and celebrated counsel for the defense," Ippolit Kirillovitch could not resist adding, "whatever eloquent and touching appeals may be made to your emotions, remember that at this moment you are in a temple of justice. Remember that you are the champions of our justice, the champions of our holy Russia, of her principles, her family, everything that she holds sacred! Yes, you represent Russia here at this moment, and your verdict will be heard not in this hall only but will re-echo throughout the whole of Russia. All Russia will hear you, as her champions and her judges. She will be encouraged or disheartened by your verdict. Do not disappoint Russia and her expectations. Our fatal troika dashes on in its headlong flight to destruction. All over Russia, for long years past, men have stretched out imploring hands trying to halt the troika's furious reckless course. And if other nations stand aside from that troika it is not from respect, as the poet would believe, but simply from horror. From horror, perhaps from disgust. And well it is that they stand aside, but maybe they will cease one day to do so and will form a firm wall confronting the hurrying apparition and will check the frenzied rush of our lawlessness, for the sake of their own safety, enlightenment and civilization. We have already heard voices of alarm from Europe; they already begin to sound. Do not tempt them! Do not heap up their growing hatred by a sentence justifying the murder of a father by his son!"

Though Ippolit Kirillovitch was genuinely moved, he wound up his speech with this rhetorical appeal—and the effect produced by him was extraordinary. When he had finished his speech, he went out quickly and, as I have mentioned before, almost fainted in the adjoining room. There was no applause in the court, but serious people were pleased. The ladies, however, were not so well satisfied, though even they were pleased with his eloquence, especially as they had no fears as to the outcome of the trial. They had full trust in Fetyukovitch. "He will speak and carry all before him."

Dmitri sat silent through the whole of the prosecutor's speech, clenching his teeth, with his hands clasped, and his head bowed. From time to time he raised his head and listened, especially when Grushenka was spoken of. When the prosecutor mentioned Rakitin's opinion of her, a smile of contempt and anger passed over his face and he murmured "the Bernards!" When Ippolit Kirillovitch described how he had questioned and tortured him at Mokroe, Dmitri raised his head and listened with intense curiosity. At one point he seemed about to jump up and cry out, but controlled himself and only shrugged his shoulders disdainfully. People talked afterward about the conclusion of the speech, about the prosecutor's examination of the prisoner at Mokroe. They jeered at him. "The man could not resist boasting of his cleverness," they said.

The court was adjourned, but only for a short interval, a quarter of an hour or twenty minutes at most. There was a hum of conversation in the audience. I remember some of the things that were said.

"A weighty speech," a gentleman in one group observed gravely.

"He brought in too much psychology," said another.

"But it was all true, the absolute truth!"

"Yes, he has great ability."

"He summed it all up."

"Yes, he summed us up, too," chimed in another voice. "Do you remember, at the beginning of his speech, how he said we were all like Fyodor Karamazov."

"And at the end, too. But that was all nonsense."

"And obscure too."

"He was a little too much carried away."

"It's unjust, it's unjust."

"No, it was well done, anyway. He's had long to wait, but he's had his say, ha-ha!"

"What will the counsel for the defense say?"

In another group I heard: "He had no business to attack the Petersburg man like that; 'appealing to your emotions'— do you remember?"

"Yes, that was wrong of him."

"He was in too great a hurry."

"He is a nervous man."

"We laugh, but what must the prisoner be feeling?"

"Yes, what must it be like for Dmitri?"

In a third group: "What lady is that, the fat one, with the lorgnette, sitting at the end?"

"She is a general's wife, divorced. I know her."

"That's why she has the lorgnette."

"She is not good for much."

"Oh, no, she is an interesting little woman."

"Two places beyond her there is a little blonde. She is pretty."

"They trapped him at Mokroe, didn't they, eh?"

"Oh, it was not too clever. We've heard of it before. How often he has told the story at people's houses!"

"And he couldn't resist doing it now. That's vanity."

"He is a man with a grievance, he-he!"

"Yes, and quick to take offense. And there was too much rhetoric, such long sentences."

"Yes, he tries to frighten us. He kept trying to frighten us. Do you remember about the troika? Something about 'They have Hamlets, but we have, so far, only Karamazovs!' That was cleverly said!"

"That was to appease the liberals. He is afraid of them."

"Yes, and he is afraid of the lawyer for defense, too."

"Yes, what will Fetyukovitch say?"

"Whatever he says, he won't influence our peasants."

"Don't you think so?"

A fourth group: "What he said about the troika was good, that piece about the other nations."

"And that was true what he said about other nations not standing for it."

"What do you mean?"

"Why, in the English Parliament a Member got up last week and speaking about our Russian Nihilists asked the Ministry whether it was not high time to intervene, to educate this barbarous land. Ippolit was thinking of him. I know he was. He was talking about that last week."

"Not an easy job."

"Not an easy job? Why not?"

"Why, we'd shut our ports and not let them have any wheat. Where would they get it?"

"In America. They get it from America now."

"Nonsense!"

The bell rang. All rushed back to their places. Fetyukovitch mounted the dais.

10. The Speech for the Defense.
An Argument That Cuts Both Ways

ALL WAS HUSHED as the first words of the famous orator rang out. The eyes of the audience were fastened upon him. He began very simply and directly, with conviction, and without the slightest trace of conceit. He made no attempt at eloquence, at pathos, or emotional appeal. He was like a man speaking to a circle of intimate and sympathetic friends. His voice was sonorous and sympathetic; there was something genuine and simple in the very sound of it. But everyone realized that at any moment he might suddenly rise to genuine pathos and "pierce the heart with untold power." His language was perhaps more irregular than Ippolit Kirillovitch's, but he spoke without long phrases and with more precision. One thing did not please the ladies; he kept bending forward, especially at the beginning of his speech, not exactly bowing, but as though he were about to dart at his listeners, bending his long spine in half, as though there were a hinge in the middle that enabled him to bend at right angles.

At the beginning of his speech he spoke rather disconnectedly, without system, one might say. He dealt with facts separately, though at the end these facts formed a whole. His speech might be divided into two parts: the first consisted of criticism in refutation of the charge, sometimes malicious and sarcastic; in the second half he suddenly changed his tone and manner and rose to pathos. The audience was waiting for this and received it with enthusiasm.

He went straight to the point, and began by saying that although he practiced in Petersburg, he had more than once visited provincial towns to defend prisoners, of whose innocence he had a conviction or at least a preconceived idea. "That is what has happened to me in the present case," he explained. "From the very first accounts in the newspapers I was struck by something which strongly prepossessed me in the prisoner's favor. What interested me most was a fact which often occurs in legal practice, but rarely, I think, in such an extreme and peculiar form as in the present case. I ought to formulate that peculiarity only at the end of my speech, but I will do so at the very beginning, for it is my weakness to go to work directly, not keeping my effects in reserve and economizing my material. That may be unwise on my part, but at least it's sincere. What I have in mind is this: there is an overwhelming chain of evidence against the prisoner, but not one fact will stand criticism, if examined separately. As I followed the case more closely in the papers my idea was more and more confirmed, and I suddenly received from the prisoner's relatives a request to undertake his defense. I hurried here at once and here I became completely convinced. It was to break down this terrible chain of facts, and to show that each piece of evidence when taken separately was unproved and fantastic, that I undertook the case."

So Fetyukovitch began.

"Gentlemen of the jury," he suddenly protested. "I am new to this district. I have no preconceived ideas. The prisoner, a man of turbulent and unbridled temper, has not insulted me. But he has insulted perhaps hundreds of people in this town, and so prejudiced many people against him beforehand. Of course I recognize that the moral sentiment of local society is justly excited against him. The prisoner is of turbulent and violent temper. Yet he was received in society here; he was even welcome in the home of my talented friend, the prosecutor."

At these words there were two or three laughs in the audience, quickly suppressed, but noticed by all. All of us knew that the prosecutor received Dmitri against his will. He received Dmitri solely because he had somehow interested his wife—a lady of the highest virtue but capricious, and given to opposing her husband, especially in trifles. Dmitri's visits, however, had not been frequent.

"Nevertheless I venture to suggest," Fetyukovitch continued, "that in spite of his independent mind and just character, my opponent may have formed a mistaken prejudice

657

st my unfortunate client. Oh, that is so natural; the unfortunate man has only too well deserved such prejudice. Outraged morality, and still more outraged taste, is often relentless. We have, in the prosecutor's speech, heard a stern analysis of the prisoner's character and conduct. His severe critical attitude to the case was evident. And, what's more, he went into psychological subtleties into which he could not have entered if he had a malicious prejudice against the prisoner. But there are things which are even worse, even more fatal in such cases, than the most malicious and consciously unfair attitude. It is worse if we are carried away by an artistic instinct, by a desire to create a romantic story, especially if God has endowed us with psychological insight. Before I started on my way here, I was warned in Petersburg, and was myself aware, that I would find a talented opponent whose psychological insight and subtlety had gained him renown in legal circles. But profound as psychology is, it's a knife that cuts both ways." (Laughter among the public.) "You will, of course, forgive me my comparison; I can't boast of eloquence. But I will take as an example any point in the prosecutor's speech.

"For instance, the prisoner, running away in the garden in the dark, climbed over the fence, was seized by the servant, and knocked him down with a brass pestle. Then he jumped back into the garden and spent five minutes over the man, trying to discover whether he had killed him or not. And the prosecutor refuses to believe the prisoner's statement that he ran to old Gregory out of pity. 'No,' he says, 'such sensibility is impossible at such a moment, it's unnatural. He wanted to find out whether the only witness to his crime was dead or alive. By doing this the prisoner showed that he had committed the murder, since he would not have stopped for any other reason.'

"Here you have psychology. But let us take the same method and apply it to the case the other way around and the result will be no less believable. The murderer, we are told, jumped down to find out, as a precaution, whether the witness was alive or not, yet he had left in his murdered father's study, as the prosecutor himself argues, an amazing piece of evidence in the shape of a torn envelope with an inscription that there had been three thousand roubles in it. 'If he had carried that envelope away with him, no one in the world would have known of that envelope and of the money in it and that the money had been stolen by the prisoner.' Those are the prosecutor's own words. So on one side you see a complete absence of precaution, a man who has lost his head and run away in fear leaving that clue on the floor, and two minutes later, when he has felled another man, we are to assume the most heartless and calculating foresight in him. But even admitting this was so, it is psychological subtlety, I suppose, that discerns that under certain circumstances I become as bloodthirsty and keen sighted as a Caucasian eagle, while under other circumstances I am as timid and blind as a mole. But if I am so bloodthirsty and calculating that when I kill a man I only run back to find out whether he is alive to bear witness against me, why should I spend five minutes looking after him at the risk of being seen by other witnesses? Why soak my handkerchief with blood wiping off his head so that it may be used as evidence against me later? If he were so cold-hearted and calculating, why not hit the servant on the head again and again with the same pestle so as to kill him outright and relieve himself of all worry about the witness?

"Again, though the prisoner ran to see whether the witness was still alive, he left another witness on the path, that brass pestle which he had taken from the two women, and which they could always identify as theirs. And it is not as though he had forgotten it on the path, dropped it through carelessness or haste, no, he had flung away his weapon, for it was found fifteen paces from where Gregory lay. Why did he do this? Just because he was so distressed at having killed a man, an old servant; because of this he flung away the pestle with a curse, as a murderous weapon. That's how it must have been, what other reason could he have had for throwing it so far? And if he was capable of feeling grief and pity at having killed a man, it shows that he was innocent of his father's murder. Had he murdered him, he would never have ministered to another victim out of pity; he would have felt differently; his thoughts would have been centered on self-preservation. He would have had no thoughts to spare for pity, that is certain. On the contrary, he would have broken old Gregory's skull instead of spending five minutes looking after him. There was room for pity and good feeling because his conscience was clear. Here we have a different psychology. I have purposely resorted to this method, gentlemen of the jury, to show that you can prove anything by it. It all depends on who makes use of it. Psychology lures even serious people into romancing and quite unconsciously. I am speaking of the abuse of psychology, gentlemen."

Sounds of approval and laughter, at the expense of the prosecutor, were again heard in the court. I will not repeat the speech in detail; I will only quote some passage from it, some leading points.

659

11. There Was No Money.
There Was No Robbery

THERE WAS ONE POINT that struck everyone in Fetyukovitch's speech. He denied the existence of the fatal three thousand roubles, and consequently the possibility of their having been stolen.

"Gentlemen of the jury," he began. "Every new and unprejudiced observer must be struck by a peculiarity in the present case, namely, the charge of robbery, and the complete impossibility of proving that there was anything to be stolen. We are told that money was stolen—three thousand roubles—but whether those roubles ever existed, nobody knows. Consider, how have we heard of that sum, and who has seen the notes? The only person who saw them and said that they had been put in the envelope, was the valet, Smerdyakov. He had spoken about it to the prisoner and his brother, Ivan Karamazov, before the tragedy. Madame Svyetlov, too, had been told about it. But not one of these three people has actually seen the money, no one but Smerdyakov has seen it.

"Now the question arises, if it's true that the money existed and that Smerdyakov saw it, when did he see it for the last time? What if his master had taken the three thousand roubles from under his bed and put them back in his cash box without telling him? Note, that according to Smerdyakov's story the notes were kept under the mattress; the prisoner must have pulled them out, and yet the bed was absolutely unrumpled; that is carefully detailed in the record. How could the prisoner have found the money without disturbing the bed? How could he have helped soiling with his bloodstained hands the fine and spotless linen with which the bed had been made?

"But I shall be asked: what about the envelope on the floor? Yes, it's worth saying a word or two about that envelope. I was somewhat surprised just now to hear the highly talented prosecutor declare of himself—of himself, observe—that but for that envelope, but for its being left on the floor, no one in the world would have known of the existence of that envelope and the money in it, and therefore of the prisoner's having stolen it. And so that torn scrap of paper is, by the prosecutor's own admission, the sole proof on which the charge of robbery rests, 'otherwise no one would have known of the robbery, nor perhaps even of the money.' But is the mere fact that that scrap of paper was lying on the floor a proof that there was money in it, and that that money had been stolen? Yet, it will be stated that Smerdyakov had seen the money in the envelope. But when, when had he seen it for the last time, I ask you? I talked to Smerdyakov, and he told me that he had seen the money two days before the murder. Then why not imagine that old Fyodor Karamazov, locked up alone in impatient and hysterical expectation of the object of his adoration, might have whiled away the time by breaking open the envelope and taking out the notes. 'What's the use of the envelope,' he may have asked himself. 'She won't believe the notes are there. But when I show her the thirty rainbow-colored notes in one roll, it will make more impression. . . . It will make her mouth water.' And so he tears open the envelope, takes out the money, and flings the envelope on the floor, conscious of being the owner and untroubled by any fears of leaving evidence.

"Listen, gentlemen, could anything be more likely than this? Why is it out of the question? If anything of the sort could have taken place, the charge of robbery falls to the ground; if there was no money, there was no theft of it. If the envelope on the floor may be taken as evidence that there had been money in it, why may I not maintain the opposite, that the envelope was on the floor because the money had been taken from it by its owner?

"But I shall be asked what became of the money if Fyodor Karamazov took it out of the envelope since it was not found when the police searched the house? In the first place, part of the money was found in the cash box, and secondly, Fyodor Karamazov might have taken it out that morning or the evening before to make some other use of it, to give or send it away. He may have changed his plan completely, without telling Smerdyakov. And if there is the barest possibility of such an explanation, how can the prisoner be so positively accused of having committed murder for the sake of robbery, and of having actually carried out that robbery? This is approaching fiction. If it is maintained that something has been stolen, the thing must be produced, or at least its existence must be proved beyond doubt. Yet no one but Smerdyakov claims to have seen these notes.

"Not long ago in Petersburg a young man of eighteen, a peddler, went in broad daylight into a moneychanger's shop with an ax and killed the shopkeeper and carried off fifteen hundred roubles. Five hours later he was arrested and the whole sum was found on him, except for fifteen roubles which he had already spent. Moreover, a clerk on his return to the shop after the murder, informed the police not only of the exact sum stolen, but even of the notes and gold coins of which that sum was made up, and those very notes and coins were found on the criminal. This was followed by a full confession on the part of the murderer. That's what I call evidence, gentlemen of the jury! In that case I know, I see, I touch the money, and cannot deny its existence. Is it the same in the present case? And yet it is a question of life and death.

"Yes, I shall be told, but he was carousing that night,

squandering money; he was shown to have had fifteen hundred roubles—where did he get the money? But the very fact that only fifteen hundred could be found, and the other half of the sum could nowhere be discovered, shows that the money was not the same, and had never been in any envelope. By strict calculation of time it was proved at the preliminary inquiry that the prisoner ran straight from those women servants to Perhotin's without going home, and that he had been nowhere else. So he had been with people all the time and therefore could not have divided the three thousand in half and hidden half in town. It's just these facts that have led the prosecutor to assume that the money must be hidden in some crevice at Mokroe. Why not in the dungeons of the castle of Udolpho, gentlemen? Isn't this supposition really too fantastic and too romantic? And observe, if that supposition breaks down, the whole charge of robbery is scattered to the winds, for in that case what could have become of the other fifteen hundred roubles? By what miracle could they have disappeared, since it's proved that the prisoner went nowhere else? And we are ready to ruin a man's life with such suppositions!

"I will be told that the prisoner could not explain where he got the fifteen hundred, and everyone knew that he was without money before that night. Who knew it? The prisoner has made a clear and unflinching statement of the source of that money, and if you will have it so, gentlemen of the jury, nothing can be more probable than that statement, and more consistent with the temper and spirit of the prisoner. The prosecutor is charmed with his own fictional inventions. A man of weak will, who had brought himself to take the three thousand so insultingly offered by his fiancée, could not, we are told, have set aside half and sewn it up. But if he had done so, it is claimed, he would have unpicked it every two days and taken out a hundred, and so would have spent it all in a month. All this, you will remember, was presented in a tone that allowed for no contradiction. But what if the thing happened quite differently? What if you've been weaving a romantic story about quite a different kind of man? That's just it, you have invented quite a different man!

"I shall be told, perhaps, there are witnesses who swear that he spent on one day all that three thousand given him by his fiancée a month before the tragedy, so that he could not have divided the sum in half. But who are these witnesses? The value of their evidence has been shown in court already. Besides, in another man's hand a crust always seems larger, and not one of these witnesses counted that money; they all judged simply at sight. And the witness Maximov has testified that the prisoner had twenty thousand in his hand. You see, gentlemen of the jury, psychology is a two-edged weapon. Let me turn the other edge now and see what comes of it.

"A month before the murder the prisoner was entrusted by

his fiancée, Katerina, with three thousand roubles to mail to Moscow. But the question is: Is it true that they were entrusted to him in such an insulting and degrading way as was stated just now? The first statement made by the young lady on the subject was different, completely different. In the second statement we heard only cries of resentment and revenge, cries of long-concealed hatred. And the very fact that the witness gave her first evidence incorrectly, gives us a right to conclude that her second testimony may have been incorrect also. The prosecutor will not, dare not (his own words) touch on that story. So be it. I will not touch on it either, but will only venture to observe that if a high-principled person, such as that respected young lady unquestionably is, if such a person, I say, allows herself suddenly in court to contradict her first statement, with the obvious motive of ruining the prisoner, it is clear that this evidence has not been given impartially. Have not we the right to assume that a revengeful woman might have exaggerated? Yes, she may well have exaggerated, in particular, the insult and humiliation of her offering him the money. No, it was offered in such a way that it was possible to take it, especially for a man so easygoing as the prisoner. Besides he expected to receive shortly from his father the three thousand roubles that he felt was owing to him. It was unwise of him, but it was just his irresponsible want of judgment that made him so confident that his father would give him the money, that he would get it, and so could repay the debt.

"But the prosecutor refuses to allow that the prisoner could have set aside half the money and sewn it up in a little bag. That's not his character, he tells us. He couldn't have had such feelings. But yet he talked himself of the broad Karamazov nature; he cried out about the two extremes which a Karamazov can contemplate at once. Dmitri Karamazov has just such a two-sided nature, fluctuating between extremes. Even when he is moved by the most violent craving for riotous living, he can suddenly control himself, if something strikes him on the other side. And on the other side is love—that new love which had flamed up in his heart, and for that love he needed money; oh, far more than for carousing with his mistress. If she were to say to him: 'I am yours, I won't have Fyodor Karamazov,' then he must have money to take her away. That was more important than carousing. Could a Karamazov fail to understand this? That fear was just what he was suffering from— what is there improbable in his laying aside that money and concealing it in case of emergency?

"But time passed, and Fyodor Karamazov did not give the prisoner the three thousand; on the contrary, the prisoner heard that his father meant to use this sum to seduce the woman he, the prisoner, loved. 'If my father doesn't give me the money,' he thought, 'I will be a thief in Katerina's eyes.'

And then the idea occurred to him to go to Katerina, lay before her the fifteen hundred roubles he still carried around his neck, and say, 'I am a scoundrel, but not a thief.' So here we have a twofold reason why he should guard that sum of money, why he shouldn't unpick the little bag, and spend it a hundred at a time. Why should you deny the prisoner a sense of honor? Yes, he has a sense of honor, granted that it's misplaced, granted it's often mistaken, yet it exists and amounts to a passion. He has proved that.

"But now the situation becomes even more complex; his jealous torments reach a climax, and those same two questions torture his fevered brain more and more: 'If I repay Katerina, where can I get money to go off with Grushenka?' If he behaved wildly, drank, and made disturbances in the taverns in the course of that month, it was perhaps because he was wretched and strained beyond his powers of endurance. These two questions became so acute that they drove him at last to despair. He sent his younger brother to beg for the last time for the three thousand roubles, but without waiting for a reply, he burst in himself and ended by beating his old father in the presence of witnesses. After that he had no hope of getting the money from anyone; his father would certainly not give it to him after that.

"The same evening he struck himself on the breast, just on the upper part of the breast where the little bag was, and swore to his brother that he had the means of not being a scoundrel. He said that because he foresaw that he would not return the money, that he wouldn't have the character, that he wouldn't have the will power to do it. Why, why does the prosecutor refuse to believe the testimony of Alexey Karamazov, given so genuinely and sincerely, so spontaneously and convincingly? And why, on the contrary, does he try to force us to believe in money hidden in a crevice, in the dungeons of the castle of Udolpho?

"The same evening, after his talk with his brother, the prisoner wrote that fatal letter, and that letter is the main proof of the prisoner having committed robbery! 'I will beg from everyone, and if I don't get it I will murder my father and will take the envelope with the pink ribbon on it from under his mattress as soon as Ivan has gone.' A full program of the murder, we are told, so it must have been he. 'It has all been done as he wrote,' cries the prosecutor.

"But in the first place, it's the letter of a drunken man and it was written in great irritation. Secondly, he writes of the envelope from what he has heard from Smerdyakov, for he has not seen the envelope himself. And thirdly, he wrote it, but how can you prove that he did it? Did the prisoner take the envelope from under the pillow, did he find the money, did that money really exist? And was it to get money that the prisoner ran off, if you remember? He ran off not to steal, but

664

to find out where she was, the woman who had crushed him. He was not running to carry out a plan, to carry out what he had written, that is, not for an act of premeditated robbery. He ran suddenly, spontaneously, in a jealous fury. Yes! I shall be told, but when he got there and murdered his father he took the money, too. But did he murder him? The charge of robbery I repudiate with indignation. A man cannot be accused of robbery, if it's impossible to state accurately what he has stolen. But did he murder his father without robbery, did he murder him at all? Is that proved? Isn't that, too, a romantic invention?"

12. And There Was No Murder Either

"ALLOW ME, GENTLEMEN OF THE JURY, to remind you that a man's life is at stake and that you must be careful. We have heard the prosecutor himself admit that until today he hesitated to accuse the prisoner of a full and conscious premeditation of the crime. He hesitated till he saw that fatal drunken letter which was produced in court today. 'All was done as written.' But, I repeat again, he was running to her, to seek her, solely to find out where she was. That's a fact that can't be disputed. Had she been at home, he would not have run away but would have remained at her side, and so he would not have done what he promised to do in the letter. He ran unexpectedly and accidentally. By that time he probably did not even remember his drunken letter. 'He snatched up the pestle,' they say. You will remember how a whole edifice of psychology was built on that pestle—why he was bound to look at that pestle as a weapon, to snatch it up, and so on, and so on. A very commonplace idea occurs to me at this point. What if that pestle had not been in sight, had not been lying on the shelf from which it was snatched by the prisoner, but had been put away in a cupboard? It would not have caught the prisoner's eye, and he would have run away without a weapon, with empty hands, and then he would certainly not have killed anyone. How then can I look upon the pestle as a proof of premeditation?

"Yes, but he talked in the taverns of murdering his father. And two days before, on the evening when he wrote his drunken letter, he was quiet and only quarreled with a workman in the tavern, because a Karamazov could not help quarreling! But my answer to that is that, if he was planning such a murder in accordance with his letter, he certainly would not have quarreled even with a workman and probably would not have gone into the tavern at all. A person plotting such a crime seeks quiet and retirement, seeks to efface himself, to avoid

665

being seen and heard. He does this not from calculation, but from instinct. Gentlemen of the jury, the psychological method is a two-edged weapon, and we, too, can use it. As for all this shouting in taverns throughout the month, don't we often hear children or drunkards shouting: 'I'll kill you'? But they don't murder anyone. And that letter—isn't that simply drunken irritability, too? Isn't that simply the shout of the brawler outside the tavern: 'I'll kill you! I'll kill the lot of you!' Why not, why isn't it that? What reason have we to call that letter 'fatal' rather than absurd? Because his father has been found murdered, because a witness saw the prisoner running out of the garden with a weapon in his hand and was knocked down by him? Because of this, we are told, everything was done as he had planned in writing, and the letter is not 'absurd,' but 'fatal.'

"Now, thank God, we've come to the real point: 'Since he was in the garden, he must have murdered him.' In those few words: 'Since he *was*, then he *must*' lies the whole case for the prosecution. He was there, so he must have. And what if there is no *must* about it, even if he was there? Oh, I admit that the chain of evidence—the coincidences—are really suggestive. But examine all these facts separately, regardless of their connection. Why, for instance, does the prosecution refuse to admit the truth of the prisoner's statement that he ran away from his father's window? Remember the sarcasms in which the prosecutor indulged at the expense of the respectful and 'pious' sentiments which suddenly came over the prisoner. But what if there were something of the sort, a feeling of religious awe, if not of filial respect? 'My mother must have been praying for me at that moment,' were the prisoner's words at the preliminary inquiry. And so he ran away as soon as he had convinced himself that Madame Svyetlov was not in his father's house. 'But he could not convince himself by looking through the window,' the prosecutor objects. But why couldn't he? Why? The window opened at the signals given by the prisoner. Some word might have been uttered by Fyodor Karamazov, some exclamation which showed the prisoner that she was not there. Why should we assume everything as we imagine it, as we make up our minds to imagine it? A thousand things may happen in reality which elude the keenest imagination.

" 'Yes, but Gregory saw the door open and so the prisoner certainly was in the house, therefore he killed him.' Now about the door, gentlemen of the jury. . . . Observe that we have only the statement of one witness as to that door, and he was at the time in such a condition, that . . . But supposing the door was open; supposing the prisoner has lied in denying it from an instinct of self-defense natural in his position; supposing he did go into the house—well, what then? How does it follow that because he was there he committed the murder?

666

He might have dashed in, run through the rooms; might have pushed his father away; might have struck him; but as soon as he had made sure Madame Svyetlov was not there, he might have run away rejoicing that she was not there and that he had not killed his father. And it was perhaps just because he had escaped from the temptation to kill his father, because he had a clear conscience and was rejoicing at not having killed him, that he was capable of a pure feeling, the feeling of pity and compassion. It was perhaps just because of these things that he jumped down from the fence a minute later to help Gregory after he had, in his excitement, knocked him down.

"With terrible eloquence the prosecutor has described to us the dreadful state of the prisoner's mind at Mokroe when love again lay before him calling him to new life, while love was impossible for him because he had his father's bloodstained corpse behind him and beyond that corpse—retribution. And yet the prosecutor allowed him love, which he explained by comparing him to a criminal being taken to execution, about it being still far off, and so on and so on. But again I ask, Mr. Prosecutor, have you not invented a new personality? Is the prisoner so coarse and heartless as to be able to think at that moment of love and of escaping punishment, if his hands were really stained with his father's blood? No, no no! As soon as it was made plain to him that she loved him and called him to her side, promising him new happiness . . . Oh then, I protest he must have felt the impulse to suicide doubled, trebled, and must have killed himself, if he had his father's murder on his conscience. Oh, he would not have forgotten where his pistols lay! I know the prisoner; the savage, stony heartlessness ascribed to him by the prosecutor is inconsistent with his character. He would have killed himself, that's certain. He did not kill himself just because 'his mother's prayers had saved him,' and he was innocent of his father's blood. He was troubled, he was grieving that night at Mokroe only about old Gregory and praying to God that the old man would recover, that his blow had not been fatal. Why not accept such an interpretation of the facts? What proof have we that the prisoner is lying?

"But we shall be told again: 'There is his father's corpse! If he ran away without murdering him, who did murder him?' Here, I repeat, you have the whole logic of the prosecution. Who murdered Fyodor Karamazov, if not he? There's no one to put in his place.

"Gentlemen of the jury, is that really so? Is it actually true that there is no one else at all? We've heard the prosecutor count on his fingers all the persons who were in that house that night. They were five in number; three of them, I agree, could not have been responsible—the murdered man himself, old Gregory, and his wife. There are left then the prisoner and Smerdyakov, and the prosecutor dramatically exclaims that the prisoner pointed to Smerdyakov because he had no one else to fix on, that had there been a sixth person, even a phantom of a sixth person, he would have abandoned the charge against Smerdyakov at once in shame and have accused the other. But, gentlemen of the jury, why may I not draw the very opposite conclusion? There are two people—the prisoner and Smerdyakov. Why can I not say that you accuse my client simply because you have no one else to accuse? And you have no one else only because you have determined to exclude Smerdyakov from all suspicion.

"It's true, of course, that Smerdyakov is accused only by the prisoner, his two brothers, and Madame Svyetlov. But there are others who accuse him: there are vague rumors of a doubt, of a suspicion, an obscure report, a feeling of expectation. Finally, we have the evidence of a combination of facts very suggestive, though, I admit, inconclusive. In the first place we have on the day of the tragedy that epileptic fit, for the genuineness of which the prosecutor, for some reason, has felt obliged to make a careful defense. Then Smerdyakov's sudden suicide on the eve of the trial. Then the equally startling evidence given in court today by Ivan Karamazov, who believed in his brother's guilt, but has today produced a bundle of notes and proclaimed Smerdyakov as the murderer. Oh, I fully share the court's and the prosecutor's conviction that Ivan Karamazov is suffering from brain fever, that his statement may really be a desperate effort, planned in delirium, to save his brother by throwing the guilt on the dead man. But again Smerdyakov's name is pronounced, again there is a suggestion of mystery. There is something unexplained, incomplete. Perhaps it may one day be explained. But we won't go into that now. Of that later.

"The court has resolved to go on with the trial, but, meantime, I might make a few remarks about the character of Smerdyakov as drawn by the prosecutor. While I admire the prosecutor's talent I cannot agree with him. I have visited Smerdyakov. I have seen him and talked to him, and he made a very different impression on me. He was weak in health, it is true; but in character, in spirit, he was by no means the weak man the prosecutor has made him out to be. I found in him no trace of the timidity on which the prosecutor insisted. There was no simplicity about him, either. I found in him, on the contrary, extreme mistrustfulness concealed under a mask of naiveté, and an intelligence of considerable range. The prosecutor was too simple in taking him for weak-minded. He made a very definite impression on me; I left him with the conviction that he was a distinctly spiteful creature, excessively ambitious, vindictive, and intensely envious. I made some inquiries: he resented his parentage, was ashamed of it, and would clench his teeth when he remembered that he was the son of 'stinking Lizaveta.' He was disrespectful to the servant Gregory and his wife, who had cared for him in his childhood. He cursed and jeered at Russia. He dreamed of going to France and becoming a Frenchman. He often said that he hadn't the money to do so. I believe that he loved no one but himself and had a strangely high opinion of himself. His conception of culture was limited to good clothes, clean shirts and polished boots. Believing himself to be the illegitimate son of Fyodor Karamazov (there is evidence of this) he might well have resented his position, compared with that of his master's legitimate sons. They had everything, he nothing. They had all the rights, they had the inheritance, while he was only the cook and valet. He told me himself that he had helped Fyodor Karamazov to put the notes in the envelope. The destination of that sum—a sum which would have made his career—must have been hateful to him. Moreover, he saw three thousand roubles in new rainbow-colored notes. (I asked him about that on purpose.) Oh, beware of showing an ambitious and envious man a large sum of money! And it was the first time he had seen so much money in the hands of one man. The sight of the rainbow-colored notes may have made a morbid impression on his imagination, but with no immediate results.

"The talented prosecutor, with extraordinary subtlety, sketched for us all the arguments for and against Smerdyakov's guilt, and asked us in particular what motive Smerdyakov had in feigning a fit. But he may not have been feigning at all. The fit may have happened quite naturally, and it may have passed off quite naturally. And he may have recovered, not completely perhaps, but still regaining consciousness, as happens with epileptics.

"The prosecutor asks at what moment could Smerdyakov have committed the murder. It is very easy to point out that moment. He might have waked up from deep sleep (for he was only asleep—an epileptic fit is always followed by a deep sleep) at that moment when old Gregory shouted at the top of his voice: 'Parricide!' That shout in the dark and stillness may have waked Smerdyakov whose sleep may have been less sound at the moment; or he might have waked up an hour before.

"Getting out of bed, he goes almost unconsciously and with no definite motive toward the sound to see what's the matter. His head is still clouded with his attack, his faculties are half asleep. Once in the garden, he walks to the lighted windows and he hears terrible news from his master, who would be, of course, glad to see him. His mind sets to work at once. He hears all the details from his frightened master and gradually in his disordered brain an idea takes shape—terrible, but seductive and irresistibly logical. To kill the old man, take the three thousand roubles and throw all the blame on to his young master. A terrible lust of money might seize him as he realized the safety of his position. Oh! these sudden and irresistible impulses come so often when there is a favorable opportunity, especially with those who have had no idea of committing a murder beforehand. And Smerdyakov may have gone in and carried out his plan. With what weapon? Why, with any stone picked up in the garden. But what for, with what object? Why, the three thousand which means a career for him. Oh, I am not contradicting myself—the money may have existed. And perhaps Smerdyakov alone knew where to find it, where his master kept it. . . . And what about the torn envelope on the floor?

"Just now, when the prosecutor was explaining his theory that only an inexperienced thief like Dmitri Karamazov would have left the envelope on the floor, and not one like Smerdyakov, who would have avoided leaving a piece of evidence against himself, I thought as I listened that I was hearing something very familiar. Would you believe it, I have heard that very argument, that very conjecture, of how Dmitri Karamazov would have behaved, precisely two days ago, from Smerdyakov himself. What's more it struck me at the time. I felt that there was an artificial simplicity about Smerdyakov; that he was in a hurry to suggest this idea to me so that I might imagine it was my own. He insinuated it, as it were. Did he not insinuate the same idea at the inquiry and suggest it to the prosecutor?

"'I shall be asked, 'What about the old woman, Gregory's wife? She heard the sick man moaning close by, all night.' Yes, she heard him, but that evidence is extremely unreliable. I knew a lady who complained bitterly that she had been kept awake all night by a dog in the yard. Yet the poor beast, it appeared, had only yelped once or twice in the night. And that's natural. If anyone is asleep and hears a groan he wakes up, annoyed at being disturbed, but instantly falls asleep again. Two hours later, another groan, he wakes up and falls asleep again; and the same thing again two hours later—three times altogether in the night. Next morning the sleeper wakes up and complains that someone has been groaning all night and keeping him awake. It is natural that it seems so to him; the intervals of two hours of sleep he does not remember, he only remembers the moments of waking, so he feels he has been awake all night.

"But why, why, asks the prosecutor, did Smerdyakov not confess in his last letter? Why did his conscience prompt him to one step and not to both? But, excuse me, conscience implies penitence, and the suicide may not have felt penitence, but only despair. Despair and penitence are two very different things. Despair may be vindictive and irreconcilable, and the suicide, laying his hands on himself, may well have felt redoubled hatred for those whom he had envied all his life.

"Gentlemen of the jury, beware of a miscarriage of justice! I have put before you just now a number of questionable
670

points. Find the error in my reasoning; find the impossibility, the absurdity. And if there is but a shade of possibility, but a shade of probability in my propositions, do not condemn the prisoner. . . . I swear by all that is sacred, I fully believe in the explanation of the murder I have just presented. What troubles me and makes me indignant is that of all the mass of facts heaped up by the prosecution against the prisoner, there is not a single one which is certain and irrefutable. And yet the unhappy man is to be ruined by the accumulation of these doubtful facts. Yes, the accumulated effort is awful: the blood, the blood dripping from his fingers, the bloodstained shirt, the dark night resounding with the shout 'Parricide!' and the old man falling with a broken head. And then the mass of phrases, statements, gestures, shouts! Oh, this has so much influence, it can so bias the mind! But, gentlemen of the jury, can it bias your minds? Remember, you have been given absolute power to bind and to free, but the greater the power, the more terrible its responsibility.

"I do not draw back one iota from what I have said just now, but suppose for one moment I agreed with the prosecution that my luckless client had stained his hands with his father's blood. This is only an hypothesis, I repeat; I never for one instant doubt of his innocence. But, so be it, I assume that my client is guilty of parricide. Even so, hear what I have to say. I have it in my heart to say something more to you, for I feel that there must be a great conflict in your hearts and minds. . . . Forgive my referring to your hearts and minds, gentlemen of the jury, but I want to be truthful and sincere to the end. Let us all be sincere!"

At this point the speech was interrupted by loud applause. The last words were pronounced with such sincerity that everyone felt that what he was about to say would be of the greatest importance. But the President, hearing the applause, threatened in a loud voice to clear the court if such an incident were repeated. Every sound was hushed and Fetyukovitch began in a voice full of feeling quite unlike the tone he had used before.

13. A Corrupter of Thought

"IT's NOT ONLY THE ACCUMULATION OF FACTS that threatens my client with ruin, gentlemen of the jury," he began, "what is really damning for my client is one fact—the dead body of his father. Had it been an ordinary case of murder you would reject the charge in view of the triviality, the incompleteness, and the fantastic character of the evidence, if you examine each part of it separately. In the face of such evidence you would hesitate to ruin a man's life simply from the prejudice against him which he has, alas, only too well deserved. But it's not an ordinary case of murder, it's a case of parricide. That impresses men's minds, and to such a degree that the very triviality and incompleteness of the evidence becomes less trivial and less incomplete even to an unprejudiced mind. How can such a prisoner be acquitted? What if he committed the murder and gets off unpunished? That is what everyone, almost involuntarily, instinctively, feels at heart.

"Yes, it's a fearful thing to shed a father's blood—the father who has begotten me, loved me, not spared his life for me, grieved over my illnesses from childhood up, troubled all his life for my happiness, and has lived in my joys, in my successes. To murder such a father—that's inconceivable. Gentlemen of the jury, what is a father—a real father? What is the meaning of that great word? What is the idea enshrined in that word? We have only indicated in part what a true father is and what he ought to be. In the case in which we are now so deeply occupied and over which our hearts are aching—in the present case, the father, Fyodor Karamazov, did not correspond to that conception of a father to which we have just referred. That's the misfortune. And indeed some fathers are a misfortune. Let us examine this misfortune rather more closely; we must shrink from nothing, gentlemen of the jury, considering the importance of the decision you have to make. It's our particular duty not to shrink from any idea, like children or frightened women, as the talented prosecutor happily expresses it.

"But in the course of his heated speech my esteemed opponent (and he was my opponent before I opened my lips) exclaimed several times: 'Oh, I will not yield the defense of the prisoner to the lawyer who has come down from Petersburg. I accuse, but I also defend!' He exclaimed that several times, but forgot to mention that if this terrible prisoner was for twenty-three years so grateful for a mere pound of nuts given him by the only man who had been kind to him as a child in his father's house, might not such a man well have remembered for twenty-three years how he ran in his father's back yard, 'without boots on his feet and with his little trousers hanging by one button'—to use the words of the kind-hearted Doctor Herzenstube?

"Oh, gentlemen of the jury, why need we look more closely at this misfortune, why repeat what we already know? What did my client meet with when he arrived here, at his father's house, and why depict my client as a heartless egoist and monster? He is uncontrolled, he is wild and unruly—we are trying him now for that—but who is responsible for his life? Who is responsible for his having received such an unseemly upbringing in spite of his kind disposition and his grateful and sensitive heart? Did anyone train him to be reasonable? Was he enlightened by education? Did anyone love him in his childhood?

672

My client was left to the care of Providence like a beast of the field. He thirsted perhaps to see his father after long years of separation. A thousand times perhaps he may, recalling his childhood, have driven away the loathsome phantoms that haunted his childish dreams and with all his heart he may have longed to embrace and to forgive his father! And what awaited him? He was met by cynical taunts, suspicions and wrangling about money. He heard nothing but revolting talk and vicious precepts uttered daily over the brandy. And at last he saw his father seducing his mistress with his own money. Oh, gentlemen of the jury, that was cruel and revolting! And that old man was always complaining of the disrespect and cruelty of his son. He slandered him in public, injured his reputation, brought up his unpaid debts to get him thrown into prison.

"Gentlemen of the jury, people like my client, who are fierce, unruly and uncontrolled on the surface, are sometimes, most frequently indeed, exceedingly tender-hearted, only they don't express it. Don't laugh, don't laugh at my idea! The talented prosecutor laughed mercilessly just now at my client loving Schiller—loving the sublime and beautiful! I would not have laughed at that. Yes, such natures—oh, let me speak in defense of such natures, so often and so cruelly misunderstood—these natures often thirst for tenderness, goodness, and justice, as it were, in contrast to themselves, their unruliness, their ferocity—they thirst for it unconsciously. Passionate and fierce on the surface, they are painfully capable of loving woman, for instance, and with a spiritual and elevated love. Again do not laugh at me. This is very often the case in such natures. They cannot hide their passions, sometimes very coarse. These passions are conspicuous and are noticed, but the inner man is unseen. Their passions are quickly exhausted. But, by the side of a noble and devoted woman that seemingly coarse and rough man seeks a new life, seeks to correct himself, to be better, to become honorable, 'sublime and beautiful,' however much the expression has been ridiculed.

"I said just now that I would not venture to touch upon my client's engagement. But I may say half a word. What we heard just now was not evidence, but only the scream of a frenzied and revengeful woman, and it was not for her—oh, not for her—to reproach him with treachery, for she has betrayed him! If she had had but a little time for reflection she would not have given such evidence. Oh, do not believe her! No, my client is not a monster, as she called him!

"The Lover of Mankind on the eve of His Crucifixion said: 'I am the Good Shepherd. The good shepherd lays down his life for his sheep, so that not one of them might be lost.' Let not a man's soul be lost through us!

"I asked just now what does 'father' mean, and exclaimed that it was a great word, a precious name. But one must use words honestly, gentlemen, and I venture to call things by their ght names; such a father as old Fyodor Karamazov cannot be called a father and does not deserve to be. Filial love for an unworthy father is an absurdity, an impossibility. Love cannot be created from nothing; only God can create something from nothing.

"'Fathers, provoke not your children to wrath,' the apostle writes, from a heart glowing with love. It's not for the sake of my client that I quote these sacred words, I mention them for all fathers. Who has authorized me to preach to fathers? No one. But as a man and a citizen I make my appeal! We are not long on earth, we do many evil deeds and say many evil words. So let us catch a favorable moment when we are all together to say a good word to each other. That's what I am doing: while I am in this place I take advantage of my opportunity. Not for nothing is this tribune given us by the highest authority—all Russia hears us! I am not speaking only for the fathers here present, I cry aloud to all fathers: 'Fathers, provoke not your children to wrath.' Yes, let us first fulfill Christ's injunction ourselves and only then venture to expect it of our children. Otherwise we are not fathers, but enemies of our children, and they are not our children, but our enemies—we have made them our enemies ourselves. 'What measure ye mete it shall be measured unto you again'—it's not I who say that, it's the Gospel precept, measure to others according as they measure to you. How can we blame children if they measure us according to our measure?

"Not long ago a servant girl in Finland was suspected of having secretly given birth to a child. She was watched, and a box was found in the corner of the loft behind some bricks. It was opened and inside was found the body of the newborn child which she had killed. In the same box were found the skeletons of two other babies which, according to her own confession, she had also killed at the moment of their birth.

"Gentlemen of the jury, was she a mother to her children? She gave birth to them; but was she a mother to them? Would anyone venture to give her the sacred name of mother? Let us be bold, gentlemen, let us be audacious even; it's our duty to be so at this moment and not to be afraid of certain words and ideas like the Moscow women in Ostrovsky's play, who are scared at the sound of certain words. No, let us prove that the progress of the last few years has touched even us, and let us say plainly, a father is not merely he who begets the child but he who begets it and does his duty by it.

"Oh, of course, there is the other meaning, there is the other interpretation of the word 'father,' which insists that any father, even though he be a monster, even though he be the enemy of his children, still remains a father simply because he begot the child. But this is, so to say, the mystical meaning which I cannot understand with my intellect, but can only accept through faith, or better, *on faith*, like many other things

674

which I do not understand, but which religion bids me believe. But in that case let it be kept outside the sphere of actual life. In the sphere of actual life, which has its own rights, but also lays upon us great duties and obligations, in that sphere, if we want to be humane—Christian, in face—we must act only upon convictions justified by reason and experience. We must act rationally, and not as though in dream and delirium, that we may not do harm, that we may not ill-treat and ruin a man. Then it will be real Christian work, not only mystic, but rational and philanthropic . . ."

There was applause at this from many parts of the court, but Fetyukovitch waved his hands as though imploring them to let him finish without interruption. The court relapsed into silence at once. He went on.

"Do you suppose, gentlemen, that our children as they grow up and begin to reason can avoid such questions? No, they cannot, and we must not impose on them an impossible restriction. The sight of an unworthy father involuntarily suggests tormenting questions to a young person, especially when he compares him with the fathers of his friends. The conventional answer to this question is: 'He begot you, and you are his flesh and blood, and therefore you are bound to love him.' The youth involuntarily reflects: 'But did he love me when he begot me?' He wonders more and more: 'Was it for my sake he begot me? He did not know me, not even my sex, at that moment, at the moment of passion, perhaps, inflamed by wine. And he has only transmitted to me a propensity to drunkenness—that's all he's done for me. . . . Why am I bound to love him, simply for begetting me when he has cared nothing for me all my life?'

"Oh, perhaps those questions strike you as coarse and cruel, but do not expect an impossible restraint from a young mind. 'Drive nature out of the door and it will fly in at the window.' And above all, let us not be afraid of words, but decide the question according to the dictates of reason and humanity and not of mystic ideas. How shall it be decided? Why, like this. Let the son stand before his father and ask him: 'Father, tell me, why must I love you? Father, show me that I must love you.' And if that father is able to answer him and show him good reason, we have a real, normal, parental relation, not resting on mystical prejudice, but on a rational, responsible and strictly humanitarian basis. But if he cannot answer, there's an end to the family tie. He is not a father to him, and the son has a right to look upon him as a stranger, and even an enemy. Our tribune, gentlemen of the jury, ought to be a school of true and sound ideas."

Fetyukovitch was interrupted by irrepressible applause. Of course, it was not the whole audience, but a good half of it that applauded. The fathers and mothers who were present applauded. Shrieks and exclamations were heard from the gallery, where the ladies were sitting. Handkerchiefs were waved.

he President rang his bell with all his might. He was irritated, but did not venture to clear the court as he had threatened. Even important people, old men with stars on their breasts, sitting on specially reserved seats behind the judges, applauded and waved their handkerchiefs. So that when the noise died down, the President confined himself to repeating his threat to clear the court. Fetyukovitch, excited and triumphant, continued his speech.

"Gentlemen of the jury, you remember that awful night of which so much has been said today, when the son climbed over the fence and stood face to face with the enemy and persecutor who had begotten him. I insist most emphatically it was not for money that he ran to his father's house; the charge of robbery is an absurdity, as I proved before. And it was not to murder his father that he broke into the house, oh, no! If he had planned to do that he would, at least, have taken the precaution of arming himself beforehand. He picked up the brass pestle instinctively without knowing why he did it. Granted that he deceived his father by tapping at the window, granted that he entered the house—I've said already that I do not for a moment believe that story, but let it be so, let us suppose it for a moment . . . Gentlemen, I swear to you by all that's holy, if it had not been his father, but an ordinary enemy, he would, after running through the rooms and satisfying himself that the woman was not there, gone off without doing any harm to his rival. He would have struck him, pushed him away perhaps, nothing more, because he had no thought and no time to spare for that. What he wanted to know was where she was. But his father, his father! The mere sight of the father who had hated him from his childhood, had been his enemy, his persecutor, and now his unnatural rival, was enough. A feeling of hatred came over him involuntarily, irresistibly, clouding his reason. It surged up in one moment! It was an impulse of madness and insanity, but also an impulse of nature, irresistibly and unconsciously avenging the violation of its eternal laws.

"But the prisoner even then did not murder his father—I maintain that, I cry that aloud!—no, he only brandished the pestle in a burst of indignant disgust, not meaning to kill him, not knowing that he would kill him. Had he not had this fatal pestle in his hand, he would only have knocked his father down perhaps, but would not have killed him. As he ran away, he did not know whether he had killed the old man. Such a murder is not a murder. Such a murder is not a parricide. No, the murder of such a father cannot be called parricide. Such a murder can only be labeled parricide by prejudice.

"But I appeal to you again and again from the depths of my soul; did this murder actually take place? Gentlemen of the jury, if we convict and punish the prisoner he will say to himself: 'These people have done nothing for my upbringing, for

676

my education, nothing to improve my lot, nothing to make me better, nothing to make a man of me. These people have not given me to eat and to drink, have not visited me in prison and nakedness, and here they have sent me to penal servitude. I owe them nothing now; I owe nothing to anyone. They are evil and I will be evil. They are cruel and I will be cruel.' That is what he will say, gentlemen of the jury. And I swear, by finding him guilty you will only make it easier for him; you will ease his conscience, he will curse the blood he has shed and will not regret it. At the same time you will destroy in him the possibility of his becoming a new man, for he will remain in evil and blindness all his life.

"But do you want to punish him fearfully, terribly, with the most awful punishment that could be imagined, and at the same time to save him and regenerate his soul? If you do, then overwhelm him with your mercy! You will see, you will hear how he will tremble and be horror-struck. 'How can I endure this mercy? How can I endure so much love? Am I worthy of it?' That's what he will cry.

"Oh, I know, I know that heart, that wild but grateful heart, gentlemen of the jury! It will bow before your mercy; it thirsts for a great and loving deed, it will be won over and mount upwards. There are souls which, in their limitation, blame the whole world. But subdue such a soul with mercy, show it love, and it will cure its past, for there are many good impulses in it. Such a heart will expand and see that God is merciful and that men are good and just. He will be horror-stricken; he will be crushed by remorse and the vast obligation laid upon him in the future. And he will not say then: 'I owe them nothing,' but will say: 'I am guilty in the sight of all men and am more unworthy than all.' With tears of penitence and poignant anguish, he will exclaim: 'Others are better than I, they wanted to save me, not to ruin me!' Oh, this act of mercy is so easy for you, for in the absence of anything like real evidence it will be too awful for you to pronounce: 'Yes, he is guilty.'

"Better to acquit ten guilty men than punish one innocent man! Do you hear, do you hear that majestic voice from the past century of our glorious history? It is not for an insignificant person like me to remind you that the Russian court does not exist for the punishment only, but also for the salvation of the criminal! Let other nations think of retribution and the letter of the law, we will cling to the spirit and the meaning —the salvation and the reformation of the lost. If this is true, if Russia and her justice are such, she may go forward with confidence! Do not try to scare us with your wild troikas from which all nations stand aside in horror. Not a runaway troika, but the stately chariot of Russia will move calmly and majestically to its goal. In your hands is the fate of my client, in your hands is the fate of Russian justice. You must defend it, you must save it, you must prove that there are men to watch over it, that it is in good hands!"

14. The Peasants Stand Firm

THIS WAS HOW Fetyukovitch concluded his speech, and the enthusiasm of the audience burst like a storm. It was out of the question to stop it; the women wept, many of the men wept too, even two important people shed tears. The President submitted and did not ring his bell. The suppression of such enthusiasm would be the suppression of something sacred, as the ladies cried afterward. Fetyukovitch was genuinely touched.

At this moment Ippolit Kirillovitch got up to make certain objections. People looked at him with hatred. "What? What's the meaning of it? He dares to make objections," the ladies babbled. But if the whole world of ladies, including his wife, had protested he could not have been stopped at that moment. He was pale, he was shaking with emotion, his first phrases were even unintelligible, he gasped for breath, could hardly speak clearly, lost the thread of his argument. But he soon recovered. Of his new speech I will quote only a few sentences.

". . . I am reproached with having woven a romantic story. But what is this defense if not one romance on the top of another? All that was lacking was poetry. Fyodor Karamazov, while waiting for his mistress, tears open the envelope and throws it on the floor. We are even told what he said while engaged in this strange act. Is not this a flight of fancy? And what proof have we that he took out the money? Who heard what he said? . . . The weak-minded idiot, Smerdyakov, transformed into a Byron-like hero, avenging society for his illegitimate birth—isn't this a romance in the style of Byron? And the son who breaks into his father's house and murders him without murdering him is not even a romance—this is a sphinx setting us a riddle which he cannot solve himself. If he murdered him, he murdered him. What's the meaning of his murdering him without having murdered him—who can make head or tail of this kind of reasoning?

"Then we are admonished that our tribune is a tribune of true and sound ideas and from this tribune of 'sound ideas' is heard a solemn declaration that to call the murder of a father 'parricide' is nothing but a prejudice! But if parricide is a prejudice, and if every child is to ask his father why he is to love him, what will become of us? What will become of the foundations of society? What will become of the family? Parricide, it appears, is only a bogey of Moscow merchants' wives. . . . The most precious, the most sacred guarantees for the destiny and future of Russian justice are presented to us in a perverted and frivolous form, simply to attain an object—to obtain the justification of something which cannot be justified. 'Oh, crush him with mercy,' cries the counsel for the defense. But that's all the criminal wants, and tomorrow it will be seen how much he is crushed. And is not the counsel for the defense too modest in asking only for the acquittal of the prisoner? Why not found a charity in the honor of the parricide to commemorate his exploit among future generations? Religion and the Gospel are corrected—that's all mysticism, we are told, and ours is the only true Christianity which has been subjected to the analysis of reason and common sense. And so they set up before us a false semblance of Christ! 'What measure ye mete so it shall be meted unto you again,' cries the counsel for the defense. And he instantly deduces that Christ teaches us to measure as it is measured to us—and this from the tribune of truth and sound sense! We look into the Gospel only on the eve of making speeches, in order to dazzle the audience by our knowledge. We use the Gospel to produce a certain effect—all to serve our purpose! But what Christ commands us is something very different. He bids us beware of doing this, because the wicked world does this, but we ought to forgive and to turn the other cheek, and not to measure to our persecutors as they measure to us. This is what our God has taught us and not that to forbid children to murder their fathers is a prejudice. And we will not from the tribune of truth and good sense correct the Gospel of our Lord, Whom the counsel for the defense deigns to call only 'the crucified lover of humanity,' in opposition to all orthodox Russia, which calls to Him, 'For Thou art our God!' "

At this the President intervened and ordered Ippolit Kirillovitch not to exaggerate, not to overstep the bounds, and so on, as presidents always do in such cases. The audience, too, was uneasy. The public was restless; there were even exclamations of indignation. Fetyukovitch did not reply. He only mounted the dais and with an offended voice, laying his hand on his heart, spoke a few words full of dignity. He touched again, lightly and ironically, on "romancing" and "psychology," and in an appropriate place quoted, "Jupiter, you are angry, therefore you are wrong," which provoked a burst of approving laughter in the audience, for Ippolit Kirillovitch was by no means like Jupiter. Then referring to the accusation that he was teaching the young generation to murder their fathers, Fetyukovitch observed, with great dignity, that he would not even answer. As for the prosecutor's charge of uttering unorthodox opinions, Fetyukovitch hinted that it was a personal insinuation and that he had expected in this court to be secure from accusations "damaging to my reputation as a citizen and a loyal subject." But at these words the President interrupted him, also, and Fetyukovitch concluded his speech with a bow. He received the approval of the audience, and Ippolit Kirillovitch was, in the opinion of our ladies, "crushed for good."

The prisoner was then allowed to speak. Dmitri stood up but said very little. He was exhausted, physically and mentally. The look of strength and independence with which he had entered in the morning had almost disappeared. It seemed as though he had passed through an experience that day, which had taught him for the rest of his life something very important he had not understood till then. His voice was weak, he did not shout as before. In his words there was a note of humility, defeat and submission.

"What am I to say, gentlemen of the jury? The hour of judgment has come for me, I feel the hand of God upon me! The end has come to an erring man! But, before God, I repeat to you, I am innocent of my father's blood! For the last time I repeat, I did not kill him! I was at fault but I loved what is good. I tried to reform but I lived like a beast. I thank the prosecutor, he told me many things about myself that I did not know; but it's not true that I killed my father, the prosecutor is mistaken. I thank my lawyer, too. I cried listening to him; but it's not true that I killed my father, and he should not have assumed it. And don't believe the doctors. I am perfectly sane, only my heart is heavy. If you spare me, if you let me go, I will pray for you. I will be a better man. I give you my word before God I will! And if you condemn me, I'll break my sword over my head myself and kiss the pieces. But spare me, do not rob me of my God! I know myself, I shall rebel! My heart is heavy, gentlemen . . . spare me!"

He almost fell back in his chair. His voice broke. He could hardly speak the last phrase.

Then the judges proceeded to put the questions and began to ask both sides to formulate their conclusions. But I will not describe the details. At last the jury rose to retire for deliberation. The President was very tired, and so his last charge to the jury was rather feeble. "Be impartial, don't be influenced by the eloquence of the defense, but yet weigh the arguments. Remember that a great responsibility is laid upon you," and so on and so on.

The jury withdrew and the court adjourned.

People got up, moved about, exchanged their impressions and refreshed themselves at the buffet. It was very late, almost one o'clock in the morning but nobody went away. All waited with sinking hearts; though that is, perhaps, too much to say, for the ladies were only in a state of hysterical impatience and their hearts were untroubled. An acquittal they thought was inevitable. They prepared themselves for the dramatic moment. I must admit that many men were also convinced that an acquittal was inevitable. Some were pleased, some frowned,

while others were dejected, not wanting Dmitri to be acquitted
Fetyukovitch himself was confident of his success. He was surrounded by people congratulating him and fawning upon him.

"There are," he said to one group, as I was told afterwards, "there are invisible threads which bind the counsel for the defense with the jury. One feels during one's speech if they are being spun. I was aware of them. They exist. Our cause is won."

"What will our peasants say?" asked a stout, cross-looking, pockmarked gentleman, a landowner, approaching another group.

"But they are not all peasants. There are four government clerks among them."

"Yes, there are clerks," said a member of the district council, joining the group.

"And do you know Nazaryev, the merchant with the medal? He's on the jury."

"What about him?"

"He is a man with brains."

"But he never speaks."

"He is no great talker, but so much the better. There's no need for the Petersburg man to teach him; he could teach all Petersburg himself. He's the father of twelve children. Think of that!"

"You don't think they will condemn him?" a young official exclaimed in another group.

"They'll acquit him for certain," said a voice.

"It would be disgraceful not to acquit him!" cried the official. "Suppose he did murder him—there are fathers and fathers! And, besides, he was in such a frenzy. . . . He really may have done nothing but swing the pestle in the air, and accidentally knocked the old man down. But it was too bad they dragged the valet in. That was a stupid theory! If I'd been in Fetyukovitch's place, I would have said straight out: 'He murdered him; but he is not guilty, damn it all!'"

"That's what he did, only without saying 'Damn it all!'"

"Yes, he almost said that," put in a third voice.

"Why, during Lent an actress was acquitted in our town after having cut the throat of her lover's lawful wife."

"Oh, but she did not finish cutting it."

"That makes no difference. She began cutting it."

"What did you think of what he said about children? Good, wasn't it?"

"Excellent!"

"And about mysticism, too!"

"Oh, drop mysticism!" cried someone. "Think of Ippolit and his fate from this day forth. His wife will scratch his eyes out tomorrow for Dmitri's sake."

"Is she here?"

"What an idea! If she'd been here she'd have scratched

em out in court. She is at home with a toothache. He, he, e!"

"He, he, he!"

In a third group: "I think they will acquit Dmitri, after all."

"I won't be surprised if he turns the 'Metropolis' upside down tomorrow. He will be drinking for ten days!"

"Oh, the devil!"

"The devil's bound to have a hand in it. Where should he be if not here?"

"Well, gentlemen, I admit it was eloquent. But still it's not a good thing to break your father's head with a pestle! What are we coming to?"

"The chariot! Do you remember the chariot?"

"Yes. He turned a troika into a chariot!"

"And tomorrow he will turn a chariot into a troika, just to suit his purpose."

"What sharp lawyers there are nowadays. Is there any justice to be had in Russia?"

The bell rang. The jury deliberated for exactly an hour, neither more nor less. A profound silence reigned in the court as soon as the public had taken their seats. I remember how the jurymen walked into the court. At last!

I won't repeat the questions in order, in fact I have forgotten them. I remember only the answer to the President's first and main question: "Did the prisoner commit the murder for the sake of robbery and with premeditation?" (I don't remember the exact words.) There was a complete hush.

The foreman of the jury pronounced in a clear loud voice, amidst the deathlike stillness of the court: "Yes, guilty!"

The same answer was repeated to every question: "Yes, guilty!" There was not the slightest extenuating comment. This no one had expected; almost everyone had counted upon a recommendation of mercy at the very least. The deathlike silence in the court was not broken—all were still; those who desired his conviction as well as those who had been eager for his acquittal. But that was only for the first moment. This moment was followed by a wave of confusion. Many of the men were pleased. Some rubbed their hands with no attempt to conceal their joy. Those who disagreed with the verdict seemed crushed, shrugged their shoulders, whispered. But how shall I describe the state the ladies were in? I thought they would create a disturbance. They could scarcely believe their ears. Suddenly the whole court rang with their voices: "What's the meaning of it? What next?" They jumped up from their places. They seemed to think that the decision could be reconsidered and reversed.

But suddenly Dmitri stood up and cried in a heartrending voice, stretching his hands out before him: "I swear by God and the dreadful Day of Judgment I am not guilty of my

682

father's blood! Katerina, I forgive you! Brothers, friends, ha
pity on the other woman!"

He could not go on and broke into a terrible sobbing wa
that was heard all over the court. It was a strange, unnatural
voice unlike his own.

Then from the farthest corner at the back of the gallery came
a piercing shriek—it was Grushenka. She had succeeded in
gaining admittance to the court again before the beginning of
the lawyers' speeches.

Dmitri was now taken away. The passing of the sentence
was deferred till next day. The whole court was in confusion
and I did not remain any longer. I remember a few exclamations I heard on the steps as I went out.

"He'll have a twenty years' trip to the mines!"

"Not less."

"Well, our peasants have stood firm."

"They have condemned our Dmitri."

EPILOGUE

1. *Plans for Dmitri's Escape*

VERY EARLY, at nine o'clock in the morning, five days after
the trial, Alyosha went to see Katerina to talk over a matter
of great importance to both of them, and to give her a message. She sat and talked to him in the very room in which she
had once received Grushenka. In the next room Ivan lay unconscious in a high fever.

Katerina had immediately after the scene at the trial ordered
the sick and unconscious man to be carried to her house, dis-
regarding the inevitable gossip and general disapproval of the
public. One of the two relatives who lived with her had left
for Moscow immediately after the scene at court, but the other
remained. If both had gone away, Katerina would still have
held to her plan and would have gone on nursing Ivan and sitting by him day and night. Doctor Varvinsky and Doctor
Herzenstube were attending him. The famous doctor had gone
back to Moscow, refusing to give an opinion as to the probable outcome of the illness. Though the doctors encouraged
Katerina and Alyosha, it was clear that they could not give
positive hopes of recovery.

Alyosha came to see Ivan twice a day. But on this particular day he had specially urgent business, and he foresaw how
difficult it would be to broach the subject, yet he was in a
hurry. He had another engagement that could not be put off
for that same morning.

They had been talking for a quarter of an hour. Katerina was pale, terribly tired and in a state of hysterical excitement. She had a presentiment of the reason why Alyosha had come to her.

"Don't worry about his decision," she said, with emphasis, to Alyosha. "One way or another he is bound to come to it. He must escape. That unhappy man, that hero of honor and principle—not he, not Dmitri, but the man lying the other side of that door, who has sacrificed himself for his brother," Katerina added, with flashing eyes, "told me the whole plan of escape long ago. You know he has already entered into negotiations. . . . I've told you something already. . . . You see, it will probably come off at the third prison station from here, when the gang of prisoners is being taken to Siberia. Oh, it's a long way off yet. Ivan has already visited the superintendent of the third prison station. But we don't know yet who will be in charge of the prisoners; it's impossible to find that out so long beforehand. Tomorrow perhaps I will show you in detail the whole plan which Ivan left me on the eve of the trial in case of need. . . . That was when—you remember—you found us quarreling. He had just gone downstairs, but seeing you I made him come back; do you remember? Do you know what we were quarreling about?"

"No, I don't," said Alyosha.

"Of course he did not tell you. It was about the escape. He had told me the main plan three days before, and we began quarreling about it at once and quarreled for three days. We quarreled because when he told me that, if Dmitri were convicted he would escape abroad with that creature, I was furious. I can't tell you why, I don't know myself why . . . Oh, of course, I was furious about that creature, and that she would be going abroad with Dmitri!" Katerina exclaimed suddenly, her lips quivering with anger. "As soon as Ivan saw that I was furious about that woman, he imagined I was jealous of Dmitri, and that I still loved Dmitri. That is how our first quarrel began. I would not give an explanation. I could not ask forgiveness. I could not bear to think that Ivan could suspect me of still loving that . . . And when I myself had told him long before that I did not love Dmitri, that I loved no one but him! It was only resentment against that creature that made me angry. Three days later, on the evening you came, he brought me a sealed envelope, which I was to open at once, if anything happened to him. Oh, he foresaw his illness! He told me that the envelope contained the details of the escape, and that if he died or was taken dangerously ill, I was to save Dmitri alone. Then he gave me money, nearly ten thousand—those notes to which the prosecutor referred in his speech, having learned from someone that Ivan had had them changed. I was terribly touched to find that Ivan had not given up his idea of saving Dmitri and was entrusting the plan of escape to me, although

684

he was jealous of me and still convinced that I loved D
Oh, you cannot understand the greatness of such self-sacr
Alyosha. I wanted to fall at his feet in reverence, but I
afraid that he would take it only for my joy at the thought
Dmitri's being saved. I was so exasperated at the mere poss
bility of such an unjust thought on his part that I lost my
temper again, and instead of kissing his feet, flew into a fury!
Oh, I am unhappy! It's my nature, my awful, unhappy nature!
Oh, you will see, I will end by driving him to abandon me for
another with whom he can get on better, like Dmitri. But
. . . No, I could not bear it, I will kill myself. . . . And when
you came in then, and when I called to you and told him to
come back, I was so enraged by the look of contempt and
hatred he turned on me that—do you remember—I cried out
to you that it was he, he alone, who had persuaded me that his
brother Dmitri was the murderer! I said that on purpose to
hurt him. He had never, never persuaded me that Dmitri was
the murderer. On the contrary, it was I who persuaded him!
Oh, my temper was the cause of everything! I paved the way
to that hideous scene at the trial. Ivan only wanted to show me
that he was an honorable man, and that, even if I loved his
brother, he would not ruin him for revenge or jealousy. So he
came into court . . . I am the cause of it all, I alone am to
blame!"

Katerina had never made such a confession to Alyosha before, and he felt that she was now at that stage of unbearable
suffering when even the proudest heart crushes its pride and
falls vanquished by grief. Oh, Alyosha knew another terrible
reason of her present misery, although she had concealed it
from him during those days since the trial. She was suffering
for her "treachery" at the trial. Alyosha felt that her conscience was impelling her to confess it to him, to him, Alyosha,
with tears and cries and hysterical writhings. But he dreaded
that moment and longed to spare her. It made the mission on
which he had come even more difficult. He spoke of Dmitri
again.

"It's all right, it's all right, don't worry about him!" she began sharply and stubbornly. "All that is only momentary. I
know him, I know his heart only too well. You can be sure he
will consent to escape. It's not as though it will happen immediately; he will have time to make up his mind. Ivan will be
well by that time and will manage it all himself, so that I shall
have nothing to do with it. Don't worry; he will agree to
escape. He has already agreed. Do you think he would give up
that creature? And they won't let her go with him, so he has
to escape. It's you he's most afraid of, he is afraid you won't
approve of his escape on moral grounds. . . . But you must
allow it," Katerina added emphatically. She paused and smiled.

"He talks about some hymn," she went on again. "Some
cross he has to bear, some duty. I remember Ivan told me a

deal about it, and if you knew how he talked!" Katerina ⟨said⟩ suddenly, with feeling she could not repress: "If you only ⟨kne⟩w how he loved that wretched man at the moment and ⟨ho⟩w he hated him at the same time! And I heard his story and ⟨sa⟩w his tears with disdain. Brute! Yes, I am a brute. I am re⟨sp⟩onsible for his illness. But that man in prison is incapable of ⟨s⟩uffering," Katerina concluded irritably. "Can such a man suffer? Men like him never suffer!"

There was a note of hatred and repulsion in her voice. And yet it was she who had betrayed him. "Perhaps because she feels how she's wronged him she hates him at moments," Alyosha thought to himself. He hoped that it was only "at moments." In Katerina's last words he detected a challenging note, but he did not take it up.

"I sent for you this morning to make you promise to persuade him yourself. Or do you, too, consider that to escape would be dishonorable, cowardly, or something . . . unchristian, perhaps?" Katerina added, even more defiantly.

"Oh, no. I'll tell him everything," muttered Alyosha. "He asks you to come to see him today," he blurted out suddenly, looking steadily at her. She drew back a little from him on the sofa.

"Me? Can that be?" she faltered, turning pale.

"It can and ought to be!" Alyosha began emphatically. "He needs you. I would not have said this and worried you, if it were not necessary. He is ill, he is beside himself, he keeps asking for you. It is not to be reconciled with you that he wants you to come; he only wants you to show yourself at his door. So much has happened to him since that day. He realizes that he has injured you beyond all measure. He does not ask your forgiveness. 'It's impossible to forgive me,' he says. He only wants you to come to his door."

"It's so . . ." faltered Katerina. "I had a feeling that you would come with this message. I knew he would ask me to come. . . . It's impossible!"

"Let it be impossible, but do it. Only think, he realizes for the first time how he has hurt you, the first time in his life; he has never grasped it so fully before. He said: 'If she refuses to come I will be unhappy all my life.' Do you hear? Though he is condemned to penal servitude for twenty years, he is still planning to be happy—isn't that pitiful? You must visit him; even though he is ruined, he is innocent," broke like a challenge from Alyosha. "His hands are clean, there is no blood on them! For the sake of his infinite sufferings in the future visit him now. Go, greet him on his way into the darkness—stand at his door, that is all. . . . You must do it, you must!"

"I must . . . but I cannot . . ." Katerina moaned. "He will look at me. . . . I can't."

"Your eyes ought to meet. How will you live the rest of your life, if you don't make up your mind to do it now?"

"Better suffer all my life."

"You must go, you must go," Alyosha repeated with less emphasis.

"But why today, why at once? . . . I can't leave Ivan

"You can for a moment. It will only be a moment. If don't go he will be delirious tonight. I would not tell you a have pity on him!"

"Have pity on *me!*" Katerina said with bitter reproach. She burst into tears.

"Then you will go," said Alyosha firmly. "I'll go and tell him you will come at once."

"No, don't tell him," cried Katerina in alarm. "I will go but don't tell him beforehand, because I may go, but I may not go in . . . I don't know yet . . ."

Her voice failed. She gasped for breath. Alyosha got up to go.

"And what if I meet anyone?" she said suddenly in a low voice, turning white again.

"That's just why you must go now, to avoid meeting anyone. There will be no one there, I can tell you that for certain. We will expect you," he concluded emphatically, and went out of the room.

2. *For a Moment the Lie Becomes Truth*

ALYOSHA HURRIED TO THE HOSPITAL to see Dmitri. The day after his fate was determined, Dmitri had fallen ill with nervous fever, and was sent to the prison division of the town hospital. But at the request of several people (Alyosha, Madame Hohlakov, Lise, etc.), Doctor Varvinsky had made an exception for Dmitri. He was not with the other prisoners, but in a separate little room, the one where Smerdyakov had been. There was a sentinel at the other end of the corridor, and a grating over the window, so that Varvinsky could be at ease about the indulgence he had shown, which was not quite legal. He was a kind-hearted and compassionate young man. He knew how hard it would be for a man like Dmitri to pass so suddenly into the company of robbers and murderers; he would have to get used to it by degrees. The visits of relatives and friends were informally sanctioned by the doctor and overseer, and even by the police captain. But only Alyosha and Grushenka had visited Dmitri. Rakitin had tried to force his way in twice, but Dmitri begged Varvinsky not to admit him.

Alyosha found him sitting on his bed in a hospital dressing gown, rather feverish, with a towel soaked in vinegar and water on his head. He looked at Alyosha as he came in with an undefined expression, but there was a shade of something like

scernible in it. He had become terribly preoccupied
e trial; sometimes he would be silent for half an hour
emed to be pondering something heavily and painfully,
ous of everything around him. If he roused himself from
brooding and began to talk, he always spoke with abrupt-
s and he never spoke of what he really wanted to say. He
metimes looked with a face of suffering at his brother. He
eemed to be more at ease with Grushenka than with Alyosha.
It is true, he scarcely spoke to her at all, but as soon as she
came in, his whole face lighted up with joy.

Alyosha sat down beside him on the bed in silence. This
time Dmitri was waiting for Alyosha, but he did not dare ask
him what Katerina's answer was. He felt it was almost unthinkable that Katerina would consent to come, and at the same
time he felt that if she did not come, something inconceivable
would happen.

Alyosha understood his feelings.

"Trifon Plastunov," Dmitri began nervously, "has pulled his
whole inn to pieces, I am told. He's taken up the flooring,
pulled apart the planks, torn up the gallery, I am told. He is
looking for treasure—the fifteen hundred roubles which the
prosecutor said I'd hidden there. He began playing these tricks,
they say, as soon as he got home. Serves him right, the swindler! The guard here told me yesterday; he comes from
there."

"Listen," began Alyosha. "She will come, but I don't know
when. Perhaps today, perhaps in a few days, that I can't tell.
But she will come, she will, that's certain."

Dmitri wanted to say something, but was silent. The news
had a tremendous effect on him. It was obvious that he would
have liked to know what had been said, but he was again afraid
to ask. Something cruel and contemptuous from Katerina
would have cut him like a knife at the moment.

"This was what she said among other things; that I must be
sure to set your conscience at rest about escaping. If Ivan is
not well by then she will see to it all herself."

"You've spoken of that already," Dmitri observed.

"And you have told Grushenka of the plan?" observed Alyosha.

"Yes," Dmitri admitted. "She won't come this morning."
He looked timidly at his brother. "She won't come until evening. When I told her yesterday that Katerina was taking
measures, she was silent. She only whispered, 'Let her!' She
understood that it was important. I did not dare to try her further. She understands now, I think, that Katerina no longer
cares for me, but loves Ivan."

"Does she?" asked Alyosha.

"Perhaps she does not. She is not coming this morning,"
Dmitri hurried to explain again. "I asked her to do something

688

for me. You know, Ivan is superior to all of us. He ought to live, not us. He will recover."

"Would you believe it, although Katerina is worried about him, she has no doubts about his recovery," said Alyosha.

"That means that she is convinced he will die. It's because she is frightened she's so sure he will get well."

"Ivan has a strong constitution, and I, too, believe that he will get well," Alyosha observed anxiously.

"Yes, he will get well. But she is convinced that he will die. She has a great deal of sorrow to bear . . ." A silence followed. A grave anxiety was disturbing Dmitri.

"Alyosha, I love Grushenka terribly," he said suddenly in a shaking voice.

"They won't let her go out there to join you," Alyosha said quickly.

"And there is something else I wanted to tell you," Dmitri went on with a sudden ring in his voice. "If they beat me on the way or out there, I won't submit to it. I will kill someone, and will be shot for it. And this will be going on for twenty years! They speak to me rudely as it is. I've been lying here all night, passing judgment on myself. I am not ready! I am not able to resign myself. I wanted to sing a 'hymn'; but if a guard speaks to me, I have not the strength to bear it. For Grushenka I would bear anything . . . anything except blows. . . . But she won't be allowed to join me there."

Alyosha smiled gently.

"Listen, Dmitri, once and for all," he said. "This is what I think. And you know that I would not tell you a lie. Listen; you are not ready, and such a cross is not for you. What's more, you don't need such a martyr's cross when you are not ready for it. If you had murdered our father, it would disturb me that you should reject your punishment. But you are innocent, and such a cross is too much for you. You wanted to make yourself into a new man by suffering. I say, only remember that other man always, all your life and wherever you go; and that will be enough for you. Your refusal to carry that great cross will only serve to make you feel all your life an even greater duty; that will do more to make a new man of you than if you went there. You could not endure it and would weaken and perhaps say: 'I am through.' The lawyer was right about that. Such heavy burdens are not for all men. For some they are impossible. This is how I feel about it. If other men have to answer for your escape, officers or soldiers, then I would not 'allow' you," smiled Alyosha. "But they say—the superintendent of the prison station told Ivan himself—that if it's well managed there will be no inquiry, and that they can get off easily. Of course, bribing is dishonest, but I can't judge about it, because if Ivan and Katerina asked me to do this for you, I know I should go and give the bribes. I must tell you the truth. And so I can't judge you. But let me assure you that I will never condemn you. It would be a strange thing if I judged you in this. Now I think I've gone into everything."

"But I do condemn myself!" cried Dmitri. "I will escape, that was settled without you; could Dmitri Karamazov do anything but run away? But I shall condemn myself, and I will pray for my sin forever. That's how the Jesuits talk, isn't it? Just as we are talking now?"

"Yes," Alyosha smiled gently.

"I love you for always telling the whole truth and never hiding anything," cried Dmitri with a laugh. "So I've caught my Alyosha being like a Jesuit. I must kiss you for that. Now listen to the rest: I'll open the other side of my heart to you. This is what I planned and decided. If I run away, even with money and a passport, and even to America, I will be cheered up by the thought that I am not running away for pleasure, not for happiness, but to another exile as bad, perhaps, as Siberia. It is as bad, Alyosha, it is! I hate America, damn it. Even though Grushenka will be with me. Just look at her; is she an American? She is Russian, Russian to the marrow of her bones; she will be homesick for the mother country, and I shall see every hour that she is suffering for my sake, that she has taken up that cross for me. And what harm has she done? And how will I put up with the rabble out there, though they may be better than I, every one of them. I hate America already! And though they may be wonderful at machinery, every one of them, damn them, they are not of my soul. I love Russia, Alyosha, I love the Russian God, though I am a scoundrel. I shall choke there!" he exclaimed, his eyes suddenly flashing. His voice was trembling with tears. "So this is what I've decided, Alyosha, listen," he began again, mastering his emotions. "As soon as I arrive there with Grushenka we will set to work at once on the land, in solitude, somewhere very remote, with wild bears. There must be some remote parts even there. I am told there are still Indians there, somewhere, on the edge of the horizon. So to the country of the *Last of the Mohicans,* and there we'll tackle the grammar at once, Grushenka and I. Work and grammar—that's how we'll spend three years. And by that time we shall speak English like any Englishman. And as soon as we've learned it—good-by to America! We'll return to Russia as American citizens. Don't worry—we won't come to this little town. We'll hide somewhere, a long way off, in the north or in the south. I will be changed by that time, and she will, too, in America. The doctors will make me some sort of wart on my face—what's the use of their being so mechanical! Or else I'll put out one eye, let my beard grow and turn gray, yearning for Russia. They won't recognize us. And if they do, let them send us to Siberia —I don't care. It will show it's our fate. We'll work on the land here, too, somewhere in the wilds, and I'll make believe I'm an American all my life. But we shall die on our own soil.

That's my plan, and it won't be altered. Do you approve?"

"Yes," said Alyosha, not wanting to contradict him.

Dmitri paused for a minute and said suddenly: "And ho they distorted the truth at the trial! Didn't they distort every thing!"

"If they had not, you would have been convicted just the same," said Alyosha with a sigh.

"Yes, people are sick of me here! God bless them, but it's hard," Dmitri moaned miserably. Again there was silence for a minute.

"Alyosha, put me out of my misery at once!" he exclaimed suddenly. "Tell me, is she coming now, or not? Tell me? What did she say? How did she say it?"

"She said she would come, but I don't know whether she will come today. It's hard for her, you know." Alyosha looked timidly at his brother.

"I am sure it is hard for her! Alyosha, it will drive me out of my mind. Grushenka keeps looking at me. She understands. My God, calm my heart; what is it I want? I want Katerina! Do I understand what I want? It's the headstrong, evil Karamazov spirit! No, I am not fit for suffering. I am a scoundrel, that's all one can say."

"Here she is!" cried Alyosha.

At that instant Katerina appeared in the doorway. For a moment she stood still, gazing at Dmitri with a dazed expression. He jumped impulsively to his feet, and a scared look came to his face. He turned pale, but a timid, pleading smile appeared on his lips and he held out both hands to Katerina. Seeing this, she flew impetuously to him. She seized him by the hands, and almost by force made him sit down on the bed. She sat down beside him, and still holding his hands pressed them tightly. Several times they both tried to speak, but stopped short and gazed speechless with a strange smile, their eyes fastened on one another.

"Have you forgiven me?" Dmitri faltered at last. Then turning to Alyosha, his face bright with joy, he cried: "Do you hear what I am asking, do you hear?"

"That's what I loved you for, that you are generous at heart!" said Katerina. "My forgiveness is no good to you, nor yours to me; whether you forgive me or not, you will always be a sore place in my heart, and I in yours—so it must be . . ." She stopped to take a breath. "What have I come for?" she began again nervously. "I have come to embrace your feet, to press your hands like this, till it hurts—you remember how in Moscow I used to squeeze them—to tell you again that you are my god, my joy, to tell you that I love you madly." She moaned in anguish and suddenly pressed his hands greedily to her lips. Tears streamed from her eyes. Alyosha stood speechless and confounded; he had never expected to see what he was seeing.

"Love is over, Dmitri!" Katerina began again. "But the past

painfully dear to me. I want you to know that will always ... so. But now let what might have been come true for one minute," she faltered, with a drawn smile, looking into his face. "You love another woman, and I love another man, and yet I shall love you forever, and you will love me; do you know that? Do you hear? Love me, love me all your life!" she cried almost with menace in her voice.

"I shall love you, and . . . do you know, Katerina," Dmitri began, drawing a deep breath at each word, "do you know, five days ago at the trial . . . even that same evening, I loved you. . . . When you were overcome and were carried out . . . All my life! So it will be, so it will always be . . ."

So they murmured to one another frantic words, almost meaningless, perhaps not even true. But at that moment it was all true, and they both believed what they said implicitly.

"Katerina," cried Dmitri suddenly, "do you believe I murdered him? I know you don't believe it now, but then . . . when you testified. . . . Surely, surely you did not believe it!"

"I did not believe it even then. I've never believed it. I hated you, and for a moment I persuaded myself. While I was giving evidence I persuaded myself and believed it, but when I'd finished speaking I stopped believing it at once. Don't doubt that! I have forgotten that I came here to punish myself," she said, with a new expression in her voice quite unlike the loving tones of a moment before.

"Woman, yours is a heavy burden," came, as it were, involuntarily from Dmitri.

"Let me go," she whispered. "I'll come again. It's more than I can bear now."

She was getting up, but suddenly she uttered a loud scream and staggered back. Grushenka walked noiselessly into the room. No one had expected her. Katerina went quickly to the door. But when she reached Grushenka, she stopped suddenly, turned as white as chalk and moaned softly, almost in a whisper: "Forgive me!"

Grushenka stared at her and, pausing for an instant, in a vindictive, venomous voice, answered: "We are full of hatred, you and I! We are both full of hatred! As though we could forgive one another! Save him, and I'll worship you all my life."

"You won't forgive her!" cried Dmitri with reproach.

"Don't be anxious, I'll save him for you!" Katerina whispered rapidly, and she ran out of the room.

"And you could refuse to forgive her when she begged for your forgiveness?" Dmitri exclaimed bitterly.

"Dmitri, don't blame her; you have no right to!" Alyosha cried.

"Her proud lips spoke, not her heart," Grushenka said in a tone of disgust. "If she saves you I'll forgive her everything . . ."

She stopped speaking, as though suppressing something. She

had come in accidentally, with no suspicion of what she w
meet.

"Alyosha, run after her!" Dmitri cried. "Tell her . . . I do
know . . . don't let her go away like this!"

"I'll come to you again in the evening," said Alyosha, an
he ran after Katerina. He overtook her outside the hospital
grounds. She was walking fast but as soon as Alyosha caught
up with her, she said quickly: "No, before that woman I can't
punish myself! I asked her forgiveness because I wanted to
punish myself to the bitter end. She would not forgive me. . . .
I like her for that!" she added, in an unnatural voice, and her
eyes flashed with fierce resentment.

"Dmitri did not expect this in the least," muttered Alyosha.
"He did not know she was coming."

"Let us not speak of that," she said. "Listen. I can't go with
you to the funeral. I've sent flowers. I think they still have
money. If necessary, tell them I'll never abandon them. . . .
Now leave me, leave me, please. You are late as it is—the
bells are ringing for the service. . . . Leave me, please!"

3. Ilusha's Funeral.
The Speech at the Stone

ALYOSHA WAS LATE. They had waited for him and had finally
decided to bear the little flower-decked coffin to the church
without him. It was the coffin of poor little Ilusha. He had died
two days after Dmitri was sentenced.

Alyosha was met at the gate of the house by the shouts of
the boys, Ilusha's schoolmates. They had all been expecting
him and were glad that he had come at last. There were about
twelve of them; they all had their schoolbags on their shoulders. "Father will cry, be with father," Ilusha had told them
as he lay dying, and the boys remembered it. Kolya Krassotkin was the leader.

"How glad I am you've come, Karamazov!" he cried, holding out his hand to Alyosha. "It's awful here. It's really horrible
to see it. Captain Snegiryov is not drunk, we know for a fact
he's had nothing to drink today, but he seems as if he were
drunk . . . I am always brave but this is awful, Karamazov. Let
me ask you one question before you go in?"

"What is it, Kolya?" said Alyosha.

"Is your brother innocent or guilty? Did he kill your father
or was it the valet? I can believe you. I haven't slept for the
last four nights for thinking about it."

"The valet killed him, my brother is innocent," answered
Alyosha.

"That's what I said," cried Smurov.

…o he is an innocent victim!" exclaimed Kolya. "But even …gh he is ruined he is happy! I envy him!"

What do you mean? How can you? Why?" cried Alyosha, …rprised.

"Oh, if only I too could sacrifice myself some day for …ruth!" cried Kolya.

"But not in such a cause, not with such disgrace and such horror!" said Alyosha.

"Of course . . . I would like to die for all humanity and as for disgrace, I don't care about that. I respect your brother!"

"And so do I!" the boy, who had once declared that he knew who had founded Troy, cried suddenly and unexpectedly and he blushed like a peony as he had done on that occasion.

Alyosha went into the room. Ilusha lay with his hands folded and his eyes closed in a blue coffin with a white frill around it. His thin face was hardly changed at all, and strange to say there was no smell of decay from the corpse. His expression was serious and, as it were, thoughtful. His hands, crossed over his breast, looked particularly beautiful, as though chiseled in marble. There were flowers in his hands and the coffin, inside and out, was decked with flowers, which had been sent early in the morning by Lise Hohlakov. But there were flowers too from Katerina, and when Alyosha opened the door, the captain had a bunch in his trembling hands and was strewing them again over his little son. He scarcely glanced at Alyosha when he came in. He would not look at anyone, even at his crazy weeping wife, who kept trying to stand on her crippled legs to get closer to her dead boy. Nina had been pushed in her chair by the boys close up to the coffin. She sat with her head pressed to it and she too was quietly weeping. Snegiryov's face looked eager, yet bewildered and exasperated. There was something crazy about his gestures and the words that came from him. "Old man, dear old man!" he exclaimed every minute, gazing at Ilusha. It was his habit to call Ilusha "old man," as a term of affection when he was alive.

"Father, give me a flower. Take that white one out of his hand and give it to me," the crazy mother begged, whimpering. Either because the little white rose in Ilusha's hand had caught her fancy or because she wanted one from his hand to to keep in memory of him, she moved restlessly, stretching out her hands for the flower.

"I won't give it to anyone, I won't give you anything," Snegiryov cried callously. "They are his flowers, not yours! Everything is his, nothing is yours!"

"Father, give mother a flower!" said Nina, lifting her face wet with tears.

"I won't give away anything and to her less than to anyone! She didn't love Ilusha. She wanted his little cannon and he gave it to her." The captain broke into loud sobs at the thought of how Ilusha had given up his cannon to his mother. The poor,

crazy creature was bathed in noiseless tears, hiding her f.
in her hands.

The boys, seeing that the father would not leave the coffi.
and that it was time to carry it out, stood around it in a close
circle and began to lift it up.

"I don't want him to be buried in the churchyard," the captain wailed suddenly. "I'll bury him by the stone, by our stone!
Ilusha told me to. I won't let him be carried out!"

He had been saying for the last three days that he would
bury him by the stone, but Alyosha, Krassotkin, the landlady,
her sister, and all the boys interfered.

"What an idea to bury him by an unholy stone, as though
he had hanged himself," the old landlady said sternly. "There
in the churchyard the ground has been blessed. He'll be prayed
for there. One can hear the singing in church and the deacon
reads so plainly that it will reach him every time just as
though it were read over his grave."

At last the captain made a gesture of despair as though to
say: "Take him where you will." The boys raised the coffin,
but as they passed the mother, they stopped for a moment
and lowered it that she might say good-by to Ilusha. Seeing
that precious little face, which for the last three days she had
only looked at from a distance, she trembled all over and her
gray head began twitching spasmodically.

"Mother, make the sign of the cross over him, give him
your blessing, kiss him," Nina cried to her. But her head still
twitched and with a face contorted with bitter grief she began,
without a word, beating her breast with her fist. They carried
the coffin past her. Nina pressed her lips to her brother's for
the last time as they bore the coffin by her.

As Alyosha went out of the house he begged the landlady
to look after those who were left behind, but she interrupted
him before he had finished.

"To be sure, I'll stay with them, we are Christians, too."
The old woman wept as she said this.

They had not far to carry the coffin to the church, not more
than three hundred yards. It was a still, clear day, with a slight
frost. The church bells were ringing. The captain ran fussing
and distracted after the coffin, in his short old summer overcoat, with his head bare and his soft old wide-brimmed hat in
his hand. He was in a state of bewildered anxiety. At one minute he stretched out his hand to support the head of the coffin
and only hindered the bearers, at another he ran alongside
and tried to find a place for himself there. A flower fell on
the snow and he rushed to pick it up as though everything in
the world depended on the loss of that flower.

"And the crust of bread, we've forgotten the crust!" he
cried suddenly. But the boys reminded him that he had taken
a crust of bread and that it was in his pocket. He pulled it
out and was reassured.

695

Ilusha told me to, Ilusha," he explained at once to Alyosha. "I was sitting by him one night and he suddenly told me: 'Father, when my grave is filled up crumble a piece of bread on it so that the sparrows will fly down. I will hear them and it will cheer me up.' "

"That's a good idea," said Alyosha. "We must remember to scatter breadcrumbs over his grave often."

"Every day, every day!" said the captain quickly, happy at the thought.

They reached the church at last and set the coffin in the middle of it. The boys surrounded it and remained reverently standing all through the service. It was an old and rather poor church. Many of the ikons were without settings but such churches are the best for praying in. During the mass the captain became somewhat calmer, though at times he had outbursts of the same unconscious and, as it were, incoherent anxiety. At one moment he went up to the coffin to set straight the cover or the wreath. When a candle fell out of the candlestick he rushed to replace it and was a long time fumbling over it. Then he stood quietly by the coffin with a look of blank uneasiness. After the Epistle he suddenly whispered to Alyosha, who was standing beside him, that the Epistle had not been read properly but did not explain what he meant. During the prayer, "Like the Cherubim," he joined in the singing but did not go on to the end. Falling on his knees, he pressed his forehead to the stone floor and lay that way for a long while.

At last came the funeral service itself and candles were distributed. The distracted father began fussing about again, but the touching and impressive funeral prayers moved his soul. He seemed suddenly to shrink together and he broke into rapid, short sobs, which he tried to smother. At last he sobbed aloud. When they began taking leave of the dead and closing the coffin, he flung his arms about, as though he would not allow them to cover Ilusha, and he began greedily and persistently kissing his dead boy. At last they succeeded in persuading him to come away, but suddenly he stretched out his hand and snatched a few flowers from the coffin. He looked at them and a new idea seemed to dawn upon him, so that he apparently forgot his grief for a minute. He seemed to sink into brooding and did not resist when the coffin was lifted up and carried to the grave. It was an expensive one in the churchyard close to the church. Katerina had paid for it.

After the customary rites the grave diggers lowered the coffin. The captain with his flowers in his hands bent down so low over the open grave that the boys caught hold of his coat and pulled him back. He did not seem to understand fully what was happening. When they began filling up the grave, he suddenly pointed at the falling earth and tried to say something, but no one could make out what he meant, and

he stopped suddenly. Then he was reminded that he
crumble the bread. He was awfully excited, snatched up
bread and began pulling it to pieces and flinging the mor
on the grave.

"Come, fly down, birds. Fly down, sparrows!" he called anx
iously.

One of the boys saw that it was awkward for him to crumble the bread with the flowers in his hands and suggested he
should give them to someone to hold for a time. But he would
not do this and seemed alarmed for his flowers, as though they
wanted to take them from him altogether. And after looking
at the grave and, as it were, satisfying himself that everything
had been done and that the bread had been crumbled, he suddenly turned and made his way homewards. His steps became
more and more hurried, he almost ran. The boys and Alyosha
kept up with him.

"The flowers are for mother, the flowers are for mother! I
was unkind to mother," he cried.

Someone called to him to put on his hat as it was cold.
But he flung the hat in the snow as though he were angry and
kept repeating: "I don't want the hat, I don't want the hat."
Smurov picked it up and carried it after him. All the boys
were crying. Kolya and the boy who had found out about
Troy were crying most of all. Though Smurov, with the captain's hat in his hand, was crying bitterly too, he managed, as
he ran, to snatch up a piece of red brick that lay in the snow
to fling it at the flock of sparrows that was flying by. He
missed them, of course, and went on crying as he ran.

Halfway home the captain suddenly stopped, stood still for
half a minute as though struck by something, and turning back
to the church, ran toward the deserted grave. But the boys
overtook him and caught hold of him. He fell helpless on
the snow as though he had been knocked down, and struggling,
sobbing, and wailing, he began crying out: "Ilusha, old man,
dear old man!" Alyosha and Kolya tried to make him get up,
soothing and persuading him.

"Captain, buck up, a man must show fortitude," muttered
Kolya.

"You'll spoil the flowers," said Alyosha. "And your wife is
expecting them, she is sitting crying because you would not
give her any before. Ilusha's little bed is still there . . ."

"Yes, yes, mother!" the captain suddenly remembered.
"They'll take away the bed, they'll take it away," he added as
though alarmed that they really would. He jumped up and
ran homewards again. It was not far off and they all arrived
together.

The captain opened the door hurriedly and called to his
wife: "Mother, poor crippled darling, Ilusha has sent you these
flowers." He held out to her the little bunch of flowers that
had been frozen and broken while he was struggling in the

But at that instance he saw in the corner, by the bed, ...a's little boots, which the landlady had put tidily side by . Seeing the old, patched, rusty-looking, stiff boots he ...hed to them, fell on his knees, snatched up one boot and, ...essing his lips to it, began kissing it greedily, crying: "Ilusha, ...ld man, dear old man, where are your little feet?"

"Where have you taken him? Where have you taken him?" the crazed mother cried in a heartrending voice. Nina, too, broke into sobs. Kolya ran out of the room, and the boys followed him. At last Alyosha too went out.

"Let them weep," he said to Kolya. "It's no use trying to comfort them just now. Let us wait a minute and then go back."

"No, it's no use, it's awful," Kolya agreed. "Do you know, Karamazov," he dropped his voice so that no one could hear them, "I feel dreadfully sad, and if it were only possible to bring him back, I'd give anything in the world to do it."

"Ah, so would I," said Alyosha.

"What do you think, Karamazov, had we better come back here tonight? He'll be drunk, you know."

"Perhaps he will. Let us come together, you and I, that will be enough, to spend an hour with them, with the mother and Nina. If we all come together we will remind them of everything again," Alyosha suggested.

"The landlady is laying the table for them now—there'll be a funeral dinner or something. The priest is coming. Shall we go back, Karamazov?"

"Of course," said Alyosha.

"It's all so strange, Karamazov, such sorrow and then pancakes after it. It all seems so unnatural."

"They are going to have salmon, too," the boy who had found out about Troy observed in a loud voice.

"Don't interrupt again with your idiotic remarks! No one is talking to you and no one cares whether you exist or not!" Kolya snapped out irritably. The boy flushed crimson but did not dare to reply.

They strolled slowly along the road. Suddenly Smurov exclaimed: "There's Ilusha's stone, under which they wanted to bury him."

They all stood still by the big stone. Alyosha looked at it. The whole picture of what the captain had described to him, of how Ilusha, weeping and hugging him, had cried: "Father, father, how he insulted you!" rose in his imagination. A sudden impulse came to his soul. With a serious and earnest expression he looked from one to another of the bright, pleasant faces of Ilusha's schoolmates and said to them: "Boys, I would like to say one word to you, here at this place."

The boys stood around him and listened.

"Boys, we shall soon part. I shall be for some time with my ... brothers, one of whom is going to Siberia. The other is lying at death's door. But soon I shall leave this town, perh for a long time, so we shall part. Let us make a compa here, at Ilusha's stone, that we will never forget Ilusha and on another. And whatever happens to us later in life, even if w don't meet for twenty years, let us always remember how we buried the poor boy at whom we once threw stones. Do you remember, by the bridge? Afterwards we all grew so fond of him. He was a fine boy, a kind-hearted, brave boy. He felt for his father and resented the cruel insult done to him and stood up for him. And we will remember him, boys, all our lives. And even if we are occupied with important things, even if we attain honor or fall into misfortune—still let us remember how good it was once here, when we were all together, united by a good and kind feeling which made us, for the time we were loving that poor boy, better perhaps than we are. My little doves—let me call you doves, for you are very like them, those pretty blue birds, at this minute as I look at your faces. My dear children, perhaps you won't understand what I am saying to you, because I often speak very unintelligibly, but you'll remember it all the same and will agree with my words sometime. You must know that there is nothing higher and stronger and more wholesome and good for life in the future than some good memory, especially a memory of childhood, of home. People talk to you a great deal about your education, but some good sacred memory, preserved from childhood, is perhaps the best education. If a man carries many such memories with him into life, he is safe to the end of his days. And if one has only one good memory left in one's heart, even that may sometime be the means of saving him. Perhaps we may grow wicked later on, may be unable to refrain from evil, may laugh at men's tears and at those people who say as Kolya did just now: 'I want to suffer for all men.' We may even jeer spitefully at such people. But however bad we may become—which God forbid—yet, when we recall how we buried Ilusha, how we loved him in his last days, and how we have been talking like friends together, at this stone, the cruelest and most mocking of us—if we do become so— will not dare to laugh inwardly at having been kind and good at this moment! What's more, perhaps, that one memory may keep us from great evil and we will reflect and say: 'Yes, I was good and brave and honest then!' Let him laugh to himself, that does not matter, a man often laughs at what's good and kind. That's only from thoughtlessness. But I assure you, boys, that as he laughs he will say at once in his heart: 'No, I do wrong to laugh, for that's not a thing to laugh at.' "

"That will be so, I understand you, Karamazov!" cried Kolya.

The boys were excited and they too wanted to say something, but they restrained themselves.

I say this in case we become bad," Alyosha went on. "But ...re's no reason why we should become bad, is there, boys? ...et us be, first and above all, kind, then honest and then let ...s never forget each other! I say that again. I give you my word that I'll never forget one of you. Every face looking at me now I shall remember even for thirty years. Just now Kolya said to one of you that no one cares whether he exists or not. But I cannot forget that all of you exist. Boys, my dear boys, let us all be generous and brave like Ilusha; clever, brave and generous like Kolya (though he will be ever so much more clever when he is grown up). But why am I talking about those two! You are all dear to me, boys, from this day forth, I have a place in my heart for you all, and I beg you to keep a place in your hearts for me! Well, and who has united us in this kind, good feeling which we shall remember and intend to remember all our lives? Who, if not Ilusha, the good boy, the dear boy, precious to us forever! Let us never forget him. May his memory live forever in our hearts!"

"Yes, yes, forever, forever!" the boys cried in their ringing voices.

"Let us remember his face and his clothes and his poor little boots, his coffin and his unhappy father. Let us remember how boldly he stood up for him against the whole school."

"We will remember, we will remember," cried the boys. "He was brave, he was good!"

"Ah, how I loved him!" exclaimed Kolya.

"Ah, children, ah, dear friends, don't be afraid of life! How good life is when one does something good and just!"

"Yes, yes," the boys repeated.

"Karamazov, we love you!" a voice cried impulsively.

"We love you, we love you!" they all caught it up. There were tears in their eyes.

"Hurrah for Karamazov!" Kolya shouted.

"And may the dear boy's memory live forever!" Alyosha added again with feeling.

"Forever!" the boys chimed in again.

"Karamazov," cried Kolya. "Can it be true as they teach us in church, that we shall all rise again from the dead and shall live and see each other again, all, Ilusha, too?"

"Certainly we shall all rise again, certainly we shall see each other and shall tell each other with joy and gladness all that has happened!" Alyosha answered, half laughing, half enthusiastic.

"Oh, how wonderful it will be!" cried Kolya.

"Well, now we will finish talking and go to his funeral dinner. Don't be disturbed at our eating pancakes—it's a very old custom and there's something nice in that!" laughed Alyosha. "Well, let us go! And now we go hand in hand."

700

"And always so, all our lives hand in hand! Hurrah for Karamazov!" Kolya cried once more. And once more the boys took up his cry.

"Hurrah for Karamazov!"

SELECTED BIBLIOGRAPHY

Works by Fyodor Dostoyevsky

Poor Folk, 1846
The Double, 1846
An Honest Thief, 1846
White Nights, 1848 (Signet Classic 0451-520130)
Uncle's Dream, 1859
The Friend of the Family, 1859
The Insulted and the Injured, 1861
The House of the Dead, 1862
Notes from Underground, 1864 (Signet Classic 0451-520130)
Crime and Punishment, 1866 (Signet Classic 0451-519957)
The Gambler, 1866
The Idiot, 1868-69 (Signet Classic 0451-517997)
The Eternal Husband, 1870
The Possessed, 1871-72 (Signet Classic 0451-519183)
A Raw Youth, 1875
The Dream of a Ridiculous Man, 1877 (Signet Classic 0451-520130)
A Diary of a Writer, 1873-81
The Brothers Karamazov, 1879-80 (Signet Classic 0451-514645)
Letters of Fyodor Dostoyevsky

Selected Biography and Criticism

Bakhtin, Mikhail. *Problems of Dostoyevsky's Poetics*. Trans. R. W. Rotsel. Ann Arbor: Ardis, 1973.

Berdyaev, Nicholas. *Dostoyevsky*. Trans. Donald Attwater. New York: Meridian Books, 1960.

Blackmur, R. P. *Eleven Essays in the European Novel*. New York: Harcourt, Brace & World, 1964.

Carr, Edward H. *Dostoyevsky, 1821-1881: A New Biography*. London: Allen and Unwin, 1949.

Coulson, Jessie. *Dostoyevsky: A Self-Portrait*. London: Oxford University Press, 1962.

Gide, André. *Dostoyevsky*. Trans. Arnold Bennett. New York: Knopf, 1926.

Grossman, Leonid. *Dostoyevsky: A Biography*. Trans. Helen Mackler. Indianapolis: Bobbs-Merrill, 1975.

Ivanov, Vyacheslav. *Freedom and the Tragic Life: A Study in Dostoyevsky*. Trans. Norman Cameron. Ed. S. Konovalov. New York: The Noonday Press, 1957.

Jackson, R. L. *Dostoyevsky's Underground Man in Russian Literature*. New York: Humanities Press, 1959.

———, ed. *Twentieth Century Interpretations of Crime and Punishment: A Collection of Critical Essays*. Englewood Cliffs, Prentice-Hall, 1974.

Lavrin, Janko. *Dostoyevsky*. New York: Macmillan, 1947.

Magarshack, David. *Dostoyevsky*. New York: Harcourt, Brace & World, 1963.

Mirsky, Dmitri. *History of Russian Literature*. Ed. Francis J. Whitfield. New York: Knopf, 1949.

Mochulsky, Konstantin. *Dostoyevsky: His Life and Work*. Trans. Michael A. Minihan. Princeton, N.J.: Princeton University Press, 1967.

Modern Fiction Studies (Dostoyevsky Number), 4 (Autumn, 1958).

Muchnic, Helen. *Dostoyevsky's English Reputation*. New York: Octagon Books, 1969.

Seduro, Vladimir. *Dostoyevsky in Russian Literary Criticism: 1846-1956*. New York: Columbia University Press, 1957.

Simmons, Ernest J. *Dostoyevsky: The Making of a Novelist*. London: Oxford University Press, 1940.

Steiner, George. *Tolstoy or Dostoyevsky*. New York: Knopf, 1959.

Wasiolek, Edward, ed. *Crime and Punishment and the Critics*. San Francisco: Wadsworth Publishing Co., 1961.

——. *Dostoyevsky: The Major Fiction*. Cambridge, Mass.: M.I.T. Press, 1964.

——, ed. *The Brothers Karamazov and the Critics*. Belmont, Calif.: Wadsworth Publishing Co., 1967.

Wellek, René, ed. *Dostoyevsky: A Collection of Critical Essays*. Englewood Cliffs, N.J.: Prentice-Hall, 1962.

Yarmolinsky, Avrahm. *Dostoyevsky: His Life and Art*. New York: Criterion Books, 1957.